It 'll be over long before noon silver Mercedes will arriv van are there to strip the room of my possessions after I'm gone. Some morning in the future you can look out one of these windows and see how it happened, too late for me—and for you.

I hope I'm not alone, I hope there are others. Many will be arguing, begging, screaming, but some will walk out unaided, with quiet dignity. If I have to, that's what I want to do.

Not that it matters.

I crush out a cigarette. I open another bottle of beer, reach for another cigarette. I don't have to go to the window to see what is happening outside. There is light in the sky.

Look for me.

WORLD OF HURT

SELECTED TALES

BY THOMAS TESSIER

For Kylie and Sabrina and Ryan and Zoey

ACKNOWLEDGEMENTS

Some of these stories were first collected in *Ghost Music and Other Tales* (Cemetery Dance, 2000) and *Remorseless: Tales of Cruelty* (Sinister Grin Press, 2013).

CONTENTS

WORLD OF HURT: THOMAS TESSIER S NOCTURNES

John Langan

As with so many of the writers who came to mean so much to me, I first encountered Thomas Tessier's name in the pages of Stephen King's groundbreaking non-fiction study, *Danse Macabre*. There, Tessier was identified as the author of *The Nightwalker*, which King described as "perhaps the finest were-wolf novel of (what was then) the last twenty years." In those pre-internet days, it took me a long time to find the book (in the aisles of The Bookworm, as I recall, which was the best of the local used book stores). When I did, it was between copies of two of Tessier's other novels, *Phantom* and *Finishing Touches*. Flushed with the feeling of success that comes with discovering not only what you were looking for, but more, besides, I grabbed the three books and hurried to the cash register.

What I experienced when I sat down with *The Nightwalker* was a narrative unlike the horror novels I was used to. This was during the later 1980s, in the midst of the so-called horror boom. The predominant form of the horror novel was a version of what Dale Bailey has called the social melodrama—which is to say, a story whose large cast of characters is drawn from different socioeconomic strata, and which occurs in a naturalistic setting rendered mimetically, and which concerns a growing supernatural threat to the established social order, and which concludes with the threat vanquished and the social order reaffirmed. While he didn't call it by this name, Stephen King discussed this strain of the horror narrative in *Danse Macabre*, noting that its underlying sociopolitical orientation tends toward the conservative (which doesn't mean that its characters necessarily have to be). In addition to King's own novels of the time, my bookshelves were crowded with a host of examples of the social-melodrama variety: Peter Straub's *Ghost Story*, Robert McCammon's *Swan Song*, and Dan Simmons's *Carrion Comfort*.

Thomas Tessier's novels were something else. Take *The Nightwalker*, which I read soon after I purchased it. The book focuses on a single character, an American veteran of the Vietnam war living in London. During the war, Bobby Ives was declared dead by the Army, a fact seemingly at odds with the vigorous sex he enjoys with his girlfriend, but which appears connected to a recurrent dream he has of dying on a Caribbean island and being reborn as a zombie—a dream which may be a memory of a previous existence. He is subject to fits of rage, which eventually lead him to murder, and which cause the reader to wonder if Tessier is writing an early version of the "traumatized vet goes berserk" narrative. But the extremes of his behavior are accompanied by dramatic changes in his appearance, making him more wolf-like, and we realize that he is transforming into something akin to the Wolf-Man. Unlike Lon Chaney, Jr., however, Ives has not been bitten by another monster. Rather, as he learns when he consults a reluctant psychic for help, the experience he is undergoing is of a piece with the one of which he has dreamed (and which turns out to be an actual event from a past life). In both instances, the monstrous supernatural is the manifestation of a process of existential becoming. He is developing into something other than human, something singular, and therefore pretty much by definition, something monstrous. While Bobby meets his end at the novel's climax, thus fulfilling the requirements of the story's genre, there's a suggestion that the larger cycle of which he's been a part will continue beyond the last page. Depending on the reader's perspective, this may be the truly horrifying portion of the narrative, or it may approach the sublime.

Either way, *The Nightwalker* is a singular accomplishment. I should probably add that I didn't understand most of what I've written about the book here the first time I completed it. I had been anticipating a werewolf novel in the mode of one of King's books. Needless to say, Tessier had overturned my expectations thoroughly. I had the sense that there was a good deal more to the narrative than I had understood. In this regard, if there was any book from the group of social melodramas *The Nightwalker* reminded me of, it was Straub's *Ghost Story*. Upon finishing that novel, I had been left with the same feeling of a substantial portion of it having evaded my grasp. This had not discouraged or upset me; instead, the suggestion that there were additional elements to a narrative which had so enthralled me was thrilling. As was the case with Straub's book, this quality would send me back to *The Nightwalker* numerous times in the succeeding decades, to the point that it remains one of the novels I've read the most.

While they were different in execution, both *Phantom* and *Finishing Touches* were equally distinctive. Written from the perspective of a young boy, the former related his encounter with and ultimate struggle against vast, malevolent supernatural forces. It was possible to find in it similarities to the children-confronting-monsters plot that animated novels from Bradbury's *Something Wicked This Way Comes* to Straub's *Shadowland* (and that would later be the engine driving King's *It* and Simmons's *Summer of Night*), but Tessier had focused his narrative on the point of view of a single child, one possessed of very real fears about the physical safety of his asthmatic mother. In so doing, he had allowed the reader to remain in doubt about the exact nature of the unearthly forces his protagonist was encountering, specifically, what their relationship was to his psyche. Then during the book's climactic sequence, he plunged the boy into a supernatural extravaganza worthy of a novel five times this one's length. The result was a work of visionary power not unlike some of the great weird stories from earlier in the twentieth century, works by Hodgson and Blackwood.

Finishing Touches was something else, again. This time, the protagonist was an American physician on an extended visit to London before beginning his practice of medicine. While it shared *The Nightwalker*'s plot device of a young American adrift in a foreign country (and therefore participated in a larger American Gothic tradition stretching back through Henry James to Nathaniel Hawthorne), the narrative eschewed the supernatural in favor of more fleshly, but no less horrifying, concerns. In the book's early pages, Tessier's protagonist, Tom Sutherland, makes the acquaintance of an apparently benign older doctor, Nordhagen. A specialist in cosmetic surgery, Nordhagen invites the American to visit his offices. When Sutherland takes him up on his offer, though, the doctor is absent; instead, he encounters Nordhagen's assistant, Lina Ravachol, to whom Sutherland is immediately and intensely attracted. Lina shares his feelings, and in short order, the two of them have acted on their mutual desire, starting an affair that is powerfully physical. Soon, Sutherland's erotic adventures are accompanied by explorations of a much darker nature, as Lina and Nordhagen bring him into the surgeon's underground chambers, in which the man conducts secret experiments upon the human form. Rather than being horrified, however, Sutherland is intrigued by Nordhagen's work, and in essence becomes his apprentice. In the character of Nordhagen, it's possible to recognize the figure of the mad scientist. Yet this mad scientist story takes place post-Freud, and specifically, the late Freud of Beyond the Pleasure Principle, for whom the two great, primal drives of Eros and Thanatos, sex and death, are fundamentally intertwined. It's this double-helix that winds through the center of what grows into a very dark novel, indeed.

Bundle these three novels with Tessier's later masterpiece, *Fog Heart*, and you would have a powerful argument for the variety and power the horror novel can achieve. (This is not to scant the accomplishment of the other books he's written, only to offer this quartet as exemplary of the restlessness and range of his work in the form.) In no small part because of his willingness to thwart genre expectations (and especially those of the social melodrama), these slender novels lingered in the memory well after considerably longer books had been forgotten. And if I found his novels distinct from the rest of what was being written, then that went doubly, triply so for his shorter work, the best of which has now been collected in the volume you're holding in your hands, *World of Hurt*.

Consider "Nocturne," which debuted as the original story in Tessier's first major collection, *Ghost Music*. This short narrative details the night-time wanderings of its protagonist, O'Netty, which take him from his home on the outskirts of a nameless city into its heart. There, he visits The Europa Lounge, located through an unassuming door which leads down several flights of stairs, deep underground. Its patrons speak a language that he does not know, but whose sound points to an origin in eastern Europe. After enjoying a couple of beers in pleasant solitude, he, along with the other patrons, is witness to a strange performance. A young man steps forward, strips, produces a knife, and engages in a shocking act of self-mutilation, which reaches a surreal conclusion. Afterward, when O'Netty is about to depart the lounge, the bartender directs him to an exit that takes him out on the street. Unsure of how exactly he should think about everything he has seen, O'Netty heads for home.

His uncertainty concerning the story's events is shared by the reader. For sheer weirdness, Tessier's story evokes the work of Robert Aickman; albeit, with a concentration of scene and effect the English writer did not achieve. It's easy enough to write a short horror story of what I call the trap variety, which is to say, an abbreviated tale of a character who suffers a gruesome fate. It's much more difficult to construct a narrative of equivalent length that leaves the reader with a feeling of expanding mystery. This is precisely Tessier's accomplishment here. Of course, we can't resist trying to (re)solve the story's puzzle, and in this regard, a number of its details are suggestive. The name of the lounge, its subterranean location, the weird language the other patrons speak, all hint that the establishment O'Netty has stumbled into caters to a vampiric clientele. Yet the entertainment he observes, the doorway that takes him out of the lounge, push the story from the realm of Bram Stoker into that of E.T.A. Hoffman. There's a temptation to read the narrative as O'Netty's dream, but none of its details support such an interpretation; there's no moment we can point to when O'Netty either falls asleep or awakens. We may look to the story's title for assistance. "Nocturne" refers to a piece of music written to evoke the particular feeling of night-time. (It's relevant here to note that for several years Tessier wrote a monthly music column for Vogue's British edition.) This seems applicable, as the world of the story is a night-time one, which is to say, one in which dreams and the irrational have free reign. In such a setting, the eminently civilized and the horrifyingly savage, the mundane and the surreal, rub elbows. This does not preclude the possibility that O'Netty has stumbled into a bar full of vampires enjoying their own bizarre diversion, but it presents the event in an oddly formal manner which foregrounds its strangeness. The name of the lounge, of course, is in an American context indicative of the foreign, the unfamiliar, but there may be additional significance to it. In Greek mythology, Europa is the girl stolen from Crete by the god Zeus in his disguise as a bull. It's thus a name associated with the supernatural, with transformation. According to the classical writer, Lucian of Samosata, the goddess Europa was identified in some quarters as a guise of the moon goddess. This would be consistent with the story's overall night-time setting and, given that the moon is also connected to sorcery, another link to the supernatural. And, at the risk of committing that most egregious of critical sins, the stretch, the name of the Lounge, with its evocation of the continent that saw some of the twentieth century's worst horrors, lends the display O'Netty sees within it a kind of symbolic power, as if what he observes is a horrifying pantomime of European culture's mid-century self-destruction, enacted, perhaps, by those driven from their homes by it.

There's a great deal packed within the story's few pages, and it's little surprise that Peter Straub selected "Nocturne" for inclusion in the second volume of his Library of America series, American Fantastic Tales. But there are numerous other stories he might have chosen, several of them considerably longer. For example, "The Dreams of Dr. Ladybank" explores Hawthorne's idea of the unpardonable sin, which is to say, of cutting oneself off from humanity by treating people as things (which features in Finishing Touches, too). Tessier begins with a conversation between two friends about what will become the central concern of the story, specifically, whether it might be possible to control others telepathically. It's a narrative gesture that evokes the conventions of the nineteenth century; though the story that follows would have shocked Hawthorne and his fellows. Finding himself possessed of this power, the titular doctor, a psychiatrist, explores its parameters, then begins to abuse it. As far as he can tell, Dr. Ladybank's control is limited to a pair of young men, a patient and the boyfriend of a patient, whose behaviors he redirects in ever-more-sadistic ways. There's a bit of the conte cruel to the story, but because Tessier develops it at length, it grows into something more than an exercise in gratuitous violence. The figure of the psychiatrist picks up on the anxiety surrounding matters of the mind, its diseases and those who treat them, present throughout the Gothic (as well as the noir) tradition. Given the class divide between (affluent, cultured) Dr. Ladybank and his (lower-class, blue-collar) subjects, there's an element of social commentary at play, too. As an illustration of the truism about absolute power corrupting absolutely, the story could hardly be more pointed; the acts its hapless subjects are compelled to commit are frequently horrifying, but they pale in comparison to the crimes of Dr. Ladybank. In this regard, the story's title seems charged with irony of the most bitter sort. What is a dream for the psychiatrist is a nightmare for those at his mercy.

As with "Nocturne," "The Dreams of Dr. Ladybank" is marked by Tessier's measured prose, his adherence to the point of view of a single character at a time, his steadfast refusal to engage in any narrative explanation or editorializing. If this gives the former story its mystery, it makes reading the latter one an uncomfortable experience. There's no moment when, as it were, the narrator takes the reader's hand and murmurs words of reassurance, tells us that yes, this character is good, and yes, that one is bad, and the good was rewarded, the bad punished, and all right with the world. Instead, we are drawn uncomfortably close to characters puppeted by a power they do not understand, as well as to the sinister intelligence tugging their neurons.

In the novella, "Father Panic's Opera Macabre," Tessier's

shorter work reaches a particular brilliance. It's exemplary of many of his stories. There's an American wandering a foreign land: in this case, Neil O'Netty (there's that name again), driving through the Abruzzo region of Italy when his car gives up the ghost. Author of two unsuccessful novels and one successful one, he's headed nowhere specific, so when his car stops in sight of a large remote house whose front is decorated with ceramic tiles cunningly painted to dazzle when the late-day sun strikes them, he has time to spend at the place. Neil soon encounters a young, beautiful woman, Marisa Panic, who informs him that the house and its surrounds are the property of her and her brother, Hugo. She is a recent university graduate, Marisa says, including a year of study in Boston, which coincidentally is where Neil hails from. He is immediately attracted to her, and when she tells him that her workmen cannot begin repairs on his car until tomorrow and invites him to enjoy the hospitality of her house, he is less reluctant than he might be otherwise. The house into which he is lead is a maze of hallways and rooms, including one whose moldy interior threatens to trigger his asthma, and from which Marisa rescues him in the literal nick of time. Outside, the house's grounds are occasionally concealed by a dense fog, which Marisa calls "il morbo," a name Neil translates as "sickness, illness, the plague." The house is situated next to a deep ravine, near whose slopes Neil and Marisa will walk the following day, on their way to picnic. By then, they will have consummated their mutual attraction repeatedly, as they will once more after they reach the site Marisa has selected for their meal. Neil will have met and supped with Marisa's elderly parents and grandparents, who serve him a soup in which float the delicate skulls of small birds, as well as her uncle Anton, a Catholic priest who expresses interest in the subject of Neil's most recent novel. Inspired by a short novel of Stendhal's, Neil's book re-tells the story of Beatrice Cenci, the 16th century Italian girl executed on orders from the Pope himself for having killed the father who had been sexually abusing her. Father Panic's concern is with Neil's portrait of the Pope and his decision, about which Neil politely equivocates. Later, Marisa tells him that her uncle is staying at the house with them while he works on a paper on the history of conversions.

Caught in the midst of an apparent sexual idyll, Neil looks forward to writing his next book, also inspired by Stendhal's work. He thinks that what he really wanted was to write tales that were like operas—gaudy, full of intensity, screaming emotions, high drama, sudden action, and troubled characters driven by primal human desires. That was the big stuff, as he thought of it. History itself wasn't the point.

It's a curiously self-reflective moment in the narrative; indeed, it's one of the few moments in Tessier's stories we encounter so direct a statement of aesthetic principal. Certainly, the intensity of situation and emotion Neil values describes his own story, up to this point. And although he has written a novel about Beatrice Cenci, he is not overly worried about history. Indeed, his sense of the region through which he has been driving is incomplete, vague.

It's worth noting here that the events operas treat are, to put it mildly, less than happy. (Again, recall Tessier's music column.) Even during his brief stay at the house, Neil experiences a couple of incidents which hint that all is not well here. The first happens immediately after his arrival. Neil sees a diminutive figure he takes for a child playing with a puppet. Upon closer inspection, she turns out to be an old woman, her puppet a child's desiccated remains. But he is distracted from this grotesque discovery by the appearance of Marisa Panic. Later, while wandering the house, he visits an alcove which he takes for the family chapel. Upon a low shelf within it, he discovers the form of a young man, his skin cold and blue, his pulse and breathing nonexistent. Spooked, he flees the space. For a second time, though, Marisa's arrival, and the steadily-increasing promise of sex with her, draws Neil's attention away from his disturbing find.

When Marisa takes him down into the house's cellar, Neil expects further erotic play. Nor is he disappointed, although the details of their lovemaking are somewhat more outré than before. Marisa requests they make love while each wearing one of a collection of wax masks she shows him. Paper-thin, the masks are strikingly accurate replicas of the faces of an assortment of men and woman. Neil is happy to oblige; in fact, the disguises seem to add intensity to the experience. Afterward, he falls asleep with the mask still tied to his head.

He awakens to a nightmare. The mask has fused with his face. A group of uniformed and armed men seize and beat him. No longer in the cellar, he is outside, in an unfamiliar location. His assailants hustle him to an open area in the midst of several large, barn-like buildings, where he sees more men in the same black uniforms as his attackers guarding a large group of men, women, and children. As he watches, the guards abuse their charges, murdering them with barbaric inventiveness. A few of the prisoners are provided the opportunity to perform what Neil thinks is an act of conversion to Catholicism and then they, too, are killed. Neil identifies Fr. Panic and Marisa among the guards, but neither knows him. He succeeds in fleeing from the slaughter into one of the surrounding buildings, but what he finds in them is just as bad, a continuation of the carnage. Eventually, he escapes into a nearby river, in which float the corpses of those he has seen butchered. He loses consciousness, and when he regains it is back at the Panic house, now revealed to be a ruin.

Although his ordeal is not yet over, we might pause here to consider this sequence of events. In a moment, Tessier has taken us from the profoundly erotic to the extravagantly violent, with the presence of Marisa in both contexts embodying the link between Eros and Thanatos we've encountered in Tessier's work previously. Although Neil is half-certain he has suffered a psychotic break, the vivid brutality of the situation into which he is plunged argues against it as anything but real. If he is not hallucinating, then some type of supernatural mechanism would appear to be at work here. Neil's confusion regarding the means by which he has arrived at this human abattoir is compounded by his inability to understand anything about the situation beyond its immediate violence. The reader may share his bewilderment, especially if they have not paid attention to the titles of the chapters detailing Neil's entry into this horror show: "By the River Sava" and "Stara Gradiska." It's with these that Tessier clues us in on where and when Neil has awakened. The River Sava forms the border between Croatia and Bosnia-Herzegovina; while Stara Gradiska was a notorious concentration camp constructed on the Stava's banks by the so-called Independent State of Croatia during the Second World War. Allied with the Nazis and Italian fascists, these Croats, self-christened Ustaše, followed the Nazis' lead in imprisoning, torturing, and murdering hundreds of thousands of undesirables, from Orthodox Christian Serbs, to Roma, to Jews. Part of a larger complex called the Jasenovac concentration camp, Stara Gradiska gained a reputation as the worst of the worst. On the night of August 29, 1942, the camp's guards engaged in a barbaric contest to see who could murder the most prisoners, and it seems likely that this is the night upon which Neil finds himself transported there.

It was a peculiarity of the Jasenovac camps, and of the actions of the Croatian fascists in general, that they placed a certain emphasis on the conversion of their opponents from Orthodox Christianity to Roman Catholicism. For the Ustaše, religious faith and national identity were inextricably linked. To force an enemy to abandon their faith in favor of Catholicism was defeat them ideologically as well as militarily. The extent of the Vatican's knowledge of these forced conversions remains a matter of some debate—though they maintained diplomatic relations with the Croatian fascists until almost the end of the Second World War—but there is no doubt local Catholic clergy knew, approved, and in some cases participated in the activities. It's not the only example of the church allying itself with repressive forces, but it may be the most damning, at least in the last century. Viewed in this context, Fr. Panic's interest in the history of conversions takes on a new, sinister aspect, as does his concern about Neil's portrayal of the pope in his novel about Beatrice Cenci. What matters for the priest is preserving the church and its authority. In the character of Fr. Panic, Tessier may well have in mind Miroslav Filipović, a Franciscan friar who became the chief guard at the Jasenovac camp, and who was nicknamed by the inmates "Brother Satan." Similarly, Marisa may be drawn from Nada Luburić, an infamous guard at Stara Gradiska, while the young dead man Neil sees in the chapel may be modeled on Maks Luburić, Nada's half-brother and the first commandant of Janesovac.

Neil will encounter that young man one more time, inside the Panic house, into which he staggers in search of Marisa and of answers to the ordeal he has undergone. This time, the young man does not remain in his alcove, and when Neil struggles against him, the young man draws strength from his touch. By now, it's apparent that Marisa and her family are some form of supernatural creature, likely vampires, and that their house and its surrounds are a kind of pocket hell over which they reign. In this place, there is no hope, there is only il morbo, the fog that is disease, that descends without warning. Here at the narrative's crushing end, the fog appears a trope for the savagery that has enveloped different portions of Europe throughout its history, and that has all too often been aided and abetted by members of one of its oldest institutions. (It seems relevant to note that Tessier published the narrative in 2000, when the most recent wars in the Balkans, with their attendant atrocities, were fresh in the collective memory.)

A novel, Kafka famously wrote, should be an ax to break the frozen sea within us. "Father Panic's Opera Macabre" is such an implement; indeed, its final image lands with the force of a physical blow. There's an unrelenting irony at work in the story, starting with the title. "Opera Macabre" sounds as if it's describing one of the grimmer operas, yet at root it translates as "death work." It's an accurate way to characterize the slaughter the priest oversees during the scene at Stara Gradiska, the nature of his interest in religious conversion, his every existence. In similar fashion, Neil looks to opera for his aesthetic model without considering the horror finding oneself in such an environment would entail. A novelist whose most successful production has been a historical novel, he remains largely ignorant of history. In particular, he knows perilously little of the role organized religion has played in the perpetration of Europe's greatest atrocities. His desire to be with Marisa blinds him to the hints that all is not well in the house, until, at the narrative's conclusion, his wish is granted in a horrifying fashion. And depending on the extent of the reader's ignorance of the history on which Tessier is drawing, the story's irony may catch us in its coils, too.

There's still more that might be said about "Father Panic's Opera Macabre," as there is about "The Dreams of Dr. Ladybank" and "Nocturne," and there is about the stories I have not had the time to address: "Food" and "Blanca" and "Ghost Music" and "Lulu" and—

But this is why *World of Hurt* is in your hands.

Writing this introduction, I've been reminded all over again of just how fine a writer Thomas Tessier is, of his ambition and his skill, each of which complements the other. It's hard to find many interviews with him; by and large, he has preferred to let his work speak for itself. Based on what is collected here, the voice of his stories is precise, elegant, and incisive. It's frequently lyrical, occasionally funny, and often deeply disturbing. It's capable of shuttling from terrors psychological to those supernatural, from the familiar to the foreign. It's the voice of an American master of the horror story short and long, and I'm honored to introduce this selection of his work to you.

John Langan

IN THE DESERT OF DESERTS

Drive at night, somebody told me in Laghouat, and at first I did. But that advice was only good as long as I knew where the road was. The road was quite fair over some stretches, but then it would peter out, fading into the surrounding terrain, becoming invisible until it reappeared a mile or two farther on. That was all right too, if I didn't stray dangerously. A sensitive driver can tell where the road ought to be even when it isn't.

But I found it maddeningly difficult to follow the trail at night. My vision was restricted to the range of the headlights, and I had no useful sense of the landscape. At one point on my first night out I was driving along cautiously when the powerful beams of an oil supply truck lanced the darkness. The truck went by, nearly a mile away from me. *That* was where the road was, I realized unhappily. A trucker could make the desert run at night because he'd done it so many times he knew the way instinctively, but it was impossible for a first-timer to travel like that. I decided to travel the rest of the way by daylight.

Besides, there was more to the challenge than just making it all the way to Niamey. I wanted to experience the Sahara at its most difficult, as well as to enjoy it at its beautiful best. It would be a shame to drive through the desert mostly at night, and come away like some empty-handed thief.

I spent much of the second day in Ghardaia, where I topped up the water and petrol tanks. I gave the Range Rover a careful examination, and was satisfied. I checked the spare parts list, but I already had everything on it. I had done these same things the day before, at Laghouat, only a hundred miles away. But this was my last chance to correct any problems or pick up something I might need. Ghardaia has supplies, equipment, skilled mechanics and even cold soda. The oil pipeline runs nearby. It's a fairly busy town, considering the fact that it's located out on the edge of the edge.

I don't distrust people but I slept with one eye on my Rover and its load of supplies. I was up before dawn, feeling as eager as I was nervous, and I left Ghardaia when the first infiltration of gray light began to erode the blackness. Now the crossing was truly underway.

I was traveling south through the Great Western Erg, and my next stop was In Salah, more than three hundred miles away. This would be the easy part of my journey, I reckoned. The desert was immediately fierce and formidable, but I knew there was an oasis at El Golea and some kind of a military outpost at Fort Miribel, both of which were on my route.

South of In Salah the terrain would become much rougher, the climate even more hellish, and although in theory there were more villages in that part of the country I knew that they would prove to be fly-speck settlements that offered little. I had been told that in the Sahara what you think you see on a map is usually not what you find on the ground. I had no fear of dying of thirst or starvation, nor even of heat, but I did worry about a mechanical breakdown that could strand me indefinitely in some heat-blasted cluster of huts on the far side of nowhere.

At first I made relatively good time, but by midday the road deteriorated predictably and I had to drive more slowly. After a break for lunch I proceeded, and soon got stuck. The sand in the Sahara can be deceptive and treacherous. One moment it may be as firm and hard-packed as an old gravel road, and then it will turn into something like dry water, all but impossible to stand in or move through. My right rear tire slid into just such a hole, and it took me nearly two hours to extricate myself with the help of aluminum tracks.

Even so, I felt reasonably pleased by the time I decided to stop for the night because I had experienced no major trouble and nothing unexpected had come up. I picked a place where the road was clearly visible, then pulled off about a quarter of a mile to set up camp.

That last night of peace I fancy I absorbed something of the remorseless clarity of the Sahara. This is a world composed of a few simple elements—sand, air, the disappearing sky, then the blue, red, yellow and white stars—but each one of them is huge in its singularity. They are so vivid and immediate that after a while they begin to seem unreal to the human observer, like stage props for a drama that never happens and involves no one. In the Sahara, it is said, God talks to himself. I had not come to the desert looking for any mystical fix or tourist inspiration, but I did find something like joy in the loneliness and insignificance it constantly threw in my face.

I ate, cleaned up, drank a single neat scotch and then slept well. It was chilly, but I had of course expected that and was warmly wrapped, and if there was any night wind it didn't disturb me at all.

Before dawn, as I prepared to leave, I found the footprints. I knew at once that they were not mine.

I almost laughed. I felt a bit like Robinson Crusoe, shocked, amused, fascinated. After the initial wave of reaction passed, I began to feel uncomfortable. Crusoe had a pretty good idea of what he was up against, but the footprints I'd discovered made no apparent sense. For one thing, they shouldn't have been there at all.

They formed a counter-clockwise trail, roughly in the shape of a circle, around my little camp. They looked like the tracks of a solitary adult male wearing ordinary shoes and walking at an ordinary pace. The footprints stopped twice, overlapping tightly before continuing, as if at those two points the unknown visitor had paused to stare and think for a moment. It was disturbing to know that he could only have been looking at me as I slept just a few yards away, inside the circle.

I calmed down after a few minutes. The headlights of an oil company truck passing by on the road must have caught part of the Rover in the darkness, and the driver stopped to investigate. It was so obvious, I felt silly. The fact that I could see no trail to or from the circle was strange, but a breeze could have hidden them or perhaps the driver had walked a particularly hard-packed stretch of ground that would show no footprints.

Once I was on the road again I thought no more about it. My progress was slow because the wind started up and the road became more difficult to follow. It was a long day, hot and demanding, but late in the afternoon the conditions changed abruptly, as so often happens in the Sahara. The wind died away and at the same time I hit a good section of the road. I covered more ground in the last four hours than I had in the previous eight.

This time I camped a little farther from the road, beyond a ridge, where no headlights could spot me. I didn't like the idea of anyone sneaking up on me in the middle of the night, out there in the depths of the desert. My vehicle and equipment were worth a small fortune, and the next person might not think twice about bashing my head in and hiding them. He could always return later with a partner to collect the goods. The chances of anybody else finding my remains would be virtually nonexistent.

I felt so secure that I was not at all prepared to come upon anything unusual the next morning, but I did. The same unmarked heels and soles, coming from nowhere, going nowhere, but circling my ground, stopping once or twice.

I was shaken. I didn't want to be there anymore, and yet I sat down. It was as if I could not bring myself to leave. I had to reason my way out of this threatening situation. Whoever had left those tracks couldn't have followed me on foot because I had come too many miles yesterday. He could have followed me by car, or truck, or even on a camel, but surely I would have seen him at some point, and if he stayed too far back he couldn't be certain of finding the point where I left the road for the night.

Besides, why would anyone bother to shadow me like this? To approach me in the darkness, but then do nothing? If he intended to attack me he could have done so twice by now. The whole thing made no sense at all. It was precisely the fact that nothing had happened that worried me most. It seemed somehow more menacing, as if I were being monitored.

Could it be a Bedouin, a nomadic Arab? It seemed unlikely. I'd been told that they travel in clans and that they seldom come through this part of North Africa. There's nothing for them here and it isn't on any of their usual routes. Besides, I doubt that the Bedouins wear ordinary Western-style shoes.

I put my hand to the ground and touched one footprint. Yes, it was real. I was not hallucinating. I traced the indentation in the sand. He had big feet, like me. I placed my right foot next to one of the footprints. Nearly a perfect match. However, my high-top camping shoes had corrugated soles, and no heels.

It was theoretically possible that I had made the footprints in the middle of the night, because I did have a pair of ordinary shoes packed away in the Rover, but I simply couldn't believe it. I had absolutely no recollection of taking them out, putting them on, walking the circles, obscuring my tracks back to the van, and then packing the shoes away again. Not the slightest glimmer of any such memory. If it was my doing, asleep or awake, I was well on the way to losing my mind.

But isn't that what the desert is supposed to do to a person who wanders through it alone? Madness creeping in, like the sand in your socks. I told myself it wasn't possible, at least not in the first three days out of Laghouat. All that desert mythology was nothing more than a load of romantic rubbish.

Nonetheless, I decided to push on all the way until I got to In Salah. I stopped only to eat and drink, and to let the engine cool down a little. I got stuck a couple of times but never lost the road, and I made pretty good time. The changes in the Sahara were largely lost on me, however. When my eyes weren't fixed on the road ahead they were glancing up at the rearview mirror. But I never saw another vehicle or person.

When I reached In Salah I was so exhausted that I slept for eleven hours. I spent another day working on the Rover, stocking up on supplies, and enjoying the break in my journey. I even had a stroll around the town, what there is of it.

And I decided to change my plans. Instead of heading south, through the moderately populated mountains of the Ahaggar, as I'd originally intended, I would now turn west to Zaouiet Reggane and then drive south through the Tanezrouft all the way to Mali, and from Bourem I would follow the course of the Niger River on into Niamey. The net effect would be to shorten my journey and make it less scenic but also perhaps more challenging. The Tanezrouft is vast, empty and closer to sea level, therefore hotter than the Ahaggar. The oil trucks don't run in that part of Algeria. Some people believe that the Tanezrouft is the worst part of the whole Sahara Desert.

So why do it? I don't know. I must have been thinking that no one would dare follow me across the Tanezrouft. Before I left In Salah I bought a gun, an ugly Czech pistol. I don't know if I was indulging my own crazy delusions, or pursuing them.

These actions and decisions of mine had an irrelevance that I could not completely ignore. It was as if I sensed that I was merely distracting myself with them, and that they didn't really matter. If the man was real, he'd be there. And if he was other than real, well, he might be there anyway.

One hundred miles south of Zaouiet Reggane, I awoke. I went out about fifty feet, looking for the footprints. Nothing. So I went a little farther, but again found nothing, no sign, no mark, that didn't belong to that place. I broke into a trot, circling my camp site, scouring the ground as I went. Still nothing of an unusual nature.

I ran right past it, then stopped sharply, one foot skidding out from under me as I turned back. Even then I didn't see it, I smelled it. And, as the saying goes, I thought I saw a ghost. A pencil-line of blue fluttering in the air. It was smoke. In the sand were two footprints, just two, not my own. The same shoes. The heel marks were so close they almost touched each other, but the toes were apart, forming a V on the ground. It was as if the man had squatted on his haunches there, staring at me while I was sleeping. Nearby, a discarded cigarette. It was still burning, almost to the filter now, and it had an inch-long trail of intact ash. I don't smoke.

I touched the smoldering tip just to convince myself that it was real, and it was. I jumped up and looked around, but there was no one in sight for half a mile in any direction. I'd chosen a natural basin, so there was nowhere to hide and even if someone was lying flat and trying to insinuate himself into the sand he'd still be easily seen. There was no one. No tracks. Just me and those two footprints, and the cigarette.

I picked it up and examined it carefully. Any trademark had

already burned away, but there was enough left for me to see that the cigarette had the slightly flattened, oval shape that is more common to the Middle East than Europe or America. But that told me nothing. I wish it had lipstick on it.

I say that, but I drove scared, and the farther I went the more frightened I became. There was nowhere on the entire planet I could feel safe, because I could drive until I passed out and I would still be in the middle of the Sahara. When I reached Bidon 5, a desperate little waterhole, I sat off by myself and let the engine cool for three hours. They thought I was another of those wandering Englishmen who go to the most awful places in the world and then write articles about it for *The Sunday Times*.

I considered driving on, but common sense finally prevailed and I stayed the night. I must have been even more tired than I thought, for I slept late into the morning and no one bothered to wake me. Early starts are like a matter of religion to me, but I felt so much better, refreshed, that I wasn't annoyed. Besides, I had plenty of time. The change of route gave me an extra three or four days.

I was also encouraged by the fact that I was approaching the southern limits of the Sahara. Another three hundred miles, and I would be rolling through the grassy plains of Mali. When I got to Bourem I might even take a side trip and visit the fabled city of Timbuktu, a center of Islamic teaching in the 15th century. I have heard that Timbuktu is just a dull and decayed backwater of a place nowadays, but I was tempted to take a look. How could I come to within a hundred miles or so of what was once regarded as the remotest spot on earth, and pass it by?

But I still had the last of the Sahara to deal with, and the road soon disappeared. My progress was slow, I got stuck and had to dig my way out several times, and the heat was devastating. I pushed on, regarding the desert now as nothing but an obstacle to be overcome as quickly as possible. Mileage is deceptive because the road, when you haven't strayed from it, meanders this way and that in its endless pursuit of firm ground, and one hundred miles on the map is usually a hundred and twenty-five or thirty on the clock. I think I reached the border, or even crossed it, when I had to stop for the night. Another day, a day and a half, two at most, and I would leave the Sahara behind me.

This time I parked only a few yards off the road. There was no traffic at all this far south so I had nothing to fear in that respect, and the sand was too treacherous to risk venturing into any farther than necessary. I checked the air pressure in all of the tires, checked my gun, had a glass of scotch, and got into my sleeping bag.

It was still quite dark when I awoke. Just like in a film, my eyes opened but the rest of my body didn't move. I was lying on my side, and I knew immediately that I was not alone. My mind wasn't working yet, I was still in a fog, and at first I thought I saw a single red eye staring at me from some distance away. It was the glowing tip of a cigarette, I realized dimly. I couldn't make out anything of the person who held it. I was overcome by a wave of choking fear that seemed to be strangling me from within. A dozen hungry lions circling closer wouldn't have frightened me as much as that burning cigarette did.

I had the gun in my hand, my elbow dug into the sand. I was still lying there in my sleeping bag, and I forced my drowsy eyes to focus on the tiny red speck of fire. A moment later it traced a gentle arc, came to a stop, and then brightened sharply. As he inhaled, I squeezed the trigger. The explosion seemed distant, a curiously muffled noise that might have come from another part of the desert. I shut my eyes, having no idea what had taken place, and I fell back into sleep.

The brightness woke me later. I didn't believe anything had actually happened during the night because my memory was blurred, dream-like, unreal. The gun was where I had put it when I got in the sleeping bag last night, between carefully folded layers of a towel on the ground nearby. If I had fired it at some point in the night, surely I wouldn't have put it back so neatly.

But when I sat up and looked around, I saw the body. I felt calm, yet desolate. He was about twenty yards away. I got to my feet and walked slowly toward him. My shot had been true, like a sniper in one of the old European wars. The slug had smashed his face into a bowl of bloody mush.

His hair was black and curly, his skin olive-colored, and he wore a plain white short-sleeved shirt, faded khaki slacks, and a pair of ordinary shoes. A man so dressed, on foot, wouldn't last more than a few hours in the desert. His presence there was such a vast affront to sanity and nature that I felt a flash of anger. It gave way, a moment later, to cold helplessness.

I found a few loose cigarettes and a box of matches in his shirt pocket, but he carried nothing else on his person. I don't smoke, but I took them. I checked inside the shirt collar but it had no label or markings.

It seemed to me that I would never know who this man was, or how he came to be in the desert with me, what he wanted, or why I had been compelled to kill him, so I got my shovel and buried him on the spot. Dead bodies are supposed to be heavy and cumbersome but he felt as light as a bundle of sticks.

Somewhere along the way in Mali I gave up thinking about it. There was nothing to do, there were no answers to be discerned in the lingering confusion of fact and fear. Guilt? No. I've seen enough of the world to know how superfluous human life really is. I drove, losing myself once again to the rigors and pleasures of simple movement.

Bourem offered little, Timbuktu less. I looked at the dust, the mud, the crumbling and overgrown buildings that seemed to be receding into prehistory before my eyes, and I left. In Niamey I relaxed, celebrated and got laid. I made my way eventually down to the beaches at Accra. I ate with Swedish and German tourists who fretted about the unofficial fact that ninety percent of West African whores are HIV-positive.

That didn't bother me. I drank bottled French water with my scotch, but I also busied myself with the women. Day after day, night after night. There's not much else to do, except drink and lie about. Besides, there are moments in your life when you just know you're meant to live.

"Why?"

Ulf was a well-meaning, earnest and somewhat obsessive Swede who had developed a spurious concern for my reckless behavior. I shrugged absently at his question. He wanted an answer but I did not care to mislead him.

"Regardless."

Ulf had money and nothing to do, nowhere to go, like me, and so we drove to Abidjan, then Freetown, finally Banjul. I enjoyed his company, but by the time we were in the Gambia the charm wore thin and I was eager to be alone again. Still, I agreed that Ulf could tag along as far as Dakar. He was still with me days after that, as I approached Tindouf far to the north.

"I'm heading east," I told him.

"But it's just a short run to Marrakesh now." Ulf was quite disturbed. He consulted the map. "There's nothing to the east, only the Sahara. No road. Nothing."

"There's always a road."

Ulf hired someone to drive him to Marrakesh. I stayed on in Tindouf for a couple of days, working on the Rover and restocking my supplies. I was serious about driving east. True, there was no road, but I believed I could make it anyway. I had it in mind to reach Zaouiet Reggane, four hundred miles away, and then take the road south until I found my campsite near the border. It was the last arc in a big circle.

Why indeed? At times I was crazy with disbelief. I thought I had to return to the spot and dig up the dead man, just to make sure that he was real. The missing bullet in my gun was not good enough, nor were the stale cigarettes I still carried with me. I had to see the body again. In some strange and unfathomable way, the rest of my life seemed to depend on it.

But there were moments of clarity too. I was caught up in a senseless odyssey. I could ramble around Africa until I died, of old age or stupidity. I argued with myself, dawdled, hung on for days in the soporific dullness of Tindouf. I dreamed of the dead man's hands reaching up out of the sand to strangle me, like some corny turn in a horror movie. I dreamed that the grave was still there, and I found it, but it was empty. Most of all, I imagined that I would never locate the place again, that I would just burn and blister myself to a blackish lump as I dug pointless holes in the desert.

I did, after all, drive east. A few miles from the village, the ground became tricky. I pushed on, often swerving one way or another on an immediate impulse. Progress was slow. Late in the afternoon, I had a sense that I would never make it anywhere near Zaouiet Reggane. Then all four tires sank into a trough of very fine sand. I got out. The Rover was in it up to the axles, with no chance at all that I could extricate it by myself. I reckoned I was between twenty and twenty-five miles east of Tindouf, which was a long one-day walk. I prepared to spend the night there. I would set off early and reach the village by nightfall. I would return the day after, with helpers, and we would haul my vehicle onto solid ground. They would laugh, I would pay, and later I'd drive to Marrakesh, perhaps catch up with Ulf, and that would be the end of it.

I woke up in the middle of the night. Unable to get back to sleep, I pulled on my jacket and walked into the chilly darkness. I didn't go far. When the dim outline of the Rover began to fade in my vision I stopped. This is what he saw, I realized.

I was still fogged with sleepiness. I sat on my haunches, with my heels together and toes apart. It's often rather bright in the Sahara at night, when the stars form a brilliant skyscape, but some high thin clouds now cast everything in shades of black. The Rover was an inky lump against the charcoal expanse of sand. This is what he saw.

Without thinking, I took one of his crumpled cigarettes from my jacket and lit it. I didn't inhale, but puffed at it, and the glowing red tip only seemed to emphasize the surrounding blackness. I imagined a shape stirring out there, mysterious and unknowable, secure in the anonymity of the night. I imagined it noticing me behind my tiny pinpoint of fire, fixing on me. As if I were the only stain on all that emptiness. And then I thought that maybe I had been wrong from the beginning.

It was like looking deeply into your own eyes, and finding nothing there.

THE VACANT LOT

1

A certain sense of unease begins to infiltrate your thoughts and feelings when you see something that is not quite right. George Prior had endured some unfortunate setbacks in the last few months that resulted in his relocating to a small third-floor apartment on the top floor of a beat-up old triple-decker in a run-down old neighborhood of the city, a place where the valley wall rose up steeply and you could catch a glimpse of the highway and river in the distance below.

There was the little matter of his wife, Laurie, who left him, or to be more precise, threw him out of the house, after twenty-odd years of quiet discontent on both sides. She had him on certain uncomfortable points—like the time she was getting in his face and he shoved her back once or twice, and she tripped over something on the floor and fell and broke her wrist. She called the cops and he spent a night in jail. They made peace of a sort and she dropped charges, but it was there, on the record. She also knew about a few of the not quite so legal things he'd dabbled in now and then, so it was not worth his time and money to fight things out in court. Cut your losses, leave. It was not a happy matter to have to swallow that, but he did.

George knew some people around town, including Jeannie Blake, who owned a number of rental properties. He had done a little work for her from time to time, helping to encourage certain difficult tenants to vacate the premises. It was thanks to Jeannie that he landed in this barely furnished apartment. The stairs to the third floor were a drag, but he could handle it. Like so much else in his past, this was meant to be a temporary situation, another way-station on the road to something better. Best of all, it was cheap, and that mattered in his current circumstances.

George was between jobs, or anything that could be construed as regular work that you went to most days of the week. He had skills—roofing, sheet-rocking, putting in windows and doors. On and on, stuff like that. He still had his tools, he just had less and less chance to use them lately. He was in mid-50s now and at that age you can't compete for long with the young guys. You can be a lot smarter than them, but they learn fast and you will fall away as your body starts to let you down.

Next to the house George lived in was a vacant lot, at the top of Fifth Street. He had a clear view of it while he sat at the kitchen table. He would sit there in the morning, drinking coffee, listening to sports talk on the radio and watching the traffic going by on Congress Avenue, his eyes scanning back regularly to the vacant lot.

There was a cheap stockade-style wooden fence around the perimeter. It tilted and sagged in places but appeared to be unbroken. Much of the lot was filled with tall field grass, overgrown weeds and thickets of stunted wild shrubs. There was a dwarf ornamental tree, of some unknown variety, that appeared to be near death, riddled with suckers and engulfed in choke cherry vines. There was garbage, mostly litter—fast food bags and pizza boxes that had been tossed over the fence.

And there was a hole, or rather in remains of a hole, since it had filled in quite a bit in the course of years with dirt, dust, soot, autumn leaves and other natural debris. A few cemented stones were visible poking up in various spots and marked the lines of the cellar and the foundation of a building that was long gone. A sprawling cluster of what appeared to be rusted cables extended out of one corner of the hole.

It was an ugly, wild mess of a lot, an empty remnant of a vanished home, and it didn't seem the least bit out of place in the neighborhood now.

2

One Friday morning when Jeannie came around the collect the weekly rent and chat for a few minutes as usual, George asked her if she knew anything about the vacant lot next door. Looking out at it every day, he had grown curious as to why it was there, neglected, undeveloped. Turned out, she knew the property well and had considered buying it at one time. Standing by the kitchen window, looking down at the vacant lot, Jeannie told him this story.

There had been a small single family home on the site, built in the 1920s by the Mikaitis family, Lithuanian immigrant parents and their children. The father and three sons all worked in the brass and copper mills in town. There were also two daughters, and by 1990, give or take a couple of years, they were the only surviving members of the family. They still lived in the family home, never married, never left it. They had worked in the factories too and in their later years apparently survived on Social Security and whatever family money might have had been left to them.

Sometime, ten to fifteen years ago, one of the sisters died in a fall down the stairs to the deep basement. That is, she fell, or was pushed or thrown—this possibility arising from the fact that people in the neighborhood reportedly had often seen the two women arguing on the street or in the yard or in voices from the house at night, on quiet summer nights when the windows are open and sound carries, voices in the dark. But the result of the brief investigation was a ruling of accidental death.

A few months later, there was a fire in the middle of a night. The last Mikaitis sister died in her sleep, in her bed upstairs, of smoke asphyxiation. Much of the house was destroyed in the fire and what was left had to be torn down, as it posed a danger to anyone living next door or passing by on the street. It was determined that the fire was caused by faulty old electrical wiring that dated back to around 1930.

There were no heirs and there were unpaid taxes, so the lot eventually became the property of the city. Over the years there were attempts to sell it, and at one point Jeannie looked into the possibility of buying it, but the city couldn't move it. From a potential buyer's point of view, it was a small lot and the cost of building a new duplex or even, at most, a triple-decker, would not be justified by what you could get for it either in terms of rent or resale, give the prevailing property values in that neighborhood.

After listening to this, George said, "My guess would be that she threw her sister down the stairs. It didn't happen by accident and it wasn't just a push."

"Why would you say that?"

George shrugged. "Just guessing. An old eastern European family. Grudges run long and run deep."

"A grudge over what?"

"Who knows? But sometimes, the smaller it is, the bigger it gets."

3

George had moved into the apartment in March. Over the following months, as spring wound its way toward summer, he noticed the curious absence of animal life in the vacant lot. Never once saw a squirrel foraging there. There very plenty of feral cats in the neighborhood, but he never saw a single cat prowling for mice in the lot. And it was an everyday occurrence for him to see a flock of sparrows perched on the telephone pole and wires on the other side of the street. Sometimes two or three big crows would scatter the sparrows and take their place for a couple of minutes. But George never saw any birds fly in and land in the lot—not on the ground, not in the tree branches nor on any of the larger bushes. Not even on the fence posts.

4

There was one time, however, when George saw something move in the vacant lot. Or, he thought he did. It was nothing so simple as plants or branches waving in the breeze. It was the large cluster of what looked like rusted old BX cable that sprawled up out of the cellar and over some of the remaining foundation stones. He had wondered about it. Did BX cable even exist back at the time the house had been built, or had they used some other form of armored wiring? There seemed to be too much of it for one small house, but perhaps he was wrong about that. And how had it all ended there in one very large clump? Had it simply happened to tumble down that way in the fire? And it all somehow had survived there after the rest of the building had been demolished and removed?

Whatever the explanation might be, the cables were still there now, and one lunch-time George glanced down at them as he was eating a sandwich. And they moved. The cables moved. That is, the entire mass of them suddenly heaved upward a couple of inches—not much, but distinctly. Then it settled right back down as it had been.

George had no doubt that he had seen this—perceptible movements up and then down again. Until a minute or two later, when he began to wonder if his mind somehow had fooled itself into imagining the incident. At the time, there couldn't have been more than a light breeze in the air, and you would think it would take hurricane force winds to shift those heavy cables.

And then there was the distance to consider. He was looking down from a third floor window next door. Could he really be sure had had seen a movement as small as just a few inches? Yes, he thought he could. His eyesight was still pretty good, better at distances than close up. He replayed the moment in his mind several more times, and each time it was the same: the cables moved.

5

Things did not get much better for George over the course of the summer. It would normally be his best work season, but nothing had been normal for a while now. The economy stunk, building work was down all over. He managed to pick up a few short jobs—a few days here, a few days there. But nothing substantial. Just to have something to do and fill in some of the empty time, he began to make some weekly pickup runs for an old acquaintance, Ralph Fortunato. These were money collections from various business interests Ralph had, some of which were even legitimate. It was not work that George actually liked, but it brought in some extra money. Though, in fact, there was no such thing as extra money in his life now.

One day early in September—in a week in which he had nothing lined up, not even a pickup for Ralph, who was out of town on a short trip somewhere—George was at his kitchen table, sipping coffee and gazing idly at the vacant lot. It occurred to him that he had never seen the fourth side of the stockade fence that enclosed the lot. It wasn't visible from his window, blocked off by tall bushes at the back end.

It was something to do, if only to kill a few minutes in a day that looked long on television and little else. George pulled on his work boots, went downstairs and out into the side yard. One side of the fence bordered the house he lived in, the front was out on Congress Avenue, and the third side was right up against the sidewalk on Fifth Street. He crossed the yard and came to the fence, then followed it down the slope to the corner. He stepped around to look at the fourth side of the fence. It was smack up against a long row of tall, raggedy old hemlocks. George found it easy enough to brush the shrub branches back and make his way along the fence.

He came across a faded, partially torn notice that had been pasted to the wood a long time ago but still survived: CITY PROPERTY, it said, NO TRESPASSING.

Just a couple of feet away, several of the fence staves had been prised loose and torn away, creating an opening just wide enough to slip through. George smiled. Kids, no doubt, teenagers who wanted to get into the lot and make their own secret little place where they could drink beer, smoke weed and do whatever else they did without being seen or bothered by anyone.

George hadn't expected this, but he immediately edged his body through the opening, pushed through a thicket of tall bushes and weeds and almost fell forward into a more open area where the field grass only came up to his knees. Now he could see the house he lived in next door, and the kitchen window of his apartment. Alright, he had his bearings.

He waded through the tall grass, heading back up the slope of the hill. He almost fell again when his foot hit something hard and unyielding, but he caught himself. It was one of the foundation stones of the house. Using it as a marker, he made his way forward a few more yards, tapping the side of his boot against hidden stones as he went.

Then the grass thinned out—he had reached the spot where the enormous tangle of rusted cables sprang up out of the old cellar. Only—they weren't BX cables, or any kind of electrical wiring. They were briars or brambles of some kind, inch-thick vines studded with thorns.

Now George could see part of the cellar wall, exposed down a couple of feet. No doubt that cellar had been largely filled with a lot of ash and debris from the fire, but also with years of falling leaves and other organic matter. At some point, the briar vines had taken root there, and thrived.

George walked around to get a better look at them. He glanced back up over his shoulder, and the sky had gone gray and featureless. He looked toward his apartment but it was not to be seen, as if blocked by some unmoving mist in the air. He looked to the other side, toward Fifth Street, but the telephone pole and wires were not visible, nor was the triple-decker that was located on that corner. George blinked his eyes, wondering if he was having some kind of unfortunate medical moment. But when he looked again at the briars and the tall grass and the rest of the lot surrounding him, it all seemed clear and normal.

Then he heard something behind him, close by. George turned around and saw a woman coming right at him. The sight of this woman startled and froze him. A woman who looked kind of like Laurie, but older, or maybe not Laurie at all but someone else, a woman he may have known at some time ago or never known at all. Her hands were at her sides but she ran right into him like one car banging into another. The expression on her face was featureless, her eyes wide open but vacant.

George felt her body hit him and he stumbled back as she wheeled away out of his vision. His foot hit a foundation stone and he fell into the briars. The force and direction of his fall caused him to roll over on his side, then face down. He could feel the thorns cutting through his clothing, into his flesh, as the vines were wrapped onto his arms and legs and around his head. In some abstract way, he began to notice wetness on his body in various places—blood? Yes, his own.

He yelled, but he was yelling downward, into the cellar. He turned his head back up, to shout out toward the street for someone to come and help him. But as soon as he opened his mouth, he bit into a thick vine that cut across his face, thorns piercing his lips and tongue. He tried to twist away, but that only drove him deeper down, into another cane of the briars, and then a thorn slicing into one of his eyes.

6

The following Friday, Jeannie Blake showed up at the usual time to collect her weekly rent payment from George. He didn't answer the door. A bit odd, because they had known each other for years and he was very reliable, he would call her if something had come up and he couldn't be there. Just to make sure nothing had happened to him, she pulled out her keys and opened the door to his apartment.

Inside, everything seemed to be in order. George kept the place neat and tidy, unlike many of her other tenants. She checked all the rooms, nothing, no George, and that was a bit of a relief. It was a drag when a tenant died on your property, especially if you kind of liked the person.

She stopped by the kitchen window and glanced down at the vacant lot next door. She had seen it countless times over the years and it always looked the same. But now something seemed out of place. She wasn't sure what, so she scanned the area again a couple of times, and then she saw it. In the big brown tangle, something sticking up in the air, as if on a stick. Or a foot. She couldn't be sure at this distance, but it kind of looked like a work boot.

EVELYN GRACE

So Evelyn Grace was dead from a drug overdose at the age of thirty eight. Her body was found on the floor of the studio flat in east Los Angeles where she had been living for the last seven months. She had been a model, an actress, a singer, and she was unemployed at the time of her death.

Evelyn Grace. Dead. An accident, or so the coroner had ruled. But it was not impossible to imagine that Evvy had known exactly what she was doing with her last needle. Or that she had been murdered for some bizarre California-type reason. In fact, it was easy to imagine all sorts of things about Evvy. She had always been the kind of girl who made a guy's blood run away with his mind.

Tim LeClerc refolded his newspaper and set it aside. He lit a cigarette. He knew her, but they had never met. He and Evelyn Grace had been in the same graduating class at high school, back in the late sixties. They had been in different groups, however, and they didn't live in the same neighborhood, so for four years they passed each other in the corridors at school but their paths never really crossed. Tim had been aware of her, it was hard not to be, but she had probably never even known that he existed. In a class of nearly two hundred there were bound to be quite a few strangers, even after all that time.

Bitter early March, the land still frozen, locked up beneath steel clouds and day-old snow that was already tarnished with the grime of Utica. The wind hit Tim's face like cold fire as he ran from the diner to his car. It was then, while he sat huddled and shivering, waiting for the engine to idle down and the heater to generate some feeble warmth, that the idea came to him. He would go to Evvy's wake.

Why not? He was curious to see her again, even if she was dead, or maybe *because* she was dead, and that was morbid. But on the other hand her parents would appreciate the gesture. You can never have too many visitors at a wake. It was only about twenty miles away, in Rome. Besides, he had no one to rush home to, nor anything better to do with his evening.

That was how far he'd gotten, Tim thought. Twenty-odd miles in twenty-odd years. Never mind. He'd seen enough of the world when he was in the army to realize that upstate New York was the place for him. He came back alive and whole, and settled into a modest but clean apartment on the eastern edge of Utica. After a few false starts he had landed a decent job at the bottling plant and had been there ever since. Nothing to crow about, but it was a life and it did have its occasional moments, although Tim would be hard-pressed to enumerate many of them. When he wanted female company he could always find it. Somebody's neglected wife, or a divorcee on the wrong side of thirty, or any of the women at work who were still single because they were overweight or ugly or too crushingly dull to snag a mate. Nothing romantic, but the years had given Tim a rather functional attitude to sex.

His was just an ordinary life, but he never regretted it or felt sorry for himself. He liked it the way it was, uncluttered and straightforward, low-key but comfortable. At least he would never be shipped home in a steel box in the cargo hold of a jet plane while strangers drank cocktails overhead. Funny, how he'd been to Vietnam and escaped that fate, while Evelyn went to L.A. and hadn't. Poor Evvy.

Tim polished his dress shoes. He put on his best shirt and tie, and his only suit. He had second thoughts while driving to the wake, but promptly dismissed them. If he felt awkward when he got there he would just take a quick look at her, mumble some words to the parents and then leave. That's what he'd probably do anyway, no sense in sitting around once his juvenile curiosity had been satisfied.

But what actually happened was shockingly pathetic. Mr.

and Mrs. Grace were the only people there when Tim arrived. He felt very odd indeed as he crossed the room and knelt down at the open casket. For a few moments he was occupied with Evvy. She looked lovely still, her face virtually unmarked by the years and events of her life. The mortician had done a good job, applying no more make-up than was absolutely necessary. Even now she retained her girlish good looks, the ghostly afterimage of a beauty you never forget once you've encountered it.

Tim was touched by her haunting appearance, saddened by the fact that her life had plummeted to this abrupt end, and he found himself wishing that he *had* met her when they were in high school together. How different everything might be now—for the both of them—if they had. It was an idle fantasy, of course, but Tim believed there was a kernel of truth in it. Don't all lives have at least one turning point that's fluky, or accidental, or capricious? Too bad, too bad...

At last he stood up and turned to Evvy's parents. Leonard Grace was small and wiry, with a scattering of white fuzz about his largely bare scalp. His manner was bright and alert, though he nodded his head too often, as if to emphasize his agreeable and understanding nature. Charlotte Grace was plump, with a moon face and a distracted air. It took Tim a few minutes to notice that now and then she would fade right out of the conversation, like a distant radio signal drifting in the ether. She had run the family for as long as it had existed, was Tim's guess, but now she was probably an Alzheimer's case.

Tim explained that he had been to high school with Evelyn, and her parents were very grateful to him for taking the time to come to the wake. He didn't actually say that he'd been a friend of their daughter, but they somehow got that idea and he saw no need to clarify the matter. It was such a sad situation, two old people, one of them not quite all there, alone with the dead body of their only child.

And hardly anyone came. The calling hours were from seven to nine, and in that time perhaps half a dozen people appeared to pay their respects. They were older folks, acquaintances of the parents, and none of them stayed more than ten minutes.

It was amazing, shocking, to Tim, who had expected a rather

large turnout. A lot of people would have moved away over the years, but there still had to be plenty of former friends and classmates of Evelyn's left in Rome, so where were they? It was as if nobody wanted to admit knowing her. But why? Just because she'd been something of a bad girl, running off to California, living a wild, silly, rotten life? Because she'd met her squalid death at an age when she should have been organizing bake sales and ferrying kids to Little League games? *I see Evelyn Grace is dead. Tsk, tsk, tsk. Well, it was to be expected.* Smug, self-satisfied bastards. I didn't even know her, Tim thought, but I'm a better friend to her now than all those people ever were.

"She never wrote to us," Mrs. Grace said to Tim.

"Oh, she did too, Mommy," Mr. Grace put in gently.

"Never wrote, never called," Evelyn's mother continued. "We never knew where she was or what she was doing."

"She sent postcards," Mr. Grace said. "And she did call up on the telephone every now and again. Let us know she was okay."

"Once a year?" his wife asked challengingly. "Once a year, at best," she explained to Tim.

"Some people are like that," Tim rationalized. "Me, I can't write a letter to save my life."

It was a terrible choice of words, he realized immediately, but fortunately Mrs. Grace was already on another wavelength, and Mr. Grace merely nodded agreeably.

A few minutes before nine, when no one else had arrived for more than half an hour, Mrs. Grace whispered something urgent to her husband.

"Tim, would you mind hanging on here a minute while I take Mommy to the can?"

"Uh, sure."

No sooner had the old couple left the room than one of the young funeral home flunkies glanced in, checked the wall clock against his watch, and left. Charge by the minute, Tim thought sarcastically. He stood up and walked to the casket. It seemed very strange to be alone with Evvy—at her wake. Once again he was struck by how attractive she looked. And death shall have no dimension, he vaguely recalled, a line from a poem in high school English class.

Without thinking, Tim reached to Evvy with his right hand, knowing that his body shielded the gesture in case anyone came into the room. He hesitated briefly, afraid he would make a mess of the cosmetics if he touched her face, afraid her fingers would grasp at his if he touched her hands. Trembling, he let his palm settle on her breast. The experience was so confused between the real and the imagined that he wasn't at all sure what he actually felt, a pleasantly firm young female breast, or something harder and dead, a mixture of sawdust and embalming chemicals. When he removed his hand he felt a jangling rush of guilt and excitement, but he was more pleased than ashamed. He'd had his little moment of intimacy with Evvy, who had always been not only untouchable but unapproachable to him.

"You *will* be there tomorrow," Mr. Grace said when he and his wife returned. It was a plea, not a question. "Won't you."

"Yes, of course," Tim replied, although he hadn't planned to attend the funeral as well.

"We had to pay the funeral home for pall-bearers," Evelyn's mother said. "Twenty-five dollars apiece."

"Mommy, please."

"I'll see you in the morning," Tim said, trying to smile comfortingly as he shook hands with them.

"Thank you," the Graces both said as he left, "thank you."

Tim called the bottling plant in the morning and told them he was taking a sick day. It was crisp and clear outside, with a hint of thaw in the air. He felt good, and had slept well, which Tim attributed to the kindness he'd shown Mr. and Mrs. Grace by sitting with them for two hours and promising to attend the Mass. It wasn't often he had the chance to do something nice like that for a couple of old folks. His own parents had died within three months of each other several years ago, and his only living aunt and uncle were in Scottsdale, Arizona. Mr. and Mrs. Grace needed him last night, and this morning, almost as if he were a son or a nephew, or an old family friend.

But it was not just altruism on Tim's part that pleased him. The bleak circumstances of Evvy's death, the fact that virtually no one came to her wake, the way her parents had *assumed* him into their tiny circle, and the feel of her breast in his hand—all of these things combined somehow to bestow on Tim a curious share in Evvy's life, and, however peculiar that might be, he genuinely liked it.

There were more people at the funeral Mass than had attended the wake, but Tim was sure that most if not all of them were just the usual band of daily churchgoers. One of the pall-bearers wore a green bowling league jacket. Aside from the funeral home crew and the priest, Tim and Evelyn's parents were the only ones at her graveside. Mrs. Grace turned wobbly and started to moan when it was time to leave, while Mr. Grace struggled to maintain a semblance of glassy-eyed composure. Tim helped them both walk along the gravel path to the cars.

"You will follow us back to the house, Tim," Mr. Grace said as he stood by the door of the funeral home Cadillac.

"Oh, no, thank you, but—"

"Please, Tim, come on along for a little while. We'll have some coffee and pastry." He put his hand on Tim's shoulder and gave a beseeching squeeze. "Mommy was up till after midnight, cooking. She couldn't sleep at all."

Tim sighed inwardly. It didn't seem right that Evvy's folks should have to return directly home alone. It was bad enough for them to have to forego the normal post-funeral reception with its sustaining presence of family and friends, but to have no one, no one at all, even to share a cup of coffee with, after they'd just buried their daughter—that was simply too much.

"Sure," Tim agreed. "I'll follow you."

The Grace home was a cramped little asbestos-shingled house of the working class thirties vintage. Not much, but no doubt it had seemed palatial, even miraculous, when it was built and first occupied during the Depression. Easy to imagine a girl like Evvy desperate to escape from here. But for Tim there was something nostalgically comfortable about it—he had grown up in much the same sort of place, and not nearly so far from this one as he had thought. When you go back to the old neighbor-hood the distances collapse, the yards shrink, and houses that once looked big turn into boxy chicken coops.

Tim and Mr. Grace sat in the living room and chatted, while

Mrs. Grace brewed the coffee and prepared a platter of pastries. It was desultory, inconsequential talk about Rome, the old days, and the rapidly changing times that had overtaken everyone. Tim and Mr. Grace were in agreement that most of the changes were not really for the better. Astroturf, for instance.

It was not until Mrs. Grace had rejoined them, and they were all sipping fresh-perked coffee and nibbling delicious sesame-rum sweetcakes, that the conversation finally gathered itself around the subject of Evelyn. It was soon clear to Tim that there was a huge, aching mystery at the center of their existence and that it had to do entirely with the missing years of Evelyn's life, from the day she'd left home years ago until the day before yesterday, when she'd been air-freighted back to her parents. Everything in between was a cloud of unknowing, a dense fog broken only by the occasional spark of a phone call here, a post-card there—which, perversely, enhanced the darkness rather than illuminated it.

Evvy was a riddle to Tim as well, but he had been thinking about her quite a bit these last couple of days. Not logically, but intuitively, since they'd finally crossed paths only because of her death and his curiosity. There were some things he knew, others that he deduced or reasoned out for himself, and, most of all, there was everything he found himself wishing, imagin-ing—it amounted to the same thing in the end. Evvy was in the purely residual phase of her incarnation, so it was up to him.

"I didn't want to go into it last night, at the wake," Tim said. "There wasn't enough time, and I didn't know how you would take it, but I do want to tell you. Evvy and I were good friends for many years. Ever since high school, in fact, and..."

"Evvy? Who's Evvy?"

"Evelyn, Mommy. Hush now, let the boy talk."

Mr. Grace leaned forward in the seat, every aspect of his presence fixed intently on Tim. Mrs. Grace was annoyed at her husband for his rare show of assertiveness, but she said nothing about it, and made an effort to pay attention.

"Well, what can I say," Tim went on hesitantly. "Evvy and I were good friends, ever since high school. Of course, we did lose track of each other for while after that, but when I got out of the army I thought I'd stay on the West Coast for a while, see if I could find a good job there, and we ran into each other again. We went out a lot, had fun together, that kind of thing. She was busy trying to make a career for herself, and in the meantime I'd found decent work at a defense plant, but we still managed to get together a couple of nights a week, and on weekends. And…well, we got pretty serious, and there were times when I was sure we'd get married and settle down to a more normal life, you know? But something or other always seemed to get in the way of it. So, it was an off-again on-again type relationship, but even when it was off we were still great friends. I always loved Evvy, no matter what, and I think she loved me most of the time. I know she did. But we never managed to get it to the next stage. I wish that we had. We stayed in touch up until a couple of months ago, when I decided that it was never going to work out, and I was ready for a change in my life, so I made up my mind to move back here. We talked maybe once or twice on the phone, right after I moved, but that was it."

Mr. Grace's mouth was slightly open, and his throat muscles worked mightily either to shut it or to say something, but he did neither. Mrs. Grace appeared to be no less fascinated by what Tim had said, but she didn't look as completely surprised as her husband did.

Tim had paused to catch his breath—and his wits, he could only hope. He had said enough, too much, and it had taken off on him at once. It had seemed harmless enough. All he wanted to do was to give them something to cling to, a few dressed-up facts to fill in some of the vast blank spot that Evvy had left them. But no sooner had he started then the story took on a life of its own and became an account of *his* long love affair with Evvy. Is that crazy or what, Tim wondered.

But he had enjoyed it, too. Such an extraordinary thrill, to hear those things, to know that they were rising from a buried part of his brain. That they put him into Evvy's life, and Evvy into his. Tim marveled that he hadn't contradicted anything he had said previously to Mr. and Mrs. Grace. But it was clear to him that they'd accept whatever he told them. They just wanted to hear as much as they could about their daughter, and that was the problem. Tim had merely opened the door.

"Go on," Mrs. Grace prompted.

"Yes, please, Tim. Tell us more."

Reluctant, feeling trapped by his own good intentions, but at the same time secretly delighted, Tim continued to elaborate his impromptu saga of Evelyn Grace's missing years. Her efforts to make it as a folk singer, then as a rock singer, finally as a country- and-western singer. Her two or three non-speaking parts in forgettable movies. The picture of Evvy perched atop a Harley that was used for the front cover of a biker magazine. Another one, showing her menaced by a man with a knife, that appeared in a true-crime magazine. The in-between jobs, waitressing in some pretty good restaurants and nightclubs, serving drinks in an L.A. airport bar, that sort of thing. The occasional respite taken in the unemployment line, recharging her batteries for the next time around. Nothing too shabby, nothing unrespectable, but never any breakthrough. The long hard road of a pretty young woman chasing her ambition down the years in Los Angeles.

Woven throughout, like a bright gold thread, was Tim's love for Evvy and her sometime love for him. Tim went on about how he was still sad that they'd never been able to make it a permanent relationship, a marriage, how he had learned to accept that. Now he consoled himself by thinking of the happier memories he had of Evvy and by reminding himself that in spite of her weaknesses and failings she had been a good person.

Tim wanted to finish there, on the kind of life-affirming note people strive for in funeral situations. He felt tired, and it seemed as if he had been talking for hours. But Evvy's mother and father were not quite through with him yet.

"The end, Tim," Mr. Grace said softly. "You have to tell us what happened to her at the end."

"Yeah, what about the drugs," Mrs. Grace demanded.

"Oh, well. Some of the movie people she knew, I guess they introduced her to cocaine somewhere along the line, and then the harder stuff. I tried to get her off it, but once you're hooked it's rough. You have to make a total commitment, and Evvy could never bring herself to that point, where she was willing.

That's the main reason why I had to give up, at last, and get out of the scene altogether. I couldn't change her, and I couldn't bear to watch what was happening to her, so I packed up my stuff and came back here. And she let me go. The guy who was supplying all her drugs meant more to her than I did."

"Did he use her?" Mrs. Grace asked. "They get them hooked, and then they use them."

"I don't know about that," Tim replied. He didn't like this because it tainted his own newly developed feelings for Evvy. It was probably unavoidable—she *had* died of a heroin overdose—but it seemed so distasteful. "All I know is I lost her. We all lost her in the end."

Mr. Grace looked subdued and thoughtful in the long silence that followed. Mrs. Grace seemed to be formulating some response but it never reached the stage of spoken words. Tim was about to leave when Evelyn's father took him aside.

"Come with me a minute," he said, leading Tim up a narrow flight of stairs. They went into a small bedroom. Obviously it had been Evvy's. "Tim, they sent back these two boxes of things with her. Personal effects. Not much, as you can see, but I was thinking maybe you'd like to take a minute and look through them. You might find something in there, some little keepsake, to take home and remember her by."

Tim was going to refuse, but it would probably be rude to do so. Besides, he liked the idea too much.

"Thank you," he said.

"Feel free, take your time," Mr. Grace added. "Come on down when you're finished."

"Okay."

Tim waited as the old man's footsteps faded away. Then he sat down on the bed, Evvy's bed. For a moment he pictured her as the most gorgeous girl in high school, the way she had been then. In this room. In this bed. He remembered seeing her at the lake on the day after the senior prom. She was with her crowd and she was wearing a bikini that would be demure by today's standards. No one had a tan in June. Evvy had snowy blonde hair, long pale thighs…It was sweet for Tim to pause there, to enjoy once again the permanence of her beauty.

Not much was right. The two cardboard cartons were filled for the most part with cheap clothes. Sneakers, jeans, T-shirts, socks. No dresses, no jackets, nothing very good. Evvy had had very little left at the end, her flimsy life stripped down to the minimum. He had to find something he could show to Mr. Grace and thank him for. The cheap plastic barette would do nicely—and it still smelled of Evvy's hair (or at least her hairspray).

Tim reached down to the bottom of the second box and pulled up a handful of bras and panties. Startled, he dropped them, but then he relaxed, smiled and allowed himself to examine them. Red and blue and lavender, not a white in the bunch. Evvy's bra size was 36C, for breasts that were ample but not excessive. Tim had been aware of that as far back as ninth grade and as recently as last night. He held a pair of delicate purple cotton briefs to his face—God in Heaven, they still had the delicious unwashed scent of her in them!

Tim quickly shoved the panties into his jacket pocket, and then carefully rearranged the other things back in the boxes. He held the barrette conspicuously in his hand and went downstairs. Mrs. Grace was still sitting where he had left her. She gave him a strained smile as he came into the living room. He started to say something to her.

Bong! and *Bong!* again, before he even hit the carpet. *Bong! Bong! Bong!* His hands were useless floppy things and his vision skittered away like marbles on a hardwood floor.

"The flat part, the flat part," Mrs. Grace warned. "Not the edge. That's my best skillet."

Tim's empty hands were bound together behind him with some sticky plastic stuff, packing tape, he realized dimly. And then his feet. His head wouldn't clear, but he tried to speak; it was impossible to put words together. He tried to focus his sight on the plastic barrette, which he was aware of, somewhere, near his face on the floor.

"Son of a bitch," Mr. Grace wheezed, his voice high-pitched, almost strangled, but with a nervous edge of triumph in it. "You could have saved her. You were the only one who could have saved her. We couldn't talk to her, we couldn't do anything with her. That's the way it is sometimes between parents and kids, you just can't do anything. No matter what you try, it doesn't work. But you could have saved her. You loved her, but you walked away and left her there to die. You left her there with that other son of a bitch, who was pumping dope into her."

"Least he could've done was make her call home once a week," Mrs. Grace remarked.

"Washed his hands of her, that's what he did."

Again Tim tried to speak, but as soon as he opened his mouth he was kicked in the jaw. His tongue hurt and he tasted his own blood. He felt the old man's hands on his body, emptying each of his pockets. Oh no, don't do that.

"Where's his car keys? Here we go…Look at this, Mommy, look. The son of a bitch was trying to steal Evelyn's underwear. Didn't want to bring *her* home, no. Just her underpants'd do."

"Whispering Jesus," Mrs. Grace responded.

Tim listened as Mr. Grace explained to his wife that he was going to drive Tim's car into downtown Rome, leave it there, and then walk back to the house. She was to do nothing until he got home, except hit Tim with the skillet again if he tried to cause trouble for her.

Move his car? That was bad. But I can get out of this, Tim told himself. Even if she is half gone, I can talk to her, I can distract her, confuse her, and work myself free. I should have known, he thought. The one thing he had steered clear of in his story was why Evvy had cut herself off from these people, to the point where she communicated with them only once or twice a year, and then by postcard or telephone. It had seemed too delicate to mention, and he had no idea of what might be involved, but now it came to him: Evvy might have had her reasons. Tim's mistake may have been to assume, like everyone else, that Evvy had been a bad child, selfish, uncaring, neglectful of her parents. Now he knew that there must have been another side to the story, Evvy's side, and he was stuck in it.

"Doesn't he need his car to drive home?" Mrs. Grace saw fit to ask as her husband was about to leave.

"He isn't going home. Tomorrow we'll drive him up to Canada and dump him there in the woods. I don't even want that son of a bitch in the same country."

When he heard his car being driven away, Tim looked at Mrs. Grace. He gathered himself, tried to clear his throat and speak.

But the old woman rose from her seat and approached him. She had the roll of tape in her hand. "I don't want to see you," she said. "I don't even want to hear you, and I sure don't want you looking at me."

Ah, no, Tim thought as he saw her yank a length of tape from the roll. She bit it loose, and he noticed a couple of fugitive sesame seeds clinging to her dentures. She slapped the tape over Tim's mouth to keep him from talking. Then, at a more leisurely pace, Evelyn's mother began to wrap the rest of his head in tape.

He thrashed his body as wildly as possible, but he couldn't stop her, and when his head was done she proceeded on down around his arms, eventually securing his knees. It was a big roll of tape, and Mrs. Grace used all of it.

"Now, that's better," she said.

Grotesque, Tim thought, grotesque. He pictured himself as a kind of slapdash mummy, rotting away in the Canadian woods. Say, fifty yards from a back road—the Graces wouldn't be able to drag him any farther than that—but would he ever be found? It was such an outrageous and unreal image that Tim was, even now, incapable of feeling mere panic or terror. Instead, his mind was overwhelmed by a profound sense of exasperation.

If only his story had been true, and he and Evvy had been in love for a while. Then he wouldn't be where he was now, and Evvy would still be alive—because Tim never would have walked away from her. He never would have settled for an unhappy ending with Evvy, not in real life.

Tim's lungs felt like they were being clamped in a waffle iron, the oxygen slowly burning out of them. The last conscious thought he had was a rich and vivid recall of the last conscious smell he had experienced, Evelyn Grace's cunt.

THE BANSHEE

He didn't mean to hit her—hard. But she went down like a toy made out of flimsy sticks, and she began crying in a loud and piercing screech. Even then she didn't stop talking. Bubbles of compressed words burst forth intermittently between heaving gasps of breath. Her features were distorted with anger and pain, her face corkscrewing tightly into itself.

"For the love of Jesus," Dermot muttered, turning away in a state of barely controlled rage. This is how murder happens. He finished the whiskey in his glass, poured a little more. She was still lying on the chipped lino, making noise. "I'm warning you, stop that racket.

You hurt me."

"It was just a shove. You didn't have to fall down, you did that on purpose. Besides, if you don't shut up my flatmates will throw me out of here. And if that happens, I swear I'll fuckin' well kill you.

They're not here," she pointed out infuriatingly.

"It's the neighbors," Dermot told her. "They'll complain to the lads again, and I'll be in trouble. They're fed up with this kind of carry- on. You can't keep doing this to me."

The noise diminished slightly. That was so typical of her, and so annoying. If he was reasonable, if he was willing to talk to her about it, then she quieted down. But there was nothing to talk about anymore. There never had been. So much trouble, and he'd never even been inside her drawers.

"Come on, now."

"No." Resentful. She made a disgustingly liquid sniffling sound. "I don't want to go yet."

"I want you out of here. Now."

"Dermot, please."

"I told you," he said. "It's pointless."

"*Dermot...*"

She began to cry again. He never should have let her in his door. Not the first time, not ever. But what could he do? Call the police? That'd be funny. And if he had to argue with her it seemed better to do it in the relative privacy of his room rather than out in the hall way. You couldn't ignore her. She would put her finger on the bell and hold it until you answered. She would pound the door with her other fist at the same time.

It wasn't his fault. True, he had smiled at her and chatted freely that first night she appeared at Dolan's, but that was all part of the job. True, when she began coming around almost every night he could see that she was developing a special interest in him, and he did nothing to discourage it, but they saw each other only at the bar and they never actually did anything together, so it all seemed quite harmless. You liked it when she told you that you were the best barman in the best bar in Southie, didn't you? You silly great eejit. And yes, it was true that the time came when he invited her back to his place for a nightcap, but he didn't so much as touch her knee.

By then he knew something was wrong. She drank a little too much and spoke a little too forcefully. Her cheerfulness had the sharp edge of desperation, and he began to realize that she was a person with a problem. She was lonely. No crime in that, but it had apparently reached the point where it affected her mind. She would say something every now and then that was— wrong. And it made you think you were in the presence of a sick soul.

Dermot instinctively sympathized with her. He sometimes had his own bouts of loneliness and he often felt painfully homesick. But he decided not to get involved, perhaps sensing that he could never fill the emptiness in her life. Probably no one could. It had gone on too long now and was rooted in her.

Besides, she didn't really attract him, so he had no desire even to try. In the face of fearful odds, Dermot had managed to get to America. He had a job. He had a room. He had plans. He was there to make money, not collect problem hearts.

By then, however, it was too late. They talked for a while that first night and then she left. But she came back to Dolan's night after night. She usually stayed until closing time so that the two of them could walk home together. Like Dermot, she lived in the neighborhood. The rear exit of Dolan's led to a dead end alley, so he couldn't easily avoid her. He made excuses—going for a plate of spaghetti with the lads, a poker game—but there were too many times when he had to put up with her chatty company over the few blocks to home.

What kind of life did she have that she could stay out until three almost every morning? She claimed she worked in an office. More than that, Dermot didn't care to know: she might mistake his idle curiosity for significant interest. He occasionally walked her to her door; she always invited him in and he always declined politely. Most of the time he went straight to his place and she tagged along. The last twenty feet were the trickiest, from the sidewalk to the door. It required finesse or rudeness for him to get inside without her. He didn't always succeed, but a glass of whiskey and another forty minutes of forgettable talk usually did the job. If you satisfied her craving for company and attention, then you could ease her out.

The funny thing was, she never made a move on him either. A flash of leg was invariably accidental; the chair slid. When she bumped into him, breasts against his arm, it was the result of an innocent tipsiness. At first Dermot saw these minor incidents as erotic overtures, but he soon realized that they weren't. It was the hour, the booze, nothing more. She was happy just to be with him, to have his company. In his more charitable moments, Dermot thought of her as an eccentric.

"Get up, you stupid cow."

"I don't want to go."

"If you don't shift yourself, I'll drag you by the scruff of your neck and toss you in the gutter."

"Dermot!" A shriek, really.

"I mean it. Come along now."

She didn't stir. Whimpering, huddled to herself. Dear God, how did it get to this point? It was actually worse than if they were lovers, because lovers do split up and vow never to see each other again. The clean break sort of thing. Dermot's mistake had been to let this situation develop to the point where it was friendship, at least in her mind, and that was somehow harder to terminate neatly.

He had underestimated her every step of the way. How had he deluded himself .into believing that he was in control? The alarm bells didn't start ringing until the first time she came visiting on one of his nights off. She had finagled his work schedule out of someone at Dolan's. The line was truly crossed. Dermot began calling her names, yelling at her, anything to drive the wretched woman away.

But his insults and verbal abuse didn't seem to matter. It was possible that she found some perverse pleasure in it, taking it as a form of attention. No matter what he did, he only seemed to implicate himself more in this imaginary relationship. Dermot felt helpless and trapped, and that made him angrier. If it took physical force to get rid of her, so be it.

"Come along," he said firmly, grabbing her by the shoulders. "Time to push off."

"You promised me a drink," she protested.

"I did no such thing."

"Why not?"

"Because I don't want to give you a drink," he said, hauling her to her feet. "I want you to go home and leave me alone. I'm tired and I have to write a letter to my father back in Ireland. He's not very well, and—"

"What about your mother?" she asked quickly, grasping at the slim conversational opening.

"She's fine, thanks. Come on now."

"My mother's dead."

"Ah, you'll be seeing her again soon enough if you don't get out of here in a flash, you drunken old sow."

She smiled at him. "Oh, Dermot..."

He opened the apartment door and gently started to steer her toward the hallway. She resisted, tilting in his direction. She had never really fought him before. Dermot regarded this gesture as an escalation on her part, a clear attempt to move things to a new level. It had to be squelched immediately. He yelled at her as he gave her a stiff-arm to the shoulder. She fell back, tried to steady herself, and pulled a picture off the wall. It crashed to the floor as she landed on a plain wooden chair—the back of it popped loose. Somehow, she straightened up on her feet as the chair cracked to pieces beneath her.

The picture was just a cheap print in a cheap frame, and the chair was worthless tag-sale junk. But they weren't his. Now he would have to replace them. Dermot gazed at the broken glass and wood on the floor. Enough is enough, he thought dimly.

She was about to say something, but he wouldn't let her. He grabbed her by the hair and yanked her out of the flat, through the front door and down the walk. She was screaming now. Dermot swung her by the hair and sent her reeling across the sidewalk. She banged into a car parked at the curb, and sank to the ground. The cries of pain continued, but the volume was down.

"And stay away, you stupid old slag."

Dermot turned and marched back inside. Mr. and Mrs. Thwaite glared down at him from the upper landing. He would apologize to them, but it was useless. They were the kind of people who would tell a leper it was his own fault when his lips fell off. Dermot knew they would complain to the lads, maybe even to the landlord. But he might survive—if your woman never came back.

He topped up his glass of whiskey and tried to calm himself. He sat down at the desk in his room and took out a sheet of lined paper. *Dear Dad*, he began. The old man wasn't well, that was an honest fact. Dermot hadn't written home in ages. No excuses, he just hadn't done it. There were times when his head felt like an anvil of guilt. He would fail again tonight. He was too jangled and distracted to concentrate.

If only he could ring them up on the telephone. Impossible. Der- mot's home was on the outskirts of a small village a few miles from Kilkelly, itself no metropolis, in the bleak heart of County Mayo. There were still some places where the lines didn't reach, or the people couldn't be bothered to hook on. If you absolutely had to use a phone, you went to a pub in town. In all the years of his growing up, Dermot could remember about half a dozen such telephone expeditions.

Yes, it was a bleak corner of the world, but he did miss it. He missed the folks, his sister Naimh. He missed the grim beauty of the stark countryside. It was all so—empty. While here in Boston, everybody lived like matchsticks in a box. All he wanted was a few years here to raise enough money so that he could buy a decent pub back home. Then he'd be away like a shot. Of course, Dermot knew there was many an Irishman who said as much, and then never returned. They went to America and stayed. But he—

"Dermot. Derrrmmmmot..."

The voice was so close he jumped. She was in the side yard, outside his window. Not even six feet away from him, across the desk and on the other side of the wall. Jesus, Mary and Joseph. He couldn't move. His body shook. He saw a splash of whiskey on the barren page. Thank God the shade was drawn. Her voice rose, becoming a scream, and she hammered the wall of the house, but he didn't move. It soon got worse, much worse. If I move I'll kill her, Dermot realized, this time I'll fuckin' murder her.

The next thing he knew, the police were at the door. He let them in, catching a glimpse of the Thwaites outside. Trouble. A couple of cops had been scratched and bitten as they subdued her. She'd gone round the twist. The police knew her, it seemed. The one who talked to Dermot was quite sympathetic, and after a while it occurred to him that he was in pretty good shape after all. A statement would be required. Fair enough.

It got better in the weeks that followed. She had abraded a cornea, detached a retina and chomped a hole in a cheek. Not the kind of thing the police are quick to forgive. She got her licks in, give her that. She had no real job, she was a welfare cheat. When it came to psychiatric testing, she made a poor impression. They found a place for her, and Dermot was told that she wouldn't be turned loose for some little while.

It was the best thing, really. She was lonely, desperate, a disturbed person. She needed care and attention, and now she was going to get it. Perhaps not in the circumstances she would have desired, but it was care all the same. It was far better for her to be where she was, than to continue along the way she had been going until something worse happened.

When the machinery of the state took over, Dermot discovered that he didn't even have a walk-on role. It was surprising, but a relief. Events occurred on the strength of their own momentum. She was the only issue, who she was and what she'd done. Dermot had to remind himself that he had in fact once been involved. He wouldn't have been surprised to get a letter from her, or a bunch of them—lonely, impassioned, repentant, pleading, reflecting a new knowledge of her past weaknesses, some such approach. But he never heard from her again.

The lads seemed to think it was all good crack, and even the Thwaites acknowledged that he was not entirely to blame—he got a civil nod from them, at any rate. Dermot drew pints at Dolan's and gathered his tips, dispensing equal measures of genuine Irish nostalgia and nationalism to boo2y Yanks who'd never been east of Revere. So it went until the morning the telegram arrived.

FATHER DYING / NIAMH / TOBERCURRY / EIRE

The back of beyond. He expected things to look different in some ways, and they did. But still, he was shocked. He had been in America for less than a year, and already home seemed so dark, chilly and cramped. His perspective had changed forever. But it was great to see his mother again. She was in fine form, as was Naimh, a lovely young woman of nineteen. And the kitchen was the same warm and cozy room Dermot remembered, the heart of the house where the fire never went out.

His father was not in good shape. The old man smiled at him but couldn't speak. There was barely enough strength left in him to change his position in bed. Dermot told him all about Boston, Southie, Dolan's ("a bar, not a real pub") and the lads ("they're not bad for Kerrymen"). After a while he noticed that his father had fallen asleep, though his eyes were still partly open.

"Why isn't he in the hospital?" Dermot asked his mother over tea in the kitchen.

"They can't do anything more for him," she replied with calm and resignation. "He wants to be here when the end comes."

"He has pills to make it better for him," Naimh added.

"What are they, painkillers?"

"Yes, it's a morphine compound."

Dermot nodded. His sister had grown up so much in the last year. She had an air of efficiency and purpose now. No sign of the immature teenager. After two years of looking, she'd finally been lucky enough to land a regular job at a stationer's shop in Tobercurry. She owned a beat-up old Mini and she changed the oil and plugs herself.

Dermot went to bed early and slept late, recovering from the effects of jet lag. His mother cooked a grand breakfast for him: fried eggs, fried bread, rashers of real bacon (not that scrawny American rubbish), sausages, black pudding, grilled tomatoes and mushrooms, all washed down with plenty of strong tea. After that Dermot was ready for some fresh air and an eventual pint. He and Naimh went out for a walk, circling across the fields toward the village.

"How long can you stay?" she asked.

"Just the week." He'd told them that last night. "I had a hard time getting that. Things are nearly as bad over there as they are here."

He knew everyone in the village, of course. They were happy to see him back, and they told him they were praying for his dad. He also got a few nudges and sly winks, as if he had been away on a long weekend in Dublin with the lady representative of the Turf Board.

"Is that your Cadillac parked out front?" Gerry Byrne teased when they went into his pub.

"Of course it is. I flew it over in my Lear jet."

Last year Dermot and Naimh had gathered in Byrne's with some friends for farewell drinks. The jokes had been much the same—all about getting rich in America, fast women, buying huge houses with swimming pools, going to Disneyland. Good for a giggle, but now Dermot could see the black edge in such humor. It took three pints of catching up before he and Naimh were able to move to the corner table and talk alone.

"How long does he have?"

"Days," she said.

"Could it be weeks?"

"It's possible, but not many. And don't you worry about it if he does hang on a bit longer. You don't have to come back for the funeral. He's seen you again and that's the important thing. You were great with him yesterday."

"What about you?"

"What about me?"

"How long are you going to stay on at home?"

Naimh shrugged. "Until something better comes along."

That could take ages, given Irish courtship rituals. *If* she found someone. He knew the local routine. Saturday nights. The twenty-mile drive to the Crystal Ballroom, the one alternative to drinking in a pub. And even then, she would sit around for hours or dance with other women while the lads tanked up. And who were they? The ones not bright enough to go off to technical college, much less the university. It was a desperate business, in such a desperate place. Dermot didn't want to marry Naimh off in a rush but it pained him to think of her growing older alone, working by day and taking care of their mother the rest of the time, passing the prime of her youth in a barren place.

"You should consider Dublin, or at least Galway. And when I get established, the States. There's nothing for you here in the long term, Naimh."

"You could be right about that."

"I know I am."

When they got home they learned that their father had died. Their mother had gone into the bedroom to check him a few minutes earlier, and he was gone.

The next three days were busy with the wake and the funeral, and the other details attendant to an ordinary human death. When it was all over—the prayers said, the papers signed, the booze consumed, the old man in the ground, the last mourner departed—Dermot occupied himself with chores around the house. There were a lot of things that needed doing, things his father had not been able to do these last few months. Dead at sixty. His mother not even that. She would want to stay on at the house until the day she died. There was no reason why she shouldn't, as long as her health was good. With a little financial assistance from Naimh and Dermot—not much, her needs were few—she'd manage all right.

If things went half-well for him, he'd be back in plenty of time to give her some grandchildren and look after her in her old age. And if he eventually changed his mind and decided to remain in America and raise a family there—if things went that well, then he could bring his mother across to live with them. And his sister, if she hadn't gotten married and had a bunch of babies in the meantime.

"Dermot."

His eyes opened in the dark. Chill air. Silence. It was a moment before his mind began to form thoughts. I am home, County Mayo, Republic of Ireland. Mother in her room and Naimh in hers. The peaty smell of turf burning, the fire still alive downstairs. The day after tomorrow—no, it would be tomorrow, in fact—he would get on a plane at Shannon and fly back to Boston.

"Dermmmmmmot..."

The bitch. Had her voice come from outside the window, or a window in the back of his brain? The sound of his own breathing. Nothing else. Dreaming—he must have been dreaming about that terrible woman. She was a good three thousand miles away, having all her neuroses and psychoses totted up by bored state employees who would move on to better things in due course.

Amazing, the quality of her voice. Like a moan from outside his window, and at the same time like a whisper in his ear. Real enough to wake him. It must have been a bad dream—he wouldn't have any other kind about that one.

The rest of the night was ruined. Dermot drifted in and out of sleep, never enjoying more than a few uninterrupted minutes of peace. Not that he heard her again, not that he'd ever heard her in the first place. He just kept waking, dozing, and soon waking again. Useless. Untracked. He grew more tired.

He must have slept again because at some point he opened his eyes and the room was brighter. Day outside, gray light: cloudy as usual. He felt as if he'd been in bed for a long time but the house was still quiet. Perhaps his mother had gone down to the shop for eggs or milk. Was Naimh returning to work today? Most likely. Life goes on—work, anyway.

Dermot couldn't move. Or it might have been that he didn't want to move yet. Some combination of the two, no doubt, inertia and laziness. His body was like a heavy weight, a solid material that encased him. He wiggled his toes a little—that's better. He tried to turn his head a little, and was surprised at how much effort it took to budge an inch. He felt okay. But then again, he didn't feel right at all.

A while later Dermot opened his eyes. Was I asleep? He had no desire to move now, no will to get out of bed and do something with the day. He had a foreign taste in his mouth, and his teeth tingled unpleasantly—as if he were biting tin. What was wrong with him, he wondered abstractly. It did seem to be a matter of interest, but not a real concern. Thoughts came and went, but he couldn't make anything of them. They were inconclusive, they had the random quality of accidents. Just thinking about what he was thinking about had the effect of exhausting him. Dermot realized his eyes were closing this time, and he felt happy about it.

He was drowning. He gagged, his tongue working furiously to retrieve something that was already halfway down his throat—he woke up spitting. It made a sound like dice on the lino. Dermot swallowed blood as he pushed his face toward the edge of the bed. He saw it on the floor across the room—a tooth. Yes, it's one of mine. The empty socket began to hurt, a deep, throbbing pain. What is this now, a toothache after the fact? Bloody unfair. It dug into him.

His face was wet. That was how he discovered that he'd been asleep again. The old woman was washing blood and dribble off of his chin. She was familiar. He wanted to tell her that she was in severe danger of scrubbing his skin down to the next layer but when she finally let go he was too weak to utter a word. Then he saw the man standing nearby. He looked unfamiliar, but he had to be a doctor. Of course—Dermot was sick. That explained a lot of things. He felt better. Still sick, but better. Where were they? Why was he alone? They were here a minute ago, he was sure of that. He hadn't seen them leave, but now the room was empty. He was too alone. It was stifling, suffocating. He tried to sit up, but failed; the old muscle tone was somewhat deficient. He opened his mouth and tried to work up some saliva. He called out feebly.

"Haaaaaaa…" Almost a wheeze. They shouldn't leave him on his own like this. Dermot was aware of pain. His insides etched with acid. His throat choking him. Even his arse, God help him, felt as if it had hot coals embedded in it, from not being moved. He couldn't move himself, so it was up to them—and they'd done a disappearing act. He tried to think of anything else, to dodge the pain. Had they picked up that tooth? He was curious to take a look at the rotten bugger.

"Haaaaaaa…"

He looked up and the girl was holding his hand. By God, she was beautiful. He knew her. Naimh. Don't leave. Stay with me. Don't even let go of my hand or I'll fall off the edge. He tried to tell her these things but the words remained stuck in his mind and all he could do was look at her.

Then the boy. The boy? If he'd come such a distance, this must be serious. Oh yes. It had been a while, and he was happy. If only I could tell you that. The boy looked just like him. It was difficult even to understand what he was saying.

"…not a real pub."

Yes, yes, but it's work, it's real money, and you'll be able to build on it for the future. There's nothing for you here.

"…for Kerrymen."

Gone again. Everything goes so fast. You are left alone in a stark room with a view of nothing much. The pain scouring away at his insides had nearly reached the surface. Anytime now. And when it gets here, with any luck I'll dissolve completely.

Dermot's mind was flooded with clarity. This is dying. The hour, the minute. A surge of strength in his arms. He pushed up on his elbows, and then, painfully, his hands. He had to see, to see—but what? Not this mean, damp bedroom in which so much of his life had been spent. Out the window, away. Two people were walking across the field, toward the house. A young man, a young woman. Dermot and Naimh.

"Haaaaaaa..."

First their father, then their mother. It happened that way more often than you might think, when they'd been very close. Or so the doctor said. Dermot went to sleep, and she never woke up. At least with the old man it was expected. But this was a shock. He'd only had a little while to speak with each of them, and even then it was minor, trivial. Dear God. You've put us all in such a lonely, desperate country.

But that was a while back.

He moved. That is, he thought he moved. Dermot couldn't be sure about it. He was dreaming. The whole thing was just a long bad dream. *Yes, it often seems that way, doesn't it?* But Dermot knew better. He made an effort to move. He put his foot down.

Clutch in.

Shifted up coming out of the bend.

He knew this road. He'd had a few drinks, but that wasn't a cause for alarm. If the Garda stopped him, it meant nothing. He was Dermot Mulreany, bound for Shannon, bound for Boston. He had somehow gotten better, overcome tragedy and loss and reached this point in his life where he—

Clutch in.

Shifted down going into a sharp bend.

He knew this road. Another Saturday night at the Crystal. The band sang "Roisin Dubh," nearly as good as the Thin Lizzy version. The black rose. He would keep that in mind—it was a good old name for a pub.

You're so good-looking. So why do you live alone? Why do you sleep alone at night?

The lads reeked of stout and Carrolls cigarettes, as usual. They couldn't dance to save their lives, and all they ever wanted to do was get a hand up your jumper, but—

He glanced down at himself, trembling with sudden aware-ness. Female breasts inside that blouse. Stocking-clad legs, two knees poking out from beneath the plain skirt that had hitched up a bit in the car. He couldn't take his eyes off them, as if they were the most amazing thing he'd ever seen.

"Dermot..."

The car—watch out. Too late, the road was lost, the tree racing unnaturally toward him—no, her. No! his mind screamed. Not Naimh! *This time O God please let me be the one who dies not Naimh not Naimh let me die!*

Even worse, he lived.

He saw her on Boston Common. He wanted to turn and run when he saw her coming toward him, but his legs went stiff and he felt swamped with helplessness and inevitability. He simply could not avoid her. Hatred boiled up within him, but at the same time it was crushed with fear. It had to be two years now, more or less. Somehow she had got out. Done her time, had her treatment. They couldn't hold her forever.

He was the only one left.

She looked pathetic, shuffling along aimlessly. Raggedy old clothes, hair a mess, face wrecked by life. Still a young woman, for all of that. Dermot stopped. Couldn't move. She glanced at him. Their eyes met. She had the same look, searching, vacant, lonely, as if she peered out at the world from some awful place. Dermot shriveled inside. Sweat misted his face, turning cold in the sharp November air.

But she showed no sign of knowing him, not even a flicker of subconscious recognition. As if he were invisible and she didn't even see him there. Then she passed through Dermot like a sudden paralyzing spasm of anguish, and was gone.

BLANCA

When I told a few close friends that I was going to Blanca their reaction was about what I had expected. Why? they asked. There's nothing to see in Blanca. Nothing much to do, except disappear. Sly smiles. Watch out you don't disappear. Maybe that's why I chose it, I said with a smile of my own. It might be nice to disappear for a while.

For a travel writer who has been on the job ten years, as I have, it isn't so easy to escape. The good places have been done, the mediocre ones too. You name it and I've probably been there, evaluating the hotels, sampling the cuisine, checking out the facilities and amenities, chatting up the locals. It's a great job, but I was tired of the regular world. What I needed was a therapeutic getaway, to spend a couple of weeks in an obscure backwater doing nothing more than sipping cold beer on a terrace and reading a good book.

I knew people in the business who'd been to Blanca. It's boring, they told me. Miles and miles of rolling plains and rangeland. There was a dead volcano somewhere in Blanca, but it wasn't worth climbing. Yes, the towns were neat and the people were pleasant enough. There's never any difficulty getting a clean room and bed for the night in Blanca. But nothing happens, there's nothing to do. No monuments or ancient ruins. No lively carnival, no festivals or feasts. The nightlife is said to be fairly low-key, so if you're looking for that kind of action, which I wasn't, there are much better places to go. Blanca was cattle country, and the only good thing I ever heard about it was that the steaks were excellent.

Blanca is not a nation but a territory, overlapping several

borders in that region of the world. The native Indians were crushed nearly two centuries ago. They still survive, a sullen minority now thoroughly domesticated by generations of servitude as cheap labor cowhands, meatpackers and household help. The European settlers tried to create Blanca as an independent state but numerous rebellions failed and it was eventually carved up by its larger neighbors. But Blanca is Blanca, they say, regardless of the boundaries that appear on maps.

Because Blanca has comparatively little to offer the visitor it is not on any of the main routes. I had to catch two flights, the second of which stopped at so many featureless outposts along the way that it seemed like days before I finally got to Oranien. With a population of nearly one hundred thousand it is easily the largest city in Blanca.

I checked into the Hotel des Vacances, which was within walking distance of the central district but just far enough away to escape the noise. My room was large and airy, and had a small balcony that overlooked two residential streets and a park. It was comfortable, and not at all like a modem luxury hotel. I slept for nearly eleven hours that first night, had steak and eggs for brunch and then took a lazy walk around the center of Oranien. The narrow side streets had a certain pioneer charm—the original hard clay tiles had never been paved over, and remained neatly in place. But the most remarkable feature of the city was its state of cleanliness. I began to look for a piece of litter, and couldn't find so much as one discarded cigarette butt. It reminded me of Switzerland, or Singapore.

On the top floor of a department store I caught a view of the southern part of the city, a vast stretch of stockyards, abattoirs and railroad tracks. All the beef in Blanca passed through Oranien on its way to the outside world. I'd come to a dusty, three-story cowtown, and it was the tidiest, best-scrubbed place I'd ever seen.

But then, I'd heard stories about the police in Blanca. They *were* the law, and if you had any sense at all you never challenged them. Littering ranked close to treason by their way of thinking, and while that might seem harsh to some I had no problem with it. I've seen immaculate places and I've seen squalor; on the whole, I prefer the former. Besides, it had nothing to do with me. I was on vacation, recovering from a personal mess, exorcising old demons (including a wife). The first few days I was in Oranien the only cops I saw were chubby little men in silly uniforms, directing traffic. They looked like stage extras in some Ruritanian operetta.

"Not them," Basma said quietly. "The ones you must worry about are the ones you can't see. The people in plain clothes. They are everywhere."

"Even here?" I asked, amused but intrigued.

"Yes, surely."

We were in the small but very pleasant beer garden behind the Hotel des Vacances. There were perhaps two dozen other people scattered about the umbrella-topped tables in the late afternoon sun. A few neighborhood regulars, the rest visitors and hotel guests like myself, passing through. Everyone looked fairly happy and relaxed.

My companion was both a foreigner and a local resident. Basma had taken it upon himself to join me at my table the day before, when I had just discovered the beer garden and was settling into *The Thirteenth Simenon Omnibus*. At first I resented the intrusion and tried to ignore the man, but he would not be denied. Finally I gave in, and closed my book.

We spent two hours or more, drinking and chatting, with Basma carrying most of the load. But he was easy company. A middle-aged Lebanese, he had reluctantly fled Beirut while he still had a cache of foreign currency. The city had become unbearable, impossible, and he believed he was a target of both the Christians ("Because I am a Muslim") and the Shiites ("Because they think all international businessmen are working for the C.I.A."). Besides, business had pretty much dried up. Basma had been in Oranien for the best part of three years, doing the odd bit of trade and otherwise depleting his capital. He was eager to move on to more fertile ground, but had not yet decided where that might be. By then I was tired and tipsy, and went to bed early. But we agreed to meet again the next day and have dinner in town, which is how we came to be discussing the police.

"Who, for instance?" I asked.

"Let's not be looking around and staring," Basma said softly. "But that couple at the table by the wall on your right. I've seen them many times and wondered about them."

A handsome man and a beautiful woman, both in their late twenties. He wore a linen suit, a white shirt, and no tie. He had dark hair and a strong, unmarked face. She was dressed in a smart, obviously foreign outfit—skirt, matching jacket and a stylish blouse. I imagined her to be the daughter of a local bigshot, she had that air of privilege and hauteur. They made me feel old, or perhaps just envious of their youth and good looks.

"I don't care," I said. "I'm just passing through. All I want to do is relax for a couple of weeks."

"Of course." Basma smiled.

So that night he gave me the grand tour of Oranien, such as it is. After the mandatory steak dinner we strolled through the main shopping arcade, which was full of the latest European fashions and Asian electronic equipment, all carrying steep price tags. We took in a couple of bars, briefly surveyed a dance hall that doubled as an economy class dating service and then stopped for a while at a neon-riddled disco called Marlene's where the crowd was somewhat interesting. There the sons and daughters of local wealth came to dance, flirt, play their social games and get blitzed. Basma called them the second-raters, because the brightest of their generation and class were away in America or England, at the best private schools and universities.

By the time we'd squandered some money at a posh gaming club and had a disturbing glimpse of a very discreet place where you could do whatever you wanted with girls (or boys) as young as thirteen, I'd seen enough for one night. Oranien's dull and orderly exterior masked the usual wanton tendencies. It didn't bother me, but it didn't interest me.

Back in my room, I poured one last nightcap from my bottle of duty-free single malt and lit a cigarette. I'd had a lot to drink, but it had been spaced out over many hours, with a meal thrown in somewhere along the line. I wasn't drunk, just tired, reasonably buzzed. I know this for sure, because whenever I have gotten drunk in the past I've never dreamed, or at least I've never remembered it. That night I did have a dream, and it was one I wouldn't forget.

I was sleeping in my bed, there in the Hotel des Vacances. It was the middle of the night. Suddenly I was awakened by a loud clattering noise. I jumped out of bed in a fog. I was at the window, looking out on what seemed to be a historical costume pageant. It confused me, and I couldn't move. The street below, brightly lit by a three-quarters moon, was full of soldiers on horseback. They carried torches, or waved swords. The horses continued to make a dreadful racket, stamping their feet on the clay tiles. Every house in sight remained dark, but the soldiers went to several different doors, roused the inhabitants and seized eight or ten people altogether. They were thrown into horse-drawn carts, already crowded with prisoners. The night was full of terrible sounds—the soldiers shouting, men arguing or pleading in vain, their women and children wailing, a ghastly pandemonium. It seemed they had finished and were about to move on, when one of the soldiers, obviously an officer, turned and looked up directly at me. Now I was standing out on the little balcony, gripping the wrought iron tightly. The officer spoke to one of his comrades, who also looked in my direction. Then the officer raised his sword, pointing to me. I knew his face—but I had no idea who he was. A small group of soldiers, apparently responding to instructions, hurried across the street toward the hotel. Still, I couldn't move. A terrible fear came over me as I realized they would take me away with the others. The rest is sensation, the twisting, falling, hideous sweetness we all dream more often than we would like before it actually happens—our moment of dying.

I slept late—it was becoming a welcome habit—and woke up feeling remarkably cheerful and energetic. I remembered the dream, I thought about it all through my shower, over brunch and during my walk to the newsstand for the most recent *Herald Tribune*. I sat outdoors at a quiet cafe, had two cups of gritty coffee, smoked cigarettes and read the sports scores from a few days ago in my distant homeland.

It felt great to be alive. Any sense of menace or fear had dissolved out of the dream. It had already become a kind of mental curio that I carried around with me. Maybe I was happy simply because I knew I could never have had that nightmare in New York. What it seemed to say to me in the light of day was: *Now you know you're in Blanca.*

"It's local history," Basma agreed when we met in the beer garden later that afternoon and I told him about the dream. "You must have known about it before you came here."

"Sure. Well, vaguely." I lit a cigarette while an Indian waitress delivered our second round of beers. "I've heard the jokes about people being taken away in the dead of night, never to be seen again."

"Yes, but they are not jokes. What you dreamed is exactly how it used to happen—and by the way, it still does, from time to time."

"Really?"

"Of course."

"Well, that's politics, which never interested me. I'd just as soon get back to dreaming about sex."

Basma smiled broadly. "No need just to dream about it."

"Dreaming will do for now."

Basma shrugged sadly. I knew I was doing a pretty poor job of living up to his mental image of American tourists as people hellbent on having an extravagantly good time. We had a light dinner together and then I disappointed him further by deciding to make an early evening of it. I was still a bit tired from our night out on the town, and I wanted nothing more than to read in bed for a while and then get about twelve hours of sleep. I had it in mind to rent a car the next day and see a bit of the nearby countryside, however flat and dull it might prove to be.

Simenon worked his usual magic. I was soon transported to rainy Paris (even in the sweltering heat of August, Simenon's Paris seems rainy), where Inspector Maigret had another nasty murder to unravel. It was bliss, but unfortunately I drifted off to sleep sooner than I expected. I woke up a little after four in the morning, still dressed, the paperback in my hand. I dropped the book to the floor and crawled under the covers. But it was no good. Finally I sat up and groaned, realizing that I would not be able to get back to sleep. For a while I simply stayed there, lying still.

I got out of bed when I noticed a strange flickering of light reflected on the half-open window. It came from the street below, a lamp-post or car headlights most likely. But when I stepped onto the balcony and looked down, I was paralyzed by what I saw. They were all there again. The horses, the carts, the soldiers with their swords and torches, the pitiful souls being dragged from their homes, the mothers and wives, the children. It was a repeat performance of the grim nightmare I'd had only twenty four hours ago, but this time I was wide awake. I forced myself to be sure: I took note of the cold, harsh wrought iron beneath my bare feet, I sucked in huge breaths of chilly night air, and I looked over my shoulder into the hotel room to reassure myself in some way. But when I turned back to the street below they were still there, the scene continued to play itself out. I was awake, and it was happening.

I realized there were certain differences. Noise—there was none at all. The horses stamped, the soldiers shouted, the men argued and their families sobbed, but I heard none of this, I could only see it taking place. Silence ruled the night. And then there was the officer, the one in charge who had pointed his sword at me in the dream. I spotted him again and he still looked familiar to me, but I didn't know who he was. This time he never once glanced in my direction. He and his troops went about their business as if I didn't exist, though they could hardly fail to notice me standing there on the second floor balcony, the room lit up behind me. The fact that they didn't may account for the other difference, the lack of fear in me. The scene had a terrible fascination, I was transfixed by it, but at the same time I felt detached from it, uninvolved. I didn't know what to make of it. I felt puzzled rather than threatened.

Finally I did something sensible. I looked up the street, away from the scene, and sure enough, I saw the usual line of parked cars that I knew belonged there. It was a comforting sight. But then, when I turned back, the dream drama was still just visible. The soldiers and the carts had formed a wavy line and were marching away from me toward the main road, a hundred yards or so in the distance. I watched them until they reached the intersection with that broad avenue, at which point my eyes could make out nothing more than the bobbing, meandering flow of torch flames.

It took another few minutes for me to realize that what I was looking at was a stream of headlights. Then I became aware of the sound of that traffic; the silence was broken. The early shift, I told myself. Hundreds of workers on their way to the abattoirs, stockyards and packing plants on the south side of the city. The newsagents, short order cooks and bus drivers. All the people who open up the city before dawn every morning. Any city. I stepped back into the room, sat on my bed and lit a cigarette, wondering how yesterday's nightmare could turn into today's hallucination.

"Do you take drugs?" Basma asked me casually.

We were walking through the park, toward a bar I'd never been to in my life. It was about five that afternoon, and I'd blurted out the story of the hallucination—which was what I still took it to be—as soon as we met for our daily drink and chat. I laughed.

"No, it's been a few years since I did any drugs, and even then it wasn't much."

"You are quite certain that you were fully awake when you saw this—whatever it was?"

"Yes."

"And you were awake *before* you saw it?"

"Definitely. I was lying there, feeling sorry for myself for waking up so early. I saw the orange light flickering on the window—it's a glass door, actually, to the balcony."

"Yes, yes," Basma said impatiently.

"Well, like I told you, I sat up and went to the window, I stepped out onto the balcony, and there it was."

"I see."

Basma didn't speak again until we reached the bar, a workers' grog shop that offered only the locally brewed beer, Bolero. Once we got our drinks and I had lit a cigarette, Basma returned to the subject.

"So you think it was hallucination."

"Yes, of course," I said. "What else would it be?"

"Ghosts." Basma smiled faintly, not as if he were joking.

"Perhaps you saw the ghosts of history."

"Oh, I doubt that very much."

"Why? It makes perfect sense. What is more, I think you may have been awake the first time you saw them, two nights ago. You only thought it was a dream, you were less certain because it was the first time and you had been drinking more—yes?"

"Yes, I had been drinking more, but I still think that I was dreaming. It ended in a panic and I was lost in sleep in an instant. No sensation of getting back into bed or thinking about it." I stubbed out my cigarette and lit another. I didn't like disappointing Basma again, he seemed as eager as a young child to believe in ghosts. "Besides, even if I were awake, that doesn't mean it was not a hallucination.

The same hallucination, two nights in a row." Basma gave this some thought. "You have a medical history of this?"

"No, not at all," I had to admit.

"Then why do you think it should suddenly start happening to you now?"

I shrugged. "Maybe the stories I'd heard about Blanca. The emotional distress from the break-up of my marriage. Throw in the mild despair I sometimes feel at the approach of my fortieth birthday." I finished the beer and I realized how self-pitying I sounded, and it annoyed me very much. "To tell you the truth, I really have no idea at all why this kind of thing should suddenly be happening to me."

"Hallucination?" Basma asked again, quietly.

"That makes a lot more sense than an army of ghosts."

"As long as it makes sense to you."

It didn't, in fact, but I was fed up talking about it, fed up even thinking about it, so I fetched two more Bolero beers and then changed the subject. I told Basma about my day trip. I'd hired an Opel Rekord that morning and driven past miles and miles of cattle ranches, through small but impeccable villages, in a wide looping route north of Oranien. Altogether, I was out of the city for about five hours, and I'd seen quite enough of the countryside. There was nothing wrong with it—it was agreeably unspoiled rangeland—but it was bland, featureless, lacking in charm or interest. Just as I'd been told.

"Yes," Basma nodded. "I have heard that once you leave the city it's much the same in every direction for hundreds of miles. Although I've never seen for myself."

"You've never left Oranien, since you got here?"

"Why should I? There's nothing to see or do." His smile broadened into a grin. "Is there?"

"Well, no."

"Do you still have the car?"

"Yes, until tomorrow noon," I told him. "It's parked back near the hotel."

"Good. If you don't mind driving, I would like to show you something. Not exactly a tourist attraction, but I think you'll find it worthwhile."

He wouldn't tell me where we were going, but there was still plenty of daylight left when Basma and I drove away a few minutes later. I followed his directions and it was soon obvious that we were heading toward the south end of the city.

"The stockyards?" I guessed.

"Ah, you've seen them."

"Only from a distance." I told Basma about the view from the department store.

"Now you will see it all close up."

I was mildly curious. We passed through the commercial district, and then a residential area not unlike the one in which I was staying. The houses and squat apartment buildings became shabbier and more dilapidated the farther we went from the center of the city. The middle class in-town neighborhoods gave way to the worker-Indian tenements on the outskirts. I wanted to drive slowly so that I could see as much as possible, and in fact I had to because there were so many people out on the streets. Kids playing games and ignoring the traffic, grown-ups talking in small groups (men to men, women to women, mostly), and the old folks sitting stoically wherever they could find a quiet spot. Most of the local social life, including the cooking and eating of food, seemed to take place outdoors.

Almost before I realized it, we were there. The industry and the workers' lodgings had sprung up together over the years, without benefit of design or long-term planning. There were row houses right up to the open doors of an abattoir, apartment buildings wedged between a canning factory and a processing plant, and a vast maze of corrals holding thousands of cattle bumping against dozens of tiny back yards. After we had cruised around for a while I began to understand that these people lived in their workplaces—they would go home when their shift was finished, but home was hardly any different. The interminable stupid bawling of the cattle, the mingled stench of blood, raw meat and cowshit, the constant rattling of trains, the drumming vibrations of the factories—everything here, everything you saw or heard or felt or smelled was about decay and death. You could taste it in the air and feel it as a slickness that settled on your skin.

We reached the worst of it, a mean stretch where finally the people themselves seemed only marginally alive. They stood or sat about in front of their shacks, looking dazed. The streets, no longer paved, had become increasingly difficult to navigate. Ditches ran along both sides, and they ran red with blood from the slaughterhouses. In the absence of traffic and other human noises, the steady shriek of power saws carving animal flesh was piercingly clear. At every pile of garbage vicious cats and scarred dogs competed with huge brown roaches and gangs of rats for whatever was going. It was getting dark fast.

"I hope you know the way back."

"Yes, of course."

Basma gave me a series of directions and it wasn't too long before we were on a better road. Neither of us had spoken much in the course of our slumming tour. As soon as I caught a glimpse of the lights in the center of the city my stomach began to relax a little. I had been to some of the worst refugee camps in the world, but never felt so tense. Refugee camps are at least meant to be temporary, and there was always the hope, however slim, of eventual movement. The people I had just seen were never going anywhere.

"I suppose I've had Blanca beef many times, in my travels," I said, just to say something.

"I'm sure you have," Basma agreed promptly. "They ship it out in every form. Brains, tongue, heart, kidneys, liver, as well as all the usual cuts, prime rib, steaks and so on, all the way down to hot dogs and Vienna sausages. If it isn't tinned or wrapped in plastic, it's frozen."

We began to joke about becoming vegetarians, describing the best salads we could remember having, and we kept at it until we were comfortably settled with drinks in Number One, which was supposedly the better of Oranien's two topless joints. It was expensive but otherwise all right. That kind of bar, where the music was loud and the women occasionally distracting, was just what Basma and I needed, since our excursion into the south end had left us in no mood for serious conversation. We drank until the place closed, by which time we were both unfit to drive, so we left the rental car parked where it was and took a taxi.

I wasn't surprised when Basma got out of the cab with me at the hotel. I didn't know exactly where he lived but I assumed it was in the neighborhood because we'd met in the beer garden and we always said goodnight outside the hotel.

"Would you like to have a nightcap in my room?" he asked me as the taxi pulled away.

"No, thanks very much. I couldn't take another drink."

"Are you sure? I have a bottle of Teachers, pretty good stuff, and I live right there, across the street." Basma pointed vaguely to the first or second building on the opposite corner. "Come on, one more.

No, really, thanks. I'm going to fall down and pass out, and I'd rather do that in my bed than on your floor."

Basma shrugged. "Okay. See you tomorrow."

"Sure. Good night." I turned away, but then stopped and looked back at him. "Hey, you know what? Your building is one of the ones those ghost soldiers raided."

"Don't be telling me such things," he said from the middle of the street. "I don't want to know that."

"Why? It's just ghosts and history. Right?"

"Don't be saying that."

Basma wagged a finger at me and kept going. I somehow made it upstairs, locked my door and even managed to get my clothes off before spinning dizzily into sleep. It was nearly noon when I opened my eyes again. The first thing that came to me was how nice it felt not to have had another hallucination, nightmare or ghostly apparition to brood about. I'd been truly out of it and I'd slept straight through, unbothered. On the negative side, however, I felt terrible the moment I stood up. I took a long shower, which made me feel cleaner but did nothing for my head, and I was going to get some food when I remembered the rental car. I didn't want to pay another day's charges but it was already late. When I got to the car I found a parking ticket under the wiper blade. I shoved it in my pocket, wondering if I could safely tear it up or if the vaunted Oranien police would catch up with me before I flew out next week. The car rental agency wanted me to pay for the second full day, naturally, since I was well over an hour past the deadline when I finally got there. I had no luck arguing until I pulled out my *Vogue* credentials, at which point the manager became obsequious and sympathetic. No problem: no extra charges.

Then I got some much-needed food into my stomach. I went back to my hotel room, tore up the parking ticket and fell asleep again on the bed while trying to read the *Herald Tribune*. It was after four when I dragged myself down to the beer garden. I held off on the alcohol, cautiously sipping a flat mineral water while I waited for Basma. An hour later, I began to wonder if I'd made a mistake. We *had* agreed to meet in the usual place at the usual time, hadn't we? But maybe he had things to attend to elsewhere, and I'd misunderstood him in the boozy fog last night. I wasn't disappointed or annoyed, because in truth I really wanted a break from Basma's company, for one evening anyway. I stayed a little longer, out of courtesy, and then returned to my room. He'd know where to find me if he turned up later. But he didn't, and I had a very welcome early night.

The next day I felt great, and I did what I'd really wanted to do all along. I sat in the shade in the beer garden, reading Simenon. I had breakfast there, followed later by more coffee, then lunch, and, in the middle of the afternoon, lemonade and a plate of watermelon chunks. By five o'clock I'd knocked off both Maigret novels in the volume, and I was ready to allow myself a glass of cold Bolero beer. It was a very light pale lager, but I was beginning to develop a taste for it.

Where was Basma? I had a sudden guilty flashback to our drunken parting. I'd teased him about the ghost soldiers, as he thought of them, and now it occurred to me that I might have annoyed him. Perhaps that was why he was staying away. What you do when you're drunk always seems much worse when you reconstruct it later. I was tired of sitting there, but once again I stayed on for another hour or so, until it was obvious that my Lebanese friend was not going to put in an appearance.

I went looking for him a little while later. I started with the comer building diagonally opposite the hotel. Inside the unlocked screen door was a small entry foyer with a tile floor and a rickety wooden table. The inner door was locked, so I rang the bell, and kept ringing it for nearly five minutes before a heavyset, middle-aged woman answered.

"I'm looking for Mr. Basma," I told her.

"He go."

"When do you expect him back?" She shrugged, and shook her head at this. "Well, can I leave a message for him?" I took out a pen and a piece of paper I'd brought for that purpose. But the woman continued to shake her head.

"He go," she repeated emphatically.

"When will he be back?"

"Men come. He go with men."

Simple enough, and apparently the end of the story as far as she was concerned. I wasn't ready to give up, however.

"What about his things?"

"What."

"Things. Clothes, belongings." Most people in Blanca can speak English because the local dialect is one of those clotted, homegrown curiosities of limited use, like Afrikaans. But this creature's English was marginal at best. "His possessions, his personal—his *things*, damnit."

"Gone."

"When did he go?"

"Yesterday."

"Can I see his room?"

"Room?"

"Yes. Basma's room. Please."

"Room—yes, yes. Come."

It took a while to get there, because the woman moved only with difficulty. She showed me into the front room on the first floor. It was a dreary little place with a couch, a couple of chairs, a table, a hideous wardrobe and a single bed. There was a small bathroom and, behind a plastic curtain, an even smaller galley kitchen. The few items of furniture were old and worn, the walls faded and unadorned, the carpeting thin as newspaper. I went to the window and looked out at the park and the quiet streets. I looked at the balcony and window of my room in the hotel across the way.

"Nice view," the woman said.

I nodded absently. There was no doubt in my mind that Basma was gone for good. The room had been completely stripped of all personal items. What was there was what you got when you rented a very modest furnished room.

"Three hundred crown," the woman said.

"What?"

"Three hundred crown. One month." She waved her hand in a gesture commending the room to me. "One hundred U.S. dollar."

"No." I hurried away.

That night I slept by the balcony window in my room. I used the big armchair, and stretched my legs out on the coffee table. It was not a comfortable arrangement, but it wasn't unbearable, and I wanted to be there. It seemed important not to miss the apparition, if it should occur again.

I tried to read for a while but I could no longer keep my mind on the words. Basma wouldn't have left so suddenly without saying goodbye, I told myself. From what the woman had said in her skeletal English, he had been taken—and that surely meant taken against his will. But by whom, and why? It seemed highly unlikely that his Lebanese enemies would come such a distance to exact revenge, and he'd been so insistent in cautioning me about the Blanca police that I couldn't imagine he'd ever set a foot wrong here. Certainly not in the realm of politics. But Basma was an entrepreneur, so it was not impossible that he'd gotten involved in some shady deal that had landed him in trouble with the authorities.

Could I help him in any way? He had been good company, a friend. He hadn't tried to con me. He'd been a useful guide to the city. It seemed wrong just to shrug it off mentally and forget about him. But I couldn't think of anything to do, other than ask the local police about him—and I was reluctant to do that.

It was dawn when I awoke to the sound of car doors slamming. The first thing I saw was a silver Mercedes with black-tinted windows, parked at the corner across from my hotel. The car's yellow hazard lights were flashing. Four men wearing sunglasses and linen suits entered Basma's building. While they were inside a van with the similarly darkened windows pulled up behind the Mercedes and waited. A moment later the four men reappeared, with a fifth man in their custody—he wasn't even handcuffed, but it was obvious he was their prisoner. I stood up, swung the window open and stepped out onto the balcony.

"Basma."

I had spoken to myself, barely whispering the man's name in stunned disbelief. But the five of them stopped immediately and looked up at me. Basma looked terrified. I thought I recognized one of the other men. I was so shocked and frightened, however, that I took a step back involuntarily and stumbled, and I had to grab the window frame to catch my balance. Then the scene below was finished, gone as if it had never happened, and I was looking down at an empty street corner.

I sat on the bed and lit a cigarette. My hands shook, my head clamored. The smoke was like ground glass in my throat but I sucked it in deeply, as if trying to make a point with my own pain. I'd been so many miles, seen so much of the world, the best and the worst and the endless in between, but now for the first time in my life I felt lost.

Then I became angry with myself. My feelings didn't matter in this situation. Basma was the one in trouble, and I had to try to help, or at least find out what was happening to him. For all I knew, I was the only friend he had in Blanca. I didn't want to—it scared the shit out of me to think about it—but I had to do something. And now I knew where to start.

They came into the beer garden just after four o'clock that afternoon, as they had several times during the past week. The woman was as beautiful as ever, cool and formidable. The kind of woman you would fear falling in love with, but love to watch. It was her man, however, who interested me. The man in the linen suit. Basma had warned me about them. I was pretty sure the man was the officer on horseback I had seen twice. I *knew* he was one of the men I had seen take Basma away.

Dreams, nightmares, hallucinations, ghosts. Take your pick. But maybe the simplest, truest explanation was that I was in the middle of a breakdown, caused by the collapse of my marriage and my abrupt flight to this miserable place. It made sense, and I hesitated, clinging to my own weakness. But I was there, Basma was gone, and that man in the linen suit was very real. I got up at last and went to their table.

"Excuse me," I said. "I'm sorry to intrude, but I wonder if I could speak to you for a moment."

"Yes, why not. Please."

He gestured for me to take a seat. They almost looked as if they had been waiting all along for me to approach them— which made me feel even more uncomfortable.

"I've seen you around here almost every day since I arrived—I'm on vacation—and the thing is, I can't find a friend of mine. He seems to have disappeared. His name is Basma. He's a Lebanese businessman. He had a small flat in the corner building across the street. Do you know him?"

"I don't think so."

"Can you suggest how I might find out about him?"

"Go to the police."

They both seemed to regard me with an impossible mixture of curiosity and disinterest. I was getting nowhere.

"He thought maybe you were a policeman."

At last, something. The barest flicker of an eyebrow, then the man smiled, as if at some silly misunderstanding. The woman was keenly attentive now, and it was hard for me not to return the all-consuming look in her eyes.

"I do work in the government," the man told me. "I am not a

policeman. But you are our guest here. Let me ask some people I know about your friend."

"Thank you."

"Of course, I cannot promise you anything."

"I understand."

"Are you staying here?"

"Yes." I gave him my name and room number, and told him I would be staying five more days. "Thank you for your help. I'm sorry to trouble you."

"No trouble."

Later, I felt disgusted at how deferential I'd been, all but groveling for a scrap of information. The man knew Basma, knew the whole story far better than I did; he was a primary player. *Thank you for your help.* But how else could I have handled it? It would have been crazy to confront the man and accuse him of arresting Basma. It would have been absurd to tell him that history replays itself every morning on that street corner, and that I'd seen what he and his colleagues had done.

So the possibilities for action on my part were extremely limited. I'd done what I could. I began to think that I should let it go, that it was just one more thing in my life to put behind me. Basma was rotting in some filthy prison cell, if he wasn't already a ghost. In any event, nothing I could do would make the least difference. I might try to write about Basma and Blanca, something political with teeth in it—but not here, not until I was safely back in New York. I'd never written anything like that before.

I slept well that night and did very little the next day. I took a couple of short walks, but mostly hung around the hotel, reading and relaxing. The government man and his beautiful woman did not put in an appearance. I enjoyed another peaceful night, no dreams or ghosts. It was pleasant to idle away afternoons in the beer garden, sipping iced tea and nibbling slivers of chilled melon. I was actually glad that the man in the linen suit failed to show up for the second day in a row.

I did think about Basma now and then. I missed his company, but in my line of work I meet so many people, all over the world. Already he was slipping away from me. I had calmed down enough to realize I would never write that article. I wasn't equipped to do it properly. Tourism was my beat, not politics or ghosts or mysterious disappearances. To hell with Blanca. Maybe it was a surrender of sorts, but by admitting these things to myself I felt I was on the way to a kind of mental recovery, and that had been the whole purpose of the trip in the first place. That evening I intended to find some new restaurant and have anything but steak for dinner. Then scout a few bars. I was in the mood for serious female contact at last. It was a little past seven when I stepped out of the hotel. At that instant the silver Mercedes braked sharply to a halt and the man in the linen suit jumped out. He came right at me. I was determined not to let this nasty little hood intimidate me anymore.

"Do you want to see your friend?"

"Yes, of course. Where is he?"

"I will take you." He gestured toward the open car door. "Please. It is still light."

I was aware that the other people on the street all stood motionless, watching. Calmly, at my own pace, I walked to the car and sat down inside. I was in the back seat, between the man I knew and another fellow, who regarded me warily. I wasn't too surprised to see the beautiful young woman in the front seat, along with the driver. She glanced at me once, then looked away. We raced through the center of the city. We were heading south, I knew that much. I asked a few questions but the only answers I got were vague and unsatisfactory.

The driver never slowed down. If anything, he pushed the car a little faster when we reached the crowded working class district. People and animals sometimes had to jump out of the way at the last second to save themselves. I could sense the others in the car trying not to smile. We passed the factories, the slaughterhouses, the tenements, the stockyards, the grisly processing, canning and freezing plants. We ripped through the sprawling shantytown and continued beyond the point where Basma and I had ended our exploration. Finally we were on a dirt road, crossing a vast scrubby wasteland. We had gone a couple of miles when I saw that we were approaching a cluster of vehicles parked with their headlights on, pointing in the same direction. They walked me to the edge of a long ditch, about eight feet deep. It was dusk, not yet too dark to see, but spotlights had been hooked up to a generator to illuminate the scene. It was all so bright it hurt my eyes. Perhaps a dozen other men stood about, smoking, talking quietly, taking notes and photographs. When my eyes adjusted, I forced myself to look carefully.

There were a lot of bodies in the ditch, I would estimate at least twenty. All the same: hands tied behind the back, the back of the head partially blown away, bloating features. I noticed the swarming insects, the ferocious smell. I stood there for a while, staring, but so help me I could not put together a single thought. A couple of men wearing goggles and masks were getting ready to spray the ditch with some chemical.

"Can you identify that person?" the man in the linen suit asked me, pointing to a particular corpse. "There."

"Yes, that's him." In spite of the puffed face, parts of which had already been nibbled at by animals, I had no difficulty picking out my late friend. "That's Basma."

"I am so sorry," he said quite casually. "It is a terrible way to die."

As if there are any good ones.

"Why did this happen to him?" I asked. "He was a harmless little man, a foreign guest in this country. Why should they," I almost said *you* but managed to avoid it, "do this to him?"

"Come here, please."

He led me back to the car, where the young woman waited. She looked smart as ever, this time in a tropical pants suit with a white blouse open three buttons deep. The man nodded to her. She reached into a leather briefcase I hadn't noticed and handed him something. He held it up for me to see. My eyes lingered on hers for a moment, but her look gave nothing away.

"Did you do this?"

I could feel the blood vacating my cheeks, then rushing back as I tried to muster a sense of embarrassed contempt. He had a large rectangle of cardboard, on which were pasted all the torn pieces of my parking ticket.

"Yes, we do that all the time back in New York. I hope it's

not a felony here. I'm willing to pay the fine, whatever it is, and I'll pay it now, if you like."

"Did you refuse to pay a late fee to Bolero Rent-a-Car, and did you threaten to write negative comments about that agency in your travel articles in foreign publications?"

I took a deep breath, exhaled slowly. "I was about an hour late, but I explained the situation to them and they seemed to be satisfied. If they're not, I'd be glad to pay the fee."

"May I have your passport?"

I gave it to him. "Why?"

"You can get in the car now. An officer will drive you back to your hotel. Thank you for your help."

"I need my passport," I told him. "I'm flying home in three days. Sunday afternoon."

"I know," he replied. "We will contact you."

I tried to talk to the driver on the journey back into town, but he ignored me. I was furious, but frightened as well. The whole thing was a grotesque charade. They didn't need me to identify Basma but they made me go through with it, knowing that I wouldn't have the courage to accuse them of his murder. Take a good look in that ditch, they were saying to me, this is the kind of thing we can do. They were toying with me, because it's their nature to toy with people.

What, if anything, could Basma have done to bring about his own destruction at the hands of these people? Perhaps he'd been involved in some way with a radical faction in Lebanon. Did the authorities here think they were eliminating a Muslim terrorist? Was he a crook or a smuggler, a charming criminal who had escaped from Beirut only to run out of luck in Blanca? To me he seemed a pleasant, fairly idle fellow with an agreeable manner and a taste for godless liquor. But, in fairness, I hardly knew him. We had a few dinners together, a lot of drinks, that was all. It was a brief acquaintance. Our backgrounds and our circumstances were totally different. They couldn't do *that* to me.

Common sense told me I had nothing to fear. The parking ticket and the rental agency were trivial matters that could be settled with a little cash. I was an American, a travel writer for a major international magazine. They might push me around, but they wouldn't hurt me.

All the same, I decided to take certain precautions. The next morning I tried to contact the nearest American consulate, which was some four hundred miles away. At first the operator of the hotel switchboard told me that all long distance lines out of Oranien were engaged. After an hour of fruitless attempts she said she had learned that they were "down," and that she had no idea how long it would be before they were working again. I went to the main post office and tried again—same result.

I tried to rent another car—at a different agency. I'm not sure what I intended to do with it—drive away, I suppose, right out of the country—but I was refused one because I could not produce my passport.

I didn't bother with lunch. I drank a couple of beers and smoked a lot of cigarettes. I wandered around until I found the railroad station. I bought a ticket on the next departing train, although I wasn't even sure where it was going. Then a uniformed policeman confiscated the ticket, smiling.

"We don't want you to disappear on us, sir."

Of course not. They got the parking ticket from the waste basket in my room. They had talked with the rental agency about me. They'd been watching and following me all the time. It was pointless to wonder why. I went back to the hotel and, as calmly as possible, I wrote a letter to my lawyer in New York, telling him where I was, that I had a problem with the authorities, and that if he hadn't heard from me—my voice on the telephone—by the time he got the letter he was to do whatever it took to get me out of Blanca—press conferences, congressmen, the State Department, the works. I wrote more or less the same thing to my editor. I used hotel stationery and did not write my name on the envelopes. The hotel was unsafe and so were the streets, but I thought my chances were a little better outdoors. I went for a walk and slipped the letters into the mailbox on the corner as inconspicuously as possible. I crossed into the park and sat on a bench for a while, smoking. Nothing happened. I got back to my room—just in time to glance out the window and see a silver Mercedes pull away from the mailbox.

This is my last night in Blanca. Tomorrow I am supposed to be on the noon flight out of here. I still have that ticket. I still do not have my passport. For two days and two nights I've waited. Nothing happens. I am waiting. There's nowhere to go, nothing to do, except smoke and drink and wait.

I think of them all the time, the handsome man in the linen suit and the beautiful young woman. Mostly I think of her, with her blouse open three buttons deep. Her breasts are not large because I saw no cleavage, but I know they are perfect. Her skin finely tanned with the faintest trace of sun-bleached down. I would like to have her, to lick her, but she is impossible to touch. You can only look at a woman like that, and wonder what it would be like to fuck death.

Tonight when I ask at the desk for a wakeup call they smile and say yes, of course, and smile some more. No one writes it down. The porter says I don't look well. Would I like dinner in my room? Some company? Clean, he adds encouragingly.

It'll be over long before noon. Around four or five in the morning the silver Mercedes will arrive, the van right behind. The men in the van are there to strip the room of my possessions after I'm gone. Some morning in the future you can look out one of these windows and see how it happened, too late for me—and for you.

I hope I'm not alone, I hope there are others. Many will be arguing, begging, screaming, but some will walk out unaided, with quiet dignity. If I have to, that's what I want to do.

Not that it matters.

I crush out a cigarette. I open another bottle of beer, reach for another cigarette. I don't have to go to the window to see what is happening outside. There is light in the sky.

Look for me.

A GRUB STREET TALE

"I still don't think he was that good," Geoffrey Wilson said as he charred the tip of a panatela. "Obviously he had a talent, but the fact is he never knew quite what to do with it."

"He's being compared to Hawthorne now."

"Ridiculous, isn't it." Geoffrey smiled and shook his head. "The same people who say that wouldn't deign to review his novels if he were still alive."

Judith Stockmann nodded hesitantly, as if she almost agreed with him. Geoffrey rather liked her, this dark-haired, dark-eyed young beauty. The perfect companion for a lovely summer evening. They were sitting on the terrace of a pub in Chiswick, discussing the short life and varying literary works of Patrick Hamm.

"You think he's overrated?"

"Oh yes, of course." Geoffrey flicked his lighter again and puffed until the cigar was properly lit. "No question."

"What was he like as a person?"

"He had a certain charm. We had some good times together in Soho, early on. He drank too much, needless to say."

"Especially in the last year?"

Geoffrey considered that. "All along the line, really. It did get worse toward the end, I suppose, but by that time Patrick and I saw very little of each other. Alas."

A sore point, that falling-out, but one that could hardly be avoided. It was a part of the unfortunate history. Geoffrey was reluctant to discuss Patrick Hamm with anybody, and at first he'd tried to fend off Judith Stockmann. But she had persisted, with notes or phone calls every week. Geoffrey eventually realized he couldn't put her off forever.

So he had agreed to this meeting on neutral ground. Dredge up a few moth-eaten tidbits for her critical biography of Patrick Hamm and try to cast things in a positive light. Geoffrey didn't care about her project, but why not see what Judith Stockmann was like in the flesh? So far, she seemed fair and objective. Quite attractive, as well.

"Were the two of you friends before—"

"No, it was strictly business at first. Our friendship grew out of our work together, over the course of time. I had serious hopes for Patrick and I genuinely liked him as a person. When he wandered off-track I did my best to help him right himself. But it's difficult for an editor and an author to hang together when there are serious disagreements."

Judith nodded again. "Commerce and creativity?"

"That was one part of it, yes," Geoffrey replied, "but there were other problems. Patrick could never bring himself to decide exactly what kind of writer he wanted to be."

"Don't most writers work through that?"

"It isn't easy to market an author who jumps from one genre to another and mixes them together. Booksellers have a hard time dealing with that, and so do readers."

"But the consensus now seems to be that Hamm found his true voice toward the end, with *The Lime-Kiln* and *The Varna Schooner*." Judith sipped her wine. "He was only forty-one, you could say he was just hitting his stride when—"

"I know, I know," Geoffrey cut in. "Everybody seems to love those two books, and of course it's all very tragic, the way that it ended. But I thought at the time that those books were really very pretentious, and I honestly still do."

"You prefer his earlier work."

"Yes, I do. *Our Lady of Heavenly Pain* and *Nightmare in Silk* are my two favorites. I published them both, and I believed that Patrick was onto something new. It was brilliant erotica, it was elegant and stylish. It used elements of the thriller and horror fiction to good effect. I loved it, and I can remember thinking, he can't miss." Geoffrey shrugged sadly. "But he did."

"Critics now tend to see those works as potboilers," Judith said. "Efficient, but limited. Finger exercises, part of Hamm's mastering the craft of fiction."

Wilson scowled. "They would, wouldn't they."

"After the first two books—"

"That's when he started to drift," Geoffrey answered before he heard the rest of the question. "He wrote that ill-conceived family gothic, *The Weybright Curse.* God, I hated that. I'd just moved up to Pell House then and I was eager to bring Patrick with me. But I couldn't accept that book. He stayed at Bingley, they published it, and it promptly sank like a rock."

"Were there hard feelings?"

"Some, yes." Geoffrey reflected for a moment. "But I still wanted to publish Patrick, so I encouraged him to get on with the next novel. *Ill-Met by Gaslight,* which I did publish. It was an odd book, a modern murder mystery with time travel, but it worked in some bizarre way, and he was back with me."

"Was that about the time he turned to short fiction?"

She had an exquisite neck, Geoffrey noted. Honeyish tanned skin set off by a brilliant white blouse and tiny pearls.

"Yes, and it was infuriating. Nasty little stories, full of disagreeable people doing disagreeable things. He put together a volume called *Micronovels of the Dead,* and that was soon followed by a second one, *Tales of Extreme Panic.* But nobody would touch them. Patrick eventually lost his agent over that short fiction. No one knew it at the time, sad to say, but he was well into his final phase by then."

"Now those stories are highly regarded."

"Patrick would appreciate the joke."

"Did he discuss the last two novels with you?"

"Oh yes, and I advised him as best I could. But there were some serious problems to overcome." Geoffrey put his cigar down on the ashtray. "You see, by that time his name and sales record in the book business meant nothing. He'd frittered away whatever identity he had managed to create for himself. He was getting to be old goods, a maverick, and nobody cared. Careerwise, Patrick was in big trouble."

She had gorgeous legs, long and slender. Geoffrey could see and enjoy them properly, now that Judith was leaning back on the sofa in his sitting room. They'd had a couple of polite drinks at the pub, and then she accepted his invitation to dinner. He took pride in his cooking ability and he intended to broil two superb Wiltshire steaks—assuming they got around to food.

He could dole out boring old Patrick Hamm anecdotes for days if that would keep her happy. Days, nights. First, he dug out a file of old letters from Patrick. Harmless stuff, often amusing, none of the final anger and anguish. Judith scanned them quickly and murmured with delight at certain passages. She gave Geoffrey a warm smile when he offered to make copies for her.

She knew the books quite well, but not the man's life. Her knowledge of personal details was limited to the kind of material that had appeared often in the press. Geoffrey was the first of Hamm's personal acquaintances that Judith had approached—so he had clear sailing and could set the tone. They had more wine as he talked and she listened.

The Soho clubs, Hamm's assorted and equally hopeless lovers, a brief stint working in an East End soup kitchen, Hamm's writing habits, his appalling taste in food, his uninformed love of music and art—Geoffrey told Judith all sorts of odd details as they came to mind. It might not be significantly illuminating of the man's work, but it certainly had the authentic feel of firsthand experience. Geoffrey could see that Judith was loving every word of it, and that pleased him.

"To get back to his books," she said. "He did stop writing the short stories and started a new novel, *The Lime-Kiln*. And he showed it to you as he was working on it, didn't he?"

"Yes, that's right," Wilson replied. "I thought it started off in very promising fashion, but at about two-thirds of the way through it Patrick lost the thread. I don't think he liked his own characters. He killed them all off, every one of them, which resulted in a book that ended as a damp misfire. What was it all supposed to be about, and who cared anyhow?"

"What did he do then?"

"He went back over it from scratch, just as I suggested. It wasn't the plot so much as the characters, the heart of the book. And the ending, of course."

"But that first version is essentially the same one that has since been published and acclaimed everywhere."

"Oh yes, yes." Wilson still ground his teeth at the notion. "After his suicide, all of that gloom and despair no doubt seemed more convincing. You could say it gave him literary credibility. I know that must sound awfully cynical, but that's how the world works sometimes. If Patrick had remained here in the land of the living, the living would have continued to ignore him."

It was sickening, really. Three years after Patrick's death *The Lime-Kiln* was published to sudden acclaim. A year later, *The Varna Schooner* followed to an equally enthusiastic response. The collected stories. And the literary community embraced a corpse, made a fallen hero of him. To Geoffrey it was all so hypocritical and crass. Trading on the dead. Sickening.

Patrick's suicide had occurred a decade ago, and the bubbles had diminished somewhat in recent years. It was bound to subside even more in time, Geoffrey was convinced. Patrick's writing was often interesting, striking and disturbing, but it was not great. Not truly classic. No matter what anyone said.

"You didn't publish the second version either," Judith said. "Can you tell me about that?"

"It was no better," Geoffrey replied promptly. "And in some ways it was actually worse. Revision was never Patrick's strong suit, and he was almost relieved when I suggested that he set *The Lime-Kiln* aside for a while and start something new."

"*The Varna Schooner.*"

"Yes, and a great idea it was. The full-length treatment of an episode merely hinted at in *Dracula.* What went on aboard that ship carrying Dracula's coffin to England? What if there were a few passengers, as well as the crew? I loved the idea. But once again, Patrick had problems. He had a very hard time getting the period atmosphere right. He wouldn't do the research, he had no interest in the kind of details that would make a book like that convincing. Instead, there was more of that fancy philosophical talk, endless pretentious babble. The same thing that I believed was the cause of all the trouble in *The Lime-Kiln.* It got in the way of the story, just totally flattened it." Geoffrey continued quickly, "Now, I know what you're thinking. That what

I disliked is exactly what people now praise in those books, it's what makes them so good. Right?"

Judith smiled. "Well, that is true."

"Yes, it is." Geoffrey turned his hands palms-up and gave a helpless shrug. "What can I say? Perhaps I was wrong. Mistakes do happen in the book business. Eighteen publishers rejected *The Day of the Jackal*. Everybody knows DeGaulle wasn't assassinated, so who cares? Twenty publishers rejected *Watership Down*. Nobody wants to read about a bunch of bloody rabbits."

Judith laughed. "So, those things do happen."

"And that was when the two of you had your final break?" she asked cautiously.

Geoffrey nodded tightly. "It was an honest disagreement. I told Patrick that his characters weren't real enough. He was too interested in using them as ideas, as symbols. That and the lack of attention to period atmosphere ruined both books."

"For you."

"For me, yes," he agreed reasonably. "If I could just give you my capsule view of Patrick's last two novels, I honestly feel that they fall between two stools. They're too sophisticated and good for the commercial market, category fiction, but they're not quite brilliant enough for literary acceptance."

"Hmm." Judith appeared to consider that.

"Patrick didn't care whether he was a commercial success and made a lot of money, or achieved literary stature. But he wanted one or the other, if not both, and that's the sad part. He never experienced either of them in his lifetime."

"That's certainly true."

They were in Geoffrey's study. He had remembered a box of old photographs from his days at Bingley and he knew that several of them showed Patrick. The Thursday afternoons when some of the house authors would drop by and the booze flowed, the fierce talk about literature and the book trade. Great times. Unheard of in this new era, with the business driven by accountants.

Judith loved the snapshots and thought one of them might be reproduced satisfactorily in her eventual book. Geoffrey agreed, happy to please her. It might never happen, anyway. Most books died before they reached hardcovers, and he was far from certain that there was enough event in Patrick's gloomy life to justify a proper critical biography. But why discourage her?

Geoffrey sat close to her on the sofa in his study, looking down her blouse while he explained who people were in each photo. Very minor writers, most of them, sorted out and silenced by the marketplace over the years. Decent folks, and they all had their two or three published volumes, now yellowing on a shelf at home, to comfort them in the genteel failure of their advancing years. Even one forgotten book—is still something.

"Did he—"

"Enough," Geoffrey interrupted softly. He took the box of photographs and set them on the coffee table. "I think I've done enough talking for one session. We can always return to Patrick Hamm another time. I'd like to hear more about you now."

"You would?"

"Yes."

Judith smiled. "But should I tell you?"

"Yes, you should."

Patrick caressed her cheek with the back of his fingers, and she liked it. She didn't do anything but he could see it in her eyes, and he suddenly thought: she may be in love with a dead man but she will sleep with me tonight. Judith smiled at him, rested her head on his shoulder and then gazed absently at the wineglass that she still held on her lap.

"Where to start?"

"It's your story. Anywhere you like."

He felt her laugh silently and managed to use that moment to slip an arm around her shoulder. Geoffrey thought he noticed her body respond by settling closer against his.

"We came from Russia. It was quite an adventure, actually," Judith said. "But at the time it was very frightening."

"Is that so?"

"Oh, yes. Our family name was Bronstein but my father took the name Stockmann, from Ibsen's *An Enemy of the People.* He was opposed to the government, he wrote pamphlets and tracts, he went to prison twice, they beat him. We lived in constant fear, never knowing when the police might come. But father was a man of real integrity. He was an anarchist, in the truest sense of the term. An idealist, really."

"A Russian anarchist" Geoffrey mused. "Fantastic."

"Anyhow, the regime was very shaky," Judith continued. "My father believed that real change, revolution, was bound to happen soon. Perhaps my father went too far in his papers and speeches, or it was just another crackdown. The Tsar's secret police had my father's name on a list of people to be arrested, and everyone knew that this time the accused would never come back from prison alive. So we had to flee the country."

"Good Lord." Still, something was not right there.

"There was no time to spare. We left everything behind, and had to sneak out of Moscow in the middle of the night."

"And you made it, thank God."

Geoffrey stroked her neck lightly, tracing lines down toward the collar of her blouse. The Tsar? She meant the KGB, clearly, but this was not the time to play editor.

"Only just," Judith said, "and not all of us. We managed to get across the border, into Romania, and then on to Bulgaria, but police agents stayed on our trail. We had a couple of very close escapes along the way."

"Of course the Romanians and Bulgarians would cooperate with the Russians, wouldn't they."

"Or at least look the other way, yes. But we made it to the coast and my father had enough money to bribe an official and buy passage for us on a cargo ship to England."

"Aha. Very good."

"Can you guess where we sailed from?"

"I have no idea." Geoffrey laughed at himself. "In fact, I didn't even know Bulgaria had a coast."

"It's on the Black Sea."

"Yes, yes, of course. The Black Sea, the Caspian. They're all somewhere in that neck of the woods, aren't they."

"We sailed from the port of Varna."

"Va—you're joking." With his free hand he took Judith's chin and turned her face so that she was looking at him. She was smiling, but not as if she'd made a joke. "You weren't serious, were you. Varna? Really?"

"Yes," she said simply. "It really happened. I know it's incredible, but it is the truth."

"Incredible? Not half. Ah, now I understand it," Geoffrey went on. "You grew, up here in England. Later, you saw Patrick's book, *The Varna Schooner*; and so you read it because you'd passed through Varna. That's how you first came to know Patrick's work, you fell in love with it, and—here we are."

"That's not entirely wrong."

"What do you mean?"

"You're right—here we are."

God, sometimes he was bloody slow on the uptake. There she was, lips parted, eyes half shut, offering herself to him, and he was still trying to carry on a conversation. Nitwit! He quickly pulled Judith closer and kissed her. It was long, slow, deep and utterly wonderful. Geoffrey's hand slipped inside her blouse and touched skin that felt like warm silk, like some rare gold liquid that seemed to welcome and embrace his own flesh. Her whole body seemed to melt into his and that somehow made him feel profoundly alive, vastly more aroused.

Her tongue—no, a tooth, surely—entered his tongue, and it was like smooth sex, a painless, exhilarating penetration. He was puzzled and startled by it, however. He opened his eyes as he tried to pull back a couple of inches—and he couldn't move. It was as if Judith held him by the tongue, with some part of her mouth. Her eyes were locked on him, but she didn't appear to see him. His tongue throbbed, but not unpleasantly. Geoffrey had an odd sense of his mind slipping out of focus, drifting hazily. It was difficult to form thoughts, they seemed to keep falling beyond his grasp. He didn't mind. Much easier to drift, to float along in a delicious fog. It was so comforting.

He didn't hurt, but he felt weak. He was still on the sofa in his study, but now he was lying flat on his back. Judith sat on the floor beside him. The golden glow of her cheeks was now suffused with a faint pink blush. He felt so tired. He smiled, glad she was still there with him, though he wasn't exactly sure what had happened between them.

"You never even read *The Varna Schooner,*" she said almost in a tone of regret. "You thought *The Lime-Kiln* was a waste and you were sure *The Varna Schooner* would be just as bad."

"No, I read it." Now he knew something was wrong.

"You didn't even remember my name," Judith told him. "Years ago. Ten, at least. More."

"Patrick gave me life," she continued. "He created me, and at the end of the book he saved my life. I lost my entire family on the schooner *Demeter,* and the crew died as well. Patrick gave them all to Dracula, who came out of his coffin in the hold. But Patrick allowed one person to survive, a child, a little girl. I escaped ashore at Whitby."

"Mad."

"But there's a price to pay for life," Judith went on. "Any form of life. Patrick made me one of those who live forever. He was a good man, strong in many ways, but hopeless at dealing with the outside world. Hopeless at career-building. He trusted you, in spite of the times you let him down. And when you had no use for him or his last two books, he finally gave up. He knew he'd done his best work, but he had no hope left for it."

"He was a baby."

Geoffrey felt good saying that. It took all his strength to get the words out. He could barely move.

"I won't take all of your blood. That would be too easy. I can keep you this way for days." Judith smiled at him. "Days on end. Until you eventually die of hunger. Like Patrick."

"Compound organ failure," Geoffrey corrected stubbornly.

"Brought on by malnutrition. Starvation. When Patrick died in that awful flat in Hackney, he had no money, nothing."

"It was a Simone Weil stunt," Geoffrey railed angrily. "The ultimate career move. He had friends he could have gone to, he'd done so many times before. And he had money."

The exertion nearly knocked him out.

"Friends?" Judith said. "You were the only one, and you let him down. Money? He had seventeen pounds, that's all."

"Enough to eat. To work, to live another day." He tried to

push himself up on one hand. He was shaky, but he thought he was beginning to regain some of his strength. "He didn't have to die the way he did."

"No, he didn't."

"He had friends. I told you. He had money."

"Yes, Geoffrey." Judith smiled again as she leaned forward, her mouth approaching his. "And I'm sure you do, too."

GHOST MUSIC

Inever wanted to tell this story, but there's no longer any point in sitting on it. I'd like to think that it might serve as a very small footnote to a very small entry in music history, but that seems rather unlikely.

Does anyone still remember Eric Springer?

Do you know who Mandy Robbins was?

A couple of months ago I was skimming *The Times* and saw the brief news item about the train wreck south of Cairo. The usual disaster in an under-developed country, dozens of people dead. I took it in and quickly passed on without a second thought, but a short while later I received a telephone call from an old friend in London. Did I know that Mandy Robbins was on that train, and had died in the crash? I was stunned. No one had heard from her in ages, though at various times rumor had it that she was living in a dark apartment in Buenos Aires, or a tiny cabin in a remote Norwegian fishing village, or a villa on a resort island in the Adriatic. But no one really knew, and after a while the stories dried up. We all more or less forgot about her, or we filed her away among our less happy memories—with Eric.

Mandy Robbins was en route to Luxor when the train accident occurred. Twenty years later, she was still running.

I live in Dutchess County now, about seventy miles north of Manhattan. I edit (and write most of) *Tonal/Atonal*, a monthly newsletter. My articles and reviews also appear in several other publications that cover 20th century music, and my monographs on Hartmann and Lutoslawski have sold well to libraries throughout the world. I'm working on Arvo Part now, and I teach a course at the local high school. It all adds up to a reasonable income and I suppose I'm happy enough in my A-frame. I own about 5,000 CDs, records and tapes, as many books, a superb stereo system, and I occasionally have an affair with a divorcee.

You know, it is a life.

But in 1976 I was living in London and I sincerely believed in the importance of great art, literary and musical. There were classics, old and modern, and they truly mattered—perhaps more than anything else. A new composition by Berio was greeted as an event of quasi-religious significance. Art was in some ways more real than life itself, I thought. Back then, I hadn't yet given up on myself, though I was already beginning to cobble together a sideline career as a commentator rather than a composer.

Eric Springer was an old friend with more talent and better luck. I was thrilled when he wrote to say he'd be coming to stay in London for several months. We hadn't seen each other in a while, though we kept in touch with postcards. Eric's Variations for Piano and Oboe had been heard on a late-night FM station in California by a young producer who decided to use it in his next film. *No-Hopers* was a cult success and the soundtrack sold quite well. Eric had already earned a measure of critical praise as a promising young composer, but now he had the added pleasure of an unexpected payoff from the world of popular entertainment.

He was coming to London to write a quartet, commissioned by the Claymore Foundation, and to be with the new love of his life. Mandy Robbins was then 23, attempting a comeback in a career that had never quite happened. She'd been a bright young prospect as a violinist at the age of 14, but the assorted stresses of high expectations, touring, and family problems had combined to derail her. At 18, she packed it all in and took a couple of years off to put her life in order. Then she began slowly and carefully to make her way back as a performer.

By the spring of 1976 she had done well enough to have a new agent and a challenging but very sweet job: she would perform the Berg Violin Concerto at the upcoming Proms. A friend and wealthy patron offered her the free use of his house in London, and she intended to spend four months mastering the technically difficult and emotionally taxing composition. It would be her breakthrough concert. There was talk of a live recording, and a contract for studio albums later. Mandy would also be the star soloist at the debut of Eric's quartet, sometime in the future.

Eric and Mandy, Mandy and Eric. When I met them at Heathrow in late April of 1976 the air seemed charged with the excitement of their romance and the dazzling music they were setting out to create. It all seemed to be coming together for both of them and I was swept up in it as well—happily so. I felt privileged to be the friend at hand.

They quickly settled into their new home, a Georgian brick house in one of the narrow streets behind Edwardes Square, on the edge of Kensington and Earl's Court. The owner had spent a small fortune renovating and redecorating, and it featured a music room with a Bosendorfer grand on which Eric could help Mandy rehearse, using a piano reduction of Berg's orchestral score. There was a separate den with a spinet in the converted basement, where Eric could work on his own composition.

It was ideal for them, and by happy coincidence I was living in a tiny flat behind the Olympia, a short walk from their place. We spent a lot of time together in the early going, as I showed them around London, took them on pub outings, introduced them to Indian food, and helped them find some of the less obvious sites that they were interested in seeing—like the modest house in Chelsea where Peter Warlock came to his sad and lonely end, and the rather dreary old pile that Edward Elgar had lived in, near the North End Road.

Eric and Mandy both took to London at once, they loved going for long walks around the city, and they soon began to talk about the possibility of finding an affordable place of their own after the Proms and staying on indefinitely.

I liked Mandy from day one. She was obviously intelligent, especially about music, though she wasn't nearly the compulsive talker on the subject that Eric and I were. She was petite, and still had a look of girlish prettiness about her, but you would occasionally catch a brief glimpse of adult sadness in her eyes when something was said that brought an unhappy memory to mind. I knew that she had struggled to escape a possessive father who'd attempted to control every aspect of her life and career; she was eventually successful in breaking away, but she still carried the emotional scars.

Most of the time, however, Mandy was buoyant and energetic, fun to talk to and be with, and it was very clear to me that she cared deeply for Eric—and that he felt the same about her. He had found her at exactly the right time in his life.

Eric was fast approaching thirty. He'd been something of a playboy for rather too long, and was in danger of being written off as an underachiever. He had never produced as much new music as some people felt he should. Now he was apparently making real progress at last. The movie success and the Claymore commission both helped enormously, but Mandy was the vital factor. She gave him love and a sense of stability, for what was perhaps the first time in his life. The two of them shared an ambitious vision—they wanted both greatness for each other in music, and to have a great love affair together forever.

Well, why not? At that age we all want everything, and we can't imagine why we shouldn't get it. I was beginning to sense my own limitations, but I still believed in Eric. And the first time I saw Mandy strike the violin strings with the edge of her hand in the famous "warm-up" of the Berg piece—a kind of firm but very delicate chopping motion, an incredibly difficult thing to do properly—I believed in her as well.

Eric and I were sitting on the small patio outside the Lord Edwarde one balmy evening a few weeks into their stay when I got the first indication that there were problems. Eric seemed to be distracted and had little to say. Mandy, who was not one for the drink anyway, had stayed home to take a hot bath; lately, she was being bothered by aching muscles in her shoulders and legs. Eric said she was rehearsing too much, and there may have been a minor disagreement between them.

I was sympathetic, but I sensed there was something else on Eric's mind. He was a tall, sturdy guy, but that evening he sat hunched over his pint in a way that suggested defeat. He looked like one of the dazed old-timers at Ward's. He had even gone for three or four days without shaving, which was not his style. We chatted fitfully for a while, and then I asked about his quartet. If there was trouble, it had to be with the music.

"Want to read some of it?"

"Of course, I'd love to."

I'd been looking forward to the moment when Eric would show me some of his new work. He reached down and unzipped the slim briefcase he always carried with him, fished out a few sheets of music paper and handed them to me. He had a smile on his face, but there was something sour in it.

The first page bore the hand-printed title "Quartet" and the dedication "for Mandy." My eyes scanned down the page and across the staves. I was amazed. It was pre-Serial, in fact it seemed to be pre-Romantic—an altogether astonishing turn back to the past for a composer like Eric. Another shock: the quartet opened with a *bassedanse*. It was incredible. Nothing in his previous work had ever looked in this direction. But I was going too fast to hear it in my mind. I started over again, caught it—and a tremendous sense of confusion washed through me.

"You're quoting Warlock," I said without looking up.

"Am I," Eric said with a hollow laugh.

"This is his Capriol Suite."

"I know."

It continued for the next five pages, what was then the only fairly well-known piece of music composed by Peter Warlock, circa 1926. The restless flurry of notes ended abruptly in the middle of the seventh page, with a large "X" scrawled across it, and the words SHIT SHIT SHIT.

"I don't understand," I said.

"Neither do I."

"Surely you don't mean to quote at this length, and here at the very beginning of your own work."

"No, of course not."

"Well...?"

"I'll tell you what's really kind of scary about it," Eric said, staring at his pint. "I've worked on that for weeks, ever since we got here, but it was only the other day when I realized what it was. Until then I had no idea." He looked up at me. "I honestly thought it was all mine."

I let that pass for the moment because I couldn't think of a thing to say. All composers and writers are influenced by those who came before; as they mature they outgrow their influences and find their own voices, or else they come to a dead end. But this was not a case of excessive influence. Eric had Peter Warlock's music note for note, as far as I could tell.

"That's not scary. Embarrassing, maybe."

"Yes." He smiled sheepishly. "It is embarrassing."

What *was* scary, I thought but did not say, was that this was all he had to show for a month of steady work.

I told him not to listen to any other music (except the Berg that Mandy was practicing) and to begin again on his quartet. We both knew that the history of great works of art is littered with false starts. Or as Edward Albee said, you nose around and nose around like a dog, until you find the right place to squat. Eric was clearly relieved when I brushed aside the incident.

Privately, I was disturbed, and I knew he was too. Why else would he even show me those self-damning pages? And how could it be explained? Eric had been living quietly with Mandy for all of that month, up to nothing worse than a few pints at night after a long day's work—and who could begrudge him that? I understood influence, but how anybody could virtually transcribe the work of another person and not know that they were doing it is beyond me. Yet I had no doubt Eric was being truthful.

A few days later, on the weekend, the three of us went up to Portobello Road and poked around among the flea market stalls. I didn't find anything, but Eric bought Mandy a lovely silver charm of a cat, sleek and vaguely Egyptian, with a fleck of amber inset as an eye. It came on a thin chain, and Mandy immediately put it on around her neck. Mandy was very fond of cats, and if she and Eric stayed on in London they intended to get one.

We had a pleasant pub lunch on Church Street, and while Eric was at the bar buying another round I asked Mandy how her work on the Berg concerto was coming along.

"The music's fine, and I love it, but it's so demanding, and my body is behind schedule." She sipped her spritzer (as usual, the only one that she would have). "My legs get very sore after I've been standing for a while, and I seem to get tired quickly." I nodded. For the concert soloist, physical training and stamina are every bit as important as they are for the athlete. "But I'm following an excellent program of exercises, so hopefully I'll be in peak condition by the end of August."

"Good. I'm sure you'll be fine," I told her. "And how is Eric's work? He seems cheerful enough, but he hasn't said very much to me about it."

Mandy's face brightened. "I heard some of it last night and it was gorgeous. And I'm not just saying that, it really was the most beautiful music I've heard in ages."

"What was?" Eric asked before I could speak. He was back at the table with two fresh pints.

"The theme you were working on last night," Mandy said.

"Oh, yes." Eric smiled at me, looking pleased with himself. "She's right, too. It's the best thing I've ever done."

"Great," I responded. "I can't wait to hear it."

By the time we got back to their place Eric and I were quite jolly with beer and Mandy was tolerantly amused. I insisted that they both give me at least a brief preview of their work before I tottered off home. Mandy took out her violin while Eric poured a very ordinary scotch for the two of us.

Some people don't like Alban Berg. They just don't get that whole second Viennese school. But I find his music heartbreaking, especially the Violin Concerto, his own farewell to life. Mandy nearly had me in tears within a few moments. She only played the final part, the adagio, but that was enough. She sat down with a wince and a groan, and put her feet up on a hassock. I told her how good she was, several times. Then Mandy and I badgered Eric to play a bit of his new music. It didn't take much. He seemed genuinely eager and he stepped briskly to the piano.

"Remember, it's just an idea I'm fooling around with," Eric told us. "And you must hear it in strings."

He began to play, taking up his theme and exploring it, much as a jazz musician will improvise around a song line. It was far from developed, still spare and skeletal—but Mandy was right, it was a gorgeous idea that just hinted teasingly at rich colors and deeply moving harmonies.

Eric played for about ten minutes. Mandy and I clapped, and he grinned as he flopped down in the armchair and reached for his whiskey glass. I came up with some encouraging words and somehow managed to hide the huge distress I felt.

I still wasn't quite sure what he'd been playing, but I knew that I knew it—and it wasn't Eric Springer's music.

My knowledge of 20th century music is far from encyclopedic. I'm patchy on the Americans, Scandinavians, Russians, the Spanish and much of the rest of the world. But in 1976 I was really into British composers, particularly the more obscure ones lost in the enormous shadows cast by Vaughan Williams and Britten (since then I've concentrated on the Germans and East Europeans).

The next day I could still hear the theme in my head, and I began to work out what it might be. By late that afternoon, I at least had a pretty good idea of who the composer was. I dreaded speaking to Eric about it, but there was no choice in the matter. I rang and asked if I could stop by, knowing that was the time of day he usually finished working.

When I got there, Mandy was out and Eric was ready to go for a walk and a pre-dinner pint. That was fine with me, but first I had him play the theme for me again. He had developed it quite a bit in only twenty four hours, but hearing it again merely served to confirm my suspicions. While we were out walking I spoke in a general way about the music and how it was so different from his previous work. We went to the Britannia in Warwick Road.

"Now," I said after we'd taken our first sip of Young's, "I have to tell you what I don't like about it."

"Okay, fire ahead."

"It's by Ernest Moeran," I said. Eric stared at me as if he couldn't believe what I'd just said. "I'm pretty sure it's from his String Trio, composed in 1931. That, or his Violin Sonata of 1923. Anyhow, I'm certain it's E.J. Moeran."

"I've never even heard of him," Eric insisted anxiously, his face flushed and agitated. "And I'm damn sure I've never heard a note of his music."

"I believe you, but..."

"You must be wrong, you've got to be."

"Check it out yourself," I said. "And do it before you play or show that music to anyone else, because you'll be embarrassed, and you might even find yourself with legal problems."

"Jesus." Eric sat back, worried and subdued. "What's going on here?"

"I don't know."

"Who the hell is Ernest Moeran?"

"A minor English composer," I explained. "Born 1894, died 1950. A few of his works are of real, lasting quality. He's the kind of composer I love to find, overlooked by most people." At that point, I hesitated. But I had to go on. "When I first got into Peter Warlock seriously a couple of years ago, I came across Moeran. He and Warlock were very close friends."

Eric stared at me.

I did not tell him the saddest details of all about Ernest Moeran. We never got around to them, or maybe I just didn't want to risk making matters worse for Eric. That in 1950, at the age of 55, on one of his many trips to Ireland, Moeran was found dead in a river, apparently the victim of a heart attack. Or that in 1926 Moeran had a colossal failure—he could not complete work on a symphony that had been commissioned by the Halle Orchestra. Or that his friendship with the remarkable but very strange Peter Warlock had nearly destroyed Moeran's life while he was still a young man. In fact, there were people who knew them both and who believed that the best thing that ever happened to Moeran was the mysterious death of Warlock himself in 1930.

I didn't see Eric again until the end of the following week. I knew he would need some time to sort himself out, and I had to put my own thoughts in order—or at least try. I used the time to do a bit of research on Peter Warlock, but that didn't help me understand what was happening with Eric. The only explanation I could come up with was that he had to be going through some kind of mental breakdown. That he did know the Moeran piece, as he'd admitted he knew the Warlock, and he had begun to re-compose them both in the mistaken belief that they were his own—as a result of some deep confusion or psychological crisis.

But, aside from the music itself, I had seen nothing in his habits or behavior that would support such a theory. He appeared to be fine in all other respects, and Mandy had given no hint of troubles with him. All I could think was that something bizarre happened whenever he sat down at the piano to compose—perhaps the pressure to justify such an important commission became too great to handle, and his mind lurched off on its own, dredging up music he knew but dissociating it from its source.

Every Friday I spent a couple of hours at Bush House editing and polishing the English translations of emigre texts broadcast on the BBC World Service. It was a handy job, and it eventually led to my interest in the so-called dissident composers from the Eastern Bloc, like Gorecki.

Eric phoned, knowing I'd probably be there. He asked me to meet him at a place called the New Ambassador Club, which turned out to be a humble drinking den up one flight of stairs on Orange Street. I have no idea how Eric found such a place, or became a member, but he was at the last table at the back.

I almost didn't recognize him. The four-day stubble was now about two weeks old and had been shaved down to form an emerging goatee and a disconnected mustache. That was startling enough in itself, because Eric had never sported facial hair. But he also looked thin and gaunt, his skin was gray and his eyes were tired. Obviously he wasn't eating or sleeping properly.

"All right," he said, after fetching some ale. "I've got a

problem. I know I heard Warlock last summer at the Hartt School. Maybe it was the music, or his odd name, but I was curious to see the place where he died shortly after we got here."

"Yes."

"And maybe Moeran was on the same concert program. I don't remember it, but maybe he was. That has to be what happened—how else would I pick up their music?"

"I'm inclined to agree."

"But that kind of music doesn't even interest me," Eric said with exasperation. "It never has. Tone-color, lyrical harmonies and the old modes. It's an *old* language."

"I know," I said. "That's never been your style."

"So why is that all I can do now? When I sit down and write or when I fool around on the piano, the only thing that comes out is that kind of music. And then I realize what it is, and I have to throw it out and start all over again."

"Do some exercises in dissonance," I suggested.

"I've tried," Eric told me. "But whenever I consciously try to set off in a particular direction I immediately come to a dead end. I get nowhere." He leaned across the table and spoke in an urgent voice. "I've been here going on two months now, and I've written nothing of my own. Not one note."

"It sounds like writer's block," I said sympathetically. "I guess the only thing you can do is to keep working until you work your way out of it. And you will, sooner or later."

Eric looked as if he didn't entirely believe me. In fact, I wasn't sure I believed it myself. Eric had another theory. The success of the movie soundtrack had somehow leached away at his self-confidence. He was afraid of not being taken seriously, of being dismissed as a popular hack. His quartet would be an easy target for that charge from people who resented his windfall, and fear of this was now blocking him creatively.

There may have been a small grain of truth in what he said, but there was also a large blob of paranoia. The music community didn't follow him that closely. Eric was just one of many young composers with true potential but a tenuous hold on the art, and he was not yet the focus of widespread interest.

"That's a stretch," I told him. "The movie money started to

come in a couple of years ago. It's in the past now, so you can forget about it. And there's no point in worrying about what the critics will say about the quartet until you finish it. You have a massive case of self-consciousness, that's all, and the way out of it is to keep working. You'll break through."

Eric thought about that for a few moments, and then he said, "Tell me more about Peter Warlock."

"This is not really about Peter Warlock," I said. "This is all about you, and your music."

"I know," Eric replied. "Still..."

"Well, he was a brilliant scholar and a very good composer," I said. "Some of his songs are among the best in English music. He was born in 1894, and his real name was Philip Heseltine. But his music criticism offended so many people that when he came to the point of publishing his own music he decided it would be best to use a pseudonym. No one—"

"Look at that," Eric interrupted. "He was so worried about what people would say that he took another name."

"Yes, but it didn't work. People soon knew that Warlock was Heseltine. By the way, nobody seems to know how he came up with that name, but he had a strong interest in the occult, and there were stories about experiments with Satanism and drugs. Warlock certainly had his darker side. Some people remember him as being distinctly sinister and he was prone to extended drinking binges. E.J. Moeran was so much under Warlock's influence that he shared a place with him for a while, but eventually he realized that the lifestyle was destroying his work and ruining his health, and he had to get out. But there were other people who said that Peter Warlock was essentially warm and caring, a very good friend, and that his occasional outbursts of wildness were merely a release from the intense pressure of work. When it came to his music, it seems he was a hard taskmaster on himself."

"Why did he kill himself?" Eric asked.

"We can't be sure he did. The gas valve was very loose, and it may be that he stretched out for a nap, and a leak did him in. On the other hand, his personal life was troubled, his finances were always in bad shape, he suffered bouts of depression, and he thought he was a failure. His music bucked the trends of the day—this was 1930—and he thought he was going nowhere. He did mention suicide to a few friends, and later they regretted not taking him seriously. The inquest returned an open verdict, but that was probably an act of kindness. From all the evidence, it certainly does look like suicide."

"He was what, thirty six?"

"Right, and it's only just in the last few years that people started listening to him again and liking what they hear. He had an intense, charismatic personality, there's no doubt about that. Most people who met him either hated and feared him, or else they simply adored him."

"Hmm." Eric shrugged. "Sometimes I think there's a weird story behind every composer who ever lived—except Sibelius, of course." I laughed. "Warlock sounds as peculiar as they come, but what he has to do with me, I have no idea."

"I'll tell you one more thing about him."

"What?"

"He was tall, like you," I said. "Some people described him as Mephistophelean in appearance. I've seen a photograph of him, and they're right about that. He had a mustache and goatee, just like the ones you've sprouted."

Events got in the way and I wasn't able to see Eric or Mandy for another two or three weeks after that. I did speak to him on the phone once and he assured me that he was at last beginning to make a little headway with his work. He sounded distracted, and I took that to mean that his mind was entirely on his music. The next time I called I got Mandy. Eric was out. He went out every day late in the afternoon and came back late at night, usually in a boozy state. When he worked, the music she heard was not music at all, just doodling at the keyboard. She was worried.

A few days later she rang and asked if I knew where he might be. She was in a state, and I got the impression that he had not been home at all the night before—or if he had, he'd gone out again. It was early evening and she couldn't stand waiting there alone, not knowing where he was or when he might return. I tried to calm her down and promised to look for him.

I didn't think there were very many places Eric might wander to, since he still wasn't terribly familiar with London. I tried his little drinking club in Orange Street first. He wasn't there but the large woman behind the bar told me that he had left about an hour ago, with a lady friend.

I tried the French and a couple of other pubs in Soho before I found him at the Colony Club. It was even drabber than the New Ambassador, but it had a better clientele—literary publishers, freelancers, the art crowd arrayed lovingly around Francis Bacon and Lucian Freud.

Eric was off in a corner at a typically rickety table with a woman dressed entirely in black. She had a long, horsy face, and long, straight blonde hair. Her name was Gillian, or Francesca. They were both moderately pissed and they each thought the other was wonderfully amusing, I most amusing of all. It took me one round of drinks and not much effort to detach Eric, and I got him into a taxi. He was humming like a tractor, but unfortunately it was nothing more exalted than the refrain from "Lola."

"What the hell are you doing?"

"I'm turning into Peter Warlock." He laughed.

"No you're not," I told him. "You're just acting like a big child—dodging your work, leaving Mandy alone for hours on end. It's stupid, Eric, stupid and uncalled for."

"Maybe he's taking me over." Another laugh.

"Why would he bother?" I snapped. "Peter Warlock is resting happily in his grave, his reputation is secure."

It turned out to be a vicious remark, and I was immediately sorry I'd made it. We were miserably silent the rest of the way. I went in with him to say hello to Mandy. Eric smiled and gave her a kiss on the cheek, and then sloped off down to his study in the basement. Mandy was in tears, obviously not in the mood for much talk. The front room was a bit messy and I noticed that she was still moving very stiffly.

"Where was he?"

"Having a drink at a club with Francis Bacon." It's amazing how you can find the gloss when you need it. "Wait till tomorrow to have a chat with him. I'll do the same in a day or two.

He's just having a hard time getting going with the quartet, but he'll snap out of it soon enough."

"I hope so."

"You'll see."

"George, thank you so much."

"Not at all. How're you feeling, love?"

"Otherwise?" A faint sardonic smile. "Still sore and achy, but I'll be okay. As soon as Eric gets back to normal."

I went straight round to the Black Hart in Earl's Court Road and had two quick shorts. There is a natural instinct to assume the best about our friends, and a concern about how much you can interfere in their lives before you go a little too far, and they shut you out. I feared greatly for Eric—that he was using his music troubles as an excuse to fritter away his time on clubbing, boozing and chatting up the dollies. He could easily wake up one morning soon and find that he'd blown the Claymore commission and lost Mandy, and I couldn't imagine how he would recover from two such devastating, self-inflicted failures.

I walked home that night trying to figure out how I might be able to get through to Eric, to shake him out of his funk without alienating him. I had no idea that it was already far beyond me. Even now, looking back twenty years later, I wonder. Weren't the signs all there, waiting to be seen? Shouldn't I have known what was really going on? But I didn't see, I didn't know—or if I did, some part of me must have been unwilling to face it.

Eric seemed subdued when I met him two days later. He had a slightly disheveled look about him, his clothes were rumpled and his hair was brushed back in slick clumps that tended to separate and dangle down on the side of his face until he shoved them back again. Eric wanted to go for a pint but I wouldn't, so we sat in the sun at Holland Park, which only made him look more bedraggled and forlorn.

I can't remember much of what we said, but it wasn't of any special importance. I was going to Italy for a few days to do an interview with Luigi Nono. Eric gave me some very good questions to ask, which showed that his critical thinking was still in fine form, and that cheered me somewhat.

He didn't attempt to explain or apologize for the evening I brought him home from the Colony. He didn't refer to it at all, and neither did I. I've never seen any point in rehashing boorish or childish behavior. Since then, of course, I've often wondered about everything we left unsaid.

I wish I'd given in a little and gone along to the Britannia or the Black Hart with him for a pint. But I wasn't in the mood, I was trying to discourage him from the beer, and we always want to believe there will be time for another pint, another day. But when we parted on the High Street a short while later, it was the last time I saw Eric Springer alive.

I rang them two or three times after I returned from Italy, but no one answered the phone. I meant to go around, but I had a number of assignments to catch up with, and so the days stretched into a week. It was about eleven o'clock one morning when I got the call. At first the voice was so faint that I almost hung up, thinking no one was there. But then I caught it—not much more than an exhalation.

"Mandy? Is that you?"

"Can you...help me."

"I'll be right there."

I'd never heard a human voice sound so weak and helpless. I think I ran all the way from my flat to their house. I tried the door at once, and found it unlocked. I shouted for both of them as I went into the front hallway, but got no response.

The front sitting room was empty, and the main music room as well—I hesitated there just long enough to glance at the loose pages of sheet music scattered around the place, hoping that some of it might be Eric's quartet, but it was the Berg score. Plates of half-eaten fast food had been left on the floor and perched on the arms of chairs, looking as dry and hard as wax imitations.

I hurried downstairs to the room where Eric worked. It was dark, and there was a damp chill in the air. It reeked of stale tobacco. I turned on a table lamp and saw some ashtrays full of cigarette butts. There were a couple of virtually new pipes on a side table. Eric had never smoked, and I was sure I'd never told him that Peter Warlock did, both cigarettes and a pipe.

There were no books, tapes or records in the room, it was as simple and austere as a monk's cell. A chaise—for one frantic second I thought I saw Eric stretched out on it, the thin blanket tucked up under his chin, just as they found Peter Warlock. Eric wasn't there, but there were more loose sheets of music scattered all over the place. Each page was clean and unmarked, lined with blank stares that lanced my heart.

Just as I got back to the ground floor, I heard a noise from upstairs. I found Mandy in the main bedroom. She was curled up beneath a sheet, barely conscious. Her face was desperately pale and her hair clung to her face in sweaty snarls. She saw me, but she didn't seem to register who I was.

"Help…Eric…"

"It's all right, love," I told her. "Eric's not here at the moment. He must have gone out."

"Eric…"

"No, it's George," I said with a grin. I sat on the edge of the bed and stroked her face lightly. "You're not well, are you? Have you seen a doctor?"

"George." Her eyes found me then. "I can't move."

"Why—"

At that moment I noticed Mandy's legs poking out from under the sheet, and I was horrified. Her toes were curled tightly and her calves appeared to have shriveled. I pushed the sheet up and saw the same slack and wasting flesh all along the lower part of her thighs. I could barely find words to speak.

"Mandy, what—"

It was absurd, but thoughts of Berg and his Violin Concerto suddenly swarmed in my mind. The piece Mandy had been preparing to play in the last week of the Proms. I've always thought of it as Berg's farewell to life, since it was all about both life and death, and Berg died (his own bizarre, absurd death) within a few months of completing it.

But there was another person involved. Manon Gropius, the lovely young daughter of close friends and a special favorite of Berg's. At the age of 18, just before Berg was commissioned to write the Concerto, Manon lost her long and heroic battle against the ravages of polio. Berg was deeply moved, and dedicated the Concerto to her—"to the memory of an angel."

Now, staring at Mandy's legs, I felt a confusion that seemed to boil up out of my bones and surge through me, leaving me dazed and paralyzed. Finally I heard Mandy's faint voice again. "Save Eric."

"He's not—"

"The kitchen."

I seemed to come back into my own body then and I raced down the stairs. I hadn't even thought of checking the kitchen at the rear of the ground floor. It had a gas stove. The door wouldn't budge. I was sure I could smell gas. As I rattled the doorknob uselessly, I noticed something hanging from it. The thin silver chain with the charm that Eric had bought for Mandy at Portobello Road, the Egyptian cat with the amber eye.

In a moment of awful certainty, I knew I'd never told Eric the single most revealing detail about Peter Warlock's death, the sign that strongly pointed to suicide rather than an accident. A few minutes before he stretched out on the chaise and tucked the blanket up beneath his chin, Warlock had taken his cat and put it safely outside the room. It was the cat's frightful wailing and mewing that eventually drew the landlady's attention.

I got Mandy out first. While the neighbors looked after her and alerted the police and fire brigade, I went back for Eric. I expected the house to blow up at any moment. I took a chair and smashed the kitchen window, unlocked the outside door, got in and turned off the gas. I waved a towel around, trying to clear the air. I had to step outside twice to overcome dizziness, but then I was finally able to go to Eric.

He was slumped back in a chair, his head pointing north, his feet crossed at the ankles and propped on the edge of the wooden table. He looked for all the world like someone who'd just dozed off while waiting for the kettle to boil.

But his lips and cheeks were as red as a tanager, and there was about his mouth the slightly bemused smile of the dead.

I visited Mandy at St. Mary Abbot's Hospital, and I saw her

again shortly before she left London. She recovered quickly from what the doctors said was probably a psychosomatic illness. She wasn't having any of that, and neither was I, but there seemed no point in trying to argue otherwise—with anyone. Mandy and I, sadly, found that we had little to say to each other. It was as if we both wanted, or needed, to retreat from a terrible experience we had shared unwillingly. I felt more than a little guilty for not paying serious attention to what had been happening to her, so preoccupied was I by Eric's situation. She scratched the Proms, of course, and disappeared. I have no idea whether any of the rumors I occasionally heard about her over the years were true, but she never performed in public again.

If Eric Springer is remembered at all today—by people who never knew him—it is probably not as the promising composer of the plaintive and Webernist Variations for Piano and Oboe, but as the composer of a sweetened-up movie theme based on it.

Notes:

"(his own bizarre, absurd death)"

Not long after he completed his great Violin Concerto, Alban Berg (1885-1935) suffered an insect bite on the back. From neglect or mistreatment, it formed an abscess. Berg was so poor at the time that he and his wife attempted to lance it themselves. They used toenail scissors. Berg's condition worsened steadily and he died soon after he finally entered a hospital. No effort was made to determine the exact cause of his death but it was most likely due to blood poisoning.

"To those whom God has forsaken is given a gas-fire in Earl's Court."—Patrick Hamilton, *Hangover Square*.

I came across this line several years after Eric's death, and for obvious reasons it made a deep impression on me.

Hamilton is probably best-known as the author of the plays *Rope* and *Gaslight*. He hated the movies that were based on them. His novel *Hangover Square* is set in Earl's Court on the eve of World War II. It ends with the hero killing two people and then taking his own life—by gas—after leaving a note asking the police to look after his cat. Oddly enough, when the novel was filmed this character, who had nothing whatsoever to do with music, was transformed into a homicidal composer.

Years earlier, Hamilton had been struck by a car and seriously injured. He recovered, but his face was disfigured. He took to wearing a grotesque artificial nose for a while. This accident contributed enormously to the alcoholism that eventually killed him. It occurred in the narrow side street directly behind the house in which Eric Springer died, years later.

LA MOURANTE

"You need something new," Lawrence said.

"Yes, but what?"

Alex had been a member of Feathers for more than a year when Lawrence made the suggestion. They were sitting in the piano bar just off the grotto, wrapped in towels, their hair still damp. A lovely little nymph brought them Sapphire martinis.

Feathers was one of the most exclusive private clubs in the world. You couldn't buy your way in. You had to be nominated by a current member, and membership was limited to four hundred very wealthy individuals who were profoundly devoted to the pursuit of pleasure. In the age of AIDS, the club was both an arc of safety and an Eden of erotic license. It was located in a sedate brick building near Park Lane, London W1, but its members came from all around the globe to check their fears at the door and to unleash their transcendent fantasies.

Alex couldn't believe his good fortune when he learned that his membership had been approved. He and Lawrence had known each other since their schooldays together at Charterhouse. They were an unlikely pair, Alex the restless Yank from Westchester County and Lawrence the jaded last son in a played-out line of Wiltshire landowners. But they got along well and stayed in touch over the years. Lawrence made a fortune in the City and Alex did at least as well on the Street. Now in their mid-thirties, they each had the freedom and the means to do whatever they desired—and they suffered no illusions to hold them back.

Alex had just been complaining about the fact that he seemed to be running out of exotic places and females to try.

Last year he'd done the hill tribes of India and Southeast Asia, and it was for the most part a disappointment. As he'd found so many times, reality can't compete with the imagination. Which, of course, was why retreats like Feathers existed for those of privilege. But the urge to travel and explore, the need to test himself against raw experience—were powerful forces in the composition of Alex's character. Thus, the constant weighing of new possibilities, however dubious.

"Do you know about a place called Fado?"

"Fado." Alex shook his head. "Never heard of it."

"Aha." Lawrence smiled. "It's an island, somewhere off the northern coast of South America. The Caribbean, or perhaps it's out more in the Atlantic, I'm not sure which. Anyhow, it's very private, very hush-hush."

"What's the attraction?" Alex had done island paradises two years ago: the Andamans, Polynesia, East Africa—enough.

"Well." The smile on Lawrence's face had turned into a foxy grin. "Have you ever made love with a dead woman?"

"No. It sounds revolting."

"Yes, it does," Lawrence agreed. "But apparently it's not. In fact, I'm told by very reliable sources that once you've tried it, nothing else will do."

"I was told that about the Bushman girls in southern Africa. And other women, in other places. It's never true."

Lawrence nodded. "Still, you have to wonder."

"I'll pass."

But the idea wouldn't. Necrophilia. Ugly word, it conjured up grisly images of dead meat splayed on a cold slab, stiff limbs and pale waxy skin. How could anyone possibly sell that, and who (aside from a few demented souls) would want it?

Lawrence provided a name and an address on a scrap of paper, typical of the kind of highly prized information that passes from one hand to another in a place like Feathers. Alex still had no intention of actually going to Fado, but he was curious enough to visit M. Alain Gaudet in an anonymous office on a pleasant street not far from the center of Lausanne.

M. Gaudet extracted a good deal of information from Alex

and provided very little in return. He described Fado as unique, an island resort privately maintained and operated, dedicated to the enjoyment of "individual practices unfettered by national laws or treaties or international conventions."

Fado was located off the coast of Blanca and was protected by the military government (for a price and perks, no doubt). In addition to the staff, it had a small permanent population with a mixed background: English, Dutch, Portuguese, Italian, French and African. The island was only a few square miles in area, but had "features of great natural beauty."

So far, so boring. M. Gaudet promised nothing. He allowed a few questions but answered them evasively. There was something in his expression that seemed to suggest that Alex should use his imagination. Alex was good at that.

Two months later, presumably after he'd been investigated in great detail, Alex was notified that he had been cleared to visit Fado. A local New York resident, a Mr. Worboys, could handle the arrangements. But did Alex want to go? Mr. Worboys proved to be only a bit more forthcoming with information.

"There are several hundred women on Fado, all shapes, sizes and shades, and they're all available to you at any time, in any number or circumstance you want. Some will be otherwise engaged at any given moment but you'll have as much variety and choice as you can handle. There's also a wide selection of living quarters to choose from—bungalows, cottages, cabanas, suites—you can change them as often as you like. The facilities operate day and night, you can have dinner at four in the morning..."

Alex listened patiently until Mr. Worboys was finished, and then asked if it was true that Fado provided for even the rarest and most peculiar tastes, as he'd heard. Mr. Worboys was silent for a moment, gazing evenly at him. He glanced briefly again at the papers on his desk, as if to reassure himself that Alex had indeed been properly cleared.

"Behavioral guidelines will be issued to you on arrival, but you can take my word for it that they're minimal." A tight smile flickered at the corners of his mouth. "None of the clients I've dealt with—and there have been a good many of them—has ever expressed the slightest hint of disappointment."

"Is that a yes?"

"Let me put it to you this way, dear boy. If you don't know why you're going to Fado, you shouldn't go."

Alex took that as a yes.

As the helicopter rose and quickly swung back toward Blanca, Alex sat in the lounge and studied the glossy arrivals kit he had just been given. How to get about. Living quarters. A detailed map of the island and its many delights. Restaurants, bars, some intriguing theme houses, woodland trails, jungle paths, caves and ornate gardens, a crater lake, waterfalls and black sand beaches.

All of which was fine, and predictable.

Alex then came across the behavioral guidelines Mr. Worboys had mentioned. There were only two of them, printed on a plastic card attached to a small round keyholder.

* *Respect your fellow guests. Do not violate their privacy or interfere with their activities unless specifically invited to participate. Disputes to be settled by staff.*

* *Respect those who serve you. Mutilation, decapitation and dismemberment are prohibited, and will result in severe financial penalties and expulsion.*

Alex smiled faintly. He rode a jitney from the heliport to an Iberian-style village square. Along the way he saw only a few guests and staff members, but plenty of women. Most of them were young, though some were a little elder. Most of them were pretty and attractive, though some had average or even plain looks. All were nicely dressed in a variety of styles and outfits.

They didn't stand around, vacantly posturing. There were no lewd gestures, but most of them did seem to notice the jitney and its handful of passengers—with a glance and an innocent smile. Welcome, stranger. Yours for the taking, Alex thought.

They all looked very much alive.

Alex chose a simple three-room bungalow nested in a wooded pocket just off a hillside trail. He sipped a drink and nibbled some fruit while he unpacked, then he took a shower and dozed for a couple of hours. It was late afternoon when he opened his eyes at the sound of someone singing softly nearby.

There was a small garden at the rear of the bungalow. Alex saw a young woman with long dark hair and golden skin. She sang to herself and occasionally clipped ja flower, which she put in a wicker basket. She was dressed in a flimsy sleeveless top and a short pleated skirt, both white. Her back was to Alex, who stood at the window and watched her for a moment.

The young woman glanced briefly in his direction and smiled when he stepped outside. She continued to sing, though her voice was so muted and indistinct that it amounted to little more than a light melodious humming, a lilting murmur—but Alex was quite enchanted; he'd never heard anything quite like it before.

He crossed the patch of thick lawn and placed his hands on her shoulders. The woman leaned back against him, eyes shutting, her face half-turned toward him. She put the pruning shears into the basket and let her hand fall to her side, brushing his thigh. The air was full of a delicious scent, a subtle perfume from this lovely creature mingling with the smell of the flowers.

Alex kissed her hair and neck. He stroked her breasts, felt her nipples responding through the thin fabric. He put his other hand beneath her skirt, encountering silky flesh, sleek and firm, and baby fine hair. When he kissed her open mouth he didn't want to stop because she tasted so sweet and felt wonderfully cool and moist.

There was a cushioned wooden bench tucked beneath a wall of arcing shrubs, and Alex took her to it. He put the basket on the grass under the bench as they sat down. Her eyes were deep brown and had delicate hints of amber. She sat patiently, waiting for him to say or do something, but there was a lively brightness in her eyes that suggested playful anticipation.

Alex put his fingers to her lips and pushed gently, and she gave him a wide smile—he saw that her teeth were very white, but not perfect; they were her own, unstraightened.

He held her hand in both of his for several moments, but he could find no pulse. He slid the thin straps off her shoulders and admired her breasts—they were round and neither too large nor too flat, but they weren't flawless. Alex moved closer and rested his head on her chest. She held him there, stroking his hair, and he concentrated—but heard no heartbeat.

Alex sat up again and looked at her. "What is your name?" But she merely gave a slight shrug and a wordless rolling murmur of sound. "You do understand me," he said. She nodded once with a quick smile. "But you don't speak." Again, the faint murmur, and this time Alex noticed that her throat and mouth barely moved as she made it.

He wasn't sure what to think. He knew that there were some languages, Thai among them, that consisted largely of vowels used in extraordinary combinations and tones. These languages sounded like flashing water, and were very difficult to master unless you learned them from childhood.

Perhaps that was it, but Alex didn't think so. The strange sounds this woman made seemed almost older than language itself. Besides, if she could understand what Alex was saying then surely she could manage a few words of English in response. But if she were not breathing, if there was no significant passage of air to cause and convey voice—Alex took her hand and pinched the fleshy spot between her thumb and first finger. The skin didn't turn pale, nor did color rush back into it when he let go. It stayed the same.

Alex was vaguely aware of his own heartbeat, increasing at a rapid pace now. His hand shook as he reached down to the basket of flowers and found a rose. He turned it carefully, located one thorn that looked large and strong enough, and jabbed it into the soft pad of the woman's thumb. She sat patiently, watching him. She didn't flinch or show any trace of pain. When Alex withdrew the thorn, the small wound it left was clearly visible but there was no spot of blood. No blood at all.

The surge of desire within him was deeper and richer than he had experienced in a long time, blinding in its sudden intensity. He took the woman in his arms and pulled her to the ground. They rolled over once, to the edge of the grass, and Alex dimly sensed the nodding ferns and shrubs touching his back as he wriggled out of his pants and pushed into her. He hadn't known such youthful eagerness in years. It was almost a new experience for him. His orgasm was so powerful and hallucinatory that Alex felt as if he were driving into the earth itself. Dazed, barely conscious, he rested in her comforting arms, his head between her breasts. The barest whisper of a happy sound emanated from her—but her body didn't rise or fall with a single breath, there was no heartbeat. She seemed perfectly still, at peace.

At first he tried to explain it to himself, to make sense of it in a way that seemed plausible. Alex was certain that she was not some kind of robot or android. The technology involved would be too advanced and sophisticated, in several different areas, to keep secret. From his work on Wall Street he knew about robotics and artificial body parts, he knew what the best companies could do at present—and not do. They made advances all the time but they were still light years from constructing a mouth that could kiss like this woman's mouth did. Alex had no doubt that she was entirely human—in body, at least.

Nor did he believe for an instant that a microprocessor had been implanted in her brain, somehow controlling everything that she did. The necessary hardware and software might be possible, but not the incalculable linkage to brain and body.

A much simpler and more plausible answer came to mind. The explanation had to be pharmacological. Alex knew that drug firms spent a good deal of time and money seeking useful new compounds in the unique plant life of the world's rapidly diminishing rain forests. There was a theory that the zombies of Haitian legend, people who were dead but still ambulatory and who could carry out certain basic functions, were in fact the product of a drug which had its origins in ancient African medical lore.

That was possible. The necessary refinements were possible. With the right resources, one lab with a small staff could do the job. Thus, the knowledge could be controlled and protected, even as it was put to use in a pet project as large as Fado. This was a line of thought with extraordinary implications but Alex had no particular interest in pursuing them.

He didn't care. It didn't matter *how* a woman could be dead but somehow still living. It was enough that *she was.*

He had sex with her twice more that evening, before travel fatigue caught up with him and he fell asleep in her arms in bed. She was awake when he opened his eyes the next morning, ready and available, still sweet. She sang to him as his body sang inside her. The sound she made was so tiny and elusive it almost seemed like a ghost in his mind.

Two days later, they were still together. They had gone out only to take short walks, to make love in a mossy clearing in the woods and later in a stream-fed rock pool. Alex was satisfied to remain with her at the bungalow most of the time. The world fell away, and he didn't miss it.

When his meals were delivered, she sat patiently with him. She dipped large raw prawns in a fiery sauce and fed them to him, but she neither ate nor drank anything herself.

Enough time had gone by, and Alex had to face the new facts of his life. He loved having sex with this woman, and his desire seemed to increase every day. This was a complete turnabout from his usual experience. For years he'd been quick to lose interest and move on in search of something, someone new. Now Alex wanted to keep this woman to himself. He felt no urge to sample any of the others on Fado. Besides, if he went off alone she might hook up with another guest, and then he might never get her back. She was sufficient, she was everything Alex wanted and needed—that was the other huge change in him.

It astonished him that the sex was never the same. The best experiences in his long sexual history now seemed like the merest biological asides. Compared to what he enjoyed with this woman, they vanished in significance. It was as if a previously unknown part of him was suddenly revealed, a primordial dimension of vast power and richness.

"Gina," he said to her. "I want to call you Gina."

She cocked her head and smiled. He was ready again.

He seemed to be flying into her, into the earth and beyond, into space and glittering dust. It was as if he were witnessing the birth of stars and galaxies, the universe itself, a million universes—through the window of his body and Gina. Then Alex would swirl together again within his body. There was something sweet and wonderfully sad about it. His whole being felt blurred and hazy. He would find himself in her arms again, tears in his eyes, his face nestled on her breasts. And he thought—if God had sex, it would be like this.

The world continued to fall away, and he didn't miss it. He had a lot of money back there, somewhere. He had done so much on the Street, and could do so much more—but it meant little. It was numbers flickering on a screen, it was nothing.

There were people in his life. A lot of them, in fact. But how many of them did he care about? They were acquaintances, not true friends. Colleagues, mostly. Women? He went through them on a regular basis, but none had ever tempted him into what might be termed a relationship. His life for the most part was made up of glancing encounters, by his own choice.

Until now. How could he continue—after Fado? Was there anything left worth his doing? Was there any place on the planet worth seeing that he hadn't already visited? Alex thought of his splendid apartment on Manhattan's East Side, and he was not happy at the prospect of returning to it. His adult life could be seen as one long, restless search for the new and the exotic, but Alex was tired of that now. Tired of always being driven by pointless expectation to ever diminishing returns.

He didn't travel to visit museums or stare at scenery. Alex went places to have women. Where next? Who next? But now there was no itinerary, no next stop in the quest—because the quest was over. No other women beckoned in his mind. The awful hunger was gone, replaced by a need to keep what he now had, regardless of what the cost might be.

There was only Gina. Sex with Gina took him right into the secret heart of this world, and beyond, and Alex couldn't bear to think of losing it.

He tried to get Gina to write, but she apparently had never learned how. He gave her a blank pad and a pen, and asked her to show him where she was from. She drew a crooked circle, and Alex assumed that was meant to be Fado. He kept at it, but she had no skill and very little understanding of what he expected from her, so he soon abandoned the attempt.

It didn't matter. He seldom spoke to her because it seemed as if he had nothing truly worth saying. Besides, they had found their own special language—eye contact, facial movements, the subtle varieties of touch and gesture—which served them better than words ever could. And it wasn't long before Alex started to answer the occasional burbles of sound that Gina made with little clicks and murmurs of his own.

Time was running him down. He could stay on Fado until his funds were exhausted, and then go back to the world, rebuild his fortune and hope one day to return to Gina. But would she still be there—for him? The magic might be lost forever in the long interlude. It might be just as good with any woman on Fado, but he was almost afraid to find out. And the work, the need to make money and do business, would be so much drudgery— assuming that Alex could still concentrate on the task, which was by no means a sure thing anymore.

Or he could stay on Fado permanently, by becoming like Gina. That would force their hand. They could hardly risk letting him wander around back in the regular world if he'd been *transformed*. No doubt they'd be unhappy, no doubt they'd find work for him to do. But Alex would still be on Fado, he'd still have Gina.

The funny part was, it seemed more like choosing life than a form of death. He thought that Gina, in her own way, was so much more alive than he'd ever been. The years spent making money he never cared about, *that* was a zombie-like existence. The dreary hours spent hanging out with people like Lawrence in places like Feathers, how vacant and pathetic it all seemed. His quest, that sad and lonely search from Mexico to North Africa to Taiwan and a hundred other forlorn outposts, looking for the next thrill, the next 'ultimate' erotic experience—pointless, all of it.

He'd had everything that world could offer. It would not be hard to give it up: he no longer had any use for it, anyway. The real thing—the true *ultimate*—was right in front of him. In a way, his whole adult life had been a rehearsal for this moment. If Alex could make the leap. The decision was easy.

"Gina, would you like me to stay here with you always?" Her face lit up and she snuggled closer in his arms. "You must help me become like you." She looked up at him, uncertain, perplexed. "It's the only way," Alex said. "You must."

She was gone when he awoke the following day. He stayed in, had brunch and a couple of drinks, and waited for a member of the staff to come along and explain to him that his request was quite out of line, impossible.

But Gina returned alone, late in the afternoon. Alex was so desperate for her by then that he felt like a cloud of fire as he flew across the room to take her in the doorway.

A while later, Gina reached into the pocket of her discarded skirt and came up with a vial of oily brown liquid.

Dear Lawrence, he would write if he could be bothered to sit down and write, *It's true. What I've found on Fado is far better than words can tell. To live forever—abandon life! It isn't hard to do and the next level is the last—is GOD. And YOU are that GOD. Believe me. And God is sex and the sex is fantastic! Of course it takes loads of infrastructure but that's all laid on here—no bother at all.* Alex started laughing, and he couldn't stop for several moments. Gina didn't know what it was all about but she joined in his mirth. She smiled so strenuously that she ended up burying her face in his lap. *Tell the crowd at Feathers I said: Get a death! Adieu and adios Lawrence old chum. It was fun. Or so it seemed for a while. But the next world is not the hereafter it's the HERE and NOW. Honest!*

Alex drained the vial. Butterscotchyish. He looked at Gina and smiled, but she had her hands clapped over her eyes.

Seventy four paces to the corner.
Seventy three the last time.
He would get it right one of these days.
Hey, no big deal!
Alex turned the corner and walked the next lane.
A breeze and a blue sky and always the sun.

But no, sometimes there was a sudden downpour.
Nice shade trees down this way.
Always something new to notice, very nice too.
Let the breeze whistle through your teeth.
And sometimes it will, for fun.
Nod hello, why don't you.
A nod and a smile, hello.
Well done, very nice too.
Eighty seven paces.
A different matter, this lane.
Hullo hullo, what's this.
Coming his way—Gina?
A nod, a smile, hello.
They pass by each other.
Used to know her, didn't you?
Around another corner, the road.
Aha! Aha! Aha!
A jitney, women getting off.
When you've had a live woman, nothing else will do.
But they like the younger ones.
Smile and nod, hello in hope.
A breeze and blue sky and always the sun.
But no, the night too, the dark.
A nod to the live women.
A smile to the live women.
Me! Me! Me! he sang in the breeze.

THE INFESTATION AT RALLS

After the unpleasant incident in Regensburg, Van Helsing returned to his home in Amsterdam but stayed only two nights before journeying on to London. He was still angry and shaken, and he felt an urgent need to escape the European mainland, at least for a little while. He believed that a dose of England and his dear English friends would soon restore his spirits and his will—as indeed it did. Within a matter of a few days his nerves settled down and his better humor was in evidence once again.

Late the following week, Van Helsing traveled to Margate to spend a few days with his former colleague and longtime friend, Dr. Charles Pollard. They had not seen each other in nearly three years. Pollard had moved from London and gone into semi-retirement, more out of personal inclination than in any bow to the exigencies of age—he was still a healthy, vigorous man. Pollard had a curious, open outlook and a lively intelligence. He was quite familiar with Van Helsing's unique perspective on life and the struggles of this world, and he was sympathetic to it in the main.

Beyond Herne Bay, just a couple of miles from Margate itself, the train stopped at a tiny, unmanned station. The windows were broken, slate tiles had been torn from the roof, and the grounds were strewn with clumps of litter, green leaves, small branches, and countless twigs. All of this, no doubt, was the result of the unusually fierce thunderstorm that had blasted through the immediate area two days earlier. The storm had skirted clear of London, but Van Helsing saw a brief report in one of the papers about the swath of wind and flood damage it had caused in the southeast.

The platform was deserted, with no one waiting to board the train or to greet an arriving passenger. Nor did anyone step off at this battered destination. The name on the sign was Ralls, which Van Helsing thought he had heard before, although he could not summon any precise recollection to mind. The train idled there for a minute or two and then continued on to Margate. Pollard was at the station to greet Van Helsing. They dined at a very agreeable chophouse in town that evening, and they continued talking well past midnight in the warm comfort of Pollard's book-lined sitting room.

In the morning, after a fine breakfast prepared by Pollard's housekeeper, the two men were about to set off on a stroll about the town, including a visit to a dealer in rare books and private manuscripts, when a breathless lad appeared at the door. Pollard clearly knew him, and sighed.

"What is it, Harry?"

"Mr. Wingrove, sir. Asks you to come right away. Urgent, he said to tell you. Sent me in the carriage to bring you."

"I cleared the day, and now this," Pollard said to Van Helsing. He picked up his medical bag. "I'm afraid I must attend to it. Do you want to potter about on your own and we'll meet here later, or accompany me on this errand?"

"Of course I'll come with you," Van Helsing replied. "Then we may carry on as we had planned, all going well."

As they rode away from the center of Margate, Pollard explained that his medical duties, though now reduced in time and the number of patients, included treating any illnesses or injuries that occurred among the resident staff and pupils at the Ralls School for Young Ladies. *Ah yes*, Van Helsing thought. No doubt Pollard had mentioned Ralls to him some time in the past, and that was why the name seemed familiar to him at the train stop.

Situated in the former country home of a wealthy family that had died out years ago, the Ralls School accepted a small, select group of girls each year and taught them how to be interesting. The emphasis was on a *useful* knowledge of the arts, history, world events, and social behavior—especially the latter, which included the art of conversation and how to be just witty and vivacious enough. The young ladies were the daughters of nobility and privilege, diplomats and statesmen, occasionally of mere politicians or captains of industry. They were supposed to win and marry sons of the same, and the Ralls School was meant to increase their overall attractiveness.

"They tend to be highly strung. Too much expectation."

Van Helsing nodded, smiling. "From within and without."

"Exactly."

"But you do enjoy this work?"

It was as much a challenge as a question, and Pollard recognized that. He didn't answer for a moment. "Bram, sometimes, often, I think everything is both interesting and uninteresting in more or less equal measure."

Van Helsing didn't respond, and the rest of the journey elapsed in silence. Soon the carriage passed through open gates in a high stone wall. Minutes later, the Ralls estate appeared ahead of them. The main house was a familiar model of the English country home, a long two-story rectangle, two wings attached to the central, communal rooms. There were a few outbuildings, one of which caught Van Helsing's attention—a church. It was small, no doubt originally the family's chapel, but its exterior had been built as a precise replica of a Gothic cathedral. The detail was impressive. Those who have wealth often indulge in such follies. Van Helsing found it not without a certain endearing quality, the orphan of a lost idea. It appeared that a corner of the roof had collapsed, and three workmen were struggling with pieces of broken stone to repair it.

A round man with a round head, Dean Wingrove greeted them anxiously at the bottom of the front steps. Van Helsing wasn't sure if Dean was the man's first name or his title. He had wispy white hair, and he dabbed a cloth at the perspiration on his brow. He quickly led them inside to his office. He accepted Van Helsing's presence as easily as if Van Helsing were not there at all, ignoring him. Wingrove settled himself behind his desk. He tried to speak calmly, but it soon turned into an anxious torrent of words.

"Charles, one of our young ladies, Miss Emily Barber, confided in a friend of hers, another of our young ladies, that she was carnally assaulted two or three nights ago. In her room, in her bed. The friend saw certain signs, blood on the bedclothes, bruises and scratches on Miss Barber's limbs, some swelling in her face, and a change in her usual manner. The past two days, Miss Barber kept to herself in her room, attributing it to her time of the month. Earlier this morning, Matron and some of the young ladies who live in the adjoining rooms heard Miss Barber moaning and crying. Matron investigated. Something is wrong, seriously wrong. Miss Barber is now showing."

Pollard was momentarily confused. "Showing what?"

"*Showing*," Wingrove answered in a stifled screech.

"That's impossible," Pollard said with sudden impatience. "She may be showing, but it's not from any assault that occurred the night before last. It could only be from some previous—event."

"And I tell you," Wingrove went on, "that a few days ago Miss Barber's physique was perfectly trim, even sylph-like. Her build is naturally slender as it is. There was no suggestion of roundness in her—in that region. Everyone here will tell you that, including Matron and the other students. The ladies each have their own room, but living in the same part of the house together, they inevitably see one another in states of partial dress at times."

"How much is she showing?" Pollard asked.

Wingrove swallowed hard. "Matron says it is as if Miss Barber were in her sixth or seventh month."

"Good Lord—that much in just a few days?" Pollard shook his head. "It may be that her imagination has run riot. Certain people do imagine attacks or other experiences with such vivid immediacy that, unknowingly, they produce the very signs of it on their own person. And certain women do become so convinced they are with child that their bodies act as if they were, though they are not."

"Doctor, I pray you are correct in that."

"Or it could be," Van Helsing now suggested in a grave tone, "that some other terrible but genuine affliction has befallen Miss Barber. Please, my dear sir, take us to her immediately."

They went to the upper floor of the wing opposite the one

that housed the students. Miss Barber was isolated in a room there. Wingrove summoned Matron, who was sitting watch at the girl's bedside. A stout, middle-aged woman with a worried expression, she stepped into the corridor.

"Any change?" Wingrove asked anxiously.

"Yes, sir. She's bigger."

"God help us."

"She sleeps fitfully, wakes for a while, then drifts off again."

"Matron, the doctor must examine Miss Barber now. I will need you back here again in forty-five minutes."

As Matron left, the three men entered the room and closed the door. Miss Barber's eyes widened when she saw them. She was on a narrow bed, reclining on a bank of thick pillows at the headboard. Her legs were splayed out beneath a sheet and a thin blanket. She was indeed quite petite, but for her belly, which was alarmingly evident.

"Miss Emily, how are you feeling now?"

"Big," she replied with a laughing groan, like a child who had eaten too much. "Very, very big."

"Yes, well," Wingrove continued, "that's why we're here. This is Doctor Pollard, our school physician, and his associate, Doctor Hazelton."

"Van Helsing," Pollard corrected.

"Van Helsing. I do apologize, sir. Now, Miss Emily, the good doctors are going to ask you a few questions and examine you. Please cooperate and answer them as fully as you can, so that they may prescribe the best treatment to relieve you of this—condition."

She stared at him in disbelief for a few seconds and then began to laugh. Pollard ushered Wingrove out of the room. When the girl stopped laughing, she regarded Pollard and Van Helsing with wary interest. Pollard placed the back of his hand to her forehead and then to her cheeks.

"Normal, low-normal."

While Pollard checked the girl's eyes and throat, Van Helsing pulled a small wooden chair around to the other side of the bed and sat down on it. He leaned closer. Pollard had his stethoscope out and was about to listen to Miss Emily's heartbeat.

"Matthew, open the top of her nightdress."

Pollard did so and then listened intently.

"Strong, regular. Racing a bit."

"But what do you see?" Van Helsing asked.

Pollard was surprised, then puzzled. "What do I see?"

"Matthew, expose her breasts."

Miss Emily observed this with a look of detached curiosity on her face, as if it were all happening to someone else. Pollard undid more buttons and pulled the upper part of the Miss Emily's white garment wide open. The girl's breasts were small but perfectly formed, with flat, pale pink nipples.

"Aha, no lactation," Pollard said. "No engorgement."

Van Helsing nodded approvingly. "So we see."

Now Pollard pulled up the lower portion of the nightdress and moved his stethoscope from one spot to another on her abdomen, listening carefully. Miss Emily's navel was almost completely flattened out by the bulging of her flesh. A minute later, Van Helsing took the instrument and listened.

"Nothing, right?"

"Agreed," Van Helsing answered. "Nothing at all."

"You're both wrong!" Miss Emily's loud outburst startled both men, and she laughed. "There's three of them, and you'll meet them soon enough. Sooner than you may think. Why don't you do your job properly, Doctor, and see if I'm telling you a lie or not?"

"I was about to do so, Miss," Pollard replied sharply.

The girl laughed again. "Be careful! They bite!"

Pollard removed a pouch of antiseptic cloths from his bag and washed his hands with one of them. He reached between Miss Emily's open legs. Several seconds later, he cleaned his hands again and led Van Helsing out of the room. Wingrove approached, but Pollard waved him away, taking Van Helsing down to the far end of the corridor.

"It's not a matter of months or days, it's a matter of hours. Tonight, or in the early hours of the morning, I should say."

"Ah, remarkable," Van Helsing said in a low voice.

"But what is it? Not a foetus, not even a dead one. How could she grow so large, as if with child, in a matter of a few days?"

"Perhaps an unnatural growth in the uterus."

"What, a cyst?" Pollard asked in disbelief. "That large?"

"Or something similar to a cyst," Van Helsing said. "A fibrous body, an errant growth, some malformation of tissue that reached a certain point, a certain degree of mass, and thereby caused this rapid and inordinate swelling in reaction, as her body prepares to expel it."

"Then she should be removed to a hospital," Pollard said.

Van Helsing shook his head doubtfully. "But we don't know for certain. If this guess proves to be incorrect, a hospital might only make matters worse, far worse. Here, you maintain complete control, without any risk of interference on the part of others. You must also consider whether the rigors of a journey might exacerbate her condition or even precipitate disaster."

Pollard nodded.

"Do you have a nurse you can rely on in service?"

"Yes. Miss Feeney. In the town."

"Perhaps you should instruct Mr. Dean Wingrove to send the boy Harry in the carriage to find Miss Feeney and bring her here. Also to give him a list of any supplies you may want her to bring. We have some time yet, if you decide Miss Emily must be moved, but you should prepare to act here."

"Yes, I quite agree. Wingrove needs a bracing, too."

"While you are attending to these matters, I wish to speak again with Miss Emily. Perhaps I can learn something more that will help us."

Pollard nodded once and went off to deal with Wingrove. Van Helsing found that Miss Emily was now drifting in and out of consciousness. But when she noticed his presence, her eyes brightened and she came awake.

"Miss Emily," he said, smiling at her.

"Are you the Jew?"

Van Helsing was hit by an unexpected wave of emotion—surprise, anger, and disappointment—but his features remained impassive.

"No, my dear. I am a Christian man," he said. "But please tell me, what made you ask such a question?"

She gave a slight shrug. "Someone."

"Someone? Who?"

"I can't remember. I heard someone say it."

"Say what? That I'm a Jew?"

"Well, no. Not necessarily you."

"My dear Miss Emily," Van Helsing said, allowing an indulgent smile to show at the corners of his mouth, "I am an old man. Please explain and clarify for me, so I understand exactly."

"Oh, you're not so old," Emily responded. "You are older, I will say that. But you don't look old. Your friend looks old. His hair is white, yours still has a strong color about it. A manly color."

Van Helsing laughed gently. "Lined with silver."

"It makes you look distinguished, sir." She changed her voice for the last sentence, so that she suddenly sounded like an adoring and compliant schoolgirl of fourteen who was infatuated with her poetry tutor.

"Miss Emily, please. I insist you answer my question."

"Yes, sir," she said immediately, continuing in the same affected girlish voice. "Someone said that a Jew was coming here to Ralls on a mission of great and terrible importance."

"What would that be?"

"To kill us."

"To kill you. Dear God. You say *us*. You and who else?"

"Us, sir. All of us."

"Why would someone kill you—any of you?"

"Because."

"Because is not a reason."

"Yes it is, sir. Because. *Be cause.*"

He gazed evenly at Miss Emily but said nothing more for a moment. In the matter of conversing with young ladies, Van Helsing's patience was vast, but the present situation allowed no time for the game of pleasant dawdling.

"Please tell me what happened to you."

He expected a show of reluctance, but Miss Emily surprised him again. She pulled herself up a little more on the bed, eagerness flaring in her eyes. Her nightdress still hung partly open. Van Helsing regarded her keenly.

"I can tell you because we are alone," she said, "and I can

see in your eyes that your interest is in *me*."

"You see well, and correctly."

"The storm passed early in the evening," she continued. "It was fearsome and beautiful in equal measure. So much lightning, such brilliant displays, purple or bluish-white daggers stabbing the air. It even blasted away part of our church. The thunder was deafening at times, the windows hummed and we thought they would explode! The rain sounded like thousands of tiny pebbles hurled at the glass again and again, one volley after another. From the front entrance we could see it spattering up gobs of muddy gravel on the drive."

Miss Emily paused a second to catch her breath, and then went on. "The air was so sweet and clean afterward, a delicious taste. The temperature was cool but not unpleasant, so I left my window open when I retired for the night. In the darkness, some hours later, My Lord came to me through that window. He scaled the wall and possessed me. I could not resist, nor did I wish to do so."

The expression on her face was proud and defiant.

"Who is he?" Van Helsing asked.

"I could see little of his features, but he was *beautiful*. His skin was like leather, his body far stronger than a man's. His tongue was long and thin, but wonderful in the sensations it awoke within me. His male part was as large as I could bear, and it was as smooth and hard as polished stone. Doctor, I adore him. And I bear the fruit of his seed."

"I ask you again. Who is he?"

"One of those blind to God's light. Set free!"

"Miss Emily—"

"Look, Jew!"

She pulled the blanket and sheet aside, tugged the hem of her nightdress up until the round expanse of her belly was visible. Van Helsing stared at her and he saw the movement in her flesh, like a strong ripple in placid water. He put his hand on it and felt its kick, its strength. Miss Emily smiled boldly at him, but her eyes closed almost at once and her head fell back on the pillows. After a moment in which Van Helsing sat still, watching as she breathed quickly, her body tossing restlessly, he put her clothing back in place, covered her again with the sheet and blanket, and left the room.

In the corridor, Matron approached. Van Helsing told her to resume her bedside vigil. He also asked her how he could find Miss Emily's room. It was on the same floor, but in the opposite wing. Van Helsing made his way there and let himself in. It was not large, but comfortable, by no means spartan. After a quick look around, he went to the window. A simple latch to open it, a spiked arm to hold it in place. He leaned out and looked down. Two floors below, the ground fell away sharply from the house, providing insufficient angle and hold for a long ladder. The construction of the exterior wall was such that any man would find it exceedingly difficult, if not impossible, to climb. Van Helsing looked closer at the stonework immediately beneath the window. He saw separate rows of thin but clear and sharply incised lines at certain intervals. He turned and leaned out of the window so that he could look upward. He saw the same scattered marks on the stone above, shallow but unmistakable.

Finally, Van Helsing took in the general view from Miss Emily's window. The rolling, park-like grounds, the long gravel drive, the reflecting pond, and the church. For a moment, he watched the workmen in the distance. They stared at pieces of broken stone on the grass, stared once again at the damaged corner of the church roof, and then conferred among themselves.

It seemed likely that Wingrove and Pollard could be found in Wingrove's office, but Van Helsing was in no mood to join them yet. He made his way down the stairs, out of the building, onto the grounds, and he walked toward the church. He sat down on a flat, protruding rock near a clump of birches, and lit a cigarette. His hand shook. He watched the workmen beside the church.

In Regensburg he had encountered evil masquerading as reason and enlightenment. Van Helsing had been invited to address the philosophy faculty. He had nearly reached the midpoint of his discourse on the many guises of evil in the present time when some of the students—and teachers, he recalled bitterly—began to chant and shout at him, accusing him of promoting old superstitions and "Jewish thought." He was "a Jew" or "a Jew-lover," who wanted to drag Europe back into the Dark Ages. Van Helsing's heart felt crushed, to hear such things in a Faculty of Philosophy. His attempts to answer them were lost in the growing derisive clamor. They were blind to their own ignorance and unreason. Finally, he abandoned his futile efforts to communicate with them and walked out of the lecture hall.

Evil came in many shapes and guises, sometimes human and sometimes other than human. Christians and Jews were allies in the struggle against evil, but the ancient division between them was the devil's own playground. Evil nurtured the growth of ignorance, fear and suspicion, the better to spread hatred across the face of the land and turn the day itself into unending night.

Was it a coincidence that Miss Emily asked him if he was a Jew, so soon after his bitter experience at Regensburg? Or was the demon who possessed her speaking through her, taking the measure of Van Helsing and trying to stir up a turmoil of emotions within him, thereby distracting him and diffusing the precise focus of his attention? He could not allow it.

Van Helsing stood up and crossed the lawn to the church. He gazed down at the scattered pieces of broken stone. He slowly walked around the church from one side to the other and back to his starting point, studying it closely. He was again quite impressed by the fineness of all the Gothic detail incorporated in the outer structure. There was no need to look inside.

"There you are!" Pollard approached. "What are you doing? I looked for you throughout the building. I'm concerned—"

"Matthew, look here," Van Helsing interrupted, pointing to the damaged area of the church. "In the storm, a lightning bolt struck there, and it shattered a stone gargoyle similar to the ones positioned at the other three corners. As you know, in times gone by, there were fervent and devoted members of the faithful who believed that using such stonework served to trap and imprison local demons as firmly as if they were in the grip of God Himself."

Pollard stared, thinking for a moment. "You're not suggesting—"

"I am stating it to you. Evil can take many different forms.

It hides now because the light of day blinds it. But it will emerge again, soon, and its spawn is what grows within poor Miss Emily."

Pollard struggled visibly within himself. "My instinct is to reject what you say, but I know better than to doubt you. If you're wrong, it won't matter, as we would treat Miss Emily to the utmost of our abilities in any event. If you're right, what action must we take?"

"First, we shall hunt down and destroy the beast. We have time yet, but we must hurry and do it. He cannot flee into daylight."

"But, where?"

Van Helsing pointed to the main house. "You can see one small window there, and another there, just below the line of the roof. An attic."

In Wingrove's office they learned that there was indeed an attic floor at the top of the house. Wingrove did not accept that "an intruder," as Van Helsing put it, could be hiding there, because only one door provided access, it was kept locked and Wingrove had the key. Nonetheless, he agreed to let them conduct a search. He reluctantly complied with Van Helsing's further request for the help of the three workmen outside and the provision of whatever weapons might be at hand on the estate. Within the hour the group was assembled. Two of the men had pitchforks, the third a shotgun. Van Helsing and Pollard took hatchets. Each of the five also carried an oil lamp, burning at its brightest.

The staff had already been directed to take the students to a garden that was set away from the house. They were to remain there until Wingrove sent for them. The only other people left in the house were Matron and Miss Emily, who were locked in the same room. Van Helsing instructed Wingrove to lock the attic door behind them and to open it only if he was certain he recognized the voice on the other side.

"Are there many windows in all?" Van Helsing asked.

"One or two on each side," Wingrove replied. "I can't remember, since we never use the space. The basement is adequate for our storage needs, and it's much easier to take things in and out of."

"You mean there is nothing in the attic?"

"Hardly anything, as I recall. The family whose home this was used it to store their mementoes and extra possessions, but all of that was removed before the school was established."

"Excellent," Van Helsing said. "This part will soon be done."

He led the party up the inner stairs and heard Wingrove dutifully lock the door below. They were in the central area between the two wings of the building. Empty, the attic seemed vast. It ran the entire length of the house, and the few low windows in it provided pockets of light that extended only a short distance inside. Most of the attic was cast in a murky grayness.

"Gentlemen, we should stay within a few paces of each other so that we can focus the strength of our lamps," Van Helsing told them. "We want to drive him into a corner. The light will blind him and allow us to complete our work. I caution you, the one we seek may not appear as any ordinary man, but you must not falter or turn away. Use your weapon well."

Van Helsing led the way and the group advanced slowly into the portion of the attic that was above the students' rooms. They had not gone very far when they heard a noise ahead of them, a vague scuffling. They immediately steered toward the area it seemed to come from, fanning out a little more but keeping the rays of their lamps in a tight focus. They heard a noise as of something running, off to the side and away from them.

"Quickly," Van Helsing shouted. "Cut him off!"

The men broke into a trot. A shape appeared at the edge of the light and then veered nimbly, circling back into the dark. Then the sound gained speed in a sharp burst, the sound of heavy leatherish feet loudly smacking bare floorboards. The men turned and tried to recover, but their quarry raced past them, beyond the reach of their light.

"He's going into the area above the other wing," Van Helsing said. "We must make better use of our lamps. The light blinds him, he fears it. Spread out more. When you hear him again, run toward him, but try to stay in front of the sound so as not to let him get past us again. If we can force him to run through us, not around us, then we have a chance to converge and spear him or trip him up with the forks."

They moved ahead steadily, their lamps now sweeping the entire area in front of them. They moved farther apart, forming a longer, looser line across the width of the attic. They passed the opening to the stairs again and a few moments later Van Helsing calculated that they were into the other wing. There was a rank odor in the air, like the stench of rotting animal flesh. "Be ready," Van Helsing told them. "He must be close now." Then they heard the sound. It came from a place directly ahead of them, it wasn't moving. It was a harsh breathing noise that conveyed a clear warning. It was softer and deeper than a hiss, similar to the throaty sound that certain Asian and African snakes are able to produce, but much stronger.

The demon leapt out of the darkness, charging them in a bounding motion, like a tiger. The shotgun blast did nothing to slow it, the pellets lodging in the surface of the thick hide. But the men with pitchforks set down their lamps and seized it, one by the upper leg and groin, the other by the shoulder and neck. They struggled to hold it as the creature lashed at them with arms that were long and surprisingly thin but tightly muscled.

Van Helsing jumped in and swung the hatchet at the gargoyle's skull, but it turned and the blade slashed less effectively along its prominent jaw. It was about the size of a small man, and it thrashed violently, at the same time letting out a hideous sound, a shrill high skirling wail. The man with the shotgun leaned in and fired again, this time the muzzle just inches from the demon's face, and the blast gouged a much deeper, circular wound. Dark liquid oozed out, the creature shrieked even more and continued to struggle. Van Helsing struck again and again with the hatchet, now aiming at the throat. He chopped through the tough outer skin, which was a mottled black and gray in coloration and beady in texture. He hacked at tendons as resistant as braided wire cables, through muscle layered in plates. Pollard dropped his hand ax to the floor and held his lamp close to the grotesque creature's face. The light revealed a pair of eyes like unmarked stone, full of wild nothingness. The demon's body did not stop moving until several minutes after Van Helsing had cut its head away completely.

"Observe the claws in its hands and feet," he said. "So strong and sharp it could scale a smooth stone wall as easily as a dog runs across a field." He set the head down beside the body, now still and lifeless. "You will find that one of the windows here is in need of repair."

"A fiend from Hell," one of the men gasped.

"Truly it is," another said in awe.

Van Helsing nodded. "And we have sent it back to Hell. You must wrap it in some cloth, remove it from here and burn it. Burn it until the last ember dies and then crush any pieces of bone that remain. Shovel up all the ashes into a pail and dump them into a river or stream—it must be running water. Tell no one of what you have seen and done here today. They would only believe you have lost your reason. God bless you, men."

Pollard, who stood nearby, gazed in fascination at the remains of the gargoyle. "And this beast was hiding here for three whole days since the storm, in the same building as Miss Emily—and the other young ladies." He turned anxiously to Van Helsing. "You don't think...?"

"Let us hope not," Van Helsing said grimly. "Come along now, Matthew. Pick up your ax. The worst part of our work here remains to be done."

Downstairs, he spoke to Wingrove. "It would be better if you ask us no questions at this time. You must allow the workmen to finish what they are doing now, and do not interfere. When they leave, you may have the students and staff return and go about their normal business. Now please, dear sir, direct the lad Harry to bring some boards to the room where Miss Emily is, also a hammer and nails. If Harry has not returned with the nurse yet, bring those things yourself, as we need them without delay. Ah, and some rope and a knife as well, thank you. No, *please*. I will not discuss this now. For the sake of everybody, and for your school itself, you must do as I say."

Wingrove glanced down once more at the hatchet in Van Helsing's hand. The blade was wet with blackish gore and bits of gristle. He looked at Pollard, who simply nodded once. Wingrove hurried away.

The doctors found that Miss Emily's time was very near. Matron was asked to leave as soon as Nurse Feeney arrived.

Pollard took her aside to let her know what to expect—she turned quite pale, but then nodded firmly. It was dark outside when Van Helsing finished boarding up the only window in the small room. He checked the lock in the door and found it adequate. Miss Emily was now in a state of restless delirium, her body twisting and shuddering. She cried and moaned in an unnerving high-pitched voice. Van Helsing cut two pieces of the rope and tied her wrists to the bedposts on the headboard to ensure that she would not be able to attack them.

"Keep your wits and remember this," he said quietly to Pollard and Nurse Feeney. "Whatever is born here tonight must not leave this room alive." Then he sat on the wooden chair beside the bed and watched the girl in silence.

Shortly after eight, Miss Emily's water broke—a sickly grayish fluid that gave off a foul smell. Layers of towels absorbed most of it. The girl shrieked and struggled against the ropes, kicking wildly. Pollard and the nurse each took hold of a leg and used their bodies to pin them back.

A black-speckled gray hand reached out of Miss Emily, dug its tiny claws into her flesh, drawing blood, and pulled itself from her body. The vile creature emerged quickly, about the size of a small dog, but with the grotesque look of a willfully deformed human. Van Helsing seized it before it was completely free of its host-mother and smashed it on the floor. Holding it down with his shoe, he cut it in half with one blow of the hatchet.

He turned back to the bed in time to see the second one leap at Pollard's face. The doctor fell away, screaming. Miss Emily began to kick her free leg at Nurse Feeney. Van Helsing stepped around the bed and snatched the gargoyle away from Pollard's face—his cheek was torn and blood flowed from the ragged wounds. The second demon squirmed, bit, and clawed savagely at Van Helsing's hand, but he dispatched it as he had the first.

Then he swung the hatchet and hit Miss Emily in the head with the flat side of the blade, rendering her unconscious for the moment. The third beast was not yet free, emerging feet first. Van Helsing used a hand towel to grasp it and pull it out. He was horrified to see a mortal rush of blood pour out with the ugly creature, splashing into the air and onto the floor. The claws of both the demon's hands had clutched and dragged a portion of Miss Emily's entrails with it in its birth. Van Helsing hammered it several times, then turned the hatchet around and chopped it in two.

For a few moments the three of them stood as if stunned and paralyzed by what they had just seen and done, and the ghastly remains around them. Whether it sprang out of the darkness to prey on the weak and innocent, as here at Ralls, or it coiled its tendrils from within to shrivel and corrode the hearts of ordinary men, as at Regensburg, evil was the same— unforgiving, savage, and utterly relentless in the pursuit of its own fulfillment. And what is that ultimate impulse of evil, Van Helsing thought, if not a profound, incalculable hatred of life itself. The days will dawn, the sun will still shine, but the invisible darkness will slowly leak through and gather strength, until it shows itself again.

He looked around. Nurse Feeney had been kicked several times but was not seriously injured. Pollard might bear scars, but he was not in danger. Van Helsing went to the bed and checked Miss Emily, though he already knew it was pointless; her heart had stopped beating.

INFIDEL

"And how is me dear old friend Andy these days?"

"He's fine. He's in good health, and he said to tell you he plays golf at least once a week."

"Tsk." Monsignor Comerford shook his head in mock annoyance but couldn't keep from smiling. "It's a grand racket, the parish priest. Marry 'em and bury 'em, and count the weekly take. Tell Andy I said that, would you?"

"I will," Caroline replied.

"Did you know Andy and I were in college together in Dublin? University College. That was ages ago, of course."

"Yes, he told me that's where you met," Caroline said. "And UCD was where James Joyce went too, wasn't it?"

"That's right, Earlsfort Terrace. Great writer, Joyce," the monsignor added perfunctorily, as if he did not quite agree with his own statement. "A fine feel for the city back then, I'll say that much for him."

Caroline reached into her purse. "I took this snapshot of Father Andy a couple of weeks ago," she said as she passed it to the elderly priest.

"Ah, will you look at that chubby little bugger," Monsignor Comerford exclaimed with glee as he took the photograph. "He was always first at table, now that I think back on it. Mind you, he never shied away from a gargle either, but you'd better not tell him I said *that*. He might worry about his image. Parish priests tend to fret about such things in America."

"You can keep it, Monsignor," Caroline said as he attempted to return the photograph. "It's for you."

"Thank you very much." He set the picture down on his

desk, next to the letter of introduction that Father Andy had written for Caroline. "But let's skip that 'Monsignor' business, shall we? Gerry will do nicely." Caroline smiled and nodded. "Good. Now then, how long have you been in Rome?"

"Four days."

It came as a mild surprise for Caroline to be reminded that she was sitting in an office in Vatican City, not in a rectory in some leafy suburb of Dublin. Monsignor Comerford, she knew, had been stationed at the Vatican for nearly two decades, but he was still thoroughly Irish in his appearance, accent and manner. The pink, well- scrubbed complexion, the curly white hair, the steady cascade of Carroll's cigarette ash down the front of his black jacket, the gentle singsong voice—all seemed to belong more in a cluttered Georgian sitting room with peat blazing fragrantly in the fireplace and a big bottle of Powers on the sideboard than in this obscure corner of the papal bureaucracy. Caroline had no clear idea what the monsignor *did* at the Vatican, but neither did Father Andy.

"And it says here," tapping the letter, "you're a librarian. Is that right?"

"Yes," Caroline answered.

"Very good, and what exactly is it you'd like to do?"

"I'd love to spend some time just looking through the books, the archives. It probably sounds silly, but I've always dreamed of having a chance to explore the Vatican library. I love books and manuscripts, all forms of writing."

Caroline hoped he wouldn't ask if she had been to Trinity or the Bodleian or the Sorbonne, because she hadn't. How could she explain to the priest that it wasn't just books, but the Vatican itself, that had drawn her? She really did dream of the Vatican—bizarre images of capture, of anonymous torture, of being trapped forever in an endless maze of barren hallways. Nothing was ever said, there were no signs, but somehow Caroline always knew that she was in the Vatican. At times she wondered if the recurring dreams were a form of sickness, but they never frightened her; on the contrary, she had come to feel almost comfortable with them.

"Is it the dirty books you're after?" Monsignor Comerford's

eyes had turned steely. "We've a regular army of these so-called scholars that come trooping through here, most of them American I might add, and all they want to do is study the dirty books. Why we even keep them is beyond me, but nowadays destroying a book is almost a mortal sin. To some folks, anyway."

The monsignor was apparently finished, so Caroline answered his question. "No. History and the history of the faith, are my favorite subjects." Faith, she thought, and the loss of it.

"Ah, that's a welcome change." The monsignor beamed at her. "If all the fine young women of the world felt that way, there'd be a lot less bother taking place."

There was a barb in the compliment, for Caroline noticed how the monsignor glanced at her unadorned ring finger. History and books were all well and good, but he believes I should be married and taking care of a bunch of babies, she thought. That was fine with her. Caroline might disagree with Monsignor Comerford as to what a woman should or should not do but she was actually pleased that he was a priest from the old school. She hadn't come to the Vatican looking for trendiness or progressive attitudes. Her own faith had been blasted by the winds of modernism swirling through the Church in recent years.

"Well, you'd better get started," the monsignor said, rising from his seat. "You can have the rest of the afternoon, just get yourself back here by five. That's when I leave, and I wouldn't want you getting lost."

"Neither would I."

"And if you haven't had enough, you're more than welcome to come back tomorrow. There's so much of that clutter downstairs a person could spend years poking through it all, if he had nothing better to do with his life. And contrary to what you might have heard, none of it is off limits." The priest paused, then winked at her. "Of course, it's not everyone that gets in."

Monsignor Comerford left Caroline with Father Vincenzo, who was apparently in charge of 'the collection.' A short, thin man who wore wire-rimmed glasses and spoke excellent English,

Father Vincenzo showed her some of the noteworthy documents and volumes in the official library. Air-conditioned, computerized, it was a completely modern operation in a centuries-old setting. And yet, it was a good deal smaller than Caroline had expected. But then Father Vincenzo took her on a tour of the three main levels below ground, where one room grew out of another and the number of them ran into the dozens before she lost count. There were books and manuscripts and tottering heaps of papers piled on every inch of shelf space, from floor to ceiling. Tiny corridors appeared, and then abruptly ended. On the third and lowest level the floor was made up of large stone slabs, long since worn smooth. The rooms were small and boxy, and seemed to have been carved right out of the earth. The passageways were quite narrow and the only lights were strung along the low ceiling with electric cable.

There were no labels, no numbers, no signs, nothing at all to indicate order. If you wanted to find something, where would you start, Caroline wondered. But she was delighted, because she finally felt she had arrived where she was meant to be.

"These are the oldest stacks," Father Vincenzo explained. "Everything valuable or important has been removed, but otherwise it is not very organized."

"There's so much of it," Caroline said.

"Yes, it extends under most of Vatican City. The equivalent of two or three square blocks in New York City, I think." Then a smile formed at the corners of Father Vincenzo's mouth. "You are a book-lover. This, I think, is what you came to see."

"Oh yes, yes. I'm amazed. It's so much like I pictured it in my fantasies." The word seemed too personal, almost sexual in its intensity. Caroline felt her cheeks flush, and all she could do was add weakly, "But more so."

Father Vincenzo brought Caroline back to the stairs in order to show her how easy it was to find the way out, and then he left her alone to pursue her curiosity. She appreciated the fact that he didn't feel it necessary to warn her against damaging, copying or tracing over anything.

Caroline wandered aimlessly for a while, stopping to look at one item or another, and then moving on. Her knowledge of French and Latin was excellent, and she had a smattering of Italian, but most of the pages on the third level were handwritten, and sooner or later the calligraphy defeated her. Caroline simply could not concentrate, her mind refused to focus. *What am I doing here?*

Somewhere in a far corner of the third level, Caroline found a battered footstool in one room. She sat down on it, and leaned back against a wall of large, leathery tomes. She was tired, and her feet ached, the usual tourist curse, but she felt very happy. Pennsylvania seemed a billion miles away. She let her eyes close for a moment, and she sucked in the musty air. To Caroline it was like a rare and delicious perfume.

Books were the center of her life, and it had been that way ever since she was a small child. She liked to believe that she could still remember fumbling to open her very first picture book of nursery rhymes—but Caroline knew that was probably more her fancy than an actual memory. Books were mysterious, frightening, thrilling, disturbing, uplifting, nurturing, endlessly available and always accommodating. Caroline had dated many men over the years, but she had yet to find one who offered the same array of valuable qualities. Most of the time that didn't bother her. If you had to have something other than a relationship for the focal point of your life, what better than books?

Books, and belief. But belief was an increasingly elusive notion. For years it had been a natural part of Caroline's life, but lately it seemed irrelevant, or not even there. Nothing specific had happened to cause this change, yet it seemed as if the deep well of her faith had gradually evaporated to the point where it was now not much more than a thin, moist residue. But you can't control faith, anymore than you can choose your dreams.

Caroline stood up and resumed her wandering. In one large room she came across signs of fairly recent activity. There were stacks of bound papers on a table, many more on the floor around it. A prospectus announced the publication of the *Annals of the Propagation of the Faith* in five hundred volumes over a period of twenty years. Caroline knew that the *Annals* were regular reports to the Vatican from Catholic missionaries all over the world. It was a staggering thought. How many centuries of this tedious and obscure paperwork had accumulated by now? And yet, Caroline was sure that some of it must be quite fascinating. However, clipped to the prospectus was a laconic handwritten note, dated November, 1974, which stated that the project was abandoned because of the bankruptcy of the publisher. And of course the Vatican wouldn't squander its own funds on such an improbable commercial venture, Caroline thought, smiling as she left the room.

She walked until she came to the lowest (the floor had a way of gradually winding down into the earth) and most remote corner of the third level. Certainly this was where the overhead reach of electric cable and lights ended. About twenty feet away, just visible in the gloom, was a stone wall that marked the end of the passageway. The books and manuscripts, stacked from the floor to the ceiling on each side, were wedged together so tightly and had been undisturbed for so long that they appeared to have hardened into a solid mass, and Caroline was afraid she would damage them if she tried to remove any one item for scrutiny. She started to turn away, intending to make the long climb back up to the street level, but then she stopped, as she thought she noticed something odd about the far wall.

It was an optical illusion, aided by the feeble light. Yes, she realized, moving closer. There was not one wall, but two, at the end of the aisle. The outer wall, which came from the right, stopped just short of the stacks on the left, and the inner wall receded almost imperceptibly behind it. Caroline approached the gap, barely a foot wide, and peered around the corner.

Total darkness. She reached into it, and felt nothing but cool air. The passage continued. Caroline didn't know what she should do. She wanted to follow it, to find out where it went, but she had nothing to light her way. She could trip and tumble down a hole, or walk into a den of snakes or vermin—too many bad things could happen. Buy a flashlight and return tomorrow.

Yes, but first...Caroline slid her foot along the ground and edged herself behind the wall. Just a step or two, she promised, to see if it ends abruptly. Her outstretched hand bumped against something hard, not stone. A metal bar. Caroline gripped it and harsh rust flaked loot in her hand. It had to be a gate, which meant that the passage *did* go on. Caroline shook it firmly once, and the whole thing broke free. It was too heavy and unwieldy to control, so she shoved it away from her. The sound that came in the darkness told her that the gate had hit a wall and then slid down to the left. Firm ground, and a turn.

Caroline worked her way along the narrow passage. The wall swung back to the left, as expected. She moved cautiously around the turn, probing the air with her hand. Caroline stopped. This was as far as she could safely go without a light. She stared at the uniform blackness ahead of her. Beyond this point she could easily get lost in a maze of passageways. Okay, she thought, you found something interesting; come back tomorrow with a flashlight and a sack of breadcrumbs.

Caroline hesitated, her mind dancing with possibilities. It could be a long-forgotten catacomb, or a burial chamber that held the mummified remains of ancient Romans. She might even discover some manuscripts that dated back two thousand years. She should discuss it with Father Vincenzo, and together they could organize a proper exploration. But even as Caroline considered this, she found it impossible to turn back. The priest's office was so far away, such an enormous climb—and Caroline felt too tired. The cumulative effects of travel and touring and the miles of walking had finally caught up with her. The dead air didn't help either. She would have to rest for a few minutes before leaving.

As she stood there, leaning against the wall, Caroline began to notice the quality of the darkness. You could say that it had no depth at all, or that its depth was endless. But it was not a perfect darkness, she realized. Somewhere in it, close by or off in the distance, there was—not light, but the subtlest texture of light. I must look like someone on drugs, Caroline thought as she stared ahead. Pupils dilated wide as drift nets to sweep any random photons across the threshold of visibility. I look like a freak, but that's okay because it's a freaky situation. Caroline felt dizzy and disoriented, as if she could no longer tell which way was up, and yet there was nothing she could do—except fall down, if that's what was going to happen—because she was just too tired, too damn tired to care. But she was not wrong. There was light, or something like it.

Caroline was aware of the fact that she was walking. Toward the light, into the dark, it didn't matter which. She felt oddly detached from what was happening, as if her body had decided to move and her mind was simply floating along with it. Probably no one still alive in the Vatican knew of this hidden area, Caroline thought dreamily. Which means, *No one in the world knows where I am now.* But that didn't frighten her. On the contrary, she felt caught up in something of real importance out on the boundary of faith and uncertainty, and dreams.

A suffusion of light infiltrated her right eye, knocking her off balance. It wasn't that strong, Caroline saw as she steadied herself and her eyes re-adjusted. It was a glow, a hazy cloud of cold light some distance away, too weak to illuminate this place. Yet it had confused her for a brief moment. Caroline crossed the intervening space and walked into the faint light. She looked at a flight of crude stairs that coiled down and away from her, deep into the chilly earth.

For just an instant Caroline's mind slid toward the idea of leaving, but just as quickly it skittered away. Her body had no strength for going back now. It was as if she were caught on an electric current that carried her only forward, and down. And so Caroline descended the wet and slippery steps, pressing her hands against the close walls and bending her head beneath the low rock ceiling. Count the number—but the numbers bounced around like a flock of billiard balls clicking in her brain, and the momentum of her descent increased rapidly, flooding her with apprehension, so she couldn't.

Almost brightness. Caroline's knees sagged as her feet hit bottom suddenly and there was nowhere to go. She had arrived in a small room, really nothing more than a landing. Then she saw the gate, another gate. No, it was a door. Through the bars, a square cell, empty but for the old man lying in the middle of the floor. A clutch of tattered rags. The man looked ancient. What light was this?

Ah, child.

—Who…are you?

The words formed in her mind but never escaped her lips. It didn't matter. The old man smiled, and it felt, disturbingly, as if he somehow made Caroline's face smile with him.

Mani.

—What?

Caroline's brain swirled sickeningly, and it took an effort of the will to remain on her feet. The old man kept smiling that near-death smile. A sack of dead skin. But the smile, and those eyes were very much alive. He moved slightly, the muted sound of dusty parchment rustling.

Ma-nee.

The first syllable prolonged, the second quite crisp despite the long vowel. Caroline shook her head slowly.

—No...

Manicheus, if you wish.

Impossible, Caroline thought. It was all wrong and she knew she should leave at once, but instead her body sank down the wall until she was sitting on the bottom step.

—The holy man?

Paraclete. Yes.

—No. Manicheus died in 275 A.D.

Was put to death.

—As a heretic.

Yes, as a heretic.

The old man's laughter simmered uncomfortably in Caroline's brain. This is crazy, she thought, I'm hallucinating, the dreams are pushing up and breaking the surface.

No.

She struggled to recall what she knew of Manicheanism. It was one of many heretical sects that had sprung up in the early years of the Church, and perhaps the most dangerous. The Church had spared no effort to wipe out the Manicheans, although some of their beliefs still lingered on in the despair and cynicism that permeated so much of modern life. They claimed that the universe was made up of two equal forces, light (good) and dark (evil), in eternal conflict. God was good, but God did not reign supreme in this universe. If you put evil on a par with good, then all else is permanently diminished and faith becomes a matter of arbitrary choice. Human beings were just insignificant players in a cosmic struggle without beginning or end. So the gap between the Church and the Manicheans was a vast theological chasm that could never be bridged. But it was an issue of purely academic interest now, or at least it should be, Caroline thought.

—How could you be here?

They brought me back and locked me in this place.

—But why? Didn't they kill you?

Yes, but to them I was a heretic.

—I still don't understand.

The laughter came again, rippling through Caroline's mind in a very unpleasant sensation.

They believed that heretics return to this world, possessing terrible powers. The power to draw the lifeblood of faith out of other souls. To control the feeble human mind. That is why they burned heretics, and tore the bodies to pieces.

But that was another time, centuries ago, and now not even the Church believed in such things. Beliefs change, but do they ever matter?

The Pope had to see me, to see for himself that I really was dead, and so they brought me back from Persia.

—And put you down here and forgot about you?

Oh, they played with me a while, using their knives and hot irons. Dry laughter, like whistling sand. *But then the old Pope died, and yes, I was forgotten.*

—When did you last…

See someone? A charming young novice in the 13th century. I haven't been able to move from this spot in about perhaps three hundred years now. Easy to find souls, but not to bring them all the way into this place.

The old man was crazy, Caroline had no doubt. But whatever the truth about him might be, he obviously needed care, and maybe medical attention. He certainly did not belong down in a clammy dungeon. It was a miracle he wasn't already dead. He looked so frail and helpless, and there was such sadness in his eyes.

—I'll get help.

Don't leave me, child.

—What should I do?

The door. Come to me.

Caroline approached the cell door. The hinges looked as if they wouldn't budge. She put her hands around one of the bars in the center of the door, and shook it. The hinges held, but there was some give inside the lock. Caroline shook the door again and the corroded latch crumbled steadily beneath the pressure. Rusty flakes showered down to the floor. The hinges shrieked painfully as Caroline forced the door open.

The old man looked up hopefully as she slipped into the cell and went to him. She wasn't sure what to do next. He looked too weak and fragile to move.

Hold me.

Caroline sat down on the floor beside him, took him by the shoulders and carefully lifted him up. His head lolled against her shoulder, then slid a little, resting over her heart, and he smiled gratefully. Caroline had no desire to move.

Touch me with your skin.

Caroline stroked his cheek lightly—it felt cool and dry, like one of the old manuscripts she had examined. Regardless of who he was or why he was there, the old man responded to her hand on his cheek. His eyes brightened and his features became more animated. He was certainly old, but so small and shrunken, like some lonely, withered child.

I need to be closer.

Caroline didn't understand. Her mind felt tired, lazy, and remarkably tranquil. She didn't want to move at all. She hugged the old man closer to her.

To your warmth.

Her mind couldn't follow a complete thought anymore. Nothing mattered but the moment, and her part in it. Caroline unbuttoned her blouse and the old man quickly pressed his face to her skin. *More.*

Her bra was in the way. Caroline pulled it down, uncovering her breasts. The old man rubbed his face against them, burrowed between them, and then she felt his tongue, like fine sandpaper, seeking her nipple. Caroline was paralyzed with delirium, dazed with a sense of giving. It felt as if her body was a vessel full of precious liquid, a kind of inner sea of living warmth that was now flowing through her skin into him. But there was nothing to replace it, and Caroline's heart quickened with a sudden surge of useless alarm.

—Holy man...

Once.

—You brought me here?

In a way, yes.

—You spoke to me in dreams...

In dreams you spoke with yourself, and I am what you found.

—You took my faith...

What we let go, was never there.

—Help me...

Become what you become, as I did.

—They were right...

Well, yes.

—You became...

What they made me.

—God help me...

And who is that, child?

Caroline reached up to touch her own cheek and was amazed to find that it already felt as cool and dry as onion-skin. Too weak to move, Caroline rested her hand on the man's bony shoulder. She was vaguely aware that she ought to push him away. There was no muscle strength left in her arm. Then Caroline was unable even to remain sitting up, and she fell back flat on the floor. She felt so light there was no pain when her head hit the stone. The old man moved lower and rested his face in the warm softness of her belly. He left no mark on her, for the touch of her skin was enough. An image flickered across her mind—she was buried beneath a million books, and it was not an unpleasant experience. Then the books began to fall, tons of them raining silently down through the darkness, and Caroline fell with them, a fading ribbon of liquid heat that spun and swirled as she flew gloriously out of herself.

She wakes in darkness. Disoriented for a moment, she shoves the dead bones off her bare skin. Now she knows where she is and what comes next. She stands, buttons her blouse and leaves. She knows the way. So much time has gone by. It's late, and she has a million things to do.

THE WOMAN IN THE CLUB CAR

for Dennis Ferado

By the time he reached Grand Central, Phil had got himself around to thinking that the entire day had been a bit of a waste. He checked his watch and saw that he had enough time for one more cigarette before he went inside to catch the 1:15 a.m. Metro-North New Haven line train that would deliver him to the station in Hawleyville on the Connecticut shore. A short drive from there and he would be back home in his condo about 3 o'clock. He looked forward to sleeping late, maybe until noon. He pulled out a cigarette and lit up.

He had walked all the way from the Tavern on the Green, thinking that the exercise and the crisp autumn air would do him good. And it did feel okay, but he was tired now. Phil had come in to the city to have lunch with his agent, Lloyd, who was as enthusiastic and effusive as ever. But there were detectable undercurrents. Phil had made a career writing feature-length and shorter articles about the arts for magazines, newspapers, and websites, and he even had a couple of minor syndications. He wrote about music, movies, theater, visual and performance art, anime and manga, whatever caught his eye and attention. He covered the waterfront, or at least he tried to. People want to label you, peg you in a specific hole, and he naturally resented that. Phil cherished the opportunity to discover something tomorrow and be able to write about it immediately, and to have Lloyd sell it a few days later. Besides, a huge number of potential new venues for his work had emerged in recent years on the Internet. So Phil should be doing just fine, at least in terms of his work.

But it didn't feel just fine, it hadn't for a while now. Today
Lloyd had suggested, gently but insistently, that Phil's longer
and more thoughtful pieces were becoming a little trickier to
bring to market. Attention spans are dropping, people want
more instantaneous, impressionistic writing. People, meaning
those mysterious, possibly-tapering-off buyers of his articles.
As for the Internet—the money was a joke, so far.

Fuck it. He threw his cigarette into the gutter, and entered
the station. Growing older wasn't something you necessarily
felt first in physical terms, of your body failing you. It could be
a taste in your mouth or a faint scent in the back of your nostrils, suggesting fruit that has grown a little too ripe around the
edges. It could be a shade being drawn down over a whole corner of your mind that seemed vital until yesterday. Phil had left
forty behind a year ago. Keeping up seemed to take more and
more of an effort. It had been three years since he and Claire
had divorced—it was mutual at the time, but decreasingly so (to
him, at least) in retrospect. Since then, scrambling to scribble for
a living began to seem less and less palatable. Or desirable. Or
tenable. Whichever.

Won't you tell me, where have all the good times gone?

The train pulled out on time, and Phil made his way to the
club car. It could appear that he had been drinking all day—
several glasses of wine over lunch with Lloyd, a few beers with
Maggie from www.lostcauseways.com at the Royalton late in
the afternoon, and then the party for Au Revoir Simone at the
Tavern, where he'd knocked back a measured but steady stream
of George Dickel, while scarfing down shrimp and other lus-
cious tidbits in quantities that would add up roughly to a dinner of sorts. Time to decelerate. He bought a can of Heineken
and sat at one of the small window tables.

He had taken this late train back to Connecticut a number
of times over the past couple of years. He'd seen some funny
things—couples with their hands inside each other's overcoat,
guys waking up two or three stops past their station and being
angry about it, a very tipsy priest blessing a teenage-looking
girl's new tongue stud, her boyfriend taking pictures.

But tonight there was only one other passenger in the club

car, a young woman sitting two tables away from him. A small handbag on the table in front of her, no drink. She stared at the table, or the handbag, but her focus was obviously somewhere else. Somewhere way else. Phil watched her in glances for a few moments. Mid-twenties, dark hair, medium length, kind of frizzy. Pale skin, angular facial features with high cheekbones and a slender nose. One hand rested on the table, long, thin fingers. Not beautiful, but attractive in some odd way. But then, Phil had reached the point in life where most women younger than he was looked attractive to him, one way or another.

Time to make a jackass of himself. More confident than he had any reason to be, he took his beer and his laptop case with him, and approached her table.

"Excuse me."

She looked up at him, but said nothing.

"You're in the club car, so you really should have a drink. May I get you one?"

"Oh. No, thank you." But not entirely discouraging.

"Please," he insisted gently. "If the club car doesn't do enough business, they'll do away with it, a great train tradition will die, and people like me will be all bollixed up. They've got spirits, wine, beer, iced tea, soda. Water. Have something, even if you don't drink it."

She almost smiled. "A gin and tonic?"

He set his beer and laptop down. "I think they can manage that."

Her name was Rachel and her stop was Hawleyville, as well but she was rather cautious and evasive beyond that. *Understandably so*, Phil thought. Stranger on a train, etc. He told her a bit about himself, his work, and how he'd lived in Manhattan but moved out to Connecticut a while back.

"You're divorced," she said.

"It shows that much?" he asked, smiling.

"Something does—life experience. Relief, maybe."

He found that disarming. "You might be right." This was no time to express the doubts that nagged him constantly. "And you?"

She sighed, not theatrical. "No relief, anyway."

"You still miss him, you want to be back together?"

"God, no."

"Then, what?"

She gave a slight shrug. Looking at the table.

After a while, he asked again, "What?"

She shook her head, as if to shrug it away. "People are at their worst in situations like that. It leaves a bad taste."

It took some more poking around to find out that her ex was an architect who had never actually had a building of his own design built, who worked as a cog in a large firm and passed his days clarifying details that no one ever noticed. Missed opportunities, in-house politics, for whatever reason, Rachel's husband had grown bitter early. He found someone else, quit his job, and moved to North Carolina. Married the Other, now ran a landscaping business.

They were starting to drift into the territory that Phil thought of as more than he needed, and wanted, to know. He made some mildly dismissive comment about her ex and Rachel gave a small nod of appreciation.

Then she prodded him, and since he had the vent down pat, he delivered it again. They had a great apartment in Brooklyn, had been there since before the huge property boom hit the Borough, and he didn't really want to leave. But Claire made a lot more money than he did, she had a rising career as an investment analyst. She got a big offer from a hedge fund in Greenwich, she wanted to get out of the city, and she did dangle the possibility that if things went as well as she expected, they might eventually be able to afford a small apartment in Manhattan. Money is persuasive, and he didn't put up much resistance.

But within a year of moving into the house in Darien, things fell apart. He hated it there and was not very good about hiding that fact. Looking back, Phil could see that he and Claire had been moving away from each other for some time. Should have been obvious to him, as it no doubt was to her much earlier. He'd had vague intimations amounting to a kind of lingering dread, but the actual breakup still came as a shock to Phil. The other guy, who lived in "the real world." The countless little things that made her feel Phil was "a drag to be around." Well, he had written worse things about other people, so he took it all as just a bad review. And soon the house was sold, and he made his next mistake.

"I should have moved back into the city, found an apartment and gone back to living and working the way I had in the past."

Rachel nodded sympathetically. What he had done was to throw most of his money into a condo unit in Hawleyville. There was something seductive about being within easy reach of the city, still being able to do most of your work from home, but not having to put up with all the draining little everyday demands and hassles of city life.

Even as he was blathering on about this, and Rachel was making a good show of being interested, Phil could feel a tide pulling in part of his brain—*you just sound old*, it said. And he could not argue with that. No mental energy to do so, for one thing—ha!

They chatted a bit aimlessly the rest of the way. She seemed to be there, and sometimes not quite there. But then, he assumed the same was true for him. It was one of those occasions when it's easier to be there in the presence of someone else than it would be to be sitting alone, even if there's no real *connect*.

They stopped at Greenwich, scene of several crimes. And Darien, scene of a few more. Phil had talked enough, he felt he could push her a bit more now.

"Do you live in Hawleyville, or nearby?"

A head-shake. "No. Just visiting a friend."

That could make sense, he thought. *Late flight in from somewhere.*

"They meeting you at the station?"

"I hope so." A wan smile.

"Did you call them? They know you're coming? I mean, *now*?"

"I think so." Another smile, and a shrug.

Phil was tired, but it just got a little more interesting. Rachel now seemed to be in a mode he thought of as female-semi-helpless. In other words, things should be okay and all set up, but maybe they're not quite. I thought you knew this, I thought you

knew that, I said this, you said, I told you and you answered...
and nothing goes right at all. Later, there would be a ton of dis-
cussion to determine what went wrong, and nothing would be
resolved.

Some of which happened. The station was closed at that
hour, and the only car in the parking lot was Phil's. No one
waiting for Rachel. Phil watched the train disappear up the line
toward New Haven. She huddled in her light jacket against the
chill.

"I'll wait with you," he said.

"No, that's all right, you don't have to."

Phil made a face. "I'm not leaving a young woman alone at
a deserted train station at this hour of the night."

She smiled. "Thank you."

"Do you want to call them?" He reached for his cell phone.

"Thanks." She punched in some numbers and listened, then
closed it and handed the phone back to Phil. "Straight to voice
mail."

She declined his offer of a cigarette, he lit up. They waited
five minutes, ten, no passing traffic at all in the immediate area.

"Have you been here before, to visit them?"

"Yes."

"How far is it?"

"A couple of miles, maybe."

"Do you know how to get there?"

Quick nods. "I think so. In the daytime."

"Come on, I'll drop you off," Phil said. "You can wake them
up and chew them out for not being here to meet you on time.
Probably fell asleep."

She shifted from one foot to the other, hesitating. "You don't
have to."

"Come on," he said. "I'm going, and if you want to stay here,
I'm calling the cops to let them know there's a woman alone at
the station, and they'll send a car by to make sure you're okay
and your ride shows up."

That decided it for her. "No, don't do that."

"Fine, let's go."

"Thank you."

"No problem, I'm sleeping late in the morning anyhow."

He followed her directions, and they headed out of town. They hadn't driven far before she pointed to a dirt road coming up fast on them.

"Here, this one, take this one."

Phil braked and swung the car onto the gravel path. He proceeded slowly, and they went another half-mile or so before the road ended in an open pasture. He put the car in park and made a bit of a show of looking around in the darkness.

"Is there a house here?"

"I think I picked the wrong turn," Rachel said quietly. "I'm sorry."

"Okay, no problem."

He reached for the shift, but she took his hand, to stop him.

"Can we wait here for a minute?"

He looked at her, and had no idea. "O-kay."

She kept his hand in hers.

"Would you—hold me?" she asked, moving across the seat, leaning her upper body against his. He put his arm around her shoulders and hugged her, his hand rubbing her back consolingly. He sensed some great sadness in her. But at the same time Phil couldn't help responding to how good she felt in his arms, how good it was to touch her.

"Thank you," she murmured in his ear, and the light brushing of her lips sent a charge of gorgeous sensation through his body.

"It's okay," he told her. "It's okay."

Rachel pulled her head back a little and looked up at him, and they kissed for a long moment. She put his hand inside her jacket, on her breast, then moved it down a little, pressing his index and middle fingers through some oddly spaced openings in her blouse, and then into her flesh. At first he didn't understand what was happening, but it felt as if he were reaching right into her body—at her direction. He had the sensation of feeling her heart on his fingertips, the pulsing beat of it, and then—not there. He felt her wetness moving over his fingers and down his wrist. She exhaled, eyes rolling, and sank against him.

Phil pulled his hand away from her, and saw that it was

covered in blood. He saw the two gashes cut in her blouse, the bloodstains that darkened it. In a rush of panic, he shoved her limp body away from him, got out of the car, went around to the other side, and pulled her out, letting her body down onto the ground. He held his hand in front of the headlight and stared at it again, but it was still the same—red and sticky wet.

Later, standing in a scalding shower at home, still trembling as he tried to scrub himself clean, he couldn't remember whether he had checked her pulse, whether he had tried to revive her or not. Maybe. But maybe not, because he had been possessed of some inner, immediate certainty that she was already dead.

For days Phil could barely sleep, expecting the police to show up at his door or grab him in the supermarket parking lot. Some such scene kept foliating in his brain, and he watched the local TV news compulsively, kept the nearest AM station on the radio all the time. But nothing happened, there was no story of any woman found or missing or dead.

I didn't do anything, Phil kept telling himself uselessly.

A couple of months later, he went to see Ray Davies perform at Roseland. It was a great show and he came away from it feeling exhilarated. He could have stayed overnight with some friends in the city, but he was no longer spooked, and he wanted to show himself that. He got to Grand Central and caught the late New Haven line train for Hawleyville.

He went directly to the club car, glancing around as he approached the bar. A thirtyish couple chatting at one table. A few solitary business types with their suits, briefcases, and tired eyes, scattered about the car, each one off on his own little island. And then he saw her, alone at a corner table, head down. A stab of panic, but it quickly faded. She glanced at him, and her eyes lingered.

"Sir?"

"I'll have a beer," Phil said. "And a gin and tonic."

CURING HITLER

My name is Jurgen Bausch and I was born in 1893 near Aachen. My medical studies were interrupted by the Great War, and in the summer of 1918 I was re-assigned to the military hospital located in Pasewalk. Until that time I had served as a medical assistant in field hospitals not far behind the front lines.

The hospital at Pasewalk was designated for the treatment of military personnel who were mentally and emotionally disturbed as a result of their exposure to the horrors of combat. These cases ranged from mild and transient shell-shock to deep and permanent psychosis, and they exhibited a variety of behavioral symptoms that in their own way were every bit as devastating as the sheer bloody carnage I had witnessed in the field.

Unfortunately, the hospital served in practice as more of a processing center than a true treatment facility. New patients arrived daily, so there was never enough time and space to give proper attention to them. The shortage of skilled practitioners resulted in long work hours for everyone. Much of our time was spent merely trying to prevent outbreaks of the grossest abuse among the patients—including violent aggression, degradation, mutilation, and self-destruction.

It was essential that we transfer patients out as quickly as we received them, otherwise we would have been overwhelmed by the tide of human debris. Thus, a patient would first be stabilized with a sedative, if necessary, and a diagnosis would be rendered, often based on the most superficial observations. The paperwork would be completed and then the patient would be pushed on to any appropriate destination we could find—the immediate family or closest relatives, a rehabilitation center, another hospital, or, in the worst cases, an asylum.

Nonetheless, a certain small number of patients remained at Pasewalk for a few weeks, even a month or more. Those cases were neither too degenerative and hopeless nor too slight, or for some other reason had been deemed worthy of more substantive treatment by the presiding medical officer.

One such case, in which I played a small role, was that of an enlisted corporal, Adolph Hitler, who came to us in October of 1918 and stayed until the end of that fateful November. By then, of course, the war was over and Germany had lost.

My chief duty at Pasewalk was to assist Dr. Albert Stadler, who was in charge of Ward 2. Stadler was an able physician and a good man whose special interest was disturbed states of mind. He was thoroughly familiar with the emerging theories of psychology, and had acquainted himself with the techniques of psychoanalysis, some of which he tentatively approved. He had not taken a formal training course in it, but he had read widely and in some of our private conversations he expressed a belief that after the war it would become the dominant force in the diagnosis and treatment of most mental disorders.

Stadler was unsparing in his devotion to work, and he could be found on the floor or in his little office on the ward at all hours of the day or night. He once told me that he found it hard to sleep, no matter how tired he was, because he hadn't been able to see his elderly parents, his wife, or his children in more than a year. Life was very difficult in Germany, and like the rest of us, he worried constantly about his loved ones. The conditions at Pasewalk were debased, the work tedious and demoralizing, but for a man of Stadler's undoubted abilities the ward was his only escape from worry and insomnia.

I was familiar with Hitler. He had distinguished himself in the modest role of messenger between units along the front lines, and he had been blinded by an exploding gas grenade. At a field hospital they found that there was nothing organically wrong with his eyes. He could see if he truly wanted to, therefore he must either be a malingerer or have some other—mental, emotional—disorder that was complicating his recovery. There was no valid medical reason to discharge the patient to civilian life, so our task was to resolve the matter and return him to his unit.

There was no question about his blindness. Both Stadler and I had observed instances of Hitler's being the unhappy victim of minor abuse occasioned by his inability to see. Once, a group of patients tricked him into falling down the stairs leading to the lower floor. Another time, a patient urinated on Hitler's face while he sat on his bed staring vacantly into space. Malingerers know how to avoid suffering such indignities.

It wasn't long before Hitler became a nuisance, and the ward officers began urging us to move him out. He was "difficult," he spent much of his time haranguing his fellow patients on whatever subject crossed his mind—the evils of tobacco and alcohol, the Jews, the war, communism, history, and so on. Much of it was the usual litany of complaints heard from soldiers of nationalist or rightist beliefs, and in a way they mirrored those voiced by the left. The common room in every ward was a bedlam of conflicting views and factions, much as the whole of Germany would become in the following years.

After a few unpleasant experiences, Hitler assembled around himself a small group of protectors and admirers. They enjoyed his rants and approved of what he said. They read the newspaper aloud to him and relished his sarcastic comments. Keeping all of the cliques like this from each other's throats was a significant part of our everyday work.

But perhaps what most unsettled us about Hitler's presence were his nocturnal ramblings. The man seldom slept, only nodding off for a few minutes now and then, accumulating at most between two and three hours of "false sleep" over the course of a twenty-four-hour period. At night, when the ward was much quieter and most of the patients were either asleep or lacked the energy to leave their beds, Hitler wandered alone. Up one corridor, down another, around the empty common room, through the aisles of beds and cots. It was as if, having nothing better to do, Hitler had decided to memorize the place and thus circumvent the limitations of his blindness.

Stadler and I had noticed this behavior. We would be taking care of paperwork in his office, late into the night, or relaxing for a few minutes, and we would hear the slow, deliberate shuffle of Hitler's flimsy slippers on the linoleum down the hall. Then, a moment or two later, he would appear, standing like a ghost at the open door of the office. Stadler and I would remain silent, perfectly still, staring at him. Hitler's gaze would be fixed on nothing. He would stop for a couple of seconds, and then resume his meandering way.

"He isn't ready to be cured yet," Stadler told me.

"Why not?"

"His blindness is hysterical in origin and the insomnia is a secondary effect. He's usually uncooperative when I question him but I've managed to learn a few things. Before the war he had no skills, no talent, no prospects, nothing. He lived poor, in city parks and culverts, occasionally at a men's shelter. But the war changed all that. For the first time he had a sense of purpose, and he performed well enough to be decorated, which gave him his first taste of genuine accomplishment. But after four years it's not so easy to maintain the same perspective. And then, suddenly the war strikes directly at him. He's gassed, blinded. But he's not regarded as a hero or a victim, which is probably what Hitler expected. No, they tell him he's malingering. And so, now, he's lost his sense of place and his focus. The problem, I think, is that some hidden part of him secretly enjoys this nowhere state he's in, and so his mind refuses to address the difficult issues he faces. We must bring him to that point. When we do, he will see again."

It wasn't my place to disagree, but I had my own thoughts on the possible nature of Hitler's affliction. An encounter I'd had with him one night made a strong impression on me. It was after Stadler and I had shared a late drink. As sometimes happened, he dozed off on the sofa in his office, so I headed to my own bed in the hope of finding a few hours' sleep. Hitler was near the doors to the common room, and he stopped when he heard me.

"Who's that?"

"Bausch."

"Bausch." I had reached him by then, and beneath the light in the ceiling I saw a smile on his face, not a pleasant smile at that. "How can you cure me if you can't sleep either?" "I can sleep," I said. "What are you doing?" He gave a slight shrug. "Waiting?" "For what?" "If you know, my dear Herr Bausch, please tell me."

He delivered these few phrases slowly but in a rhythmic flow that was almost musical, his voice soothingly bemused— and yet, there was a gravelly undertone, an implicit taunt.

What disturbed me more, however, was the sight of his vacant eyes in the glow of the ceiling light. Hitler was standing with his face slightly upturned, as he usually did when moving around the ward. I knew that he had particularly bright blue eyes, but that was the first time I'd observed them so closely. They made me think of the eyes on Greek statues—blank, empty of any human expression or depth, but somehow so arresting we find it hard to turn away from them. The cold gem-like blue fire that shimmered in Hitler's eyes only enhanced the strange effect.

I finally realized that I'd been standing there for several minutes, simply staring at him, or his eyes. Hitler hadn't moved at all in that time, as if he knew exactly what was happening and liked it. I felt weak, drained, almost too tired even to breathe anymore. I felt that if I stayed there any longer I might sag to the floor in a coma. I forced myself to wake up a little, enough so I could brush past him and find my way to bed.

"Bausch," he said with a soft laugh. "Get some sleep."

I was exhausted after a sixteen-hour workday, followed by a few glasses of wine, and now I was further unsettled by the eerie emptiness of that brief encounter. And yet enough of my mind was still functioning. I had noticed something and would remember it the next day. Hitler had stopped at exactly the place where his blind upward gaze was pointed directly at the light fixture built into the ceiling. Without realizing it himself, he was beginning to respond to shades of darkness. He was beginning to see again. On his own.

A few days passed before I had the time to give this matter

proper consideration and discuss it with Dr. Stadler. He tended to discount its importance, but he did conduct a new examination of Hitler's eyes. The tests, which I observed carefully, showed no organic damage—and no apparent reaction at all to a variety of light stimuli. Hitler was surprisingly cooperative throughout and seemed quite disheartened by the results.

So my theory was shot down, but Dr. Stadler was delighted by Hitler's reaction. For him to be discouraged was a sign of hope. It meant that the patient had reached the point where he wanted, at least subconsciously, to be cured. Now, perhaps, he could be led across the threshold.

A few days later, Dr. Stadler instructed me to retire to my bed early in the evening and sleep. He would need me later that night, and I had to be fully rested, awake, and alert. I met him in his office at two a.m. As instructed, I had taken care not to go near Hitler on the way in or inadvertently let him know that I had returned to the ward. I settled comfortably on the sofa just behind and a little to one side of the desk. I was not to betray my presence by any movement or sound.

"Here we are now," Dr. Stadler said gently as he steered the patient into the room a few minutes later. "Here's a chair. Sit facing forward. That's it."

Dr. Stadler took his own seat. The only light in the room came from a gooseneck lamp on the desk, and now Stadler turned it around so that it was shining directly on Hitler's face. Stadler and I were in darkness. The light had no effect on Hitler, who sat with his face turned slightly upward. I had a clear view of him from just a few feet away, and already I found it hard not to stare at those brilliant eyes.

"Are you all right?"

"I would be, if I could see."

"Yes, and the time has come for the two of us to sort things out. You can't remain here indefinitely. They've got you pegged as a malingerer and probably a coward."

Hitler's cheeks flushed with anger.

"But your service record is exemplary," Dr. Stadler went on. "No one with a history like yours suddenly turns into a coward or a malingerer. Their diagnosis is wrong on all counts."

Hitler relaxed slightly, as his sense of honor was restored. "And yet," he said, "the condition persists."

"Your blindness is real."

A tremor of anxiety. Hitler now appeared oddly vulnerable. "Will I ever see again?"

"Only if you truly want to. Physically, there is nothing at all wrong with your eyes."

"Of course I want to see. But—how?"

"Hold out your hands. That's it, lean forward a little and rest your arms on the desk."

Dr. Stadler reached across the small desk and took Hitler's hands in his own. I could see that he held them tightly.

"Now listen carefully. I can't give you a full and proper course of treatment here, but I can give you the key. Then it's up to you, if you decide to use it. Life has failed you. First the world around you, and now more recently the war itself. The gas grenade was the final straw, triggering your blindness. But this blindness is in fact a defensive mechanism, a kind of shield constructed by your mind to protect you from further insult. We know that such reactions are a form of hysteria, but they can be overcome. Most of all, it requires will and courage, and I know from your record that you have the will and the courage necessary to succeed. To *see*. And then *not* to resume your past life, but to create a new life for yourself, your *real* life."

What increasingly alarmed me about all of this was not that I thought it was incorrect—I did, but that only meant it would be a waste of time—but the reactions occurring in the patient and the physician. Hitler appeared to shine with new confidence, while Dr. Stadler's speech grew slower and more disconnected. It was as if he were drunk, or drowsy, and in the process of falling asleep. I recognized this as the same thing that had happened to me the night I met Hitler outside the common room, and even then I could feel the same effect within myself, though it was weaker, probably because I was seated several feet away.

"It's there within you," Stadler continued. "Find the will to break through the curtain that blinds you. Summon the courage to see what you face, and then to face down what you see." After another pause, Stadler asked, "Do you hear me?"

"Yes," the patient replied.

"Do you understand it?"

"Yes."

"Will you..."

But at that point Dr. Stadler's head nodded forward onto his chest. I couldn't move. Hitler gently pulled his hands away and turned his head in my direction. His eyes appeared as vacant and unseeing as ever. I couldn't tell if he sensed my presence, not that it really mattered anymore. Slowly, he swung his head back toward the desk and the still form of Dr. Stadler.

"Get some sleep."

Then he stood up and walked out of the room. As a matter of fact, I fell asleep right there, on the couch. Dr. Stadler and I were both awakened a few hours later by the usual morning chaos breaking out across the ward. We didn't get a chance to discuss the session. Hitler, for his part, continued to move around like a blind man, delivering his endless harangues by day, roaming the corridors like a ghost at night.

Three days later, everything changed. As it happened, both Stadler and I were in the common room. An NCO rushed in, a piece of paper in his hand and the look of death on his face. He read the announcement of the armistice. The war was over. There were tears of joy, of sorrow, of anger. We all feared for the future, knowing not what it would be but that it would be difficult. My eyes scanned the room and I spotted Stadler. He gave a shrug and a forlorn smile. He made his way across the room to me, took me by the elbow, and invited me to his office for a drink to mark the mixed blessings of the occasion. The ward officers and patients could fend for themselves. The noise was ferocious.

As we were leaving the room, we noticed Hitler in his usual corner, surrounded by his set of chums. Copies of the armistice announcement were being passed around. Hitler snatched one. He read it, his face coloring. He tore the paper to shreds and then launched into one of his loud rants.

"...Germany in ruins..."

"Well, he can see again," Dr. Stadler said as we stepped out of the room. "That's something, anyway. I wonder if he realizes that he's about to become unemployed again."

Years later, Dr. Stadler died in mysterious circumstances. His offense, I believe, was telling Hitler that he suffered from hysteria. To Hitler that was a grave insult.

For myself, I still believe Hitler was blinded by that gas grenade. It was a genuine injury, but his eyes were not damaged permanently. His system recovered at its own pace. The attitude of a patient is a critical factor in determining whether recovery will be speedy or slow. Clearly, Hitler's attitude was no help in regaining his sight—until someone or something came along, enabling him to find the inner strength and will that would carry him across the final barrier.

Whether it was Dr. Stadler and his mistaken "cure," or if it was the armistice ending the war, the horror of defeat—I don't claim to know. Maybe Hitler simply recovered on his own.

It probably doesn't matter.

All I know is that there are still moments when I lie in the dark and see those beautiful and unbearably empty blue eyes, and slowly I feel the life begin to drain out of me again, and I hear that low, insistent voice as surely as if it were happening to me all over again, and it says, "Bausch, get some sleep," and I wish I could.

THE GREEN MENACE

I was weeding one of the flower beds out front when the black Cadillac came up the gravel drive and stopped just a few feet away from me. With its hooded headlights and the two huge chrome bullets mounted on the wide grille, it looked like some giant mechanical land shark. At the time—this was in May of 1955—I thought it was one of the most beautiful cars I'd ever seen.

The man who got out of the Caddy dropped a cigarette to the ground and crushed it with his shoe. He was wearing a plaid flannel shirt, not tucked in, and khaki slacks. He didn't look like someone who spent a lot of time outdoors. The skin on his face was chalky and I could see that he had office hands. It was still the middle of the afternoon and he already had a shadow filling in along both sides of his jaw.

"Hey, kid," he said to me. "Give me a hand here."

I dropped the hoe I was working with and followed him around to the back of the car. He opened the trunk. There were two suitcases inside, one a little smaller than the other, as well as a black briefcase. He immediately grabbed the smaller suitcase and took that one himself.

"Get those other two for me, would you."

"Sure. How long are you staying?"

He ignored that, slammed the trunk shut and stomped up the wooden steps to the veranda and through the front door, like he knew the place. Which he didn't, I was sure he'd never been to Sommerwynd before. Though, I do remember thinking there was something vaguely familiar about him, like maybe I had seen his face on a baseball card a while back—not one of the keepsies.

My father was at the desk and quickly fell into conversation with the man as he signed in. I wasn't really paying attention, just standing there, waiting to find out which room he was given. But then my mother came out of the office, followed by my grandfather, and I saw the adoring look on their faces as my father introduced them. And then my father gestured toward me.

"And you have already met Kurt, our son. Kurt, this is our distinguished guest, Senator Joe McCarthy."

So that was why he looked familiar. I'd seen his face in a newspaper or on the television. But I was still a couple of months shy of 16 at the time and had no interest at all in politics. The only thing I knew about him then was that he was a Commie-hunter and was loved for it by a lot of people, especially in our home state of Wisconsin. I nodded and mumbled something incoherent when McCarthy glanced at me and shook my hand. He had a so-so grip and cool, dry skin.

"Kurt," my father continued, "anything the Senator needs or wants while he is our guest, please see to it at once, or tell me or your mother."

"One thing," McCarthy said, raising a hand, his index finger extended. "I am here to get away from Washington and all that for a little while. So, I'd appreciate it if all of you would skip the 'Senator' stuff and just call me Joe." He looked at me again and gave a thin smile. "That includes you, kid—Kurt."

He was in room number 6, the best of the nine guest rooms at the lodge. It had the widest view of the lake, its own little balcony and the largest bathroom. He kind of exhaled when he stepped inside and looked around, like he was not impressed. I heard an odd clunk when he set down the smaller suitcase he carried. He reached into his pants pocket, pulled out a money clip and peeled off a dollar bill. He handed it to me.

"When you get a chance," he said, pointing to the coffee table in the sitting area, specifically to the clamshell ashtray on the table, "I'll need a bigger ashtray. And a bucket of ice."

"Yes, sir."

Knotty pine. He was surrounded by knotty pine, floor to ceiling on every wall, and it made him feel kind of edgy. Joe was

fifteen minutes into his escape-from-the-rest-of-the-world, as he
thought of it, and he was already wondering if he had made a
mistake. Just one more in a long list of them, ha ha.

He was at Sommerwynd, a small fishing lodge on a small
lake in a remote corner of northwestern Wisconsin. It didn't
have a telephone, and the nearest town was twenty-odd miles
away. It was the perfect place to go to ground for a while, to
relax, recharge his batteries and think about what he wanted to
do next, to plan his next moves. If there were any. Billy O'Brien
knew the Wirth family, who ran Sommerwynd. Billy made the
arrangements for Joe. Billy was a friend who stayed a friend—he
didn't drift away, like so many others had. But now Billy had
landed Joe out in the back of beyond, and Joe was not sure it
was such a great idea after all. Still, give it a go. He could always
leave whenever he felt like it.

Joe reached both hands behind him and up under his loose
shirt to unhook the holster and the .22 clipped to his pants belt.
He set them down on the bedside table. Then he pulled his left
pant-leg up and unbuckled the holster and the snub-nosed .38
he wore above his ankle. He put them on the table next to the
big armchair on the other side of the room. He'd never had to
use either gun—yet. But Joe knew he had millions of enemies
out there and he was not about to go down without a fight if any
of them decided to come hunting for him.

He pulled the smaller suitcase close to the writing table,
where he was sitting. He flipped the latches and carefully
opened it on the floor. Inside, securely wrapped in cloth hand
towels, were eight bottles of Jim Beam, along with Joe's favorite
Waterford crystal whiskey tumbler. He put the drinking glass
and one bottle of the bourbon on the desk, closed the suitcase
and set it down on the floor, right next to the night table beside
the bed. He cracked open the bottle, poured a couple of fingers and took a good sip. That helped. He lit a cigarette, then
took another gulp of the whiskey, savoring the mixed flavors
of bourbon and tobacco in his mouth. That's more like it, he
thought, feeling a little better already.

I fetched a heavy glass ashtray from the supply cupboard and then went to the ice house, where I chipped off enough small chunks of ice to fill a large thermos. I wasn't expecting another tip, and didn't get one. He took the ice and the ashtray from me at the door of his room, muttered thanks and kicked the door shut with his foot.

I saw him again that first evening when he came down to the dining room for supper. The season at Sommerwynd didn't really start until after the Memorial Day weekend, so the only other guests there were an older couple, the Gaults, who visited every year. McCarthy nodded politely to them when he entered the room, and then sat as far away from them as he could. He looked like a man with a lot on his mind—more than once I saw him wipe his hand down across his face and give a slight shake of the head, as if he were trying to change the subject of his thoughts.

My mother explained to me how McCarthy had been a kind of national hero, rousting out Reds who had infiltrated the American government, leading the fight to preserve the American way of life and protect our country from the threat within. But his enemies struck back and somehow managed to get the U.S. Senate to censure McCarthy in a vote the previous December. So that was what he had come to Sommerwynd to get away from.

At the time, I didn't understand much of it and I wasn't curious to learn more. I just nodded as my mother went on about what a good man McCarthy was and my father chimed in to say how gutless, shameful and treasonous the Senate was in their action against him. I remember trying to translate it into baseball terms. He was like a pitcher who made it to the big leagues, a rising star, but then his opponents figured out how to hit him, and beat him. Guys like that—if they don't learn a new pitch or change their delivery, they don't often make it back to the top.

It was a nice evening to sit out on the front veranda or back patio, or for a stroll down to the boat dock, but McCarthy finished his meal, skipped dessert and coffee, and went back upstairs to his room. I did catch a glimpse of him a little while later, about the time when the frogs start up their chorus. I was taking the day's food scraps out to the compost heap near the vegetable beds. On my way back to the house, I saw him sitting at the table on the small balcony off his room. McCarthy didn't appear to notice me, he was probably just staring off at the view across the lake and the rising moon. I saw a curl of smoke in the dusk light, and a sudden glow from his cigarette as he inhaled.

The frogs were having a party, somewhere down the right shoreline some distance from the lodge. They began croaking and thrumming away even before the sun's descent reached the high tree line on the far side of the lake. At first, Joe kind of enjoyed listening to them. It was the kind of nature sound you would expect to hear in a place like Sommerwynd—frogs croaking, owls hooting, bats flapping in the night air, a fish jumping and slapping back into the water. Sounds that felt right.

But after an hour and a half of it, Joe began to wish they would shut up. "Come on, give it a rest, guys," he muttered as he poured another drink.

It amazed him how loud they were. The frogs didn't appear to be close to the lodge, their ribbity croaking seemed to come from a fair distance away—and yet, the volume they produced was quite strong. And the numbers of them. It didn't sound like a group of six or eight frogs, more like dozens and dozens of them. As darkness settled in for the night, their noise and numbers actually appeared to increase. Maybe the sound just carried very well in the deep stillness of the location, with the lake surrounded on all sides by forest.

Joe finally had enough of it and went inside, shutting the door to the balcony. He could still hear the frogs, but their sound was greatly diminished. He fixed another drink, pulled out *Triumph and Tragedy*, the final volume of Winston Churchill's history of the Second World War. He knew he would need something to occupy time like this at Sommerwynd, and he figured that Churchill was a good man to read when you were in a tough spot. He had already tried the radio in his room, but the only station he could pick up faded in and out of static—he caught a bit of a song that sounded like Patti Page being electrocuted.

Joe read for a while, then set the book aside. It was one of those moments—occurring more frequently of late—when he felt he had little or no patience left for anything. Not the book he was reading, not the room he was sitting in, not the building or place he was, nobody he knew or encountered, not the weather, the season, the time of day or night. Nothing, nor himself.

He picked up one of his pistols and toyed idly with it in his hands. There was a certain comfort to be found in the kind of inanimate object that is simple in design and serves its purpose, and needs other reason to be. A spoon, a fork, a knife, a shovel, a clay tile, a garden hose. A gun. Like this one. There had been moments in the past year when he was almost tempted to go that route. But his enemies would have loved it if he did, and he would never give them the satisfaction.

He could still hear the frogs. Jesus Christ, didn't they ever stop? It was a low throbbing sound, boombadaboombadaboom in an endless beat. Fat, slimy creatures rumbling in the muck. Joe undressed, crawled into bed and turned off the table lamp. He quickly fell asleep, but drifted back up very close to consciousness some while later, again dimly aware of the frogs—still going at it.

Croak—you're croaked.

Croak—you're croaked.

Joe didn't turn on the light. In the darkness, he got out of bed, got a hold of his tumbler and the bottle of Jim Beam, poured one more large one, fumbled for a cigarette and the matches, and eased himself into the armchair. He did all this without opening his eyes, because to do so would make him more awake, and the whole point of getting up was to maintain this state of semi-consciousness, drifting along the edge of the one and the other, not quite awake or asleep. He knew without forming the thought that it would take two cigarettes to finish this drink. Then he would transport himself back to bed, and sleep would come again, and then it would finally hold.

Croak—you're croaked.

Joe made a kind of sighing, humming noise, not much more than a low, droning murmur within himself. It didn't sound like anything, but he knew what he meant by it. He meant: Fuck you. Fuck all of you.

McCarthy didn't come downstairs for breakfast the next morning. He did just make it in time for lunch, but all he wanted was coffee, and a lot of it. Mom brewed up a fresh pot for him and he drank most of it while sitting on the front veranda, one cup after another, each with its own cigarette.

I was nearby, working again on the flowerbeds, but I didn't say anything to him. It seemed pretty clear that he wanted to be left alone. He looked as washed-out and beat-down as anybody I'd ever seen. I tried not to keep glancing up at him, but it wasn't easy. Just knowing he was somebody important, or had been,

When he'd had enough coffee, McCarthy went back inside and I didn't see him for almost an hour. Then he came on the veranda again, this time with a little bounce in his step. He clattered down the front stairs and came over to me.

"Tell me something, kid," he said. "What's with those frogs?"

"You mean their croaking at night?"

"That's exactly what I mean. They kept me up all night."

He said it almost as if it was my fault, and his blue eyes bored into me like I knew something I wasn't telling him. Which I didn't.

"It's the time of year when they do that," I replied with a shrug. "It can be annoying at first, but you get used to it and don't even notice after a while."

"If they make that kind of racket every night, I won't be here long enough to get used to it." McCarthy started to step away, but then he turned back to me. "I'm going to go for a walk. Are there any good trails here, so I don't get lost?"

"Sure. There's one that goes all the way up to the top of that ridge," I said, pointing off to the rising tree line to the east. "There's a nice view at the top, and then the path circles down and around, back here to the lodge."

"Uphill," McCarthy said. "That sounds kind of strenuous."

"There's another trail that goes all the way around the lake," I told him. "It sticks pretty close to the water and it's mostly level ground."

"That sounds better."

I gave him directions to find the path—out behind the

house, beyond the generator building, the boat dock and my grandfather's workshop. McCarthy nodded his head and set off on his hike.

A little less than an hour later, I heard the gunshots.

Joe took note of his surroundings as he walked. It was an odd kind of place, Sommerwynd. The lodge itself was nice enough. The lake was small but picture-perfect, and had no other development on it. According to Billy, some well-connected and well-off people visited Sommerwynd from June through September, valuing it for its remoteness and natural setting. Free use of a canoe or rowboat, fishing, swimming, hiking. There was supposed to be a tennis court, though Joe hadn't seen it yet, and would not be interested anyhow. Still, he wondered how the Wirth family managed it all, with just the four of them there at present. But then he figured that they probably just hired a few temporary workers to help out in the busy months.

He passed the first cinderblock building, which had four large propane tanks attached, and he could hear the generator humming inside, providing the electricity that kept the lodge going. A little farther on, he found the second cinderblock building, also painted white. It had no windows. The kid had referred to it as his grandfather's workshop. In other words, Joe thought, that's where Grandpa goes to get away from his family for a while. Have a drink in peace, flip through the few issues of *Playboy* he had smuggled in, and remember what it was like back when.

He soon found the trail, and before long it swung in with the shoreline of the lake, so that the trees behind him cut off any view of the lodge, and he was alone in the woods. A fly or a bug of some kind buzzed him for a couple of seconds—he swatted at it and kept walking, and it went away. Joe thought, not for the first time in his life, that Nature is over-rated.

The path hugged the water for a good stretch, and there were a couple of times when Joe spotted small fish in the shallows. That was nice. Then, maybe a half hour into his hike, he came to a spot where the trail swung to the right, away from the lake and into the woods. He stood on a large flat rock that sat at the edge of the water and he studied the scene for a moment. He figured it out. A stream entered the lake here, but over time enough silt had accumulated to back up some of the flow, which created a small, swampy lagoon. The path went inland to get around this obstacle.

Joe was about to continue his walk, but then didn't. The lagoon itself was kind of pretty. It was too early for lily pads, but the glassy black water was already laced with duckweed. The rock he was standing on was in the shade, making this a good spot to take a break. He pulled the hip flask out of his back pocket and sat down on the rock, his feet dangling a few inches off the ground. A sip, a cigarette. There was a cool breeze coming off the lake, and he sat facing into it, enjoying the way it felt on his skin, the way it rippled the water. Yeah, Nature was over-rated, but it did have its moments.

Part of him wanted to go back to D.C. And resume the battle. Or restart it, more accurately. But another part of him said that the battle was over, finished, and that he had lost it. Forget it, move on. But, move on to what? What was left? For a while, it was as if the whole world watched him and listened to him— how do you get that back? Because now, he was invisible.

An odd sensation crept over him, that he was not alone. He turned around, wondering if someone from the lodge had come with a message, but there was no one on the trail. Then Joe looked at the lagoon—and he saw a pair of eyes in the water. Dozens of pairs of eyes, just breaking the surface, looking at him. It startled him, but he quickly realized that this lagoon was where those noisy frogs lived, and there they were, looking at him. The lagoon was full of them, more than he could count.

Joe stood up, flicked his cigarette into the water and stepped down, off the rock. A few feet away, a frog crawled forward, partly out of the water. It was huge, the size of a watermelon. *Jesus.* Joe looked around, spotted a pebble, picked it up and flung it into the lagoon. It splashed close to one frog, but the creature didn't move. A couple of frogs had emerged from the lagoon and were now crawl-hopping toward him. Joe pulled his right foot back and kicked one of them back into the water. The frog was so heavy that Joe felt the strain in his ankle muscles.

The frog flopped backward, just a couple of yards away, righted itself and began to move forward again. The other frog now on the ground, jumped and caught Joe's ankle in its mouth. Teeth, the damned thing had teeth! Joe tried to shake it off, but the frog held on. Joe raised his other foot and slammed it as hard as he could down on the frog's head.

Nothing—that was what he got for wearing sneakers in the woods. And that was when he noticed that the frog had whiskers around its mouth, which shot out like small blades, one of them piercing Joe's calf. What kind of frogs were these, that had teeth and sharp barbels like a catfish?

Think about that later. The pain began to hit him. Joe reached behind his back, got his .22 out, held it to the side of the frog's head and squeezed the trigger. Blood and flesh flew, and the frog at last dropped off his ankle. But Joe was astonished to see that other frogs were coming forward, at him. Calmly, he aimed the pistol and shot them in the head or face, until the gun was empty. He had a couple of boxes of bullets back at the lodge. He reached down to get the .38 from his good ankle, and proceeded to empty that into another bunch of frogs as they got closer to him.

Then, he knew it was time to leave. Joe grabbed one of the dead frogs by the leg and hurried away with it, back to the lodge.

Well, we'd seen these frogs, of course, and thought nothing of them. They never bothered us and we never bothered them. My grandfather, Klaus Wirth, claimed to have refined some of their unusual features through cross-breeding. He was a biologist, a great admirer of Luther Burbank. He had returned to Germany in the 1920s to continue his research work. He was not a Nazi, but after Hitler came to power he was not allowed to leave the country, and was pressed into government scientific service. In my family, none of us ever seemed to know quite what that meant. In any event, my grandfather returned to Wisconsin after the war, refused to seek work at any university, and declared himself in retirement. Still, he conducted what he called "research." He and my father converted the old chicken coop into what became my grandfather's workshop. We knew that he had scientific equipment, and animals imported—even that he had obtained frogs from Africa, with teeth. Still, whenever my grandfather hinted at a "breakthrough," my mother and father rolled their eyes.

Now we had Senator Joseph McCarthy sitting on the patio, one bare foot propped up on a chair, my mother carefully wiping his wounds with disinfectant, me and my father standing nearby, not knowing what to say. My grandfather hung back a couple of yards from the rest of us, looking as if he hoped that this would all blow over and he wouldn't have to move to Argentina.

And on the flagstone, a dead frog. With half of its head blown off. With nasty-looking teeth and whiskers. I'd seen them, but never one close up. It was very big, green and black, and it looked heavy, although I didn't try to lift it. The animal looked so slimy and ugly, I wanted nothing to do with it.

My parents were endlessly apologetic, but McCarthy kept going on and on, asking questions they couldn't answer, suggesting that there was some actual plot or plan in place—yes, there, in the middle of nowhere in northern Wisconsin—to somehow create a vicious creature that would eventually wreak havoc on the land.

"This is the goddamn *uber*-frog," McCarthy shouted.

At that point I actually reached down and ran my fingers along the teeth in the open mouth of the dead frog. They were not large, but felt very sharp. I stood up and backed away, wiping my fingers on my pants. My grandfather gave me a little nod of the head and I stepped back to see what he wanted. He whispered in my ear.

"They eat fish and bugs, nothing more." But then he added, "That I know of, so far."

My mother had McCarthy's leg all cleaned and wrapped by then, and he did seem to be a little more composed. Still, he glanced at my grandfather and said, "I'd like to take a look at that workshop of yours, Pops."

My grandfather suddenly turned icy—something I cannot remember ever seeing until that moment. His narrowed and he spoke quietly through a slight smile.

"I do not believe you have security clearance for that."

McCarthy did a little double-take at that, but before he could come up with a response, a woman screamed. I knew right away it was Mrs. Gault, since she and her husband were the only two people not on the patio. Sure enough, the Gaults came around one of the hedges screening off the generator building, Mrs. Gault limping, sobbing, and assisted by her husband.

"She's been attacked," he said. "By a frog!"

"They're coming," Mrs. Gault wailed.

"Masses of them," her husband added.

I took off while he was rambling on. I ran down across the lawn, around the line of hemlocks, past the generator building, and then I saw them. They hadn't reached my grandfather's workshop yet, but they were closing in. Hundreds of huge frogs, hopping fitfully through the tall grass—toward the lodge, us. I turned around, ran back to the patio and told my father what I'd seen. He just kind of went into a distant stare for a few moments.

My mother, who was already wiping and dressing Mrs. Gault's ankle-bite, said, "Perhaps we should all go inside."

"Or just leave," Mr. Gault snarled.

That was when McCarthy raised his hand and wagged his fingers at me. I went over to him. He pulled a key out his pocket and handed it to me.

"In my room, in the large suitcase, there's a couple of boxes of bullets. Go get them for me. Quick"

Looking back, I was caught up in it. I flew.

The lodgekeeper, Karl Wirth, looked frozen, but Joe knew what had to be done. They could ran like rats, or they could stop this in its tracks. It wasn't really a choice.

"Do you have any guns?" Joe asked.

"A rifle, a shotgun," Wirth replied.

"That's it?"

"Yes."

"I thought this was a hunting lodge."

"Fishing, swimming, boating," Wirth said. "A bit of hunting in season, but that's for the guests. Hey bring their own rifles. I'm not a hunter myself."

"Get them," Joe ordered. "And all the ammo you've got."
Wirth hurried away obediently. Joe told Mrs. Wirth and the
Gaults to go inside the lodge. He walked out on the lawn, toward
the lake. His leg throbbed, but the pain was not unbearable. He
was a little past the generator building when he spotted them, a
black and green wave surging forward. Ugly bastards. Oh yes,
he'd put a stir in them, no doubt about it. But it was inevitable.
These people, the Wirths, were living in a dream—oh, we don't
bother them, they don't bother us. Just drifting along, until the
time came when it was too late, and the moment became one of
their choosing, not yours.

The kid was back, with the bullets. "Ever use one of these?"
Joe asked, handing Kurt the .22.

"I did target shooting a couple of times."

"Good enough. Load up, and aim for the ones in front. Take
your time, they're not exactly fast on the ground."

Joe led the way and when they got to the old man's workshop, they began plunking frogs along the advancing front line.
It shook him, how many there were of the beasts. He knew then
that they didn't have nearly enough bullets. At some point, they
would have no alternative but to run for their cars and flee. But
Joe noticed that as he and the kid moved laterally, so did the
frogs. Vicious, but very dumb creatures. Where could he lead
them?

I admit, I was into it. Maybe because it didn't seem to be that
dangerous a threat, really. We always had the option of leaving,
and coming back later with some kind of professional or state
help to eradicate the frogs—or, whatever would be done with
them. But I got a kick out of picking them off, one at a time, seeing their fat bodies pop in blood and pus. It was like, suddenly
you're in a movie, and you're playing this part, and it's more fun
than what you'd normally be doing at that time of day.

Unfortunately, we ran out of bullets fast, and there were *a lot*
of frogs still coming. My father arrived then, with his rifle and
shotgun and a couple of boxes of cartridges. McCarthy grabbed
the rifle and started snapping in shells. He moved us away from
the direction of the house, and the frogs followed, coming after

us—I thought that was so smart of him, but I didn't know what good it would do. McCarthy directed my father's fire, a shot gun blast here, there, almost as if he were steering the flow of the frogs as they came at us. Whenever one edge of the wave appeared to be moving closer, McCarthy fired a couple of shots himself, picking off frogs that he took to be leaders in the throng.

We got to the generator building, and the frogs had come around both sides of my grandfather's workshop. My father and stood there, waiting for McCarthy to say or do something, but he was standing there, letting the frogs get closer and closer. Finally, he turned to me.

"You run that way around the building, back to the lodge," he said. "If they start getting close, pack everybody in the cars and get out." He turned to my father and said the same thing, except that he pointed my father in the other direction around the building. He slapped us both on the back. Go!"

"Wait," I said. "What are you going to do?"

"Just gonna let them get a little closer and make sure they're coming on both sides, then I'll be right behind you."

Except that he wasn't right behind us. My father and I met up on the patio, and moved out into the driveway area on the other side of the hedges, so that we could see what was happening. We saw the frogs closing in on the generator building, and then McCarthy scrambled out on the side away from the house, running toward the edge of the woods. He was limping, but made good time. The frogs were coming around both sides of the generator building, toward the house. Some peeled off, to go after McCarthy. He dived into the brush at the edge of the tree line, and a moment later, rifle shots rang out. I was slow when it came to following his line of thought, but it became clear a few seconds later when he hit one of the propane tanks, and it went off, and the others followed almost immediately. *Whoomph! Whoomph-whoom-whoom-whoomph!*

It took me years to decipher the visual images I have in my head. Yes, the fireball dominated, but eventually I began to see that a flat sheet of flame also spread out at the same time. Lower to the ground. It was lost for a time—I kept seeing sheet metal fly off the roof, cinderblocks blasted into chunks. We stood there for a long time while the smoke and dust and debris settled. Then we could see a lot of scorched frogs, dead on the ground, and I spotted a few others still alive, retreating toward the lagoon.

Son of a bitch, it worked. Joe stood up and walked toward the house. He looked all around, but couldn't see a live frog that wasn't heading the other way. It would do for now, but the problem remained, and would have to be dealt with.

He found the kid and his father on the patio, both looking shell-shocked, though the kid had a smile lurking on the edges of his mouth. Joe liked that, and slapped the kid on the back.

"You did good."

"Thanks!"

Joe turned to the father, was it Karl or Klaus? He wasn't sure, but it didn't matter. The guy was just standing there, hoping that normal life would somehow be restored to him. Joe smiled reassuringly.

"You've got insurance, right?"

It took a few seconds, but then the man nodded.

"Ah, good, you'll be fine then."

Joe went inside, packed his things, came downstairs and tried to check out. Mrs. Wirth wouldn't let him pay a cent. She was very apologetic, as was Joe. The lodge had no electricity now, so everyone was preparing to move out until repair work could be arranged and carried out.

"Just a thought," Joe said before he left. "I wouldn't try to explain this in too much detail. An accidental explosion is an accidental explosion."

Tell her husband the same thing, and he probably wouldn't get it, but Mrs. Wirth nodded immediately. When Joe was turning away from the front desk, he saw the kid crossing the other side of the lobby.

"Kurt, would you grab a couple of these bags for me?"

We got over it. We spent a few days at our winter house 40 miles away while Dad got the insurance and repair stuff taken care of, and the investigation went the usual path of least resistance.

An accident is an accident, there was no question of gain in the case. And we went back, and had a good season. The new generator was a beauty and actually saved money.

My grandfather never went back to his workshop. When he died a couple of years later, some people came in and took away his equipment, and my parents just let the empty building rot. As was always the case in my family, when there was no need to talk about something, we didn't.

I've learned a lot about McCarthy since then, and it's hard to find anything in it that I like. I think he grew up at a time and in a place where he learned that if you didn't beat up the other guy, he'd beat up you, and he lived accordingly. I know what it's like to grow up feeling alone. When I heard a year or so later that McCarthy had died in a hospital, that he was an alcoholic and had struggled with all kinds of health issues, I thought it was a very sad end to an important life. Later, after I got to know more about him, I came to think that it was just a sad end to a life. He was not a likeable man, but I have to say that I kind of liked him at the time.

My father died of a heart attack a few years later. My mother had to sell Sommerwynd. For a long time nothing much happened out there, but there are a lot of very expensive summer homes on that lake now.

The frogs? The state killed them off, as an invasive species. At least, I think they killed them all off. I don't live there anymore. I'm in sales, in Madison. No wife, no kids, not sure how I ended up here. But I'm doing okay.

Still a long drive ahead. Joe decided to kill it now. He pulled into a place called The Valley Inn while the sun was still visible in the sky. A string of bungalows in the middle of nowhere, on the road to nowhere. Let's say nothing about the room, but that it had a television and got two snowy channels. He poured a couple of fingers of Jim Beam in a plastic cup, and lit a Pall Mall.

Might as well have done this in the first place.

IN PRAISE OF FOLLY

He drove north in air-conditioned comfort, a road map on the seat beside him, Satie's piano music rippling pleasantly from the stereo speakers. Thank God for the little things that make human life bearable when summer's on your neck.

It was August. The stagnant heat and humidity were so heavy they no longer seemed like atmospheric phenomena, but had assumed a suffocating gelatinous density. People moved slowly if at all, dazed creatures in the depths of a fungal deliquescence.

It had to be better up in the Adirondacks, cooler and drier. But Roland Turner was not just another vacationer seeking escape. He was on a mission of discovery, he hoped, a one-man expedition in search of a serious folly.

Roland was one of the very few American members of the Folly Fellowship, an organization based in London that was dedicated to "preserve and promote the enjoyment and awareness of follies…to protect lonely and unloved buildings of little purpose…unusual, intriguing or simply bizarre structures and sites." Roland first learned about the group two years earlier, when he came across an issue of their quarterly magazine in a Connecticut bookshop. The photographs were fascinating, the text charming and witty.

A typical English eccentricity, Roland thought at the time, the sort of thing that lasts for a year or two and then dies away as enthusiasm and funds decline. He wrote a letter to ask if the Fellowship was still going, and was surprised to get a reply from the president and editor himself, one Gwyn Headley. Not only was the Fellowship still active, it was thriving, with more than five hundred members worldwide (most of them, naturally, residents of the United Kingdom).

Roland immediately mailed off a bank draft to cover the cost of membership, a set of back issues of the magazine, a folder of color postcards, and a copy of Headley's definitive work, *Follies: A National Trust Guide* (Cape, 1986).

There was something romantic and mysterious about monuments, castles, and old ruins that had always appealed to Roland. He saw the past in them, and he loved to imagine what life had been like so long ago. Perhaps it was because his own day-to-day existence was placid and humdrum. Roland owned a printing company, a small outfit that produced trade newsletters and supermarket fliers for the Westchester County market. Over the years he had worked long and hard to build up a reliable trade, and now he presided over a solid, secure business operation. On the negative side, Roland's personal life was somewhat threadbare.

He'd been through a number of brief intimate encounters, but none of them even came close to marriage. Now in his middle age, Roland could take it or leave it. He enjoyed a good book, mainly history or historical fiction, as well as classical music, and he had a special fondness for follies.

A genuine folly was a building, garden, grotto or other such architectural construct that had been designed with a deliberate disregard for the normal rules. A folly was something literally "to gasp at," as Headley put it in his massive tome. Roland had not yet been able to travel to Britain, due to pressure of work, but he had managed to track down a few American follies, such as Holy Land in Waterbury and the Watts Towers in Los Angeles. He'd also visited a fully functional house that had been built out of beer bottles in Virginia, a four-acre Sahara located in the Maine woods, and a home designed as Noah's Ark in the Tennessee hills. American follies tended to lack the air of lost grandeur that was the hallmark of classic British follies, but they often displayed a kind of heroic zaniness that was utterly endearing.

Roland could only look forward to the time in his life when he would at last be free to spend two or three months journeying around England, Scotland, and Wales, leisurely inspecting some of the remarkable things he could only read about now—such as the rocket ship in Aysgarth, the "house in the clouds" at Thorpeness, Clavel's Tower, and Portmeirion, not to mention all the splendid follies that could still be found in and around the great city of London itself.

Follies are the dizzy, demented lacework on the edge of the vast human tapestry, Roland had written in a letter that for some unknown reason Mr. Headley had not yet seen fit to publish in the magazine of the Follies Fellowship. In his spare hours, Roland continued to hone his thoughts and write up notes on the American follies he came across.

Then, two weeks ago, the message had arrived from London. A "rather spectacular" folly was rumored to exist on the grounds of the old Jorgenson summer cottage in Glen Allen, New York. Would Mr. Turner be able to check it out and report back? If it proved to be a worthwhile site, photographs and notes would be welcome. Roland immediately faxed his answer: "Absolutely."

It took a while to find Glen Allen on the map. Apparently a rural village, it was some two hundred miles away, a little north of Big Moose Lake in the Adirondacks. Definitely a weekend trek.

Get up there and find a rustic inn Friday evening, spend Saturday investigating the Jorgenson property, and then drive back down to Rye on Sunday. Roland fled the office at noon, and a few minutes later hit the turnpike.

As far as anyone knew he was enjoying a short getaway in the countryside. Roland had mentioned his interest in follies to one other person, Patty Brennan, a robust divorcee who had worked for him briefly last year. Roland thought he fancied Patty, but they never got beyond the talking stage.

"You mean like Coney Island, or Grant's Tomb," had been her reaction when he told her about follies.

"Well, no, not exactly..."

Perhaps Roland had explained it badly. He decided then and there to keep the world of follies to himself, his little secret. Patty soon fell in love with the man who cleaned the heads of her VCR, and quit to take a position in his business. It was all for the best, Roland convinced himself. When you share something you treasure with another person, it's no longer quite so special; it inevitably loses a little of its magic aura.

Roland made fairly good time, but the actual journey clocked in at closer to three hundred miles, so it was a little after six in the evening when he reached Glen Allen. He passed by the Glen Motel on his way into town but found no other accommodation, and eventually circled back to it. A satellite dish, a room full of vending machines, three other cars parked in the lot. Nothing at all like a rustic inn, but it would have to do. Roland went into the office and paid for a room.

The middle-aged woman on duty took his cash, gave him a key and some brochures about the boating and fishing opportunities in the vicinity.

"Where's the best place to eat in town?" Roland asked.

"Bill's Friendly Grille, right on Main," the woman replied. "By the way, there's an electrical storm supposed to come through tonight. If the power goes out, you'll find some candles in your closet."

"Thanks. I was thinking of taking a look at the Jorgenson estate tomorrow. Is it hard to find?"

"The Jorgenson estate," she repeated carefully, as if giving the matter some thought. She was a large woman with bland, empty features. "No, it's not hard to find but it might be hard to get to. It's just a couple of miles up the glen, but nobody's lived there in about thirty years, so the private road's all overgrown. You'd have to hike some." Then added, "From what I heard, there's nothing much left to see."

"Oh."

"Are you in real estate?"

"No, no, I represent the—well, it's a British fellowship, you see, and we're interested in neglected sites of architectural distinction." He was upset with himself for hesitating and then failing to utter the word *folly*, but there was no point in trying to explain it to this woman. As it was, she made a vague sound and appeared to have no interest whatsoever.

"Well, I could be wrong but I don't think you'll find there is any architecture up there."

"None at all?" Roland asked in disbelief. Until now, he hadn't even considered the possibility that he might have come all this way on a wild goose chase. "There's nothing left?"

The woman shrugged blithely, seeming to take pleasure in his distress. "Place burned down ages ago." She picked up the book she had been reading—a paperback account of some lurid murders in Texas—and found her place.

"Ah. Well..."

His room was adequate, just. There was mildew on the shower curtain, and the air had a damp, musty smell that some city people regard as the authentic flavor of the countryside, but the sheets were clean and the air conditioner worked. Outside, the heat and humidity were nearly as oppressive as they'd been in Rye.

Roland decided not to linger in his room. He was hungry and a storm was coming. He left his overnight bag, still packed, on a rock maple armchair, left his camera locked in the trunk of his car, and set off to find Bill's Friendly Grille.

Glen Allen, what there was of it, had the peeling, outdated look of a town still stuck in the Forties or Fifties. It was not unpleasant—the weathered clapboards, the old Flying Red Horse gas pumps, the rusty cars and battered pickups, the general store with a group of kids hanging around out front—a curious mix of what was genuinely quaint and what was merely Tobacco Road.

But it wasn't what was there, Roland realized as he parked. It was what wasn't there—no trendy boutiques, no video stores, no T-shirt joints, no fast-food chains, no blaring boomboxes, not even one odorific Chinese takeaway—that was somehow pleasing. The present had not yet arrived in Glen Allen, at least not with the full force of all its tawdry enterprise.

Roland sat at the bar and had the cheeseburger deluxe, which was suitably greasy and rather good. The fries were on the soggy side, but the coleslaw was tangy and delicious. Roland washed it all down with a large mug of cold beer—the first of several he would enjoy that evening.

There were a handful of other customers, regulars it seemed, who clutched their glasses, kept an eye on the Yankees game on the TV at the far end of the bar, and chatted easily with each other. None of them showed any particular interest in Roland, which was fine with him. Most of them were young and probably knew nothing firsthand about the Jorgensons. But Roland did eventually manage to learn something from Bill, the elderly owner of the place, who also presided over the bar.

"Old man Jorgenson made it big in steel, right up there with Carnegie. Lot of money. My father worked on the house when they built it, back in the Twenties. Oh, it was beautiful. Wood from South America, marble from Italy, you name it. French furniture, big paintings on the walls. No expense spared. They lived there about two months a year, every summer. They called it a cottage, you know, because it only had about twenty rooms."

Roland nodded, smiling. Bill had a way of saying something and slapping his hand lightly on the bar as if to signal that he was finished. He would turn and drift away, tending to his other customers, but sooner or later he would wander back to Roland and continue, gradually filling in the rest of the story.

The Jorgenson clan came and went year after year. They kept pretty much to themselves. Nothing memorable happened until the winter of 1959, when the house burned down mysteriously. It was gutted, a complete loss. The only people there at the time were the caretaker and his wife, both of whom died in the blaze. Some people thought it was an accident, others that local vandals were responsible—the rich are always resented. There was a lengthy investigation, but no final verdict.

The place was abandoned, the Jorgensons never came back. It wasn't until a few years ago that the estate was in the news once more. A new generation of Jorgensons had seen fit, no doubt with tax considerations in mind, to deed the hundred-plus acres to the state of New York. The surrounding Adirondack forest had already reclaimed it, and now it was a legal fact.

"Weren't there any other buildings, besides the main house?" Roland asked anxiously. "Any other structures?"

"Oh, sure," Bill said. "There was a big garage, a gazebo, a few sheds, and an icehouse. And, uh, Little Italy."

"What?" Roland's hopes soared. "Little Italy?"

"Yeah, my kids used to play there when they were growing up back in the Sixties. Crazy thing."

It was a folly, no question. It seemed that the old man had been in love with Italy, so much so that he decided to create a garden that featured miniature replicas of famous Italian sights: the Trevi fountain, Vesuvius and Pompei, the Blue Grotto at Capri, and the Colosseum, among others. Jorgenson had added to it every summer for nearly three decades, and by the time of the fire the Italian garden was said to cover nearly four acres. Roland was both encouraged and depressed. Yes, there was an authentic folly, but it had been rotting away since 1959, exposed to hot summers, freezing winters, and the random violence of local kids. Whatever still survived was no doubt crumbling in the grip of the forest. It was sad, and Roland thought he would be lucky to get one halfway decent photograph. But it was certainly worth writing up—and publishing—it would be Roland Turner's first appearance in the pages of the Fellowship magazine.

It was well past ten when he finally left the bar. The heat had eased considerably and a breeze blew through town. The storm was closer. Roland could only hope it would be long gone when he went looking for the Jorgenson place in the morning. He caught a glimpse of lightning in the sky, but it seemed far away and there was no following rumble of thunder.

Main Street was now deserted, and Roland thought it looked a bit like an abandoned movie set. Signs swayed, windows rattled, leaves and dust swirled about, and everything was cast in the dim yellow glow of a few widely spaced streetlamps. The bright neon Genesee sign at Bill's stood out in welcome contrast.

Roland was about to get into his car when he first heard the sound, and he stopped to listen to it. Choir practice? No, this was not musical in the sense that it followed any pattern; it was not even human. Roland slowly turned his head, trying to figure out which direction it came from, but it was too diffuse, and the wind in the trees frequently overwhelmed it.

Back at the motel, Roland heard the sound again as soon as he stepped out of his car. It was stronger and clearer, yet just as hard to define as it had been in town. An Aeolian chorus that sang in the night, rising and fading, shrilling and moaning. The wind was part of it, but there had to be more, some unusual local feature that produced this effect. Roland actually liked it. He was reminded of certain ethereal passages from Debussy and Vaughan Williams. In his room, he turned off the air conditioner, opened a window, and listened to it a while longer.

The storm passed by a few miles to the north, crackling and thundering in the distance like a transient war, and the village of Glen Allen took an intense strafing of rain. But it was gone in a quarter of an hour, and its aftermath was a humid, dripping stillness.

In the morning, as he was about to set off for the Jorgenson place, Roland spotted the woman who ran the motel. She came out of the vending machine room with a full garbage sack in one hand. Roland crossed the parking lot and asked her about the sounds he had heard the previous night.

"That's the wind coming down the glen," she told him. "When it blows a certain direction, you get that."

"Yes, but what exactly causes it?"

"The wind coming down the glen," she repeated, as if he were dense. "You don't notice it so much in the winter."

"Ah."

He stopped at Colbert's Store, a few doors up from Bill's on Main Street, to buy a grinder and a carton of juice for lunch. A few minutes later, he nearly drove past what had been the entrance to the Jorgenson summer estate. As Bill had explained, it wasn't hard to find: about two miles up North Street, which was the only road north out of town, and look for it on your left. There were two stone columns flanking a single-lane driveway. Roland backed up and studied the scene for a moment.

The stone columns bore the dead pastel blue and green stains of lichen, and their caps were severely chipped and cracked. The wrought-iron gate was long gone—only a pair of deeply corroded hinges remained. Then Roland realized that Jorgenson had planted a wall of arborvitae along the road in both directions. It could still be seen, but barely. It must have reached twenty or thirty feet high, but now it was a skeletal ruin, shot through with tall weeds, young maples, choke cherries, wild grapes, and other vines and parasites. The entryway itself was so thick with brush that Roland couldn't even park in it; he had to go another fifty yards before he found a grassy spot on the right. He slung his camera around his neck, took his lunch cooler, locked the car, and walked back down the road.

The original dirt road to the house was thoroughly overgrown with weeds and field grass, but it wasn't hard to follow. Roland wandered off it twice and immediately noticed the change from the firm gravel base to a more yielding soil underfoot.

He passed through a tunnel of trees, a landscape effect that may well have been quite lovely once; now it was ragged, dark, and gloomy, devastated by secondary growth. He came out of it on the edge of a large clearing, and sensed that he was now close to the site of the house. It was no longer "cleared" at all, of course, but the perimeter was unmistakably marked by the much taller pine trees of the surrounding forest.

Roland's pants were soaked. The sky was overcast, so all of the plants he waded through were still wet from the rain. But he preferred it that way to a blazing hot sun. He followed the road as it climbed a very gradual rise and then leveled off. *Yes,* he thought excitedly, *this has to be it. Where else would you build a house?* The three or four acres of flat high ground he stood on provided a gorgeous southern view.

Roland gazed down across the old clearance, looking for any human traces. There was a small lake—perhaps Jorgenson had it created for him—and the stumpy remnants of a wooden pier. The lake was nearly dead now, choked with algae, reeds, and silt, but it must have been beautiful once.

Roland found it easy to visualize the Jorgenson children out on the lake canoeing, or jumping from the pier and swimming. The family might well have had picnic lunches in the shade of the big sugar maple that still stood by itself not far from the water. A view of the past. The lives, the dreams, so much effort to build a little world within the world. Were the Jorgensons haughty and unbearable, or decent and worthy of what they had? But it didn't matter, because what they had here was gone and so were they.

Roland turned and snagged his toe on a rock. It was part of the foundation of the house. He walked it, leaving his own trail in the tall grass and wildflowers. The fire, and the years, had left nothing but a rectangle of stones that barely protruded from the earth. The outbuildings had vanished as well; maybe some of the locals had dismantled them for the lumber and fittings. Roland took a photograph of the ground on which the house had stood, and then another of the broad clearance, including the lake. He ate his lunch quickly, eyes scanning the landscape for a sign, a clue. If the Italian folly was hidden somewhere in the forest, he could spend a week looking for it. There was only one other possibility—somewhere up behind the house. Beyond a low ridge only a hundred yards away, the land seemed to hollow out as steep walls formed on either side. That was north. That was the beginning of the glen, or the end of it.

Roland trudged up the rise, and gaped. There it was, Little Italy, Jorgenson's folly. He was so excited he nearly broke into a run, but then he steadied himself and clicked off several shots of the whole panorama. There were all kinds of houses—country villas, farmhouses, squat urban blocks—scattered in clumps and clusters. There were statues, many statues, fountains, archways, piazzas, towers, churches, stables, barns and much more. It went on into the glen as far as Roland could see.

The land on which most of the folly had been built was low, but it was marked by any number of little hillocks that enhanced the visual effect. In addition, the walls of the glen had a way of jutting out and cutting back that created niches, defiles, and recesses of varying size and depth. Every wacky detail somehow worked, and it all came together to create a remarkable illusion at first sight.

In fact, it looked its best at a distance. When Roland came down the slope to it and began to make his way through the narrow passages, the decay was all too obvious. Most of the structures had been built with cinderblocks, or plaster on chicken wire, and then coated with paint or whitewash. Tin roofs had been painted a reddish-brown to suggest tile. Cheap stuff for a rich guy, and it showed the effects of age, neglect, and intermittent vandalism. Whole walls had been knocked down or worn away. Much of the tin was corroded, the paint blistered and peeling—what there still was of it. Statues were missing hands or heads, sometimes both. Everything was severely chipped or cracked.

Brambles and vines proliferated, often making it difficult for Roland to move about. But in that respect, the folly had been spared worse damage. The ground was rocky and the soil thin, so not much else managed to grow there.

Roland advanced slowly, taking pictures as he went. He knew little about Italy but he recognized most of the famous landmarks Jorgenson had chosen to replicate. He was particularly impressed by a fifty-foot section of the Aqueduct high enough to walk under without ducking his head. It was broken only in three places and actually dripped a tiny residue of last night's rain. Roland had to smile when he noticed that the plaster Aqueduct was lined with cast-iron half-pipe.

What really made the whole thing work was the dizzy range of scale—or rather, the complete lack of scale. A two-foot house stood next to a three-foot statue of a dog. Mt. Etna was somehow smaller than the Duomo, while the Spanish Steps were larger than all of Venice. Nothing matched anything.

That, and sheer quirkiness. Working only two months a year, Jorgenson obviously felt compelled to add a number of ready-made items to his dream world. The statues, for instance. And Roland especially liked the birdbath—a common garden birdbath—that utterly dominated St. Peter's Square. There were other birdbaths to be seen, as well as birdhouses that could be purchased in any garden shop or nursery even today; perhaps in the extreme reaches of his obsession Jorgenson saw an ideal Italy populated solely by birds. Roland grinned a few moments later when he came across a statue of Saint Francis of Assisi, surrounded by birdhouses that were mounted on sections of lead pipe—with the entire tableau situated between a *trattoria* and a bizarre little maze apparently meant to suggest the catacombs.

Roland came into a small clearing with a stone bench. Maybe this was where old man Jorgenson sat, pondering his extraordinary creation and dreaming up more additions to it. Roland rested his feet for a moment and changed the film in his camera.

It was easy to lose track of the size of the folly. Many of the structures were only three feet high, but quite a few were as tall as man, and with the gently undulating flow of the ground it was impossible to see ahead to the point where the folly displays finally came to an end. But it was also impossible to get lost, since the walls of the glen were always visible.

Roland had to keep moving. The sky seemed to be darker now, not from the lateness of the hour but from the appearance of more storm clouds. He hadn't thought to check the weather report, and he had no idea whether a new storm was due or it was the same one circling back. Roland didn't like the idea of having to hike all the way back to the car in a downpour, but it might come to that. He wasn't going to leave until he had seen and photographed every part of the folly.

Jorgenson had saved his most astounding flight of fancy for the last. Roland stepped through a gap in a wall, and he thought that he was standing in a courtyard. A stretch of ground roughly one hundred feet square had been covered with large paving stones that had subsequently buckled and heaved. Now the whole area was shot through with tufts of dull green weeds, laced with some kind of wild ground ivy.

There was a line of columns along the left edge and another on the right. They were ten or twelve feet high and some of them had fallen over, but they created a sudden impression that still had power. Roland found himself thinking of the Pantheon, but he had no clear mental image of the original to compare.

All this, however, was peripheral to the set piece straight ahead. Where the paving stones ended, the ground rose up slightly before it leveled off, creating a rough natural platform. It was as wide as the courtyard, and it was full of statues. There were dozens of them. Roland stumbled forward.

Several interesting features, he thought in a daze. All the statues were positioned to face the center of the glen. They all had their arms raised and their faces uplifted, as if acclaiming the gods or seeking their merciful help. None of them had hands. They had open mouths but otherwise there were no facial features, not a nose or an eye or an ear in the entire assembly. They had no feet, unless they were buried in the ground, for the legs rose up out of the soil, converging in thick, trunk-like torsos.

The statues were crude and stark, and yet they seemed to be possessed of a terrible poignancy.

They weren't presented as Romans in togas and robes. There were no gods or creatures of myth, not even a Venetian gondolier. They were like golems, clad in stone. Roland climbed the rise to inspect them close up. The surface was brownish in color, rough but firm in texture—like partly annealed sand. Perhaps there was an underlayer of plaster or cement. Roland had seen nothing else like it in Jorgenson's Little Italy. It was an improvement; these statues showed very little evidence of erosion.

But what madness!

Roland was in the middle of his final roll of film, snapping medium shots of the amazing statuary, when the first hand grabbed him by the belt in the small of his back. Then there were others on his body, pulling him down from behind. Something banged him along the side of the head, stunning him briefly.

How much time had passed? Roland's vision was blurred, and would not correct. His head throbbed painfully. It was dark and the air was somehow different. Maybe he was in a cave. He could just make out flickering firelight, and the busy movements of his captors. Roland couldn't move. They held him to the ground, his arms outstretched.

They were like kids—not yet fully grown, voices unformed. He thought there were about a half-dozen of them. He had no idea what was going on, he couldn't understand anything. An unnatural silence alarmed him. Roland tried to speak to them, but they sat on his chest and legs, pinned his head in place, and stuffed foul rags in his mouth. Then he saw the dull glint of an axe blade as it began its downward descent to the spot where his left hand was firmly held. Same thing on the right a few seconds later, but by then Roland was already unconscious.

Searing pain revived him; that, and perhaps a lingering will to struggle and save his life. He was alone for the moment, but he could hear them—their squeaky murmurs, and a disturbing wet scraping noise.

Demented teenagers. Maybe some weird sect or cult. Or they could be a brain-stunted, inbred rural clan that preyed on anyone who was foolish enough to stray into their territory.

How could this happen? Was the whole town in on it? What could they want? Perhaps in exploring and photographing Jorgenson's Italian folly, he had somehow violated their sacred ground. But it seemed most likely that they were insane, pure and simple.

Roland still couldn't move. His wrist-stumps were bandaged. The bastards had actually chopped his hands off. The realization nearly knocked him out again but Roland fought off total panic. He had to think clearly, or he was surely lost. The rest of his body from the neck down seemed to be wrapped in some kind of wire mesh. His mouth was still clogged with the hideous rags, and he had to breathe through his nose. He tried to lever his tongue to push the rags out, or to one side, so he could speak, but at that moment they came back for him.

They dragged him, and it became clear to Roland that some of the monstrous pain he felt was coming from where his two feet had been. They threw him down in a torch-lit clearing. They spread his legs, held his arms out, and began to smear some thick, gooey substance on him. Roland flipped and squirmed like a fish on the floor of a boat until they clubbed him again.

Fresh air, dusk light.

The same day? Couldn't be. But overcast, the wind whipping loudly—and that choral sound Roland had heard his first night in town. They carried him out of the cave, and the wailing noise seemed to fill his brain. He was in the center of it, and it was unbearable.

Only his head was exposed—the rest of his body now stone. It came up to his neck in a rigid collar and forced his head back at a painful angle. Roland caught sight of them as they propped him in his place on the third rank of the statuary. They weren't kids, they didn't even look human—pinched little faces, stubby fingers, a manic bustle to their movements, and the insect jabber that was all but lost in the boiling wind.

Like caricature scientists, they turned him one way and then another, tilting, nudging and adjusting. They finally yanked the rags out of his mouth. Roland tried to croak out a few words but his tongue was too dry. Then the final mystery was solved as his captors thrust a curious device into his mouth. He saw it for an instant—a wire cage that contained several loose wooden balls. They were of varying sizes, and Roland thought he saw grooves and holes cut in them. It fit so well that his tongue was pressed to the floor of his mouth. A couple of strands of rawhide were tied around his head, securing the device even more tightly.

A last corrective nudge, and then the wind took hold and the wooden balls danced and bounced. Another voice joined the choir. Satisfied, they went on to complete their work, covering the rest of his head with the sticky cement and then applying the exterior finish. Only his open mouth was left untouched.

Roland thought of insects nesting there. He pictured a warm mist billowing out on cool mornings as he rotted inside. And he wondered how long it would take to die. *They must do repair work later, to keep the cages in place after the flesh disappeared.* A strangely comforting thought in the giddy swirl of despair.

The wind came gusting down the glen. Empty arms raised, his anonymous face lifted to the unseeing sky, he sang.

THE VENTRILOQUIST

Robbie had heard about this woman. Annemarie. Nobody knew her last name. She could see things. She could tell you things about yourself that you didn't know. Something good or bad maybe coming your way. He had heard all kinds of talk about her, at least since back in his freshman year at the high school. It was a small city. People get to know.

He knew some who'd gone to visit her. Girls who thought she was for real, and kind of scary. She knew right away that my grandmother was in the hospital, they'd say, that my brother was in a car crash. That I was pregnant. That kind of stuff.

Guys who laughed it off as a joke, or who hinted that if you paid extra the woman would do a lot more than just read your cards.

His grandparents were a bit superstitious that way. His mother too, though less so. Robbie had never really given it much thought. Probably he would say he didn't believe in it. But here he was, twenty-one years old, on his way to see the woman. Scraping the bottom of the barrel for a glimmer of hope. That showed better than anything else ever could how thoroughly screwed up he was by Suzy Schneider. He resented it, bitterly, but now he knew what it was like to feel that you have to try anything.

Robbie knew that Annemarie lived in a trailer park on the northern edge of town, out on the old turnpike that used to be the main thoroughfare up and down the Brass Valley. There wasn't much traffic on it anymore, since they put Route 8 through on the other side of the river a few years ago. Many of the businesses had subsequently relocated. A scattering of them remained, but the pike was a half-forgotten backroad now.

Cedar Glen was about half a mile past the shooting range. Robbie slowed down and swung his '59 Fairlane onto a dirt road that wound slowly through the trees. Most of the trailers were old and on the small side, round like snail shells, relics from the Thirties and Forties. They showed their age, too, with stains, faded paint, and patches of rust. There were potted flowers, lawn chairs, barbecue grills, folding tables, and other small signs of lingering effort, but overall it struck Robbie as the kind of place where people end up when they have nowhere else left to go. Most of the ones he saw—and they scarcely even glanced at him as he passed by—looked as if they were at the back end of middle age, or older. Not a kid in sight.

The road meandered and looped around, but it always came back to the main stem, and the place wasn't that big anyway—it was hemmed in by the rising valley walls and the pike along the Naugatuck River. Robbie had checked with a friend and he knew more or less where he was going and what he was looking for. Just beyond the communal picnic area—itself a sad joke—the road curled over a small rise and then down into a lower flat area where the trees were thinner and the sun penetrated.

Hers was the newer trailer, parked alongside a narrow stream. It was long, intended to look like a ranch house, but with a flat roof. Powder blue and white, with a couple of sporty diagonal yellow bars up near the front end. What clinched it were the two cars parked nearby. The beat-up Impala with the Connecticut plates would be hers, and the shiny new Cadillac with the New York plates would belong to some other fool who thought that the woman could tell him something important.

Robbie pulled in, turned his engine off, lit a Lucky, and waited. It was a beautiful afternoon, the air sweet and mild. It wasn't bad down here, where she was, but he couldn't imagine living in one of those boxy things. Though, to be fair, the rooms he shared with his mother and kid sister on the ground floor of an old triple-decker seemed cramped enough. He had to get out, find a place for himself. He was working on that, but it took time to put the money together. Meanwhile, the days dribble away like piss on a bad morning.

He could feel the anger smoldering and sparking up within him. It was September 17th, 1969, exactly thirty-four days since he'd last seen Lori face to face, and seventeen since she'd changed her telephone to an unlisted number. Oh, Suzy had some bitch in her, all right.

He was getting to the end of his second cigarette when a colorfully dressed hippie couple emerged from the trailer. Expensive boutique shit. In the music business, Robbie figured. They hopped into the Caddy and roared off with a spray of dust and gravel.

A chunky woman with steel-gray hair opened the door even before Robbie could knock. He had to pay twenty-five dollars. Then she steered him into a small room off to the right, the shorter end of the long trailer, and told him that Annemarie would be with him in a couple of minutes. Twenty-five was kind of steep, he thought, but he hadn't objected to it. If they could charge that and get it, she must be pretty good after all.

Robbie sat on one of three plain wooden chairs that were arranged around a small circular table with a maroon velvet cloth. Dark blue curtains covered the windows and light was provided by a trio of wall fixtures with parchment-like shades that gave the room a pleasingly warm golden glow. There wasn't much else—a soft thick carpet that matched the curtains, and a wicker wastebasket off in a corner. The lack of atmospheric touches was mildly disappointing, but on the other hand, maybe it simply meant that she didn't need to rely on typical fortune-teller props.

The door opened and Annemarie entered the room. Robbie stood up and nodded awkwardly at her. She had dark hair that extended below her shoulder, a slim figure, powerful eyes in a narrow face, and she was wearing a thin gray caftan that hung loosely on her body. Thirtyish, and still pretty. But she looked tired, very tired, and sad. She had some small object in her hand. She hesitated for a moment as she stared at him, her eyes widening slightly, her lips tightening.

"Why have you come here?"

"I was hoping you could help me."

Her body seemed to sag a little as she sighed. Her expression now was almost sorrowful, but she gestured for Robbie to sit down and she took the chair directly across the table from him. She handed him a new deck of ordinary playing cards, still wrapped in cellophane. "Open it, take out the jokers, and shuffle the cards several times," she instructed. "Take your time, do a good job touching and mixing them, and while you're doing that, I want you to think about the reason you came here. The person or situation that most concerns you."

Robbie did as he was told. As a kid he had learned how to make the cards flutter and whirr perfectly when he shuffled, and he was pleased to see that he still had that ability, though he hadn't actually played cards in quite a while. He concentrated on Suzy. How they had known each other for years, living in the same neighborhood and going to the same schools. How their romance had come as an astonishing surprise to both of them, overpowering them late in their junior year. And then how right it seemed, how very right and good, and what a fine happy couple they made. Going steady, going out and doing things together. Their passion and dreams.

"That's fine," Annemarie said. "Now I want you to deal three cards face down. The next card also goes face down, but to one side. Then keep on dealing the whole deck into those two groups, three in one pile, then one in the other, and so on."

Robbie's fingers moved swiftly and the cards fell. Not long after high school, the trouble began. Small stuff at first, just a hint now and then, a pout, a look of dissatisfaction. Suzy went fulltime at the perfume counter at G. Fox. Robbie worked for Ray Palumbo, who had his own nursery and landscape business. It was hard, sweaty work, but Robbie liked it. He liked working outdoors. If you owned your own business and built it up, like Ray had done, you could earn a pretty good living doing something you enjoyed. That's what Robbie had in mind for himself, down the road.

Annemarie took the pile of thirteen cards and held them tightly in her hands. She had Robbie reshuffle the rest of the deck and then separate them again, this time putting two in one pile and one aside, and continuing in that way.

Suzy moved into an apartment with a couple of girlfriends. It wasn't always comfortable to spend time with her there, the others hanging around, coming and going. He suspected that they were telling Suzy he wasn't good enough for her. He sensed that she didn't enjoy being with him as much as she had, that he was losing her, and it ate him up inside. Never had he felt so helpless, bewildered, and incapable of righting things.

Then it turned into soap opera. The evening she wasn't home when he called, and one of her roommates was a little too curt. Somehow it told Robbie that he was finished, only Suzy hadn't gotten around to telling him yet. He went out with Ray's nephew Teddy. They hit a few bars in town, and ended up later at the Music Box out on Bantam Lake. Suzy was there with Artie Huff. Couldn't get a date in high school, but now Artie was a college boy, a prick with better prospects, apparently. By then Robbie was buzzed enough to make a scene, and that really was the end of it.

The next day it sunk in, and he cried. Then the desperate attempts to see her, to speak with her—just once more. Nothing worked. And the hurt didn't let go, it only seemed to get worse, festering with anger.

Annemarie took the second group of thirteen cards and held them for a moment before setting them down on the table in front of her, with the first group. She had Robbie divide the remaining cards into two groups of thirteen, and again she took the discards.

Now she directed him to lay out the final thirteen cards he held, in this way: one card face down, five cards face up, another card face down, horizontally in front of him; a second line of five cards face up, directly above the first; the last card face down, at the top, forming a triangle with the other two cards that were facing down. The other ten cards were a mix of numbers and suits, with a queen of clubs, an ace of diamonds and a king of hearts in the mix. It seemed pretty ridiculous to Robbie, a meaningless rigmarole cooked up to look mysterious and impressive.

Annemarie stared at the cards for a couple of minutes, and then she looked up at Robbie. "There are three things you want."

He was confused. All he wanted was to get Suzy back, or at least to know if he ever would. "No, I—"

"Don't tell me," she interrupted. "If you think about it, you'll find that what you want presents two other possibilities, depending on whether or not it is fulfilled."

"Huh." She was right, almost. Two other thoughts did immediately come to mind, when she put it like that. "Okay."

"These cards are very favorable," Annemarie told him, waving her hand over the ten cards that were facing up. "Two threes and two nines, that's very good. The king of hearts represents you. The queen of clubs is the one you want, isn't that so?"

"Yeah, that's right," Robbie found himself replying. "Who's the ace of diamonds?" Thinking it might be Artie Huff.

Annemarie's fingers waved dismissively. "It only means that you're good at what you do. Your talents, your work."

"Oh." Robbie felt vaguely pleased.

"There are no indications of internal conflict," she went on. "You're not hesitant or doubtful. You're certain within yourself of what you want in this situation, isn't that so?"

"Yeah, definitely."

"All right. What you want most is always at your left hand. Touch the card there with your fingertips, the one facing down."

Robbie did so. Annemarie then reached forward, took the card and pulled it gently out from under his fingers. She turned it over for him to see. It was a dinky little four of diamonds. *Can't hurt*, he thought.

"You're completely stopped," she said. "I'm sorry."

"What? Stopped? What's that mean?"

"You will never have her. The four is completely disruptive of your numbers. It's impossible."

Robbie exhaled slowly. He thought he was beginning to catch on to some of this. The numbers didn't work, and maybe the fact that the four was a diamond referred to Artie having better career prospects. It was hard to take, but it made sense.

"Now focus on your second thought," Annemarie told him. "Touch the card facing down on your right."

Whatever else happens, don't let Artie have her. Not that little jerk. Robbie pressed his fingertips to the card and held them there.

Annemarie reached across the table again and carefully took the card, turning it over in the air. A six of spades.

"The number is yours, there is no resistance, but the outcome is not necessarily conclusive."

"What's that mean?"

"It means that what you wish in this circumstance will most likely come to pass, but it won't resolve the matter. In spite of what many people think, spades are the most ambiguous suit."

This was more like it, this was the kind of thing he wanted to hear. And yet it wasn't quite good enough. "So...?"

"You have one more thought."

He sure did. He wanted Suzy to feel the pain he had felt, to know what it was like to see everything come crashing down—and yet not be able to do anything to stop it. A current of anger hummed and buzzed within. Robbie put his fingers on the card facing down at the top of the triangle. Annemarie removed it and turned it over—the jack of spades. She gazed at him, her eyes giving nothing away.

"What's it mean?" he asked. "Jack of spades."

"What you want is unopposed."

"You mean it'll happen?"

"Nothing external prevents it."

"And what's that mean—exactly?"

"If you truly want it to happen—"

"Well, I do."

"—then it will."

"What about it's a spade? What's that mean?"

"Uncertainty—when, where, how. Things like that."

"And what about—"

"Thank you for coming to see me."

Robbie was still thinking about it five weeks later. What a crock. He might have known. Kind of spooky the way she got some things right. But that was part of the act. She knew how to carry it off. Only later, when you get out from under the spell, could you see it for what it was.

First off, Annemarie told Robbie he would never have Suzy. But the very next day, Suzy spoke to him on the phone when he called. It was kind of cool, no breakthrough, but it was a step in the right direction. It seemed to him that she sounded almost unhappy.

They talked a couple of more times on the phone, but then Suzy cut him off again. He started following her, and discovered that she and Artie liked to go to Vito's Steak & Seafood in Torrington. Sneaky, a little out of the way. Popular, judging by the cars in the lot.

Two weeks, and more. She talked, always vague, uncertain. But at the same time, Artie wasn't going away. Artie Huff was still the man, and whenever Robbie saw her with him, she looked like she was truly enjoying herself. The bitch. She felt like broken glass in Robbie's bowels.

The proof that Suzy was just stringing him along, playing with him, came when she lost interest in the game. She stopped taking his calls again, and this time he knew at once that it was final.

It was a rainy Saturday evening in November, the last time Robbie followed them up Route 8. Vito's, of course, why else would you drive to Torrington? The temperature was in the thirties, not quite freezing, and the road was slick. Just north of Thomaston, near the Northfield exit, the road passed over a deep ravine and stream. The drop had to be a hundred feet or more. Robbie hadn't even thought about it, but when he saw it coming he sped up and pulled alongside Artie's car. They looked at him. Both of them. He saw the blank look on their faces. They saw him but they didn't get it, none of it, not at all. Robbie swung the wheel, and loved the contact. Artie's car bounced, and then flew directly into the steel overpass.

He caught a glimpse of the wreck in the mirror as his car spun across the road. Artie wouldn't have her. Suzy had seen her own end coming and must have felt the same great anguish he knew....

Robbie's car plowed through the wooden posts on the other side of the highway, just beyond the main overpass, and then dropped off, tumbling down into the ravine. He didn't mind at all.

TORCHING THE ESCALADE

Lloyd hadn't seen Dickie Smith in oh, a year, probably longer, so when he ran into him in the parking lot at an auto parts store, he was startled by what he saw. Dickie was a successful businessman, always on top of things, a deal-maker in commercial real estate and development projects up and down the valley. But now Dickie looked like a beaten man, his hair grayer and thinner, his face older and puffy, unshaven in a couple of days—clearly not a guy on his way to or from the office.

Still, he affected an upbeat manner in the few moments they chatted. Lloyd and Dickie had known each other since high school, when they were the double-play combo at short and second for the only St Ann's team ever to reach the state championship final, a game they lost on a wild pitch in the bottom of the ninth. They shook hands and were about to go their separate ways when Dickie hesitated.

"Hey, Lloyd."

"Yeah?"

"You free for lunch sometime? On me," he added.

"Sure."

"In the next few days? There's something I want to talk to you about."

"Uh, yeah. I'm off this Saturday."

Dickie nodded. "That works for me."

As planned, they met at the bar of The Cantina, a casual Tex-Mex restaurant tucked away just behind Library Park. They got a couple of beers and then moved outdoors to one of the tables on the deck. Dickie looked better, clean-shaven, dressed in a crisp sports shirt, khaki slacks and loafers.

"Where are you living now?" Dickie asked after the waitress took their food orders. "Still in town?"

"Yeah, up off Highland Avenue. One side of a duplex."

"Renting?"

"Yeah. It suits me," Lloyd said. "Quiet street, good neighbors, good Italian deli and other shops just around the corner."

"Good."

"You?"

"We moved to Westbury a couple of years ago," Dickie replied.

"Nice." Lloyd was familiar with Westbury, a well-off little town about ten miles away. "More country-like out there."

"Yeah, there's a working farm down at the end of our street."

"Nice."

"You still running the tire shop?"

"Yep."

"For your—?"

"My uncle Frank," Lloyd said, nodding. "That's right."

"How's that working out for you?"

Lloyd shrugged. "He built up a good business over the years, and I think I do a pretty good job managing it. So, it's a living."

"He make you a partner?"

Lloyd smiled. "Not yet."

"Any chance a piece of it might come your way at some point?"

"Put it this way, he'd like me to think so and I'd like to believe it. He has no sons, I'm his only nephew, and I do run the joint for him. I know the business."

"That's good," Dickie said. "I hope it works out for you."

"How about you? Business good?"

Dickie looked at him like he was nuts. "Lloyd, the whole friggin' economy is in the friggin' toilet."

At that point, their food arrived. Lloyd tucked into a cheeseburger platter while Dickie picked at a large bowl of chili, fries and slaw. The chat shifted to sports, the Red Sox, and updates on old mutual acquaintances. Toward the end of the meal, Dickie set his fork down and leaned forward a little.

"Lloyd, I am screwed six ways from Sunday."

"Why?"

Dickie's tale of woe came spilling out in a rush. The property market was crashing and he had virtually no income for the foreseeable future. A couple of years ago, he and his wife Mary had upgraded to a $600,000 home in Westbury that was now worth barely half that amount, making it impossible to refinance. Not that there credit anywhere, with the credit market frozen and banks teetering left and right.

"Jeez, I'm sorry to hear you're in such a bind," Lloyd said.

"It gets worse," Dickie continued. "Our daughter, Michelle, is entering college in September—Fairfield. So that's another boatload of money, right there."

"Wow."

What money Dickie had put aside in investments over the years had dropped fifty percent in value when the stock market crashed last fall, and he had been selling off the rest at the market's current rock-bottom prices. His wife was a nurse, a good job, but she now had to work double shifts to keep them— barely—afloat in their house.

"The economy will pick up again," Lloyd said, knowing it sounded lame.

"Yeah, eventually. A year or two, they're saying, but nobody knows. But even when it does turn around, I may be dead in the water. I can't get back in business if I don't have an excellent credit rating."

"But it sounds like you and the wife are still getting by."

"Right," Dickie said. "But there's one more millstone around my neck. Did you happen to see what I was driving when we bumped into each other a few days ago?"

"No, you were on your way in and I was on my way out."

"I bought an Escalade last year. Signed the papers about three weeks before the world went off the cliff." Dickie smiled ruefully. "It cost eighty five grand, of which I still owe seventy. You know what the monthly nut on that is?"

"Oh, man."

"Oh yeah, I drank the Kool-Aid. Here's the thing, Lloyd. If I default on that loan, my credit rating will be destroyed." Dickie signaled the waitress for two more beers and pushed on. "But if the car is stolen by some punks and set on fire, the insurance company picks up the tab, and I'm okay."

"That's not a good idea," Lloyd said.

"It's the *only* good idea left. Just hear me out on this."

Lloyd sipped his second beer and listened. In fact, Dickie had worked it all out pretty well. A place near the local mall where the vehicle could be parked and "stolen" without being caught on a security camera or necessarily attracting attention. Where to torch the Escalade. How he could explain what he was doing during the hour or so before he reported the theft. It involved a certain amount of carelessness and foolishness on his part—he may have accidentally hit unlock instead of lock, he did keep a spare key and pass-key in the storage compartment inside—but those are routine factors when cars are stolen. Plausible, plausible, plausible. Yes, the cops would question him closely, it was a lot of money. But Dickie knew a lot of the local cops. They wouldn't press very hard. In the good money days, he'd been a generous donor to the Police Activity League programs for the kids in town. So had Lloyd, for that matter—he wrote out a check every year on behalf of the tire shop.

There was a grand in it for Lloyd. Half an hour of his time, give or take. Just be there to drive Dickie away from the scene and drop him off near the mall. Lloyd thought about it. Thursday evening would be perfect. Everybody at work knew he stayed on for an hour or so after closing to do paperwork.

"Where's this place you want to do it?"

"South End. Ten minutes. Let's go in your car."

"You got a girlfriend, Lloyd?"

"I've got a friend, and she's a she. I wouldn't call her a girl, and I wouldn't call her a girlfriend. But we have our moments."

"That's all that matters."

"I haven't been in this part of town in ages," Lloyd said.

"It's been a commercial dead zone for ages."

"Are you sure you want to do this, Dickie?"

"Certain. Okay, just past this building on the left, there's a lane coming up. Turn down there and we'll get to a large vacant lot. Pull in there."

Lloyd followed Dickie's directions. It was almost like arriving at a courtyard. A cinderblock building on the left and another one on the right, a two-story brick building straight ahead, and a line of scraggly trees engulfed by brush behind them. A large open ground in between, old concrete now buckled and pot-holed in places, weeds thick in the cracks. As soon as Lloyd put the car in Park, Dickie jumped out. Lloyd followed, but he left the engine running. It was a 10-year-old Malibu and the starter had been clicking on him lately.

"That's the back of what used to be a cheap-goods store called Arlan's," Dickie said, pointing to the right. "Up front, that was a tool-and-die shop, and over here," he said, waving his hand to the left, that was a used car lot for a while. They kept most of their cars back here."

They were approaching the middle of the lot when a very loud, shrill series of screeches pierced the air, repeating itself several times.

"What the hell is that?" Lloyd asked.

Dickie chuckled. "After the used car guys left, a couple of other businesses came and went, and the last renter I know of was a motorcycle gang called the Doomsters. It was their headquarters, club, whatever—they hung out, partied here, and they'd have 40, 50 bikes parked out back here. I don't know if it was the car dealers or the bikers, but one of them got tired of pigeons and seagulls dumping on their vehicles, so they installed a speaker system that broadcast bird distress calls, or maybe that's the sound of hawks and falcons screeching. Predators. Anyhow, it was to scare away any other birds."

"Why would it still be operating?" Lloyd asked.

"Because it's illegally wired?" Dickie asked in return, with a grin. "And they didn't bother to dismantle it when they packed up and left. But look, here's what I want to show you. On that side, across the river, you've got Baldwin Street, but you can't see a house for the trees. On the west side, all trees up the valley hill. And north and south, there are no houses. Just vacant buildings. Look around, it's a sunny Saturday afternoon, and you can't see a human being anywhere."

The mechanical bird screeches continued to rip the empty air. Even in broad daylight, this godforsaken place had the creepiest, loneliest feeling about it, the kind of place that even homeless people would avoid, because it wasn't close to anything. Lloyd began to feel physically uncomfortable.

"Thursday evening. Around six-thirty?"

Dickie smiled. "Perfect. Thanks, Lloyd."

"Let's get out of here."

It drizzled for much of the day on Thursday, until late afternoon, when the rain finally subsided. But the area remained humid and overcast, and according to the radio, patches of fog were forming in low-lying parts of the valley.

A little after six, Lloyd locked up the tire shop and got into his car. Even though it was June, it was such a dark day out that everyone was driving with their headlights on. There was a time, years ago, when driving down South Main at this hour of the day would be very slow going, the street clogged with traffic as the mill-workers headed home. But then the brass and copper mills shut, one after another, and the highway came through, and everything was forever different.

When Lloyd arrived at the vacant lot, he drove all the way to the far end of it, at the back of the old Arlan's building, and swung his car around so that he was facing the lane—his way out. He switched the headlights off but kept the car idling in park.

He wondered if Dickie would get cold feet at the last minute and fail to show up. Lloyd checked his watch. He would wait fifteen minutes. But only a few moments later, he saw the headlights and then the Escalade as it turned onto the lane. Dickie pulled up near Lloyd's car and hopped out of the SUV. Lloyd lowered his window.

"Did you think I wasn't coming?" Dickie asked.

"I was just starting to wonder."

Dickie laughed. "No, it's all systems go. I'm going to take it to the middle of the lot, open all the doors and windows, douse the interior real good, and touch it off. It'll probably take a couple of minutes before the fire sets off the gas tank."

"You fill her up?"

"This afternoon."

"Dickie, I'm not driving out onto the lot, I'm staying over here, as far away as I can be. Just in case that things goes off early and there's shrapnel flying around. I'm not worried about getting hurt, but if something hits my car and we're stuck here—see what I'm saying?"

"Right, that's okay. I'll be jogging my ass as fast as I can."

"Dickie, you want to pay me now?"

"Why? I'll pay you when we get to the mall."

"I know you would," Lloyd said. "But, say something goes terribly wrong and you incinerate yourself out there."

"Okay," Dickie said, reaching into his pocket. He handed an envelope to Lloyd. "Now, let's get this done and get the hell outta here."

Lloyd folded the envelope of bills in half and shoved it into his pants pocket. He watched as Dickie drove out to the middle of the lot and brought the Escalade to a stop. That horrible screeching racket started up again. Dickie had the windows and doors all open, and was pouring gasoline from a red plastic container—looked to be 5 gallons. Dickie splashed the fuel all over the interior, then some more over the roof and around the tires. When he was finished, he tossed the container into the back seat. Then he moved a few yards away and pulled something out of his jacket pocket, about the size of a softball. White. Probably a rolled-up wad of cheesecloth, Lloyd figured. Dickie lit the object, held it carefully for a few seconds, until it got burning good, and then lobbed it right into the front passenger seat—just like a perfect shovel toss from second to short, to start a double play. The Escalade went right up in flames with a whoosh, and Dickie was jogging away. Lloyd put the car in gear and started to edge down the lane.

But then stopped. He saw something moving in the distance—in the air, behind Dickie and the burning SUV. A dark shape, sweeping down through the air. As it got closer, Lloyd could see that it looked like a huge bird of prey, bigger than any bird he had ever seen. And different from a bird—dark brown leathery hide, not feathers. It had a lethal crescent beak and visibly large talons—now extending forward.

Dickie never saw it coming. The creature hit him from behind, seizing Dickie's entire head in his mouth, lifting him off the ground, shaking him violently. Dickie's headless body dropped onto the concrete. The bird—whatever it was—flew up and out of sight for a few seconds. Lloyd just sat there, unable to do anything but gaze at the scene. Then the creature swept back down, clutched Dickie's body in its talons and flew away as easily as if it were carrying a beach ball. The mechanical screeching continued to play.

It wasn't until the Escalade's gas tank detonated with a deep *whummph* and a fireball, that Lloyd began to think and act again. He sped down the lane, onto the street, and drove away—too fast, at first, but then he forced himself to slow down. He made it home. He drank Jim Beam until he had a nice buzz going and he finally began to feel a little calm.

But his brain kept replaying what he'd seen. And something else, something that his eye might have seen without his mind focusing on it. It was a crumbling old factory, boarded up on the ground floor, it's upper floor windows are broken and gone, the place open to the elements. And what could be nesting inside on the top floor.

There was nothing about it on the local TV news at eleven that night, nor did it make the newspaper the following morning. But the next day, there it was. The Escalade found, totally destroyed. Owner missing. Financial worries. Feared suicidal.

Lloyd thought, *That's all more or less correct.*

FOOD

"It's almost over now," Miss Rowe said, more to herself than to him. There was a faraway look in her eyes, but she smiled and her voice was bright with anticipation. "Don't worry, though. It'll be all right."

Almost over? What did that mean? Mr. Whitman would rather not think about it. As far as he was concerned, it was a typical summer Saturday. The August heat had eased off a bit, and there was a sweet breeze in the air. Other people would go swimming or shopping or would watch a baseball game, and Mr. Whitman and Miss Rowe would do what they usually did every Saturday afternoon, or so he hoped.

"But you aren't well," he was compelled to say. "I mean, it looks like you're in real pain now. I can see it."

"No," she replied without much conviction. "It's not that bad, honestly. I know what I'm going through better than you do, and it's all right." Miss Rowe quivered as she adjusted herself on the mattresses and tried again to change the subject. "What did you bring for me today?"

Mr. Whitman ignored that. "I do think you should let me get a doctor. You ought to be in a hospital, but the least you can do is have a doctor examine you."

"Absolutely not. If you do anything like that, I'll never speak to you again."

Miss Rowe said this not harshly, but more as a verbal pout. Unfortunately, Mr. Whitman knew it was also probably the truth. He was simply incapable of dealing with her on any terms other than her own. His sense of duty wasn't as strong as his fear of damaging the friendship they shared.

Mr. Whitman crossed the room, threading his way carefully through the piles of debris, and stood for a few moments by the open French doors. He enjoyed more of the breeze there, but the backyard was a distressing sight. The lawn hadn't been mowed in weeks. As if on cue, someone's power mower started up and whined steadily in the distance. The garden at the far end of the yard didn't quite exist. Mr. Whitman had cleared and spaded a patch for peppers and tomato plants, but he had never gotten around to putting them in. Now, the bare black soil sprouted a few weeds instead. But he had been busy, he reminded himself. Miss Rowe had taken over his life that summer.

"What have you brought?" she asked again.

"Oh, Balzac," Mr. Whitman answered distractedly. He had almost forgotten the book he held in one hand. Every Saturday afternoon he read a story to Miss Rowe. Balzac was one of her favorites, and his. Today he intended to recite "Facino Cane," a tale he practically knew by heart but which never failed to move him deeply.

He could see that Miss Rowe was pleased, but she was unable to speak. At that moment she was eagerly cramming a thick slice of Italian bread into her mouth. The sight was too distressing for Mr. Whitman to bear, so he turned to the volume of Balzac and flipped through its pages. It wasn't the bread, nor the generous layers of brandy pâté and cream cheese that were slathered on it. Food, all food—that was the whole wretched problem. Miss Rowe was a compulsive eater. Most of her waking hours were devoted to the consumption of food. She was half his age, if that, and by his conservative estimate, more than triple his weight.

Their strange relationship had begun six months earlier when Mr. Whitman moved in and became her neighbor. They were a couple of solitary refugees from the outside world. They occupied the two ground-floor apartments in a converted Victorian house on the outskirts of Cairo. Not the Cairo in Egypt, but rather a country village in the central part of eastern Connecticut, where many towns have grandly incongruous names, like Westminster, Brooklyn, and Versailles.

Mr. Whitman had never married, but he had saved and

invested his money shrewdly over the years, and when he reached the age of fifty he was finally able to retire from his editorial job in New York and leave the city behind him. He could please himself now, and do what he wanted—which was to buy and sell rare books. Mr. Whitman's specialty was crime, true and fictional, though he loved all literature. He had a respectable collection which he kept in the two-room shop he rented in the village. He also had a dozen or so truly valuable books in a safe-deposit box at the bank. Mr. Whitman didn't make much money at this business. He actually disliked selling any of his books and so he invariably overpriced them. But money had ceased to be an important factor in his life, and he was happy to spend several hours a day in his shop, surrounded by his collection, listening to public radio on the FM and tending to a very small mail order trade.

He discouraged off-the-street customers by keeping the door locked and the shades drawn. He was in the process of compiling a catalogue of his collection, but in a leisurely fashion. More often than not, he would push the lists aside and settle back to lose himself in a book. Mr. Whitman knew he would never be able to read everything he wanted to in one lifetime.

Miss Rowe was something of a mystery to him. She disliked talking about herself, but she did drop an occasional hint. Her only living relatives were a couple of cousins on the West Coast. However, Miss Rowe had come to Cairo from Boston, where something unspecified had apparently rocked her life about a year ago. An accident, an assault, some emotional trauma? Mr. Whitman had no idea. Perhaps she would tell him in time. Whatever it was, Miss Rowe had come to stay in Cairo with just enough money in the bank to pay her rent—and eat.

When Mr. Whitman first met her, she still moved around a bit, going out to buy what she wanted or to drive the back roads and take in the countryside. But now it was virtually impossible for her to leave her apartment. These last few months had seen Miss Rowe put on weight at an astonishing rate. Clearly she had gone past the six-hundred-pound mark, and she showed no signs of slowing down. She had arranged for several local food stores to deliver groceries to her. Fresh supplies arrived daily.

Her apartment had been transformed into the nerve center for this remarkable consumption. Furniture was literally pushed out to make room for the essentials. A schoolboy with a perpetually dazed look on his face came around every afternoon to dispose of the piles of trash that Miss Rowe produced, while she spent most of her time reclining on an arrangement of king-size mattresses, stacked two across two, and an array of pillows. She covered her epic bulk with overlapping sheets.

Around her, within easy reach, like a ring of sophisticated equipment in the intensive-care unit of a hospital, she had a hot plate, a microwave oven, three small refrigerators, a toaster, a blender, a can opener, and shelves for paper plates and plastic tumblers, forks, spoons, and knives. Then there were the garbage sacks and cartons of food.

Mr. Whitman was used to all this because he had become a frequent visitor, as fascinated as he was appalled by Miss Rowe's extraordinary way of life. At first they had argued about it, often heatedly. He would tell her she simply had to go on a diet and get help—whatever it took to stop her from gorging herself incessantly. But Miss Rowe wasn't having any of that. She was happy, positively cheerful about her habits. Mr. Whitman took to reading to her from articles and books on the subject of bulimia, compulsive eating. But she refuted these expertly, pointing out that she never vomited, never purged herself with laxatives, and never suffered any attacks of guilt or depression. In short, she wasn't bulimic.

She enjoyed eating, pure and simple.

Mr. Whitman persisted, explaining to her over and over the dangers, the very real threat to her heart and health. But again Miss Rowe smiled at him and dismissed his warnings. "Your body tells you," she would reply calmly while devouring another can of spiced apple rings. "Most people really don't pay attention to their bodies, but I do. I really do. When it tells me to eat, I eat. When it says enough, then I'll stop." Her body, it seemed, urged her only, always, to eat.

Mr. Whitman then adopted a rather different tactic. He told her about his past travels throughout Europe and Asia, vacations in Mexico and the Caribbean. He went on eloquently and at length about the sights he'd seen and the people he'd met. But travel seemed to hold little interest for Miss Rowe, and in desperation he began describing some of the exotic foods he had eaten abroad. He didn't like doing it, but his reasoning was that if she were sufficiently intrigued she might want to do some traveling of her own, if only to sample foreign cuisine—and then she would have to impose some dietary discipline simply to be able to undertake any trip. That also failed, however. Miss Rowe loved food, but quite indiscriminately. The thought of toad in the hole, coq au vin, Arnold Bennett omelets, prawn vindaloo, Creole crayfish, and five-snake soup aroused no excitement in her. She was perfectly happy to zap three or four chicken pot pies in the microwave, and tamp them down with pickled herring, a few hot dogs, and a quart of applesauce. Miss Rowe was not averse to good food but she had no time for extraneous effort.

Although his concern never diminished—on the contrary, it continued to grow—Mr. Whitman began to concede the struggle after a month or so. The arguments were pointless, in the sense that they achieved nothing. Miss Rowe's confidence was perfect, unbreakable, her appetite supreme. Mr. Whitman could see himself turning into a nag, and that wouldn't do. Besides, by then he liked the girl too much to fight with her. He would still try, with a remark here, a caution there, to get through to her, but he had come to accept her as she was. He hardly realized it, but she had quickly become very dear to him. She was practically the only other person in his life.

The power mower continued to drone down the street, but the breeze had died away for the time being. Mr. Whitman sat on the room's only chair and found his place in the book. As always, a few words of Balzac healed much in life.

"'I was living at that time in a little street you probably don't know...'"

Miss Rowe closed her eyes and listened contentedly. She chewed marshmallows because they were quiet. Books had never interested her, but she loved to hear Mr. Whitman read stories to her. He was very good, seldom stumbling over a word, and he could be dramatic without sounding hammy. No one

else had ever read to her, not even when she was a small child.
"'I don't know how I have been able to keep untold for so
long the story I am about to tell you...'"

He lit a cigarette when he finished the tale. He had made
a point of telling Miss Rowe the very first time they chatted
that he limited himself to ten smokes a day, thinking she might
find a way to apply his example to her own situation. She told
him that she admired his willpower but she did not take up the
suggestion. Now they talked about the story and the author,
with Mr. Whitman carrying most of the conversation and Miss
Rowe saying that "Facino Cane" was beautiful but so sad—and
how many cups of coffee did he say Balzac drank every night?
Finally Mr. Whitman was ready to conclude his visit.

"Please come back and see me this evening," Miss Rowe
said when he stood up.

"Sure, I'll look in later," he promised. Then it occurred to
him that there was something slightly odd in the way she had
spoken. Some hint of urgency. "Are you all right?"

"Oh, yes," Miss Rowe replied, but with pro forma assurance.
"It's just that I'd like to see you again. This evening."

"Fine. Well." Mr. Whitman started to go.

"Something's happening," she whispered breathlessly, to
hold him there a moment longer.

"What is it?" Mr. Whitman asked. Now he was worried.

"I don't know. I just feel...different. Like something is changing inside me. But it's not bad," she added hastily. "It feels good,
in a funny kind of way."

"You can't judge things like that by yourself," he told her
sharply. "I really do think you need to see a doctor. It could be
your heart. Funny signs often mean there is something not at all
funny just around the corner."

"No, no." Then Miss Rowe made an effort to restrain herself
and went on daintily, "I will not be poked and prodded and
tested and otherwise treated like a freak. Next thing you know,
I'd be in the *National Enquirer*. As it is, I worry all day and half
the night that word will get out through one of the delivery
boys and I'll be besieged by reporters, photographers, curiosity seekers, and self-important doctors. I couldn't bear it." She

hesitated, then brightened. "Anyway, I told you: I feel good, not sick. In fact, I've never felt better. I'm tingly all over."

Mr. Whitman sighed unhappily. It would be nonsensical if it weren't fraught with danger. Tingly all over. He couldn't begin to imagine what that meant in terms of her general health. Or in any other way.

And the remark that something was happening—what on earth was he supposed to make of that? He knew that Miss Rowe had a penchant for the dramatic and was always trying to make something out of the sheer uneventfulness of her daily life. That's all there was to it, he tried to persuade himself.

But she did look somewhat different. Miss Rowe's face had a little more color to it than usual. She appeared to be slightly flushed; her cheeks were pink, whereas they were usually rather sallow because she spent all her time indoors.

Mr. Whitman and Miss Rowe touched each other rarely, and then only when their hands met to exchange something. But now Mr. Whitman had to be decisive. He sat down on the edge of the mattresses and held the back of his hand to her forehead.

"Are you running a temperature?" he asked out loud, to make his intentions clear.

"Oh," she said, perhaps a little disappointed. "I don't think so."

"Hmm." Mr. Whitman marveled silently at the feel of her skin. Miss Rowe's head was not as large as a beach ball but gave the impression that it was. He expected it to be soft and spongy with so much fat, but it was surprisingly firm. Although there were layers of jowls pleated below the jawline, her forehead was smooth, nearly taut. The texture was almost silky, and supple. Mr. Whitman discovered he was reluctant to take his hand away. "Perhaps just a slight temperature," he announced, though he was not at all certain.

"I think you're imagining it," Miss Rowe said with a girlish smile. "But it's nice that you care. I don't know what I'd do without you."

You'd just keep on eating, Mr. Whitman thought sadly. But he smiled back, for he was truly fond of the young woman.

"Take it easy," he advised her. "You know, I wish you would

eat more fruits and vegetables and go easier on that junk food."
He had delivered this message countless times.

"Oh, but I do," Miss Rowe insisted enthusiastically. "Did I
tell you that I made a nice big green salad this morning? I did,
all by myself. Greens, and cherry tomatoes."

"Well, that's good," Mr. Whitman responded, his face forming an amused grin. She seemed so proud of herself for managing such a trivial feat. There was something endearingly child-
like about Miss Rowe when she was in this kind of mood.

"I'm surprised more people don't realize how good a salad
can be for breakfast," she went on.

"Yes."

Mr. Whitman left then; otherwise, he would be stuck there
for a long and expanding rhapsody on salads, breakfasts, and
food in general. He went directly to his shop in town, fussed
around the shelves for a little while and then selected Rufus
King's *The Lesser Antilles Case* and Kirby Williams's *The C.V.C.
Murders* for his Saturday night and Sunday afternoon reading
treats.

Back in his apartment, he filled a pilsner glass with cold
beer and looked through the few items of mail he had found at
the shop. There was nothing of much interest except a catalog
from a dealer in St. Paul. He pushed the catalog aside and lit
another cigarette.

Miss Rowe worried him. If something happened to her, if
her heart suddenly gave out, he would be morally responsible.
Now he wondered if he wouldn't also be legally at risk for failing to bring her to the attention of some medical authority. He
had no idea what the law said, if anything, about a situation
like this. Would he be liable to a charge of negligence? Or even
negligent homicide? What was he supposed to do?

It didn't seem fair. Miss Rowe was, after all, an adult, and
as such she was responsible for herself. She was compulsive but
not mentally incompetent. Should his loyalty be directed to her
as a personal friend, accepting her as she was, or to her health
and well-being? The two should not be mutually exclusive,
though in this case they seemed to be. Mr. Whitman thought
that sooner or later he might have to discuss the matter with a

physician—or even a lawyer. But he would mention no names, at least until he had received some guidance. It was now a matter that demanded clarification.

Later, when the sun had gone down but darkness had not yet settled in completely, Mr. Whitman tapped on Miss Rowe's door and entered her apartment. There were no lights on and it was hard to see, but he was aware of her stirring as the sheets rustled softly. Perhaps she had dozed off for a while.

"Turn on the lamp." Groggy, she struggled to hoist herself up against the pillows.

"Am I disturbing you?"

"No, not at all. Come in."

Mr. Whitman switched on the light and took his seat. Her eyes were somewhat puffier than usual, he thought, her complexion even more flushed than it had been that afternoon.

"Come closer," she said. He slid the wooden chair nearer to her bed, wedging himself between one refrigerator and the shelves of paper plates. "No, not there. Here. Sit next to me on the bed, please. I'm feeling kind of down."

Mr. Whitman perched himself cautiously on the edge of the mattresses. He was surprised that Miss Rowe didn't suffer blue moods more frequently. It wasn't right that a young woman in her early twenties should lead such a solitary, reclusive existence. And no matter how strongly she denied it, the constant eating had to take a psychological toll. Mr. Whitman wondered if her usual high spirits were finally beginning to weaken.

"You're so good to me." Miss Rowe took his hand, squeezed it, refused to let go. Her grip was warm and strangely inviting. "I wish I could thank you in some way."

"Oh, don't be silly," Mr. Whitman responded with a nervous smile. "The funny thing is, only a few minutes ago I was telling myself that I've really been quite negligent about you."

"That's not true. Far from it. You've been just the person I needed. Without you, I don't know if I could have…well, you have made all the difference, believe me."

"It's nice to hear that."

She squeezed his hand again. Odd, Mr. Whitman thought. It was almost as if she were comforting him.

"I must look awful," Miss Rowe went on. "I haven't looked in a mirror in ages. Do I...look awful?"

"No, of course not." She wasn't begging for a compliment, but Mr. Whitman naturally wanted to answer as positively as he could. "You do look tired, though, and as I've told you before, you need to make some changes in—"

"I *am* changing," she interrupted, looking away from him but also tightening her grip on his hand. "I *am* changing."

"Good. Well, good." Mr. Whitman didn't know what else to say because he didn't understand what she meant. He had a vague feeling that she was trying to edge him closer to something. "Can you tell me—would you like to tell me—what happened?"

"When?"

"In Boston."

"Oh." She looked at him again and smiled. "Does it make a difference? What if I told you that I killed someone, my family, for instance?"

"I wouldn't believe it," he scoffed. The idea was absurd.

"You see? It doesn't make any difference."

"But something did happen," he insisted. "You must tell me, Frances. It would be good for you to talk about it with a friend you can trust."

They rarely addressed each other by their first names, and Miss Rowe seemed touched. But she merely shrugged and gave him a bewildering smile.

"That's just it," she said quietly. "Nothing happened."

Mr. Whitman found that hard to believe, although there was nothing deceptive or evasive about her manner and tone of voice. On the contrary, they carried the weight of truth.

"I want to talk to someone about you," he told her finally. "I'm sorry if it upsets you, but I have to, and this time I mean to do it."

To his surprise, Miss Rowe didn't object. She nodded slowly as if to say she understood, and she even pulled his hand closer to her. "Not tonight, though," she said. "You won't do anything about it tonight."

"Well, no," he allowed. It was the weekend, after all, and he had no reason to think another day or two would hurt. "First thing Monday morning, though."

"That's all right."

It seemed too easy, and for a few moments Mr. Whitman wasn't sure that he'd actually said what he intended, or that Miss Rowe had fully grasped it. Not that it really mattered; he knew what he was going to do on Monday morning and already he felt a little better about things.

"Lawrence."

"Hmm?" He had to swallow to clear his throat. "Yes?"

"Would you lie down here next to me on the bed?"

Her voice was tiny and distant, painfully vulnerable.

"I just need you to be here with me and to hold me for a few minutes."

Mr. Whitman couldn't speak, but he felt an emotional surge that made his body tremble and his cheeks redden. He slipped off his loafers. *She must be terribly lonely,* he thought. *She needs comfort, a little human warmth.* He stretched out on the mattress and moved tentatively closer to her enormous bulk. Miss Rowe pulled him closer still, until the length of his body was pressed against hers. She handled him easily, almost like a toy doll, so that he had one arm across the expanse of her middle and his head resting on her breast. Then Miss Rowe seemed to sigh and settle, and they stayed that way for some time.

Mr. Whitman was glad that she was under the sheet and he was not. He was more or less paralyzed, caught in a state of diffuse but undeniable erotic tension. Maybe he needed this human warmth, too, and the contact seemed all the more exciting because it was essentially chaste. He stopped thinking about it and let himself enjoy it like this, drifting along dreamily, half awake, until it eventually occurred to him that he had been lying in her embrace for quite a while.

The air was cooler now. The French doors still stood open, and it was dark outside. Miss Rowe's breathing was slightly congested but regular, and her arm slipped away from him when he stirred. She was asleep. He moved carefully, gathered up his shoes, turned off the lamp, and returned to his apartment.

He had another beer and smoked a cigarette. He couldn't sit

in one place for more than a minute. His feelings were alarming, exciting, intense, and above all mysterious to him. Did he love her? Yes, but not as a lover—although he had to admit, there was a disturbing new physical element to it now. The feel of her body and her touch lingered on him like a tactile afterglow. He almost believed that if he looked in the bathroom mirror he would see it on his hand and cheek, a radiance, an aura.

Then a shocking thought came to him. She was *beautiful.* Miss Rowe—Frances. All six hundred-plus pounds of her. She was truly beautiful. And not in spite of her massive size, but because of it. The one thing about her that had frightened and even repelled him now struck him as nothing less than miraculous. Perhaps she did suffer from a dangerous compulsion, but wasn't it also a sign of her strength and courage, her character?

Mr. Whitman drank two more bottles of beer and didn't bother to count the cigarettes. His mind raced, uncovering pockets of illumination where there had been only uncertainty before. Yes, he did love her. In all ways. He would take care of her, more devotedly than ever, but without trying to change her. He would keep her alive, healthy, happy; there were ways. The discipline of love, a better diet.

Somehow it could be made to work.

And in some way, it seemed, he had to surrender to her for her to surrender to him.

Mr. Whitman glanced at the clock, but he didn't care that it was after eleven. He had to see her again, and tell her things. He had to be with her again—for the warmth and the great peace he had found in her embrace.

In the doorway of his apartment, he hesitated one last time. Was he making an idiot of himself, a pathetic middle-aged fool? Was he drunk, deluded, hysterical? He didn't care.

Mr. Whitman listened at her door and heard faint sounds of movement. He tapped, got no response, and then knocked a little louder. Still nothing—but those peculiar noises, muffled and unfamiliar. He turned the handle and went inside. The room was dark, but moonlight through the open French doors provided a bit of definition. His eyes began to adjust.

Miss Rowe was writhing on her makeshift bed like a person

lost in an increasingly uncomfortable dream. She appeared to be asleep, but Mr. Whitman felt a shiver when he noticed that her eyes were half open, glassy, unseeing. She made sounds that were half-strangled in her throat. *A fever,* he thought. *Convulsions?* Something terrible was happening. He banged his knee against a refrigerator and crushed a carton of cheese crackers underfoot as he approached the bed, but Miss Rowe gave no indication that she recognized his presence. Her movements were becoming sharper and more violent by the minute, thrashing and jerking.

Mr. Whitman put his hand on her forehead and was startled to find that she was not feverish at all, but unnaturally cold. Her skin was slick with moisture, her hair smeared back on her skull. More than anything, he was frightened by how cold she felt—but there was something else. Her skin felt different. It was hard, layered, almost scaly.

"Frances?"

Then her head turned again and caught the meager light. Mr. Whitman saw that her eyes had changed. They were closed now, and swollen so tightly that it was all but impossible to make out the thin slits on either side of her nose—itself so broad and flat that it looked as if it had been pressed or squashed to her face. She continued to toss and squirm, but with her arms tight to her body and her legs rigidly straight together, as if she were bound in cord from her head to her feet.

The noises emanating from her grew in intensity, and as she struggled free of the sheet, Mr. Whitman saw that her jowl-ringed flabby neck had altered. It melded smoothly into her shoulders, as if there were no real human neck there at all. And the skin, like that of her face, was so pale that it was almost a brilliant white, shiny as glass.

Mr. Whitman shook with fear, but he could hardly move. He managed to place a hand on her shoulder—the round slope where her shoulder had been—and again he was shocked at how cold she felt. He had to do something, but the idea was nothing more than a disembodied thought in his brain. Miss Rowe escaped the sheet. *Naked,* he realized dimly, *she's naked.* But her body had lost its features—breasts, hips, buttocks—and become a long, large, tubular thing. She was not Miss Rowe. She was something more or less than herself. Something—*larval*.

She struggled mightily on the bed, heaving and shrugging her entire body as if she were trying to escape from that place. Mr. Whitman clambered across the lower part of the bed as he realized she was trying to move herself away from him. It seemed that the most important thing was for her to remain where she was, and to get expert help. It was the only way she might overcome whatever terrible illness has seized her. But Miss Rowe would not remain still. She squirmed vigorously, rolling and flipping, advancing off the edge of the bed. She was so large—for an instant, Mr. Whitman was deeply frightened by the sheer, naked size of her as she reared up at him.

I love you, he thought hopelessly. He threw himself at her, arms spread wide, his legs pushing with all the strength he could muster. He hoped to embrace her and get through to her, to force her back onto the bed. Their bodies met and froze together for a moment, Mr. Whitman clinging to Miss Rowe.

"Frances," he gasped, dizzy with love and fear.

The moment lasted barely a second or two, but it seemed much longer to Mr. Whitman—it was his last. He thought that she recognized him in some way—his warmth, his physical presence, some part of his being. But then whatever forces held her drove Miss Rowe over him with irresistible power, and Mr. Whitman was bent back like a slender blade of grass as she surged and slid on her way. The appliances around the bed, the cartons of food and the shelves—now everything in the way was knocked easily aside like hollow stage props. Picking up speed, Miss Rowe moved into the night and was gone.

In the morning the delivery boy found the French doors wide open. There was a trail of sticky wetness across the back lawn, a wide unbroken ribbon that snaked through the dew on the grass to the unused garden plot. It looked like a tunnel had been dug there, and then had collapsed in on itself. A huge mound of soil had been turned up, and this dirt had the round, nodal appearance of digested earth.

Of Mr. Whitman, there was no trace.

NOCTURNE

In the calm of his middle years, O'Netty made it a point to go for a walk at night at least once a week. Thursday or Friday was best, as there were other people out doing things and the city was livelier, which pleased him. Saturdays were usually too busy and noisy for his liking, and the other nights a little too quiet—though there were also times when he preferred the quiet and relative solitude.

He enjoyed the air, the exercise, and the changing sights of the city. He enjoyed finishing his stroll at a familiar tavern and sometimes seeing people he knew slightly in the neighborhood. But he also enjoyed visiting a tavern that was new to him, and observing the scene. O'Netty was by no means a heavy drinker. Two or three beers would do, then it was back to his apartment and sleep.

O'Netty went out early one particular evening in September and found the air so pleasant and refreshing that he walked farther than usual. A windy rainstorm had blown through the city that afternoon. The black streets still glistened and wet leaves were scattered everywhere like pictures torn from a magazine. Purple and gray clouds continued to sail low across the darkening sky. Eventually he came to the crest of a hill above the center of the city.

He decided it was time to have a drink before undertaking the long trek back. He saw the neon light of a bar a short distance ahead and started toward it, but then stopped and looked again at a place he had nearly passed. The Europa Lounge was easy to miss. It had no frontage, just a narrow door lodged between a camera shop and a pizzeria. The gold script letters painted on the glass entrance were scratched and chipped with age. But the door opened when O'Netty tried it, and he stepped inside. There was a small landing and a flight of stairs—apparently the bar was in the basement. He didn't hesitate. If it turned out to be something not for him, he could simply turn around and leave, but he wanted at least to see the place.

The stairs were narrow and steep. The one flight turned into two, and then a third. O'Netty might have given up before descending the last steps, but by then he saw the polished floor below and he heard the mixed murmur of voices and music. The bottom landing was a small foyer. There was one door marked as an exit, two others designated as rest rooms, and then the entrance to the lounge itself. O'Netty stepped inside and looked around.

The lounge could not have been more than fifteen feet by ten, with a beamed ceiling. But there was nothing dank or dingy about the place. On the contrary, at first glance it appeared to be rather well done up. It had a soft wheat carpet and golden cedar walls. There were three small banquettes to one side, and a short bar opposite with three upholstered stools, two of which were occupied by men a few years younger than O'Netty. Along the back wall there were two small round wooden tables, each with two chairs. Table lamps with ivory shades cast a creamy glow that gave the whole room a warm, intimate feeling.

There were middle-aged couples in the back two banquettes but the nearest one was empty, and O'Netty took it. The bartender was an older man with gleaming silver hair, dressed in a white shirt, dark blue suit and tie. He smiled politely, nodded and when he spoke it was with a slight, unrecognizable accent. O'Netty's beer was served in a very tall pilsner glass.

The music playing on the sound system was some mix of jazz and blues with a lot of solo guitar meditations. It was unfamiliar to O'Netty but he found it soothing, almost consoling in some way. He sipped his drink. This place was definitely unlike the average neighborhood tavern, but it wasn't at all uncomfortable. In fact, O'Netty thought it seemed rather pleasant.

After a few minutes, he realized that the other people there were speaking in a foreign language. He only caught brief snatches of words, but he heard enough to know that he had no idea what language it was. Which was no great surprise. After all, there were so many European languages one almost never heard—for instance: Czech, Hungarian, Rumanian, Bulgarian and Finnish. O'Netty concluded that he had come across a bar, a social club run by and for locals of some such eastern European origin. Before he left, perhaps he would ask the bartender about it.

Although he couldn't understand anything the others said, O'Netty had no trouble catching their mood. Their voices were relaxed, lively, friendly, chatty, and occasionally there was some laughter. It was possible for O'Netty to close his eyes and imagine that he was sitting on the terrace of a cafe in some exotic and distant city, a stranger among the locals. He liked that thought.

Some little while later, when O'Netty was about halfway through his second glass of beer, he noticed that the others had either fallen silent or were speaking very softly. He sensed an air of anticipation in the room.

A few moments later, a young man emerged from the door behind the bar. The music stopped and everyone was still and quiet. The young man came around to the front of the bar. He could not yet be thirty, O'Netty thought. The young man swiftly pulled off his T-shirt and tossed it aside. He was slender, with not much hair on his chest. He kicked off his sandals and removed his gym pants, so that he now stood there dressed only in a pair of black briefs. The other two men at the bar had moved the stools aside to create more space.

The young man reached into a bag he had brought with him and began to unfold a large sheet of dark green plastic, which he carefully spread out on the floor. He stood on it, positioning himself in the center of the square. Then he took a case out of the bag, opened it and grasped a knife. The blade was about eight inches long and very slightly curved. The young man's expression was serious and purposeful, but otherwise revealed nothing.

What now, O'Netty wondered.

Let's see.

The young man hooked the tip of the blade in his chest,

just below the sternum, pushed it in farther, and then carefully tugged it down through his navel, all the way to the elastic top of his briefs. He winced and sagged with the effort, and he used his free hand to hold the wound partly closed. Next, he jabbed the knife into his abdomen, just above the left hip, and pulled it straight across to his right side. He groaned and dropped the knife. Now he was hunched over, struggling to hold himself up, and he could not contain the double wound. His organs bulged out in his arms—liver, stomach, the long rope of intestines, all of them dry and leathery. There was no blood at all, but rather a huge and startling cascade of dark red sand that made a clatter of noise as it spilled across the plastic sheet. The young man was very wobbly now, and the other two at the bar stepped forward to take him by the arms and lower him gently to the ground. The young man's eyes blinked several times, and then stayed shut. The other two carefully wrapped his body in the plastic sheet and secured it with some tape they got from the bag. Finally, they lifted the body and carried it into the room behind the bar. They returned a few moments later and took their seats again. Conversations resumed, slowly at first, but then became quick and more animated with half-suppressed urgency.

After a while O'Netty finished his beer and got up to leave. No one paid any attention to him except the bartender, who came to the end of the bar for O'Netty's payment and then brought him his change.

"By the way, sir, in case you don't know. You can use the fire exit. There's no need to climb all those stairs."

"Ah, thank you," O'Netty replied. "It *is* a lot of stairs."

"Good night, sir."

"Good night."

The fire exit opened onto a long metal staircase that brought him to a short lane that led to a side street just off one of the main avenues in the center of the city. It was already daylight, the air crisp and fresh, the early morning sun exploding on the upper floors of the taller buildings. O'Netty stood there for a few moments, trying to regain his bearings and decide what to do.

Then he saw a city bus coming his way, and he realized it

was the one that went to his neighborhood. It must be the first bus of the day, O'Netty thought, as he stepped to the curb and raised his hand.

CLUB SAUDADE

He followed the woman's directions and had no trouble finding the place, but Jay was disappointed when he got there and actually saw it. The Platts Mills neighborhood was small and isolated, hemmed in by Route 8 on one side and the Naugatuck River on the other, an unpromising location for a club featuring live music. He crossed the bridge, passed under the railroad trestle, and there it was, just as she'd told him—the abandoned brick factory building at the bottom of Bristol Hill.

Jay pulled into the vacant lot across the street and parked. He sat there for a few moments, staring at the three-story building, which stretched halfway up the street. Most of the windows were broken, and some still had rusted old air-conditioning units mounted in them—as if one day everybody had suddenly been given five minutes' notice to leave. The outside walls were engulfed in ragged ivy that reached all the way to the roof of the building in some places. Shrubs that had once no doubt added an attractive decorative touch, now stood more than ten feet tall and the lower branches sprawled across the sidewalk to the curb. Hardly any graffiti, another sign of how abandoned the place was.

Jay checked his watch—he was five minutes early. He got out of his car, locked it, and lit a cigarette. The woman's name was Mimi Grenier. She had approached him the previous Friday night in the bar at Lloyd's Lounge on Route 7 in Danbury, a few minutes after Jay and his band, Nightblue, had finished their set. She told him that she owned and ran Club Saudade in Waterbury, which had grown passably successful over the last few years by appealing to specific audiences—they had assigned nights for Portuguese/Brazilian music, jazz, blues, and one night a week for the metalheads and bikers. That last one would pay for the jazz and blues nights, Jay figured.

The Saudade had lost its lease and been closed for about a month now, but Mimi had just secured a deal to use part of the basement in this old factory building as the new location for the club. She had teams of plumbers, electricians, and carpenters lined up to come in and transform the place, and she hoped to re-open in another month or two. She was insistent that Saudade's following was strong and loyal—when the bookings went well, people came from as far away as Hartford and New Haven—and they would come back again to the new venue.

All of which sounded fine. Though, now that he was there, Jay saw no trucks or vans, no sign of any electricians, plumbers, or builders coming and going. There wasn't even another car in the lot where he was parked, which made him wonder if Mimi herself was even there, waiting for him. But he could see a narrow lane off the street, running along the bottom end of the building. That was where she told him he'd find the entrance. Maybe she had parked her car up that lane.

What really hooked him was what she had said to him about his music, the band's sound, the mix of blues and jazz, rock and other influences from around the world. Since he composed all of Nightblue's original music and chose most of the covers they did, she was in fact praising him for who he was—the creativity, the intelligence, the skill and judgment, for bringing all that together and making it work.

On stage. Live.

And he was ready to hear that—from someone, anybody. Jay had been pushing Nightblue for more than ten years now. His day job in customer service for a big health care insurance company, at the call center in Danbury, was not what anyone would regard as a career. But it allowed him the luxury of working on Nightblue, which he thought of as his true career, his real life's work. Someone would *hear* them. Him.

There were other burdens—the regular personnel hassles, losing his keyboards guy or drummer or guitarist—people do give up, move on—and the difficulty in finding replacements who could fit in and also dug the music. Jay played bass and knew he wasn't anything more than an adequate singer. Over the years, he'd never been able to find a decent vocalist, so Nightblue evolved primarily as an instrumental band, a bit of the blues, a jazz influence, a techno flavor—and then Danny, the synth ace, had a little meth issue come up that landed him inside. It was always the same, kind of like trying to patch a leaky tire while out you're driving around on it.

Oh, and the personal side of it wasn't brilliant either. Jay had pushed on through one failed marriage and two terminated relationships. Nina told him—

—Arrrggh, forget that.

So, what Mimi said to him mattered, the possibility of a regular weekly gig in a place where people came—and listened. That would be so good. He knew that he was probably reading too much into her words, but reading too much into anything that sounded good was par for the course in this business.

If you didn't believe, why bother?

Jay tossed his cigarette to the ground, crushed it out with his heel, and crossed the street. He found the doorway a few steps up the lane. A cardboard sign was tacked to the top of the wooden door, hand-printed, wobbly, in marker pen:

CLUB SAUDADE COMING SOON!

He pulled on the door handle and it opened easily. A steep flight of wooden stairs down to the basement level. He entered the building. The second or third step from the top, the stairs simply collapsed beneath him and Jay fell to the floor below.

Broken boards hit him, the wind was knocked out of him, and pain sprouted up all over his body—dull, sharp, achy, in his bones and muscles. His head throbbed and blared angrily. He didn't move for a long time, lying there gasping, his brain trying to take in all the negative feedback, sort it out and understand.

Dust in the air. Dim light. A heap of pain. A bad memory always turns up when you least need it, and now he heard Nina saying, *You don't live in the real world.* Well, if you could see me now. How real is this? But she was right. Take hope one step too far, and it will fuck you over. That memory wanted to be heard again by him, while Jay was still upstairs, out on the street, and he hadn't listened to it.

Nina would have a sad smile on her face, and turn away.

Someone turning away from you—is not casual.

Jay gathered his breath and slowly pushed himself up from the cement floor. He expected people to come rushing to his aid—Mimi, some workers, anybody. But no one appeared, he was alone. He looked up and saw that the stairs were gone, a pile of loose, rotting lumber jumbled all around him. A couple of dangling, jagged fragments of wood stuck out in the air up by the door. He had fallen twelve, maybe fifteen feet, but at least it didn't feel like he had broken any bones.

A yellow light bulb glowed dimly in the ceiling high above him. So there was electricity here, anyhow, and that vaguely encouraged him. But he could also see that he had no chance of climbing up to the door and getting out. He tried his cell phone, but couldn't get a signal. So he would have to find another door or a window, or stairs.

Jay stumbled into the large room that opened up off the stairway, kicking up dust. But it was not merely dust, it was some silky, very fine powder that blossomed in the air around him, filling his nostrils and lining his throat, choking him. It obscured his vision, burning his eyes, and rubbing them only made it worse. He caught a glimpse of a door in one of the walls, and moved quickly toward it, kicking up more plumes of the noxious gray powder.

Coughing, spitting, he stumbled down three steps and found himself in a much larger room. More yellow bulbs in the ceiling provided the only illumination. Jay looked around, trying to understand what he had gotten himself into. Did Mimi even remember that she had an appointment to meet him there today, at this hour? This room was large enough to serve as the main area for a club, with a stage in one corner, lots of tables, and a bar—he could see that it would all fit. But nothing had been done, no one was here, and it didn't look as if anyone had actually visited the place since it had closed.

He walked around, looking for any possible way out. But

the basement windows had been blocked off with sheet metal, to keep out intruders. Jay thought he might be able to pry or kick the metal loose on one of the windows, if he could reach it—but the sunken floor made that impossible. Perhaps he could find a crate or something to stand on, and a board or a piece of scrap to help work the sheet metal loose.

But, as large as the room was, it was empty. Nothing but dust and long sheets of cobwebs that hung in the dead air. Jay spotted an opening in the wall at the far end of the room. It looked like a corridor or passageway of some kind, but when he got to it he could see that it was more like a tunnel, presumably to some other part of the factory's basement. The yellow lights in the tunnel ceiling tilted at odd angles, and Jay saw that portions of the ceiling had rotted away. Electrical cables dangled, the insulation cracked and fallen away in places, exposing bare, live wires. It baffled him that the power was still on in this deserted building.

He heard a liquid sound, spattering, and then he saw what it was—some thick, whitish fluid dripping from numerous spots in the ceiling, hitting the concrete floor. Jay bent over to touch it, but as he did so, one drop from above landed on the back of his neck, some kind of acid or alkaline pain burning, eating into his flesh. He cried out and jumped away, wiping at it with his hand, then brushing it away on his jacket.

He tried his cell again, again nothing.

Jay sat down on the floor just outside the tunnel and lit a cigarette. He tried to picture how the factory was built, particularly how the basement was structured. There must be separate areas that were used for different purposes, each of them connected by passages like this tunnel. But somewhere, there had to be more access points to and from the outside, as well as stairs to the next floor up.

He stubbed the cigarette out and stood up. The only way to go was forward. *Say goodbye to one London Fog windbreaker,* Jay thought as he pulled his jacket up over his head to protect him from the dripping waste liquid. He ducked low to avoid the dangling wires, and ran through the tunnel—into darkness.

The floor disappeared and he fell another three steps down,

hitting the ground with a thump and a grunt. Okay, so this was another area, a little deeper into the hillside. Jay waited a few moments so his eyes could adjust to the dark. No light seeping in from any blocked windows. The light from the tunnel barely penetrated a few feet. But after a while, Jay picked out what he thought was a very faint glow in the distance.

He began moving cautiously in that direction, one arm held out to detect any floor pillars or other objects he might bump into, his feet slide-stepping along.

You're delusional. That's what Amy had told him. About Nightblue's prospects. Granted, that came shortly before she left him and was part of the process of her making up her mind to do so. She wanted him to get serious. He was in his thirties and had next to nothing to show for it. What, a CD that he'd paid for himself to make, and that nobody wanted? Yes, it was great to follow your dream, but what if your dream led you to a dead end? Jay understood her point, and Jay disagreed. But now, in his present circumstances, it was hard not to recall Amy's words and wonder how he had come to be in this place, this trap. More to the point, how to get out of it.

He continued to move toward the dull suggestion of light—he could still see it ahead of him, though he had gone some little distance already, and it was no brighter. Jay had a shaky sense of up and down in this darkness, but he did get the impression that the glow he saw was closer to the ground, not on a wall or the ceiling. And it was too diffuse to be a light bulb.

His right foot hit something. He reached down to touch it and realized that it was a piece of broken glass. He cautiously patted around the area just in front of his feet, and the stuff was everywhere he touched—broken, jagged shards of glass covering the floor, sticking up dangerously, and it was several inches deep. He tried to move around it, first to one side, then the other, but heaps of glass ranged from one wall to the other.

Jay stood there for a moment, staring at the cloud of pale light ahead, wondering if it would be better to go back to where he had started and try to scale the walls to reach the door. Even if he failed, he could sit there and wait, somebody was bound to come and investigate his car. Sooner or later. He could call out when he heard someone in the area, even if it was just a passing car. Maybe homeless people had broken into the floor above and would return in the evening. Someone was bound to hear him, or find him. It made a certain sense, it was as good an option as any other at this point.

But. Find him. Something about that sounded too—final.

And the glow of light was not that far ahead now. Jay decided that he had to see what it was. If it turned out to be a bust, then he would make his way back and take his chances there. Oddly—it seemed to him—he still felt no sense of alarm, just annoyance at what he was going through, and a certain detached wonderment.

He stepped forward, wagging each foot as he placed it down slowly, to knock aside any pieces of glass that were sticking up. The glass crunched under him, and he could feel bits of it biting into his sneakers at times, but he always raised his foot and shook them off before proceeding the next step. It wasn't quick or easy, but he adjusted, and soon got to be pretty good at knocking the glass down or aside as he walked on it. The pale glow of light drew closer. Jay's confidence bounced back.

You're one of the good guys.

Thank you, Lisa.

I loved you from the first time we met and talked.

Same with me, for you.

But, man. You really want to be a loser.

Jay didn't think that was fair, or accurate. Just because he'd referred once or twice to this great bluesman or that jazz titan, who'd spent entire decades of their lives playing in cheap joints and never making any real money, didn't mean that he wanted to live like that himself. He had no martyr-to-art complex. He was paying his dues, and he believed that would eventually come back to benefit him, and the band.

But Lisa might have been right about one thing. She told him that he was burying himself and the group by staying in Danbury, playing bars and clubs up and down Route 7 and just across the state line in New York. The sound he was working, he needed to be somewhere else—Brooklyn or Boston, Philly or D.C.

Maybe. Probably. But that's just not on. Moving four guys,

five, who have day jobs and girlfriends, one toddler. On spec? Ten years ago, maybe. Jay could do it, but the others couldn't, not ever. Did that make him *true*, or just a wanker?

His right foot came down, and he felt no glass. A firm surface, one angled slightly downward. He stepped forward, left foot down, and both feet went flying out from under him. Jay banged down on something very hard and smooth and slick, as if it were coated with oil, and his body slid on it with astonishing speed. Then it was gone, and he shot off into the air.

Falling.

Hitting something soft, moist, yielding. Stunned, he couldn't move for several moments. He had landed. On something like soil. But looser. Something that smelled richer and riper, like compost.

He looked up. The walls seemed terribly high, and he could tell that they were walls because they were encrusted with chemical deposits that gave off a phosphorescent glow, the only light source. Jay could even make out the dark shadow of the metal ramp that he had stepped on and slid down. It was far, too far above.

Baby, let's give it one more go. He reached into his pocket. It was worth a try, but the deeper you go, the less likely you are to get a signal.

He stayed where he was, lying on his back in the muck, not knowing what to do. Random corners of his brain opened briefly, asking *Okay?* or *Close?* and then shutting by themselves, as if they didn't in fact care what he wanted to do. It interested him a bit, but Jay didn't exactly care either, because caring wouldn't make any difference.

It wasn't long before he felt the movement—something going on that vibrated in the ground and hummed into his body. He put his hands down to push himself up—and his fingers closed around some bones. It was the lower arm and hand of a human being. He dropped it, and it occurred to him that the most amazing thing about him might be that he was so calm, could look at things and think about them without getting shook. While at the same time, he could be so hopeful and expectant about what he did.

The soil rose up in front of him, a creature emerged, something like an enormous salamander, wet and black, iridescent gold streaks and splotches on its back, claws on its rather small front paws, something with a history and nature about which Jay knew nothing. Bands of teeth were exposed as the beast opened its mouth and moved toward Jay, who didn't even try to move now. The monster lunged at him, its jaws plucking him off the ground, clamping down across his chest, lower abdomen, and hips. Jay could feel himself giving in, no longer even caring. He tried to rally, uselessly.

The women were right.

FOR NO ONE

Frank was eighteen, a year older than Gregory, and this deal was his idea in the first place, so Gregory had little say in how they would do it. If Frank wanted to wait another twenty minutes, they would wait. Gregory stood and bounced on one foot, then the other, but the movement didn't help his nerves. Frank sat on a tree stump, looking calm and unconcerned, as if it were just another empty afternoon.

"You really think this guy has money?"

"Bound to be something," Frank replied. "No wife, no kids, not even a dog. He's middle-aged, been working all his life, but he lives in a house that's, like, an overgrown shack. He drives an old car and he never goes anywhere except places like the supermarket and the post office. This guy was always a little weird, okay? So, you tell me: what does somebody like that do with his money?"

"I don't know," Gregory said. "Put it in a bank?"

Frank's laugh was like a loud bark. "You hear the story about that guy who died in his armchair? It was on the news."

"No, what guy?"

"Some old fool," Frank said. "He died alone in his shitty apartment somewhere in New York and they didn't come find the body until the smell got real bad. The place was a cesspool. It turns out this guy was living on dog food and crackers. He kept the heat and lights off most of the time, he wore an overcoat indoors and he slept in his armchair. That was how they found him—dead, in his overcoat, sitting in the armchair. But here's the thing. There's half a million bucks stacked up in the fridge, stuffed in the sofa cushions, in the vacuum cleaner bag—anywhere you could hide wads of bills."

"*Half a million?*"

"Really."

Gregory stopped bouncing on his feet and thought about it for a few moments. Yeah, you heard stories like that now and then, but he still had his doubts. He'd seen the guy's place the week before, when he and Frank scoped it out from the woods behind Lyons Court. It was a dumpy old house with curling shingles and tarpaper on the outside, rusted appliances in the small yard, and a one-car garage with a saggy roof. It wasn't the kind of place where you'd expect to find anything but loose change.

Still, it was an easy target. Anything they took away from it would be that much more than they had when they went in. And Frank knew what he was talking about. He'd grown up on that narrow dead-end street, Lyons Court. Frank had seen the guy at close range for years.

The man's name was Halloran. He kept to himself, he seldom said more to anybody than hello and maybe a few words about the weather. He went to work in the morning and came home between five-thirty and six in the evening. He worked at the newspaper office downtown, several miles away. He never had any visitors. That was as of three years ago, when Frank's family moved into half of a duplex over on Mercier Boulevard, but Halloran's routine was probably still the same.

"Isn't it time yet?" Gregory asked. "Seems like an hour ago we saw him drive by on his way to work."

Frank checked his watch. "Yeah, close enough."

They picked up their backpacks, crossed Ferguson Avenue and walked down the long alley behind the abandoned Bonder Nickel Plating mill. A patch of rubble-strewn waste ground, then up the wooded hillside. A few minutes later they reached the crest, and the back of Halloran's house was less than thirty yards away. None of the other houses on Lyons Court were visible, which also meant that none of the neighbors could see them. Even so, Frank and Gregory crouched at the edge of the woods for a few minutes, watching to be sure nobody was in the immediate area.

"Okay," Frank said at last. "Let's take this sucker down."

On Northbury Avenue, Halloran unconsciously eased up on the gas pedal as he drove past Ponzillo's. He'd taken Sylvana there for pizza once and she liked it so much they went back several more times that same month, now nearly a year ago. He had such good memories of her being happy there with him, smiling, laughing, chatty, her unpredictable sense of humor lighting him up inside.

But there was also an evening at Ponzillo's when she first hinted to him that she might not stay, after all. Sylvana could say certain things in an offhand way, as if she had no understanding of what they really meant or how the words pierced him. It would be easy for Halloran to take another route to and from work each day, but he never did.

The heavy mist had given way to a steady rain by the time he swung the car into Lyons Court and parked in front of his garage. Halloran dashed from the car to the side door that opened into the kitchen. He slid the key in, turned it, and started to push. He immediately felt the door hit something on the other side. He stood there for a moment, stunned by what he saw. The kitchen was a mess, with every drawer and cupboard door hanging open. The floor was strewn with broken dishes, cups and glasses, utensils, cans and packages of foodstuffs. An empty canister, sugar dumped on the scarred old linoleum.

Details blurred. Halloran was only dimly aware of himself as he stepped through the kitchen. Not much damage in the dining room that he seldom used anyway. Cushions slashed in the living room, tufts of stuffing yanked out, and scores of books tossed from the shelves.

He kept moving. Up the narrow flight of bare wooden stairs. Not to his bedroom first—although he caught a glimpse of the shambles in there through the open door—but to the small front room where he would sit in his armchair for a while each night, smoking cigarettes, drinking a couple of bourbons, alone with his thoughts.

He rushed into the room, and the daffodils he was carrying slipped from his hand. Halloran felt as if he were sinking through the floor, and the floor below, down into the earth itself.

Right away it looked like a loser to Gregory. They got in through the cellar door, below a hatchway. Frank popped the simple hook lock with his shoulder. There was a workbench and a lot of tools, a laundry area, and an oil furnace with a hot water tank in the middle of the cellar. They found no hiding places and nothing of value.

They went upstairs and Frank started in on the kitchen. He was working himself into an angry state, swearing and throwing things around carelessly, so Gregory got out of the way and busied himself in the adjacent dining room. It didn't contain much, just table linens and dishes in two corner cabinets. There wasn't even any real silverware.

It was the same everywhere they searched on the ground floor—no money, nothing of any use to them. Frank was cutting open sofa cushions in the living room with a steak knife. Gregory found the vacuum cleaner in a closet in the passageway nearby. There was a bag half-full of dust inside it, nothing else.

"Hey, the books," Frank said with sudden excitement. "People hide money in the pages of books."

Gregory looked around the living room. There were some built-in bookcases containing hundreds of books. But it didn't take long for the two of them to pull every one, flip the pages and toss it aside. All they came up with were a few bookmarks and funeral cards.

"Fucker's pissin' me off," Frank snarled.

"People usually keep their valuables in their bedroom," Gregory said. "If he's got anything, that's probably where it is."

Frank went at it in Halloran's bedroom while Gregory took the other room upstairs. It was smaller, and on the front side of the house. It was probably meant to be a second bedroom, but now it was almost empty. There was nothing in it except for a few items in the back corner, behind the door. A fat, overstuffed old armchair, and hassock, and a floor lamp. Beside the armchair was a rectangular coffee table, only about two feet by three. A few books on the floor. An end table stood on the other side of the armchair, and it held several bottles of liquor—at last, something they could take away. But Gregory's gaze went back to the glass-topped coffee table and the items that had been carefully arranged on it.

It was a kind of shrine. In the center was an 8x10-inch photograph, standing in a cheap cardboard frame. It was a close-up of a young woman with long black hair, dark eyes, and honey skin. Gregory thought she might be Hispanic, in her twenties. Good-looking, but the expression on her face and in her eyes was what grabbed and held him. She wasn't smiling. She looked intense, defiant, maybe even a little angry. It was a face full of powerful feelings, not easy to read. You could look at her, and just keep on looking. Yeah, she was hot, but trouble, Gregory figured.

Candles of different heights and colors surrounded the photograph, and there was a vase with a small bouquet of somewhat droopy flowers. A number of snapshots were laid out flat on the table. She was in every one. An older man appeared with her in a couple of them. It had to be Halloran. You could tell that he'd held the camera at arm's length, aimed it as best he could, and clicked. Gregory thought at first that maybe she was his daughter but then he remembered Frank saying that the guy had no family. Besides, in one photo they both had their mouths open and their tongues were playing together. They looked wicked happy.

Gregory exhaled. *Fuck me.*

Also on the table, off to one side, was a small folder. He picked it up and quickly looked inside. More snapshots, and the negatives. Gregory took the pictures halfway out of the sleeve and flipped through them—all of them with that girl. *Her, her, her.*

From the other room came the whirlwind sounds of Frank's growing rage, the grunts, things being thrown. Gregory snatched up the 8x10 in the cardboard frame along with the loose snapshots and the folder with the rest of the pictures and the negs. He shoved them all into his backpack, then he walked across the landing to the wreckage in the other room.

"Anything?" Gregory asked.

"Yeah, a fuckin' ten-dollar bill on the bureau."

"There's booze in the other room," Gregory said. "Maybe eight or ten bottles, some of them unopened. Let's wrap them in towels and then get the hell out of here."

You are the best thing that ever happened to me, she said. Her eyes were brimming with tears but the look on her face was one of great joy. *I want to stay here with you forever.*

Now, that was all he had left, a hoarding of words remembered and scenes replayed in his mind. Nothing could be worse than the agonies he'd suffered when he lost Sylvana, the days and nights when raw physical pain ran riot throughout his body. But this, to have the last tangible signs of her presence taken away from him, closed him out. Halloran was alone, lost in his own home. He had nothing left of her to hold onto, nothing to gaze at in moments of bittersweet recollection. His loss was complete now, and all he saw ahead for himself was barren, a desert.

It was like a fairytale, and it began on a Saturday afternoon early in September, last year. Halloran was in the backyard stacking firewood when he heard screams coming from the woods. He took a piece of oak and ran toward the sound—they were the cries of a woman. He came into a small clearing and saw two young women beating a third one, who was trying to break away. Halloran yelled and rushed toward the group. The other two women turned and fled into the woods, down the hill.

He approached the one who had fallen to the ground. She gasped and sobbed, her body shuddering. She had cuts and bruises on her arms, forehead, and face.

"It's okay now. They're gone."

"Don't leave," she pleaded. "They'll come back."

"Don't worry. Come on, I'll get you out of here."

He managed to calm her somewhat, and led her to the house. They sat at the kitchen. While he cleaned her wounds and applied disinfectant, she gave him a jumbled, confused explanation—that those women wanted to kill her because of a man who she was not even involved with, at least not anymore. Halloran would have thought it silly and incredible if he had not actually seen them attacking her. Crimes of passion, soap opera. But here she was, injured and clearly frightened, telling him she had nowhere to go, that she'd spent the previous night hiding in the abandoned nickel mill. The other women spotted her on the street and chased her into the woods. He nodded but didn't know what to think or say.

"My name's Jim."

"I'm Sylvana."

Sylvana from the woods, he thought. She had beautiful skin and eyes, and long dark hair. She was wearing a Simpsons T-shirt, dirty jeans, and sneakers. When he finished treating her wounds, he heated some soup and made grilled cheese-and-tomato sandwiches. She ate everything eagerly. Then she sat back in the wooden chair and peered anxiously across the table at him. She looked meek and fearful.

"You saved my life."

He had to smile at that. It seemed far too dramatic. "Oh, I don't think they would have gone that far."

"They would!" she insisted. "You don't know them."

"Well, I'm glad I was able to help."

She looked down at the plate still in front of her and was silent for a few moments. Her hair fell forward, partially masking her face, though he could still see her eyes when she looked up at him. Halloran guessed that she was in her mid-twenties, but she still looked girlish. Finally, she spoke again, her voice tiny and desperate.

"Can I stay here tonight? In a chair, or on the floor? I don't have anywhere else to go, except that factory. Tomorrow morning I'll figure out what to do. Get a bus out of town, maybe."

"You have *nowhere* to go? No family or friends?"

She shook her head forcefully. "Nobody I can trust."

Halloran felt no instinctive doubt or suspicion, no sense of danger in her presence. It might be a mistake but he didn't care. More than twenty years ago, the woman he was in love with told him that they were through—only a week before they were to be married. He was utterly crushed, and he knew that he'd never entirely recovered from the experience.

Since then his life was uneventful, routine and empty,

largely by his own choice—as if he had sentenced himself. He didn't care too much about anything. He did his job and he even enjoyed it to a certain extent—he was in charge of the archives and library department in the basement at the city newspaper. He kept mostly to himself. But now, after going so long with nothing, there was nothing to consider.

"Yes, you can stay here."

Sylvana let her breath out in a rush, her shoulders relaxing in relief, and then a lovely smile erased all the apprehension from her face. "Thank you. Thank you, Jim."

She didn't talk much that evening because she was tired, yawning constantly from lack of sleep. They watched television, but she nodded off several times, waking with a start, apologizing, then drifting off again. He gave her a spare set of his pajamas and she spent some time in the bathroom while he removed the back cushion and laid out sheets, a pillow, and blanket on the sofa for her. The pajamas were too large for her and she looked very cute when she padded into the room, the cuffs folded back at her ankles and wrists. She could hardly keep her eyes open. She came and hugged him, smelling of soap and toothpaste.

"Thank you, Jim. You're so nice to me."

He turned the lights off and sat there, watching TV with the volume down low. Watching her on the sofa. Sylvana fell asleep almost at once, and her breathing assumed a steady rhythm. He stayed there for another half hour or so, then turned off the television and quietly went upstairs. He read a William Trevor story. He lay awake in the dark for a while, hearing only the sounds of the house itself.

Halloran was a light sleeper and he heard her moving when she was still on the stairs. He turned his head toward the door, opened his eyes, and tried to focus. Not yet dawn. Gray light filtered in around the shades and faintly illuminated the room. Sylvana appeared, moving like a child who is not really awake. She groped at the blanket on his bed, slid in between the sheets, and snuggled close to him, her body pressed against his. Halloran expected to hear her breathing fall back into its sleep rhythm again, but he didn't. After a few moments Sylvana moved even closer to him and he felt the warmth of her breath on his cheek and his ear.

"You're trembling. It's okay, Jim. *I want you.*"

Out of dreams, into his life. Sylvana changed everything. Halloran had been sleepwalking his way through a colorless life for more than twenty years, but now he was awake again, and he savored every minute of it.

They made love each morning, sleepy, fast, then luxuriating in the gorgeous afterglow. And again each night, more slowly, elaborately, often playfully—Sylvana loved to tease him and to play at sex, embellishing and heightening their passion.

She had nothing but the clothes she was wearing in the woods, so he took her out and bought her a skirt and blouse, a few more T-shirts, an extra pair of jeans, sandals, socks, underwear, and even a couple of pieces of lingerie.

They cooked together, teaching each other simple dishes, comfort foods. They watched movies, lying together on the big old sofa, feeding each other popcorn, licking and sucking butter from each other's fingers. It was like playing house, Halloran occasionally thought in moments of secret doubt and worry. It was exciting, it was enormous fun, and it brought him constant joy, pleasure, and a lot of laughs. She brought him happiness. He also knew there was something unreal about it, but he didn't care. He loved it and he wanted it never to end.

Sylvana seemed to enjoy it as much as he did. She told him that she had never been happy or felt safe until the first morning when she woke up there with him. Early on, Halloran didn't know how much to believe her when she spoke like that—she told him she loved him that first Sunday, and it startled him at the time. The words seemed to come too easily, or perhaps she just used them more casually. But the expression in Sylvana's eyes was always persuasive, her manner compelling and endearing. Before long, he believed everything she said.

Halloran went to work each day fearful that she would not be there when he returned home in the evening. He called her during his two breaks and at lunchtime. Sylvana answered promptly, and each evening she was at the door, bouncing on her toes, eager to jump into his arms. She seemed so happy that Halloran sometimes felt humbled and even unworthy.

"Are you sure?" he asked her one night when they were on the sofa, kissing and cuddling, not really watching television.

"Sure about what?"

"Me. Living here. Everything."

"Yes, yes, yes."

Sylvana's answer was immediate, and the look of love on her face had a fierceness that moved him deeply. He would not doubt this woman. He had not thought of love for so long that it almost seemed like a foreign language, one that he would never know or even need to know.

"Are you sure?" she asked.

"Yes. Totally."

"You won't get tired of me and throw me out?"

"Sylvana, I love you."

There it was. The words felt natural and necessary, clamoring to be released. Halloran's heart was racing, and the power of his feelings awed and thrilled him. Sylvana gasped and stared at him, tears welling up in her eyes. She hugged him tightly and kissed his face again and again, speaking his name with each kiss.

He wanted to know all about her, but that was one subject she would not go into, waving away her past as of no importance. Apparently, most of it was unhappy or difficult in varying degrees, a life she was glad to escape and had no desire to discuss. Halloran didn't push it. In time she might feel more comfortable and be willing to talk about it. For now, he was content to let the situation remain as it was, so their love could continue to unfold and grow.

One day when they were picking up a few things at the drug store, he slowed as he passed a rack of disposable cameras. He hadn't owned or used a camera since the romance and engagement that had ended so painfully and abruptly. Later, he destroyed every picture of them. He hadn't mourned or languished in self-pity. He'd drifted off to a place by himself, and never really left. The bitterness faded some. You can't forget, but you can learn to live as if you have forgotten, and get by.

That was a very long time ago. Halloran stared at the rack for a moment, and then he picked up one of the camera packs.

I was so fuckin' horny for you this afternoon, man, I wanted to take the bus into town and go right into your office and drag you into the bathroom or a closet, anywhere, and pull your clothes off and suck your dick until it's real big and hard and you're dyin' because it feels so good, and then I jump on it and you slam deep into me and we rock and bang like thunder, and we scream like crazy when we come.

Halloran poured another three fingers of Wild Turkey and lit another cigarette. He had replayed every scene in his mind hundreds of times, knew them all by heart, and could recall huge chunks of their talk verbatim. He'd spent nearly a year reconstructing that month, day by day, hour by hour, and he always thought the same thing: it had been glorious.

Until that evening at Ponzillo's. He raised the possibility of looking for a new house. A cute little Cape in a better neighborhood, perhaps. He had never considered moving until Sylvana entered his life. Now he liked the idea of providing them both with a much nicer setting. A place with a real yard and a lawn, with flowerbeds. Halloran had been thinking about it for a couple of days before he mentioned it to her. But as he was speaking he saw a troubled look cross her face.

"What's the matter?"

"Nothing."

But the corners of Sylvana's mouth were slightly turned down and she avoided his eyes.

"No, tell me. What's wrong, sweetie?"

She shrugged helplessly. "It just seems so—big. A big thing to do. Buy a new house. I mean, wow."

Halloran changed the subject, and soon she was as cheerful and buoyant as usual. But he worried. He knew that it wasn't the idea of a new house that seemed so "big" to her. It was her life with him and the years ahead that were implied by a new house. Perhaps it occurred to her that she didn't really want all those years with him, with the age difference. Perhaps Sylvana was already losing interest in him.

I love you so fuckin' much, man.

The evening after Ponzillo's, he was broiling steaks and he noticed her regarding him with a strange look. He asked her what she was thinking about. Her face turned sad and she looked away.

"I was thinking I don't deserve you."

"That's silly," Halloran said, feeling helpless.

She didn't respond.

Maybe she just got tired of playing house with him, of sitting alone there for hours every day, trying to keep busy tidying up, watching TV, but always cut off, alone. At first it was probably easy for her, but maybe it had become tedious. She may have thought she wanted everything he offered, but was incapable of accepting it and living with it.

It was a Friday and they had simple weekend plans: dinner that evening, some shopping Saturday afternoon, followed by dinner out and a movie, brunch out and a drive in the country Sunday. Was that too simple and dull? He got home, and she was gone. It was final—she'd taken all her clothes and things, leaving only the packet of snapshots. She had placed it on the kitchen table, like a farewell message.

Later, he found another wordless gesture upstairs. A clothes hanger left on the bed, the closet door open. Sylvana had taken one of his shirts, the dark blue one that she liked most. A few times she'd been wearing that shirt, and nothing else, when he arrived home from work.

Halloran fell into a pit of misery. He missed a week of work, his body ravaged by violent reactions, like a drug addict in withdrawal. He could hardly eat anything, it wouldn't stay down, and he smoked and drank too much, trying desperately to numb himself. In a remarkably short period of time, she had threaded her way through the entire fabric of his being.

He felt scoured out, gutted. Eventually, he started to function again. He went back to work, back into the old arid existence he'd known before Sylvana. He still hoped, foolishly, that she might return or at least call him on the phone.

That notion was demolished three weeks after she left by an item in the newspaper. A young woman killed at a nightclub in the South End. Her name was Sylvana Ramos. She was there with a man, and she was stabbed repeatedly by two other women when she went to the ladies room. It was a love triangle, the exact details still unclear. Sylvana bled to death before the ambulance arrived.

You're a wonderful lover, a beautiful man with a beautiful heart, so full of kindness and love.

"My heart is yours," he told her.

As long as you love me and take care of me, I'll love you and take care of you.

At first his pain was suffused with bitterness and anger. Even if she meant such words when she said them, she must have known that sooner or later she would betray him. He hated her for those lies. He hated himself for believing her. Most of all, Halloran hated the fact that he had let himself believe in love again.

With the terrible news of Sylvana's death, most of the anger seemed to evaporate out of him. His pain diminished to a persistent low ache that would probably never disappear. But other feelings emerged that gave him strength and solace. Astonishment at how much happiness, joy, and pleasure they had created together in that one month. Halloran felt oddly bewildered and grateful—like a diseased man who has experienced a miracle without actually being healed.

He had an enlargement made of the snapshot he liked the best, the one that captured some of her fierce love and hunger for life. He set it up on the coffee table with some of the other pictures laid out around it. He added a few candles and a vase of daffodils, which he always replaced as soon as they started to wilt. Every night he sat there for a while, had a drink or two, and thought about her. Sometimes his anger smoldered and flared again, but most nights he found comfort in the photos of Sylvana and his memories of their time together.

You're the first man who makes me happy to be alive. I love, love, love you, I love you so fuckin' much, man.

But now, every physical trace of her was gone. Halloran sat in the armchair and stared at the empty spaces on the coffee table. All that he had left of Sylvana was inside his head, and that scared him. He feared that he would begin to forget—small details at first, floating away like specks of dust plucked up by a lazy breeze, thinning out slowly in the air, vanishing. What did they do on the fourth day? The fifth, the eleventh? Would he begin to lose the clear mental image he had of Sylvana's face? That thought was in itself enough to bring new desolation to him, a sense of the blackness gathering around.

Halloran splashed a little more Wild Turkey into the glass. He lit a cigarette and shot a jet of smoke out into the air. It came back to him again, something she said the night before she left him. He didn't pick up on the sorrow in her eyes at the time. Four beautiful words. Four words that also signified the end.

I'll always love you.

Gregory shut his bedroom door. He had a plastic grocery bag balled up in one hand. He took the backpack out of the closet and sat down on his bed, up against the headboard. Several days had passed since he and Frank broke into the house. He took the pictures out. He'd looked at them before, at least once a day, in fact.

He'd been having some weird reactions lately, and it was because of these damn pictures. Last night he dreamed that a bunch of soldiers kicked down his bedroom door and pointed automatic rifles at him. They found the backpack and they dragged him away. It ended at that point, but he woke up gasping and terrified.

And the feeling that people, maybe the cops, were watching him. He knew that nobody was going to question him about a break-in that netted ten bucks and a little booze, but Gregory got the point. The photos linked him to Halloran's house and they were the cause of all his uneasiness. He had to get rid of them.

Not that he wanted to. He liked looking at them. At her. Oh, she was hot, with full juicy lips, burning eyes, and all that hair. One shot was mildly revealing. It showed her kneeling on a bed, her legs wide apart. She was sitting back on her upturned heels. She was naked from the waist up, but her long hair hung forward, so that only the inner curves of her breasts were visible. She was wearing a half-slip, and it rode up so high you could see her pale pink thong and even make out the bulge of her pussy. She had a wicked smile on her face.

But Gregory felt something more than desire when he looked at the photographs, especially the large close-up of her face. He saw pain, hurt, and anger not far below the surface, and in some way he recognized them as his own, but his feelings disturbed him. *You want to fuck her, but she could be your twin sister, your twin self. Crazy shit like that!*

He tore the photos into shreds and put them in the plastic bag, along with the negatives. The 8x10 was the last one. He stared at it, still reluctant to part with it. *Who are you? Come over here and fuck me sometime.* He ripped up the picture and the frame, and then tied the bag tightly. Later, he shoved the bag into a litter box on Division Street.

After Gregory disposed of the photographs, he walked a few blocks to the Mohawk Market and hung out by the video games at the back of the store for a while, drinking soda. He and Frank met there every afternoon, unless they'd made other plans. Though, the last couple of days, Frank had not shown. *What's up with that?* Gregory wondered.

He hoped that Frank hadn't found a new bitch, because then Frank wouldn't be around until he got tired of playing with her. Couldn't blame him if that was the case, though. It had been a while since Gregory'd gotten any, and he was definitely missing it. He had stopped going to high school back in the spring. Maybe that wasn't such a good idea after all, because he got more in school than he did out of it. Gregory waited a while longer and played a couple of games. Back home, he called Frank's house.

"Hello, who is it?" Frank's mother shouted into the phone a moment later. She sounded annoyed and impatient.

"This is Gregory, Frank's friend from school."

"He's not here. Hasn't been here for two days." She didn't sound the least bit concerned or even interested.

"Oh. Where did he go?"

"How would I know that?" *Click.*

Two days now. Gregory was pissed, and he still felt uneasy.

Mist hung in the air all morning but the sun burned it away as the sky cleared early in the afternoon. Gregory hated living at home and was glad to get out of the house. He checked the Mohawk, but Frank was still a no-show. Three more days had passed. Gregory called Frank's house again that morning but his mother said they still hadn't heard from him, and she still didn't seem to care.

Gregory was hanging around outside the Music Den when his heart jumped for a second and his mouth opened. The woman—the one in the photographs—was walking along the sidewalk in his direction. There was no doubt in his mind. He tried to act casual, as if he were paying no special attention to her, just scoping her in a glance the way men do. Yeah, she had the same hair, the same eyes, and the same strong expression on her face. She was wearing black jeans, a plain light blue T-shirt, and sneakers. She also had a man's dark blue shirt draped over her shoulders and back, its long sleeves tied loosely over her breasts.

She was a little shorter than Gregory would have guessed from the pictures. Slightly older too, and as of right now rather tired and drawn, as if she hadn't slept much lately. Still, she was a woman of striking appearance. She walked past Gregory. He didn't think twice, and fell in step a few yards behind her, curious to find out where she was going.

It took him a couple of minutes to get over his surprise. He had no idea that she still lived around here. From the way that poor bastard had the table set up, with the candles, flowers, and pictures, Gregory figured that she had either died or gone far away.

He didn't follow too closely, but kept her in sight. She walked at a deliberate pace and never slowed down to look in a shop window. Fifteen minutes later, she turned right onto Cormier Boulevard. Gregory realized that she must be going to see Halloran. Lyons Court was off Cormier, at the crest of the hill about a hundred yards ahead. He trudged along behind her and barely hesitated before entering the narrow lane.

Lyons Court angled to the left and then curled around to

the right, along the ride of the hill, a bit like a reversed question mark. Gregory moved more quickly when he lost sight of her briefly. He figured it was almost three in the afternoon. Maybe Halloran was already home, or she had a key and would let herself in. Gregory's curiosity was stoked. He had no idea until now that the two of them were still happening.

She stood at the edge of the property, looking at the house. The whole yard was cordoned off with yellow police tape. Then Gregory saw that the upper floor and roof of the house were gone, collapsed. The house was burned out, only the ground floor walls still stood. The interior was visible through the empty windows and doors, filled with rubble, ash, and jagged pieces of charred lumber and shingles.

The sight so startled Gregory that he walked right to the spot where the chick was, almost without noticing her. She glanced briefly at him, then looked back at the ruins of the house.

"What happened?" he asked.

"The man who lived there was sitting in a chair in one of the rooms upstairs. It was late at night. He'd been drinking. When he fell asleep, or passed out, he dropped a lit cigarette. The chair caught fire. He died from the smoke. You know, suffocated."

There was something kind of dark and smoky about her voice that got right inside Gregory's head, and he liked it.

"You know him?"

She appeared to hesitate, and then all she said was, "I saw the story about the fire. It was in the paper a few days ago."

"You live around here?"

"No, but I'm staying down there." She pointed toward the trees and bushes beyond the burned house.

"What?" Gregory was confused. "In the woods?"

"No, the empty factory at the bottom of the hill."

"You're shittin' me. Why're you staying there?"

"I had to get away from some people and I had nowhere else to hide. They want to kill me."

"That sucks," he said.

"You want to see where I'm staying? Hang out a while?"

All right. "Sure."

"My name is Sylvana."

"Gregory."

"Come on," she said, ducking under the police tape.

As they made their way through the woods and down the hillside, she babbled on, telling him some complicated story about this guy she loved and some other bitch who was also crazy about him. That was the one who wanted to kill Sylvana, Gregory figured, whatever. He was not paying too much attention to what she said. His eyes were on her ass, nicely rounded and tight in those jeans. He loved the way it bounced as she moved.

At one point the path opened into a small clearing. He grabbed her arm and pulled her around into his arms. He kissed her—and she kissed him right back, her tongue jumping into his mouth. Then she pushed loose and grinned at him for a second or two before turning away and continuing on toward the factory. Gregory hurried to keep up with her.

She led him to the main office building in the abandoned Bonder Nickel complex. They went in through a boarded-up basement window that had been kicked in. He followed her upstairs to the second floor, to an office at the end of one corridor. The room was dark because the windows were covered outside with sheet metal, but Sylvana struck a match and lit a couple of candles on the floor. Gregory saw a sleeping bag nearby, a backpack that looked full, and some juice bottles. Otherwise, the room was empty. It wasn't a great place to stay but it wasn't nearly as bad as Gregory had expected.

"My friend Maria brought me a few things."

"Why don't you stay with her?"

"No, that other bitch would soon find out. I can't bring trouble to my friend's house."

"Why don't you call the cops?"

Sylvana laughed. "Yeah, the cops. Hey, maybe I could stay with you? In your room? What do you think?"

Gregory chewed his lip and thought about it. Wow, this fine bitch in his bedroom. "I'd have to ask my father. I could talk to him tonight."

She gave him an odd smirk. "Yeah. Maybe tomorrow."

Sylvana unzipped the sleeping bag and opened it out on the floor. She untied the man's shirt she had on her shoulders, folded it neatly and set it down as a makeshift pillow. Then she stretched out on the sleeping bag and looked up at Gregory.

"Come here, baby."

"You know what love is?"

"Yeah, sure," Gregory said.

He was lying flat on his back. Sylvana sat beside him, one hand between his legs, slowly stroking him. She kissed him repeatedly, though none of her kisses were as long or as deep as he wanted. Gregory figured they were just warming up. He played with her tits.

She laughed. "No, I meant, have you ever been in love? Do you know what love really feels like?"

"I think I'm falling in love right now."

Sylvana laughed softly again. "You're sweet. But love isn't always easy. Sometimes love hurts."

"So I've heard."

"Love makes your blood pound and your hands shake. Look, I'll show you. Hold your hand close to my breast, but don't touch it."

Gregory raised his hand an inch or two from her left tit. He noticed that his heart was beating faster and his fingers were moving—he couldn't hold them perfectly still.

"You see? And there's a tightness in your chest."

Gregory felt a sudden weight across his upper body, as if he had a heavy iron chain wrapped tightly around him.

"Your eyes get red because you can't sleep, or from crying so much, and they hurt even when you keep them closed."

His vision turned blurry and he felt tiny threads of fire burning from his eyes back into his brain.

"Sometimes you have no feeling in your arms and legs."

Gregory's hand fell away from her breast, as if his muscles had turned to jelly, and he couldn't move.

"One time I was in love," Sylvana continued, "and I had it so bad I couldn't sleep at night. I'd drift off but then wake up a few minutes later, always with a vicious headache. Sometimes love is a sickness."

He winced as a bolt of pain shot through his head. Then it felt as if his brain was pulsing, pressing against the sides of his skull, as if it wanted to explode out of his head and escape.

"And I broke out in spots," Sylvana said. "Thousands of them. It was a rash of some kind. The itching drove me crazy. I'd sit there and dig up my own flesh, scraping it raw and bloody."

Gregory felt his skin writhing, all over his body—but worst of all on his face, one eruption after another, then fiery cascades of them. He wanted to rub and scratch all over but he couldn't move his hands. He opened his mouth and made a short, strangled sound.

"Yeah, I had crying attacks, too," she said. "You know what they're like? You can be anywhere, at work, buying food at the store, and in an instant your face balloons up with blood and the tears are just pouring out of you, and you can't stop sobbing."

Gregory's body heaved and shuddered with violent gasps. Hot tears blinded him and streamed across his face.

"My stomach was eating me alive, man."

His guts churned and raged, as if jets of boiling acid had been turned on inside of him.

"And along with that, you feel like you're choking on yourself, you can't even breathe, and you suddenly feel so awful that you have no control left at all, and your stomach—"

Gregory gagged, vomit filling his throat and mouth, clogging his nostrils, a bilious fire inside his face.

"Gregory," Sylvana said with a sad smile. "Do you still think you're falling in love with me?"

He couldn't speak, could hardly breathe, his body was rocking and jerking on the floor. But, helplessly, like a man condemned always to act against himself, Gregory nodded.

"Ah, you're a sweet boy. Like the other sweet boy I met not long ago. He wanted me, too, and he felt the pains of love."

Sylvana touched him and her hand felt like hot metal searing his forehead. Then she seemed to be floating in the air directly above him, her face inches from his. The look in her eyes was fierce.

"The worst part about love is losing it," she told him. "You think you have it, you think you have everything you need and want. But then it's gone. Just like that. Gone."

Sylvana was fading out, becoming transparent.

"I have to go now, so that you will know loss, too."

Gregory was terrified and he struggled to speak. Puke bubbled out of his open mouth. His body still twitched spasmodically. He was getting no air. Black patches spotted his vision, more and more of them, blotting out the light. Now he couldn't see her at all. Or the room, anything. He was thrashing in blackness.

"Your heart will burst, your brain will stop. And you will die alone, because love is merciless."

Her voice came and went, her words sounded brittle and faint, like specks in an ocean of radio static.

"Any minute now."

LULU

It seems to me that there can no longer be any choice between enduring the torment of reality, of false categories, soulless concepts, amorphous schemata, and the pleasure of living in a fully accepted unreality.

—Joseph Roth, *Flight Without End*

I never met my grandfather, Leo Kuhn. He refused to come to America and live with us, despite repeated invitations from my father (his son), preferring to spend the last years of his life in the small Vienna apartment that had been his home since the end of World War II. Leo still had a few old friends there, and he lived with his memories. My father visited him twice, the second time accompanied by my mother. While they were there, late in January of 1961, my grandfather passed away quietly in his sleep one night. He had been in gradually declining health for some time. He was 66-years-old.

Leo Kuhn, according to my father, was "a half-assed writer" who had published a lot of things back in the '20s and early '30s, but had never quite amounted to anything. He wrote short stories, articles, poems, topical essays and impressionistic sketches that appeared in the ephemeral press. What my father meant, I learned much later, was that Leo was impractical and never really earned a steady income. He was one of the many who, when young, manage to survive on the fringe of the literary world. You don't get paid much but you don't need much, and money doesn't seem to matter anyhow. Your writing does appear in print, and for a while at least, that's enough to sustain the hope that you will eventually mature into a writer of lasting significance.

Once you pass into your thirties, however, and have a wife and perhaps even a child or two, it becomes much more difficult to maintain this kind of life, even if history does not intervene. Leo knew important people and he was in fact well-connected, but he never managed to produce the great novel or stage play that would transform his career in a single stroke. Most likely he never had it in him, or perhaps the immediate demand for the next short piece and the next small payment kept getting in his way.

Vienna in those days, even with all the chaos and suffering that followed the Great War and the collapse of the Austro-Hungarian Empire, was still a lively city, fermenting with rich artistic and intellectual activity. My impression is that right up until the very last minute Leo spent most of his waking time at places like the Cafe Griensteidl and the Cafe Central, seated at a table in a corner, consuming endless cups of coffees, smoking one cigarette after another, and dashing off yet another feuilleton by day, then drinking wine or pilsner on into the night with friends and acquaintances from that floating world. Over the years he came to know, at least on a nodding basis, such figures as Schnitzler, Hofmannsthal, Musil, Werfel, Perutz, Zweig and Schoenberg—a stunning array of cultural titans.

Eventually, however, history did intervene. Karl Kraus once described Vienna, that City of Dreams, as "the proving ground for world destruction." The rise of Nazism in Germany and its rapid growth in Austria made it increasingly difficult for Leo to sell or publish his work. His wry humor and sarcasm had been displayed countless times in print, making serious enemies whose day would soon be at hand. And in any event, he was a Jew.

Several months ago, I came across some of Leo Kuhn's papers. A few diaries, notebooks and files of yellowed clippings that chipped off at the edges in my hands. They were in the attic. My father had just died and I was clearing out his house. I was annoyed but not entirely surprised that he had kept the existence of these papers secret from me for so long. I'm an associate professor of German Literature, I can speak, read and write the language fluently. My doctoral thesis was on the patterns of social unreality in von Doderer's *The Demons* and *The Waterfalls of Slunj*. My father certainly had to know that this material would be of tremendous interest to me, not only for any footnotes it might add to a particularly fascinating period of European literary history but also for whatever it could tell me about my own grandfather.

Over the years, however, I had come to understand that my father harbored a lot of anger and bitterness toward Leo. It had to do with their flight from Austria. Both Leo's family and that of his in-laws were reasonably well off. They had some relatives already in America, and apparently they had few illusions about the turn history was taking. Quietly, unobtrusively, they disposed of all their major assets and managed to transfer most of their funds out of the country. Family members made their way out of Austria in small groups over a period of time, usually on what were described as "holiday" or "business" trips from which, of course, they had no intention of returning.

No doubt some very substantial bribes were paid to facilitate all of this, but it was remarkably successful. By the early spring of 1938, when Austria became a province of the Reich in the *Anschluss*, most of my grandfather's and grandmother's families had already made it to the United States. Leo was not among them. He refused to believe that such drastic action was necessary. He thought that fascism was destined to fade quickly and that he was clever enough to weather the squall. He would somehow keep his contacts, he would write under pseudonyms, and he would emerge well-positioned in the aftermath of the storm. He did agree that his wife and their three-year-old son (my father) should leave with the others, and he promised to follow them if that truly became necessary.

Just a few months later, however, when he suddenly had to flee Austria in the aftermath of *Kristallnacht*, Leo went to Paris. The Nazis would subsequently chase him from that temporary haven, but then he found shelter in the south of France and remained in hiding there until the Liberation. He never did make any real attempt to reach his family, not even after the war, when Europe was in ruins and there was no point at all in trying to persuade them to return from America. In a sense, what Leo did was effectively to abandon his wife and son—or at least that is how my father apparently grew up seeing it. All through my own childhood, no one spoke of these things. Not my father, not my mother, none of my cousins, my uncles or aunts. My grandmother died long before I was born— but even her cancer failed to bring Leo across the ocean. I'm sure my father regarded that as the final, unforgiveable sin.

Years later, shortly before her own death, my mother did tell me that Leo was a black sheep figure in the family, an alcoholic, a foolish self-centered man who cared only for himself and for his writing, who would not change himself or his ways in order to reunite his family, even when he knew that his so-called "career" was marginal and his writing had no enduring value. He preferred to remain in postwar Vienna, clinging to his ghosts and tattered illusions.

That is probably not an inaccurate portrait of Leo, but it is incomplete.

Working only in my spare time, it took me months to decipher and read all of his surviving papers. The printed matter was occasionally interesting but did nothing to change the assessment that he was a minor writer, an adequate journalist who could not shake the notion that he was destined for higher things. Leo's handwriting was cramped and hasty, his words were long dark blots that reminded me of atonal note clusters and feverish, tortured music.

After the war, he wrote and published many short trivial things, but he kept coming back to one story, which he never finished. It was meant to be an account of his friendship with Joseph Roth in Paris, particularly in the weeks leading up to Roth's death there in 1939. Leo had known Roth in Vienna years before, but they did not become close until Leo arrived in Paris in 1938. Roth had been based there since 1933, having left Germany the day after Hitler took power.

Joseph Roth was very much the kind of writer that Leo Kuhn always wanted to be, and Leo adored him. Roth's haunting, elegiac novels, such as *The Radetzky March* and *Flight Without*

End, captured both the fallen world of Austro-Hungary and the bleak estrangements of life in the Empire's wake. He was a major author, though his work has never found much of an audience in English, and, unlike Leo, Roth's extensive journalism never got in the way of his serious fiction. He wrote fifteen novels in the last fifteen years of his life, despite the fact that his personal circumstances grew increasingly nightmarish. His wife went mad, he was hounded by the Nazis, he was frequently destitute, and he was a determined alcoholic, right up until the day his heart finally gave out.

It seems to me that Leo could never make up his mind as to exactly what kind of piece he wanted to write about Joseph Roth. Some parts read like notes for a straightforward memoir, while other passages have the feel of fiction. Even with all that we do know about Roth, it is still impossible for me to be sure how much of what Leo wrote was true. At one point he cites Gautier's famous account of Gerard de Nerval as the literary model he would follow, but sometime later he appeared to change his mind, drawing black lines across whole paragraphs and scribbling brief, contradictory messages to himself.

—No, not an elegy
—This is a ghost story
—Inner story only
—Roth's ghosts were *real*
—Not right, be factual!
—Real love or mythic love

And so on. I often think of Leo Kuhn sitting alone in his small apartment, struggling through the whole drab decade of the 1950s with the numerous elements of his story, trying to force them together into a coherent whole. He failed, and I wonder why. If nothing else, Leo was a competent writer, he understood basic structure and he had a workable command of language. Furthermore, it gradually became clear to me that he had *all* of the story. Perhaps he simply could not bring himself to finish it, to let go of it. Perhaps he needed it as a continuing presence, to be worked on and lived with for the rest of his days. Or perhaps he was helpless, possessed by a story that was a kind of demon he could never exorcise.

Not surprisingly, I have the same kind of problem. This is not an essay or a memoir, nor is it fiction, though it undoubtedly contains some of all three—and I have no reliable idea which parts are which. A large part of it derives from Leo's own first-hand observations, but nearly as much of it draws on what Roth told him, and neither Leo Kuhn nor Joseph Roth were completely reliable.

I am attempting to put the pieces together now, both for Leo and for myself. I believe this is the story that ultimately cost my grandfather his family.

By the time Leo arrived in Paris in April of 1938, Joseph Roth had long since fallen into the final pattern of his life: writing and drinking, furious bouts of the one followed by furious bouts of the other. He had spent some time in Brussels and Amsterdam, but he always returned to Paris, where the largest community of exiles from Germany and Austria had gathered. They subsisted in a dreamlike state of hope, waiting for reality somehow to annul itself so that they could resume their true lives. Roth saw them—and himself—as lost ghosts who linger on, incapable of accepting the fact that they had died and this world was no longer theirs.

Roth's circle of friends and acquaintances had shrunk practically to none, by his own choice. A woman named Sonja lived with him on and off. When she was there, Roth seemed to pull himself together. He ate better and would write a great deal in a short period of time. But sooner or later Sonja would disappear for a few days, and Roth immediately lost interest in anything. He made the rounds of the cheap bars and taverns in the neighborhood, drinking away the days and nights until Sonja came back to rescue him again.

Leo had taken a single room in a house owned by an elderly Russian, just around the corner from the rue de la Vieille Lanterne, where Roth lived in a small apartment. The first few times they met, their conversations were brief and civil, but Roth clearly intended to keep to himself. Gradually, however, Roth began to accept Leo as more than just another neighbor, and to feel comfortable with him. They shared a common past, in a way. Leo was friendly but respectful, and made no demands or judgements. In fact, he was always happy to accompany Roth on his regular drinking excursions. They were the only times when Roth really seemed to relax and would allow himself to speak freely.

Their friendship was cemented on the night when the German stranger came up to them on the street as they were making their way from one tavern to another. The man wore a hat and overcoat, and he was smoking a flat Turkish cigarette. He was young, his skin was waxy smooth and his eyes were clear.

"Ah, the good Herr Nachtengel," Roth said sarcastically.

"Are you well, Herr Writer?" the German replied. "I hope you're taking care of yourself. We don't want anything to happen to you." A mirthless smile appeared on the man's face. "Someone of your great—stature." It was obviously an insult, both personal and literary. Roth was comparatively short, and he had no international profile in the way that an author such as Thomas Mann did.

Leo had barely taken in this brief exchange when the man turned to him and smiled coldly. "How nice to meet you at last, Herr Kuhn."

Roth grabbed Leo's arm and they brushed past the German. Leo was quite startled that the man knew him by name. A few minutes later, when they were alone in the back corner of a basement bar, Roth explained patiently that there were scores of German agents in Paris, each of them keeping track of numerous exiles, waiting for the time when scores would be settled. There would never be mercy for those who had committed political or cultural offenses.

"You're on their list, same as me," Roth said with a faint smile, and then he laughed. "But cheer up. At least it's a sign that you did something right somewhere along the way."

Roth, who had never known his own father, was Jewish on his mother's side, but it was his writing that singled him out for special attention. His fiction was not at all directly political, nor did it espouse a certain cause. Instead, Roth chose to examine the effects of history on the lives of individual characters.

His primary focus was always on the human. But as far back as 1923, in his very first novel, *The Spider Web*, he had written presciently about the extreme nationalist gangs and private militias forming throughout Germany, and in that serialized tale he had even made specific mention of Adolf Hitler, who was then still largely an unknown figure outside of the right-wing netherworld. The Munich Putsch, in which Hitler attempted to seize control of the Bavarian state government, did not take place until November of 1923—ten long years before he finally became *führer* of all Germany. But Roth's early reference to him was the kind of thing that Hitler would neither forgive or forget.

That night was also the first time Leo spoke with Sonja. Roth got so drunk that Leo had to help him make it back to his apartment, and she was there when they arrived. It was obvious that she had just returned, and Roth was clearly very happy when he saw her. "My lover," he said again and again, as he held her in a clumsy embrace. "My muse." However, as soon as he sat down on the chaise, he leaned back, closed his eyes and passed out, his breathing loud but regular.

"Thank you," Sonja said to Leo as she led him to the door. "He will be all right, now that's he's home."

She was short and no longer quite young, but still very attractive. Her hair was black, or a very dark brown, and it was cut short in a style that had gone out of fashion several years before. Her body was slim but pleasingly rounded. Her skin was very pale, yet as bright as alabaster. Her eyes had such a penetrating quality that Leo suddenly felt awkward and quickly turned away. He sensed some special power in her presence, a quality of strength and relentless honesty—although, the next day, he wondered if that wasn't just a wine-induced fantasy.

"I'll look in—"

"No, please don't," she told him. "He'll be writing."

"Of course."

"You're a writer, too, I can tell," she added, moving closer to Leo. "So, you understand. He needs to use his time."

"Yes." His throat was tight, he felt very warm, and he wanted to touch her, a thought—a sudden desire—that shocked him. "Of course."

"Time to do his work, to write."

Leo nodded, mumbled something, and left. The next day he woke up with his head full of dreamy, confused images of Sonja. It was difficult to understand why, since he had been with her for only a few moments. It had to be some implicit sexuality, the unspoken frankness in her eyes—the way she had looked at him. Certainly she was attractive, and he'd consumed a good deal of wine. Most likely he had gaped at her without even realizing it. Rather than act embarrassed or shy, or pretend that she hadn't noticed, her expression, her response, was to direct it right back to him—as if to say, Yes, and so?—forcing him to confront himself and his uncertain impulses.

It was disconcerting, all the more so the day after. Leo had no intentions toward the woman, and he would never want to disrupt Roth's personal life in the least way. He admired Roth so much that at times he even felt guilty about drinking excessively with him. Wouldn't it be better, after all, if Leo could persuade Roth to drink less and write more? But to do so would cost him Roth's friendship, that was quite clear. One time Roth told him, "I drink as atonement, otherwise I would not continue." Leo didn't fully understand exactly what Roth meant—that he would not continue to drink? write? live? When he asked, Roth frowned in irritation, gave a shrug and said, as if it were self-evident, "Continue."

In any event, Leo firmly believed that all serious writers sacrifice parts of their personal lives in order to accomplish what they do, and that the resulting work must justify the price paid.

That afternoon Leo made the first entry in his "Roth" notebook. But the first name that actually appears in it is Sonja.

Leo saw her again a few days later. It was growing dark at the end of the afternoon and he had just posted another pseudonymous article to Vienna. These harmless pieces on Parisian culture and social life still brought him a small return, but the market for them was vanishing quickly. Few in the Reich wanted to read or hear anything even vaguely positive about the French, no matter how non-political the topic might be. But Leo was not about to start writing the kind of anti-French nonsense that was now so much in demand in Germany. There were already plenty of literary whores working that dismal street, and it appalled him.

Leo saw Sonja emerge from the narrow Rue de la Vieille Lanterne, and he instinctively pursued her. A moment later, he caught up with her and they walked together for a while. Whether she spoke German or French, her pronunciation was exact but unaccented, almost characterless. She was at ease in both languages, so it was impossible to guess where she came from originally. But the pure sound of her voice was lovely to the ear, soft and rich. *Every time she spoke, I wanted to lean closer, to get as close as I could and let her voice wash over me,* Leo wrote.

The facts tumbled out hurriedly in his notebook. She told him that Roth had just fallen asleep after a long night and day of writing. Now he would be asleep for many hours, perhaps right through to the next morning. Roth's work was going well but it was very difficult and painful for him.

And when he slept like that, Sonja had to get out of the apartment—she had to live, breathe, relax. Roth knew, he understood her. All he wanted was for her to be there the next day, to come back to him when he had to start work again. Out of some peculiar need, he simply couldn't write without her nearby, and if she did not return after a while he would give up, go out and start drinking again.

Leo found all this fascinating, but it baffled him. Why did she leave and not come back for days on end? Their relationship appeared to have some mysterious aspect, but Leo would not dare ask either of them about it. He could only hope to learn more in time, for he was certain that it was a key element in any understanding of Roth and his great work. As for Sonja, she was quite intriguing in her own right, and Leo immediately enjoyed being in her presence. Nor did it escape his notice that she seemed quite happy to be with him.

After they had walked a short while it became apparent that Sonja had no particular destination in mind, so Leo took her to a brasserie he knew that served decent food and wine at working-class prices. It was as if he had taken her home. She relaxed at once, threw her wrap off her shoulders, and her face appeared to be lit up from within. He seldom needed to speak.

She told him that she was a singer and had performed in numerous nightclubs in Germany and France, though not so much lately. She'd had a string of lovers, each of them worse than the one before. They were businessmen, schemers, criminals, and they had led her into trouble with the police at one point. She had used many different names, mostly to do with her stage act—Sonja, Kristen, Nelly, Mignon, among others. But all of that was in the past now, and she could only be interested in men who created, not destroyed. Men who wrote or painted or made music. Joseph Roth was small and unsightly, he had somewhat bulging eyes, his hair was disappearing, and his body was a wreck from years of heavy drinking. But he created, the fire in him was true and good, so Sonja would give him whatever he wanted and needed. After all the pain and trouble she had been through, she thought that love was an illusion, a fantasy—but one that was still, sometimes, worth the imaginative effort. Leo didn't know what to make of all this. She seemed both sophisticated and naive at the same time.

But it didn't matter. By then he was completely under her spell. The fire in her dark eyes, the way her hair moved as she spoke, her voice stirring him, seeming to speak right into his mind, the line of her throat, the way her breasts filled out her simple blouse, her small delicate hands—everything about her was so soothing and pleasing to him. He felt happily drowsy, from the food and wine and the heat of the nearby coal-fire, and he didn't want to move. It had been a long time since Leo had last enjoyed the company of a woman, much less one who made him feel thoroughly at ease, as Sonja did.

His wife—and this was the only direct comment I ever found by Leo about my grandmother—was a good woman, but she understood little of who he was and what internal forces drove him.

As the evening went on, Sonja even appeared to grow younger. There was more color in her cheeks, her manner became more animated and girlish, but never loud or silly. It was delightful. *I realized that what I felt—in a genuine physical sense—was nothing less than the surging energy of life itself radiating from her like heat and light from the sun,* Leo noted without irony the next day.

"Show me something you wrote," she said when they left the brasserie and were walking along the street. "Please?"

"All right," Leo replied after the briefest hesitation.

His room was small and chilly, but he lit a fire and poured some schnapps for both of them. She stood by the fire and quickly scanned a short tale of his that had been published the year before. When she put the magazine down on the table, she smiled at him—a smile that made him feel very good since it seemed to signal her approval of what he had written. They sat on the lumpy old chaise in front of the fireplace, the only suitable furniture, and almost at once Sonja raised one leg and swung herself around so that she was sitting on his lap, facing him, her legs on either side of his. Her hand stroked his cheek and teased his hair, she sipped her schnapps and then ran the tip of her tongue along his lips. She must have noticed the sudden conflict in Leo's expression, for her smile grew wider, and there was a measure of good-natured sympathy in it.

"Don't worry," she said. "He doesn't need me this way."

"He called you his lover."

"For him, love is only spiritual now. He's fighting death."

"Even so..."

"It's all right," Sonja assured him. "And you *do* need me this way. Don't you?" Her smile now naughty and complicitous. "No point in denying it."

"Already you know me too well."

"Leo, be bad with me."

She unhooked a couple of buttons on her blouse, took his hand and slid it inside, pressing it to her breast. She leaned closer, until their foreheads touched, and her mouth licked and nipped at his. Somehow, the glasses were quickly set aside, she had his pants open, and she pulled him into her. Their passion was as fierce as it was swift in its consummation.

"Give me a name," she whispered to him, after.

"What?"

"Give me a special name, so I'm yours alone."

"Oh, I don't know..."

"No one else will ever hear it," she insisted. "All those other names I've used were spoiled by other people. Except for Sonja, but that belongs to Joseph, you know."

"Lulu, that's who you are," he said, surprising himself.

"Ah, that's the first name I remember from childhood! I used to think it was so old-fashioned, but now you've rescued it for me." She kissed him.

"Where were you born?"

He felt her body shrug in his embrace. "Orphaned, I suppose."

Then desire intervened, slower this time but more powerful than before, a long, devastating yet beautiful expression of the lonely hunger and deep need within both of them.

Leo awoke cold and alone in the gray dawn. He crawled into bed and soon fell asleep again, waking late in the morning. He fretted through the rest of the day. He was too tired to work properly, but he jotted down brief notes to himself and worried about his friendship with Roth. Leo reminded himself again and again of what she had said: *He doesn't need me this way.* Nonetheless, it was imperative to keep this sudden liaison secret. There was no way of knowing how he might react. It would be bad enough if there were an angry break between Roth and Leo, but far worse if this interfered with Roth's work.

But Leo couldn't stay away, he wanted at least to see her again as soon as possible. That evening he knocked on the door of Roth's apartment, and a shouted voice invited him in. Roth was at his small rickety table, writing. Sonja sat on the rug at his feet, her head resting against his knee. Roth stood up and crossed the room to talk with Leo. He was working, quite busy, no time to spare just now, but perhaps in a few days he would meet Leo and they would go out for a drink. Leo understood, of course, and encouraged Roth to push ahead with his work. At one moment in the brief conversation, Leo's gaze drifted past Roth's shoulder to Sonja, who was still sitting on the rug. At once, her hands moved and touched her breasts, cupping them, and her face lit up with a large smile. She was so naughty! Leo had to look away immediately, and he was relieved that Roth apparently hadn't noticed anything unusual in his expression just then.

Two days later, in the early afternoon, his Lulu came to him and stayed for several hours. This soon became the new pattern in Leo's life. She would come to him whenever she could.

Sometimes they went out to eat and drink, but time was so precious that they usually stayed in his room and made love, later resting in each other's arms before the fire, then making love again as often as they could before she eventually had to leave. She was a wild, imaginative lover, desperately needy but also infinitely giving. It was as if Leo had discovered true passion and desire for the first time in his life—and discovered, as well, that there is no end to it, no logical conclusion, that it goes on and on as long as there is life and imagination to illuminate its perpetual labyrinthine turns.

"Where did you go?" he asked her one day.

"When?"

"Those times when you used to leave Roth, and be gone for a week or more. Where were you, what were you doing?"

A child-like pout. "It doesn't matter." Then she smiled. "That's all over, finished. When I leave him now, it's only to come to you."

"Yes, but—"

"Shhh," kissing him again and again. "Just fuck me."

Leo's need was as great as hers, and the more he had of his Lulu the more he wanted. When she wasn't there with him, he soon grew restless and he found it hard to concentrate on his work. He constantly felt tired, or lazy, and could lie on the chaise for hours, half-awake, recalling previous meetings with Lulu or trying to imagine what delights the next one might include. At times he scolded himself for acting like a lovesick boy, but then he would think: *Yes, I am. So?*

Leo continued to see Roth fairly regularly, but there was a distinct change in Roth's behavior. Now that Sonja no longer left him for very long, he was able to get more writing done. But drink was still an essential part of his life, so he drank some as he wrote, and once a week he went out for an extended binge with Leo that would last from early in the evening until nearly dawn. In spite of this, he did look a little healthier, or perhaps more at peace in some way, and Leo later observed in his notebook that his affair with Lulu was, ironically, secretly, having a beneficial effect on Roth.

Like a man putting his affairs in order, Roth carefully began to share more of his past life with Leo. After the Great War, he had married—too soon, he later realized. His wife, Frieda, was a good person, not unintelligent but a middle-class daughter who aspired to a settled home life. She would make a good mother. She may have fallen in love with the idea of marrying someone who would eventually become a famous and successful writer. Roth was still at a loss to explain why he had married her, except that perhaps Frieda represented some image of stability he felt necessary in his life at that time.

In practice, the reality was quite different for both of them. He soon found her uninteresting and complacent, even tiresome in her petty ways. But Roth could always escape, and did. Frieda was trapped in their apartment, left alone for days and nights at a time while Roth roamed the countryside on journalistic assignments or simply caroused in the cafes with his friends. Fear of how others would react, and perhaps a sense of her own failure as a wife, prevented Frieda from sharing her situation with anyone or doing anything about it. The powerful social constraints of her conventional upbringing and her own fragile nature only made matters worse, and Roth returned home one morning to find her curled up on the floor, peeling and eating wallpaper. She never completely recovered, and in time had to be placed in an institution. A couple of years later she contracted some illness, and died.

Roth never forgave himself. He found a new sense of urgency in his work, but writing was not an escape. He also took to drinking in a new way. It seemed to him that alcohol was a fitting, fine and ultimately final punishment. He would yield himself to it, and carry out the sentence. From that time on, his whole life became a kind of macabre race in which the goal was to write as much as he could and also to destroy himself in the process.

If Leo saw any parallels between Roth's personal life and his own, he did not enter them in his notes. I have to believe that he thought about them, was even haunted by them, for the rest of his life. It seems to me that Roth and Leo had both sacrificed their wives (and in Leo's case his son), probably without giving it much consideration at the time. They had chosen the artistic, literary life, and had lived it exactly as they saw fit, in a typically youthful and unfettered spirit—regardless of the consequences for those who were closest to them.

Roth subsequently had one romantic affair, with a young actress and writer named Irmgard Keun. They were together for a couple of years, drifting from one European city to another (outside of Germany). Their relationship was passionate and stormy, and ultimately doomed. She couldn't bear to sit by and observe Roth's self-destructive descent, nor could she save him from it. Finally, as much at his insistence, she pulled away and left him. Roth told Leo that he thought of Irmgard as his only "true" love, but that he accepted losing her—it was a necessary part of *his* sacrifice.

[Irmgard Keun was another of those whose names were on a German list. She fled Holland when the Nazis invaded in 1940 and escaped to England, where she remained until her death in 1982. Her best novel was published in an English translation as *After Midnight*, Victor Gollancz Ltd, 1985.]

Sometime after that, Roth wandered into a dingy cellar bar in Montmartre, where he sat and drank, and watched and listened as a young woman "who was no longer quite so young" sang that most poignant and bitter song of abandoned love, *Surabaya-Johnny*. She told him later that he was the only one there who paid any attention, and that his eyes were "big and wet" when she finished. She wore a black slip. She said her name was Mimi. Before long, however, Roth began to call her Sonja.

He told Leo that without her he no longer had enough strength or will to write a single sentence.

Leo and his Lulu continued their affair, and it would seem that Roth never found out about it—or if he did, he never let on. By his own account, Leo was happier than he had ever been. She was a joy as well as a pleasure, child-like, almost innocent, but at the same time a profoundly erotic woman to whom nothing was new or forbidden. She was as much a fantasist as any storyteller, though her imagination expressed itself in who and how she was on any given day. Thus, her presence always had about it an air of anticipation and unpredictability that Leo found compulsive and addictive.

But there were certain worrying signs that he wondered about. She always came to him in a tired, pale condition. This was understandable, since she spent so much time sitting up with Roth as he wrote, and obviously there was nothing healthy about that way of life. They all were poor, ate badly and drank too much. All the same, he was shaken one time when, after making love, they were huddled beneath the blankets, luxuriating in their nakedness together, talking quietly about nothing in particular, and she suddenly murmured, "He's killing me, you know." But when he sat up in concern and asked her what she meant, she passed it off lightly. "Nothing, really. Not like that! It's just that at the end of each session, I feel like I've worked as hard as he has. I'm so exhausted I feel dead. That's all."

It pleased Leo to see how quickly she was transformed whenever she was with him. The color would begin to resurface in her cheeks, her eyes grew brighter and her whole body brimmed with new energy. It was nothing less than the power of love and passion, visible to the naked eye, the two of them drawing new life and vigor from each other every time they met. And if their trysts generally left Leo in a similar state of exhaustion, so much so that even the following day he could barely do one hour's work, he was not bothered in the least. He willingly and completely surrendered himself to *the magic of Eros*. But Leo was still capable of giving the matter some practical consideration.

"You must live with me."

For once, she looked surprised. Then sad. "I can't. I belong to him, and I wouldn't do that to him. This is all you and I can have."

"He's going to die soon," Leo said. "You know it, too."

"Don't speak like that."

"And after the war, whenever it comes—"

"Please!" Now her expression was pained. "Don't write endings for us, not even imaginary ones. You have a wife and child somewhere, another life, and sooner or later you'll want it back. That is what the end of the war will mean to you, whenever it comes."

"No, no—"

"Don't," she cut him off. "It hurts too much."

"I'm sorry. My poor Lulu."

Then she showered his face with kisses, teasing his mouth. "Think of me as your dream lover. I only want to give you pleasure. Be happy with me."

He was. He even began to think that he would be happy to die with her, as life without her had become inconceivable to him. The day after a long encounter with Lulu, he would lie in bed or on the chaise for long hours on end in a kind of daze, his body weak, his mind adrift on a sea of images. It was hard to form clear thoughts. Much of this time was a blissful quietus, the aftermath. But one small part of his brain continued to ponder the internal dynamics of their situation, and Leo's notes reflect a deep-seated uncertainty.

Today she spoke to me of Courtly Love. It is deeply carnal, its whole point is consummation in body as well as spirit. For centuries the Church and society have worked strenuously to de-sexualize Courtly Love and turn it into some harmless, chivalrous claptrap. True Courtly Love is subversive, a threat to the existing order. Tristan went against the King. Women had the power to pick and choose among men, to decide their own fate.

Courtly Love is, by definition, adulterous.

Tristan possessed Isolde in the flesh—but could not keep her.

Leo asked Lulu what all of that had to do with the two of them. She said that their love was like Courtly Love, freely given with no expectation, and thus pure in and of itself. She wanted him to know how much she cherished it.

Does she really understand? Leo asked himself later. She has her hand on the truth, but perhaps does not entirely grasp it. Any good student of medieval history knows that the ultimate goal of Courtly Love is not sexual, nor is it even spiritual. The true goal of Courtly Love is death.

Novalis: "Our love is not of this world."

Toward the end, Leo's notes were obsessive on the subject of death. He believed that talk about Courtly Love was simply part of the fantasy that Lulu spun for herself and for him, and as such he enjoyed it. But death was the kernel of truth in the fantasy, and Leo saw it differently, though in equally mythic terms. He began to ruminate about the role of the Muse. Sonja was Roth's Muse. Roth sucked the life and creative spirit out of her, which was why he could write so much and so well when she was with him, and could not when she was away. The Muse gave, but her giving was also a real sacrifice of herself.

The other part of the dynamic (to stay with Leo's term) was his relationship with Lulu. His dream lover. She was right about that, there truly was a dream-like, unreal quality to the passion they shared. It was a kind of mutual fantasy, in which he and Lulu could escape the disappointing world outside for a little while, and flee into the realm of pure desire. It was a fantasy he cherished.

But Leo could also see the weak point in the equation. His life force was being drained, and it was the only one that was not being replenished adequately. The situation could not continue this way indefinitely. The inexorable conclusion was death—his. Whether Leo truly believed this is impossible to say, but he did write this astonishing note: *If Roth were healthier I might have to decide whether to kill him, but as it is I can at least hope to outlast him.* Perhaps he was looking ahead to the prospect of Lulu becoming his Muse. But then he would have to face the question of where she would turn to draw strength in order to feed and inspire him in his work. There would have to be another "Leo," another lover. He had worked himself into an intellectual corner with heartbreaking implications. All of Leo's knowledge and understanding had turned poisonous, and he wanly noted: *If it proves necessary, I will submit. Roth is worth it. Lulu is worth it.*

All of this seemed quaint and amusing, the first time I read it. People take things so seriously, and years later it looks so different. Few of us can relate now to that time and place, that distant, dead culture. But these were very intelligent and gifted people, better-educated, thoughtful, questioning in a way that quite escapes us now—we have an answer for everything we ask, lucky as we are.

The more I stared at poor Leo's words, his clotted handwriting, the more I followed his tortured chain of thought—the more I sympathized with him and even came to believe him. Or at least to believe that he believed. If I could understand him, then I could forgive him for not being in my life. And the truth is, I wanted to forgive him, for Leo, like Joseph Roth, had chosen a remorseless faith in literature and its necessary way of life— which I secretly shared, but lacked the courage and foolishness to attempt.

Things played out his way, in a sense. On the last afternoon of what Leo called his "only genuine life," Lulu came to him and they passed a few hours in the most intense lovemaking, pressing the far edge of violence and unfathomable need, an experience that left them both in tears of joy, incapable of speaking until the time came when she had to leave. Roth would finish his book that night. He told her to ask Leo to join them the next evening to celebrate.

I understood: Roth had known all along.

The following afternoon, when he knocked on the door of Roth's apartment, there was no answer. Perhaps he had come too early. He tried the handle, and the door opened. Yes, there they were. Roth was asleep on the chaise, and Sonja was asleep in the narrow bed in the far corner of the room. Leo was about to back out quietly when Roth suddenly groaned and stirred. There was something vaguely alarming about the noise Roth made, so Leo carefully approached. Roth's eyes stared at him, and Leo had never seen such anguish. Roth's hand moved, barely. Leo interpreted it as a beckoning gesture, and he moved closer.

"I'm dead." Roth's voice was a feeble whisper.

"Lulu."

The word may not actually have escaped his lips, but Leo spoke it, and he turned immediately to the bed. He rushed across the room. She was there, he saw the blankets mounded up over her body. He recognized the beautiful curve of her hips, the correct length of her slender frame. He even saw, he was sure, the slight rise and fall of her shape as she breathed, deep in understandable sleep. When Leo put his hand on her shoulder, his memory-sensation was true, he knew exactly how her shoulder felt and recognized it again. But when he gently pulled back the layers of cheap fabric, they fell away from his hand. He uncovered nothing but the bottom sheet, which still bore the impress of a small body. Leo touched it, and he thought he could detect a fading warmth. But all the sheet held was dust and lint and bits of human grit. He pressed his face to the bed, and—oh God, yes—he could smell her in the most intimate way, as he had tasted and smelled her in love.

But she was gone, like a bed-ghost (*Bettgeist*).

Roth was still alive, and in agony. Leo hurried and performed the necessary function of getting help. Roth was taken to Saint-Jude, the nearest hospital for the poor. Strangely, Leo had no trouble sleeping that night. He left the door to his room unlocked, but he had no visitor. Lulu did not magically appear. Leo was allowed to see Roth the next morning. He was in a ward filled with dozens of patients, all from the bottom of French society. The conditions were mean and the pervasive smell was terrible. Roth had no strength left in him, almost no life at all. Only his lips and eyes moved a little. His large eyes were yellowish and his face appeared to have collapsed into itself. For several minutes he merely gazed at Leo, and his expression was impossible to decipher.

Finally, Leo found a few words. "Did you finish it?"

"Yes."

"Good. I'm so happy to hear that."

"Kuhn."

"Yes?"

"You're looking at the saddest man in Europe."

Then his eyes closed. Leo waited until he was sure that Roth's breathing continued. He smiled and patted Roth's hand. *No*, he thought as he turned away and started to leave. *Nobody so close to death can be that sad.*

Leo left his door unlocked again that night, probably still hoping somehow that Lulu would return to him. But she didn't. It was nearly noon when he awoke the following day. He felt rested, better physically now, though his heart was still sick with disappointment and sorrow.

As he was leaving to go to the hospital again, Leo almost walked right past a man lingering on the sidewalk. But there was something familiar—and then the man smiled and stepped closer.

"Herr Kuhn, how nice to see you again." The German agent.

Leo started to continue on his way. He had seen this man a number of times over the months. Leo refused to speak a word to him. But now the German reached out and took hold of Leo's arm.

"Just to save you the inconvenience," he said. "Your friend Herr Roth died this morning. No doubt you were expecting this, it's hardly a surprise, considering the foolish way he lived. One evening I saw him sitting alone in Bernier's—in the rue de Faubourg, do you know it?—and I thought to myself, this is a man who died a long time ago but doesn't realize it. Nobody reads his sort of thing anymore now, do they? What do you think?"

Leo freed his arm and hurried away.

He remained in Montmartre, living in that room, until the following year, when he left for the south shortly before the Nazi occupation of Paris. He left just before dawn, successfully dodging Herr Nachtengel.

Joseph Roth's last novel, *The Legend of the Holy Drinker*, is now regarded as one of his finest works. It is a tale of atonement and redemption. Roth was 44-years-old when he died.

My grandfather, it seems, also drank heavily until the end of his life. But I don't think his drinking served the same purpose as Roth's. It seems more likely to me that Leo used alcohol as a consolation for the loss of Lulu, and perhaps also for the failings of his career as a writer—he was never the writer he wanted to be, and surely he understood that.

Yes, yes, I know she is gone, if indeed she was ever there. And I know she will never come back—I tell myself this everyday. But the rest of me is not convinced. So I light the fire every evening and try again to put the words in order. Perhaps if I get the magic pattern right, it will summon her back. My Muse, my lover—I have no life without her.

Romantic nonsense, the delusions of an old man—I suppose

they are. But I can understand his desire to believe now. Leo never gave up on the only two things that really mattered to him after he left Germany: his Lulu and his writing. Naturally, he couldn't stop working on her story—their story. And he remained faithful to her hopeless plea: "Don't write endings for us."

Every time I sit down to write an essay, a report, or even a harmless little tale of my own (none of which has ever been published), I think of my grandfather. His irrational faith in the rightness of such work pleases me. I see it as a gift from him to me—one that certainly skipped past my father. But it is a gift of very mixed qualities. And, I remember my mother's warning to me.

Dawn is often at hand when I finish writing. I can make out shapes in the thick gray light. I go to bed, and see once again the shape of my lover beneath the blankets. I know so well the curve of her hip, the length of her body. Sometimes the lingering darkness fools me and for an awful moment I may not see her hair on the pillow, and my heart races as my hand reaches to touch her.

IF YOU SEE ME, SAY HELLO

Ted was on his way back into town, less than a mile from home, when he saw the car coming in the opposite lane. An orange Mini Cooper. It was actually called Rally Orange and it wasn't a stock color. You had to special order it. Her car, her color, she'd waited months for it to come in. A car he expected never to see again. The traffic was steady, the road wide at that point. It was early in the afternoon on a Friday in February, in an unusually mild winter.

Impossible to think it could be her. But the Mini drew closer and he saw the same racing stripe, and then the long blonde hair. No, it can't be. She sailed past, her eyes on the traffic ahead, not looking for him or his nondescript Accord. Yes, no doubt at all. In his rearview mirror, the clincher: the Pennsylvania license plate.

Ted's heart pounded and he was breathing through his mouth as he hit the horn, then the button to lower the window. He stuck his arm out and waved, but he knew it was too late then. Too many cars had passed. He couldn't do a U-turn in this traffic. Then he was in a line at a red light. He could turn left, turn around somewhere up that street, head back and try to catch up with her, but he knew it was hopeless, he'd be guessing which way she went. She would soon reach both a major inter-section and the highway. Ted pulled into a bank parking lot and sat for a moment, breathing deeply, trying to calm down.

It had been a little over a year since she decided that her life was going in a different direction and that he wasn't going to be in it any longer. She never gave him a good reason. It wasn't someone else. They were just not right together, at least not right enough for her. So she left him and moved back to the Philadelphia area, where she had family and old friends.

But now, here she was, and they'd just missed each other. He had been out driving for an hour or so, nothing important. The only reason she would have driven hundreds of miles to Connecticut was to see him. Why hadn't she called first or sent him an email? And why hadn't she waited at the apartment building for him to return? Ted tried to consider all the possibilities, but none of them made much sense. He'd seen her, she was there, she was real for a moment. But now she was gone again, and he was still lost.

He thought about the direction she was heading. He put his car in gear and started to drive. He decided to swing by the ice cream stand, the state park, and a couple of other places in the area that they used to visit. Maybe she was driving around there too, killing time, before going back to the apartment building to see if he had returned home. Maybe he would spot her. If not, perhaps he would get back to his place—their place, really—and find her there, in the parking lot, in her orange Mini, waiting for him.

Jen accelerated and pulled into the flow of traffic on I-95. She had spent a couple of hours there, but she'd allowed for it, and she would be in Boston in time for the evening reception at the comic book convention. So many things seemed to get better for her after she left Connecticut—the talented people she'd met at Blue Terror Comics, the way she walked into the job and was doing so well at it, seeming to understand everything at once. She didn't feel bad about any of it. She had grown up a great deal in the space of a year.

But sometimes she felt bad about Ted. This visit was for him. She hadn't been growing up with Ted, not enough, and maybe that was why they couldn't last. But at the same time, maybe she wouldn't have grown up at all without him, and that was why she felt she still owed him something and would always miss him. For her, he'd been both necessary and impossible.

She drove past Swirlee's, the ice cream stand, but of course it was closed until April. She swung through the state park on

the edge of town, where they'd had picnics and necked passion-
ately, but where the trees were was now bare and the parking
lots empty. She sat in her car outside the apartment building
where she had spent so many delightful hours, and felt a sense
of a loss that was still beyond her control.

She felt lonely and sad today. There were moments, now
and then, when Ted still felt like a real presence in her life.

They'd found him on his sofa, fully dressed but with his
shoes off, looking as if he had simply stretched out to take a nap.
That was about six months after she'd left.

The autopsy found no apparent cause of death and therefore ruled it was the result of natural causes. As if to say, his
heart just stopped. But she knew better. Nobody dies of natural
causes at the age of 33.

I'll always love you.

Traffic on I-95 opened up. Jen hit the gas.

IN THE SAND HILLS

It was a long way to drive, just to kill a man who might not even be there. From Denver north up to Alliance, and then another 100-plus miles east on Highway 2, until Driscoll got to a place called Skinnerville. It was shown as a small-dot town on the outdated road map he was using, but Skinnerville had since been abandoned by its residents. Now it was nothing more than a scattering of a few dozen vacant houses, barns, and other buildings in varying stages of decay and collapse. Some tilted precariously, while others had already fallen in on themselves. The former general store was built out of cinderblocks, still solid, but the large glass windows were long gone, and the metal roof and the gas pumps out front were eaten through with rust.

Driscoll pulled over for a moment. That was helpful—no one in Skinnerville. No one to see Driscoll and maybe remember his face, or the car he was driving or the license plate. No one who could even put a date on the day he passed through Skinnerville—going east at first, then later heading back west. No one with a shred of useful information to pass along to the sheriff or the state troopers, in the unlikely event that they came around later, asking about any strangers in the area recently.

Driscoll fished a crumpled piece of paper out of his jacket pocket and took another look at it. A few simple handwritten directions, along with a map that could have been drawn by a kid in kindergarten. Three to five more miles, then a dirt road off to the right, and then another mile or so. He was close now. Driscoll drove on.

A functional idiot named Walter Bopp had offended Mr. Lee,

to the tune of about $100,000. Bopp had collected and delivered money for Mr. Lee for some period of time, and was considered to be a reliable, trustworthy courier. Until, that is, the day when he finally gave in to temptation and disappeared with a bag of Mr. Lee's cash—far too much of it to be written off as an expense or a minor loss.

So it fell to Driscoll to put things right. Driscoll had put many such matters right for Mr. Lee over the years. Mr. Lee's gratitude was a good thing to have. It would be very nice if Driscoll could retrieve some of the cash, in which case he would get a slice of it. But he would be paid for his efforts regardless, and it was ultimately more important that punishment be handed out. Mr. Lee was responsible for Denver, for all of Colorado, in fact. To offend and embarrass him that way was intolerable.

Mr. Lee had friends in many places, and they helped in the search for Walter Bopp. But in due course it became apparent that he was not in Vegas or Reno, living high and gambling large. Nor were there any sightings or rumors of him in Frisco, Phoenix, or L.A. It began to seem more likely that Bopp had gone to ground in some place where he felt safe, where he thought he would never be found. There, he would just sit on the money and wait it out for a while, before making his next career move.

As if Mr. Lee would ever forget.

It took a while, but Mr. Lee was able to track down one of Bopp's former live-in lovers, Krystal Waters (now Starr). She was only too happy to tell the sorry tale of her six months with Walter, dating back several years. What a cheating, miserable rat he was, and a lot more like that. The situation got to the point where Walter was heavily involved with a married woman whose husband was a bouncer at a club, a man known to be violent and dangerous. Suddenly fearing for his life, Walter persuaded Krystal that they had to leave Denver immediately. So, they fled to his family's ranch in the Sand Hills of northwestern Nebraska. But the "ranch" turned out to be a broken-down old farmhouse out in the middle of nowhere. Walter's brother, Bob Bopp, was the only family member still living there, and he seemed a little crazy, given to long silences and occasional grunted words. He spent a lot of time staring at Krystal in a way that made her feel very uncomfortable.

They spent a month or so there before she was finally able to persuade Walter that they should return to Denver. They did, and Bopp somehow managed to avoid getting himself killed— yet. But Krystal had had enough, and dumped him.

She was very happy to draw the map and write down the few directions to the Bopp family homestead in Nebraska, and Mr. Lee was grateful to her.

The night before, Driscoll had stayed at the Palomino Motel on the outskirts of Alliance. He had breakfast at a nearby diner and was on the highway by 9 a.m. It was close to noon when he spotted the dirt road, just about where Krystal said it was. Driscoll swung the Cougar coupe onto the hard-packed surface and drove ahead slowly. He was in the Sand Hills now, not just passing through them on asphalt. It was a bizarre landscape, so arid and empty, but stitched in places with some kind of prairie grass that rippled and waved in the steady breeze. The sand itself was almost gray, kind of lunar, Driscoll thought. When a brief gust of wind blew some of it into the car, it felt granular, and it stung his cheek. He rolled up the window.

The road meandered around and through the maze of hills, which ranged from gentle, swelling rises to stark walls that towered up thirty feet or more, breaking off in sharp ridges. A few looked like enormous, frozen ocean waves, carved out by the wind. It was a mystery to him why anyone would ever want to live out there.

Driscoll kept an eye on the odometer. The way the road looped and curled, it was easy to see why Krystal had been kind of vague about the distance from the highway to the farm-house. He had driven just over two miles when he came around another bend and saw the Bopp place just ahead. The hills gave way to a wide, clear, level piece of ground, and then rose again around it. There was a very large barn, some corrals or holding pens, which suggested that at one time the Bopps had raised cattle. But the paint on the barn had peeled away, almost com-pletely, and it looked like it was no longer in use.

The farmhouse did have something of a ranch style to it,

built just a single-story tall, strung out long and low to the earth, with a couple of extra rooms tacked on to the back of it. A simple frame construction job on a concrete slab that now had visible cracks in it, crumbling in places. The whole structure was falling apart in slow motion.

More important, there was a pickup truck parked out front. Maintaining the same slow, deliberate speed, Driscoll cruised up to the house, his eyes scanning the windows and the immediate area for any signs of a person moving about. Nothing yet. He had a .38 in a shoulder holster beneath his jacket, which was half-unzipped, and he had a smaller .22 strapped under the cuff of his jeans, just above his ankle.

Before he got out of the car, he hit the horn twice, which he imagined might be the polite, neighborly thing to do in these parts. Announce yourself, signaling good will and normal behavior. But nobody opened the front door to greet him, no face peered out of a window to see who was there. Driscoll walked up the three wooden steps to the porch. He knocked firmly on the door, while standing just to the side of it.

"Hello. Anybody home?" he called. "Walter? Bob?"

He knocked again, but there was still no response. He listened carefully, but heard no sound of movement inside. He swung his head to glance briefly through one of the windows. Now, there was a nice touch you don't see often—the front door apparently opened directly into the kitchen. Driscoll chanced a longer look, and there was no one in sight. He went to the window on the other side of the door and saw what must have passed for the living room—lumpy armchairs and other very old furniture that appeared not to have been moved or dusted in quite some time. Yeah, Krystal must have loved this place.

Driscoll went around to the back of the house, but the windows there were a little too high for him to look through. He found a shed with a generator inside, a couple of propane tanks—that would provide electricity. But there were no telephone wires, nor a television antenna. Once you got here, you were here.

He went into the barn, which was very spacious but showed no sign of recent activity. Every flat surface was coated with a layer of sand. The milking area equipment was rusted, the hayloft above without a single bale. Driscoll took a deep breath through his nose—even the smell of cow shit had left this place.

He circled back around to the front of the house and took a closer look at the pickup truck. It was rusty in patches and generally beat up. Maybe ten years old, at a guess. The registration tag on the plate was dated AUG '83, two years and a week ago. One of the back tires was flat, the other three were getting there. He looked inside the cab and saw a lot of empty beer and soda cans, candy and burger wrappers, a faded issue of *Hustler*.

Driscoll started to walk back to the porch, but the wind had picked up a bit and the sand was hitting his face, so he got into his car and sat for a few minutes. He had a couple of possibilities to consider now. The first, obviously, was that Walter was not hiding out there after all, and that Driscoll's trip was a waste of time. Maybe, but the remoteness of the location and the fact that it was Walter Bopp's old family home still made it seem like the best bet, the most logical place for him to run to. Krystal's description of the house was so accurate, it only reinforced the idea.

Perhaps Walter, with or without his brother, had gone out in another vehicle earlier that morning, before Driscoll had arrived there. They might return at any time, or not until this evening. Well, Driscoll was prepared to wait. In the meantime, there was another possibility—that the money, or whatever might be left of it, was tucked away somewhere inside the house.

He got out of the car. The wind hit him hard enough to stall his movement for a second, sand peppering his cheek again. The sky was clear, but he noticed some black clouds in the distance. Driscoll hurried to the front door and had to laugh when he found it unlocked. He stepped inside with a herky-jerky motion, in case someone was lying in wait, ready to take a shot at him. But the kitchen was empty, the house still. He shut the door loudly, stamped his foot and called out another greeting, but again there was no response from within.

The room had a lingering smell of boiled food. There was a steel pot on the wooden table, containing a small heel of ham, a few chunks of potato, and some cabbage. In the sink, one plastic dinner dish, with a knife and fork. Driscoll touched the food residue on the plate; it was dry but not moldy—he judged it to be a day old, two at most. The cabinets held a few staples like salt, sugar, flour, and a can of coffee, but little else. He was startled when he opened the refrigerator, because the motor rumbled into action, the light went on inside, and he could hear the generator begin droning in the shed outside. The fridge held a gallon jug of milk, down about two thirds, and a couple of cans of Coors.

He quickly checked the rest of the rooms, first to make sure no one was there. A thin infiltration of sand crunched underfoot as he walked. Jesus, he would hate to live in a place like this, with its low ceilings, the long dark hallway that snaked through it, and the small, boxy rooms—most of them now cluttered with things accumulated over the course of what had to be several lifetimes.

Driscoll found one bedroom that looked as if it was still in use, or had been until very recently. The bed wasn't made, but the blanket and sheet had been thrown roughly back into place. The bureau was not dusty and there were some men's socks and underwear in the drawers, as well as a few folded shirts and pairs of jeans. In the closet, a couple of pairs of slacks and a sports jacket. Nothing special, but passable—the kind of clothing that Walter might wear in Denver.

He saw a small, portable transistor radio on the night table, next to the lamp. Driscoll picked it up and turned it on. A burst of static, followed by a pop song that faded in and out. So the batteries were still good. An AM station, most likely in Alliance. Reception would probably be better at night.

Other than the clothes, there was nothing personal in the room. No mail, no papers or documents, no photographs. Driscoll examined the floor, the walls, the ceiling, and the closet very carefully, but found no sign of a hidey-hole where money or other valuables might be hidden. He gave up on the idea of searching every room thoroughly because there were just too many boxes, cartons, and crates of junk in them to deal with now. It was as if the Bopps had never thrown anything away.

In the living room—maybe they called it the parlor back

when—he found a clutch of old photographs, framed and mounted on a wall. History in an eyeful. It looked as if five generations of Bopps had built and run this place, each succeeding one a little fewer in number than the last, until the family gene pool finally petered out in Walter and Bob, two runty little kids standing between their forlorn parents. The kids who wouldn't even bother to try keeping the place going, who would sell off every cow, chicken, and pig they had, and anything else they could get a buck for, and who would then hang on here—or, in Walter's case, return here now and then—while everything that was left slowly rotted.

Driscoll got back to the kitchen, and froze. He could smell smoke—cigarette smoke, no mistake. It was fresh, hadn't been there a few minutes ago. He reached under his jacket and pulled out the .38. The smoke hadn't penetrated the rest of the house, and he saw no butt in the sink or ground out on the floor. He spotted a clear glass ashtray off to the side on the counter, but it was empty.

Mindful of his back, Driscoll edged around the room to the front window and looked outside. No sign of anyone, just the wind whipping up the sand in short blasts. He opened the door and stepped onto the porch. No one in sight, anywhere. But he saw, at the bottom of the front steps, footprints in the sand. One set approaching the house, another one slightly overlapping the first, going away. He could tell they weren't his. Then his eyes caught something moving—a cigarette, propelled by the wind, scudding across the sand. Half a cigarette, still burning.

It was not good to be standing there, an open target. Driscoll quickly went back into the house and shut the door. He grabbed a wooden chair and pulled it around to the front window, sitting to one side of the glass, so that he had a clear view if anybody approached, but without exposing himself. At the same time, he had the back door covered, as well as the hallway passage into the rest of the house. His body was tense, juiced with anticipation, but his mind was calm and in focus. These were the moments in his work that he loved and lived for—the moment of confrontation, and the inevitable crushing of the other person beneath the sheer, irresistible force of Driscoll's will.

He hefted the gun in his hand, and thought about it. Someone had come into the house, someone smoking a cigarette. That person had heard Driscoll moving about, and had apparently turned around and left. Hold on, that same person would have seen Driscoll's car first. So, why enter the house, but then immediately turn and leave? And there was no third car or truck out front, so where had that person come from—on foot? Driscoll tossed those things around in his head for a few minutes, but couldn't work any of it out.

Never mind, it didn't matter at the moment. This was their house, but now he occupied it. Sooner or later, they would have to come to him. Driscoll held the gun inside the pocket of his jacket. He was patient and ready.

An hour later, he was not so sure. In that time, he hadn't caught a glimpse of anyone outside, and the only sounds he heard were the wind whipping up and bursts of sand plinking off the window glass. It was darker now, the black clouds rolling in, and there, the first rumble of thunder. He wondered how long the storm would last and whether he should sit it out there, or leave now. But Driscoll hated the idea of not finishing the job, and the fact that someone knew he was there changed everything. He could return tomorrow, but in the meantime Walter Bopp could skip off to Omaha, anywhere, just to get away. Driscoll would be all the way back to square one in that case, with no idea where Bopp was.

He was impatient now, sitting and waiting, so he decided it was time to take another, more careful look throughout the house. He went to the front door, slid the latch lock in place and, for good measure, snugged the back of a chair up under the door handle. He did the same thing with the back door. Now if somebody wanted to enter the house, they would have to make some noise to do so, and he would hear them.

Driscoll walked back down the hallway to the one bedroom that had appeared to be in recent use. This time he checked behind the bureau, under the mattress, and in the pockets of the slacks hanging in the closet. Still nothing. He tried the radio again, spinning the tuner wheel up and down, but with the storm in the air there was solid blaring static from one end of the dial to the other, all stations lost in the thicket of noise.

He sat on the bed and tried to get a sense of the life of someone living here, to feel what it was like. No telephone. No television. No useful work to be done, because it was no longer a functioning farm or ranch. No point in working on the upkeep of the house, because, really, who'd want to live here anyway? Nowhere to go, except away, forever. A transistor radio not much bigger than a pack of cigarettes—it came down to that? It spoke of a life so diminished that it barely seemed like life at all. Now Driscoll had to wonder—why would Walter Bopp come here to hide out with his loot? Of all the places in the world where he might go to escape Mr. Lee's vengeance, and start a new life. This might be Walter's old family home, it might feel safe and secure. But it was nothing, beyond nowhere.

A blast of wind shook the house, breaking Driscoll's thought. He worked his way back to the kitchen, looking through some drawers, poking through cardboard cartons and orange crates, finding nothing of value or interest. A couple of old jewelry boxes, their contents long since pawned. The same song, endless variable refrains—life devours itself to start anew, for the moment, for no other reason.

The chairs were in place, the doors still locked. But the view from the front window hit Driscoll like a kidney punch. The air outside was very dark and the sand was flying on the horizontal. Thunder continued to rumble and there were flickers of lightning, but it was not raining. Sand was accumulating around his car, already up to the bottom of the front bumper, and it was drifting higher even more quickly in the front wheel well, as he watched. He knew immediately that he wasn't going anywhere until the storm blew through and he could dig enough sand away to free his car. Tiresome thought, it took a little energy out of him. He probably wouldn't be back in a comfortable motel room tonight with a drink and a movie on TV.

Driscoll took the gun out of his jacket pocket, just to hold it for a few seconds and draw some charge from it, and it fueled his strength and sense of purpose. Because the person with the cigarette was still somewhere in the vicinity. Sheltering from the storm in the barn, or one of the sheds Driscoll hadn't bothered to check. In which case, good luck to you out there. I'll see you when the storm passes, and you come out. For Driscoll to be put in this situation, there was now only one possible outcome for Walter Bopp. *He* would turn over whatever of Mr. Lee's money he had left and then *he* would dig Driscoll's car out of the sand. Then he would die. End of job. And home to Denver.

The rain kicked in then, and right away it bucketed down. Driscoll could see the sand being splattered up as gobs of gray mud on his car. A deep sense of anger began to exfoliate within him. These are what are sometimes called aggravating circumstances. You will pay for this. You, you, *you*.

Driscoll walked down the hallway on the other side of the house, room by room, kicking over boxes and crates of things, to see if anything interesting fell out, yanking out drawers and spilling their contents. Junk, junk, junk, the debris of lives that were gone and meant nothing anyway. It infuriated him—as if he had come all this way to inspect a tag-sale in which nothing would actually sell.

He was so angry and impatient as he stalked about, that his foot slid a bit on the throw rug at the end of the corridor. He reached out to brace himself against the wall, but it was a small door he hadn't noticed or opened before. It looked like a closet door at the end of the hallway. Driscoll turned the handle, noticing that the door opened out, not in. He found an empty cubbyhole of a room, with an open metal hook mounted in the low ceiling. Then he saw a loop-handle in the floor planks—a trapdoor. He pulled it up and secured it to the hook. The first thing he noticed was the smell of stale smoke.

Below, was darkness. But there was a length of BX cable connected to an electrical switch screwed onto the wooden frame of the opening. It must have been a root cellar, a place to store produce like potatoes and apples. Or, just as likely, it had served as a storm cellar, a place to take shelter from the massive thunderstorms and seasonal tornadoes that tracked through this part of the country. Funny, at that moment Driscoll noticed that he no longer could hear the storm outside. Maybe it had blown by and was gone already.

He examined the trapdoor again. There were three sturdy slide locks on the underside, and no locking mechanism on the top side. That was as it should be—you could secure yourself in the cellar, but you could not accidentally or intentionally be locked in down there.

Driscoll took a couple of steps down the narrow wooden stairs and flipped the switch. A light went on below. Now he could see that the stairs descended fifteen feet or more, deeper than he expected. But most of the cellar was out of sight, because the bottom of the stairs ended just a couple of feet from a concrete wall. Gun in hand, Driscoll went down the steps as quickly as he could, angling his body and head so that he could scope out the whole room immediately, his shoes clomping loudly on the boards. He went into a crouch and darted a few steps to the side as he spun away from the stairs.

He saw the body of one man lying on a mattress in the far corner. A few feet away, another mattress and a second man, who was almost in a sitting posture, his upper body propped against the wall, his legs splayed out in front of him, his head slumped down on one shoulder. Neither of them moved. Driscoll was almost certain that they were dead, but he approached them slowly and with caution, his gun moving back and forth in the cool air from one to the other.

When he got close enough to them, there was no doubt. Walter Bopp and his brother George. Not only were they dead, their gray flesh looked like dried, wrinkled fruit. Their eyes had shrunk inward and been covered over by saggy pouches of skin, leaving only thin, puckered slits as markers. How had they come to such a grotesque end? There was no sign of violence, nothing that suggested murder or suicide.

Driscoll turned to look around the cellar, but there was little else to see. A small, glass-topped coffee table. A plastic baggie with a few seeds and stems at the bottom, an empty packet of rolling papers. A dozen or so empty beer and soda cans. Cigarette butts on the floor. A box of candles, a box of wooden matches. A kerosene lantern and a gallon jug of kerosene.

Nothing else. No sack full of Mr. Lee's money. Nothing.

The two nothings, Walter and George, and the nothing else they had left behind.

Driscoll heard something before he saw the movement. It was a dry, granular sound, like very fine sand sliding down a sheet of parchment. Walter had gotten up off the mattress, and George was stirring now as well. Driscoll fired one shot into Walter's chest—it made a brief *pfft* sound on impact and produced a puff of dust—but it didn't slow him at all. Walter clamped a hand on Driscoll's shoulder. Driscoll banged off five more shots directly into Walter's face, but it was like shooting into a bucket of sand—the bullets were just swallowed up without effect. Driscoll was reaching for his other gun, but George was on him too now, and the brothers dragged him to the floor. Like silent, smooth-working automatons, they dug into his body, puncturing his clothes, their fingers as sharp as blades of frozen sand. Driscoll could feel the strength flying out of him, as if in one long exhalation. Their fingers poking, puncturing deeply into his chest and belly and throat. The sudden warmth washing over him was his own blood. The Bopps were like mindless, overgrown sand creatures playing at making a mess—out of him.

Driscoll was fading in and out. He could not walk it back in his mind—the cellar, the stairs, the house, the storm, the drive, the purpose of his trip—none of it, and find one mistake or misperception on his part. It made no sense.

And yet, and yet—this.

No...no... This is not...what happens...to me....

10-31-2001

It was the saddest Halloween. There were few jack-o'-lanterns or decorations set out this time. You could see anxiety in the faces of the parents, who came in small groups and wouldn't let their kids go into any house—you had to hand the treats out to them at the doorstep. As if neighbors they'd known for years now might be—someone, something else. As if, even with the parents right outside, some unspeakable atrocity might be perpetrated in an instant on the other side of the door.

There weren't many, though it was a perfect autumn evening. In the past, they'd show up every five minutes or so from 6:00 until around 8:00 p.m. This time, it was over in about half an hour. The streets empty. Front door lights turned off down the street, one after another. Everybody was still on edge, only fifty days later.

Still, he left his light on until 8:00 as usual, and a stray girl showed up a few minutes before that. Looking twelve-going-on-teenager, unsure if Halloween wasn't a waste, that she was now too old for it, but giving it one last turn.

Not from the neighborhood, but he'd seen her a few times in the center of town, kicking around aimlessly. Probably from one of the triple-deckers clustered around the old thread factory. No friends with her, no one waiting outside. Kind of dumpy, but now dolled up like a rock star slut. A pillowcase fat with candy.

"Hi, wow, great outfit. Come on in."

He stepped to the side in the foyer, holding the door open for her.

She came in.

Ah, compliant, too.

I REMEMBER ME

Glen came out of the building on Park Avenue South and stood on the sidewalk. He wasn't sure what to do. A couple of men out by the curb noticed him, and exchanged words. One of them walked briskly toward Glen. Ah yes, he would be a pointer.

"Cab, sir?" the man asked politely. "Or directions?"

"Yes," Glen replied. "A cab, please."

The pointer raced to the curb and waved at the passing river of traffic. The other man stood by with an approving look on his face. He would be the pointer's pointer. No doubt the pointer's pointer's pointer was on patrol nearby. They did an amazing job, moving millions of people around Manhattan every day. But now the man came back, visibly upset with himself.

"What was it again, sir?" he asked sheepishly.

Glen looked at the piece of paper he discovered in his hand. "A taxi," he read aloud.

"Gotcha this time."

The pointer turned back to the road and resumed his attempts to flag down a vacant cab. A few moments later, he had one.

"Thank you," Glen said as he got into the vehicle.

"You do have your destination, sir?"

"Yes, thanks."

"Thank you."

The pointer closed the door and bustled away. Such a polite man, Glen reflected. He handed his piece of paper to the driver, who nodded gravely and consulted a plastic chart that was mounted on the dashboard before he finally entered the destination. Then the taxi accelerated smoothly, edging into the flow. The driver, meanwhile, settled back with a gaudy tabloid. Glen could see the headline on the open page: I EVEN FORGOT HOW TO MAKE LOVE!!!

As the street signs went by, Glen recognized them. But when they passed an expanse of wooded land he suddenly felt uncertain. It was big, and rather attractive. The leaves had such brilliant colors. But what was it? Glen asked the driver, who was unhappy about being disturbed.

"Central Park," he replied a minute later, when he spotted a sign that said Central Park West.

I thought so, Glen told himself. A park that big could only be Central Park. He had known all along—you can know a thing, even if the name for it slips your grasp. It was nothing to fret about, it didn't mean you were stupid or sick. Everyone has such lapses from time to time. It was—but Glen was too tired right now to think about it.

Just past 99th Street, the taxi swung around boldly and came to a stop in front of a large apartment building. The driver sat up and looked around.

"Here you are."

"Thanks."

Glen paid the fare. Money was still fairly easy, because it had numbers on it. Numbers went deep. Money went deeper. Money would last until the end, no doubt about that. He put his wallet back into his jacket pocket, and caught sight of two words penned in blue ink on the inside of his wrist:

GLEN BARNES

"And you are?" the doorman asked.

"Glen Barnes," Glen announced calmly.

The doorman checked Glen's face against the house photo bank on the desk terminal. Apparently everything was in order, as the doorman soon looked up and smiled.

"Yes sir, Mr. Barnes. You're in apartment eleven-twenty, as I'm sure you know."

"Yes, of course. Thank you." Glen hesitated, searching the wide lobby with anxious eyes. "The, uh—"

"The elevators are around there, to your right," the doorman supplied helpfully.

"You haven't moved them since this morning," Glen said in an attempt to make a joke.

"Couldn't be bothered," the doorman shot back, breaking into self-appreciative laughter. "Nice to see you again, Mr.—"

"And you, Jimmy."

"George."

"George, yes. What happened to Jimmy?"

"Jimmy? There's no Jimmy here, Mr. Glen."

"Really? I am sorry. My mistake."

"You're thinking of another place," the doorman named George suggested considerately. "Where you work, maybe."

"Yes, yes, that must be it."

What a strange man, Glen thought as he stepped into the open elevator. Eleven-twenty, wasn't it? He noticed he was sweating. It would help if everybody wore name tags. But there were others who said that would only make matters worse. Glen didn't see how that was possible.

He found a card-key in his wallet and tried it on the door. It worked. He went inside. It was a pleasant-looking apartment. It was his. And hers. She smiled at Glen, came and gave him a kiss on the cheek.

"Hi, Glen," she said sweetly.

"Hello...dear."

A lot had changed with the coming of The Flu.

Glen sat and watched the news on television. Glen's wife was in the kitchen, doing something. Glen had a small notebook in his hand. He flipped through it discreetly and in a few minutes he found the page he was looking for. Her name was Marion—but he knew that, of course!

"Marion," he called out.

"Yes?"

"How are you, Marion?"

"Fine...dear," she called back to him.

Glen quickly scanned the rest of the page, and saw much that was immediately familiar to him. You see, he thought, it's still all there. She

— has a mild case of high blood pressure
— is a lapsed Catholic
— works at a shelter for teenage girls
— likes icky French pop singers
— but does not speak or give French
— and is generally lazy in bed
— reads historical
— likes microwave cuisine
— drinks one spritzer at night
— hates smoke
— except her father's pipe
(— her father is Phil, mother invalid)

Glen slipped the notebook back into his briefcase and looked at the television again. The economic news was very good. There was virtually no unemployment now, thanks to the pointer program.

There was a dark cloud attached to the silver lining, however, as it seemed that the demand for pointers would continue to grow for the foreseeable future, the need far outstripping the supply. It didn't take a genius to see what was coming.

There was also news about The Flu. The news was that there was no news, just a new statement to the effect that its symptoms were still believed to be transient in nature, and not permanent, deteriorating alterations. A doctor told the newsperson that six years was not too long a time for symptoms to persist. Good God, Glen thought. Don't tell me we've had The Flu for six years now. That is a bit much. He got up and went into the kitchen to raise this point with—his wife.

She hastily closed a notebook she was studying and shoved it into her handbag.

Glen emerged from his apartment building and stood there. A pointer soon appeared to help him, but had trouble finding a cab. You could try to flag one down yourself if you knew that was what you needed, but the drivers gave preference to the pointers. The thing to do was to cooperate. Everyone had to change and adjust, otherwise nothing would work anymore. As he waited, Glen heard a loud metallic voice coming from the park.

When the light changed, and there was still no taxi, he went to see what was going on. A crowd had gathered around a man who stood on a red plastic crate. He had a megaphone. "The Flu is not a virus," he shouted. "The Flu is not just a bunch of bacteria. The Flu is a single organism. The biggest, most vicious creature alive on this planet. It sweeps across the continents and oceans as if they were nothing, and it feeds on us like locusts on a field of corn. It decimates us, and with every new feeding season the disaster grows far greater. Soon the dark process will be complete, the final changes wrought, and—"

"How do you know all this?" a heckler cut in.

"I know, because I worked for the government. I learned the awful truth they're trying to keep from you. I—"

"Yeah, but how do you remember it?"

This produced gales of raucous laughter. Glen smiled. What was he supposed to be doing? He had a piece of paper in his hand and he was wearing his suit for work. He made his way out of the crowd and headed toward the street. A young man approached.

"Need a cab, sir?"

"Yes. Are you a pointer?"

"Yes sir."

"Don't you have a badge?" Glen asked. "Or a uniform?"

"They abandoned that idea, sir," the young man said gently, as if speaking to an idiot. "Negative psychology. Where are you going?" He took the destination chit from Glen's hand and peered at it briefly. "Downtown. You're in luck, sir. I've got a taxi here with a couple of other downtown passengers, and there's room for one more. Hurry up, they're ready to go."

"I don't want to share a ride."

"We've all got to cooperate, sir," the man said sternly. "I hope you're not one of those selfish people who refuses to pitch in and make sacrifices like the rest of us."

"Well, no..."

"That's the spirit. Here you go."

Glen slid into the back seat of the taxi. There was a burly fellow already there, and another soon followed, sandwiching Glen in the middle. No one said anything. The taxi moved away, and a short while later it swung onto a road that ran through the park. The dying leaves had wonderful color now—it was that season of the year. Glen wished he had a window.

The man on his right suddenly hit him in the face. The man on his left began hitting him in the stomach. They kept hitting, and Glen never had a chance to say anything or resist. His mouth was full of loose teeth and blood, his vision was blurred, and he couldn't breathe. Then something hit him on the head, and he had only the vaguest sensation left in his body. He was being moved, he flew in the air—landed, fast and hard.

His briefcase was gone. His pockets were empty. His hands were empty—and bleeding; Glen must have landed on them when he hit the pavement. He wandered about for a while after coming to, and now he was sitting beside a pool of water. His head and body ached tremendously. He took off his tie, dipped it in the water, and cautiously touched his face with it. His skin stung, he knew his lips were swollen, and his teeth felt wobbly. The usual host of people moving about; they ignored him. He lowered a hand into the water and then began to pat it with a dry patch of tie. Glen sponged off some of the grit and gravel. Where the skin was only blood-stained, not torn, he rubbed harder to get clean.

Then he saw the faint ink marks swirling off with the blood, vanishing in the water—and he froze. My name was there, Glen realized too late. A few traces of ink remained, but they formed nothing. Not even a single complete letter.

This could be very bad, he told himself, but don't panic too soon. He knew a lot about himself. He had a job, he had a wife, he had an apartment. His job was downtown—that phony pointer had said so. These simple facts were hardly conclusive, but they were good to know and he was determined to hang onto them.

A little later he saw a policeman, who listened patiently to his story. The policeman explained that such muggings were quite common nowadays, and that the streets were full of people who had more or less lost their identities this way. Glen wondered if he had heard about it on the news and then forgotten it.

"What can I do?" he asked.

"You don't remember your name, not even your first name?"

"Not at the moment," he said. "I hit my head, and..."

"Yeah," the policeman said, nodding sadly. "Same thing with your address and place of work?"

"Yes."

"Okay, here's what you do. There's an Identification Center in the Plaza Hotel. That's the nearest one to here. If you ever had your fingerprints taken, or if you have any kind of criminal record, they'll have it on the computer and then they can confirm who you are."

"Otherwise?"

"Otherwise, you got a problem. There's talk about creating a national identity program but that's probably a couple of years away. In the meantime..." The policeman shrugged.

"This is terrible."

"Makes you wish you knocked over a gas station when you were a teenager, don't it? Hey, cheer up. Maybe you did."

"Why didn't they tell us it was this bad?"

"They been telling us for the last few years," the policeman said after consulting a fact sheet. "You just keep on forgetting about it. That's how this thing works."

"God, it's fiendish."

"Damn right it is. You don't notice until something happens so you get pushed off your spot, and you can't get back."

The policeman pointed him in the right direction and wished him luck. As he walked along he became aware of the large number of people who seemed to be wandering about aimlessly. Perhaps he was just imagining it as a result of his current state, but where was the sense of purpose in their stride, the glimmer of focus in their eyes? He was disturbed by the presence of so many bodies on the ground. They were lying everywhere, on the benches and in the grass, some were even sprawled on the sidewalk. Some of them almost looked dead, but surely the situation hadn't reached that point yet. Dead bodies rot, they smell, they cause disease. But he had to admit that the signs were not good.

The line of people outside the hotel was enormous. It would be hours before he got inside. The line didn't seem to be moving at all. He might have to come back tomorrow or the next day. As far as he knew, he'd never broken the law or been fingerprinted, but it was apparently his only chance. He moved along, looking for the end of the line. Then a short man took him by the elbow and leaned close.

"Looking for an I.D.?" the man asked.

"I'm looking for mine, yes."

"I got just what you need," the man went on. "Credit cards, keys, Social Security, addresses, phone numbers, everything a guy needs to get going again. The whole package."

"But is it mine?"

"You gotta start somewhere, pal."

"I don't have any money."

"Then what're you wasting my time for?"

The little man disappeared into the throng. It took a while to realize how unsettling that exchange really was. Identities for sale. But what good would it do? You couldn't just take the contents of someone's wallet and pockets, and gain the benefit of their identity. An interloper was bound to be exposed at home or at work. No, this was a scam, pure and simple. First you robbed some unfortunate person, and then you sold their useless personal papers to someone desperate enough to try anything.

There was one more aspect to this that particularly worried him. What if you walked into another person's home and the wife didn't recognize you as an impostor? She had forgotten what her husband looked like, and she had no photographs—or she thought they were photographs of someone else. You had the key, you were acting as if you belonged there. Would she accept the wrong man? Was anything like that possible? No, of course not. But when he tried to form a mental picture of his wife's face, he could not fill in any details.

Late in the afternoon the air turned very cold, a nasty wind set in and the sky was gray with wintry menace. He was in line but had advanced only a few yards, or so it seemed. If he had to come back tomorrow, where would he spend the night? He felt weak and sluggish, and it occurred to him that he was hungry. But how could he get anything to eat without money? If he had somebody's credit card at least he could get a meal in a restaurant. If the card still worked. But if he had cash to buy a card he could buy food more easily. The grave implications of his predicament were pressing in on his mind.

"This is all because of The Flu?" he asked the man tottering vacantly beside him in the line.

"What flu?"

"The Flu. You know. The Flu."

"If you say so."

It was pointless. He had to think. Perhaps he could find a safe comer in the bus station, or the train station, a doorway sheltered from the wind. Something like that. People lived that way, and survived. What shocked him to the core was how suddenly it had happened to him. One minute he was being driven to work, the next he was literally thrown away like garbage. And from the moment he came to in the park he could feel the awful change that was taking place. Terrible new facts assailed his brain. He was losing the will to resist, he could almost feel it leaching away. Helplessness was rooting itself in him.

"Mike?"

The breathless voice of a plain young woman. He had noticed her approaching, studying the faces in the line. Now she stared at him with frantic eyes.

"Oh my God, it *is* you," she exclaimed. "Mike, oh Mike."

The woman threw her arms around him. She hugged and kissed him, and told him how she had searched and searched for him. She had almost given up hope of ever finding him.

"This just happened to me today," he told her.

"That's what you think," she replied with an understanding smile. "But how do you know that the way you remember is more accurate than what you've forgotten? Besides, don't you think I know my own husband?"

"Tell me your name," he said.

"Roberta. Roberta Stone, and you're Mike Stone." She shook her head with amused delight, and laughed. "I bought that shirt for you at the Smartfellas shop."

Mike. Stone. Surely it would come ringing back to mind, if that was his name. But maybe it was symptomatic to draw a blank. There were no rules in this new situation, you had to play it by ear all the time. Mike was a short and simple name, and in that respect it did feel somehow right.

"What should I do?" he asked her.

"What do you think you should do, silly?" She put her arm through his and pulled him out of the line. "You should go home. Where you live. Now. With me."

"Should we get a taxi?" he heard himself asking.

"What're you, made of money?"

"I don't have any money," he had to admit.

"So what else is new?"

Home was a rather drab basement apartment on West 54th, near Eleventh Avenue. Roberta had the address tattooed to the back of her left hand. She had her name on the heels of her feet. There were hot dogs for supper, and a warm bed later. The next morning she took him around to Skinpainter, who made sure that MIKE STONE would never lose track of his life again.

"What can I do?" Mike Stone asked Roberta Stone.

"You were unemployed before you got lost."

"What about you?"

"I don't work."

"How do we pay the rent and buy things?"

"Interest from the sale of my mother's house."

"You mean we don't have to do anything?"

"Neat, huh?"

Until the French-cut stringbean fiasco. There was big news about a shipment of frozen French-cut stringbeans into Manhattan. Food had become a problem. Either the farmers forgot to plant it or harvest it, or the middlemen forgot to process and deliver it. Something was always going wrong, it seemed. But then a few tons of French- cut stringbeans arrived. The government had found them in a freezer. Roberta bought as many packages as she could grab. So did Mike Stone.

He was watching the news on television. The news was about how no one had heard from Europe in a long time. Well, they said it was a long time—but how could they be sure? Perhaps it was just the day before yesterday.

There was also news about The Flu. The news was that there was no news, but a doctor explained that the symptoms "continued to persist." He said that was not very unusual, even after eight years. Good God, Mike Stone thought. Have we had The Flu for as long as that? Eight years.

He got up and went into the kitchen to raise this point with Roberta (whose name was tattooed along the right side of his left index finger).

She had a wrapper in her hand. There were a couple of green blocks on the counter. Frozen French-cut stringbeans, glistening with moisture. She looked very unhappy, at a loss. He knew that something was wrong, so he didn't mention The Flu.

"What's happening?"

"I don't understand," she complained.

"What?"

"What do you do to get this stuff ready?"

"It's right there on the wrapper," Mike Stone said. He took the foil-paper from her hand and studied it. There was a picture of piping hot stringbeans with butter melting over them. "That's how you do it. Fluffy, like that."

"That's how you eat them," she said. "But how do you get to where they're like that?"

He looked at the directions. "Put them in a pot with a half inch of water. Heat to a boil. Cover, turn down the heat. Then let simmer until tender. That means test them after five minutes or so, to see if they're done. Okay?"

She nodded, but a while later he discovered that she had put the covered pot in the oven and baked it. The handle melted, and then began to burn. The beans were a dead loss.

The next day he took her out for a walk. A very long walk. He lost her in the crowd. There were crowds everywhere now. But he wasn't worried. She could find her way home if she could read her tattoos, or get someone to read them for her and give her the right directions. There were so many pointers available.

Of course, if she forgot to read the tattoos, or forgot what they meant, that would be a different matter.

Roberta failed to return. After a few days it seemed likely that she would never come back. Which was more or less what he, Mike Stone, had expected.

He managed quite well without her, and the time soon came when he stopped thinking about her at all. He had more important things to worry about by then.

Some other people moved into the apartment with him. A gang of young women, and a couple of tough men, one of whom claimed to be the actual owner of the building. He had no documentation but that was not surprising because paperwork had been in decline for a while now. Mike was allowed to sleep in the tiny front hallway every night, as long as he brought back food or firewood. It was a fair compromise, he decided.

This arrangement worked for a short while. One of the young women began to show an unusual interest in him. This was quickly discouraged by the two men, who spent most of their time each day herding the women about on mysterious missions to unknown places. When they went out, Mike had to leave too. Once, when he forgot to bring any food or firewood, they made him sleep outside in the stairwell.

That was the day he came across a storefront office that had been converted into a branch of the Federal Identity Network. It was dark and empty inside, but a great many people stood about on the street as if expecting it to open for business again.

"What's the problem?" he asked someone.

"I don't know."

Mike waited a while. Nothing happened. Then a car sped by, drawing considerable attention since there was hardly any traffic anymore. Nothing else happened, so Mike left.

The next day he saw a man hanging by the neck from an awning pipe. Pinned to his chest was a piece of cardboard, on which the letters DR had been hand-printed.

"What does that mean?" Mike asked someone.

"He was a doctor."

"How did they know?"

"I don't know."

Some little while later, on a similar day, Mike did not find his way back to the apartment. There was never a pointer around when you needed one. But then, there seemed to be less people on the streets, so the pointer program might have been discontinued. The warm weather had arrived, fortunately; shelter was no longer a major problem.

He was sitting on the curb, eating peanuts, when a woman sat down next to him. She was about his age. He offered her some of the peanuts. She took them, watched what he did and then did the same thing. They smiled at each other.

"What's your name?" she asked.

He looked at his finger. "Roberta."

She looked at her hand. "I'm Carl."

"Hi, Carl."

"Hi, Roberta."

They shook hands. They spent that night in an empty office. They hugged and kissed and did it, and he felt better than he had in a long time. But when he woke up in the morning she was gone, and so were his shoes. Why had she taken them, he wondered. You could find shoes easier than food. Besides, he was sure that she had her own shoes. He tried to picture her, and he concentrated on her feet. Well, maybe she didn't have any. Shoes.

He watched a man standing by the curb. The man swayed as if he were caught in a windstorm, though the air was calm. The man looked up the street, then down. Then up again, and down. There was no traffic to worry about, but the man stayed on the curb. A minute later, the man fell to the sidewalk.

This park overlooked the water. The big buildings were back behind him. He liked the place. There were only a few people on the ground. A nice breeze, the taste of salt in the air. A very high blue sky, some puffy white clouds, a warm sun. He bent over and snatched a stalk of tall grass. It was like a miniature tree with leaves and branches sprouting from the top of it. He placed it between his teeth—not because he was hungry, but because it was a naturally irresistible thing to do. He found that he could twirl it around easily, without opening his lips. You must have done this before, he told himself.

It was more pleasant to sit down than stand. Just for a few minutes. Then he would have to get up and do something. He knew he had something to do, somewhere to go. It had slipped his mind just what, but it would come round again. The sun felt wonderful on his skin. He hoped it would fade the peculiar markings on his hands. He had no idea how they'd got there in the first place, and they were a nuisance to think about. He studied his fingers, as if he were seeing them for the first time.

"Remarkable," he said aloud.

He stretched out on his back and twirled the stalk of grass, imagining that it was a tree growing out of his mouth. The earth was warm beneath him. Sooner or later it would rain. He thought of the rain washing him into the ground. Yes. Warm rain, sun, a deep blue sky far above. While I melt away like snow.

"Time to stand up," he says, but he does not stand up.

"Time to get up and go."

He does not.

THE DREAMS OF DR LADYBANK

A Divine Image

Cruelty has a Human Heart
And Jealousy a Human Face
Terror, the Human Form Divine
And Secrecy, the Human Dress

The Human Dress, is forged Iron
The Human Form, a fiery Forge.
The Human Face, a Furnace seal'd
The Human Heart, its hungry Gorge.

—William Blake

PROLOGUE

"It's an amusing thought, Ian, but…"
        "Impossible."
    "Well, yes."
    "Science fiction."
    "And weak on the science," Jack said.
    "But doesn't the idea itself excite you?"
    "Not really. I mean, what's the point? Everyone knows it's a dead end. Besides, even if it were possible, and I'm not for a moment admitting that it is, but if it were, you'd probably wind up with a raving psychotic on your hands, and that's not my idea of fun. Psychotics are very boring people."
    "Psychosis is by no means inevitable."

"This is a splendid malt, by the way."

"Help yourself to more."

"Thanks, I will."

"The point you're refusing to acknowledge is the simple fact of communication, establishing once and for all that it really is possible. My God, Jack, that's a huge leap and you know it. You can't deny it."

"And you can't prove it."

"Perhaps I can."

"Well, I'd love to see it."

"What would you say if I told you I've found a suitable mind for the experiment?"

"I'd say she's probably young, impressionable, quite pretty, very malleable, and a great piece of ass."

"Jack."

"But I'm afraid that your getting her in bed and fucking her brains out will not be widely accepted as scientific proof."

"All right, I give up."

"Ah, don't stop now, Ian. I'm enjoying this. I haven't had such a good mix of booze and bullshit since college, when we used to sit up late at night, trying to figure out what the hell an ethic was, and how to get around it. We called those sessions the Utica Club, because that's all we could afford to drink."

"But I'm serious."

"Okay, you're serious, and you've got this, uh…"

"Subject."

"Right, subject."

"Two of them, actually," Ian said with a hint of smugness in his tight smile. "Two young men."

"Men, huh? You must be serious."

"Yes, and the fact that there are two of them should provide proof enough to justify continuing the research, don't you think? One might be a fluke, but two different people, who are strangers to each other, who respond and meet and interact *by design*—you would take that seriously, wouldn't you?"

"Sure, but come on, Ian. You can't do that with people. If you could, somebody would have discovered it by now. It's not as if we're completely ignorant of how the brain works. What it can and can't do—and I'll tell you one thing, it can't do that."

"The human brain does generate extremely low frequency radio waves, ELF signals. That's a well-known fact."

"Yes, but you can't do anything with them."

"If you say so."

"Not like you're talking about."

"We'll see."

"So, are these guys patients of yours?"

"No, they're just a couple of losers I met."

"And they agreed to go along with whatever it is you plan to try out on them, this experiment?"

"They don't know anything about it."

"What?"

"That would ruin everything, Jack. If they knew, they would expect, and expectation would contaminate their minds. Of course I haven't told them anything."

"Uh, have *you* ever heard of ethics, Ian?"

"Which one did you have in mind?"

"Oh, the one about not experimenting on people without their knowledge and consent. Seems to me there might even be some kind of a law about that."

"Tsk, tsk."

"What exactly is it you intend to do?"

"Nothing. That's the beauty of it."

"I don't understand."

"I'll just be thinking, Jack. That's all. Thinking of them and perhaps even for them."

"Ah, that's all right. Thinking isn't against the law, not yet anyway. But how will you know if it works?"

"I'm not sure, but I imagine it will become apparent one way or another."

"Well, if it does work, let me handle the legal side of it. Maybe we can sell it to Sony, ha-ha."

"That's a thought."

"I can see it now. Everybody will go around wearing a smart little beanie on their head, with an antenna sticking up. They'd sell like Walkmans—or should it be Walk*men*?"

By the time Jack finally left, after sopping up a good deal

more single malt scotch, Doctor Ian Ladybank was almost sorry he had mentioned his little secret. But he had to tell someone, and Jack was the closest thing to a friend he had. You can't stumble across something like that and then not want to shout about it. Nor was it really a little secret; it was serious, major, an awesome challenge. He was sure it had in fact been discovered by others, in the past, although they might not have understood what it was the way he did. It was a skill, it had limits, and it was suitable only for personal purposes.

Amazing, how it had happened. Doctor Ladybank had given the matter a lot of thought over the years. The brain was his hobby, as well as his vocation. He read everything that came out and he even made a special study of radio science. His obsession wasn't his alone—there were other people active in the field. He was aware, for instance, of the theory that some UFO sightings may be triggered by localized disturbances in the earth's magnetic field that interfered with the wave cycles in the observer's brain. It was a matter of some significance to Doctor Ladybank—although few others seemed to consider it important—that the earth, the planet itself, was constantly broadcasting its own ELF waves, and that they were remarkably similar to those generated by the human brain. He devised his own mental exercises, instructing his mind to do what it had never done before.

All of this led nowhere until a young woman named Shelly had come to see him, not long ago. She thought she was stigmatic and she had the wounds to prove it. Her case was not as interesting as it had seemed at first glance but she was an attractive little creature. In his waiting room, as he was showing her out, Doctor Ladybank suddenly found himself wishing, or willing, that Shelly would reach up and touch her breast. A silly but typical erotic fancy, borne no doubt of mid-afternoon tedium. The girl did not respond, but her boyfriend, who had accompanied her to the office and was standing nearby, absently rubbed his Megadeath T-shirt at the spot where it covered his left nipple. The young man's blank expression indicated complete ignorance.

Stunned, Doctor Ladybank at first could not bring himself

to believe what had apparently just taken place. It was too easy to be true. But yes, he had felt a tiny mental spasm at the instant the thought—wish, command, whatever—formed within his mind. Doctor Ladybank was flushed with a sense of accomplishment, happy as a boy who suddenly flicks his wrist in precisely the right way and at last manages to skip a rock across water.

He stood by the window in his office a few minutes later and watched Shelly and her boyfriend walk away down the street. When they were almost out of sight, Doctor Ladybank had a parting idea for them—and sure enough, the boyfriend's hand swung around to pat Shelly's ass. That evening Doctor Ladybank thought about the boyfriend again. *You need to talk to me. Urgently.* Less than a minute later, the telephone rang. He was Alvin Doolittle, but he preferred the nickname Snake.

The other one was sent to Doctor Ladybank, like many of his cases, by the juvenile court. Tony Delgado was only sixteen, but he had his own apartment, a trick pad near the river in the south end of the city. It was a decrepit neighborhood, full of rotting old tenements and abandoned factories, a tidal basin of foundered lives, but it provided all the tolerance and anonymity needed for Tony to practice his trade.

Doctor Ladybank quickly sized the boy up as innately Machian in affect. What Tony possessed was not quite a mind, but more of a constantly shifting panorama of received images and sensations. He learned little but survived, thanks to an underlying canniness that for nearly three years had helped him dodge both the law and the retribution of the streets. A minor stupidity had led him to juvenile court, which promptly fobbed him off on Doctor Ladybank, who within a quarter of an hour had the youth uttering numbers in German while tugging at his earlobes.

It was a discovery that should be important. It should give Doctor Ladybank power, fame, wealth—all the usual prizes. The only trouble was, he didn't know how to take the next step. What to do with this fantastic skill. How could he present it in such a way that would satisfy the scientific community? He could make videotapes of sessions with Snake and

Tony, inducing all kinds of bizarre and unlikely behavior, but that would prove nothing. Not the least of Doctor Ladybank's problems was the painful fact that this skill of his simply didn't work with most people. He tried it with everyone he met now, but the original poor fools were the only two in the plus column. In spite of the odds against it, he was dogged by a fear that both of them really were flukes. Maybe it was just a freak of nature, devoid of any principle or broader application. But even if that were so, there was still a measure of personal satisfaction in what he was doing.

And it was early days yet. Doctor Ladybank was sure that he would learn much more as he pursued his experiment, and sooner or later the ultimate answers would come to him.

ONE

Tony Delgado thought he understood the problem. This Pied Piper, to give him a name, had a special kind of radio that he used to beam his infernal messages into Tony's brain. It had been going for a couple of weeks now, and the situation was only getting worse. Tony had tried to catch the Pied Piper several times before he realized that it was impossible. The Pied Piper was only about six inches tall, and could appear or disappear at will. Many times he was heard, not seen. There was no way Tony could get a hold of the little demon.

Tony was running out of possibilities. He had gone to Dorn's Connection, the largest electronics store in the city, but they told him they didn't have any kind of jamming device that would do what he wanted. They suggested that he consider buying a good radio or stereo system, and just play loud music whenever he was bothered. But Tony had already tried that with the boombox he owned, and it didn't work. Static-ridden, distorted perhaps, the Pied Piper still got into Tony's head.

Now Tony had another idea. He rooted through the underwear in the top drawer of his bureau, and came up with the stiletto he had acquired somewhere along the line. It was his best weapon in the awkward moments that occasionally arose, not so much for use as for display. In Tony's chosen line of work it was sometimes necessary to introduce a deterrent factor, that slight touch of intimidation that prevents serious trouble, and the stiletto had never failed to chill a tricky customer. He was pleased to find that it hadn't lost any of its sharpness, though for the task he had in mind now all he would require was the very fine tip of the gleaming blade.

Tony Delgado lived in a small apartment in the heart of the south end. He was sixteen, and had been on his own for the best part of a year now. He had a perfect body, which he took care of religiously because it was his bread and butter. At five-ten, he was neither too tall nor too short. His physique was slender and boyish, and he avoided the muscular look, but he exercised enough to maintain a body texture that was both supple and firm.

He had one good room, the large one where he entertained his customers. Tony had invested a lot in that room, setting it up for the fantasy scenarios that were his trademark. He sometimes had to discourage mushy johns who wanted to use his personal bed or to stay all night. He preferred it that way, keeping the rest of his place, and life, off-limits. Tony's bedroom was small and cluttered, the kitchen bug-infested. The bathroom was modest but clean, and one way or another it saw a lot of use.

The trouble started more than a month ago. Tony had always been successful at avoiding the police until then. He had picked up a john at a bar in the neighborhood, but when they got outside the asshole lost his nerve. A patrol car happened to pass by as Tony was kicking in the rocker panel on the man's shiny new car. It should have come to nothing. The asshole naturally refused to press charges. However, Tony then made the unfortunate mistake of giving the cop a hard time, even shoving him away once. Since he was still a minor, Tony was sent to juvenile court, where some drip of a judge gave him a boring lecture and then ordered him to see a psychiatrist.

What a joke that turned out to be. For one thing, the guy had a funny name, Lady-something. Ladybug would be right, Tony thought, because the shrink was the crazy one. He was straight, and even beautiful, but as the interview went on Tony began to feel like he was stuck with a creep. It was no one thing the guy did that bothered him, just a very uncomfortable feeling that got stronger all the time. Tony had never experienced anything like that, and he had met some strange people.

In the end, the shrink talked pure nonsense. He told Tony to watch out for bright lights, bright colors, and, most of all, bright flowers. What kind of shit was that? Tony decided Doctor

Ladybug was in bigger trouble than he was, and he nodded his head politely, agreeing with everything the shrink said.

It must have been the smart thing to do, because he was sent home to his mother, no additional sessions required. He was free of any legal obligations. Tony was back at work in his apartment that same night.

Tony's mother understood nothing. For thirty years she had worked at a dry-cleaning shop, and still did. Some people argued that the fumes were dangerous, and Mrs. Delgado did get headaches regularly, but it was steady work and there was a lot to be said for seniority.

She believed anything Tony told her. He was her youngest child, born when she thought her body was past all that. And he was the best when it came to calling her, visiting and giving her little gifts. So kind and considerate. She didn't like the fact that he lived away from her when he was still so young, but there was nothing she could do about it. Kids grow up quicker today, they do what they want, and Tony didn't have a father around to lay down the law. But at least the boy was good to her, and he lived less than a mile away.

So his first brush with the law had come to nothing, and his mother still lived in happy ignorance of his activities, but Tony faced other problems. AIDS had claimed or scared off some of his top customers, and to keep his income up he was forced to cruise the bars more often. That multiplied both his legal and medical risks. So far he remained clean, but business was tough, and getting tougher every week.

He had also developed a taste for coke. The good stuff, not that crack shit. But it cost money, and Tony was also convinced that it was one of the reasons he was so jumpy of late. However, these drawbacks were not enough to curb his appetite. They were simply new factors to bear in mind.

Worst of all, the Pied Piper had entered his life. At first Tony thought he was imagining things, or that it was some kind of weird side-effect of the drug. He would glimpse a trick of light or a play of shadows, but it was always on the other side of the room, and he always caught it out of the corner of his eye. When he turned to look carefully, there was nothing to see.

Then there were the sounds. Tony began to think of them as messages of some kind, though he never really understood them at all. They were like bubbles of noise that burst open deep inside his head. There was always a lot of static with it, which is how Tony finally cottoned on to the possibility that the Pied Piper was broadcasting to him. It was possible to pick out a few words now and then, sometimes a phrase or two, but none of it ever made any sense. Tony did get a certain feeling of urgency, and that only aggravated his distress.

Soon enough, the little man emerged tauntingly, letting Tony see him clearly—if only for a brief instant at a time. Now, a day never passed without one appearance, usually more. He never actually said anything, and his expression was always blank. The little fucker was a constant torment, even when he wasn't there. The only positive thing was that so far he hadn't turned up when there was a customer present.

Tony went into the bathroom and turned on the light around the mirror. He stood close to it, opened his mouth and found his targets. Tony's teeth were not perfect. Over the years he had accumulated a few plastic or composite fillings. They were okay, he figured. He wanted the two larger ones that were made of lead or silver, some kind of metal. It seemed obvious to him that the Pied Piper was using those fillings as built-in receivers for his transmissions. The metal picked up the beam and relayed it along the nerves in Tony's jawbone on to the center of his brain. So, if he could just get rid of those two fillings he might solve his problem. He had called three different dentists, but they seemed to think it was a set-up for a lawsuit, and turned him down cold. The only alternative was to do it himself.

It wasn't easy. At least he could get at the two fillings and still see what he was doing, but for the longest time the tip of the blade found no hold. Tony grew frustrated, then angry as the knife slipped off the tooth and jabbed his gums. He tasted a little of his own blood when he swallowed. His open mouth filled with saliva too fast, and some of it trickled down his windpipe, setting off a violent but useless coughing jag. Tony's eyes were bleary as he tried to refocus on the tooth. He was beginning to think it was an impossible chore, but then the point of the blade finally lodged in some tiny crevice for a second. It slipped off almost at once, but he was encouraged, and several tries later he found the spot again. Tony worked it carefully, digging the tip into the gap and trying to expand it. As long as the metal blade touched the metal filling it jangled the nerves in his tooth like a constant electrical charge, but he would endure that to get rid of the Pied Piper. Any pain would be worth suffering if it would end the daily nightmare visitations.

Tony's eyes continued to blur with tears and his jaw ached, but he was making progress. Now he had gouged enough of a crack to be able to use the knife as a lever. But whenever he relaxed or became careless, the knife would pop loose again and stab Tony in the gum or the roof of the mouth. The saliva that spilled out on his chin was distinctly pink. Worst of all, the goddamn metal filling seemed to be welded to the goddamn tooth. No matter how hard he pried at it, there was barely any movement.

"Come on, you fuck," Tony whined. "You're killing me."

Then he screamed and dropped the knife as he reached for the wall to hold himself against as a blast of pain shot through his entire body. The knife clattered in the sink. This is too much, he thought as he reached for it with trembling fingers. But then he discovered that the filling was loose. Yeah, he could move it with his tongue. It was still hooked in there, but when he poked it repeatedly it felt like it was rattling in place. Gasping for breath, Tony forced himself to re-insert the knife.

"*Ein, zwei, drei...*"

He increased the pressure, and the pain blossomed, weakening him so much that all the strength in his body seemed to be flying out of his pores. One last shove—the filling was at last torn free, but the knife blade scraped a bloody furrow across the roof of Tony's mouth at the same time. He nearly swallowed the jagged filling but managed to spit it into the sink. It bounced around like a deformed marble before coming to rest. Tony was dizzy and drained, and the hole in his tooth felt enormous, but he had done it. One down, one to go. He washed his mouth out, and then sat on the toilet lid for a few minutes to rest.

The second filling seemed to take longer, probably because

he had little patience left. His arms and neck ached, along with his jaw, but somehow the pain bothered him less. Tony pushed on, desperate to finish the job, and eventually he was rewarded when the second filling slid off his tongue and joined the first one in the sink. He felt an enormous sense of satisfaction, freedom and accomplishment. He took the two lumps of twisted metal into the kitchen, opened the window, and threw them as far as he could out into the weed-choked, trash-strewn backyard.

Tony rinsed his mouth again, this time with warm salty water to stop the bleeding. Then he poured a large scotch, to remove the bad taste and soothe his nerves. He sat down in his one good room and sipped the drink carefully. God, he was still shaking. His arms and legs felt so weak. He let his tongue dance over the two holes in his teeth. They were huge. The edges Were so sharp he would have to be careful not to cut his tongue on them.

But no dentist could refuse him now. Two fillings fell out when he was eating. Tough pizza crust, say. Or peanuts, or when he bit into a steak. It didn't matter what. That kind of thing happened all the time. Tony would insist they be replaced with plastic or porcelain fillings, anything but metal.

He smiled faintly as he sloshed the whiskey around in his mouth. It stung his exposed nerves, but he knew that it was also beginning to deaden them. The pain was fading deliciously.

Zzzzzt.

Oh no, no.

Zzzzzt.

Tony put the drink down on the table because he was afraid he might drop it. This can't be happening. He looked around the room nervously. A glimmer of movement, then gone. A shadow that passed in an instant, as if a bird had flown by the window. Then the static cleared up beautifully.

—Ah, that's much better.

The words blared inside Tony's trapped mind.

—You can really hear me now, can't you!

TWO

"Hic, haec, hoc"

"Say what?" The bartender looked puzzled, wary.

"What?"

"You said something to me?"

"No," Snake replied. "I didn't say nothing to nobody."

"You want another beer?"

"Yeah, I want another beer," Snake said, his voice brimming with defiance. "And a clean glass."

The bartender brought the drink and the glass, withdrew some money from the small pile of cash in front of Snake, and muttered to himself in Spanish as he turned away. Lousy greaseball, Snake thought as he inspected the new glass. I'm sitting here, minding my own business, having a quiet beer, and this asshole has to get on my case. Say what? Say, fuck you, bro.

At least tonight Snake knew what he was doing in this place. He was waiting for the whore, Toni. Last night he had no idea at all why he had come there. The El Greco was a pisshole of a bar, buried in the unfriendly depths of the south end. But Snake went out last night, leaving Shelly behind alone and cursing, and he'd come straight across the river to this dump. He hated the place. It had the terrible smell of food you'd never want to eat, and it was full of jabbering spies. They all had the same look on their faces too, mean and vaguely pissed off, as if every damned one of them had to go through life with a splinter up his dick.

They wouldn't bother him, though, because Snake was wearing the colors. Sure, they could beat the living shit out of him if they wanted to, but they knew he'd be back sooner or later with thirty of the hardest fuckers around who would trash the El Greco, along with every spic they could get their hands on. Nor did it matter that Snake was no longer exactly in good standing as a member of the Legion of the Lost; he wore the colors, and that was all that counted in a situation like this. The colors commanded respect, or at least fear—which wasn't very different.

Last night he sat in the same place at the bar for nearly an hour, wondering what the hell he was doing there and why he could not bring himself to leave. It was odd, but then some odd things had been happening to Snake lately. Headaches, for one, the kind that ordinary painkillers didn't cure. And, according to Shelly, he was talking to himself more and more. But that was crazy. It stood to reason that a man can't go around talking to himself and not know it. Could he? What about that latest incident, the one with the bartender a few minutes ago? No, it was impossible. In a noisy place like this, the bartender made a mistake.

Besides, Shelly had her own problems. She'd gone quite pale and spotty in recent weeks. She also scratched herself a lot, so much so in fact that it had reached the point where she had these ugly open wounds in her hands and feet and on her body. Then, as if that weren't enough, she decided they were the marks of Christ on the Cross. Snake had to take her to the doctor, who sent them along to a shrink. Dumb fucking bitch. He ought to sell her off to an out-of- state gang, but the way she was now, her sales value was scraping along the bottom. Shelly was so bad that he didn't even want to touch her anymore—unless he had to hit her.

Maybe that was why Snake had come to the El Greco, to meet a new piece of ass. He had accomplished that much last night, when Toni sat down beside him and they got to talking. She was a fine item, all right. Cute fanny, long legs, pretty face. She could be a bit fuller up front, but Snake had never been all that keen on big tits. He liked women lean and—snaky.

It didn't bother him that she was a spic. Somehow, that was okay in a woman. Toni's creamy skin was such a pleasant contrast to Shelly's newsprint surface. And the eyes—deep, round, warm and brown, with flecks of gold. Snake couldn't remember the last time he'd looked closely at Shelly's eyes, but now he thought of them as washed-out blue peas adrift in a pinkish-white glaze. No question, Toni was an exotic gem in comparison.

It did bother him, however, that she was a whore. He didn't care how many men she fucked. The problem was that he lacked the money to buy her talents. Even if he had it, it would go against the grain for Snake to spend it on something he'd always managed to get for free.

He and Toni were eventually able to work out a deal based on non-cash considerations. She liked coke, and she needed Demerol. Snake had experience and helpful contacts in the field. He was strictly minor league, but he did know how to cut himself an edge in such transactions. It was one of the many ways in which he cobbled together an erratic income.

"Darling."

"Hey, babe." Snake smiled as Toni edged close to him at the bar. "You look great."

"Buy me a drink."

"Sure. What'll you have?"

"You forgot already. Tsk, tsk."

"Yeah, well…What was it again?"

"Red Death on the rocks."

"Right."

As there were no other barstools free, Snake gave Toni his. He signaled the bartender. Toni looked fantastic in a clinging black mini-dress. Snake could hardly take his eyes off her legs, but he did turn away long enough to watch the bartender care-fully when he took the money for Toni's drink.

"You can take your sunglasses off."

"I like the dark," she replied.

"It's dark enough in this dump."

Toni sipped her drink. "Do you have something for me?"

"I told you I would."

"I know what you told me, but do you have it?"

"Of course I do."

"You're a darling. What is it?"

Snake leaned close to her. "God, you smell great."

"What do you have?" Toni repeated with an edge in her voice. "What do you have for me?"

"Demerol."

"Beautiful." Toni relaxed and smiled at him. "There is one thing I have to tell you."

"Yeah? What's that?"

"It's the wrong time to use my little pussy."

"That don't bother me, babe," Snake declared proudly. "In the Legion of the Lost we don't just poke bloody cunts, we hunker right down and eat 'em."

"Really?" Toni gave a dramatic shudder. "Sounds icky. And it would bother me, darling. But you know, I really have a great ass, and I'm sure you'd love it."

"Yeah, it looks good, and I bet it feels like velvet," Snake said. "But I ain't no butt-fucker."

"So there are some things the Legion of the Lost won't do," Toni said sarcastically.

"Damn right."

"Oh well. I guess—"

"Read my mind," Snake told her.

"I give great head."

"Right. You better, babe."

"How many pills do you have?"

"Put it this way. You owe me five blow jobs."

Toni looked rather disappointed. "But darling, you will be able to get more, won't you?"

"What do you do, eat 'em like candy?"

"I'm in pain," Toni said resentfully.

"You need somebody to look after you," Snake pointed out, a clever idea forming in his mind. Blow jobs every night. A great source of income. He would move her out of the south end and put her to work making real money, no more of this back alley boffing for bucks. "Yeah, somebody who'll take good care of you."

"I take care of myself."

"I mean a regular guy."

"I've got a hundred regular guys, darling."

"To protect you," Snake clarified firmly.

"I've never needed protection."

"That just means you're overdue for trouble."

"Oh." Toni didn't seem to care for what Snake had in mind, but then her face moved slightly as if she had just felt a twinge of pain, and then she smiled up at him. "Oh dear."

"Yeah, but don't worry about it, babe," Snake told her with a wide grin. "Now that I'm here you'll be all right. I'll take care of you and you'll take care of me, right?"

"You might decide you don't want me," Toni said. She had a peculiar smile on her face. "When you get to know me."

Snake laughed. "Oh, I'll want you, babe, you can be sure of that. Matter of fact, I want you right now."

Toni discreetly slipped her hand between Snake's legs.

"Mmm, so you do."

"Come on, let's go."

"Your old lady must not be treating you right."

"What old lady?"

"I can tell, darling."

"Yeah, well, she's on the way out," Snake said. "She just don't know it yet."

"No one ever does."

"Come on," Snake said anxiously.

"Let me finish my drink," Toni insisted calmly. "Besides, I can see that you like standing in the middle of a crowd of people and having me touch you this way. It's nice, isn't it?"

"Jesus, babe."

But she was right.

THREE

—Greetings, plasmodium.

"Hey, I've been looking for you."

—Stand by.

"Where are you?"

—Here.

"I can't see you."

—You can hear me.

"Come on out, man. Let me see you."

Tony had a large mayonnaise jar. If he could just get his hands on the Pied Piper long enough to shove him into the jar and screw the cap on…Into the trash…Into the landfill…But, only after Tony hammered a few nail holes in the cap and then steamed the brain-eating son of a bitch alive over a pot of boiling water for a couple of hours.

But maybe Tony wouldn't throw him away. Maybe he'd put the jar on a shelf in the living room and let his johns goggle at it. What the hell is that, they'd ask. Souvenir from the Caribbean, he'd tell them with a straight face. My voodoo chile.

—Slime.

"Where the hell are you?"

—Everywhere.

"Yeah? Where's that?"

—In your head.

"That's what I have to talk to you about," Tony said. "You have to let me call a dentist and get an appointment, because my jaw is killing me all the time now."

—No.

"I can't take it anymore."

—No.

"Fuck, man, why the fuck not?"

—He'll see what you did to your teeth and he'll think that you're crazy.

"I *am* crazy."

—He'll get them to lock you up.

"I'm locked up here most of the time, talking to myself."

—I am always with you.

"Then come on out and let me see you."

—See!

Suddenly Tony couldn't see anything but the Pied Piper. It was as if he were inside Tony's eyeballs, peering into his brain. He had an evil grin on his twisted face, and now his filthy hands came up and started scratching at the inner lining of Tony's eyes in an effort to shred through the membrane. Scraping, ripping, peeling the cells away with ridged fingernails that were as sharp as razorblades.

The pain was excruciating. Tony slid off the chair and fell to his knees on the floor, holding his head in his hands. He was too weak to scream, it felt like the breath had been sucked from his lungs. One hand groped blindly toward the small brown bottle on the coffee table. Tony had tried all the regular store-bought painkillers, but none of them helped. Finally he had scored some Demerol from a beautiful idiot named Snake, his new friend. The Demerol was fantastic, although it never really lasted quite long enough. Now Tony had just a few left.

—No.

The muscles in Tony's arm went dead. His fingers fumbled at the brown bottle but could not grip it. *Please*, came the whimper from the back of his skull. *Please let me*—but a shrill racket overwhelmed his feeble thought.

—Sorry.

Tony began to beat his head against the floor.

—Do you want the people downstairs to come up and find you like this? They'll call a doctor and he'll decide you're crazy. He'll have them lock you away forever.

Tony continued to bang his head on the hardwood floor in an effort to knock himself unconscious.

—Listen.

Tony could no longer lift his head; it rested face down in a smear of blood. But the pain had let up, and his brain began the laborious process of forming clear thoughts again. His breathing came back in short, shallow gasps.

—You can have your pill.

Tony tried to reach for the bottle, but couldn't.

—Not yet. Only when you have listened to what you must do for me.

"Yes."

—And accept.

The air was thin and liquid. It had a raw, unpleasant edge that reminded Tony of grain alcohol.

"What is it?"

—You must bring someone here.

"Who?"

—Someone you trust.

"I don't trust anybody, man."

—Nevertheless.

"How can I, with you hanging around?"

Business had fallen right off the table ever since the Pied Piper had taken over Tony's life. He couldn't dare bring anyone home when he longer had control of the situation. He had to go out at night all the time now, hustling quick tricks in toilets and alleys for prices he would have laughed at a couple of months ago. Tony's whole world had shriveled around him like the skin on a rotten corpse.

—You can.

"Can I take money from him."

—Yes.

"And do my job?"

—That is what you must do.

"I get it," Tony said, smiling faintly. "You can't see me when I'm outside, and you want to watch. Right?" For once the Pied Piper was silent. Tony chuckled. "That's okay, man, that's cool. But you have to understand." His voice took on a pleading tone again as he pushed himself over onto his side. "I can't go on living like this. It just won't work."

—Leave the living to me, plasmodium.

"I mean it, man. I'm dying in my socks. People will come to see what's the matter, why I'm not in touch. My family, like that, you know what I mean."

—Then deal with them.

"I can't handle it."

—Why not?

"I just can't. I'm afraid."

—Of what?

"You…"

—But, I'm you.

"The fuck you are," Tony protested. "I'm sick. I hurt all the time now. The only way I can face people is in the dark, and it's all because of you. *Not* me, I'm the one you're doing it to, and maybe I should be locked away somewhere. Maybe that'd be the best thing."

—Nonsense.

"You're killing me. Day by day, you're killing me."

—Ingrate.

"Come here, you little shit."

Tony had regained a slight measure of strength by now, so he lunged in the direction of where he thought the Pied Piper might be, but his fingers grasped empty air. The demon was gone. Tony knew it at once from the sudden lightness he felt, the release of his mind.

It was the worst attack yet. Tony's heart banged inside his chest, weak but frantic, and his skin was slick with sweat. His arms trembled, nearly buckling, as he made an effort to sit up on the floor. He looked at the thin patch of blood on the hardwood and felt a terrible anticipation of his own doom. This is how he would die, like an animal, like less than an animal. Like trash, like slime, unseen, all but invisible, stepped on, rubbed away, a smear, a tiny stain on the street.

Tony crawled up into the chair. He saw the brown bottle of Demerol, but he no longer felt the need for any. Save them. The ache in his jaw was dull and distant. If only he could manage to grab the Demerol and get it down his throat in the minute before the Pied Piper got a hold of him. It was the only thing that did seem to keep the demon from getting through, at least for a short while. But he would have to carry a loose pill all the time, or else have one installed in a special socket in his teeth, like some of the Nazis. Come to think of it, the holes were already there, waiting to be custom-fitted.

He needed more Demerol, that was the main thing. Enough to keep him safe day and night. It was so damn good, so much better than coke or weed or anything else he'd ever tried. Better even than sex. So what if it turned him into a placid addict, lolling about like a zombie? Anything was better than having that fucker inside his brain.

Tonight he would see Snake again, and he would make sure the guy was sufficiently motivated to get more Demerol. There was no way Tony could live without it now.

He noticed the mayonnaise jar on the floor, and it puzzled him for a moment. He picked it up and looked at it. The strands of mayonnaise left inside had turned into a greenish-black slime. Slime, the Pied Piper had called him.

Plasmodium. That was a word Tony knew for certain he didn't know and had never heard before. Until today. Where did it come from? Impossible. Unless the Pied Piper was real.

The pain began to swell like an infernal orchestra in Tony's head, and he reached for the brown bottle.

FOUR

"Where y'goin?"

Snake looked over his shoulder. Shelly was still on the old couch, which sagged nearly to the floor. She looked like she was sampling coffins and had found one that suited her. She had been lying there most of the day. She was out of it, brain-blitzed on those pills the shrink had prescribed for her. Shelly discovered happiness when she doubled the original dosage and now she didn't scratch herself so much. She was also a lot easier for Snake to handle, although his feelings for her did not improve. Snake was hooked on Toni.

"Out," he replied curtly.

"Out where?"

"Fuck you."

Shelly struggled to push herself up on one elbow. It wasn't a pretty sight. Scrawny arms and legs. A whining, watery voice that came from a face resembling a tombstone. She also broadcast an odor that would pit steel. He looked away from her and put on his Legion of the Lost leather jacket.

"Snake..."

"Don't wait up."

Twenty minutes later Snake parked his beat-up Dodge Colt on South Freedom, hurried around the corner and entered the El Greco bar. The usual do-nothing crowd was on hand, drinking, yammering over the soccer table and sticking their chests out at each other like animals. Snake hated them all. They seemed to smirk at him and laugh to themselves whenever he came in, but not one of them had the balls to take him on because they knew he'd kick the shit out them. Snake knew about spic fighting abilities—they were game little roosters, but hit them in the body and they all break up like a sack of sticks.

Toni was there too, as she knew she damn well better be. It hadn't taken him long to straighten her out on that score. Snake was not to be kept waiting, not for one minute. You have to make sure a whore knows her place and toes the line, otherwise she'll piss all over you. Snake was pleased, but didn't show it, though he did tell her she looked sexy when she came and wrapped her arm around his waist. They got drinks and sat down at the far end of the bar, away from the crowd. Unfortunately, the El Greco didn't run to booths or tables.

Toni smiled, gave him little kisses, murmured in his ear and touched him secretly, but for all that she seemed tense and edgy. Her face was drawn and she toyed with her drink nervously.

"What's the matter, babe?"

"I'm in pain," she said.

"Drink your drink, and have another."

"You know what I mean."

"Relax."

"You got more?"

"Sure," Snake said.

"How much?"

"Jesus, you are jumpy tonight. Enough, okay? I have enough for you."

Toni settled down a little and stroked his thigh gratefully. Nice. Snake was pleased, but not entirely happy. His efforts to advance the situation in the last ten days had so far failed. He loved the blow jobs in his car, parked in a dark lot, and he knew he had a hold on Toni, but his control over her was only partial. She had agreed to consider working exclusively for him, but still would not commit to it. Snake's dream of free sex *and* free money hovered just beyond his reach. For the moment.

"But," he said quietly.

"What?" Toni's face tensed immediately. "But what?"

"I'm not happy."

"Why?"

"Take those sunglasses off."

"Pretend I'm a stranger, hot for you, and—"

"Take 'em off," Snake demanded. "It's dark enough here."

"Okay." Toni removed the shades and blinked, wincing. Then she smiled at him. "Whatever you want, darling."

"That's better."

"Besides, I'm hot for you anyway, you know."

"Yeah, well." Snake tried to look cool, but it wasn't easy to ignore her hand between his legs. "Listen to me."

"What's the matter?"

"I want you working for me."

"I know, but—"

"You don't belong down in this part of town. I can take you to better places, fix you up with guys that have more money. You can pull a ton, and I'll take care of everything. Everything you need, I'll get it for you."

"Sounds good," Toni said in a neutral tone of voice. "Maybe we could do that, but I'm not ready for it yet."

"No? We could leave right now, head on up to the Green Door and bag a half-dozen yuppies in no time."

"But not tonight, darling. I don't feel too good."

Snake shrugged his shoulders as if it didn't bother him one way or the other, but the expression on his face tightened. "There's something else."

"What?"

"I'm getting kind of tired of doing it in the car."

"Oh."

"Don't worry, babe. You're great. But I'd like to go back to your place, where we can take a little more time and really do it right. Slow and sweet, you know?"

Toni looked unhappy. Snake knew he was walking a fine line. She had already made it clear to him that she didn't bring anyone home, that it "wasn't convenient" for some reason which she would not specify. If he pushed her too hard, she might decide to drop him and take her chances with somebody else. Whores know so many people. It might take her a few days, but sooner or later she'd find another source of coke and Demerol, and Snake would be left out in the cold. Toni was too valuable to lose. It wasn't often that you found such a hot young thing, such an unusual beauty who really could perform. Toni was a sizzler.

But damn it, if Snake was going to be her one supplier, then he was entitled to more than he was getting. She didn't even let him touch her hardly at all, aside from a little ass-grabbing and an occasional brush with her nubby tits. Snake wanted more, much more. He wanted to roll around naked with her on a bed, to watch her strip, to splash around together in a bubble bath— the kind of things he did with Shelly, when she was human. Toni was great when she put her nose to the grindstone, but Snake was determined to strike a better deal.

"Darling, I will take you back to my place, and we'll have a wonderful time—many wonderful times."

"All right."

"But," Toni said, holding her hand up, "I have to get myself organized first."

"What the fuck does that mean?"

"I told you, I'm suffering the most monumental pain, from my dental problems. That's why I need the medicine."

"Right," Snake said wearily. He knew better than to ask why she didn't just get her dentist to write a prescription. She was a no-hope junkie whore, and it wasn't hard to figure out what the future had in store for her, but at least he had found her while she was young and still had a lot of tread. She was worth taking a certain amount of bullshit to keep. "How long will that be?"

"Next week."

"Really?"

Her eyes danced vaguely, avoiding him. "I hope."

"Jesus, babe."

"You poor darling," she said soothingly, caressing him again discreetly. "I'll make it up to you, just wait and see. I will, I really will. We'll have the most fantastic time together. And in the meantime, I'll suck your brains out, I'll drink you dry."

Talk like that dazed Snake. "God, you make me hot," he told her. "Let's get out of here."

"First."

Business first, was what she meant. Snake expected that and had prepared for it. In his pockets he had two packets of pills, a larger quantity in case Toni met either or both of his demands, and a smaller number if she turned him down. It was time to yank the leash. Snake slipped her the packet containing half a dozen Demerols. Without looking at it, her eyes widened in alarm.

"That's all?"

"'Fraid so, babe."

"Why?"

"Recession. Supply and demand. Things are tight. Remember when I told you it'd be a lot easier if we worked together?"

Toni was trying to look stern, but it didn't suit her. "You know I can find other sources," she said.

"It isn't wise to take business away from the Legion," Snake countered, falling back on his last serious threat. Not that the Legion gave a damn about him. However, Toni didn't know that, so the threat was as good as real. "It makes 'em want to go out and kick somebody's face in, that kind of thing."

"All I want is a little time," Toni said pleadingly.

"What I just gave you is a little time."

Toni sighed unhappily. "All right."

"Now, let's go out to the car."

FIVE

Tony couldn't stand it anymore. The pain was too much for him to bear. Three days ago he had finally gone to a dentist and had his teeth filled with some kind of plastic. It was a hideous session, lasting hours. The dentist obviously thought that Tony was crazy because of what he had done to his teeth, and for not removing his sunglasses. It cost a lot, and since Tony was not a regular patient and had no dental coverage he was obliged to fork over the money in advance. That was smart on the dentist's part, as Tony never would have bothered if he knew the fillings weren't going to work. They didn't.

At first he thought it was just a matter of time before the pain wore off for good, but after three days it was clearly there to stay. Perhaps he should have had new metal fillings installed to interfere with the Pied Piper's broadcasts, but the originals hadn't really done the job, and it now seemed likely that Tony's teeth had little if anything to do with the strength or weakness of the torment he experienced.

He hadn't actually seen the Pied Piper in some time now, but the messages still came through several times a day. They meant little to Tony, aside from the sheer pain and terror they caused him. It had reached the point where he spent most of his time in bed or on the couch, weak from the last onslaught, trembling with dread in anticipation of the next one.

The pain usually subsided at night, and Tony would go out to eat and then hustle up some work. He tried to do what the demon voice wanted. He brought several customers back to his place and performed magnificently. They were cheap bums who didn't deserve such royal treatment but Tony would do whatever it took to please the Pied Piper. When the voice returned, however, it was always dissatisfied, and the agony continued.

Worse, Tony hadn't seen Snake since the night before he went to the dentist. He needed more Demerol, huge amounts, to get him through each day and make life somewhat bearable. Tony stabbed a glossy fingernail at the ice in his drink. It looked as if Snake would not appear at the El Greco tonight. That was bad, because Tony was completely out of Demerol. It had occurred to him that unless he got some he might kill himself tomorrow—assuming the Pied Piper would let him. Tony didn't know what to do. He left the bar, planning to return later. In the meantime, he would hit a few other places and see if he could find Snake.

The bastard was jerking his chain, that's what it was. Tony wouldn't work for him, wouldn't take him home for a long night of sex. Well, there was a problem. Somehow, Snake had yet to grasp the fact that Tony was at least nominally male. Tony could work the straight side of the street, but that was nerve-wracking, and he had no appetite for it. Nor could he bring Snake home, as it wouldn't be long before the Lost Legionnaire noticed some little something taped flat between Tony's legs.

Tony pulled a couple of quick tricks in his wanderings, but he didn't find Snake. He eventually found himself crossing the bridge into Riverside. It was a poor working-class neighborhood, virtually identical to the south end but for the fact that there were very few blacks or Hispanics in Riverside. It was for the most part unknown territory to Tony, but for some reason he felt he was heading in the right direction.

He tried a few bars along the way, looking in, then turning to leave immediately. Tony had long ago developed an ability to recognize places where he was sure to get beaten up.

He had to work out something with Snake. He could tell him the truth, and probably get beaten up for that, but at least it would clear the air. The charade couldn't go on much longer, and it might be better to get it over with sooner than later. But he had to have something to appease Snake. A share of Tony's income from gays—that might do it. Why not? It was the same kind of deal Snake wanted, except that Tony would be working his regular beat, not the cash-laden yuppie straights at the Green Door. The money might be less but it was still money for nothing. And Tony would have his steady supply of coke and Demerol. Yeah, it might just work out.

Nonetheless, Tony shuddered at the prospect of confronting Snake with the truth. Was it really necessary? Tony had enough cash on him now to buy a few days' worth of pills. Do that, just pay for the medicine, take it and go. No sex, no promises. Keep it strictly on a business footing. And if Snake insists on more? Tell him it's that time of the month. No, Tony remembered he had done that only a week or two ago. Vaginal fungus? Snake might want to eat it. Tell him you've got the clap, and you're out of action for a while. Head, yes; anything else, no.

The rattletrap Dodge Colt—there it was. Tony was amazed. He had found Snake. Almost. The car was parked in front of an aged triple-decker. On one side of the house there was a vacant lot, then a bakery and some more shops. On the other side, there was a diner, now closed, and a bar that Tony had already checked. Across the street, nothing likely. It had to be this apartment house. But which of the three apartments?

Tony started on the ground floor. He pushed the doorbell, but it didn't ring. He was about to knock when, through the side window, he caught sight of an elderly man sitting in an armchair in the front room. Doubtful. Tony went up the battered stairs. The light was mercifully dim, a single hanging bulb nearly burned out, and the air was permeated with the compressed smell of stale cooking—decades of it. The apartment on the second floor was dark and the screen door was locked. Tony caught his breath, and then continued on to the top floor. Lights, a dull noise inside. Tony knocked. Nothing. He knocked again, louder. Still no sign of a response. He knocked hard enough to hurt his knuckles.

"Yeah."

The voice was faint and distant, but Tony was certain he had heard it. He tried the door, and it opened. He entered a narrow hallway. It was dark, but light came through an archway ahead on the right. Tony took a few steps and stood, looking into a drab living room. There was a girl on the couch.

"You must be the little woman."

"Who're you?"

"I'm looking for Snake."

"He's out."

"Where?"

"I don't know."

"His car is out front," Tony said. "Would he be somewhere in the neighborhood?"

"He went with Crabs."

"What?"

"Crabs. His friend."

"Oh." Tony felt uncomfortable talking across the room. He moved closer to the pathetic girl, who made no effort to get up. She was squeezing her fingers strangely. "Are you okay?"

"No. I'm out of medicine and I'm all fucked up."

"So am I."

Without thinking about it, Tony went to the couch and sat on the edge of it beside the girl. She looked awful.

"That's a pretty dress."

"Thank you." Tony glanced at the girl's hands again and was shocked to see that she was digging her nails into the palms, and blood was oozing between her fingers. She was gouging out a hole in the center of each hand. "What're you doing?" Tony cried in a voice strangled with alarm.

"It's Jesus," the girl said. "Jesus is in me."

"Jesus?"

"These are His wounds." The girl's eyes were brighter now, lit with enthusiasm. "Look at my feet."

Tony turned his head and glanced back. "Oh my God."

"Yes, yes."

"Honey, let me—"

"And look here."

Before Tony could do or say anything, the girl yanked up her T-shirt, revealing a pancake breast. That's not much bigger than mine, Tony thought. Then he noticed the running sore in the side of the girl's body, about the size of a silver dollar. The skin around it was streaked with dried blood. She must have picked at it for hours, days. It was terrible to see, but also fascinating and even exciting. Tony felt as if he'd walked into this girl's living, ongoing dream.

"Nobody believes me," she said sadly.

"I do," Tony found himself saying.

"You do?"

"Yes. I do."

The girl smiled. "You're so pretty."

"When is Snake coming home?"

"I never know."

Tony's eyes drifted helplessly back to the bloody wound near the girl's breast. The skin had not been allowed to form a scab. The wound had the wet, puckered look of a vagina, Tony thought in a fog of wonder. You have two of them and I don't even have one. He couldn't keep from smiling.

"Put your hand in," the girl said. "Just like they did with the Lord Jesus. Go on. Please."

"My hand won't fit."

"Your finger then."

Tony hesitated, but then was astonished to see his hand move toward the girl's body. His middle finger slid effortlessly into the moist wound. It terrified him to picture the long artificial nail, hard and sharp, pushing deeper into the girl's body, but he didn't stop until the finger was in all the way.

"Tell me your name."

"Shelly." Then, "No. *Jesus*."

Tony felt as if he had plugged into a chaos of heat, turmoil and liquid. Shelly's body quaked violently, her eyes shining, an unfathomable expression on her face. Pain and peace, maybe. Her hands clutched Tony's arm, pressing it harder to her body.

The next thing he knew, he was in a squalid kitchen, washing his hands in a stream of tepid tap-water. Roaches huddled in the gap between the backsplash and the crumbling plaster wall, but he ignored them. Tony's mind couldn't seem to focus on anything for more than a second or two, and now the pain was starting to seep back in at the edges.

Where was Snake? But that didn't matter. Go away. Get out of here. Now. You can always kill yourself tomorrow, but if you stay here they'll come, and they'll think you're crazy. And then they'll lock you up, and it'll be too late to do anything.

In the living room, Shelly was still. Her eyes followed him as he approached. He imagined the faintest smile on her face, or maybe it was actually there. At the edge of his vision, where he could not quite look, he knew that Shelly had inserted her finger into the wound. Her hand twisted and poked. There was a lot of bright red, and it was spreading, but Tony looked away. Then he left as quickly as he could.

ENTR'ACTE

Doctor Ladybank chatted with Jack and his wife, Gloria, for a few minutes, and then took his drink out onto the terrace. The party was in full swing, and it was a little too hot and crowded inside for him. The evening air was pleasantly cool, sweet with a mix of fragrances from Gloria's flower garden. Nice woman, was Gloria. A bit too nice for a rogue like Jack, but they seemed to get along and had been together for years.

Doctor Ladybank normally didn't care for social gatherings, mingling with a lot of strangers, making forced conversation, but every now and then Jack threw a good old-fashioned cocktail party that simply couldn't be missed. This one came at a particularly good time. Doctor Ladybank needed a break. He'd been giving too much of himself to his experiment lately.

It didn't tire him, it wasn't stressful, there were no nasty side effects at all as far as he could tell. But it was utterly irresistible! In just a few short weeks he had become thoroughly caught up in the lives of his two subjects. He resented any time spent away from them. Work, eating, sleeping—the bulk of his normal activities had faded into dullness.

There were many problems yet to be resolved. First, was the lack of quality time with Tony and Snake. It was often difficult to get through to them, especially at night. When Tony went out, Doctor Ladybank almost always lost contact. The same applied to Snake. It was not an absolute rule, however. There were several times when he did reach them at night, including a few important moments. Doctor Ladybank had no idea whether that was because of the intensity of his concentration or merely the configuration of their surroundings.

By now he had a rough idea of the range of his effect on the two young men. It went from basically annoying them to generally influencing their behavior, and peaked at substantial control of their thoughts and emotions. It was dazzling, but also somewhat perplexing. He could hurt them, to the point of unconsciousness, but he had not yet learned how to make them laugh or feel sudden moments of spontaneous pleasure. Doctor Ladybank regretted that, as both Tony and Snake were doing so much for him, and they lived such unrewarding lives. But he didn't regret it very much; there was no place for sentiment in science.

Feedback was bliss. That was perhaps the most exciting part of Doctor Ladybank's discovery. How would he know if his efforts were really working? In practice, he found that he just knew, he sensed it somehow, without knowing quite how he knew. It was not as if he "heard" Delgado answering him, for instance. But Doctor Ladybank's thoughts and directives flowed intuitively, as if they were in fact conversing on some new level, and thus, when he held either of them in the strongest contact he was aware of what they were doing, how they responded and what his own next words should be. To Doctor Ladybank it didn't qualify as vicarious experience but there was certainly an intellectual thrill in it.

It was a bitter disappointment to him that in the four weeks since he had happened on the technique, as he thought of it, he had not found anyone else receptive to it. That was definitely a puzzle, apparently defying the laws of chance and probability.

The greatest mystery, though, was at the heart of the whole experiment. To what degree did he affect their behavior? Was it mostly his doing, or was he just providing an added mental shove, urging them along paths they would have taken anyway? So far, it was impossible to know for sure.

A mosquito buzzed close to his eye. Doctor Ladybank went in and got another drink. He was buttonholed by Margaret Zuvelia, a lawyer with the Public Defender's office. She didn't fit in with Jack's corporate law crowd but she was young and very attractive, which made her an ideal party guest. Doctor Ladybank had met her on one of his court-appointed cases, and they'd encountered each other a few times since. What a subject she'd make, he couldn't help thinking. But when he tried the technique, it had no effect whatsoever on her. Sad. They chatted about a nineteen-year-old pyromaniac they had both tried, and failed, to keep out of prison a few months ago.

"He set a fire in the library," Margaret said with obvious delight. "Then he got the prison laundry."

"Splendid. Troy's a determined lad."

At that moment Jack horned in, looking loose and well-oiled, but not at all tipsy.

"Maggie," he said, smirking like someone about to explain an inside joke. "I have to warn you."

"About what?"

"Ian here. You better watch out. He can make you take your clothes off right here, in a room full of people."

A tendril of dismay uncoiled in Doctor Ladybank's mind.

"Really," Margaret said, smiling. "How can he do that?"

Jack tapped his forehead. "Brain waves. He beams them over to your brain and makes you do whatever he wants."

"Jack." Doctor Ladybank forced himself to chuckle and shake his head dismissively.

"I'd love to see it," Margaret said.

"Honestly," Jack continued. "Ian is conducting experiments on a couple of people, doing just that. How's it going, by the way, Ian? Got them jumping through hoops yet?"

"You're not," Margaret said.

"Of course not," Doctor Ladybank replied. "Jack and I were laying waste to a bottle of malt last month, and we were talking about clairvoyance, telepathy, that kind of thing. It was just a load of idle speculation, that's all."

"Ah." Margaret nodded.

"Oh, Ian, come on now," Jack protested. "You were damn well serious about it. I wasn't, but you were."

The silly crock was pushing it. Doctor Ladybank was shaken, but he maintained an expression of placid indulgence.

"It was the whiskey talking," he told Margaret. "Then, and now, in Jack's case, I'm afraid."

"I see."

Jack gave up, and the three of them laughed politely.

"I still think it's a good idea," Jack said as he started to leave in search of others on whom he could shower bonhomie.

"What is?" Margaret asked.

"If Ian gets you to take your clothes off."

"Jack, go away," she told him, trying to suppress a giggle. "Go away and behave yourself."

Yes, Doctor Ladybank thought. Go away, Jack.

SIX

For once in his life something had gone right. If he hadn't been in the right place at the right time the cops would have put the collar on him in a flash. They knew him, they'd busted him a couple of times in the last few years, though never for anything too serious. Yeah, they'd love to hang some hard time on his ass if they could, but Snake was covered.

It was a minor miracle, looking back. Half of his life, it sometimes seemed, was spent in transit, scraping around, looking for this guy or that, hanging out—unaccountable time witnessed by nobody who would ever remember. But on the night Shelly died, Snake fortunately had been with or seen by other people for every minute of the hours in question. More amazing, they all stood up for him when it counted.

He and Crabs had gone to Rudy's early that evening. The two of them teamed up to monopolize the pool table for several hours, winning drinks until nearly midnight. Then they decided to go to a nightclub called Ravens, on the other side of town. They were turned away at the door and exchanged mean stares with—of all people—a cop moonlighting as a bouncer. Snake and Crabs were both known to the cop; he'd thrown them out of Ravens a couple of months earlier. Retreating across the road to Cher's Plus Two, a titty bar favored by area bikers, Snake and Crabs met a number of other people they knew. They stayed until closing time, two a.m. By then they were in such good spirits that they decided to drink a nightcap or two at Snake's place. Instead, they found the dead body and promptly called the police.

What a way to go, Snake thought as he drove aimlessly around town. Shelly. She had her good side, a while back. But to die like that, to carve a hole in yourself with your own fingernails, and bleed to death...Jesus. It was enough to make Snake wonder how he had put up with her for so long. She must have been stone cold loco, so far off the wall that she couldn't even see it. To tell the truth, however, he had never imagined she was that sick. Weird, sure, and the laziest damn thing on earth. But not sicko sick. Maybe Snake should have paid more attention to that shrink who saw Shelly. Maybe they all missed something then.

Oh well. It was over now. Any residual feelings that Snake might have had for Shelly disappeared when he learned that he, as her common-law husband, had to pay to dispose of her remains. If she had any relatives, he didn't know who or where they might be, and she didn't leave much more than a pile of dirty clothes. She lived light and went fast, amen. Snake didn't hesitate to choose the cheapest available cremation (the "Bake 'n Shake," according to Crabs). Shelly's ashes were in the jar on the seat beside him now. It was time to find somewhere nice for her.

The ocean was too far away. A babbling brook would be nice, but then Snake considered the fact that any moving waters in this old mill city were bound to be thoroughly polluted. What about a park? Open air, a quiet setting, flowers—shit, he could strew her ashes right in a flowerbed. That would be perfect. But then again, it wasn't so easy. The two or three city parks Snake knew of had pretty much gone to seed, neglected, overgrown, dangerous. The best one was adjacent to the public library, and it wasn't so bad, but even there the winos used the flowerbeds as a toilet and a parade of fags stalked the shrubbery.

It wasn't as if Shelly deserved a spot in Arlington National Cemetery, but Snake felt obliged to do the best he could. He hadn't been much help to Shelly in what turned out to be her last weeks alive. Plus, she had spared him the aggravation of tossing her out, so he figured that he owed her something.

There it was! Snake knew he'd found the ideal place for her as soon as he drove around the bend in the road and saw the green expanse of a fairway in the distance. The city golf course. She would like it, he had no doubt. All he had to do now was find an attractive little spot off to the side somewhere, maybe beneath a birch tree in the rough. Hell, there might even be a clear brook in a place like this.

Snake parked the car along an open stretch of the road, took the container of ashes and walked quickly through the weedy grass toward the fairway. It was the tail-end of dusk, so if he didn't find a place soon he'd end up dumping her in the dark.

There was a foursome a hundred yards away, but they were on the way in, their backs to Snake. He jogged across the fairway. The woods on the other side looked promising, but when he reached them he found the ground unsuitable. More tall grass, rocks, and bare dirt where paths had been worn. At least at the library she would have had flowers. Damn it all anyway. He was looking for the kind of scene they put on greeting cards and in Disney films, but this was just a bunch of useless country-type land.

Snake pushed on. A few minutes later he came out on the far side of the woods, and he was startled by the sudden change. He was in someone's backyard. Nice looking house, must have cost an awful lot. Beautiful grounds, too. Snake hadn't tried burglary, but this would be the kind of place to start with if he ever felt like having a go.

He had other business now. His eyes had settled on a lovely rock garden just a few yards away. Snake hurried across the lawn to it. Oh yes, the perfect resting place for Shelly. There were cascades of delicate flowers, clusters of blue, purple and white, not much pink or red. Just the colors you saw at funerals, Snake thought as he bent over and started to scoop out a hollow in the rich soil. You'll love it here, kid. The kind of folks who live in a place like this will take real good care of you, or at least the garden around you.

"What do you think you're doing?"

Snake jumped upright. He had been about to unscrew the cap of the jar containing Shelly's ashes, but now he froze, gaping at the middle-aged man who stood ten feet away, hands on hips. Must have seen me from the house, Snake thought uselessly. He wasn't worried about having been discovered by the homeowner, but he was puzzled. The guy was a stranger, and yet seemed familiar. Snake could turn and run, and he knew he'd get away easily, but somehow the urge to flee had been transformed into curiosity.

"Who are you," the man demanded, his voice more

threatening, "and what do you want?"

"Hey, Jack." Snake was surprised to hear himself say that. "How the hell are you, Jack?"

The man's head clicked back a notch. Then he stepped closer and peered at Snake.

"I don't know you."

"Sure you do, Jack. We used to hang out at the Utica Club, remember? *Agricola, agricolae, agricolorum.* Right? *Hic, haec, hoc, ad hoc,* in hock around the clock with bock beer."

Even in the gathering darkness, Snake could see the man's eyes widen as he tried to digest what he'd heard. Snake couldn't help him. He had no idea.

"Get out of here this instant."

"Jack, lighten up."

"I'll call the police."

"Why don't you crack open a bottle of Glen Grant? We can sit down and talk twat, just like the old days."

The man tottered, then turned stiffly toward the house.

"Jack, Jack..."

Snake scooped up a rock and caught the man easily. The rock crushed the back of his skull, creating a wreath of pinkish-gray jelly around the edges of the impact. The man grunted once, the last of his breath forced out of him. He hit the lawn and didn't move again.

Snake pulled the body over onto its back. Now the wife will have to sell this place, he thought. Who knows what'll happen to the rock garden? The new owners might well dig it up and plow it under. That wouldn't be right. You're going to get a real fancy burial, Shelly. Elegant casket, expensive plot. Can't beat it.

He unscrewed the jar, forced the man's mouth open, and began to pour the ashes down the throat. It soon filled. Snake tamped the coarse powder down with his fingertips. Believe me, Jack, if you saw Shelly at her best you *would* want to eat her. That would have been when she was about fifteen.

The cheeks bulged, Snake noticed when he was finished. Jack the Chipmunk. Best I could do. Time to take a *haec.*

So long, kid.

SEVEN

Tony washed down the Demerol with a gulp of Red Death on the rocks. Behind the shades, his eyes watered slightly, but he felt his body steadying. That was mental, since he knew it would take a good five minutes before serenity began to kick in and all was right with the world again...for a while.

"You look happy, darling."

"I buried Shelly."

"Maybe that's it. Where did you put her?"

"Somewhere out in the countryside," Snake said with a vague wave of the hand, as if he'd suddenly lost interest in the topic. "It's a pretty place."

"I'm sure it is."

Tony had heard about it only last night around this time, as they were sitting on the very same two barstools at the El Greco. It was boring. Tony didn't want to listen to another word about the stupid cunt who'd bled herself to death, but Snake was having a hard time putting it behind him. He kept pulling away from it, and then sinking back, like a car stuck in a rut. It was morbid, as well as incredibly tiresome.

Tony had his own uneasy feelings about Shelly. He imagined he had met her—or was it a dream? Anyhow, he had this picture of her in his mind, like he could see her dying. It was probably because Snake had given such a graphic description of what Shelly looked like when he found her. And it had stayed in Tony's head, making him feel very uncomfortable.

Part of the problem was that Snake kept him jangled up in a state of constant uncertainty, dishing out the pills in ones and twos like candy. Wouldn't sell a quantity, even though Tony had the cash. Snake wanted other things, and so he was making a move for absolute control. It was clear and simple, but Tony had yet to figure out a worthwhile response to it. Shelly's death was a minor week-long distraction that didn't really change anything in Tony's life.

The easiest thing, of course, would be to stop using Demerol or coke, period. Then Tony would be able to kiss Snake goodbye, and how sweet that would be. The big clod had lost any semblance of attractiveness he might have possessed. Not that he was ever anything but a trick and a supplier as far as Tony was concerned. The game was fun at first, but now Snake's mean and demanding way of treating Tony most of the time was simply unbearable.

And how could he get off the drugs? That was impossible, at least in Tony's present condition. They weren't drugs, they were medicine. They kept him alive. Whether that was a good idea was another matter, but as long as he wanted to survive all the pain and mental interference, he had to have his medicine.

Zzzzzt.

Oh God, no. Not now, not here. Tony had a terrible fear of the Pied Piper getting through to him in a public place. Even if it was only the El Greco, where some pretty weird things happened from time to time.

Zzzzzt.

Fucker. Get lost. Ignore him. But that never worked. The demon had continued to haunt and hurt Tony everyday over the past week, never letting up for long. The Demerol helped, but it was by no means a perfect immunity. All it did was keep the agony in moderate check for a while, so that Tony remained just this side of suicidal. The Pied Piper still got through.

—Plasmodium. Found you.

"Be right back, darling," Tony said to Snake. "I've got to make a trip to the little girl's room."

"Yeah," Snake muttered.

Tony slid off the barstool, wobbled for a second on his high heels, and then clattered quickly across the linoleum. Thank God the pisser was vacant. Tony shut the door and leaned against it, pressing his head to the blotchy particleboard.

—I want him.

"Fuck off."

—You heard me.

"For what?"

—Bring him home.

"It won't work with him. He's straight."

—Do it, slime.

"Listen, when he sees my *cojones* he'll go crazy. He'll tear them off and shove 'em down—"

Tony went blind and sagged to the damp floor, too stunned to make a sound as pain exploded throughout his body, abrading every cell in his nervous system. It felt as if sonic booms were being triggered inside his brain and the plates of his skull were about to crack open at the seams.

Yes, yes, okay. He couldn't even get the words out, but the torture died down immediately. Tony found that he could breathe again, he could think, he could see the slick of scummy water his face rested in on the floor. He was theoretically still alive, a fact of dubious value. Why is this happening? Why are you doing this to me?

—Because you are slime.

You got that right. "But you're me, right? That's what you said a while back, fucker. If I'm slime, so are you."

Silence. Relief. Goddamn, Tony thought as he struggled to his feet, I shut him up. I shut the Pied Piper up. At least for a minute or two. Turned him right off. Tony gripped the sink to steady himself and then looked in the mirror. His face was grimy and wet from the floor. He washed himself and applied some fresh make-up, regaining a little composure in the process.

It was no good. The Pied Piper was gone for now, but he had delivered his message. Tony had to bring Snake home tonight, and whatever happened from that point on—would happen. Might even be better if Snake did go berserk and kill him. That would put a stop to all this misery. He could see the newspaper stories. An anguished biker tricked by a transvestite—Snake might have to transfer to the Foreign Legion to live that one down. Meanwhile, Tony's tearful mother wouldn't believe a word they said about him and his queer life. She'd hand out pictures of him as a choirboy and talk about the perfume he gave her last Mother's Day (because she was still young and pretty).

Why the fuck not? Who the fuck cares anyway? When you live in the shadow of the curb, where else do you expect to die? Grab the best chance that has come along in years. If you don't, that little demon fucker will just come back and eat at you, rip away at you, until you do what he wants. Get it over.

Besides, Tony knew that the column inches, however lurid and distasteful, would be a kind of comfort to his mother. Maybe not right away, but in the long term. A front-page murder story was better than no obituary at all.

EIGHT

The place was a dump on the outside, but the living room was nice enough. In a spooky kind of way. The shades were drawn and the only light came from a large floor lamp with a fringed shade that cast the room in a soft golden glow. The air was humid and warm, but it had a sweet scent that added an exotic, mysterious touch, and the furniture was comfortable. It wasn't the way he'd fix up a room, but Snake decided that he liked it as he sat back in a big armchair.

Toni was on edge, nervous as a high school girl on her first date. What a riot. Snake wasn't going to make it any easier for her. Why should he? This was his payoff. He was going to enjoy every minute of it. On the way there from the bar Snake gave her explicit instructions. He was to be treated like a king, she was to wait on him, pamper him, baby him, indulge him, humor him, and above all, she was to tease him to the max. He couldn't wait for that to start. This was going to be the greatest damn fuck Snake had ever had, the one he'd dreamed of for years.

The whore looked good, real good. Her hair was quite short, and it was brushed and slicked back in a striking fashion, and it looked so wet you'd think she had just this minute stepped out of the shower. Tonight her dress was almost elegant, not at all the usual trashy glitter. She wore a white blouse that hung loosely on her flat-tish upper body, and a long wrap-around skirt that had a nice way of parting to flash her terrific legs when she walked. Toni was somewhat on the tall side, a sort of slum-pussy version of Jamie Lee Curtis without the front porch.

"What would you like to drink?"

Better already, Snake thought. Just being there had changed

her tone of voice. Gone was the barroom hustle, replaced by such a sweet desire to please—God, he loved it. Toni was standing beside the chair, close to him. Snake liked that too. He placed a hand on her leg, just behind the knee, savoring the firm flesh beneath the fabric of her skirt. It was one of his favorite sexy spots on a woman's body. You could feel those wires—now, what the hell are they called, tendons, sinews?—that run all up and down the leg. Neat.

"Do you want a drink, darling, or...not?"

"Mmmm."

Snake's hand slid higher, taking the skirt with it, but Toni stepped aside gracefully, escaping his reach. As she did so, she contrived to flap the front of her skirt open briefly. Very nice little move, Snake thought appreciatively.

"Well?"

"Got any bourbon?" he asked.

"Of course."

"Okay, let's have a large glass of bourbon, on the rocks and with a splash of water."

"*Ein, zwei, drei.*"

"Huh?"

"What?"

"What'd you say?"

"I said it's on the way."

"Okay. Fine."

A little weird, but what the hell. Snake already had a good buzz on, so nothing was going to bother him. As long as Toni did her part. From where he was sitting he could see her in the tiny kitchen, pouring the drinks. At that moment, she put the bottle down and bent over. She opened her skirt and fiddled around with the catch on her garter. It took a moment for the significance of the navy blue ribbon and the bare skin to register. Oh Jesus, she's wearing stockings, Snake realized with joy. And now she's showing me. Man, this is just like being in the foreplay part of a porn movie. Scenes like this were the best—the teasing, the slow seduction—even better than the wild sex that would follow soon enough. But now Snake wasn't just another jerk-off watching the picture; he was starring in it.

The bourbon was good and there was plenty of it in the heavy crystal tumbler Toni brought him. She sipped a pale liquid from a glass about the size and shape of a lipstick holder.

"What's that?"

"Cointreau," she told him.

"Oh yeah." None of that Red Death shit here. She was doing it all right, no question. "Nice stuff."

"Snake?"

"Yeah?"

"Do you have any metal fillings?"

"Metal—what?"

"Metal fillings in your teeth. Lead, silver, like that."

"Oh, sure. Lots. I've got a regular scrapyard in my mouth, everything but gold. Why?"

"Do you get much static?"

"Just from people who don't know better," he replied with a quick laugh. "But I soon straighten them out."

"So…You don't hear anything?"

"Like what?" Like, what the hell is this all about?

"A voice."

"Just yours and mine, babe." Snake sounded calm, but he was beginning to worry. She looked nervous, close to panic, in spite of the fact that she was sitting on the couch, drink in hand, her thigh tantalizingly visible. "Hey, relax."

As if on cue, Toni said, "Whatever they want."

"What?"

"Whatever they want."

"Who?"

"Men."

"Oh." This was an abrupt shift, but it was definitely a lot more promising, so he went with it. "Such as?"

"Come on my face. Come in my mouth."

Her voice was stiff, and her eyes seemed to be fixed on some remote inner point. However, Snake now thought he understood the game. She was going to tell him about the things she did. Dirty talk to turn him on. It was a little more open and blunt than he would have liked, but he was prepared to cut her some slack if it had the desired effect.

"That's pretty normal," he told her.

"Ride my ass."

"Some do like that. Not me, but some do."

"Tie me up. Blindfold me."

"Uh-huuh."

"Hurt me."

"Not too bad, I hope."

"Piss on me. Shit on me."

"Aw, Jeez." That was exactly the kind of stuff Snake didn't want to hear. How the hell could he lick her body now, with that stuck in his mind? "Where? On your back or stomach," Snake said hopefully. "Right?"

"And my chest. And face. And mouth."

"That really drags me down, babe." The script had gone into some other movie. Snake was not happy. The only thing that kept him from clocking her on the jaw was the fact that he didn't want to give up yet. There was still a chance Toni would snap out of her robot stare and get back on track. "I wouldn't treat you bad like that," he said. "I'd treat you like a queen."

Toni suddenly began laughing. Snake didn't understand, but he smiled at the improvement in her manner. She appeared to be much more relaxed again. He also liked that foxy look in her eye as she tuned in to him.

"Darling, would you really be a good boy?"

"Sure."

"I want you to do something for me."

"What?"

"Promise not to peek? Promise not to touch where you're not supposed to?"

"Well, I don't get it."

"Put your drink on the floor and sit forward on your seat."

"Okay."

When Snake did what she told him, Toni got off the couch and carefully stepped up onto the coffee table, inches from his face. Hey, hey, hey, Snake thought. This is more like it.

"Here," Toni said, handing him her glass of Cointreau. "I'd like you to rub it into my skin. Just the bare skin now, and you must behave yourself."

"O-*kay*."

Snake splashed the liqueur on his hand and then placed the small glass on the table. Toni pulled her skirt open, and cupped one hand modestly over her panties. The sight of that navy blue underwear against her golden skin was fantastic. Snake lovingly stroked her upper thighs, above the stocking tops.

"Mmmm..."

"Your hand is in the way," he dared.

"You don't touch there. Understand?"

"Yes."

"That's good. You're a good boy, aren't you?"

"Yes."

"And you're doing a good job. What does it smell like? You can put your face closer."

Snake went so far as to put his face between her thighs, his cheeks touching her. His forehead bumped against her hand. Toni didn't stop him.

"Oranges."

"Right." Now her fingers gently pushed his face away. "The back, too. Don't forget the back."

Snake poured the last of the Cointreau in his hand, and Toni turned slightly on the table. She pulled the skirt higher, so he had a clear view of the flimsy blue fabric stretched tightly over her ass. He rubbed the back of her legs gently and slowly, while his eyes were locked on target just above. Toni's other hand was still planted on her crotch, so deeply that her fingers curved up in sight from behind. Odd, but Snake barely gave it a thought as he had other things on his mind. His hand inevitably slid up and grazed her firm round bottom. She let him do that until he began to squeeze it energetically, insinuating his fingers beneath her panties, and then she spun around.

"I told you to behave."

"Oops."

"Never mind, you did a good job."

Toni stepped down from the coffee table and took her spot on the couch again. Snake took his drink from the floor and slurped a major mouthful. He smiled at her and let his eyes drift slowly along the length of her body, stretched out on the couch. As if responding to his gaze, one of her knees pushed up so the flap of her skirt fell away.

"Did you hear that?" she asked.

"What?"

"The voice."

"No." She was still a little crazy, he thought. "You hear voices, you better see the Doc."

"Which doctor?"

"The witch doctor, yeah," Snake said with a laugh. "Hell, I don't know. Go to a shrink, babe."

His eyes were on her legs and he didn't feel like discussing anything else. Toni's arm had fallen casually across her crotch, another peekaboo move that tickled Snake, and her thumb rolled in a small arc on her upper thigh. Lightly, back and forth. It was mildly hypnotic, very arousing.

"Tell me about him," she said.

"Who?"

"Your doctor."

"I don't have one."

"But you know one."

"No, I—"

Snake hesitated. Well, he did know one. Technically. He'd met Shelly's shrink, back a month or two ago. But he didn't know the man, in fact he couldn't even remember the guy's name.

"Go on."

As if to encourage Snake, Toni now stretched out completely on her back and raised both knees up straight. Then she let them loll open and she rubbed herself in a slowly escalating rhythm as her body squirmed with pleasure. Snake didn't know what he could say, but he didn't want to stop the show. He was caught up in it almost as much as Toni was.

"The Doc is okay."

"Yeah…"

"The Doc is good."

"Yeah…"

"He'll take care of you, but you have to trust him."

"Yeah…"

"And do what he tells you."

"*Yeah.*"

Her knees drove toward her chest, her hands worked in a last frenzied rush.

"I wish I could tell you his name."

"*YEAAAAAAAHH!*"

Her body rocked convulsively, then turned rigid. She puffed air in short bursts. You momma, Snake thought. He nearly missed his mouth as he tried to take a drink with his eyes frozen on the girl. You hot little whore momma, that was better than a sexpic. The way she had done it with her clothes still on somehow made it that much more real. It was like peeking through the window next door and watching your teen queen neighbor engage in self-service fun. Snake had a hard-on, and he was clean out of words.

Toni rolled over onto her belly, her skirt rumpled and still showing a lot of leg. Her face was pressed to the couch, her one visible eye peering brightly at Snake. There was the faintest of smiles at the corner of her mouth.

"You like to watch."

"Hey." Snake shrugged with a grin.

"You do, and you like to have someone do it for you. That's okay, darling, that's cool."

"Well, not always…"

"I'll do it for you. Special, because you're special."

"So are you, babe."

"Come on with me."

Snake followed her into the bathroom. It was dark, and Toni didn't turn on the light. Instead, she pulled the door so it was almost shut, allowing only the slightest illumination to filter in from the living room. She had Snake stand facing the bathtub and told him to unbuckle his belt and unzip his pants. She was right behind him, speaking in a low soft voice, caressing his back.

"Grab hold of the shower bar," she directed. "That's right, that's it. Now close your eyes and imagine you're in a luxurious hotel room somewhere, maybe Paris, or Rio. You're high up, maybe forty floors, and the view is fantastic. You stand at the window and gaze out at the spectacular scene. It's night, and it's like a dream, just being there. The city is far, far below, but it's all lit up like a million shiny jewels. Now, a young woman comes into the room. Women always come to you, so you don't even turn around, you just know she's there. For you. She comes right to you, her hands flowing over your body. You still don't turn, you watch the city below and you let her love you..."

Her hands snaking around him, finding his nipples, squeezing them through his shirt, then planing down, snagging his pants and taking them to the floor. Her face to the small of his back, her hands gliding up the front of his thighs. She takes his cock in one hand, cups his balls with the other, tightening her grip with expert care as her face burrows into his backside. She licks and explores until she finds the puckered rim.

"Ohhh-aaaah..."

She tongues it delicately while her hands play with him in front, the pace of her movements increasing steadily. Snake heaves with anticipation, his body shaking beyond his control, and she knows he is about to come. Her tongue plunges deeply into him.

"Oooooh-Gaaaaaahd... "

He shoots off. Little spattering sounds from the porcelain tub, but they're almost lost in the noisy rush of breath above. Snake can hardly hold himself up by the shower bar, he's so weak and dazed by this onslaught of pleasure. He still can't believe it, what she did to him. So good.

"Toni..."

She had backed away from him a little. When he glanced over his shoulder at her he caught sight of the swift movement, but he didn't understand it. Then he felt it, and it was the last thing he felt. The stiletto blade punctured his spine, paralyzing him. The tip snapped off, but she kept hammering the broken blade into his body, up and down, between the ribs, into his flabby midriff, blood blossoming in a spray of gray roses, his hands slipping off the shower bar, the slow dizzy fall through hot buzzing air, and still it came at him, that knife, *bam bam bam bam bam bam*, arcing at him, fixing him for all time, his shiny metal transport to the end of the night, *bam bam bam bam bam*, out of the gray, the gloom and the shadows and into the perfect no pain the perfect no night the perfect no light the perfect the

NINE

The silence was terrifying.

Tony was shaking so violently that he had to hold onto the sink and the wall to keep from falling to the bathroom floor. He hit the switch and the ceiling light went on. It was temporarily blinding, since Tony didn't have his shades, and he whimpered in pain. The floor was covered with blood—such a vibrant red—he could see that much as he squinted through his tears. Tony breathed deeply, sucking air in an effort to hold off panic.

Snake was in the tub. Tony had pushed him into it when he saw that the guy was about to keel over backwards on top of him. Now the only thing he could think to do was to leave him there in peace. He's draining, Tony told himself. Let him drain. It was the best place for him.

But then what? He couldn't move a big body like that on his own, and he certainly couldn't get it out of this building or the neighborhood without being seen. Not even in the middle of the night. Impossible. This is bad, bad, bad. He hazarded a glance in the mirror. A savage stared back.

"What now?"

Nothing. The little shit. Tony noticed his stiletto on the floor, and saw for the first time that the tip was broken. Where was the other piece? The way his life was going, that would turn out to be the one little thing that landed him on Death Row. The two hundred-plus pounds of incriminatingly dead meat lying in the tub suddenly seemed as vast as a continent, and somewhere in that land mass was a vital scrap of metal. He had to find it and then get rid of it.

Tony edged closer to the bathtub. Jesus, why did he have to

stab the guy so many times? But why did he even have to stab him at all? Dead, Snake looked merely pathetic. A nobody. Just one more poor stiff who wanted to live, and be loved by somebody, but who never quite got a handle on his life. Not all that different from me, Tony thought.

But, on to business. Tony picked up the stiletto and washed it under the tap in the sink. Then he wrapped it tightly in the hand towel, wiping it several times to make sure he didn't leave a fingerprint on it, and carried it into the kitchen. He dug up a plastic supermarket bag and put the knife in it, towel and all. He rolled it into a tidy little parcel, squeezing out as much air as he could, and he used the loop handles to bind it with several knots. He set it aside on the counter.

Tony wasn't ready for the next step yet, so he changed into jeans and a T-shirt, put on his sunglasses and had a large drink to settle his nerves. He didn't feel better, but at least he was somewhat calmer.

The silence was truly awful. Tony thought he could hear the cells beginning to turn rotten in Snake's body. Snake had become a factory, a death mill where billions of tiny forces worked away nonstop at the process of decay. Snake was sliming out, so there was no time to waste.

He mopped up the blood on the bathroom floor, and then began the awkward job of removing Snake's clothes. Why? It seemed the thing to do. In the pockets of Snake's cheap black pants he came across a wallet containing thirty two dollars, and a medicine jar that held fifty Demerol pills. Fifty of them! To think I almost felt sorry for you, you cheap bastard. I'm in good shape now, he thought gleefully. Tony burned the driver's license along with a few other papers in the kitchen sink, wiped Snake's wallet clean, and buried it in an empty milk carton in his garbage bag. He put Snake's clothes in another bag.

So far, so easy. Three ordinary parcels to throw away. But what about the big parcel in the bathtub? Tony needed help. The Pied Piper had gotten him into this mess, so where was he? Not a peep. The little fucker. I'll bring him here fast. Tony got on his knees and smashed his forehead against the kitchen floor. It worked immediately.

—Slime.

"Jesus, man." He struggled to his feet. The pain wasn't so bad but black spots peppered his vision for a moment. "You can't take me to a certain point and then leave me there alone."

—I can do anything.

"Then get rid of the guy in the bathtub."

—That's your problem.

"I might as well call the cops," Tony said. It was a bluff, and not a very good one, but it had just occurred to him that the Pied Piper needed him, or wanted him, in some way. He reappeared the minute Tony banged his head on the floor. For the moment, at least, it seemed to give Tony a slight amount of leverage. "I'll tell them he was a trick, and he turned nasty and pulled a knife, and I had to defend myself."

—That's the ticket.

The quick mockery worried Tony. "Why not?"

—You defended yourself by stabbing him all those times in the back?

"Well…"

—Remove the body, plasmodium.

"How do I do that?"

—Piecework.

"No way, man, no way. I'd rather call the cops, and take my chances that way."

—Yes?

"You bet yes. I'll do it right now."

Tony turned toward the telephone, but froze, and then sagged against the wall. It was as if invisible hands were wringing his liver, and at the same time a tiny neon worm burned like acid in the depths of his ear, eating its way into his brain.

—Yes?

"…No…"

—I own your mind, which means I own your body. Listen and hear, boy. I can make the acid pour into your stomach all day, I can dump adrenalin into your blood till your heart shivers so bad it knots up and can't send oxygen to your brain, I can bleed your eyes and ears. I can make your nose run so much you'll drown in your own snot. I can cover you with sores, I can make your skin itch so much you'll scratch it to bloody shreds, and I can bloat your balls so they're as big and foul as rotten apples, or I can make them as small and hard as orange pips. I can squash them, I can make you piss hot acid and ground glass, I can make your lips peel off like layers of parchment, and your muscles turn to mush. I can make you chew up your tongue and spit out the bits. I can turn the marrow in your bones to lava, I can fill your mouth with fungus and raise hordes of maggots in your arsehole. And believe me, I can keep you ticking along this way forever. Yes?

"...Yes..."

—Good little plasmodium. Now get to work. Use the Ginsu steak knives you got from that nig-nog limousine driver. They're tacky, but they'll do the job.

"You know everything in my life?"

—Your life is mine.

Then he was gone. Tony obediently got the steak knives and took them, along with every spare plastic bag he could find, into the bathroom. The pasty bulk of flesh was still there.

"Sorry man, but you're already dead."

Tony made a few tentative slices at one elbow, and promptly threw up all over the corpse. Jesus mother's tit, he'd never get through this. He made sure that the drain was fully open, turned on the cold shower and pulled the curtain around the tub. While Snake was being sluiced down, Tony went to the sink to pat water on his own face and rinse his mouth out. Then he took a Demerol, figuring it would help him through the ordeal.

A few minutes later, he hummed as he cut loose Snake's left forearm. The elbows and knees were trouble enough with all those wires to saw, but the shoulders were much worse, far messier. At least the head was easy. By then, however, Tony had filled every plastic bag he had. He would get more tomorrow, but for now the only thing he could find to put Snake's head in was the spaghetti pot his mother had given him. It had a lid. Tony squirted some wash-up liquid in with the head and added water until the pot was nearly full, hoping the detergent would delay the inevitable rot and stench. He placed the covered pot on the stove, where it did not seem too conspicuous.

He did as much as he could, eight plastic-wrapped items, the head in the pot and the torso still floating in the tub. When he woke up the next morning, Tony had to have a shower. He couldn't stand the feeling of dried blood on him, dried scum, and the bits of Snake's flesh that had lodged beneath his finger-nails. He had fallen asleep as soon as the last package was taped up. The only way he could have his shower was if he had it with the torso too, since there was nowhere to put it. Reluctantly, that's what Tony did, heaving the ghastly thing as far back in the tub as possible and then standing directly under the show-erhead. He had to clear the drain a couple of times, as it got clogged with greasy chunks of gristle and meat. Tony showered quickly, then sat on the edge of the tub and cleaned between his toes with running water.

As he had done the night before, he filled the tub until the torso floated, and sprinkled pine-scented kitchen cleanser on it. To be on the safe side, he added two-thirds of a bottle of Canoe, the last of his rubbing alcohol (which was also useful in certain sexual scenarios) and a blue toilet tablet. That should keep the smell down for a while.

Sleep had refreshed him somewhat. Tony didn't need the Pied Piper to tell him what he had to do. Fortunately it was over-cast outside. He put on his sunglasses and went to the supermar-ket to buy the largest and heaviest trash bags they had. He also bought a couple of rolls of sticky packing tape, more detergent, rubber gloves, alcohol and disinfectant. The store's fluorescent lights were getting to him, even with his sunglasses on, so he picked up a pair of mirrored clip-ons that helped considerably.

Tony had a couple of ideas. He now thought he knew the best way to get rid of the torso, and in the back of his mind he had a rough notion of how to escape the torments of the Pied Piper once and for all. But he would have to approach it care-fully when the time came, never quite letting his thoughts settle on it, or else the demon might tune in and foil the attempt.

It was a long day, taking four trips in all. A piece of arm and a piece of leg each time. He carried them in a gym bag, and he dropped them in litterbaskets, dumpsters, anywhere reasonably safe, where they were unlikely to be noticed and opened. He even managed to slip one forearm into the trash bin at Burger Billy's, along with the remains of his lunch. By the end of the afternoon Tony was exhausted from all the walking he had done, but he also felt enormously relieved that much of Snake was scattered around the center of the city. Out of my life.

Tony examined the trunk of Snake's car, to make sure it had enough room for the torso. Some people fill a trunk with garbage and then just leave it there, God only knows why. Snake's trunk had a well-worn spare tire, a jack and some small tools, and the puzzler: a beat-up copy of Elvis's *Blue Hawaii* album. Good place to keep your record collection, Snake. Tony parked the car right in front of his building.

He had a drink, though he didn't need it to relax. He felt serene, almost—*almost* in some kind of control of his life once more. Tony had sailed through this horrible day, popping Demerol whenever the wave seemed to falter.

What day was it anyway? Sunday. Time? A little after six in the evening. Good, perfect. People were eating, and in a few minutes they'd sit back to watch *60 Minutes*. There would not be many cops on patrol at this in-between hour.

Wearing the rubber gloves, Tony somehow got the torso into a large heavy-duty garbage bag. He knotted and taped it, then slid it into another one. Was a third bag necessary? Why not? There was no point in taking chances. Tony wiped a thin streak of scum from the outer plastic when he finished, and dragged the big sack into the living room. He removed the rubber gloves and carefully put band- aids on his fingertips. With the torso, at least, there would be no prints on the bags.

Now. No need to carry it, even if he could. Tony looked up and down the hallway outside his apartment. All clear, nobody in sight, no sounds of activity. Tony tugged the garbage bag by its plastic loop handles, dragging the load into the hall. He locked his apartment, and then pulled the sack to the top of the stairs. Still no one about. Gripping the loop handles firmly, he tipped the torso over the edge and followed behind, letting it bump down the stairs but holding it so that it didn't bounce noisily out of control. It was like walking the dog, Tony thought

with a smile. No sweat. When he got to the ground floor he
stepped over the bag and was about to drag it to the front door
when Leo Jenks emerged from his apartment. He was okay, a
middle-aged man who delivered bread for a local bakery, but
Tony wasn't at all happy to see him at that moment.

"Hey, Tony."

"Leo, how's it going?"

"Good, and you?"

"Okay. Just cleaning up."

"Yeah? Whaddaya got there?"

"Newspapers and magazines. You want 'em?"

Jesus, don't get cute.

"Not unless it's *Penthouse* or *Playboy* Leo said with a sly grin.
Like everyone in the building, Leo knew Tony was gay.

"'Fraid not."

"The stuff piles up, huh?"

"Sure does."

"Let me give you a hand," Leo said, bending to reach for one
end of the garbage bag.

"No, don't bother, Leo. It's too clumsy to handle that way,
but no trouble to drag, you know? Just leave the front door open
for me, will you?"

"Yeah, sure. See you, Tony."

"Yeah, thanks."

Fuck me pink, Tony thought when Leo was gone. If he had
got his hands on it he'd have known right away that it wasn't
a bunch of newspapers and magazines. But it was no time to
stand around, worrying about a near-miss. Tony hauled the
sack outside to the edge of the curb as quickly as he could.

"Jesus," he groaned, heaving it up and into the car. Fucker
must have weighed a quarter of a ton. Tony banged the trunk
shut and allowed himself a casual glance around. The old geezer
next door was sitting on his front stoop, but he was busy playing with his grandson. There were other people on the street,
but none of them seemed to be watching Tony. He straightened
his sunglasses, got into the car and drove away.

"All *right*."

With the window rolled down and the radio playing, it

wasn't bad at all, especially since the humidity had fallen. Tony liked driving but he seldom got the chance to do any, so it was a treat for him to be out like this—in spite of the load he had in the trunk. He cruised through the neighborhood, then headed into the center of town. He circled The Green, drove out to the east side and checked the action along the commercial strip leading to the mall. Nothing much happening. Well, of course. It was a Sunday night, and that's the way it's supposed to be. Quiet.

By nine o'clock Tony was ready to get it done. Better to do it while there was still some light in the sky. He drifted north into the woody hills near the highway, on the outskirts of town. There were few houses on these side roads that zig-zagged up the steep valley walls. A power company sub-station. A junkyard. A landfill transfer depot. Not much else. Aha, there it was, just what Tony was looking for: a clearing off to the side where folks dumped unwanted items. He stopped the car and got out.

Nothing, only trees for a hundred yards in either direction. Tony listened carefully, but there was no sound of an approaching car. On the ground: an abandoned sofa, several bald tires, rusty wheel hubs, a corroded hand-wringer washing machine, and the best sight of all, plenty of garbage bags similar to the one Tony had. People. Makes you wonder, Tony thought with a smile. There was a junkyard down the road, *and* a landfill station. They could bring their rubbish to either place, but no, they've got to throw it here, along this nice woody stretch of land.

Tony opened the trunk and took extra care not to rip the bag as he pulled it out. He dragged it across some of the other bags on the ground. Still no cars coming. He left the package behind a dirty but unscarred vinyl clothes hamper that had no doubt been discarded because of its ugly design.

Sorry, Snake. We had our moments, one or two.

The pot on the stove was a shock. For some reason, Tony had blanked it right out of his mind. But there it was. Okay, so he still had work to do. Tomorrow he would dispose of Snake's head, and then he would deal with the Pied Piper.

TEN

The window shade appeared to be on fire, which meant it was extremely bright outside. The sun has no mercy, he thought. Men have no mercy—not much anyway, and not often. Everything was supposed to be better now, but it wasn't. Tony thought two days had passed, but it might have been three.

Where was his brain? The sun beat him, the moon laughed at him, nothing worked. He found it hard to keep track of anything. So much time, thousands of minutes, had been spent sitting still, trying to think, trying to focus his mind. Trying to find it.

The Pied Piper had got him once—or was it twice? Hard to be sure. The Demerol helped and Tony had found some silence, but the demon voice jarred him from sleep, pried open his brain when his guard was down. No mercy.

—Open a vein.

"Fuck you."

—Get it over with. Best thing.

Like that, juiced with spasms of pain meant to keep Tony in line. But he was learning. The Pied Piper couldn't be there all the time. Even in a fog of Demerol, Tony managed to organize his thoughts into a rough plan. There wasn't much chance it would do any good, but it was worth a try. Anything was better than going along with this shadow-life, twitching between drugs and torture, barely able to function.

He remembered how he had at first been plagued with a lot of static and garbled bits of words. That had been bad enough, but not nearly as bad as the clear reception he had been getting ever since he removed his metal fillings. The metal had not aided the broadcast, as Tony originally believed, but instead had actually interfered with it, at least a little. So, a lot of metal would block out the Pied Piper completely. Maybe.

The spaghetti pot was taken, unfortunately. Tony put on his doubled sunglasses and ventured outside. The glare was so fierce that his eyes were seared with pain from light leaking in at the sides, and he was nearly blind before he even got to the corner. The supermarket was three blocks away, too far to go. Tony dived into the cool, dark interior of the Sparta Mart, a neighborhood shop that carried groceries and a few basic items. Mrs. Bandana, the wife of the owner, sold a lottery ticket to another customer and then directed her indifference to Tony.

"You got any aluminum foil?"

"Bottom left," she replied curtly, pointing toward the rear of the store.

Tony took two overpriced boxes. He also found some rolls of masking tape, which he figured should not be as harsh on his skin as the sticky packing tape he had at home. He paid, and insisted on being given a plastic bag to carry his purchases. Tony needed it for Snake's head. Steeling himself to face the glare outside, he ran all the way back to his apartment.

He put the pot in the kitchen sink and removed the lid. The smell was horrendous. He turned on the hot water and let it pour over the head, gradually rinsing away most of the muck. At least there were no worms crawling through the eyes and mouth, nor any other nightmare surprises that Tony had feared. When the water finally ran clear, he dumped the head into the sink and put the pot aside on the counter.

You don't look so bad now, he thought. What was your name? Alvin Doolittle, according to the driver's license. How the hell could a person with a name like that ever get into the Legion of the Lost? Snake sounded better. In fact, he looked better dead than alive. A bit rubbery, but the color had washed out nicely. The skin had the bleached look of white marble, Tony thought, or a fish's belly. There was no sign of trauma in Snake's face. He looked calm, an admirable quality.

Something Snake had said. The Doc this, the Doc that, trust the Doc, do what the Doc says. Hard to tell if it meant anything at all, since the whole scene had been mad, sick. But Snake told him to go see a shrink, and that seemed important. Tony had been sent to a shrink by the court, the weird guy with the weird name. *All my troubles started after that. Maybe he can help.*

—Easy, slime.

Tony shuddered. "Go away."

—Poor little plasmodium.

"The Doc'll take care of you."

—Maybe I am the Doc.

Jesus, that was a thought. "Are you?"

—You've got two heads now. You tell me.

"I'll find out, one way or the other."

—Will you indeed?

"Believe it."

But the demon was gone, his parting shot a raucous laughter that erupted in Tony's head. It took a moment to clear. *Oh yes, I'll kill you,* he thought bitterly. *If he could just get to see that shrink again, he might find an answer.*

Tony took a large, empty trash bag and dropped Snake's head into it. Then he rolled the black plastic tightly, taping it to form a rough ball. When he was satisfied with his work, Tony put the head in the Sparta Mart bag and then picked it up by the loop handles. *There.* He looked like anybody carrying home a nice big cabbage or honeydew melon from the market.

—Die, you slime.

"Oh fuck…"

—Lie down and I'll help you die. It'll be easy, it won't hurt at all. Lie down. Now.

"No, no…"

But Tony could feel the demon taking hold of him. The blood in his veins felt like broken glass, slashing him apart, churning his insides into a massive hemorrhage. As he started to fall, he grabbed the box of aluminum foil from the counter, ripped it open and fumbled to unroll a length of it. He hit the floor, rapidly losing strength. He couldn't even tear the foil, but he did yank enough of it out of the box to pull over his head—

—and suddenly the Pied Piper was silenced. Not completely gone, for Tony could still sense his presence, but substantially muffled. He pressed the aluminum foil to his skull, adjusting it to fit more tightly, and then he waited anxiously. Was the demon voice merely toying with him, allowing Tony to think he had won, before unleashing the final assault? It would be just like the sadistic bastard to do that.

But nothing happened, and Tony gradually became aware of a distant, very faint static buzz. There you are, little buddy. A minor irritation, nothing more. No pain. No words. No torture. Tony laughed out loud, shocked with relief and joy.

"It works! It works!"

Now you know you can beat the guy, Tony told himself. It's always something simple, easy to overlook or misunderstand. Like the common cold that wiped out the Martians in that old movie.

Less than an hour later Tony was ready to go. You look like a crazy, he thought sadly as he checked himself for the last time in the bathroom mirror. But that didn't really matter because he would be walking through the South End, where half the people out on the street looked damaged one way or another. Maybe he should have kept Snake's car, instead of abandoning it in the lot at the train station. No, the car was a major risk. He'd done the best thing he could with it. Now Tony would just have to walk, and if people stared—let them.

Tony had fashioned an aluminum foil skullcap, which he kept in place with an ordinary headband. For extra safety he had tied a couple of dozen thin foil strips to the headband, making a long fringe that hung down as far as his jaw on both sides, and around the back.

It would be better to wait until evening, but he was anxious to get rid of Snake's head. Besides, Doctor Ladybank wouldn't be at his office later. Now that the Pied Piper couldn't reach him, Tony was full of good ideas. He'd looked up psychiatrists in the Yellow Pages, and discovered an Ian Ladybank. His office address was in the center of the city. That was the shrink Tony had been sent to, no doubt about it. He called to make sure that Ladybank would be in all afternoon, but he didn't give his name or ask for an appointment. It seemed a safe bet that when he walked in with this headgear they'd lead him right to the shrink.

Tony's doubled sunglasses did a pretty good job, but all the light leaking in at both sides was enough to wear him down fast, so he taped the shades to his face with masking tape, overlapping the strips until he had built up a thick screen that tapered down across each of his cheeks. That should do it, he thought. Block out most of the unwanted light and you'll be okay. He could hear the Pied Piper still clamoring to get in, but faint and far away. Oddly, it was good to know the demon hadn't vanished.

Tony walked a couple of blocks with no difficulty. The tape worked fine, his eyes were still okay. No sweat. Well, no, that wasn't exactly true. It was a hot day, very humid, and Tony was perspiring already. But that was a minor inconvenience. He felt good for the first time in ages.

Was he the only person on earth being tormented by the Pied Piper, or were there others? Strange, how Tony had felt a sudden urge to ask Snake if he heard the voice. A very strange thing to do—you just don't ask other people if they hear any mysterious voices. It didn't matter, because Snake had so much metal in his head that he most likely wouldn't hear anything even if the Pied Piper did broadcast to him.

That old movie came to mind again. Was it possible that the Pied Piper was really a Martian, or some other alien? Could this be part of a plan to take over human minds, Tony wondered. Drive us crazy, turn us into slaves? *Because*, he thought, if the voice came from me, if it was all just my own craziness, then how could the aluminum foil work? So the voice had to come from someone or something outside. Ordinary people can't do that, but perhaps it was a top- secret government project. Or aliens. Tony had seen a few stories in the newsstand rags about this kind of thing, and he had always laughed about them in the past. But this was now. He knew a lot more, from bitter experience. Anything was possible.

What about Doctor Ladybank? The Doc. Was he in on it? Why did Tony feel drawn to see the man today? For help. But the Doc hadn't helped him at all last time. Just gave him some bullshit about watching out for—bright lights and colors. Jesus, maybe I was hypnotized, Tony thought. Maybe that's what this is about. If that's it, I'll kill him. Right there in his office.

How good it felt to be able to use his brain again! It had been so long since his thoughts weren't cluttered or twisted with the Pied Piper's invasive tactics. Tony felt human again.

But he was beginning to think he had made a mistake. He was approaching the center of the city and he still hadn't gotten rid of Snake's head. It was partly due to the fact that Tony had not found a suitable place to dispose of it, but even more because he was simply attracting too much attention. People— every rotten one of them—were stopping in their tracks to gawk at him as he walked along the street. How could he dump his parcel with a big audience on hand? Somebody would step up to open the bag at once and then they'd all grab him before he could get away.

To make matters worse, the aluminum foil skullcap and fringe were magnifying the heat and frying his brain. Tony was sweating like a pig now. He stopped abruptly and went into the department store he had almost passed. The air-conditioning came as a great relief. He wandered around for a few minutes, imagining that all the security people in the place were watching him.

Shit! what if they demanded to inspect his bag? He couldn't very well refuse, they'd just hold him until the cops came. Tony began to tremble with fear. Then he saw what he needed. He kept his shopping bag clutched tightly in one hand, and he went to the counter in the sports department. He paid for a New York Yankees baseball cap, which he put on immediately. It sat snugly on the aluminum foil. The clerk appeared to be in shock, but handed him his change and receipt without a word. Tony then strolled out of the store as if he hadn't a care in the world.

Brilliant idea, he thought. The fringe was still hanging in plain view, and there was all that tape on his cheeks, but he now felt somewhat less conspicuous. It would be a lot better if Tony could do away with the fringe, but that was too risky. If he let the Pied Piper back in, he'd never be free again. Maybe he could do without the fringe, maybe the skullcap was sufficient to block out the Pied Piper, but Tony wasn't about to take a chance.

Burger Billy's was crowded. Tony was pleased to see that he was indeed drawing fewer stares, thanks to the baseball cap, but there were still people watching him. He didn't feel comfortable enough to drop Snake's head in the trash bin, so he turned around and left the fast food restaurant.

The public library. That was the place. There was a large litter barrel (disguised as a piece of mod sculpture) in front of the library. Tony had already tossed one of Snake's feet into it and the newspapers had made no mention of its having been found. Best of all, it was located in the middle of a long sidewalk that went from the curb to the library, which sat back a distance from the street. That meant he could time it so that there was no one nearby when he walked past and dropped the dead man's head in the artsy-fartsy opening of the litter barrel. In spite of the heat, he pushed on in a hurry.

One more block, Tony thought. Then the park. He was sticky with sweat, tired but determined. I'm going to treat myself when this is over. A quick warm bath, followed by a long cool shower. Broil a T-bone steak, wash it down with that bottle of bubbly the TWA steward had given him, do a couple of lines and hit the bars. But tonight it would be for fun, not work.

"Hey, fuckhead."

Tony was only a little way into the park when the half dozen or so teenagers descended on him. Assholes, every one. They had nothing better to do with their time than hassle the elderly, the drifters and the gays who lingered in the park. Anyone they felt they could pester without comeback. They closed around Tony like an evil cloak, taunting him, shoving him, flicking fingers at his Yankee cap, snatching at the plastic bag.

"Fuck off, you little shits."

"Eat shit, fuckhead."

Some of them were a year or two older than he was, but that didn't matter. Tony strode on toward the library, poking elbows at anybody who got too close. They answered by bumping him, and then he was tripped. As he fell, cursing them loudly, he was hit on the head and his hat went flying. The aluminum foil skullcap was knocked loose. Oh Jesus, no. He clamped his hands on it and tried to adjust the headband. Somebody was yanking at the strips of foil that hung across Tony's face.

"Nice hair, asshole."

"What's in the bag?"

"Open it."

The kids were already pulling at the tightly wrapped parcel. Tony jumped up and lunged for it, but they pushed him down again. He had been sweating so much that the masking tape wouldn't stick to his cheeks anymore. Light flooded in, burning his eyes. Tony shrieked at them and swung out with his fists, but he didn't make contact. In return, he was pummeled from all sides. The doubled sunglasses were ripped from his face.

Tony fell to his knees, hands clapped tightly over his eyes. I'm okay, I'm okay, he tried to convince himself. But he already knew from the shouts and screams that they had discovered what he had in the bag. Now he was being kicked and punched, and when he tried to ward off the blows he was hit in the stomach so hard his eyes opened briefly. The color purple ravaged him—he was in a flowerbed full of violets.

Tony screamed.

"No! Don't touch that, not that! Please don't—"

But they did. They were ready to take his mug shot, and one of the cops calmly reached up and pulled off that stupid aluminum foil thing he had on his head.

Zzzzzt.

EPILOGUE

Life isn't disappointing, but people so often are. They may raise your hopes for a while, but sooner or later they'll let you down. People are...Doctor Ladybank pondered the matter for a few moments, seeking to find the right word. Yes, he had it.

People are unworthy.

He was not entirely sure what they were unworthy of, but the point seemed irrefutable. It was difficult to follow every train of thought to the end of the line when you were drowning in a sea of disillusionment. The gift—for that was how Doctor Ladybank now regarded it, not as a skill or a technique—was apparently gone. Radio silence. Day and night he tried to tune in someone, anyone, but he found no one.

What happened? Doctor Ladybank wasn't sure. For a few days after Tony Delgado's arrest, the boy could still be reached. But then he began to fade gradually, and after a month he disappeared altogether. It was not the effect of buildings and metalwork and power lines, or Doctor Ladybank never would have managed to reach across the city in the first place. Nor could it be a matter of distance, as he had driven the fifty-plus miles to the Bartholomew Forensic Institute, part of the state hospital for the criminally insane, where Delgado was being held pending trial. He parked in the visitor's lot and sat there for an hour, trying feverishly to regain contact with the boy. Nothing.

Doctor Ladybank wondered if the failure was his. But he did the same things with his mind, he hadn't forgotten how it worked, anymore than you can forget how to ride a bicycle. Of course, it may have been a gigantic fluke, a scientific peculiarity that had its brief moment and then passed. But Doctor

Ladybank could not believe that. He still had faith in his gift. All he had to do, he told himself, was persist. It would come back to him. And he would connect. Believe. Persist.

His favorite theory about this temporary failure centered on the inadequacy of his two subjects. Snake had always been tricky to handle, a dim prospect. Doctor Ladybank had never enjoyed the same intimacy of mind with Snake that he had with Tony. To steer him out to Jack's backyard and then get him over the hump—that was like composing the *Gurre-Lieder.* Delgado, on the other hand, was ravishing in his openness and malleability. Great potential, unlimited opportunity. But something had gone wrong, and Doctor Ladybank feared that he had gone too far with the boy. Now parts of Delgado's brain had simply shut down and were incapable of any mental reception. How else to explain it?

Of course, terrible things had happened. But no, don't say that. Terrible is an emotive word that has no meaning. It would be more accurate to say that unfortunate things had happened. He couldn't explain it, but it was hardly all his doing. When minds meet and interact in such a pioneering way the results are almost certain to be unexpected. Two minds adrift in each other, it was like—and here Doctor Ladybank took comfort in the persistence of the musical metaphor—a vast orchestra lost in the aleatoric reaches of the night. Besides, Snake and Tony were hardly innocents.

Fuck it, as they would say.

Doctor Ladybank stared at the papers in front of him, but he couldn't see the words. It was that time of day, when he usually summarized his notes on the patients he'd seen, but his mind just wouldn't focus. Such boring and squalid lives that people insist on living...Doctor Ladybank was glad when the phone warbled. "Margaret Zuvella on the line for you."

I remember the bristols, but the face escapes me.

"Yes, put her through." Pause, click. "Hello, Maggie?"

"Hi, Ian. How are you?"

"Fine, thanks, and you?"

"Busy as usual, but bearing up."

Doctor Ladybank gave the obligatory chuckle. "Now, what

can I do for you on this rainy Tuesday?"

"I was hoping you'd agree to examine a client of mine. He's indigent, of course, so it'll be at the usual lousy state rates. But he's convinced you can help."

"Oh? What case is it?"

"State versus Anthony Delgado."

"Ah."

"You know him, you saw him a while back on another case. He seems like a major league fuck-up, but what do I know? The state experts are picking his brain now, which is why we need you.

Yes."

"Yes, you remember him? Or yes, you'll examine him?"

"Both."

"Ian, you're a doll."

Not really—but Doctor Ladybank didn't say that. The tide had come in, his boat was lifted off the sand, and he was sailing again. The time would come, he knew beyond the slightest doubt, when he would make contact, and *connect*, with some other person. When that happened, Doctor Ladybank would progress with the gift, exploring new territory, achieving the unimaginable.

But for now, thanks be to the void, he had a chance to learn more from one of his mistakes. Perhaps even to save it.

Tony smiled when he saw Doctor Ladybank's fountain pen, one of those fat expensive jobs. In happier times he'd had a couple of well-off tricks who used that kind of pen. Check-writers with skinny dicks.

They were in a small consulting room at Bartholomew. It was painted the mandatory institutional shade of pastel green, and it was stuffy from a lack of air-conditioning, but it was as good as heaven—compared to the ward in which Tony was kept. The guard stood outside the door, keeping an eye on them through the sturdy wire-and-glass window. Doctor Ladybank had brought Tony a carton of cigarettes from Maggie. Tony had never smoked before, but in a ward full of wackos it seemed a perfectly natural, even healthy thing to do.

The questions were stupid and boring, but Tony tried to give polite answers. There was something eerie and unreal about this. After so much time, he was still unsure of Doctor Ladybank's true role in what had gone down. Had he been directly involved in all of Tony's suffering? Was he partially responsible for the bleak future Tony faced? It seemed unlikely, because the same man was now trying to construct a "demon voice" insanity defense so that Tony would be spared hard prison time. Not that he relished the prospect of an indefinite committal to the nuthouse.

"One problem," Doctor Ladybank said, "is your assertion that the voice stopped communicating with you."

"Yeah, it did."

"When did that happen?"

"When I was still in the city jail," Tony said. "It took me a couple of weeks, maybe more, to get rid of it."

"You stopped the voice?"

"That's right."

"And how did you accomplish that?"

"By banging my head on the bars and the cement floor," Tony explained proudly. "See, it really bothered him when I banged my head on the floor at my apartment. He said the people downstairs would put the cops on me. But I figured, maybe he was afraid I'd shake up the works." Tony tapped the side of his head. "So that he couldn't get to me anymore. In jail, I had the time to try it out, to do it everyday, as much as I could take. And it actually worked. I could feel him getting weaker, and finally I couldn't hear him at all anymore. If I'd only done that at the beginning, I'd have saved myself—my life."

"I see." Doctor Ladybank put his pen down. "Do you have to continue this behavior, banging your head, in order to—"

"Hell, no," Tony cut in. "It did the job, and that's it. I never got a kick out of knocking myself senseless, you know. I'm not crazy. I just...went through *something* crazy. And I'll tell you this too: he's still out there, man. I know he is."

"Yes. Now, tell me—"

"Doc, I have a question for you."

"Yes?"

"Why did you tell me about bright lights and colors?"

"Pardon?"

"The first time you saw me," Tony said, leaning forward, his arms on the table. "You gave me some line about watching out for bright lights and bright colors."

"I'm sure I didn't," Doctor Ladybank insisted.

"Yeah, you did. It sounded weird at the time, and I didn't give it much thought. But later, when the voice came and all the trouble really started, lights and colors began to hurt me. They got so bad I had to wear sunglasses and dark clip-ons. But I was still in agony." Tony paused. "Why did you do that?"

"I can assure you I did no such—"

"What was it, some kind of test? Or were you just having a little fun with me?"

"Anthony, you won't help your case this way."

Doctor Ladybank was trying to sound calm, but he was clearly flustered. His cheeks had more color now and his eyes cast about evasively as he droned on about Tony's "willful and naive attempt to embellish the delusion," and other uptown bullshit.

"Doc," Tony interrupted. "I'm a whore. Maybe that's why I can always tell when I'm being jived. I thought it was the CIA, or aliens from space, or that I was just crazy. I doubted it was you, I really did. Until now."

"I'll speak with your attorney."

Doctor Ladybank was trying to look annoyed. He shuffled the papers on the table, picked up his pen and began to write. As if Tony were no longer there, and had indeed ceased to exist.

Writing about me. The subject. That's what you were doing. You weren't trying to read my mind, Tony thought, you were trying to write it, to script my life like a dream or some kind of movie in your mind.

"Plasmodium."

Doctor Ladybank looked up sharply when Tony spoke the word. A ghost of a smile formed around the psychiatrist's eyes, seeming to say *I cannot be hurt by you.*

The baleful, haunting expression on the man's face triggered a profound claustrophobia in Tony. It felt as if the world, the universe itself, and every cell in his brain, was shutting down, blinking off, closing forever, and all that would be left was his sense of awareness—perpetual awareness of the dark around him.

The room itself was being blotted out.

Write this!

Tony snatched the fat pen from Doctor Ladybank's fingers and in a single swift motion rammed it nib-first through the shrink's right eye. He pushed it as far into the demon brain as he could, and then sat back, experiencing a remarkable sense of clarity and peace of mind.

Doctor Ladybank's mouth opened slightly. Otherwise, he did not move. His left eye was still open, glistening sightlessly. He appeared to be considering the matter.

SCRAMBURG, USA

For Jack Ketchum and Dallas Mayr

1

WHAT ABOUT THE BOY

Captain Frank Bell tossed his cigarette out the car window, pried a spearmint Lifesaver loose and popped it in his mouth. He'd rather not have the Hacketts catch a whiff of the two double bourbons that he had downed at the Legion a few minutes ago. Rev. Joe Hackett was the pastor at Zion Lutheran, and his wife Eileen ran the Women's Auxiliary. The Hacketts were fixtures in town—good people to be in good with.

And they had a problem. They needed his advice. Again. Captain Bell smiled as he swung his car into Oak Lane, the short dead-end passage behind the church, where the Hacketts lived. He knew exactly what he was going to say. He'd be glad to give them his advice—but he could do better than that now. He could *help* them.

Captain Bell parked in front of the trim white colonial at the end of the lane. It was a minute to four, he was right on time. A sun shower broke loose as he got out of the car, and he hurried up the gravel path to avoid the sudden rain. The minister's wife opened the front door about two seconds after he rang the bell. Middle-aged, short and somewhat plump, she had strangely colorless hair.

"Mrs. Hackett."

She nodded at him without smiling. He noticed the way she

held herself, her head and neck turned slightly away from him, her movements brief and stiff. It was a warm June day, but she was wearing a blouse with long sleeves.

"He's in his office," she said, gesturing to the first door on the right. "Go on in, he's expecting you."

"Thank you, ma'am."

She moved her head to keep the left side of her face from his view as he passed her. He knocked once and entered the office. Joe Hackett got up from the chair behind a blond wooden desk. He was tall and thin, but he had a paunch. He wore gray trousers, a white shirt and necktie. He looked like a smalltown insurance agent—which, in a way, he was.

"Good to see you." He shook hands with the cop and waved him to a brown Naugahyde armchair. "Thanks for coming by, Frank."

"Glad to."

"You want anything?" he asked as he returned to his seat behind the desk. "Lemonade? Glass of soda?"

"No thanks."

"So. How are you?"

"I'm fine, Joe. How are you?"

"Fine, thanks. Just fine."

The minister's hands fidgeted with some of the papers on his desk and his eyes avoided Bell's gaze. The cop knew what to expect. The poor helpless bastard would circle around for twenty minutes, like a dog looking for the exact right spot to dump his load.

"When did he hit her?"

Hackett was startled, but then his face crumpled and his hands fell flat on the desk. "The other night."

"Not the first time, was it?"

"No."

"He hit you?"

Hackett was breathing hard, still not looking up at Bell. Finally, he nodded. "Yes."

"You ever hit him back?"

"Of course not." Hackett looked offended. "Fighting is wrong. It's no answer to his misbehavior."

Bell sighed. Misbehavior. A better reason was, the kid was big and strong and would take the old man apart like a Tinkertoy.

"You ever spank him, over the years?"

"When he was a child, sure. God knows he needed it, he was such a handful. Right from the beginning."

"Joe, it's not your fault it didn't take."

"We've done everything we could for him."

"I know you did."

"Schramburg is a nice town," the minister continued, "a good town. We gave him a good home, all our love. We taught him right from wrong. We didn't spoil him with lots of toys and things, like other families, but he didn't go without. He wanted a train set, a bike, army men—he had those things. And vacations? We took him to—"

"You and your wife did your part," Bell interrupted. "He got it from his mother and father. Nothing you could ever do about that."

"That's why I don't like to blame him, not entirely. His father runs off, he and his mother end up in the Town Farm. And then—to live through that terrible tragedy. Dear God. None of that is Howie's fault."

Bell sighed again. "No, it isn't. But he is who he is, and that's what your problem is now. What else has he been up to lately?"

The rest spilled out quickly. The constant bullying and threats, the atmosphere of anxiety and fear that poisoned their home, the drunkenness, the cursing, the foul, vile language, the torrent of insults—all of that had been gradually increasing over the last couple of years. But now, in recent months, their adopted son had become physically violent.

"Who's he hang around with?"

"That's another thing. I don't even know their names. There's only three or four of them, but they're...."

"Just like him."

"Yes, that's right." The minister had a look of pleading on his face. "Frank, there's nothing we can do with him. I'm afraid of where this might go, what might happen. You already gave him a couple of chances."

Bell nodded. "He was what, thirteen, fourteen? Shoplifting, minor vandalism. Most boys have a little of that to burn off. I'm always glad to give a kid another chance at that age. But some of them never straighten up and fly right, no matter how many chances you give them."

Hackett pulled himself together and sat up straight. "Frank, I have no doubt whatsoever that you should be the next chief. Larkin, God love him, he's a good man, but he's past it now. It's only a matter of time, and I believe you're clearly the best candidate to succeed him. Things will get better in Schramburg with you leading the force."

"Thanks, Joe." There were two Lutherans on the Police Board, the town's civilian committee that would cast the decisive vote.

"But, back to *this*. What can Eileen and I do about Howie? He is beyond our control. He is growing up to be…."

"A monster."

"That's what I'm afraid."

"When is his birthday, Joe?"

"Last month, May tenth."

"And how old is he now?"

"Eighteen."

Captain Bell smiled. "I thought so, but I wasn't sure. That's your answer, Joe. That's your answer, right there."

"What do you mean?"

"He's eighteen, he has no legal right to live here anymore," Bell explained patiently. "He's an adult. It's time for Howie to sink or swim on his own. He sure isn't going to college, but he can join the army, join the navy, or he can get a job and pay his own way. It's your decision to make, but believe me, the best thing you could do is put him out."

Rev. Joe Hackett sat back in his chair, startled. This was something that had never occurred to him. He thought about it for a few moments and then shook his head sadly.

"We couldn't do that."

"You can and you should."

"No, I mean we could never do that. It's beyond the point where we can tell him anything. Howie would—that would just touch him off again." He glanced away, shuddering at the thought.

"Nah, he'll go." Bell smiled again. "And he'll go quietly."

"What?" Hackett was puzzled but hopeful. "How?"

"I'll be there to make sure he does."

2

THE END OF JUNE

Howie Hackett tottered slightly as he left Dr. Finsterwald's office on the third floor of the Greene Building. That hangover was still pounding in his head, *and* he'd just had a tooth yanked. There was a hole in his mouth that felt as big as Hilfer's gravel pit. It was plugged with a wad of cotton. The whole right side of his face felt like a pillow. The elevator finally arrived with a rumble and a loud clank. The old guy in the Phillip Morris costume tugged the gate open.

"Feel better yet?"

"Watch it, Dad. I'm not in the mood."

The elevator operator shut the gate, pulled the lever around to G and then sat back on his stool, smiling at the floor. Howie stood with his back against the wall of the carriage. The place stank, the whole damn building stank of cigars and old men.

Outside, it was still raining lightly. Howie stopped at Vic's Smoke Shop a little farther down East Main and bought a pack of Luckies. He cut through Kresge's and came out on Union Street. His blue '55 Chevy box was parked in the lot next to the Shamrock. Once he was inside the car, he reached under the seat, found the pint of Seagram's 7 and took a quick gulp. Some of it leaked through the cotton padding and stung like hell in spite of the novocaine. But the rest of it felt very good. He was about the turn the key when an older guy in a navy blue suit knocked on the window. Howie cranked it down a couple of inches.

"What?"

"You know me?"

"Nope."

"Captain Frank Bell." The man reached into his jacket pocket and came up with a badge. "Schramburg P.D."

Howie blew air out of the left side of his mouth. "Okay, so?"

Bell pointed to the other door. "I want to talk to you."

Howie didn't move. "So talk."

The cop's eyes narrowed. "Open the door, Howie. It's raining out here. Don't piss me off."

Howie reached across the front seat and unlocked the door. The cop went around the car and got in. He smelled of Vitalis.

"Okay, what?"

"This your vehicle?"

"Yeah. You want to see the papers?"

"Your father give it to you?"

"No, my father never gave me anything," Howie said. "Joe Hackett gave it to me." He grinned. "Got tired of me using his car, I guess."

"Let's go for a drive."

"Hey, what the hell is this all about anyhow? I just had a tooth out, my mouth is killing me and I want to go home. You got a problem with me, tell me what it is right now."

"*Drive.* Otherwise, I'll haul your ass in to the station and put you in a tiny room with no windows, no sink, no toilet, and you can sit and wait for five or six hours, however long it takes, until I'm ready to talk to you again, like I am right now. I've got about three seconds of patience left."

"Okay, okay." Howie started the car. "Which way?"

"Get on South Main, heading out of town."

"Okay, but—"

"I'll tell you when to talk."

Howie drove. He had no idea what this was about. His anger was building quickly, but the thing that worried him and held him in check was that one word—captain. This guy was no ordinary cop. There were a lot of reasons why Howie could be in trouble, but he thought it was all nickel and dime stuff, minor violations—like the bottle of booze under the seat, or the row of hedges he'd plowed through in somebody's front yard one night last week. But even if they knew about any of that, it wasn't the kind of stuff that a police captain would come and talk to you about. Like this, with *you* driving *him* somewhere. Then Howie noticed the black-and-white in the rearview mirror, two uniformed cops in it. Shit.

"Cross the river up here and then get on 212 south."

That was the old turnpike in and out of Schramburg, now more of a secondary road. "Where we going?"

"I want to show you something."

"Show me what?"

"You'll see."

Ten minutes later they were on 212 and the houses fell behind and the countryside took over, rocky hills and thick pine forest that was broken up now and then by weedy meadows or patches of swamp.

"You know that picnic area just ahead?" the cop said after they'd gone a few more miles. "Pull in there."

The rain was a little heavier now and the picnic area was deserted. Bell had Howie park near a wooden table at the far corner, screened from the road by trees. The black-and-white pulled up close behind them and the two cops got out.

"Come on."

Howie got out of his car and slowly followed the captain, walking off the dirt road, into a grassy area beneath a huge maple where they were protected from the rain. One of the uniformed men was right behind them, and then Howie saw the other one—taking grocery bags from the cop car and putting them into Howie's. He couldn't see what the bags were packed with, but they were full. Were they going to frame him with some stolen goods? He stopped and pointed back toward the cars.

"Hey, what's going on? What's he doing?"

"Putting your things in your car."

"My things?"

"Yep, your dirty underwear, crud like that."

"What for? What's—"

"Because you're leaving Schramburg. For good."

"Like hell I am," Howie yelled. "I live here."

"Not anymore you don't."

The captain grabbed him by the arm and yanked him closer. Then he drove his fist into Howie's stomach so fast and hard that he didn't have time to react. The cotton wad flew out of his mouth. He doubled over in pain, gasping. The captain grabbed him by the ears, twisting them, and pulled his face forward as he slammed his knee into Howie's nose. Blood spurted and he screamed, dropping to the wet ground. Then the uniformed cop took over, stomping on Howie's hands and knees and ankles, kicking him in the stomach, ribs and head.

"*You were in the goddamn poorhouse,*" the captain was saying as Howie moaned and writhed helplessly. "They gave you a good home, they gave you more than you ever would've had. And how did you repay them? Made their life a living hell. You piece of shit."

The other uniformed cop finished throwing Howie's things into the Chevy. He came and stood over Howie. He unzipped his trousers, pulled his dick out and began pissing down on Howie's face and head. The cop's partner started laughing.

"Man, how many coffees you have today?"

"Oh yeah, got a full tank."

"Jeez, I don't want to touch him now."

They grabbed Howie by his belt and his feet, and dragged him through the wet grass back to his car. They hauled him up and shoved him behind the steering wheel. He slid over on his side, the pain still so bad he could barely move. The passenger door opened and Captain Bell leaned in, his face close to Howie's.

"You keep heading south and don't ever come back. I have twelve patrolmen and every one of them knows you on sight. You ever set foot in Schramburg again, I guarantee you'll drop off the face of earth. You hear me?" He slammed his fist into Howie's nose, mashing it even more. "*Did you hear me, asshole?*"

"Agghh-unhh...."

"Good. From now on it's *Scramburg* to you, bud. Now get the fuck out of here and don't even think of coming back. *Not ever.*"

3

ILONA AND THE ELEGANT TWINS

He drove south, holding a T-shirt to his bloody nose, breathing through his open mouth. There were lots of ways to get back into town and he took the one that seemed least likely, circling way around to the north, sticking to back roads and then quiet neighborhood streets.

His luck held, he didn't see a cop car, and eventually he made it to the Muellers' house. Howie pulled into the rutted driveway, away from the street, and hit the horn twice. Less than a minute later, Ilona came out the front door. He smiled and almost felt better. His bundle of love, she was all of 5'1" tall. Her blonde hair was tied back in a ponytail. She wore tight blue jeans, a sleeveless white blouse and penny loafers. He loved the way her curvy little body moved as she crossed the front yard, hurrying through the rain. Ilona hopped in the car—and screamed.

He winced. "Jesus, put a muffler on it."

"Oh my God Howie they killed you baby—"

"Damn near."

"What happened?" Ilona blinked back the tears, and then her face flushed with anger. "Who did it, baby? Who did this to you?"

He started to give her the bare details of it, but he had to cut it short. He quickly rolled down the window, leaned out and puked. His head was throbbing, his whole body ached and he felt sick inside. He could still taste blood in his mouth and throat.

"I need to—"

"Come on inside," Ilona said. "You're all messed up. Don't worry, I'll take care of you, baby. You'll be alright. Just don't say anything about the cops, okay? My mother doesn't need to hear that."

"Those fuckin' bastards...."

"They don't understand you, baby."

"Fuck them. Fuck fuck *fuck them all*."

"Come on, baby," Ilona said, helping him get out of the car. "You need first aid right now. I was a Girl Scout, you know."

"You were?"

"Three years. I learned first aid, all that stuff."

"Still got the uniform?"

"Probably. Why?"

"Jeez, I'd like to see you in that sometime."

"Yeah, you'll be alright."

Mrs. Mueller's hair was stringy, as usual, and she wore the same shapeless housedress she always had on when Howie came by. She was watching Queen For A Day. When she caught sight of his face, she blinked once and then started cackling.

"Somebody finally got you, huh?"

"Leave him alone," Ilona told her mother. "He's hurt."

"Boy, they sure made a meatloaf out of you."

"Mom, shut the hell up—"

"*You* shut up."

"No, *you*—"

"I don't want him bleeding all over our things."

Ilona took Howie downstairs to the cellar. She had him sit in the old easy chair next to her father's workbench. She disappeared for a couple of minutes—he heard her and her mother yelling at each other again—and she returned with some first aid supplies. She wrapped ice cubes in a washcloth and made him hold it against his lips, which were puffy and still bleeding a little. She got a basin of warm water from the sink in the laundry area and began to wash the cuts and scrapes on his face and arms.

"They can't do this to you, Howie. This is America. You can live anywhere you want."

"You got part of that right."

"There's a bump in your nose now."

"Yeah."

She gently cleaned away the clotted blood around the nostrils. "Can you breathe through it okay?"

Howie cautiously placed a finger on each side of his nose and tried to press and work it back into shape. A tiny bit at a time, otherwise the pain lit up his whole head. But he could feel something moving.

"Better now."

"That's good. Don't try to fix it all at once."

By the time she finished, much of the pain in his body had died down to a low ache. Howie could think clearly again, and the anger blazed inside. He was not going to let them do this to him. Joe and Eileen—they gave the cops his clothes, they were in on it. In fact, they must have come up with the idea in the first place. A fucking minister, a so-called man of God. Sorry, we're all tapped out of charity. Throw the bastard out, he isn't ours anyway. From now on it's *Scramburg* to you, bud.

Not that he hadn't given them good reason, but still it astonished and infuriated him that they'd do such a thing. Well, think again, fuckers. I'm not ready to leave this little dump of yours. Not yet.

Howie looked around the basement. "Say, your old man's got some workshop here. Got more tools than a hardware store. I bet I could borrow a couple of them and he wouldn't even notice they were gone."

"Howie."

He grinned at her. "Relax. It'll just be for a little while tomorrow. You'll bring them back before he even gets home from work."

"What're you going to do?"

"Make them sorry."

"Who?"

"All of them."

Ilona flashed a wide smile. "Oh baby, count me in."

"You sure? This could be the big flame-out. I've got nowhere to go and nothing to lose. But you—"

"Hey, remember me? I'm with you."

He smiled. "You're hot stuff, you are."

"Glad you noticed."

"Oh yeah." He pulled her onto his lap. "I noticed."

Howie moved his car to the street around the corner from the Muellers' house and left it parked at the curb. If the cops spotted it, they might tow it in—he wouldn't put anything past them now. But he'd be taking a bigger risk if he drove it around town.

Howie used the Muellers' phone, and Vance and Vaughn picked him up about twenty minutes later. He often referred to them as the elegant twins, and sometimes he called one of them Cool and the other one Classy. They took it in stride. They had James Dean hair. They wore great shirts, never tucked in, collars turned up, sleeves folded back just twice—they had elegant wrists. When they were just standing around, they had a slouch that seemed like the most natural way to be. They gazed off into the distance in a way that showed how pretty much uninterested they were in whatever was around them—like the whole town. They said things like "I couldn't even work up contempt for the guy" or "That wouldn't sell in Paris," which had a magical ring to Howie. They would ride around for hours in their father's big old Hudson, sitting back, and it was like they owned Schramburg but regarded it as a minor burden and a disappointment.

Howie had known them since grammar school, but he never hung around with them until freshman year at Schramburg High. He'd been kept after in detention again, it was late winter, dark outside, and he decided to save time by cutting across the football field. Behind the Snack Shack, he saw the elegant twins getting pounded by four other kids. Howie didn't like the numbers and jumped right in. He was big then too, and he made all the difference in the fight. After that, he was in with the twins.

They had it made. Their mother had died of cancer a few years ago. Their father had his own business, a laundry. He used to beat them all the time when they were little kids, but then they got bigger and started to beat him instead. They owned the old man now. Whatever they wanted, fine. They believed he was going gaga from inhaling so much carbon tet over the years, and they were waiting him out. When he died, they intended to sell the business and move to Hawaii.

"You need a room?"

"We have a room you can use."

"Jeez, thanks. It won't be for long."

"Long as you want."

"Just don't make a mess, you know?"

"No, hey, I'm not a slob." He'd have to remember that. Howie sat low in one corner of the back seat. He was trying to straighten out a Lucky bent almost in half—the goddamn cops had even kicked his smokes. "The other thing is, I need to put my car somewhere."

"The lot behind the laundry."

"You can't see it from the street."

"Man, you guys are the best."

"Hey," dismissively.

"So, what do have in mind?"

"Kick some ass. All over this fuckin' town."

Vance and Vaughn glanced at each other, and then briefly back at Howie. They smiled, as near as they ever did. He'd never seen them look so interested in anything before.

4

SHELTER IN THE GRAVE

That night the elegant twins procured a case of Utica Club and sat up drinking with Howie in his new room. It was on the third floor over the laundry, at the back of the building. The old man lived on the second floor, so it would be easy to avoid him. The only drawback was that the room was stuffy and hot, even with the windows open. Vance and Vaughn shared the other room on the third floor, and there was a bathroom.

Howie had to call a few times, but he finally got in touch with his one other solid friend, Artie Boncal, who immediately came around to see him. Boncal was the only other surviving Town Farm child who still lived in Schramburg. He'd been taken in by a family that had three other kids of their own, who treated him as a resented outsider who didn't belong in their little nest. After fourteen years of that, Boncal stayed away from the house as much as possible. Now that he had just graduated from high school, he was trying to figure out how to move out completely. They tell you that you have to finish high school in order to get a good job, so he did, he had scraped through every damn year. And what did that get him? He didn't know how to do much of anything. The kind of jobs that he had a shot at weren't even worth taking—they wouldn't pay enough to cover a single room in the cheapest boarding house in town, let alone an apartment of his own. Boncal was trying to get a handle on this situation.

"Man, they worked you over pretty good."

"They'll be sorry they didn't do a better job."

Boncal pulled the ring on a can of beer. Vance and Vaughn were on the small sofa and there were no other chairs in the room, so he perched on the bed, a few feet away from Howie.

"Those brown spots mercurochrome?"

"No, iodine."

"How come you didn't use mercurochrome?"

"Ilona had iodine," Howie said.

"You guys use iodine or mercurochrome?" Boncal asked the twins, who were slumped back, smoking cigarettes and drinking beer. Their look of shared boredom changed slightly to one of puzzlement.

"I never used either one."

"Me either."

"Good idea," Boncal said. "Don't get cut."

"You working yet?" Howie asked.

"Nah. The other day the old man told me he heard there was a job going at Acey's, so I stop by, thinking maybe they wanted somebody in the office, you know? Paperwork, writing up orders, that kind of thing? Turns out they need another tire-changer. Fuck that."

"I could use some help," Howie said.

"Sure." Boncal nodded. "Like what?"

"I got to stay out of sight, at least for a few days," Howie explained. "So I need you to go sit in a car for me."

"Can do. Uh…is there more to it than just that?"

Howie gave a short laugh. "Well, yeah…."

At noon the next day, Ilona drove her '56 Ford into the parking lot behind the laundry. Howie quickly descended the back stairs and slipped in on the passenger side. He was wearing a baseball cap and sunglasses in an effort to make his face a little less recognizable. He gave Ilona a quick kiss and then sank down in the seat.

"How're you feeling today?"

"The hole from my tooth hurts and I'm still aching in about a dozen different places. Otherwise, okay."

"Oh, baby…."

"You bring the stuff?" he asked.

"Sure. It's on the back seat."

Howie glanced behind. "All of it?"

"Y-e-s spells yes."

"Good girl."

"Where to?"

"Get on Millville and head out of town."

"Okay. What's out there?"

"You'll see."

It took almost twenty minutes before they reached the eastern edge of the city, beyond residential neighborhoods, where houses were few and far between. Much of the remaining open land was undeveloped because it was too rocky and hilly. Some of it was still on the books as the property of the town of Schramburg.

Howie reached behind him and picked up Mr. Mueller's bolt-cutter. In the brown paper bag from Ray's Hardware was a hefty new padlock and two keys for it.

"Okay?"

"Perfect," Howie said. "Take the left, just ahead."

Ilona almost missed it because the entrance was surrounded on both sides by weeds and dense brush that stood eight or ten feet high. They were on a narrow gravel road, but had to stop almost immediately. Just ahead, a chain hung across the road from two wooden posts. A rusty No Trespassing sign dangled from the middle of the chain and two others were nailed to the posts.

"Is this..."

"Right," Howie said. "The Town Farm."

Moving quickly, he got out of the car and went to the lock that held the chain in place. The bolt-cutter sliced through it easily. Howie chucked the old lock into the woods, lowered the chain and waved Ilona on through. Then he pulled the chain back up in place and fastened it with the new lock. Ilona accelerated before he got the door completely shut.

"What do you think—one minute?"

"If that," she replied.

"Anybody drive by on the road out there?"

"Nope."

"Good."

Soon the road swung to the right, and after another hundred yards they came out in a small clearing where the weeds only reached knee-high. In the center stood the burned-out ruins of the Town Farm. Ilona parked a short distance away, and they sat staring at it for a moment.

"I never knew exactly where it was."

"You never been here before?"

"No."

"I used to come out here a lot when I was around twelve, thirteen," he said. "Looking for my mother's ghost."

"Ah, baby." Ilona put her hand on his arm. "Did you ever see or hear anything?"

"Nah."

"Why did you want to come here now?"

Howie took the other bag of things he'd asked Ilona to pick up, and looked inside. Some bottles of soda and an opener, chocolate bars, potato chips, matches and a pack of Luckies. Good. He opened the car door. "I'll show you. Let's go."

"Okay."

The Town Farm had been a long barn-like building, three stories tall. The exterior brick walls remained in place now, their windows vacant. Most of the roof and the upper two floors had collapsed during the fire, and the ground floor was still full of charred debris and crushed rooms. Years later, Howie heard the official version of what had happened—that late one night a fire had broken out in the small kitchen on the second floor, due to the inattention of somebody on the staff. The interior was a maze of boxy wooden rooms, so the fire spread very rapidly upward. It took a while for the fire trucks to get out there from downtown. The official death toll was 22, but everybody assumed it was closer to 40, since it was no secret that the town unofficially housed some harmless local mental cases there along with the poor.

That was fourteen years ago, when Howie had just turned four. He couldn't remember much at all about that night. He had a sense of noise, of clamor and commotion and terrible screams, but they were more like dream images than memories of something real. What he knew for certain was that his mother had thrown him from their third floor window. They caught him in a blanket. Flying down three floors? It seemed like one more theft that he couldn't remember a bit of it. The smoke over-came his mother, or the floor collapsed first; either way, she was lost.

Same deal for Boncal, except that he claimed he could remember the entire fall to the ground, just like in a movie. He also claimed that he and Howie had been pals at the Town Farm, playing together outside, running up and down the long dark corridors, raising hell. Howie didn't remember any of that—as far as he knew, the first time he met Boncal was a couple of years later, at Twain Elementary—but he never contradicted him. Howie liked hearing those stories, whether they were true or not. There wasn't a whole helluva lot to like about Boncal, but that was one thing.

"Baby, I don't want to go inside."

"Don't worry, it's safe." He yanked several times on the sheet of corrugated metal that blocked the front door, prying it loose. "Come on, it's okay. You need to see this."

Ilona followed him, stooping slightly to squeeze through the tight opening. Inside, they edged along the wall, hemmed in by mounds of ash, broken and burned floor joists, and other debris. They went a short distance and then Howie bent over and entered a dark tunnel-like passage.

"How-ie."

"Come on," his voice echoed out to her.

Carefully feeling her way, Ilona followed, and a few moments later she was able to stand up. It was still dark but enough light filtered through, and she saw Howie. There were in some enclosed space. The air was cool and damp, but had a bad musty taste.

"This was one of the offices," he said. "The fire was above, so it all fell down. You can see, what it was like." He pointed. "That whole side of the office was crushed, but this part along the front of the building, it's still here. Look, you can see the edge of a desk sticking out there."

"Wow." She didn't know what else to say for a few moments.

He seemed to be in such a strange dreamy state of mind. "But baby, why did you want to come here now?"

"Okay." He turned to face her in the faint light. "I wanted you to see this place, so you know where it is and how to get here. I'm staying with Vance and Vaughn right now, but if things get too hot and I have to split real fast, and I can't get in touch with you and you don't know where I am—this is where you'll find me. You'll know I need you to come for me, and we can figure out what to do then. Okay?"

"Oh, okay."

Howie rolled the bag of supplies tight, found a place for it in one of the cluttered corners and covered it with debris. "In case I need it," he said, as if to himself. Then he took Ilona's hand and placed one of the keys in it. "You'll need this to get in. Make sure you put that chain back up right away. A cop probably drives by on the main road once or twice a day and looks to make sure the chain's in place."

"Okay."

"And you don't tell anybody. 'Cause I'm not telling anybody else, not Vance and Vaughn, not Boncal. I want only you to know."

"Got it."

"I can trust them, but I don't know how far, and I don't want to find out the hard way. You're the only person I trust totally."

Ilona almost leapt into his arms and kissed him. "Thanks, baby. I'll be here for you. Anytime, anyplace."

He loved the way she clung to him, her body on his, her legs hooked around his hips, the way it felt to hold her like this with one arm under her sweet ass, the way her skin felt and smelled, her thick hair—

"But can we go now?" she said softly in his ear. "You don't want to make out here, do you? In this place? You got a room in town, remember? A room with a bed in it?"

"You're right, I do."

"Good. Let's go. I don't like it here."

Howie hugged her tighter. "Me either."

5

HOWARD DOESN'T LIVE HERE ANYMORE

Vance and Vaughn moved Howie's car, as planned. They were out for most of the afternoon, picking up things that Howie wanted, and they returned to the third floor around 8 in the evening with their girlfriends, the Apache sisters, Cindy and Cathy Grenier. The girls were one year apart in age. They both had long straight black hair and strange French-Canadian accents, which was why Howie had started calling them the Apache sisters a while back. They liked it.

Ilona had picked up some burgers and cole slaw at Duke's Drive-In. She and Howie ate the food back in his room. They made out some more, and drank a few beers. When the twins arrived with the girls, Howie stood up, an eager look on his face.

"How'd you do?"

"No sweat."

"You got everything?"

"More than everything."

"Yeah, we had a couple of ideas of our own."

"Wow, that's great. Like what?"

"Tell you later," nodding toward the girls.

"Okay. Hey, I owe you guys."

"If you do, you do."

"The show must go on, right?"

"Damn right," Howie said.

Boncal turned up a little while later. He looked quite pleased with himself, and then even more pleased to see that he had a larger audience than he had expected.

"Any luck?" Howie asked.

"Jesus, what a day I had," Boncal began. He opened a can of beer and took a deep swallow. "Man, I needed that. Anyhow, I sat there for I don't know how long, and didn't see nobody, no cops, nobody."

"Where'd you park?"

"On Meadow, across from the entrance to Oak Lane."

"Okay, good."

"I went and got a cup of coffee, came back. Still nothing. Then I went and got a grinder and soda, came back. Still nothing, still nobody. I mean, some people did go in and out, the mailman, somebody else, one of the neighbors, I guess, but not your folks, and no cops."

"Man, they're really laying low," Howie said.

Boncal held a hand up, like he was stopping traffic. "Maybe not. Because later this afternoon, he comes out."

"Joe?"

"Right, the minister. And he walks down the lane. He's got some papers in his hand, like folders? He walks out as calm as can be, turns on Meadow and heads down the street. I figured he's going to the church or maybe to see his lawyer, who knows? Something like that."

"Did you go to the house then?"

Boncal grinned. "That's exactly what I did."

"I told you to," Howie said, mildly annoyed.

"I know, I know," Boncal continued. "So I walk up the lane and go up to the front door. Before I knock, I'm tossing a coin in my hand, and I drop it, accidentally on purpose, right?"

The Apache sisters and Ilona giggled. That pleased Boncal. He smiled at them and became even more animated in his recitation.

"So I bend down to pick up the quarter, and while I'm down there I casually lift the milk box and take a quick look. Hey, you drink Brock Hall milk, huh? We drink Tranquility Farms. You really think Brock Hall tastes better, or what?"

"Was the fuckin' key there or not?"

"No, no key."

Howie frowned. "Figures. Then what'd you do?"

"I rang the doorbell. Nobody comes to answer. Now, the curtains are drawn but the front window is open, with a screen on it, and I can hear somebody moving around inside. So I wait a couple, three minutes, and I ring the doorbell again. Another wait, nothing happening. So I ring it for the third time, and a minute later I hear somebody testing the locks on the other side of the door." The girls laughed. "So I go, Hello? Anybody home in there? And this woman's voice says, Who is it? I go, Is that you, Mrs. Hackett? She says, Who is that? I go, Mrs. Hackett, it's me, Arthur Boncal, I'm a friend of Howard's. She says, What do you want? I go, I'm looking for Howard. I haven't seen him in a while. Is he home? And she doesn't say anything for a minute or so. Well, maybe less. Then she says, Howard doesn't live here anymore. He moved, she says. So I go, Oh yeah? Where'd he move to? Now, get this," Boncal alerted his audience. "She says, I don't know where. He didn't tell us." Even the twins were laughing now. "So I go, Oh. And she says, Please go now, I can't help you. And I just get back to the sidewalk when this car comes screeching up, and who jumps out? None other than your old buddy, Captain Frank Bell."

"Big Frank," Howie said quietly.

"Captain Bell?" Cindy said.

"He's a friend of our old man," Cathy added.

"He is? How's your old man know him?" Howie asked.

"They drink together at the Legion."

"The American Legion club? Over on Crescent?"

"Yeah."

Howie nodded, then turned back to Boncal. "So, what'd big Frank say to you?"

"Oh man, it's, Who're you? Let's see some ID. What're you doing here? I tell him I'm looking for you. He goes, Are you a friend of Howie Hackett's? I tell him, Hell no, not anymore I'm not. I go, He owes me ten dollars and I'm tired of waiting for it. He says, Okay, beat it. And don't be coming around here and bothering the Hacketts no more, understand? Because you won't find Howie here anymore. He's a mean-looking fucker but I'm cool, I tell him, Okay, okay. And I walk down the lane and get in my car and get out of there."

"That was this afternoon? Where you been?"

Boncal shrugged. "I went back to the house and I sat down on my bed, and then I stretched out, and fell asleep."

"You're okay, Boncal," Howie said. "Millions would disagree, but I think you're okay. Thanks."

"Hey, anytime. So, what's next?"

Howie smiled. "I'm working on it."

6

THE 4TH OF JULY

The telephone company substation in Schramburg was located on Franklin Avenue, in an area of tool shops, small factories, trucking depots and other commercial enterprises. It was a very small brick building with a fenced-in parking area behind it. Howie knew it wasn't the place where the phone operators worked—Boncal's older stepsister worked at that place, on the other side of town. *This* was the junction box, connecting the town with everywhere else. Only one or two people usually worked here, maintenance men, fixing things when a problem arose. Today the lot was empty.

Ilona swung her car into the short driveway and went to the back lot. If anybody came out and asked, she was just turning around. But there was no one in sight. Beyond the chain-link fence was waste ground. On either side, brick walls. Howie pointed to the back corner where a clutch of thick wires entered the building. Ilona pulled up along the building and backed closer, so that her car was directly beneath the wires. Howie quickly got out, climbed onto the trunk and then the roof of the car, and began swinging the ax. He was a little surprised— each one was thicker than his wrist, and they were harder than he had expected. But the ax bit into them, and they fell to the ground, one after another. Three minutes, five? He was sweating and beginning to feel edgy, but still nobody appeared, and then the last wire snapped loose and flopped to the ground. He wanted to continue chopping, cutting the wires several more times, but he and Ilona had been there long enough. He dropped the ax on the floor of the back seat.

"Let's move."

Ilona was pale, her body rigid. It wasn't until they were nearly a mile away that she said, "What's that gonna do?"

Howie put his baseball cap and sunglasses on, and sank lower in the seat. He shrugged. "Piss off a bunch of people, I hope."

The parking lot at the high school filled up early. People walked the short distance from there to Church Street and the town Green to watch the parade. Howie and Ilona were parked on a verge of grass at the back end of the lot. They sat and waited. A few more cars came in, circled around and, finding no open space, left. They were alone. And then they could hear the martial music of the marching band, as the parade approached the center of town, a couple of hundred yards away. Howie glanced around once more, to make sure there was no one in the immediate area.

"Okay." He grabbed the gym bag on the back seat and then leaned across and kissed Ilona. "See you on Fairview."

"Okay, baby. Be careful."

Crouching low, Howie got out, hurried a few steps to the nearest car, got down on the ground and then slid underneath. He waited a minute or so for Ilona to drive away. He'd thought about this, and he'd sat outside on the third floor back landing, lighting strips of cloth and counting the seconds to see how fast they burned. They didn't need to be soaked in gasoline.

He was careful and took his time, sliding on his back from one car to the next, reaching up to open the gas caps, using a bent coat hanger to push each long strip of the cloth down inside. Ten cars. Maybe that was pushing it. He had to get away. But ten—that'd sure get their attention.

Howie sat up and looked around. The only people he saw were two older folks some distance away. Their backs were to him as they walked down Hillside. He waited a few moments until they were out of sight. The band was loud now, the parade was in the center of town. Howie took his Zippo out, scooted from car to car, still keeping himself low, and he lit each piece of cloth. He walked briskly up Hillside.

Whoompf…

Whoompf…

m-whoom-whoompf…

He lost track, but it sounded like most of them. Ilona was waiting where Hillside hit Fairview. He got in and she hit the gas.

"You got 'em, baby." She was more relaxed now.

"Yeah. Big trouble in a small town."

They had to hang around behind the laundry for nearly an hour before Boncal showed up. He was driving a powder blue '54 Chevy with a cream top.

"That's so cute," Ilona said.

Howie snorted. "Jeez, where'd you find that?"

"Hey, it wasn't easy. Lotta people out today."

"You hear anything?" Howie asked with a grin.

"Yeah, I heard the boom boom booms, and the sirens. Beautiful, man, I wish I saw it. No trouble, huh?"

"Nope. Okay, let's get going." He put the gym bag on the floor in the front seat of the car Boncal had stolen.

"Be careful with that," Ilona said.

Howie nodded. "See you at Palmieri's."

"You be there."

"We'll be there, don't worry." He got in the car. Boncal stared at him. "What's the matter?"

"I can't get used to seeing you wearing a baseball hat."

"Fuck you, too."

"But the shades look cool."

"Shut up and drive."

"We're moving, we're moving."

Less than ten minutes later they cruised down Crescent and passed the Legion Hall. The meeting room and offices were on the right side of the long low one-story building, the bar was in the annex to the left. The spaces in front were full of cars, and there were more in the side lot. Two fat older guys, one dressed in a military uniform, stood outside, talking.

"Keep going," Howie said.

"Uh-huh."

"Thing I don't like about this car is, if they report it missing right away, you can't hide a car that looks like this."

"Hey, I did the best I could."

"I know, but…Jesus."

They turned around at a gas station about a quarter of a mile down the street and headed back. Howie reached into the gym bag and pulled out the two sticks of dynamite that were taped together. The twins knew a guy out of town who used the stuff the blow out stumps and ledge on his farm.

Howie had been thinking about using three sticks, but then he figured three of them might roll easier, and he didn't want that.

"You test how fast that fuse is?"

"Yeah. Don't peel out, just accelerate. Once we're out on the street again, drive steady, not fast."

"Easy does it."

"Right."

"You figure a lot of…?"

"Cuts and stuff. They'll get the shit scared out of them."

"Flag-wavers piss me off. Dunno why, but they do."

"'Cause you're not one of 'em."

"Right."

"And they're the first ones to tell you so."

"Damn, that's right."

"Well, Big Frank won't be drinking there tonight."

Boncal laughed. "Nobody will."

The two guys were gone, there was no one outside.

"Swing in."

"Yep."

Howie flicked open his lighter. As they came through the front lot and drove past the bar, he lit the fuse, held his arm out of the car window and heaved the dynamite.

"Keep going."

Howie glanced back. It must have landed on the roof, which is what he wanted. He didn't see it bounce down to the ground. Boncal had the car back out on the street. Howie twisted around in his seat just in time to see it go off, a big flash, the front

window blowing out, the whole front part of the roof shred-
ding, wood and shingles flying through the air. The blast shook
the car as they drove away.

"I think we got Bingo," Boncal said.

"Yeah. Whole lotta shakin' goin' on."

Howie pulled out a rag and began wiping down everything
they might have touched in the front part of the car. A few minutes later Boncal pulled up and parked in front of Palmieri's
Shoes, off East Main. The store was closed for the holiday and
traffic was light on the street. Boncal took the loose wires he'd
connected to start the car, and yanked them apart. He and
Howie finished wiping off the steering wheel, the shift, the
window and door handles. They got out and crossed the street
to Ilona's car.

"You do it?" she asked.

"He's got a great hook shot," Boncal said.

"There's a hole in their roof."

Ilona's face lit up. "That is *so* boss."

"What next?" Boncal asked from the back seat.

"Nothing for now," Howie replied. "What time is the fireworks show at Veterans Field tonight?"

"When it gets dark," Ilona said. "Nine, nine-thirty."

"Good."

"Drop me back where I live," Boncal said. "They're cooking
dogs and burgers, and I'm hungry. You guys want to come in
for some? It'll be okay. They're all assholes, more or less, but you
don't actually have to talk to them."

"No," Howie said. "I'd better not. Can you come by around
seven tonight?"

"Sure."

When Ilona and Howie got back to the laundry, she said,
"They're cooking out at my house too this afternoon."

"That's okay. You go ahead."

"You can come."

"No." Howie shook his head. "Your folks aren't going to
see me again. You tell them you broke up with me. You can
tell them that it was because I'm always getting in trouble and
fights. The last one was the final straw. Your mother saw me,

they'll buy it, and that'll make it a lot easier at home for you, in case all this gets worse. Which it will."

"Okay."

"Listen, here's another thing. I want you to stay home tonight, or go to the fireworks with your family. I won't need you, and it's better if you're with them tonight."

Ilona wanted to protest. "You sure?"

"Positive. I'll have one of the twins call your house tomorrow, and when you get on the phone I'll get on and talk to you."

"Okay, baby." She smiled and kissed him. "Be careful, for me, and have a great Fourth of July. The rest of it."

"Oh yeah." Howie grinned. "There's a lot left to go."

At Howie's urging, the twins had spent the 4th with their old man at a family gathering in Willow Falls, two towns south. Now the old man was up on the second floor, staring at the TV with a bottle of Rheingold in his hand, and the twins were in the garage, pouring gasoline into quart bottles, while Howie cut more strips of cheesecloth. The Hudson had a big tank, and they must have siphoned off close to half of it by now. The three of them looked up sharply when the side door suddenly swung open, but then they relaxed as Boncal stepped inside. He grinned when he saw what they were doing.

"Oh good, the war's still on."

7

AN AUDIENCE WITH THE POPE

"What the fuck is going on here?"

Police Chief Dickie Larkin winced. "Honest to God, Jimmy, it looks like random vandalism."

"Don't tell me that, we already wrote it." Jimmy Pope held up the morning edition of the *Schramburg Sentinel*, which carried a big headline: VIOLENCE MARS HOLIDAY FESTIVITIES. The sub-head: Teenage Vandals Suspected. A couple of photographs showed the damaged exterior of the Legion Hall and a line of blackened and burned-out cars in the high school parking lot on Hillside Avenue.

"You got it," Larkin said, his hands shaking.

"No, no," Pope said, seething. "The phones are knocked out for half the town for six hours, you have nine cars blown up at the high school and a lot of others damaged, you have the American Legion—*the Mother of God American Legion, for Chrissake*—blown up, *bombed*, with fourteen people injured. And then in the evening, nine stores and twelve more cars bombed. Fire-bombed. *Fire-bombed?* What the fuck is going on here? And exactly what the fuck are *you* doing about it?"

"When it rains it pours," Larkin said helplessly. "We'll run them down, Jimmy. No question about that."

Frank Bell sat quietly.

"And when we do," Larkin continued, "it'll be a nice little story for you. Couple of malcontents, mark my words."

Bell watched the Pope, as he was called. Medium height,

fiftyish, slightly pudgy. Jimmy Pope was the owner and publisher of the Sentinel, which his family had owned since the
year after the Civil War ended. He was more important than the
mayor, three out of the last four of which he had pretty much
elected by himself. If there was one person in Schramburg who
could guarantee Bell the chief's job, it was Jimmy Pope. It was
shortly after six in the morning, July 5th.

"Nice little story," Pope fumed. "Don't give me that shit.
What do you have so far?"

Larkin turned and said, "Frank, what's the latest?"

Bell kept his eyes on Pope.

"There are a few more incidents."

"What?" Larkin was surprised. "You didn't—"

"We were on the way in, a lot to talk about."

"Right, right."

"Couple more cars, a liquor store."

"Jesus," Pope said. "Who *is* it?"

"Scum," Bell said. "Local scum, is my guess, and I've got a
list of the most likely ones."

"You do?" Larkin put in.

"We're only twenty miles from the Canadian border," Pope
ranted on. "How do you know this wasn't the work of skilled
saboteurs? That's what it smells like to me? Phone lines? Since
when do kids try to cut off a whole town? We're vulnerable out
here."

Chief Larkin started to speak but then hesitated, as if he
didn't quite know what to say to that.

Bell jumped in. "Mr. Pope, that's exactly the angle I'd rather
not see in the paper, at least not right now. I do think it's quite
possible that local scum did this—with outside help on this."

"You do?" Larkin said.

"Aha." Pope leaned forward on his desk, gazing intently at
Frank Bell. "Go ahead, tell me more."

"But if that gets out, it'll probably scare them away. And we
want to catch them, *all* of them. On the other hand, if they read
the paper, and they think that we think it's just a little rash of
vandalism, that could help us in two ways. First, it could make
them relax, and get sloppy and careless, which could make it

easier for us to trip them up and find them. Second, it gives us the necessary time to do the kind of behind-the-scenes work that will eventually crack this case."

"What kind of behind-the-scenes work?" Pope asked.

"Well, we may have to knock a few heads. Not that I want to, but sometimes you have to encourage people to talk."

"Heh heh heh," Larkin laughed weakly. "He just meant that in the figurative, Jimmy."

"No, I think he's got the right idea," Pope said.

"Well, sure, whatever it takes," Larkin added quickly.

"Okay," Pope said. "I'll hold off on that angle for now. But I want you to keep me informed on a daily basis of how you're progressing."

"I'll call you myself," Larkin replied.

"No, you've got enough to do, Dickie. You're the public face of the police department. Captain Bell here can call me. Say, between 6 and 6:30 in the evening?"

"I'll be glad to," Bell said.

8

IN RESPONSE TO YOUR EDITORIAL

"Did you read this?" Boncal asked, holding up the morning edition of the *Sentinel*. "You see what they're calling us?" Howie nodded. "Yeah."

"'Cowards and bullies'," Boncal recited. "What else? Oh yeah, 'Black-hearted scum...the lowest of the low...the kind of youth who decent kids loathe and avoid at high school.' Hey, that's us." Ilona laughed and the twins were smiling. "James J. Pope, Publisher," Boncal finished. He tossed the newspaper down on Howie's bed. "That guy must think he really is the Pope."

"The real Pope doesn't talk like that," Ilona said. "He's a sweet old guy, always smiling, like you wish your grandfather was."

"The Pope of Scramburg does," Howie said. "We were the scum of town at the Town Farm, and we still are. Right, Boncal?"

"Too fuckin' true."

Howie checked his watch. It was just past two in the afternoon. Even people who went to lunch at one would be back at work by now. Busy at their desks or counters, doing whatever crap they did.

"Let's go for a ride," he said. "I want to take a closer look at that newspaper building. I've seen it plenty of times, but never really paid any attention to it. Know what I mean?"

"What do you got in mind?" Boncal asked.

"What I got is one more stick of dynamite."

"Oh yeah, right."

"You ride with Vance and Vaughn, I'll ride with Ilona. You guys just pull up on the street, down a little ways. We're gonna drive past it a couple of times, swing in through the parking lot and take a look around, see if there's a doorman or a parking guard, anybody like that. That's a three-way junction there, so if we end up going one of the other ways, see you back here later."

"Okay."

The *Sentinel* building, which housed both the newspaper offices and the printing works, was located a couple of blocks from the Green. It was big and solid, old brick, with a lot of carefully trimmed ivy growing on it. There was a small parking area in front and a much larger one to the side. It was not as busy as a store, but somebody was going in or out of the building about every fifteen seconds.

"Okay, let's go in," Howie said after two passes around the block. "Circle around slowly like you're looking for a space."

There was a reception desk inside, just visible through the glass entryway, but nobody on the door. Signs directed visitors and employees to the side parking lot, but there was no parking guard out front. The handful of parking spaces near the entrance had individual signs designating their exclusive use—managing editor, production manager, etc.

"Whoa, *here*. Look at this."

Ilona braked. They were right beside the back end of a large, shiny Cadillac. It was royal blue and the rear license plate read JJPOPE. Howie laughed as he reached under his seat and pulled out the gym bag.

"Go around once more. I need a second."

He took out the stick of dynamite and quickly sorted through some pieces of cut fuse. He found one that looked like about two minutes, which he figured should be time enough.

"You sure about this?"

"Opportunity knocks," he replied. "Okay, stop."

"What if somebody's walking by when it—?"

"Everybody has one really bad day," Howie told her. "We know not the day nor the hour."

He glanced around. One person walking away from the building, turning onto Memorial Boulevard, another one on the way inside. Howie flicked his lighter and touched the end of the fuse. He got out of the car, holding the dynamite close to his leg, and walked alongside the Cadillac. He stopped and bent down, as if he'd dropped something, and shoved the stick under James J. Pope's beautiful car.

"Okay, we're done here."

They had to wait about thirty seconds for the light to change before they could get out of the lot and onto the street. Not bad.

"You want me to go around the block, come by again?"

"No. I'd love to see it, but the traffic's gonna get jammed up in a couple of minutes and there'll be cops all over the place. Let's just get out of here."

"Fine with me."

Howie laughed. "I'll read about it in the paper."

"We saw the flames shoot up in the air," Vance explained. "The car didn't go up that far, but it jumped."

"Yeah, we were just coming back around," Vaughn added. "There was no place to stop and traffic was steady."

"It was destroyed, right?" Howie asked. "Oh God, yeah."

"Totally."

"Good."

"I thought the car'd flip up and fall over," Boncal said, sounding disappointed.

"Those Caddies are heavy," Howie said. "One stick isn't going to do that. But they've got nice big gas tanks. Neither of the cars next to it went off ?"

"No, but they got torched real good."

"Was anybody walking nearby?" Ilona asked.

"No."

"Oh good," she said.

"But then lots of people came running out of the building, and the traffic slowed right down, everybody gawking and pointing. We just made it around the corner to Water Street, and we got the hell out of there."

Howie opened a beer and walked to the back window. He looked down at the parking lot and the garage. They'd moved his car inside, just to be extra careful. It was killing him not to be able go anywhere with it. He felt mad and strong, happy about the way he'd struck back. But at the same time he was trapped, dependent on the others. He had almost no money left and it was too risky to keep breaking into joints like that liquor store, which anyhow had only been good for $25 and a couple of bottles of Jack Daniels that he gave to the twins.

Ilona appeared at his side and put an arm around his waist. "What's the matter, baby?" she asked softly.

"Nothing. Just thinking."

"Thinking about what?"

"Thinking about what next."

"What's next?"

"I don't know."

"We can leave. I'll go with you."

"Go where?"

"Anywhere away from here."

"And live on what?"

She shrugged. "We can both find work. Something. Who cares what, as long as we get out of here and can be together?"

"Yeah, maybe."

Howie put his arm around her and they walked back to sit with the others again.

"So what's up next?" Boncal asked.

"You guys just go about your business," Howie said. "I'm going to sit tight for a few days. The cops'll be jumping around this town like fleas, day and night. Best thing is, we cool it for now."

The twins nodded.

"Okay by me," Boncal said.

9

YOU KNOW ME, FRANK

"You feeling better?" Bell asked.

"Yeah, sure," Glen Fertig replied.

"Glad to hear it."

Bell sipped his drink and then took a long drag on his Chesterfield. Fertig was knocking back beers. They were in Sully's, a neighborhood bar at the foot of Crescent Avenue in the South End.

"All the same, it shakes you up."

"I'll bet it did."

"The sudden explosion, the screams, glass and wood chips flying through the air like bullets."

"Like war."

"That's exactly right," Fertig agreed. "Brought Korea right back to me, I can tell you. Jesus, it shakes you."

"Good thing people like you were there," Bell said. "You've been through lots worse, you know how to stay calm."

"Right, right."

"I'm sure that was a help to others there."

"Oh sure, we pulled people out from under, got them outside where the ambulance boys could deal with them."

"Old man Pope is spitting fire about it."

"Oh yeah, they got his car a few days ago."

Bell shook his head. "Man, he was screaming."

Fertig gave a slight laugh. "Broad daylight, right in the middle of downtown. Pretty fucking bold, huh?"

"Bold is right," Bell agreed. "The bastards."

"We had to deal with that in Korea, in the cities and towns. Agents from the other side, planting bombs, sudden shootings. Like that."

"And they weren't wearing uniforms."

"Hell no. They were dressed like everybody else, that's why you never knew who they were until it was too late."

"That's what it's like here. It's like we got this little invisible army out there, driving us nuts."

"You going to run them down, Frank?"

"Yeah, and I have an idea who it might be."

Fertig perked up. "You do?"

"Yeah, but I need some help."

"What kind of help?"

"Strictly between you and me and nobody else," Bell said, leaning closer across the table.

"Sure. You know me."

"Okay. I'm too high profile, people know me, so I can't do the kind of intelligence work that needs to be done."

A faint smile appeared on Fertig's face. "Intelligence work."

"Right, and shit, this isn't a big town, we don't have anybody else on the force who could handle that."

"Sure, of course not."

"On the other hand, nobody knows more about how to go about this sort of thing than you do."

Fertig nodded. He had a distant look in his eyes. "I could tell you some stories. I been through the book."

"Think you could...."

"What? Give you a hand?"

"Well, this conversation never—"

"No, never, come on. You know me, Frank. Of course I can."

"'Cause I could sure use it."

"You got it."

"Thanks, Glen."

"No, really, glad to. If I could help put a stop to these creeps, I'd be only too happy. But I need to know where to start."

"I'm looking for a punk named Howie Hackett."

Fertig nodded. "Okay. Name means nothing to me."

"He's suddenly become impossible to find, but I'm pretty sure he's still around here."

"He's got to have a friend," Fertig said with growing enthusiasm. "A friend, somebody. And that's who we go through."

"Right. The one friend of his I'm sure about is another punk, name of Arthur Boncal."

"You're kidding."

"No, why?"

"Hell, I know the Boncals. I used to live across the street from them until I moved out on Cedar Hill a few years ago."

"They friends of yours?"

Fertig made a face. "Nope, not at all."

"Good."

"And I can tell you about Artie. Kid's a first-class jerk-off. He was drinking when he was thirteen. No respect for nothing. A regular Little Mr. Tough Guy, as long as he could get away with it. But he's got no character inside him, if you know what I mean?"

Bell nodded. "They're all the same."

"Get him boozed up and he'll be blabbing his mouth all over here and gone. Don't worry about that."

"Good. I hope so."

Fertig thought for a moment. "That all you want to know? Where this Howie Hackett guy is?"

"I want to know everything."

Fertig nodded. "In case it's not so easy...."

"Yeah?"

"Well, I'm just saying. It might get...."

"That's why I thought of you," Bell said. He smiled. "Glen, you know what you're doing, and you know what it takes to get a difficult job like this done. You've been through it. Personally, I don't care if I never hear of this Boncal again. All I'm interested in is results."

"Okay, Frank. I'm on it."

10

JUST CURIOUS

Boncal was sitting by himself at one of the picnic tables at Duke's Drive-In, across the street from Washington Park. He was nearly finished with his burger and birch beer when a wiry guy with a buzz cut came along and stopped abruptly. He sat down on the other side of the table.

"Hey, aren't you Artie Boncal?"

"Yeah." The guy looked familiar.

"I used to live across the street from you."

"Oh yeah, Mr. uh—"

"Right. How you doing, Artie?"

"Not bad."

"Good. Everybody okay at home?"

"They're all the same as ever."

"Good. So, school's out, huh?"

Boncal laughed. "School's over, yeah."

"That right? You graduated?"

"Yeah, somehow."

"Don't matter how, long as you finished."

"So they tell me."

"Where you working?"

"I'm not, yet. Still looking."

"Oh. Well, good luck."

"Thanks."

"Say, Artie. You busy right now?"

"Nope. Why?"

"You want to make some money?"

Boncal straightened up. "Sure. I mean, doing what?"

"Since my wife died, I've got more darn things to do than I can ever catch up with around the house."

"Your wife died? Jeez."

"Thanks. Anyhow, I got a bunch of stuff up in the attic that I need to move down to the garage. Old stuff I'm going to give away or else take to the dump. Just boxes and bags, nothing too heavy."

"How long a job you think it is?" Artie asked.

Glen Fertig scratched the side of his jaw. "Oh, I'd say about four hours, maybe a little over. Figure the afternoon. But naturally I wouldn't be paying you by the hour. This ain't bagging groceries down at the Grand Union, where they pay you a buck-five an hour. This is more like a moving job or when the repair guy comes to fix your TV. You pay a flat fee for the whole job. See what I mean?"

"Uh, yeah…."

"And to me this job is worth twenty-five dollars. What do you say?"

Boncal gulped. "Sure thing. Hey, thanks."

"Thank you for helping me out. You got a car?"

"No, I'm still trying to save for one."

"No problem," Glen told him. "I'll run you back into town when you're done."

It didn't go exactly as planned. Boncal gladly accepted a beer, then a second, and a third. He seemed happy to chat with Glen about anything, all thought of work forgotten. Glen would casually raise a subject, Boncal would start talking. In due course, Glen heard it all—about Boncal's home life, the kind of cars he liked, his high school years, his favorite football and baseball teams, and even about a couple of girls Boncal had dated. Only the last part was of particular interest to Glen.

"You're what, eighteen?"

"Yeah."

"Ever had a blow job, Artie?"

"*Huh?*"

"Don't worry, I ain't queer. Just curious."

"Oh, okay. Well, uh, sure."

"Yeah? How many?"

"A couple—a few. So far, that is," he added hastily.

Glen nodded. "Take my advice, get as many as you can. And never marry a woman who won't give you a good blow job. Otherwise, you'll be kicking yourself all the way to the grave."

"No, I wouldn't. I know."

"Ready for another?"

Boncal shook his beer can. "Sure."

The one thing Boncal wouldn't open up about was his friends. He never had that many, he said, he pretty much kept to himself. And since graduation, it seemed like hardly anybody was around. Glen gently pushed him, and Boncal finally mentioned occasionally hanging out with a couple of guys named Vance and Vaughn, and their girlfriends, Cindy and Cathy Grenier.

"Oh yeah? Frankie Grenier's girls," Glen said.

"That's right. You know them?"

"I know Frankie from way back. Cute girls."

"Yeah, too bad they're taken."

"They're French, too. They'd know how to drain your pipe."

Boncal got a dreamy look on his face at that thought. Glen tried to draw him out more about his other friends, but it went nowhere. Finally, he got tired of it, and stood up.

"Artie, give me a hand, will you? I got a case of Genny down in the basement. I want to put it in the icebox in the kitchen, but my back's been acting up lately. Some kind of twinge."

"Sure, I'll be glad to." Boncal tottered just a little when he got up. "Then you want me to start work on that job for you?"

"Or we can have another beer and you can come back tomorrow and take care of that stuff then. There's no rush."

"Hey, why not?"

Glen led Boncal down the narrow stairs to the basement, and then to an area on the right. A large square of linoleum had been laid down, there was an armchair, a side table and a floor lamp.

"Hey, you fixed this up nice," Boncal said.

"Yeah, I needed a place to get away from the wife sometimes.

Yak, yak yak, you know? This way, I could sit back, have a few beers and listen to the ballgame on the radio."

"Yeah, I get you. Now, where's that beer?"

Glen pointed to a case of Genny 12-Horse sitting on the floor across the room. Boncal started toward it, stepping past Glen—who took a sock full of ball bearings out of his pocket, swung it hard and caught Boncal just behind the right ear. The kid went down and didn't move.

By the time Boncal came to, Glen had him stripped naked and tied with metal wire to a straight wooden chair in the middle of the linoleum. The armchair and side table had been pushed farther away. The wire bound Boncal's hands to the arms of the chair, his ankles to the legs, and several more strands across his stomach were lashed tightly to the back slats. The wire was sharp and had already drawn trickles of blood. There was a rope around Boncal's throat, tied in a slip knot and stretched taut to a hook in the ceiling above. Boncal could not move without hurting or choking himself. Fear and panic filled his eyes as he grasped the situation.

"Oh no...*hey*...please...."

Glen stood at the workbench on the other side of the basement. He turned and walked slowly toward Boncal. He had his army bayonet in one hand and large grooved pliers in the other.

"Artie, listen carefully now. We can do this neat and easy, or we can do it messy. Don't fuck around with me, you hear? Because I don't like it when people fuck around with me. I ask you a question, you answer me right away, and it better be the truth. You got that?"

"Y-yeah."

"Okay, good. Now, where's your pal Howie Hackett?"

"Howie Hackett? I ain't seen Howie in weeks," Boncal said in a rush. "He's not my pal, he owes me money. Somebody told me he left town not long after graduation—his mother, his mother told me. I went to the house looking for him. I—"

Glen frowned. "Artie, you're just not taking me seriously, and you should, because I'm *very* serious. Let me give you an example."

Glen clamped the pliers on Boncal's right nipple and pulled it, stretching the skin and flesh. Boncal screamed. Glen flicked the bayonet once, slicing the nipple off. He dropped it in a bucket on the floor and went to get himself another beer. He knew it'd be a minute or two before the kid got back to where he could talk again.

"Frank? Glen."
  "Hi. Any luck?"
  "You bet."
  "Yeah? What'd you get?"
  "Everything. The whole ball of wax."
  A sharp intake of breath. "How soon can you be at Sully's?"
  "Better give me an hour."

Glen walked up behind Boncal, raised his pistol and fired once at the spot at the base of the skull. He got it right—instantaneous, with hardly any blood coming out. He smiled. He hadn't lost it, he still had that touch.

11

SAME GOES FOR YOU

"Hey Ma, somebody's looking for Artie," the kid in the doorway hollered over his shoulder. *"And it's a girl—"*

"A girl?" an adult voice called back. "Our Artie?"

"Yeah."

Mrs. Boncal appeared on the other side of the screen door a few seconds later. She was wiping her hands with a dishrag and she nudged the boy aside with her hip.

"Can I help you?"

"Hi, Mrs. Boncal," Ilona said. "I'm a friend of Artie's from school. Is he around?"

"Nope. Artie hasn't been home the last two nights."

"Oh. Do you know where he is?"

"Nope. But he's done this before."

"He has?"

The woman nodded. "He and some of his buddies go on a beer binge and don't sober up for three or fours days. He'll be back."

"Maybe he went away for good—" the kid yelled.

"Don't count on it, Jess. Artie's always talking about leaving home for good," she explained to Ilona. "But he never does."

"Okay. Well, thanks."

"If you see him...."

"Yeah?"

"Oh, never mind."

Ilona returned to her car and got in. It didn't make a lot of sense. If Boncal was on a beer binge, it'd most likely be with

Howie. Maybe Boncal had some other friends she didn't know about.

She'd brought Howie some donuts this morning. He was starting to get a little stir crazy up in that third floor room, so they decided to spend the afternoon at Gorge Lake, twenty miles from Schramburg. Since she had to go back home for her swimsuit and a few things, Howie asked her to stop by Boncal's house on the way and to see if he was around.

Oh well.

Ilona was about to turn onto her street, but then she saw the police car parked outside her house. She killed the turn and drove on, somehow resisting the urge to floor it. Fear swirled inside her. Okay—maybe they only wanted to ask her some questions. But she wasn't going to face that unless she had no choice. She'd thought about it. Sometimes she thought she could be cool and would have no problem, but other times she was sure that she'd be so nervous she'd give something away.

She parked behind the laundry and ran all the way up the back stairs to the top floor. Breathless, her heart pounding, she got to the open door of Howie's room and saw him shoving some of his clothes in a bag. Vance and Vaughn stood nearby, looking anxious.

"What's going on?" Ilona asked.

"The cops were here," Howie said.

Vance: "Not two minutes after you left."

Vaughn: "We talked to them downstairs."

Ilona looked at Howie. "But you're still here, thank God. What did they say, what happened?"

"I gotta split. Fast," Howie told her.

Vance: "They're looking for Howie, alright."

Vaughn: "They said they're coming back with a warrant."

"How did all this happen," Ilona said. "The cops were at my house just now too. I saw their car and I kept driving. I drove right back here."

"The cops at your house too?" Howie echoed.

"And another thing, Boncal hasn't been home for two days."

Howie and the twins stood looking at each other.

Vance: "Boncal?"

Vaughn: "Could it be Boncal?"

"No, Boncal wouldn't squeal," Howie said after a moment. "He's in this as much as the rest of us. You don't know—it might be those Apache sisters, if they got talking to somebody."

Vance: "No, no. They're our chicks, man."

Vaughn: "They're gonna get us in trouble? No chance."

"Shit, I don't know," Howie said. "We'll figure it out later. Let's go. I gotta split this place now."

The twins helped Howie carry some bags down and put them in the back of Ilona's car. Howie handed his car keys to Vance.

"I'll give you a call in a day or two," he said. "We'll figure out a place where we can meet, and you guys can bring my car."

"You know where you're going?"

"Only that it's out of town. Thanks, both of you."

Vance: "Hey, anytime."

Vaughn: "It's been a kick."

"Yeah." Howie grinned. "I think we made our point."

"I told you so," Frank Bell said, turning the key in the ignition of the unmarked police car.

"Damn, they really are stupid," Glen said. "Very stupid, and predictable."

"Yeah, but how can anybody be that stupid?"

"They've had practice."

"You going to pick up those twins later?"

"I don't know," Bell said. "I don't really care about them right now. It's just a matter of time before they get themselves in some kind of trouble bigger than this, anyway."

"What about the Mueller girl?"

"She's in it as much as Howie."

Bell followed them across town. He knew how to fade back one or two cars and still keep the Ford in sight. They were on Millville, heading out of Schramburg, when it hit him.

"Well, fuck me pink."

"What?"

"I know where he's going."

"You think it was Boncal?" Howie asked.

"No," Ilona replied.

"Me either."

They were sitting back, resting against the trunk of a large maple tree, drinking warm beer. An empty Milk Duds box and an Almond Joy wrapper were on the ground beside them. Howie had an arm around Ilona's shoulder, his hand lightly touching her breast. He loved the way she felt, the way her body nestled against his. All the worry and fear had vanished once they got here.

"He likes you too much to do that."

"We were there together," Howie said, flicking his thumb toward the Town Farm ruins. "That's why."

"How bad was it living here?"

"I don't remember any one terrible thing, other than the fire. But it was sweltering hot in the summer, drafty and cold in the winter. The rooms were so small. I remember being scared of other people all the time. Most of 'em just sat around or stood around or walked around going nowhere. It was like they were zombies."

"What was your mother like? You never told me."

"Beautiful, like you. Fell for a loser, like you did."

"Howie, don't say things like that."

He laughed. "I don't know. She was my mom, and at that age that was good enough for me. I still miss her, so...."

"That's answer enough."

"You going home?" he asked a minute later.

"Nuh-uh."

"You'll just get in more trouble if you don't."

"Like I care. How much more trouble can it be, after the cops have been at my parents' house looking for me?"

"Oh yeah."

"Besides, if I go home, you'll just crawl into that rat hole and sleep in there. This way, at least you can sleep in the car."

"You're sleeping in the car too, right?"

"Well, of course I am."

"It'll be like the drive-in, but without the movies."

"No," Ilona said. "The one thing you never did at the

drive-in was fall asleep. Not that I noticed."

"Sit in the back seat with me?"

"Y-e-s spells yes."

Bell pulled the car up close to the chain, wondering if he had made a mistake and enabled them to get away. He was so sure they were headed for the Town Farm that he'd deliberately dropped farther back and let them get out of sight, so there'd be no chance Howie could spot them.

But now he wasn't so sure. He didn't expect the chain to be up. He figured Howie would pop it and just keep going. Bell got out of the car and examined the padlock. Oh yeah. It was shiny, practically brand new, and it was cheaper and a little smaller than the locks the town used in its parks and properties, as Bell knew from years of checking them on patrol.

"We're hoofing it from here."

"Okay," Glen Fertig said.

They closed the car doors quietly and started up the dirt road. When they got to the bend, they moved into the woods. It was slow going because the brush was thick and the ground was soggy. They were out of the direct sun, but the air was full of gnats. When it felt like they were near the crest, where the land would then begin to dip down into the meadow where the crumbling Town Farm ruins stood, they worked back toward the edge of the road. They moved very slowly and quietly now.

"There's the car," Bell said softly, pointing.

"Yeah, and there they are."

"Where?"

"The big tree, over to the right."

Bell spotted them. "Good eye, Glen."

"Looks like they're having a picnic, fer cryin' out loud."

"They almost have their backs to us. What is that, forty yards, would you say? Fifty?"

"Closer to fifty. You want to rush 'em from here? We can do that," Glen said with a crisp new air of authority. "The breeze is coming this way. Take off, keep to the right, widen their field of blindness, keep the distance, then we come up straight behind them. We fork off the last ten yards, you take one, I'll take the other."

"Right," Bell said. "I'll take him, you cover the girl. If she starts acting up or screaming, give her some knucklewurst."

Glen nodded. "Run soft, don't thump your feet."

"Yeah, and don't trip and shoot your balls off."

"Ha ha. I forgot, you were in the army too."

Guns in hand, they stepped out of the brush and trotted along the edge of the meadow. It was easy, the movement was good, and Bell felt a burst of exhilaration inside—he hadn't run across a meadow like this since he was a kid. Glen looked fierce, crouching low, never taking his eyes off the couple beneath the tree. At ten yards they slowed to a walk, since it was obvious they were undetected. They split off, circling around either side of the tree, arms extended, guns pointed. Howie and Ilona were locked in a long passionate kiss.

"He's armed with a handful of tit," Glen said.

"Hands up, Howie. *Now.*"

Howie and Ilona spun up off the ground in shock.

"Okay, okay," Howie said, raising his arms.

"You bastards," Ilona wailed in despair.

Glen grabbed her arm and pulled her a couple of steps away. "Put your hands on your head and kneel down," he told her.

"Fuck you." But Ilona obeyed.

"Same goes for you," Bell said to Howie. "Put your hands on your head, kneel on the ground."

"Okay, okay. You got me, big fuckin' deal."

"You have a gun or knife?" Bell demanded.

"No," Howie replied. "Just a buck knife, in the car."

"Let me ask you, miss," Glen said politely. "Do you blow him?"

"Two or three times a day," Ilona snarled. "And we fuck once or twice a day too."

"Glen."

"Just curious, Frank."

"Okay, Howie," Bell said. "Face down on the ground. Nice and slow. That's it. Good boy. You should've been this obedient the last time we met."

"I live here," Howie said. "I got nowhere else to go."

Bell came around behind, still holding his gun to Howie's head. He straddled Howie's hips and crouched down. He switched the gun to his left hand and reached toward his back pocket.

"Before I put the cuffs on you, Howie, tell me, are you right-handed or left-handed?"

"Right."

"Same as me."

Bell took a smaller pistol from his back pocket, leaned forward and put the barrel close to the right side of Howie's head. He pulled the trigger and the kid jerked once.

Ilona jumped, screaming, her face contorted, tears washing across her cheeks. Glen clipped her across the jaw. It wasn't enough to stop her noise, but it knocked her to one knee. Bell swung his arm slightly and shot her three times in the chest. She fell right back and didn't move.

Glen shook his head. "Damn. I liked her."

Bell stood up. He holstered his own pistol, took a handkerchief out of his his pocket and carefully wiped the other gun. Still using the cloth, he bent over and placed the gun in Howie's hand, pressing Howie's fingers to the grip, touching the index finger firmly to the trigger. Just to be sure, he checked Howie's pulse, and it was gone. Bell stood up again. He went and checked Ilona's pulse. He moved back a few paces and stared at the scene, and finally he was satisfied.

"Murder-suicide," Bell said as he and Glen walked back down the dirt road. "Same old thing. Goodbye, cruel world."

"I could see why he liked her so much."

Before he backed out onto the main road and they left, Bell gave the gas a sharp hit. The car shot forward, the cheap lock snapped and flew off, and the chain fell to the ground.

12

IT WAS IN THE OCTOBER

The Legion bar was packed and there was a current of anticipation in the air. Everybody was waiting to see what Kennedy would say and do about the missiles in Cuba. Voice grew louder and had more of an edge in them. There was a sense of gathering darkness—unfamiliar but inviting, soft and silky to touch, its flavor elusive but sweet.

"They fixed this place up real nice," Pope said.

"Yeah, they did a good job," Bell agreed.

"Who got the contract?"

"Buddy Malone."

"That right? His old man was a Democrat."

"I know, but Buddy's okay."

"Good. I haven't been here in a while."

"Yeah, you ought to come in more often, Mr. Pope."

"I'll try. I've got to get back to the office now. This is one of those big front page nights."

"Sure is. Say, what's your guess?"

Pope frowned. "This guy doesn't have the balls to go right in and get rid of Castro, but that's what he ought to do. Solve the problem once and for all. And if the boys in the Kremlin so much as twitch, take them out too. That day is coming sooner or later, so we might as well get it over with while we've still got the clear edge in firepower."

"Right."

"Nice talking with you, Frank."

"You too, Mr. Pope."

The publisher was gone less than a minute when Glen Fertig came and stood beside Bell.

"Hey, Frank."

"Glen. How's it going?"

"Not too bad. You?"

"Fine."

"Good, good." Glen sipped his beer and said nothing for a moment. "Frank, about that day."

"Yeah?"

"What if somebody saw us?"

"Like who?"

"I don't know. Anybody."

Bell sighed. "It's out in the middle of nowhere."

"Yeah, but it's a big open area, and you got all the woods around it. Somebody out hiking, going fishing, kids. Like that."

"Jeez, Glen, if anybody saw anything, don't you think we'd have heard about it by now? It's been about three months."

"Yeah...Yeah, I guess."

"It's over. Forget it."

"You don't have anybody following me, do you, Frank?"

"Following you? No. Why the hell would I do that?"

"No reason, that's why I asked."

"You think somebody's following you around?"

"I can't go so far as to say that," Glen said. "I haven't seen anybody on my tail. But lately I've had this feeling that somebody is watching me, keeping tabs on me.

"A feeling." Bell lit a cigarette.

"Right. You know how you think you're alone, but then you get a feeling that somebody's there, and you turn around and see somebody you know coming? Or you notice that somebody across the room is staring at you at just that particular moment?"

Bell nodded tolerantly. "That's what it's like?"

"That's what it's like, right."

"Otherwise, you feeling okay lately?"

"In the pink."

"Look, Glen, you want my honest opinion?"

"Yeah, of course."

"I think maybe you're spending too much time alone at that

house. Anybody's alone too much, they start seeing and hearing things. Imagining things. It's not healthy. I know you miss your wife—"

"No, not really."

"Okay, regardless. It's been a while since she died. You need to get out more, see some women again. Get laid."

"You could be right," Glen said. "I've had some dreams about that girl. I got her hair wrapped in my hand, I'm holding her head down—"

"What girl?"

"The one...you know...Town Farm."

"Jesus, Glen, I don't want to hear that. Get your head aired out and your feet back on the ground, okay?"

The place fell quiet as Kennedy appeared on the TV mounted high on the wall behind the bar. When he finished, the air filled with an instant buzz of talk and there were a lot of boos around the room.

"Gotta run, Glen," Bell said quickly. "See ya."

"Yeah, okay."

Glen Fertig stood alone. He looked around.

13

ALL HALLOW'S EVE

James J. Pope left the *Sentinel* building a little after seven that
night. The weather had been quite mild the last few days, and
still was, but some rain clouds had drifted into the region that
afternoon, and now the air was thick with a wet mist.

He had never much cared for Halloween, even as a kid.
He always felt uncomfortable dressing up in any costume,
except a suit. Now it made him smile every year to publish Joe
Hackett's slightly revised opinion piece on the pagan origins
of Halloween and why it ought to be abolished. That was not
going to happen, of course, because Halloween was also a business event. The only business Pope opposed was smut.

The last few years, he and his wife had worked out a handy
way of getting through Halloween. Pope never knew exactly
when he'd be able to leave the office; it depended entirely on the
news of the day. He didn't like to have his wife home alone, kids
coming to the door every five minutes. You can't be sure who's
out there on Halloween, so Louise would spend the evening
at their son Jay's house, with him and his family. If Pope got
away early enough, he'd join them there, otherwise he would
see Louise later, at their own house. It had been a quiet day, so
he still had plenty of time to go to Jay's and visit for a while.

Pope stepped quickly along the sidewalk in front of the
building and unlocked the door of his new ivory and gold
Cadillac. He turned the key in the ignition, pulled the headlight switch, and was startled to see a girl in front of his car. She
sat on the low brick wall between the sidewalk and the flower

and shrub bed along the front of the building. She was bent over, her face in her hands. How could he have passed so close to her, and not seen her? Pope opened the door and got out of the car.

"Excuse me. Are you alright?" He couldn't tell if she nodded or was just crying, or both. "Listen, you can't stay here. Can I help you? Do you need to use a phone?"

The girl looked up at him, her face shockingly pretty in the glare of the headlights. "My father threw me out."

"Threw you out? Of the house? How old are you?"

"Seventeen."

"He can't do that," Pope said briskly. "Come on, I'll take you home and make sure he understands."

"No, he'll just get madder."

"It's the law," Pope said dismissively. "Don't you worry, when I get through with him, he'll understand."

"But then you'll leave, and he'll beat me."

"Oh no he won't. He'll never beat you again."

The girl wiped her tears, smiled and stood up. She got in the car. She sat with her hands clasped between her legs, which pulled her skirt up a little above her knees.

"Have you been out here long?"

"A few minutes," she said. "I was walking around. I didn't know where to go or what to do."

Pope nodded. "Are you very wet? There's a blanket in the trunk, if you'd like."

"No, that's alright."

"What's your name?"

"I don't want to say yet."

"Well, your first name?"

"My first name is Betsy, for short."

"Okay. What did you do that got your father so upset?"

"That's kind of personal," she said.

"I need to know, if I'm going to talk to him."

Tears welled up in her eyes again and she looked distraught. Then she slid quickly across the seat and leaned against him, resting her cheek on his chest.

"I'm sorry," she said. "I'm so scared."

Pope awkwardly patted her shoulder a couple of times, and let his arm remain there.

"That's alright," he said. "You don't have to be afraid."

She took his left hand and squeezed it. Then she pressed his hand over her breast. "He touched me—here." For a few moments neither of them moved or said anything. Then she took his hand a put it between her legs. "And here." She left his hand there and put hers on his thigh, sliding it up. "And he made me touch him here, and he said, See how you make me feel? And he was hard, like you are. And the thing is, I liked it. I liked being touched, I liked touching." She pulled his zipper down and got his cock out of his boxer shorts, stroking it. "Like this. And then he said, Go on, go on, take it. So I did."

She took the tip in her mouth, her lips warm and wet. Pope sat frozen in arousal and anxiety. His eyes glanced around, but it was dark and misty out, and the night people were all inside, working.

"And I liked it. Like this."

"Ohhhhh…."

His head tilted back and his eyelids fluttered, half-closed. Then she moved her body slightly, and Pope had a brief uncomprehending glimpse of her hand coming up toward his face, as if to caress him.

The blade slid easily into his throat and punctured an artery. She held him tightly until his body stopped shuddering.

Before she vanished into the night, she pressed the fingertips of his right hand on the handle in several places. Then she let the knife drop naturally onto his lap.

Glen didn't like Halloween. He had to go out and buy a bunch of candy, otherwise the neighbors would all think he was a creep. He wished he could turn off all the lights and make them think nobody was home, but he couldn't do that.

Frank Bell was stopping by. It wasn't easy getting Frank to agree. He said he had a number of things he was doing that night, so he couldn't promise to meet Glen at any one place at any certain time. Finally he gave in and said he'd swing by at some point.

Kids came as ghosts and witches, cowboys and baseball players, and Glen would say "Yeah, yeah, very nice," give them each
a candy bar and usher them out as quickly as he could. The only
good moment came when two teenaged girls dressed as cheer-
leaders arrived at the door.

"Lemme see you do a cheer," he said.

They waved their pompoms and yelled "Rah rah sis boom
bah!"

Somehow it was disappointing, but he gave each three candy
bars. "If you girls need any part-time work, I could use some help
around here. Dusting, vacuuming, like that."

Their giggles turned to laughter as they hurried away.

"No, I mean it."

When he shut the door and turned around, he thought he
saw the kid again—standing at the top of the stairs to the second floor. But then he was gone again. This had been going on, a
glimpse here, a glance there, always out of focus, out of the corner of his eye. At first he thought—hoped— that it was the girl,
but it wasn't. Glen had one clear look a few days ago, just for an
instant, and it was that Boncal kid.

"You're flirting with Bellevue," Glen muttered.

He opened another can of Rheingold and sat down, trying
to think it out. He had to talk to somebody, and Frank was the
only person who would understand from whence this came. But
how could he tell Frank? In a way that would make any kind of
sense, that is.

Was he going queer? Does it happen like this. He had to
wonder. Because he'd been through war, and the dirtiest, ugliest
part of war at that. And Glen hadn't flinched or wavered—he did
what he had to do and got through it. Of course, you never forget,
but life goes on. Compared to that, the thing with the kids was
a day at the beach. But he couldn't shake it and he kept seeing
something and feeling what-the.

Frank didn't arrive until almost ten o'clock. He bustled past
Glen and sat down in the living room.

"Thanks for coming. What can I get you?"

"Nothing, thanks. I can't stay long."

"Okay, I won't keep you. How're you doing?"

"Did you have kids coming in here and getting candy tonight?"

"Sure, it's Halloween. Why?"

"With that gun out on the coffee table?"

"Oh, well, mostly they just stayed in the doorway."

"That the gun you had that day?"

"Yeah. I meant to clean it tonight."

"You ought to just get rid of it," Bell said. "Treat yourself to a new one, dump this one in a lake."

"That's a thought."

"So what's up?"

"Well, Frank...."

The girl was sitting on the floor, between his legs, smiling up at him. She rested her head on his crotch, her hair fanned out along his thigh. She kind of nestled her face against him, and he was hard right away.

"Yeah, what?" Bell said.

"He killed me," the girl said to Glen. "I could see that you were the good person there. I liked you. I knew that I could talk to you. If only we got the chance."

"Come on, Glen," Bell said with annoyance. "You just going to sit there staring at your fly?"

Glen looked up for a second. "Well, Frank. "

"But he killed me."

"You killed her," Glen said.

"Killed who? That girl?"

"Yeah."

"Damn right I killed her. And him. So what? Jesus, Glen, what the hell are you still bringing that up for?"

"See?" she said. She pressed her lips around the bulge in his khaki pants. "He did it, but you can save me."

The Boncal kid was beside Glen's chair. He nodded at Glen and took his hand. He moved it toward the coffee table. He smiled. Glen took the gun in his hand.

Frank Bell started to jump up and reach for his own gun, but a hand on his chest slammed him back in the chair. There was no hand, but that's what it felt like. He was confused for a moment.

"Glen, put that down and listen to me. You—"

"You killed her," Glen said.

"Yeah, and you killed that other kid. Who the fuck cares?"

The girl smiled up at him as she rubbed and nuzzled him with her face and mouth. Boncal was smiling, nodding yes yes yes. And without even looking, Glen turned the gun toward Frank and fired three times.

"Thank you, baby," she said.

Boncal winked. At least Glen tought he winked, but the kid was gone as soon as it happened. He looked down again and felt a great sense of relief. She was still there, still smiling up at him.

"You do care," she said. "Don't you?"

"You saw. For you."

"You want to come with me."

"Yeah…."

"You want to taste me?"

"Yeah…."

"Want me to taste you?"

"Oh yeah…."

"Lift me up, baby," she said. "Take me to you."

Glen swung his arm up and gazed down the barrel

"Mmmmm…hit me *hard…now.*"

He did.

Joe Hackett's unofficial anti-Halloween ziti dinner was a lost cause, but he held it every year nonetheless. It was a good thing to do. Some folks came, mostly the ones whose kids were grown and out of the house. A few others straggled in later, after they'd taken their kids on the rounds. But Joe didn't mind. He'd put on a couple of records—maybe some oompah music, a polka band—and there were door prizes, a funny quiz and some jokes that he found in an old volume of humorous anecdotes at the town library. God always noticed and cared, even if few others did.

Back at the house, Eileen went into the kitchen to make them both a mug of hot chocolate. It wasn't winter yet, not by a long shot, but they both liked hot chocolate before bed, even in warm weather. With a marshmallow floating in it, melting slowly.

Joe went into the living room and sat down in his chair. He picked up the Bible. This was the one book in the whole history of the world that you could read forever, and never be finished with. He opened it, and found that he was reading the story of the prodigal son. He felt a slight pang, but the words rolled on, pulling him in, as they always did whenever he turned to any passage of this book.

He tore the page out, stuffed it in his mouth and began to chew. He tore another page out, shoved it between his lips and bit into it. He felt like he was in a dreamy state—the paper and ink tasted so good, he had no idea. Now Joe was yanking off thicker clutches of pages and cramming them into his mouth, animal noises escaping in short bursts. He used his fingers and pushed, shoving the paper down.

Eileen came into the room. The tray flew through the air and made a terrible racket as it crashed to the floor. She clutched her hands together at her throat. Joe's face was purple, turning black, and his hands moved in a stiff, robotic fashion, ripping pages from their family Bible, and shoving them down his throat. She could hardly think, let alone grasp what she was seeing. She tried to cry out to Joe, but it was as if a hand was clamped to her throat. She tried to rush to him, but the hand pressed her back against the wall and held her there.

Joe moved like a wind-up toy that was near the end. He could only tear off parts of pages and push them at his mouth—most of the paper fell away to the floor now. A strangled sound of bottomless need emanated from him, an unbearable strangled grunting. Then he keeled over on the floor and, after a few spasmodic hand twitches, stopped moving.

Eileen struggled, but couldn't move. The invisible hand still held her by the throat against the wall. She whimpered, and it turned into a long hopeless wail—but it was cut off sharply when she felt warm breath on her cheek.

"*He* hit you."

She knew that voice.

The hand disappeared—she was free. For a moment she couldn't move, she just stood there shaking. The voice whispered in her ear, in a voice that shocked her because she knew it so well.

"*You* explain it."

FATHER PANIC S OPERA MACABRE

THE HOUSE OF TILES

For Anthony Glavin, and for Bora Bozic

It was late in the afternoon when the Fiat overheated. Neil had watched with a growing sense of annoyance and anxiety as the temperature gauge edged slowly upward. He still had plenty of gas in the tank, but no coolant or even plain water for the radiator. It was the time of day when, in any event, he would be looking for a town with a small hotel or a guesthouse to stay at for the night, but the last village he'd passed through was nearly an hour behind him. Surely it would be better to continue on in this direction now. He was bound to find help somewhere soon, a town, a farmhouse at least—if his car would just hold up a little while longer.

Neil wasn't sure exactly where he was anymore, but he knew that he was probably still in the Marches, most likely in the Monti Sibillini, a range of mountains once thought to be the home of the sibyls of classical myth. The dominant peak in the near distance had to be Monte Vettore. Somewhere in this area was the Lago di Pilato, where according to legend Pontius Pilate was buried, perhaps even in the lake itself. Now and then Neil glimpsed another range farther off, which he assumed to be the Gran Sasso, part of the Apennines. Tomorrow, or as soon as the car was checked out and ready to run, Neil's route would take him in that direction, and eventually back to his apartment in Rome. A breakdown would be a minor nuisance, but he knew approximately where he was, and he wasn't lost.

This was Neil's second excursion since he had arrived in

Italy, and he now felt quite comfortable driving around the country by himself. A couple of months ago he'd made the same kind of rambling tour of Tuscany. It was predictably beautiful and delightful, but perhaps a bit too familiar. Tuscany has been hosting visitors for centuries, its hill towns and byways have been endlessly written about, painted and photographed. Some of that must have seeped into Neil's mind over the years, via books, magazines, television and Italian films, because there had been moments when he felt the strange sensation of having already been in a certain town or village, though it was in fact his first visit to the region.

This time out he wanted to see some part of the country that was less well-traveled and not as heavily visited by outsiders, to avoid the obvious routes and hopefully to find here and there a little of the old Italy—assuming that it was still there to be found. A friend at the Academy had suggested that Neil try Abruzzo and the Marches, which proved to be a good idea.

He had driven east from Rome to Pescara, stopping only twice along the way. It was the shortest route to the Adriatic coast. From there he turned north and drove the A14 as far as Ancona, an uninteresting run that took him through one beach resort town after another. But when Neil finally left the *autostrada* behind and began to circle slowly inland, he soon found himself in exactly the kind of countryside he had been looking for. The land rose up steadily, wrinkling itself into steep hills and mountains.

The roads were all narrow, frequently little more than country lanes that snaked along the rims of deep canyons and gorges, plunging, rising, curling unpredictably. The towns and small villages Neil passed through were perched on high cliffs, terraced along rippling hillsides, or nestled in tiny vales.

It would be inaccurate to describe the Marches as isolated or out of touch with the rest of the country and the world, but it was somewhat out of the way, and it was definitely a little rougher and wilder than any other part of Italy Neil had experienced so far. It was old, and in some villages almost the only people he saw were elderly, the young having moved elsewhere for college or jobs.

In some places there was nothing to see other than a few ramshackle old stone houses clustered around a small central square where old men sat outdoors, drinking wine, playing cards, chatting idly among themselves or dozing in the sun. Neil spoke Italian fairly well but he found it difficult to get a conversation going with these people. They were polite, but their reticence and open but distant stares reminded him—lest he forget for a moment—that he was an outsider among them.

The needle was just touching the red band at the far right side of the gauge now. Perhaps the car needed oil, not coolant. It didn't make much difference though, since he didn't have an extra quart of oil with him either. But he had checked both fluid levels before leaving Rome, so there had to be a leak somewhere in the system.

Neil had spent nearly a week meandering around the Marches now, from Loreto to San Leo, Gradara, Macerata, Camerino, Visso. He'd taken in some of the obvious sights like the Frasassi Caves and the Infemaccio Gorge, but for the most part what he liked best was simply wandering around the old towns, taking in forts and palazzos that dated back hundreds of years but were still quite impressive, gazing at art and architecture that survived from a time when the world was completely different, but still human, still ours. At such moments Neil could almost taste the past in his mouth and feel it on his skin. The phantom sensations of half-forgotten or lost history— it still amazed him that he was actually making a fairly successful career for himself out of these unlikely and insubstantial impressions.

Now he was in the emptier upper reaches of the province, a place of black stony tarns and ragged windswept grasslands, the whole laced through with sharp ridges, rocky outcroppings and narrow dark glens. The asphalt gave way more often to longer stretches of loose and rutted gravel. It was easy to suspect that you had strayed off the road and onto a rural path that had fallen into disuse and now led nowhere, but Neil had already learned that it wasn't necessarily so—it was just the way the roads were in this area.

Still, it happened to him now. The road dipped down and

swung in a long arc around a high stone shelf. When he came out on the far side of it, he saw a large house and several low outbuildings on the hillside a few hundred yards ahead, and he could see that this was not a through road after all, that it ended at the house. No matter. Neil still felt a sense of relief. He would at least be able to get water for his car and directions back to the main road and the nearest town.

As Neil drove slowly closer, the road wound down through clumps of trees and stands of tall thick brush before rising again. His angle of view had changed so that when he finally came out into a clearing he was looking up at the house, and it suddenly exploded in dazzling light. It was catching the sun on its descent in the west, Neil realized. The house had looked a kind of dull buff color at first, but now it shimmered like burning gold.

The effect was so striking that Neil shifted into neutral and just stared at the house for a few moments. He noticed that the facade was covered with painted yellow tiles, scores of them, each about two feet square. The house was old, many of the tiles were chipped or cracked, but the clever light trick still worked. The person who conceived and built it had probably been dead for decades, but Neil silently said thanks—his pleasure disturbed only when he noticed steam billowing out from beneath the hood of the car.

STICKS AND STRINGS

Neil turned the key and got out. He put the hood up to help the engine cool off faster. Now that he looked carefully at the radiator, he could see that it was in poor shape. The fins were corroded, and in places had completely rotted away. No real surprise there. He'd known it was an old car when he bought it from the art historian Lydia Margulies, who was just finishing her stay at the Academy when Neil arrived. But the car was a bargain, and it had not given him any trouble until now. Still, this was something he should have anticipated and taken care of before he left Rome.

He started walking toward the house. For a moment Neil wondered if it was one of the many abandoned farms that could be found across the Italian countryside. There were no signs of life and the only sound was the loud hiss of the strong breeze in the trees. Three large brick chimneys protruded from the red pantile roof, each containing four separate clay pipes, but no smoke came from any of them. He noticed that several of the individual roof tiles were cracked or had slipped.

But it occurred to Neil that if the house had been left derelict, most of the windows would surely be broken by now, and none of them were. It was a large boxy building, three stories high. The windows on the first two floors were tall, wide rectangles, but those at the top level were small and circular, almost like portholes, suggesting an attic with a low ceiling.

Neil found traces of a footpath as he approached the house—he could feel and see a bed of tiny white chipped stones beneath the thick coarse grass that had claimed most of the ground. There was a long balustrade marking off a terrace immediately in front of the house. It was made from a purplish-gray stone that Neil had seen elsewhere in the region. The same material had also been used for the weed-lined paving stones on the terrace and the broad steps that led up to the front door. A few stone urns graced the balustrade, but they held no ornamental shrubs or flowers.

As he passed along in front of the house, Neil hoped to see something through the windows, but the rooms inside were blocked from view by heavy drapes. The glass panes were coated with a thin layer of grime. Up close, he noticed that the impressive tiles covering the house looked merely faded and dull when the sun's rays didn't hit them at the right angle, their gloss muted with dust. Most of them were blank, simply colored yellow, but a few, seemingly placed at random, also contained rust-brown markings or motifs. They were unfamiliar to Neil but made him think of indecipherable runes, clotted Gothic lettering and dead Teutonic languages. He knew that there was still a strong Germanic presence farther north, particularly in the Italian alps, and that in Friulia there were people who spoke something that was neither modem German nor Italian, but a vestigial hybrid of old Low German and Roman Latin. So this house seemed out of place in the Marches, but that only pleased Neil. It was just the kind of unusual thing he'd hoped to find in his meandering explorations.

A somewhat larger yellow tile was centered directly above the front door. It contained a dark red sketch of a human head, seen in profile, drawn in a few bold strokes. It was crudely heroic but striking, and it suggested a prince or a warrior. He had a flowing moustache and wore a conical helmet from the Middle Ages. Then Neil noticed the man's eye. It should have been only partly visible on the left side of the head, as seen naturally in profile, but the entire eye had been sketched in. It was not turned forward with the rest of his face, but out, directly at anyone coming to the house. It was an anatomical impossibility that made Neil smile.

There was no bell or knocker, so he rapped his fist on the wooden door. After a minute or so, he tried again, longer this time, forcefully enough to hurt his knuckles. Still, no sound came from within. He pounded the door with the fleshy side of his fist, and then with the fat part of the palm of his hand, but again to no result. Finally, he decided he would have to go around to the back of the house and try to find someone there.

As Neil turned to walk down the steps, he was startled to see a child sitting on the balustrade, at the farthest end. A little girl, maybe eight or nine years old. Surely he hadn't failed to notice her as he approached the house. She must have come out and hopped up there while he was knocking on the door. Somebody is home, Neil thought gratefully.

The girl's short legs stuck out slightly in the air. She appeared to be playing with a puppet in the shape of man, made from sticks and string. She held her hand out and walked the puppet back and forth and in tight circles on the gray stone balustrade. Her head bobbed rhythmically and her lips moved as if she were talking or singing quietly to herself as she played.

Neil didn't want to frighten her so he smiled broadly to convey his friendliness. As he got closer he could hear her voice—it was surprisingly harsh, and she spoke in a language he didn't recognize. It sounded tangled, vaguely Slavic. With each step he took toward her, the tempo and volume of her speaking ratcheted up, as if she were narrating his harmless movements into an event of absurd tension and melodrama. It was the kind of silly thing that a dreamy child would do.

She wore a black skirt that came down to her ankles and heavy black shoes that looked too large for her feet. A man's plaid outdoors shirt hung loosely like a light jacket over her grimy sweatshirt. In the declining sun her hair appeared reddish-blonde, but it was matted in a thick frizzy clump. The sun was just above and behind her, almost directly in his line of vision, so it wasn't until Neil came within fifteen feet of her that he realized she was not a child at all. Far from it, she had to be at least forty—probably older. Several of her teeth were missing, the others stained or chipped. She had blotchy red cheeks, the skin around her mouth was lined and the flesh beneath her hooded eyes was purplish and sunken. But it was the crazed look of gleeful malice in those eyes that most disturbed Neil. His smile quickly faded away.

The woman's plump stubby fingers worked the sticks faster, making the puppet dance and jump wildly. She bounced up and down on her perch, and her voice was a loud mad rant. Neil said something in Italian but it had no effect on her. The poor woman probably suffered from some mental illness or defect, perhaps genetic in origin. He felt very uncomfortable in her presence and didn't know what to do next.

The puppet distracted him. In spite of his own reluctance, Neil found himself moving closer to peer at it. The stick figure was a little over a foot in height and had been fashioned as a human skeleton. But the bones and details were so well done that Neil realized it couldn't be made out of carved sticks, it had to be manufactured. Then he noticed the naturally misshapen skull, the toothless jaw, the tiny leathery pieces that might be tendons or gristle, and the dull brownish stains in certain parts of the bones.

The woman was laughing raucously, but then she suddenly froze in silence, as if a switch had been turned. Her eyes were staring blankly past Neil. Before he had time to react, she hopped off the balustrade and scurried away from him, around the side of the house and out of sight, the gruesome puppet dangling from her hand.

MECHANICAL FIX

From the way the dwarf suddenly halted her strange act and stared past him, Neil knew that someone else had appeared. He turned back toward the house and was relieved to see a young woman standing alone at the top of the stone steps by the front door. Neil turned on the friendly smile again. In a relatively isolated spot like this he expected to be met with some caution or even unfriendliness. The dwarf had already unsettled him a bit, so he wanted to appear as harmless and unthreatening as he actually was. He held his arms out and opened his hands in a gesture of helplessness.

The woman came down to the bottom of the steps, and Neil stopped a few yards from her. She looked refreshingly normal in black designer jeans, a long-sleeved white blouse, stylish sunglasses and sandals. She didn't seem at all concerned, but merely perplexed by his presence.

Neil quickly explained the situation, pointing to his car. She nodded her head slowly while he spoke, as if she could not quite grasp his point. But then she stifled a big yawn and smiled sheepishly at him, and Neil realized that he had probably awakened her from an afternoon nap. He apologized for disturbing her, repeating that unfortunately his car could go no farther without water. He added that he would also be grateful for directions to the nearest town where he could find a room for the night. Now the woman seemed to be more awake and she gave a brief nod of comprehension.

"*Si, si. Acqua.*"

"*Si, grazie.*"

"I can tell from your pronunciation that you're an American," she then said in smooth, lightly accented English. "Am I right?"

"Ah, you speak English. Yes, you're right, I am American. I'm living in Rome for a year, as part of my work. I took some time off to drive around and explore the countryside. My name is Neil O'Netty, by the way"

"I'm Marisa Panic," she replied, pronouncing her last name *Pahn*-ik. "I'm pleased to meet you."

"And you." Neil gently shook her offered hand, which felt pleasantly cool and dry. "When I first came around the bend and saw the house, I was afraid there might not be anyone at home."

"Oh, we're always here. Onetti? That's Italian."

"O'Netty with a *y*," Neil explained. "It's Irish, but I am Italian on my mother's side, which is how I got a headstart on the language."

"I see. You do speak it well. And I think you're from Massachusetts. Somewhere in the Boston area?"

"Right again." Neil laughed. "Southie, then Medford."

"It's not that you have a very strong accent," Marisa told him. "But I spent a year at B.U. on a student exchange program."

"Aha." Neil was delighted. It had been a while now since he'd had a chance to converse in his own language.

It felt comfortable and relaxing, like getting into his favorite old clothes. "Well, I think your English sounds better than my Italian."

"Thank you." She smiled. "I don't get to use it much here."

Neil found her very attractive. Marisa's skin was milky white, with a faint rosy glow, and she had long cascading waves of very fine black hair that was not glossy but had a rich, subdued luster, like polished natural jet. She was about 5'6" tall and her body was sleek but gloriously voluptuous. Neil wondered what color her eyes were—even through the sunglasses, he could see flashes of light in them.

"Are you still studying?" he asked.

"No, I finished last year. The University of Parma."

"Really? Parma is one of the cities I plan to visit while I'm here." It was true. He loved *The Charterhouse of Parma*, and Stendhal had, in a way, been an inspiration and a small factor in Neil's recent success.

"I can tell you a couple of good places to stay, clean, not expensive," Marisa said. "And some excellent family restaurants."

"Great. Thank you."

"Are you traveling alone or with—?"

"Yes, I'm on my own."

"Let's see to your car. Then we can have some refreshments."

As they walked briskly toward the Fiat, Marisa clapped her hands sharply three or four times and called out a couple of words that Neil could not recognize. He saw a man emerge from one of the low worksheds on the nearest rise. Marisa shouted something else to him, and the man went back into the shed, reappearing a few moments later with a large plastic container and a funnel in his hands.

"What language were you speaking to him?"

"I'm not sure what you would call it," Marisa replied with a laugh. "These people have been with my family for a long time. It's some kind of local dialect from Dalmatia, I believe."

"Is your family Italian?"

"On my mother's side, like you. My father's family, well, they say if you go back far enough, they were the original Illyrians. I don't know any of that ancient history, but my grandfather and his family came here at the end of World War II, fleeing the Communists on the other side of the Adriatic. They bought this old farm, which had gone to ruin during the war."

They had arrived at Neil's car. The man came hurrying along a few seconds later. He had the rough, ruddy features and large leathery hands of somebody who had worked outdoors for decades, and he might have been anywhere from forty to sixty years of age. His clothes were stained and torn, he had the same gnarly, raggedy appearance of the dwarf, but he was of average height and build. He ignored Neil and glanced subserviently toward Marisa as he set the plastic container and funnel down on the ground. He used a rag to remove the radiator cap, which was still hot to touch. Neil stepped closer to take a look. No liquid visible, as he feared.

Neil sat inside and turned the engine over, then got out again to hold the funnel while the man angled the bulky jug and carefully poured a small but steady stream of water into the radiator. Neil watched it swirl down through the funnel. A minute later, he could see it accumulating and moving inside as the pump circulated the liquid. The system took a lot of water, but finally the radiator was full.

"All right, now let's see," Neil said.

As soon as he put the cap on and snugged it tight, the pressure inside increased and tiny jets of water appeared in several places on the body of the radiator. Soon it was hissing audibly and the rising steam was visible in the air. The man pointed theatrically. Neil frowned.

"How far is it to the nearest town?"

"Four miles back to the road," Marisa said, "and about another eight miles from there. Your car wouldn't make that, would it?"

"I doubt it. Can I use your phone to call for a tow?"

"I'm afraid there's no telephone here," she answered with a look of apology. "My brother has a cell phone, but he's away on business until the end of the week."

"Could I trouble you to drive me to the town, and then I could make arrangements to have my car picked up?"

"My brother has the car too," Marisa replied with another look of sincere regret. "It's the only workable vehicle we have."

Neil's car was boiling out clouds of steam now. As he went to switch it off, Marisa started speaking quickly to the workman. It sounded like she was asking him something. He nodded and answered her at some length. She turned to Neil and smiled.

"He thinks the radiator is ruined."

Neil gave a short laugh. "I think he's right."

"But he thinks they can patch it up enough tomorrow so that you'll at least be able to get to town and replace it."

"Oh, that'd be great," Neil exclaimed, his spirits lifting. "Thank him for me, I'm really very grateful."

"Of course you'll stay here tonight."

"That's very kind of you. I'm sorry to impose on you like this. I hope it won't be too much of an inconvenience."

"Not at all," Marisa said, smiling brightly. "We have plenty of room, and I'm so glad to have some company for a change. Come on, get your bag, whatever you need, and we'll go inside."

THE BOX ROOM

"You mentioned something about working in Rome. What business are you in—banking, finance, technology?"

"No, nothing like that," Neil said with a smile. "I have a one-year fellowship at the American Academy. I'm doing some research for a book I'm working on. And also writing it, of course."

Marisa had slipped her arm through his as they walked. It was a common practice in many European countries, so Neil knew better than to read too much into her simple gesture. But he enjoyed the closeness and the physical contact with her.

"Ah, you're a writer."

"An author, yes."

"That's marvelous." Marisa gave his arm a little squeeze. "What kind of books do you write?"

"Historical fiction, sort of." Neil always felt a little awkward trying to explain his work. "Anyhow, I've only written three so far."

"But that's wonderful. They must be very good for you to be chosen for the Academy. It's very prestigious."

"The first two disappeared almost without a trace," Neil told her with a rueful smile. "But the last one did much better."

"What is it about, what period of history?"

"The 1590s, in Italy. It's called *La Petrella* and it's a retelling of the story of Beatrice Cenci and her family."

"Oh, of course. I remember that," Marisa said excitedly. "Beatrice conspired with her mother to murder her father, and she was then tortured and beheaded in public for it, even though her father had raped her. She was only about, what—fifteen years old?"

"That's right."

"It's a famous story."

"Yes, but not in America. I discovered that there hadn't been a full-length fictional treatment of it in many years, so I decided to try it. I found Beatrice by way of Nathaniel Hawthorne, who saw Guido's portrait of her in the Barberini Gallery and fell in love with her. I read Stendhal's account of the case, and many others. But my version is quite different."

"You changed the story?" Marisa asked.

"Not the facts or the incidents," Neil said. He felt that he was talking too much about something that could not really interest her. "But the feelings and motivations of the people. Beatrice is usually idealized, portrayed as an innocent, still virtually a child."

"Wasn't she?"

"I tried to make her both innocent and knowing," Neil said. "When I did more research and read some passages from the actual court documents of the case, I found it all much more uncertain and open to interpretation in different ways. There's a moral ambiguity to Beatrice, which is probably why she fascinates me."

"I see. But her father—he really was an evil man?"

"Oh yes, he was a monster."

That seemed to please Marisa, who smiled broadly. "I'd love to read your book."

"I'm sorry I don't have a copy with me, but I'll be happy to send you one when I get back to Rome."

"Thank you. Signed, please?"

"Of course."

Marisa squeezed his arm again and Neil smiled at her. She was so attractive, pleasant to talk to and be with, and his encounters with women had been disappointingly few since he'd come to Italy.

They reached the front door, but before she opened it Marisa turned and looked around as if she were checking the weather. Then she led him into a dimly lit entrance hall. As soon as the door clicked shut, Neil noticed how quiet the house was. There were two large armoires and a couple of free-standing coat racks, along with a pair of heavy upholstered chairs made of very dark wood, and a long ornate wooden bench. All of this furniture was old, chipped and dusty. A gloomy corridor led straight into the house from the entrance area. Off to the right was a wide flight of stairs that led to a landing and then angled up toward the center again.

"I hope you won't mind waiting for a moment while I go and make arrangements for your room and bed? We so seldom have visitors, I want to make sure they open the window and change the linens."

"Don't go to any trouble for me," Neil insisted politely. "I'd be fine on a couch with a blanket."

"Oh no, we can certainly do better than that." Marisa led him into a small sitting room and turned on a floor lamp that had a battered shade with a fringe. "You can sit here. I'll be right back."

"Thank you."

As soon as he was alone, Neil noticed that it was an interior room. It had no windows, no other doors. There were two plain wooden chairs, both so dusty that he decided not to sit down. Boxes of old books were stacked up against the back wall of the narrow room. He went closer and looked at them but the titles were in a language he didn't recognize.

Neil began to feel uncomfortable in his breathing. He was asthmatic, though he had such a mild case of it that he rarely experienced difficulties. A single Benadryl capsule was usually enough to quell a reaction. But now he could taste powdery alkaline fungus in his mouth—even before he spotted the patches of it on the lower side walls of the room. Neil's lungs tightened, he could feel himself losing the ability to breathe in and out.

He turned toward the door, forcing himself to move slowly and carefully, as he had learned long ago—sudden exertions only made matters worse. Now he felt a little dizzy, lightheaded, as if he'd just been hit by a very powerful nicotine jag. This was something Neil didn't associate with asthma. His thoughts were foggy and vague, but he wondered if it was an effect of the particular fungus in that room—not mildew, it was something else, something new and deeply unpleasant to him—and he could imagine invisible toxic clouds of it being sucked in as he breathed, quickly absorbed into his blood, and then sluicing chaos into his brain.

Neil reached for the doorknob but his hand seemed to wave and flap listlessly in the air. Wow—the word formed in his mind with absurd calm and detachment—he couldn't remember the last time he had a reaction this strong and swift. He might even fall down.

But then Marisa opened the door and smiled at him.

IL MORBO

"You look pale," she said, taking his arm in hers again. "I think I'm just a little tired, that's all," Neil said. "I did a lot of walking and driving today before I got here."

"Dinner is later, but we'll have some wine and snacks now."

"That sounds very good."

She led him down the long corridor toward the rear of the house. There were any number of doors on either side, but all of them were closed. They passed three more staircases, one that went down on the left side, then farther on another that went down to the right, and at the back, one more that led to the upper floors.

"Too many rooms," Marisa said, almost to herself. "It's impossible to take care of all these rooms anymore. Most of them are closed and never used. There's no need for them."

Neil nodded sympathetically. "Do you have any brothers or sisters? I mean, aside from the brother you mentioned."

"No, only Hugo. That's part of the problem. He's away on business often and has no interest in running things here. Neither do I," she added in a lower, almost conspiratorial tone.

A familiar story, Neil thought. He couldn't imagine someone like her remaining here for very long, even if it was her family home. A bright young woman who had recently finished her university degree—work and life and love were all to be found elsewhere now, out in the world.

He felt better as they stepped outside, his breathing was almost back to normal. They walked to a stone patio with a weathered wooden table and several chairs. It was located a short distance from the house, at an angle that allowed them a very attractive view of the sharp ridges and deep vales that unfolded in the distance.

He also saw, directly beyond the yard around the house, a gradually rising series of terraces and still more outbuildings. Men were working the plots, kids were playing, and Neil occasionally caught a glimpse of a woman in a woolly jacket and long skirt peering out of one hut or another.

He and Marisa sat at the table. A bottle of red wine and two crystal goblets had already been placed there, and two older women soon appeared to set down platters of food. Neil knew immediately from their features that they were not related to Marisa.

There were slices of cold sausage, black olives, cuts of three or four different kinds of cheese, something that looked like *pate* or a meat pudding, a couple of loaves of bread, butter, a bowl of dark olive oil and a few jars and dishes that contained unknown sauces and spreads. The wine, which Marisa said they made from their own grapes, was a dark ruby-maroon in color and had a little too much of a tannic edge, but it was drinkable.

"*Robusto*," Neil managed to say.

Marisa was no longer wearing sunglasses. Her eyes were deep blue, frank, open, curious—perhaps he was reading too much into them this soon, but they were so easy to gaze at. The breeze played in her silky black hair. She had such striking features—strong cheekbones, a wide mouth, rosy full lips, a proud nose, clear smooth skin with a pearly luster—altogether, they grabbed your attention and held it.

Neil and Marisa nibbled at the food, drank the wine and talked for an hour or more about books, history, Italy, America, and their lives. He felt very comfortable and relaxed with her. He was usually not one to volunteer much information about himself, but he soon found that he wanted to tell her things, that he enjoyed her questions and interest.

When *La Petrella* was published and Neil had to give quite a few interviews, he quickly developed a brief biographical sketch that satisfied most questioners. How he had stayed on in Worcester after graduating from Assumption College. The six years of substitute teaching by day, bartending nights and weekends at the Templewood Golf Course or at Olivia's. All of the reading and writing he had done in odd hours, slowly accumulating the first novel, and then the second. How both of those books were indifferently reviewed in only a few places, and barely sold. How Neil had decided to give fiction one more chance, and—bingo. The glowing reviews of *La Petrella*, the solid sales, the trade paperback that sold even better, and the film option. It was a happy American story, neat and edifying.

But with Marisa, Neil wanted to say more. He told her about the death of his mother, which was followed only a few months later by the breakup with his longtime girlfriend, Jamie, and how those two events had forever changed him, diminishing his expectations of life and instilling in him a certain resignation to melancholy that even now, almost four years later, showed no sign of going away.

"Ha, it serves her right," Marisa said of Jamie. "She left you just before your book came out and did so well. I'm sure she has kicked herself many times since then. Better you found out sooner than later. You should be glad she left when she did."

He wasn't, but Neil laughed at Marisa's words and part of him hoped that she was right about Jamie kicking herself. Still, even after the book was published, she had never called or written, never made any attempt to revive the relationship, and he'd long ago accepted the fact that it was dead.

Marisa spoke softly but quickly, her voice fluid and pleasing to the ear. She had a way of filling any brief moments of silence that arose. Neil gradually learned more about her, and it was pretty much as he had already guessed. She had returned home after college, intending to stay for a month or two, the summer at most. Her degree was in history, which meant that she could only teach or go back to college for a postgraduate degree, neither of which appealed to her. She had been thinking of moving to Florence. She could always find a job like waitressing to earn money while she looked for an opening in a more interesting line of work—perhaps fashion, magazines, the arts. Florence was a lively creative city, there were always opportunities for bright young people who looked for them.

But she soon was caught up in "keeping things going" at

home. Her parents and two surviving grandparents were all in
varying stages of illness or frailty. It was impossible just to walk
away. Her family and the tenants needed her. Marisa's brother
Hugo was often away on business—he was a rep for a medical supply company—and his financial contributions were very
helpful to the household.

Marisa seemed to understand that the whole enterprise was
by now hopelessly outmoded, a relic of the past, and doomed to
collapse, though she didn't say so. But she apparently regarded
it as her family duty to do her part and see it through as long as
her parents and grandparents were alive. As she spoke of these
things, Neil could see that she was forcing herself to smile and
affect a light tone, but there was loneliness and sadness in her
eyes. It wasn't hard to understand why she was so grateful for
a visitor.

Neil noticed a group of six or seven men standing together
on one of the terraces. They appeared to be watching him, and
Marisa. Neil wondered what those people would do when the
farm finally went under. Perhaps they thought he was from the
bank, and wondered the same thing. Even at some distance,
they seemed alien, slightly wild, lost people.

A heavy mist was drifting across the hills and settling
around them, a low gray cloud of moisture. It came with surprising swiftness, obscuring the sunset and the views. Marisa
frowned.

"*Il morbo,*" she said.

"What?"

"This fog. It's a regular feature of the region, especially up
here at these altitudes. The local people call it *il morbo*"

Neil shivered, feeling a sudden chill. "That means sickness,
illness, the plague," he said.

"Yes, exactly." Marisa laughed. "Sometimes it blows through
and is gone in an hour, but it can linger for a couple of days—
and when it does, you do start to think of it as a plague."

On the terrace above, the men were losing their individual
definition in the mist, becoming a cluster of dark shadow figures. The air was gray and full of floating globules of wetness.

"Let's go inside," Marisa said.

PASSEGIATA

She led him up a flight of stairs and along a short corridor. They took a sharply angled turn, so that they appeared to be heading back the way they had just come, though by a different passage. They went through a doorway, across a raised gallery that was open above an empty room, and then into yet another corridor. Their footsteps made an echoing hollow clatter on the bare floorboards. The floor itself seemed to tilt slightly one way and then another, or to sag in the middle—it was never quite solid and level.

Marisa held his arm snugly against her as they walked, and Neil could feel the movements of her hip. The way their bodies touched, the way Marisa smiled at him—he wanted to believe she was seriously flirting with him, but he decided it wasn't serious. Not yet, anyway. Now that they were indoors, he noticed a sweet woodsy fragrance about her. Juniper? Whatever it was, he found it deliciously attractive.

"The layout is a bit crazy," she said apologetically. "At one time we had many relatives living with us here—cousins, aunts, uncles, in-laws. The rooms were divided and altered many times over the years to accommodate everybody and their belongings."

"I see."

"There was a story that a couple of hundred years ago this was not a farmhouse, that it was originally a monastic retreat or home for some obscure religious order that eventually dwindled away."

"Is that right?"

"You can still see religious carvings and symbols in certain places on the old woodwork, so maybe it's true."

"I like places with a mysterious history," Neil said.

"Yes, so do I, but now it's just a big nuisance."

They turned a corner and were in a wider area, a cul-de-sac. There were two doors, one on either side of the dead-end wall. Marisa opened one of them and went into the room. Neil followed.

"I hope this will be all right," she said.

The room was large, almost square in shape, and sparsely furnished, but it looked comfortable enough. The tall narrow window was swung open and the air in the room was clear, with no trace of mustiness—that was the most important thing as far as Neil was concerned.

"Oh, this is fine," he said. "Very nice."

"There's a bathroom just outside, through the other door. Perhaps you'd like a little time now to unpack your things, to rest and wash up before dinner," she suggested.

"Yes, I would."

"I'll come back for you in, say, an hour and a quarter? I don't want you to get lost wandering around this place alone."

Neil laughed. "Again, I'm sorry to impose on you like this. I'm very grateful for your kind hospitality."

"It's no trouble at all." Marisa hesitated, or lingered, for a moment in the open doorway, smiling warmly at him before she turned to leave. "Make yourself at home here. I'll see you again in a little while."

He smiled back at her. "I look forward to it."

Neil stood and listened as the sound of her footsteps faded away, and then he surveyed the room again. There was a queen-size bed with ornate dark woodwork, an armoire, a chaise and one other chair, a clothes rack and a couple of small end tables. A bedside lamp and a standing floor lamp provided the only light, but they would do. A threadbare rug covered much of the plank floor. The walls were bare, and had been whitewashed so long ago that they had turned gray. He noticed an unlabeled brown bottle and two drinking glasses on one of the tables. He removed the glass stopper from the bottle, took a sniff, poured a few drops and tasted it—grappa. He splashed a little more in the glass. A nice touch.

Neil went to the window, rested his arms on the stone casement and leaned forward to look outside. He suddenly realized that his room was in a wing that had been added on to the main body of the house at some point. It was toward the rear of the house and on the far side, which explained why he hadn't noticed it either when he first approached the place or later, when he was sitting on the patio. Directly below him now, a drop of almost thirty feet, there was only a narrow curling path of ground between the house and the rim of a deep rocky gorge.

Neil finished the grappa and set his small travel alarm for forty-five minutes. He took off his shoes and stretched out on the bed. The mattress was soft and comfortable, and the large down pillows were lightly scented with cedar. Neil shut his eyes and dozed off almost immediately. When the alarm beeped he got up, gathered a few things and went into the bathroom. There was a huge old tub, a toilet with a water tank above it, a sink and mirror. The stone tile floor felt cold through his socks. Neil washed his face, shaved quickly, brushed his teeth and changed shirts. He felt better, clean and awake again, refreshed by the nap.

As Neil stepped back into his room, he heard a noise. It struck him, because until now he hadn't heard any sounds in the house other the ones he and Marisa made walking. This sound was raspy and grating, repeated in a steady rhythm, as if one piece of metal was being scraped against another. It sounded quite close by, so Neil walked the short distance into the corridor to see if he could find where and what it was. He still had a few minutes before Marisa was due to come and fetch him. Neil vowed not to embarrass himself by getting lost.

It was almost completely dark outside and very little light penetrated this inner corridor. He saw a few widely spaced electric candles mounted in sconces on the wall, but they were not turned on and there was no switch to be found in the immediate area. To make matters worse, once he was in the corridor Neil could not get a true sense of direction on the metallic noise. It was still there, somewhere around him, but elusive.

As his eyes slowly adjusted to the gloom, he began to discern a very faint shaft of light not too far down the passage to

his right. Good enough, he thought. He would check it out and
then return to his room.

Neil was still wearing only socks on his feet. The floorboards felt weak in places, almost spongy, and they groaned
softly beneath his weight. It would be a real surprise if dry rot
and woodworms hadn't already taken over large portions of the
interior of the house, particularly in the rooms that were closed
and unused, dark and damp.

The light came from a recess in the wall. Four steps led in
and up to a landing with a wooden ceiling so low that Neil had
to bow his head slightly when he got to it. There was a very
small open area on the right, an alcove with a narrow built-in
bunk. The pale light came from several votive candles in blue
glass jars that stood in a line along a single wall shelf.

There was a young man lying in the bunk. He looked to be
a teenager still, certainly no older than twenty. His skin was
clear, his features boyish, his hair cut short and neatly arranged.
A red sheet covered him from his feet to his chin. A stark iron
crucifix was mounted on the wall directly above the boy's head.
The skeletal Christ figure looked like it might have been carved
out of ivory that had turned brownish-yellow.

Neil stood there for a moment, taking all this in, trying to
imagine an explanation. He stepped closer and studied the
youth. There was no sign of breathing—in fact, the boy's skin
looked icy blue, though that was probably an illusion caused by
the glass candleholders. Neil took one candle and held it below
the boy's cheek, illuminating his face with a clear light. Oddly,
all that did was make the blueness more apparent.

Unlikely possibilities flashed through Neil's mind. The
boy had just died and was laid out here as at a wake. But why
wouldn't Marisa tell Neil about it? Even more to the point, why
would they put the body up here in this absurd little raised
alcove instead of a proper sitting room downstairs, or the nearest funeral home? That made no sense. Perhaps the young man
had died some time ago, and the family knew a way to preserve
his body more or less perfectly, as it now appeared. But that
seemed no less implausible.

Neil leaned forward and lightly pressed the back of his

hand against the young man's gleaming forehead. It felt very cold and hard. When Neil took his hand away he saw a clear rosy-whitish impression of his fingers on the boy's skin. It disappeared in a second or two, heat vanishing.

Then Neil thought he heard a faint exhalation, and he became aware of the metal noise again, rasping somewhere nearby. He stumbled back, his socks slipped and he had to grab the wall to keep from falling on the stairs. Neil returned quickly to his room.

POCKETS

Neil had no time to think about what he had just seen before he heard Marisa's heels clicking loudly down the corridor. She appeared in his open doorway, a sudden irresistible vision. She looked gorgeous. She was wearing a fashionable short, tight, sleeveless black dress with a scooped neckline. It was a dress perfectly designed to emphasize the generous curves and elegant lines of her splendid body.

It was impossible not to stare at her—Neil realized he was probably gaping like a teenage boy. But it also occurred to him that she had obviously chosen to dress like this for him and no one else in this place. Marisa's body filled his vision—it seemed to fill the entire barren room with the explosive richness of life.

She knocked needlessly on the door frame. That was when he finally noticed the smile on her face—playful, expectant.

"You look lovely," he told her.

"Did *signore* try his bed?"

"Yes, he did."

"And was it satisfactory?"

"Yes, it was very … comfortable."

"You're quite sure?" Mock-doubtful.

"Well, I think so."

"Nothing else you need?"

"Now that you're here, I'm fine."

She laughed. "That little rest did you some good, I'm thinking. You don't look so tired now."

"I do feel much better. Refreshed."

"Good, I'm glad. Are you ready to go downstairs?"

"Sure."

Neil put on his sports jacket and Marisa took his hand in hers as they left the room. She startled him by turning to the right in the corridor, so they were bound to walk right past the steps leading up into the alcove. He was even more surprised when she stopped at the entrance and turned as if to go up the steps—but there were no steps, only an open doorway into another room, this one quite small, with a circular staircase down to the ground floor. He must have misjudged the distance, he told himself. The stairs and alcove must be a little farther along that corridor. Neil almost asked Marisa about the dead boy, but decided not to for the time being.

Now they were in a large warmly lit room that featured a regulation size English billiards table. There were several overstuffed armchairs off on either side of the room. At the far end, a sofa and a couple more chairs were arranged around a portable television set. The billiards table was in quite good condition, complete with string pockets, but the rest of the furniture was the same kind of battered old junk he'd seen elsewhere in the house.

"Do you play?" Marisa asked.

"I have played pool, but not proper billiards."

"I'll teach you later, if you want. It's not hard to learn. The rules, I mean. The game itself is another matter."

"I'd like to learn." As long as she was teaching.

'This is the room where Hugo and I kind of hang out," she explained as she went to a small bar near the television set. "He likes to play billiards, so I learned just to give him some competition. Not that I'm very good. One of my uncles was crazy about the game and had this table shipped here from Paris. He died several years ago. The television gets two or three channels on a good night."

Neil nodded sympathetically, but he didn't know quite what to say. It all seemed so dreary and depressing. Even this large room, with its clutter of furniture and its warm lamps, where at least two people spent some time and relaxed, somehow still felt dark, empty and lonely, bereft of life. Only family love and loyalty could keep somebody in a place like this, but even allowing that Marisa had an abundance of those qualities, Neil thought she was bound to go batty sooner or later if she stayed here for very long.

"The table is beautiful," Neil said lamely.

Marisa poured two glasses of wine and gave one to him— the same house red, he discovered when he took a sip. Either he was getting used to it or this was a better bottle, because he found it more agreeable now. Marisa perched herself on the fat arm of a heavy armchair, her legs open to the extent that her dress would allow. Neil's throat tightened and his heart felt like it was booming in his chest.

Jamie had a somewhat fulsome figure too, at first, though in time she had become obsessive about taking off weight. Perhaps that was part of the big fuzzy why—why it all went wrong for them.

"There are a couple of things I should warn you about."

"Oh?"

"Nothing serious." Marisa smiled. "It's just that my relatives are all still pretty much old world people. By old world I mean, you know—before the War. That was the world they grew up in and they still have a lot of those ways and attitudes. They might see rather—"

She hesitated, unable to find the word she wanted. "Different?" he offered. He was the writer.

"Yes." Marisa smiled gratefully. "Different."

"Thanks for telling me," he said. "But I'm sure it won't be a problem as far as I'm concerned. I'm always glad to have the chance to meet and talk with people who lived through that period."

"Good." Marisa was still hesitating about something. "Oh, and if you don't like the food, please, you don't have to eat it. Just have some bread and salad, and I'll fix you something else later. I can tell them we had a lot to eat on the patio earlier."

"We did, and I'm not that hungry now." Neil resisted the urge to smile at her warning about the food. "But I'm sure it'll be fine."

"Thank you."

"Not at all. I'm the guest here."

"One more thing."

"Yes?"

Marisa stood up and stepped close to him. The thin gold bracelets on her wrist gleamed in the light as she put her glass down on the bar. A vibrant blue opal the size of a quarter dangled from a black ribbon that hung tightly at the base of her slender throat. How he wanted to kiss that throat.

All of that lovely black hair, the fire in her eyes, the silky texture of her skin, the way her perfume seemed to settle around him and draw him still closer to her, the movement of her tongue moistening her lips just as she was about to speak—Neil was completely captivated by her physical presence, dazed by its power. Dazed, but still aware.

"I hope you don't mind, but I told them that you are a friend of mine from the university. Well, you're a little older, so I said you were a visiting lecturer there and we became acquaintances. That was rather naughty of me, I know. I should have spoken with you about it first."

"Oh," Neil said. "But, why?"

"Like I said, they're kind of funny that way. If they thought you were a stranger, they'd sit up awake all night, worrying, wondering—who is this man, who sent him, what does he really want? Where they came from and what they went through, a stranger at the door—you have no idea how much it could disturb them. It's crazy, I know, but I thought it best not to risk upsetting them, at their age." Her eyes peered up at Neil, her expression submissive and childlike. "I'm sorry."

"That's all right." Now Neil allowed himself to touch her, putting his arm around her shoulder, stroking her back soothingly. "I understand and I'm sure you're right that it's better for them this way."

"Oh, thank you so much."

"Besides, I really was a teacher for a while."

Marisa smiled brightly, her body resting against his, her head on his chest. God, her hair felt so good on his cheek. He felt her hand on the small of his back. She looked up at him again and opened her mouth as he leaned forward to kiss her. Marisa's tongue met his aggressively, her arm tightened across his back and pulled him closer. Neil could feel the same anxious desire and tension in her body that simmered within him. Their kiss was long and deep, lingering. Finally, Marisa pulled her head back a couple of inches. Now her smile was intimate, complicitous. She slowly ran the tip of her finger along her wet lips.

"Well, hello."

"Hi ..."

"We'd better go in now," she said.

"Mmm?" Neil kissed her neck and throat. Marisa sighed with pleasure, but then gently put her hands on his chest.

"Really. My uncle is a priest. If he were to walk in and find us like this, I'd never hear the end of it."

Neil must have frowned or pouted. Marisa kissed him consolingly, her tongue teasing him.

"Be patient," she said. "We must."

"Okay," he said, smiling. "Let's go."

Marisa took his hand and led him through a doorway into an empty enclosed passage that led to another door. When she opened it, the first thing Neil heard was the familiar sound of metal scraping on metal.

GASTRONOMICO

There were six people already in the dining room when Marisa and Neil entered. They were seated at one end of a table that could hold twelve or fourteen. They were all elderly and they looked half-asleep, propped up in their chairs, barely moving until Marisa approached and spoke to them or touched them on the shoulder. Neil held back a few steps. He couldn't understand what Marisa was saying but the gentle affection in her voice was clear enough. There were three men and three women—Marisa's parents and grandparents, he learned. Neil stepped forward and smiled and nodded to each of them when Marisa gestured toward him. They glanced briefly and vacantly at him, but none of them nodded or said anything. Handshakes were obviously not on.

One of the grandmothers had several small spoons on the table beside her plate, and she was sharpening them with a metal file. Neil stared at this curious spectacle for a few seconds before the old woman suddenly grinned at him and made a crisp scooping motion with the spoon she held.

"Fruit spoons," Marisa explained with a laugh. "You know, like for eating grapefruit with?"

"Oh, yes." Neil still couldn't imagine how he had been able to hear this persistent but not loud sound all the way upstairs. Yet he had no doubt that it was indeed the very same sound.

"Grandmother sharpens them every evening," Marisa explained, as if it were a perfectly normal activity. "It's one of the few things she can still do around the house, so I suppose it makes her feel a bit useful."

"That's good for her, then." And perhaps it was, but Neil

had never heard of anyone sharpening fruit spoons before. He took it to be an unusual but harmless display of eccentricity.

"Yes, it is." Marisa smiled gratefully.

The room was large, but aside from the table and chairs the only other furniture was a sideboard adjacent to the other door, which apparently led to the kitchen. The two long walls were hung with tapestries so faded and dusty that it was impossible for Neil to make out the scenes depicted on them. The room was lit only by candles, which didn't help. The wooden floor was bare and it sagged or tilted in places, just as it did elsewhere in the house.

The same two women who had served them on the patio now came into the room with bowls and platters of food. Marisa asked Neil to help her pour the wine, and he was grateful to have something to do. The men, who wore stiff, old-fashioned suits that almost resembled uniforms, exchanged a few quiet words with each other and then laughed briefly. Neil sensed that it was at his expense—perhaps they thought it absurd or humiliating that he let himself do a servant's work. And at a woman's bidding, no less. Not that he cared in the least about such a silly, antiquated attitude. He also noticed the women casting gnomic glances at him, but they remained silent.

A place had been set at the head of the table, though no one occupied that chair. Neil hesitated, uncertain whether he should pour wine in the glass there too, but then Marisa nodded yes.

"My uncle—ah, here he is."

The priest came in through the doorway from the billiards room—Neil noted—and walked briskly to the table. He had wiry gray hair that was cut short. Although he looked nearly seventy he stood tall and straight and he had a sturdy, muscular build that conveyed strength and energy. The standard collar and black jacket made him look like just another diocesan priest, but he also wore a purple sash across his tunic, a medallion of the Virgin Mary, and there were several small pins and medals affixed to his lapels and breast pocket. He smiled and kissed Marisa lightly on the cheek.

"Father Anton, this is my friend Neil O'Netty from America,"

Marisa said, introducing them. "Neil, this is my uncle, Anton Panic."

"I'm very pleased to meet you," Neil said.

"Thank you, thank you. So nice." The priest's head bobbed several times and he clasped Neil's hand tightly. "So nice. Thank you."

Father Anton's eyes danced behind thick lenses, and Neil wondered if the frames could actually be genuine bakelite.

"Thank you, and your family, for your hospitality," Neil said to the priest, sensing that Father Anton was the decisive figure in the household. "I'm very grateful."

"No, please. Our pleasure to have a guest."

Neil and Marisa sat opposite each other, in the eighth and ninth places at the table. One of the servant women carefully set down a large covered porcelain tureen on the table between Neil and Marisa, and then left. Neil bowed his head slightly when he saw everyone else do that, and Father Anton said Grace in Latin, adding a few more words at the end in the family's other language. The old men chorused "Amen" loudly, and then laughed again, as if at a private joke.

Food was passed around. Neil loaded up on bread and salad, as Marisa had suggested. The bread was coarse and crusty, with a fresh yeasty smell. The salad contained various greens, mushrooms, peppers, tomatoes and chunks of cold meat sausage. Neil drizzled dark olive oil and balsamic vinegar on it. He also took a helping of a soupy rice dish.

The old man beside Neil nudged him in the arm. Neil assumed this was Marisa's father, though in fact he looked only marginally younger than the two grandfathers. He must have been in his early fifties when Marisa was born, but late births were probably not unusual on remote farms. It was clear that the man wanted Neil to help himself from the tureen now. He glanced at Marisa, who nodded reluctantly.

"But we can skip it," she said quickly.

"Oh. Well, let's see."

"You can just pass it along to them."

"That's all right."

Neil didn't want to appear rude. Even as Marisa was speaking to the others, apparently explaining how much she and Neil had eaten just a little while ago on the patio, he lifted the lid of the tureen. It appeared to be some kind of stew, brownish in color. Neil took the iron ladle and swirled it once through the liquid, stirring up small bits of meat, potatoes and—skulls. Tiny skulls that must have been very young birds, probably baby chickens. There were scores of them in the stew, each one roughly the size of a misshapen marble. O-kay. Neil smiled wanly at Marisa.

"I think you were right."

As soon as Neil lifted the heavy tureen and passed it along the table, the others broke into jolly laughter, and it felt as if some tension went out of the air. They were all fully awake now.

"I'm sorry, I warned you," Marisa said. "I wasn't sure, but I thought it might be something like that. Old tastes. It's an old recipe."

"That's okay," Neil assured her. "It's probably quite good, but I think I'd have to get myself in the right state of mind to try it."

"Mr. O'Netty," the priest spoke up. "Zuzu informed me that you have written a book about the case of Beatrice Cenci. Yes?"

"Zuzu is a family nickname for me," Marisa told him. "Don't ask me what it means, but it goes back to when I was a baby."

"I like it." Then he turned toward Father Anton. "Yes, that's right, my last novel was about the Cencis."

"Aha."

The priest spoke English slowly and with difficulty, but he was eager to hear about Neil's version of the story. He seemed particularly concerned that Neil might have been critical of Pope Clement VIII, for refusing to spare young Beatrice's life. Neil babbled on about what a thorny moral problem that was, even in today's world, and how he tried not to take one side or the other. A novel was not a debate, et cetera—the usual points he had made in numerous interviews. It was strange, speaking past six people who couldn't understand a word he was saying and ignored him. But Father Anton nodded every few seconds and appeared to be listening carefully.

Neil thought he was probably speaking for too long, but he couldn't focus his mind. His words seemed to vanish immediately in the air, and the only thing he could hear—on and on—was the muffled crunching sound of all those little bird skulls being eaten.

BILLIARDS AT HALF PAST TEN

To Neil's relief, dinner in that house was a functional matter, not a social event. Marisa's parents and grandparents ate energetically and loudly, but surprisingly quickly They drank one large glass of wine each, and when they were finished they shuffled off out of the room, scarcely even glancing at him as they left. It was probably his fault, Neil thought. If he weren't there, they would chat and linger at the table as families do—or did.

Though somehow he doubted that. The priest, Marisa and Hugo were the practical, capable ones who kept things going here. Without their efforts, the farm would be sold and the old folks packed off to a nursing home. Not that they seemed to appreciate it. Neil thought they acted as if they took all this for granted, which amounted to a terrible ingratitude. But—old people, old ways. They weren't going to change now.

When the others left, Father Anton came and sat beside Neil. He had a few more questions to raise and points to make about history and literature, which was apparently a matter of some real interest to him. Neil did his best to speak sensibly and not get carried away. He had no special theories or insights. History was interesting. It provided useful plots and frameworks as well as a magical sense of distance, of stepping into another world, another time and place. He felt very comfortable with it.

But all Neil really wanted to do was write tales that were like operas—gaudy, full of intensity, screaming emotion, high drama, sudden action, and troubled characters driven by primal human desires. That was the big stuff, as he thought of it. History itself wasn't the point. The critics had seen much more

in *La Petrella* than Neil thought was there, including a few mysterious literary techniques he didn't even understand. Which
made him feel kind of like a secret phony at times, but that was
their business.

Father Anton was polite and intelligent, and after ten minutes he got up, clasped Neil's hand again, and said good night.
He went around the table to kiss "Zuzu" on the forehead, and
then left the room.

"He likes you," Marisa said. "I can tell."

"He seems very nice. But why is he living here? I mean,
priests are usually assigned to parishes or schools," Neil added.

"He could be retired if he wanted, at his age. But he is on
a kind of sabbatical instead. He is working on a paper for the
Pope."

"Really?"

"Oh yes. Father Anton has known every pope, going back
to Pius. He found a place at the Vatican early in his priesthood,
and ever since then he has been very, you know what I mean,
well-connected."

"Wow. What is his paper about?"

Marisa shrugged. "I'm not sure. Something to do with the
history of conversions in Christianity. That's why he was so
keen to hear what you had to say about how you make use of
history in your books."

"Ah, I see."

The two servant women entered the room then and began
to gather up the dishes and utensils. Neil thought he saw a sudden darkening of Marisa's expression. Then she turned to him,
and smiled again. She pushed her chair away from the table
and stood up.

"Shall we get out of the way?"

"Absolutely."

They went back into the billiards room. Marisa asked Neil
to pour some more wine for both of them. She turned on the
television and fiddled with the rabbit ears until she got a reasonably stable picture. It looked like some awful game show,
but she turned the volume off. Then Marisa went to a shelf and
picked up a pocket transistor radio that looked about forty years

old. She rolled the little tuning wheel until she found a station playing some Abba-like Europop. The relentlessly cheerful tinny sound hung in the air like a bouquet of desiccated flowers.

"They aren't necessary for me," Neil said, nodding toward the radio and the television as he handed Marisa a glass of wine.

"I know, but it looks good. In case."

"In case?"

"You know. If someone comes in on us."

"You really think they would?"

"It's possible." Marisa shrugged, her eyes sad. "Better to give them a little while to get to bed."

"You're a grown woman."

"Don't make fun." Marisa turned away, pouting. "You can see that they don't think that way. They never will."

Neil put his drink down on the bar and stepped close behind her. He put his arms around her and kissed her hair and neck. "I'm sorry. I wasn't making fun. It's hard for you here, isn't it?"

She seemed to sigh and relax a little in his embrace. She gave a slow nod and her free hand reached around to rest on his hip. Neil's hands spread across her belly. When they brushed up against her breasts he felt her quick intake of breath, then the long slow exhalation, a vibration within her body, a silent cry of pleasure and deep need.

Marisa slipped out of his arms, turned around and leaned close to kiss him. Her tongue danced and teased, licking across his lips. She pressed her hand to his chest, as if to hold him back at a certain distance, but two fingers slipped between the buttons and touched his skin. She was smiling brightly again. Then her fingers tightened on his shirt and pulled him closer for one more kiss before she moved to the sofa.

"Let's sit," Marisa said. "Just for a little while."

"Okay."

They sat just a couple of feet apart on the sofa, their bodies turned to face each other. Neil caught a glimpse of Marisa's pearl gray panties and he realized that her legs were bare. It occurred to him that all of this might be a colossal tease and nothing more, but he doubted it, and in any event he didn't care if it was. Would he rather be alone in his room upstairs, trying to finish Rose Tremain's *Restoration*? Uh, no.

"So, tell me, why haven't you found someone else?" she asked. "It has been some time since this other woman left. A handsome young author like you, and very successful. I think the women would be knocking on your door day and night."

Neil laughed. He knew he was quite ordinary looking. But it was true that after the publication of *La Petrella* some women he'd known only on a casual social basis suddenly seemed to find him much more fascinating and worthy of their attention. Not to mention the strangers.

"I haven't been a monk."

"Aha."

"But no one serious." It was time to turn the tables. "And what about you? I can't believe you didn't have plenty of boyfriends when you were at college, in Parma."

"*Boys*, yes," Marisa said dismissively. "Anyhow ..."

Neil watched the way her lips moved as she took another sip of wine, the slight tightening of the muscles in her throat as she swallowed. It was not unlike a fairy tale, he thought, or a romantic opera. Marisa was the beautiful young princess imprisoned in a remote castle by the evil queen or king, in this case by a whole van-load of elderly relatives and a bunch of tenant farmers. And that made Neil the prince who comes to rescue her, et cetera. It was the kind of old-fashioned story he liked—but it only took another momentary flash of sadness in Marisa's eyes to remind him that it was a very different matter for her, with no easy alternatives or solutions.

Still, there was nothing he could do. Invite her to Rome? Offer to take her with him when his car was fixed and he left? Sure, he could do that without any commitment on his part, but he sensed that Marisa would simply decline the offer. She had intelligence, spark, wit, and a desire to escape, but she also seemed resigned to play out the role that had been assigned to her for now by family and circumstance.

Her free hand rested across the inside of her thigh and her hair curled around her face, tumbling down over her shoulders like a gauzy wimple. She glanced at the door to the dining room and then back the other way toward the circular staircase. She leaned closer to Neil—who let his gaze linger on her cleavage. By now he was convinced that Marisa liked him looking at her this way, with voyeuristic intensity and undisguised desire.

They continued chatting for a few minutes but Neil was hardly aware of what they actually said. It was nothing important, just talk intended to pass whatever amount of time it took for Marisa to feel comfortable.

At one point she went to get the wine bottle from the bar. When she came back to the sofa, she sat right next to him. Their knees touched and she let her hand rest lightly on his leg. It was all Neil had been waiting for, the final signal. He ran the back of his fingers over her cheek, then trailed them down to stroke the inner curves of her breasts, her skin so silky and lovely to touch. Her hand moved between his legs, just brushing his cock.

Before they kissed again, he saw Marisa quickly scan the room once more. Apparently reassured, she let her eyes close and her kiss was hard and wet, full of aggressive passion. When their mouths parted, she smiled at him with her eyes—it was a look of recognition.

Marisa suddenly turned and stretched out her body, lying down on the sofa so that her head rested on Neil's lap. She nestled her cheek against his erection. She pushed her feet into the cushion and raised her legs, so that her dress slipped back and exposed even more of her thighs. Her knees swaying in the air, together, then apart.

"Ah, you want me so much," she said softly. "Don't you?"

"Yes, I do."

"Do you think that's a good idea?" Playful, teasing again.

"It's the only idea."

"But we can't rush. Desire is all anticipation, isn't it?"

"Not *all* anticipation."

Marisa laughed. "And fantasy, imagination."

"Not *all* fantasy and imagination," Neil insisted, grinning at her. "It involves action too, and fulfillment."

"But the right action."

"And what's the right action?"

"Oh, but that's where imagination and fantasy come in," Marisa said, as she continued to move the side of her face against the bulge in his pants. "I'm sorry, you're so sweet to me, but I don't want to rush. You'll be gone, you know, and I'll still be here. Remembering this."

"That's all right," Neil said, moved by her words.

"So many nights I spent in this room, on this couch, the television and the radio turned on. But I was alone and all I could do was imagine moments like this. What we would say, what we would do."

"Well, I'm here now."

"Better than any dream."

"I doubt that."

"No, really," Marisa protested. "I don't like boys. I imagined a man a little older, though not too much! A man considerate, intelligent, experienced, understanding. You're even more, you're a gift."

"So are you," Neil told her. His right hand was between her legs and he slid his finger beneath her wet panties, stroking her, gently pushing on and entering her. Marisa's body heaved and squirmed, her desire storming, barely contained. With his other hand he caressed her cheek again and rolled his fingertip along her upper lips—she took it, sucking hard. "And what did you imagine yourself saying?"

Marisa tugged on his finger, then opened her mouth as she looked up at Neil. "Two." He was confused for a second, but then understood, and he slipped his middle finger into her mouth too. Her eyes were fierce with need and desire. "Three." Three. "Four ... " Four, her face taut, her teeth biting hard on his flesh. Eyes wide, staring up at him.

He continued stroking her swollen clitoris. She was so wet and hot, and he was enthralled by the way her body responded. Then she pushed his fingers away from her mouth and grabbed his head with both of her hands, her fingers clutching his hair, pulling his face down as she lifted herself to kiss him again, her tongue thrusting, her lips squeezing and pressing and pulling on his mouth and tongue, their chins now dripping with saliva. Marisa tasted so sweet and felt so wonderful. And how utterly glorious it was to break free of thought at last and plunge into the tornado.

SOUND CHOOSES TO ECHO

They made love with gasping urgency and quickness on the scarred leather sofa. After only a few minutes of resting, Marisa slipped out of Neil's arms, sat up and straightened her dress. Her panties hung from one of her ankles. Neil reached down to remove them. He held them to his face for a second, smiling at her, and then put them in his pants pocket.

"Oh? What's that, your trophy?" Lightly mocking, playful.

"No. I just don't want you to put them back on."

"Ah, good. I'm not through with you, either."

"I'm glad to hear it."

Neil zipped his pants and buckled his belt. Marisa slid closer and leaned against him as he put his arm around her. Reckless, reckless—he knew that, but he didn't care. What really bothered him about their quick fuck was that it had been just that, a quick fuck.

"We both needed and wanted each other so much," Marisa said. "The first time had to be like that. Thunder and lightning."

"Yes." Neil gave a soft laugh. "The first time."

"And how do you know it won't be the same way the second time?" Marisa asked with a naughty grin. "And the third? We might make a lot of thunder and lightning, you know."

"That's great, if we do," he told her. "But I also want you in a bed, yours or mine, where we can take our time and really make love."

Marisa wriggled closer in his embrace, sighed happily and kissed his chin, running her hand along his leg. "So do I, and we will. But first we had to wait until they were in their rooms. And then—we couldn't wait a minute longer! But that's okay.

Every time is good in its own way."

They sat together like that for a while longer, kissing, touching each other, all tenderness, affection and dreamy smiles. Neil loved the way she felt in his arms, the softness of her skin, the fragrance in her hair, the sweet spicy taste of her mouth.

Reckless, yes—but what the hell, if she got pregnant, he would marry Marisa and they would have a child. He would still write his books, it might even turn out to be a happy marriage and—Neil almost laughed aloud, it was such a startling and improbable thought. But what surprised him most was that it didn't scare him at all. His personal life had been drifting nowhere the last few years. Before that too, probably. Perhaps he had reached the point where he secretly hoped that some outside event would force a dramatic change that sent his life in a completely new and unexpected direction, and he would have no choice but to go along with it.

Things like that happened in opera all the time. Part of Neil's brain knew that in the cold light of day he would see it differently, rationally, and that he would probably want to drive away from Marisa and this house with no complications or lingering ties. But for now that part of his brain had no voice. He only wanted this wonderful erotic interlude to continue. Let the two of them see how much pleasure and deep comfort they could give to each other in a short period of time.

Marisa took his hand and they rose from the sofa. They ascended the narrow circular staircase. She smiled back over her shoulder at him when he put his hand on her hip. How he enjoyed the way her body felt as she moved, the smooth, elegant working of her perfect flesh and taut muscles. He slid his hands under Marisa's dress, caressing her thighs. She stopped near the top of the stairs, enjoying his touch, murmuring softly to herself. She turned and sat down on the top step, and opened her legs wide to him. She pulled the front of her dress back with one hand, while the other one partly covered her lush triangle of fine black hair.

Neil leaned forward, gripping the iron stair with his hands to brace himself. He ran his cheek down along the inside of her thigh—ah, it was so silky, warm and soft. Neil imagined he could feel an electric charge building as his skin moved over hers. His tongue probed between her fingers, but she wouldn't help him. Finally he touched and had a fleeting taste of her hot wet inner flesh, so tantalizing. He felt the little jump her body gave, and heard the brief but sharp intake of her breath. Marisa gently took his face in her hands and raised it. She was smiling so warmly and happily. Her hair fell over him as she pulled his face to her breasts and held him there for a moment. Then she slid her body back a little on the floor and stood up.

"My lover. Come on. Not here."

Neil took her hand again and followed her back into the corridor. It was very dark, except for a glimmer of light farther down on the right, where his room was. Marisa started to walk in that direction, but Neil looked to the left and saw the same faint blue glow he had seen earlier. He decided it was the perfect opportunity. He tightened his grip on her hand, and wouldn't move, so she turned around.

"Your room is this way," she told him. Her voice was low, almost a whisper. She tugged his hand.

"What's that blue light?"

He started walking toward the alcove. For some reason he expected Marisa to resist, but she didn't.

"Oh, that. You want to see? It's interesting."

They carefully went up the short flight of steps. There was barely room enough for both of them on the tiny landing. The alcove was virtually the same as before, with the shelf of votive candles still lit and the crude iron crucifix on the wall, but the bunk was empty—bare wood.

"What's this all about?"

"Remember, I told you that they think this house was once a religious retreat, something like that?"

"Oh, yes."

"Okay, so. My uncle thinks that this was a special place they used, where one priest or monk could shut himself in for a while to meditate or to pray." Marisa pointed to a couple of spots on the side walls. "You can see where there might have been hinges for a door. If you were inside, it would almost be like lying in a coffin, so it would help you to think about death, and God, and the life to come. Your movements would be completely restricted. You couldn't stand up or walk around, the way you could in your room. You have no window, no view. No distractions at all. There is nothing to do but lie there and think and pray. You see? Unusual, isn't it?"

Aside from the way she kept her voice down, she reminded Neil of so many bright young guides who explained things at the many historical sites he had visited.

"But why the candles now?"

"Oh." Marisa waved her hand dismissively. "The old women keep them lit all the time. They believe this story so strongly, they want to have it ready in case the soul of some holy man ever returns. Or to honor them all, like devotion candles in a church. Something like that."

"I see."

It made reasonable sense—except for the young man Neil had seen lying there in the bunk. The red sheet on him. His cold blue skin, the way it had appeared to react to his touch. But now Neil was wondering if perhaps he had imagined all of that. He couldn't mention it now.

"I used to think the candles were dangerous," Marisa went on. "But we depend on them in this house. We only have one generator, no connection to the national grid. But there's never been a fire so far. After a while, you get used to things and don't even think about them."

"Yes."

They backed out of the alcove, made their way down the dark steps and a few moments later were in Neil's room. There was no lock in the door but he felt a little better in some vague way when he pulled it shut and the old latch clicked loudly in place. He switched on the small lamp that was on the bedside table. It created a pocket of golden light around the bed but left the rest of the room in shadows.

Neil had his back half-turned to Marisa for a moment but he felt her presence close to him, like electricity in the air, a growing force of barely contained energy. She reached around him from behind and started tugging his shirt out, unbuttoning it, quickly unbuckling his belt, unzipping his pants again.

Her hand slipped into his pocket for a second. Neil pulled his shirt and undershirt off, and immediately felt Marisa kissing his back, rubbing her face on his skin. Her mouth so wet and hot. His pants fell to the floor and he stepped out of them. He yanked his socks off, and was naked. He could feel her body give a slight shrug, he heard the rustle of her dress falling, and then he felt her bare breasts pressing against his back.

Marisa had removed her silk panties from his pocket and now she had them wrapped loosely around her hand as she took his cock and began to stroke it, sending waves of exquisite sensation through him. He reached behind with both hands, caressing her fanny, pulling her even more tightly to his body. She continued stroking him and he was very hard again. "Mmm," she murmured happily.

Neil turned and kissed her, his hands on her breasts and between her legs. He sat down on the bed, pulling her with him, but she stayed on her feet and straddled his legs. Marisa gently pushed him flat on his back, without breaking their long wet kiss, her body poised over his. She felt so wonderful and he loved the way her hair trailed across his skin. He moved farther onto the bed. She moved with him, letting her breasts hang so that her nipples just grazed along over his belly and chest. Then she swung one leg over him and lowered her hips, her body suddenly drawing him into her, seizing him in one swift, sure movement that made him gasp with pleasure.

She leaned forward, letting him kiss her breasts and suck her nipples as their lower bodies heaved violently together. Neil reached down to stroke her wet hard clitoris at the same time as their bodies were thrusting furiously, making the large bed rock and groan. Marisa's cries grew much louder, she no longer cared who might hear anything.

It was longer the second time, but not slower, and the pleasure they experienced was far more intense, ravishing both of them. Their bodies were drenched with sweat when they finally lay still together. Marisa kissed his neck, her lips moving weakly, the lightest of touches. Neil could only hold her in his arms.

He must have dozed off for a little while. Marisa was kissing him and telling him that she couldn't stay in his room all night, but that she would be back in the morning. Neil gave a little groan of unhappiness, but he smiled sleepily when he opened his eyes and saw her.

"Your face is red, all around your mouth," he said.

She grinned. "So is yours. And your lips are swollen up."

He smiled. "So are yours."

"Not just my lips!"

They laughed, kissed and hugged again, but then she left and the light went out and Neil immediately fell back into a deep happy sleep.

He was naked and cold, and he groped blindly for something to cover himself with. Then the voices entered his brain and stubbornly dragged him back to near-consciousness. Neil sat up slowly and opened his eyes. There was a little gray in the light that came through his open window. The voices were coming from somewhere outside. They were unintelligible, foreign, but surprisingly clear and sharp in the predawn silence.

Neil stood up and listened. He could still hear the voices, though they were a bit fainter now. He crossed the cold floor to the window. The air was very cool, but the cloudy fog—*il morbo*—had disappeared. It was still fairly dark outside but he could see things clearly enough.

In the distance, on one of the ridges about a hundred yards away, two men were walking. But no, there were three of them. They were moving in a direction away from the house. Their voices carried so well that it seemed to Neil almost like a ventriloquist's trick, as if they were standing on the ground just below his window. But he still couldn't understand anything they said. Their voices were gruff, angry, or so it sounded to Neil.

Then he realized dimly that two of the men were dragging and yanking the third one along. They appeared to hit and kick him, as necessary, to keep him moving. A struggle of some sort was in progress, but at such a distance it seemed merely curious to Neil, almost abstract. It went on like that for a little while longer, and then the three men disappeared beyond the downward curl of the winding ridge.

Neil stood there a moment longer, until he realized that he couldn't keep his eyes open and that he was nearly asleep on his feet. He was still so tired. He turned around and went back to bed, pulling the sheet and blankets up over him, clutching them tightly just beneath his chin.

Then he heard—somewhere in the distance, outside—a gunshot. But it was there and gone in an instant, and sleep had him.

THE SECOND DAY

A sound, a metal click too small and distant to stir him, nothing more than a transient pinprick on the otherwise blank expanse of Neil's sleep. But then something else, different and closer, a whisper of cloth, accompanied by a feeling of movement—his own. Marisa was in bed with him, he realized, suddenly aware of her warmth enveloping him, her radiant skin on his and her hair fanning across his belly as she took him in her mouth.

"It's all right," she told him when she wriggled up and settled into his arms beneath the sheets. "My uncle is in the grotto. He says Mass there for the farmers every morning and then he visits with them afterward. He won't be back for a while."

"The grotto?"

"The *grotta rossa*, they call it. It's a cave in the mountain, it's on the other side of the hill out back. Over many years, they made it into a shrine to Our Lady. I'll show it to you later."

"What about your parents and grandparents?"

"Oh they don't climb here anymore. They only one who might walk in on us would be my uncle. He would be upset and hurt."

"And angry?"

"Well maybe a bit."

"What about the—the servants?"

Marisa sighed—unhappily, it seemed to Neil. "They will stay away until I instruct them to clean your room and make up your bed. When we go downstairs."

"Do they bother you?" He had spoken without thinking, so he quickly added, "Or am I just imagining that?"

She hesitated before admitting, "It is difficult."

Neil could tell that she didn't want to talk about it. They lay still for a few more moments, but then Marisa sat up in a sudden quick movement and smiled irrepressibly again. She was so beautiful, her black hair mussed, her magnificent breasts swaying slightly as she turned her body to face him, her eyes sparkling with life. She kissed his lips, his cheeks, his neck, his ears, a quick flurry of affectionate butterfly kisses. Neil felt a fresh wave of emotion surge through him, not merely lust or desire, but something more complicated and harder to define.

Suddenly he remembered that the men there were going to patch his radiator today, and then he would drive away to find the nearest town and a repair shop. An inn for the night. At least, that was the plan. But now Neil felt no urgency about leaving. He wondered if Marisa would ask him to stay for another night. Instead of letting him take a room in town. He could hire a taxi to drive him back here and pick him up again when his car was ready—which might take two or three days, if they had to order out to get the correct replacement radiator.

"Come on, now," she said, interrupting his thoughts. "We don't have *that* much time. I want to watch you shave."

They ate breakfast on the patio. It was a mild sunny morning and the air was sweet. Neil had deliberately chosen to wait until mid-September for this trip, knowing that the hordes of the summer visitors would pretty much be gone by then. He and Marisa had fresh fruit, omelets and strong coffee. Neil felt awake again, though still a little tired.

They saw Father Anton returning to the house. He had a long brisk stride for a man of his apparent years. When he noticed Marisa and Neil on the patio, he veered off the path and stopped to say hello and exchange a few pleasantries with them, nodding and smiling. But it seemed as if his thoughts were on other matters, and he soon left them to go inside.

"It's much different today," Marisa said. "Better, easier, you know? Yesterday they didn't know you and they were kind of uncertain. But today, it's like you are part of the household."

Neil laughed. "Good. I was afraid that I was causing you

problems with them. Not to mention the inconvenience."

"No," she scoffed. Neil loved the way emotion showed in even the smallest of her facial expressions. "It's good now, it's okay."

"Well, I'm glad."

"So, I was thinking. Since it's such a lovely morning, perhaps you would like to go for a walk. There are plenty of old paths and trails, and the countryside is quite nice around here."

He smiled at her. "I'd love to go for a walk with you."

"Ah. I was hoping you would say that." Marisa moistened her lips. "I want to touch you again, right now." Then she laughed happily at her own impatience. "Damn!"

A few minutes later, equipped with a small picnic basket and a large beach towel, they set off. When they had walked a little more than a hundred yards, Neil stopped for a moment and glanced back. Now he could see the side of the house where his room was, though he wasn't sure exactly which window was his. So they had to be on the same ridge where he had seen the three men early that morning.

"Is something wrong?" Marisa asked.

"No, not at all. I just realized that the way we're going is in the view I have from the window in my room."

"Yes."

"I woke up early this morning. Just for a moment."

"You did?"

"I heard voices out here and I saw some men on this path."

"I should have warned you," Marisa said. "Those people make noise day and night. The old ones stay up late, drinking. Then the younger ones get up early to go about their work. They have no consideration. I'm very sorry, I hope they didn't disturb you."

"No, I fell right back to sleep."

"I'm glad."

"I thought I heard a gunshot."

"Yes, they hunt early in the morning," Marisa explained. "Sometimes they bring back a deer, or ducks and geese from the lake. They need the food. It's such a shame, you know."

"What is?"

"The land looks so beautiful—and it truly is. But it is *so* difficult to live on, almost impossible. All of the work that has to be done, it never ends, and it never seems like enough."

They walked for nearly an hour. It was easy going, as the path never rose or descended too sharply. They stopped a few times to enjoy the views and to kiss. Marisa told him how she and her brother had explored all of the countryside for miles around as children, and she got Neil to tell her a bit about the book he was working on. It was another Italian chronicle from Stendhal, he admitted. Marisa thought that was wonderful, but Neil knew the critics would probably tear into him for repeating himself. Oh well. For one thing, he didn't have a better idea.

The sun was almost directly overhead when Marisa led him off the faint path and through a brief stretch of high brush and small trees. A few minutes later they came out into a mossy clearing at the base of a rocky wall, an area not much larger than a good-sized living room. A clump of spindly birch trees provided some shade. A narrow stream of water flowed down the rocks and disappeared into the thick brush at the perimeter.

"We're here," Marisa announced. She spread the beach towel on the grass beneath the birches.

"Perfect," Neil said. He set the picnic basket down and went to the stream. He had worked up a light sweat, so he splashed his face with water. It was very cold and it felt great. A perfect place for a picnic.

Marisa was kneeling on the towel, sitting back on her heels. She had already removed her canvas shoes and tossed them onto the grass. She was wearing a peasant-style blouse and a loose skirt that came to mid-calf, but which was now bunched up just over her knees. Neil sat beside her, resting his back against the trunk of one of the birches.

"There's a bottle of wine in the basket," she said. "Some fresh bread, mortadella and cheese."

"Mmm."

She leaned forward on her hands, and she was like a big beautiful cat pressing against him. Still on her hands and knees, she positioned herself over his lap, and smiled up at him.

"Or would you like to play with me first?"

"*Mmmm ...*"

Neil reached under, slipping his hand inside her blouse, caressing her breasts, teasing her nipples. His other hand moved beneath her skirt and up the back of her thigh—the sudden thrill of finding that she had no panties on, that her flesh was so hot and moist already. His finger moved into her easily and stroked and rubbed her. Marisa's eyes were closed, her mouth open, and she sighed and groaned with something more than pleasure, some longing and need so great that it seemed almost heartbreaking to Neil. Then she whipped her head back, hair flying, and her mouth tightened, her breath sharp and fast, grunting with ferocity. Neil stroked and caressed her until she sagged down on her forearms and rolled her face in his crotch. Feeling how hard he was, she lithely swung her body around so that her backside faced him. She pulled her skirt up over her hips.

"Please, now ..."

Neil quickly pulled his pants down, knelt behind her, took hold of her and then thrust into her. Such dizzying pleasure, laced with a passing spasm of sharp pain. Marisa cried out urgently.

"Harder, harder ..."

She swung her head back and forth in the air again. Neil grabbed her long hair in one hand, carefully pulling it taut. She tilted her head back, and then he could see the wild smile, the roaring look on her face—her eyes open and fiery, urging him, challenging him.

"*Harder harder ... make me feel you ... more ... MORE!*"

Her cries were so loud now. Sweat stung Neil's eyes as he slammed into her again and again, and Marisa went down, her face pressed against the towel, her arms splayed out, hands clutching the cotton, her eyes closed again now, and he forced her hips down to the ground too, his body pressed on hers as he came, his face buried in her hair.

"My lover ..."

"My lover," Neil said, stroking her face.

"Ah." Marisa put on an impish smile. "I think maybe you

better not say anything more right now."

"Will you come to Rome? At least to visit?"

Her eyes widened in mock-surprise. "See what I mean?" She pressed her finger to his lips. "*Sssh*. Who knows?" She kissed him again.

It was the middle of the afternoon by the time Neil and Marisa arrived back at the house. They found two men pondering Neil's radiator, which was on a large sheet of plastic on the ground. They were daubing it with a tarlike substance. Much of the front end of the car had been dismantled, with loose parts scattered all around. One of the men launched into a long and detailed explanation—to Marisa—that involved hand-waving and pointing to various tricky places on the radiator. Neil didn't understand a word they spoke but it was quite obvious that he wasn't going anywhere that day. He didn't mind, in fact he felt a distinct sense of relief.

"It's difficult," Marisa explained. "There's so much corrosion, so many spots for them to patch up."

Neil nodded. "I can see how bad it is."

"Maybe by tomorrow?"

"Okay."

"Anyhow, if they can't get it working again, my brother will be home by the end of the week."

"Even better."

Marisa tried not to smile. "It's a good thing they don't speak English. You're very naughty!"

Neil smiled at her. "I'm trying."

THE LAST NIGHT

Neil was exhausted by the long walk and their intense love-making, so he was glad when Marisa suggested another late afternoon siesta. She led him back to his room, promising to return for him later. He was also grateful to hear that they were excused from dinner with the family that night. He had no desire to find out what might be on the menu this time. Though in all fairness to them, it was their house and he was the intruder, and Marisa's family probably felt just as uncomfortable as Neil had.

But what a bizarre, sad household it was. What would he make of all this without Marisa? As Neil stretched out on the bed and nestled his head in the soft pillow, he realized that since he had arrived there yesterday he'd had almost no time to think about anything. The one instance when he had a few moments alone, Neil had heard the unusual metal scraping sound and he had discovered that peculiar alcove, which may or may not have had the body of a young man in it. Otherwise, Marisa was with him, occupying his thoughts and attention, or else he was too tired and sleepy to think.

Marisa was wonderful. He loved the way she made him respond naturally, instinctively—without the need for thought or analysis. She had such a gift and an appetite for living, it seemed to him. It was a terrible thing that she was stuck here, so unfair and unnatural. Her own personal life was indefinitely on hold.

Neil had to find the right way to speak to Marisa about it, to make her see that she had to do something—for her own sake. She could at least try to get away for a few days every month, to

Rome, anywhere. Just to be among other people, to stroll about a city, eat in a restaurant, see a movie ...

He was about ten years older than Marisa was, but that didn't seem to matter to her and it certainly didn't to him. Maybe a real relationship would never work out, but Neil had a strong sense that he could not just drive away and let go without even trying.

He had to leave ... but he had to see her again ...

... wanted her ...

His eyes closed.

"Do we have to wait for everybody to go to bed again tonight?" Neil asked, smiling at her.

"You're so naughty, I love it," Marisa said, laughing. "No, we don't. I have a special place I want to show you."

They were finishing a light meal in the billiards room. Some vacuous Euro-techno music droned on the radio in the background. Marisa looked very pretty, very girlish in a dark blue-green plaid skirt that almost reached her knees and a white short-sleeved blouse that was somehow even sexier to Neil because it was buttoned all the way to the top. She wore several thin silver bracelets on her wrists. She had braided some of the hair on the sides of her head and tied it with beaded blue bands.

"I had to tidy it up while you were sleeping," Marisa continued. "I had not been down there for years."

"*Down* there?"

"Yes." She pointed to the floor. "There's a huge cellar beneath this house. It's full of things my family brought with them after the war and have never used since. I don't know what we'll do with it."

"But they were lucky they could take anything at all with them," Neil said. "By the end of the war tens, probably hundreds of thousands of people had nothing more than the clothes on their backs."

"Yes, I suppose. Anyhow, when we were children, Hugo and I had our own little clubhouse down there. It's buried in the middle of everything. It was a good place to hang out on rainy days. Later, I used to like to go there alone, to read or just to think. You know?"

"Sure." Neil nodded. "The childhood retreat, the adolescent haven. We all had private hideouts like that."

Marisa laughed. "Hideouts—yes, that's the word."

She took his hand. Neil thought that they were heading toward the front of the house, but as usual there were so many turns and passages that it was impossible for him to keep a sense of direction. They finally arrived at the door that led to the cellar. As soon as Marisa opened it, Neil heard the sound of an electric generator. She flicked a switch and some lights went on below. The narrow stone stairs descended along an interior wall that was made of rock and mortar, and were open on the other side.

"Watch your step," she warned him.

Neil nodded. The air was cool and damp, but he could tell from his first few breaths that it probably wouldn't bother him. The unbroken flight of stairs was steep and long—it was more like two normal floor levels down to the bottom, Neil estimated.

They had not quite gone halfway when Marisa stopped and turned to him. She pointed out across the expanse of the cellar now visible on the one side. Single light bulbs dangled from cables here and there, providing some illumination, though much of the place was cast in shadows.

"Looks good," she said, sounding exasperated.

"I see what you mean."

The place was a vast warren of storage areas, shelves and platforms, all of them full of boxes, cartons and trunks. One area contained metal racks jammed with clothing on hangers—coats, dresses, suits, shirts. Another part was given over to larger items that were covered with tarp, unusual shapes, some kind of equipment or tools.

'This is only half of it," Marisa told him. "It's the same on the other side of this wall."

"Wow, it looks like they brought everything with them."

"Oh, no, not at all. You'll never guess."

"Guess what?"

"What my families did, before they came here. Both of the families, my mother's and my father's. They worked together."

"Weren't they farmers, like here?"

Marisa laughed. "No!"

"Then I have no idea."

"Don't worry, I'll show you."

At the bottom of the stairs she led him around the wall into the other half of the cellar. At first it looked like more of the same, a maze of aisles and clogged passages through a sea of accumulated possessions. It was hard to see much because the light bulbs were widely scattered and dim, but Neil noticed a few unusual items—large rolls of canvas, for instance, a collection of grotesque puppets, some faded banners mounted on poles.

"Yes?" Marisa prompted.

"Still no idea," Neil said. "Unless they ran a circus."

"Ah, you're getting warm."

"Really?"

"Yes, they had a traveling show, not really a circus. In good weather they would go from town to town, the larger villages, throughout the entire region. They had a puppet show, they staged little plays, usually stories from the New Testament, things like that."

"Are you part gypsy?" Neil asked jokingly.

"No way," Marisa exclaimed. Neil found her sudden use of such an American expression endearing. "Those people, they call themselves Roma now, but they were trouble wherever they went. They made it very hard for families like mine. Nobody liked or trusted them. Gypsies, I mean."

"Nobody likes the gypsies," Neil echoed, trying to keep the sarcasm out of his voice. "Even today, even in America."

"Of course. But never mind them. I want to show you something that my great-grandfather did. I'm not sure if he started it. Probably not. But he was a master craftsman. Now forgotten, unknown."

The sadness in her voice struck Neil. They had come to a long table that was covered with wooden boxes, each one about the size of a medicine cabinet. Marisa went to one directly beneath a light bulb and lifted the lid. Neil stood close beside her. She carefully peeled back a sheet of something that looked like parchment or vellum, revealing a mask of a human face. The detail was remarkable.

"It's wax," Marisa said. "Look how fine the work is."

She slipped her fingers under the mask and lifted it—and Neil could see that it was almost paper-thin and translucent.

"Go ahead, it's okay," she told him. "You can touch it."

Neil took one edge of the mask between his fingers, rolling them over the filmy wax. It felt strong enough not to tear easily, but also very soft and supple. It had a slight oily slickness.

"What did they do with them?" he asked.

"They wore them in the plays they put on. And I think maybe they showed them, like an art exhibition—you know? One of the banners they used translates as 'The House of Masks.' You see, the trick is, he cast them from real people, and then he used the casts to make these masks. He had some formula he developed to make the wax like this."

"It's beautiful," Neil said. "But doesn't your grandfather know how it's done? You could do something with this, you know."

"Yes, he must know, but he won't say. He won't talk about it at all anymore." Marisa shook her head sadly. "I'm so afraid it will all be lost, because Hugo and I just don't know what to do about it."

"Your father?"

"Same thing. He probably knows, but if I try to bring up the subject, he switches off. Like *that*," she said snapping her fingers.

Neil looked down the length of the table—tables, as he realized there were three of them lined up end to end. "All of these boxes—"

"Yes, each one contains several masks."

"Do you take care of them?"

"Ah, good question, my lover." Marisa was still holding the mask in her hands. "Hugo and I are the only ones who have ever even looked at them in the last fifty years, yet this is how they are. The temperature and moisture in the air here must be just right. And wax is a remarkable substance in the right conditions. It doesn't change."

"Fifty years. God. It does feel a little oily."

"Yes," she agreed quickly. "I think they were conditioned or rubbed with some kind of plant oil to help preserve them this way."

Marisa laid the mask back in the wooden box and arranged the cover sheet over it. She closed the lid and fastened the hasp, and then looked up at Neil with a quizzical expression on her face.

"I was a history student at university," she said. "You write about history. But do you have any idea how much history is here, in this cellar? I mean real history? What they saw, what they lived through?"

"Look at them," Neil said, his voice suddenly loud. "Your parents and grandparents, all still alive. All that history. You should get them to tell you about it, everything they can remember. Write it down, or better yet, get it on tape. Marisa, you can still do this."

"Ah, they won't talk," she said with a shrug of resignation. Then she smiled again. "Come on, we're not there yet."

BETWEEN SLEEP AND DEATH

They only had to go a short distance farther. Neil noticed that they were nearing one of the outer walls of the cellar. The dark expanse of rock loomed above them, and it was laced with alkaline encrustations, which in certain places appeared to glow with a faint greenish phosphorescence. Neil could only wonder at the age of the house and the labor that must have been involved in the construction of the cellar walls alone.

They stepped out of the shadows and stood beneath a light bulb in a small clear area in front of what looked exactly like a miniature house. There were two wooden steps up to the narrow door, on either side of which was a tiny square window. The house was only about eight feet wide and not quite twice that in length. The back end stood flush against the cellar wall.

"This was one of the wagons they used a hundred years ago," Marisa told him. "Probably long before that too. Who knows."

"A wagon?" Neil was surprised, but then he could see that it made perfect sense. He saw where the wheels had been, and that the front steps, as he first thought of them, were in fact where the driver would sit when they were traveling. The house was painted in blue and gold and the curved roof was red—at one time it must have been very bright and eye-catching, Neil thought. There *was* even a small but ornate overhang above the door. It was a relic of history, as Marisa had said. Neil could easily imagine a train of these wagons making their way over the unpaved roads of a Europe that had long since vanished.

Marisa seemed to sense what he was thinking, and said nothing for a moment. Neil was still taking in details, like the small wooden box fastened beneath each window, to hold a flower pot.

"It's astonishing how much they brought over," he remarked. "I don't know how they ever managed it."

"They were lucky to get out," Marisa replied. "They told me it was the end of the war, but I believe they must have started long before that. They probably began sending the wagons overland at least a year before. And how they managed it, that's simple. They bribed their way."

"Oh, of course."

"Gold, jewels."

"You must try to get them to tell you more," Neil said. "The details, what it was like every day and night for them. Real history is not just in the big events, but in what ordinary people lived through. You should do it, not necessarily because you want to do anything with it, like turn it into a book, but for yourself. For you to know."

"Yes, I should." Marisa turned to a small table nearby. She took a wooden match and lit a candle. No electricity inside.

Neil followed her up the two steps. She opened the door and went in. She put the candle on a shelf and then lit a couple of others that were already placed around the

room. Neil had to duck his head to get inside. One of the candles must have been scented because he immediately noticed the fragrance of lavender in the air.

"Close the door," she said, smiling broadly. "Take your shoes and socks off, make yourself at home."

Neil slid the bolt in place—this door actually locked. Marisa pulled the tiny curtains across the windows.

The floor inside the wagon was covered with an old oriental carpet. There was almost no furniture, just a small low table surrounded by cushions and pillows—dozens of them, in various sizes and colors. On the table was a bottle of wine, already opened, with the cork sitting loosely in place, two glasses and a platter of antipasto covered with a glass lid. There was even a shallow bowl of water filled with floating purple flowers.

It all reminded Neil of the way that some guys he had known would prepare their apartment when they were having a girl in for the evening. But here—in this dismal pit of a cellar beneath an old house out in the middle of nowhere. His poor Marisa. It was touching, but ultimately so sad. And yet, Neil was happy to be there with her.

"It's great," he said. "You must have done a lot of work."

Marisa gestured as if she were wiping her brow, and then stifling a big yawn. "You had a nap today. I didn't!"

"Ah, baby. Let me pour you some wine."

"That sounds very good."

They stretched out together on the pillows, half-sitting, resting back, their bodies touching, Neil's arm around her shoulder. He unbuttoned her blouse enough so that he could slip his hand inside and hold her breast.

"Mmmm."

They relaxed like that in silence for a few moments. Neil was still thinking of how to phrase what he wanted to say to her when Marisa began to speak, her voice quiet, reflective.

"Do you believe in life after death?"

"What?"

"I mean, my family does. They're devout Catholics—more Catholic than the Pope, my uncle always says—and they believe in life eternal through Christ. I was just wondering, do you?"

"I was raised a Catholic too."

"And?"

Neil smiled, admiring the way she wouldn't let him dodge that one. "No, I stopped believing that a long time ago."

"Are you sure?"

"Well, yes. But you never really know. Until."

"Ah."

"Do you?"

"Do I what? Believe that?"

"Yes."

"Not the same way," Marisa said. "But I think maybe we do live on in another form. You know what I think it is like? Have you ever been just a bit awake, but still almost totally asleep? You have an awareness, but you feel like you have no body. You feel like you're floating in a vast ocean, but it's not water, it's not air. There's no color, nothing to see. You are just *being* there, and *there* is nowhere. You're alone. All alone. You don't see anything, you can't smell or hear anything. Nothing touches you, because you have no body. There is nothing you need, nothing you want. You don't even have any thoughts. No memories to please or hurt you. And yet you do have some kind of awareness. I don't know what other word to use. Awareness. Like, you know you exist. And you understand. Yourself. Everything. Your awareness encompasses all your memories and experiences, and more, but it isn't limited just to them, it never calls them up as scenes or words. Do you know what I mean? Your awareness is complete. In this—nothing. And the amazing part of it is, all you have is this awareness, but you are *content*. You can be this way forever, regardless of whether you're lying in a grave or your ashes were scattered to the wind. You still *are*, and you're content."

"What would be the point?" Neil asked after a moment.

Marisa laughed, dispelling the solemn mood. "We used to talk like this at the university, late at night. Student talk."

"That's all right. But I have no answers."

"Of course, nobody does. I was just talking, imagining out loud," she said apologetically. "I've gone so long without anyone to talk to."

"You have to get away from here."

Marisa propped herself up on one elbow. "Impossible."

"No, it's very possible."

"Never mind that now. Let's be bad. Let's fuck."

Neil smiled. He started to pull her to him to kiss her, but she slipped out of his arms, giggling. She crawled across his body and reached behind a large pillow for something on the floor. Neil ran his hand up her leg, stroking her thigh, his fingers teasing. She murmured happily and wiggled her feet in the air, but rolled off his lap and sat up.

"Here."

She was holding a wooden box. It was just like the ones on the tables outside that contained the masks.

FIGURES IN WAX

"I want to try something with you," she said, her eyes shining with promise and anticipation. "If you don't like it, that's okay."

"What is it?"

"You'll see!"

Marisa put the box down on a pillow beside them. She pulled her skirt up and swung her body so that her legs straddled his and she was facing him, half-sitting on his lap. She loved this position and so did he. Neil put his hands on her bare thighs for a moment, and then finished unbuttoning her blouse while she did the same with his shirt. She was wearing a half-bra that unhooked in front. She looked wildly sexy with her clothes hanging open like that. She kissed him teasingly, her mouth wet, her tongue dancing and licking lightly, but she pulled back every few seconds. She had his slacks open now. Her touch was tantalizing—again and again Marisa's fingers brushed slowly along his cock, and then moved away. Neil cupped her breasts in his hands, bending forward to suck and tug her hard nipples between his lips, teasing them with his tongue. Although they were still only playing—their eyes were open, smiling, widening, urging each other on—he was already completely caught up again in the long beautiful whirl of desire and arousal. But then she put her hands on his face, holding him for a moment.

"These are the most remarkable masks my great-grandfather ever made," Marisa said as she reached to open the box—Neil had almost forgotten about that box. "I put one of them on once. It was incredible. Now I want to do it again, with you. I want you to see what it's like."

It sounded kind of silly, but Neil shrugged. "Okay."

"Ah, my lover, I love your romantic soul."

"And I love yours."

Marisa carefully lifted a mask from the box. It was clearly unlike the one Neil had seen before, on the table outside the wagon. This mask hung in the air almost like some clingy, nearly transparent fabric. Marisa spread her fingers and the facial features in the mask became apparent. The eyes, nose and mouth were open, though little more than slits.

"Me first," she said.

Neil gave a short laugh. "Fine."

She tilted her head back slightly, closed her eyes and shook her hair away from her face. Then she raised the mask and let it fall gently into place on her skin. She blinked her eyes a couple of times and moved her lips open and shut, twisting them once or twice. She smiled at him. She looked almost the same, but different in some subtle way Neil couldn't immediately define. Younger? Her strong features even stronger, more dramatic? They wore these masks in Bible stories, he reminded himself. Like masks or makeup for opera singers, they were probably intended to heighten and emphasize certain basic character features or flaws for the benefit of an audience. With Marisa, he thought, the mask made her look even younger than she was, like a fierce, precocious teenager. Her expression seemed to convey even more forcefully the great depths of her powerful sensual nature.

Neil touched her cheek, and was astonished. It still felt like her skin, warm, soft and silky smooth, and yet he thought he could also feel some added vibrancy, like a wild hidden current that suddenly finds its outlet. The mask fit the contours of her face amazingly well.

Marisa picked up another mask and held it open for him. But before Neil would put it on he had to test it and make sure that it wouldn't trigger an asthmatic reaction. He thought of wax as essentially odorless, but there was no way of knowing what chemicals might have been used in the preparation of the mask. He put his face close to it, and inhaled. Again, closer and more deeply the second time. Yes, there was something, but it was not the kind of chemicals Neil had feared. Mint? Anyhow, it was all right.

"It's hard to believe this is actually wax," he said. "It's so fine and supple. It's almost as thin as plastic wrap, but it has body."

"I know, but there are dozens of different kinds of wax in nature and they are very adaptable. Are you ready?"

"Sure."

Marisa helped him position the mask over his face. It seemed to float in the air for a second before settling down on his skin. Neil blinked his eyes a couple of times—he could feel the mask close around them, but there was no impairment or discomfort. He touched his eyebrows—he could feel the mask over them, yet at the same time Neil had the illusion of touching the hair itself. It was remarkable, just as Marisa had said.

Now he caught the essence of the mask in his nostrils and mouth. He thought he detected a sweetness, like honey. As in honey, bees and beeswax? That made sense.

Something else, stronger than any of the mints. It had to be wintergreen, Neil thought. He could almost feel it shooting light into dormant and dark corners of his brain, it was so invigorating and stimulating.

Marisa ran her fingertips over his face, smoothing down a few loose parts of the mask. Her touch was exquisite, setting off tiny flares of pleasure in his skin. She smiled when she saw him react.

"Are you all right?"

"Fine," he replied.

"Are you sure?"

"Oh yes," he said emphatically.

Her face was very close to his. She touched his lips, licking along them slowly—Neil trembled with sudden delight. Her breath seemed to enter his pores. It was soft and sweet, as delicious as the air on a beautiful summer night.

"You don't want to take it off?"

"No ... not yet ... and don't stop what you're doing ..."

"I haven't even started." Marisa took his lower lip between her teeth and bit until it began to hurt him, and then she pressed it tenderly between her wet lips for just a moment before releasing him. Anticipation ...

She kissed him hard and pushed him back on the pillows, her tongue thrusting into his mouth, and it felt like their faces were merging, possessed of each other in brilliant consuming flames of desire. Energy and hunger for her roared through him, every nerve in his body seemed to pulse and buzz anxiously. He rolled Marisa over onto her back and then broke their kiss as he pulled her blouse wide open to get at her breasts, rubbing them with his face—it felt like a wonderful shower of sensation in their skin, a cascading rain of pleasure. She wrapped her legs around him and dug her heels into his backside, pulling him into her as she cried out, urging him on, her voice loud, becoming a long staccato shriek that filled the little room.

Their bodies glowed like hot coals. Everything seemed so vivid to Neil, the infinite beauty of the way their bodies fit together and how they felt in the perfect peace and silence afterward. But Marisa could not wait more than a couple of minutes. He was still in her, his face on her shoulder. She gently turned his head a little so that he could see her eyes.

"My lover."

"Mmm …"

"Now, tell me."

"Tell you what?"

"Wasn't that the best fuck you ever had?"

She put her hand over her mouth, as if she'd said something naughty, but it didn't hide her impish smile.

Neil laughed. "By far," he answered truthfully.

"But, no." Marisa shook her head contrarily. "I don't think so. The *next* one is."

She slid out from under him and sat up. He saw her hand reach back to the wooden box. Too soon, he was thinking in a haze. I'm thirty-five, not nineteen. She had another mask in her hand. She reached between his legs and began to stroke him with it.

She was right.

Neil had no idea what time it was when he awoke, but it was so quiet that he could hear one of the candles guttering. He felt cold. Then he looked around and discovered that he was alone in the wagon. His face felt tight and somehow unnatural—the mask, he remembered. He pulled at it and he could feel it with his fingertips, but he couldn't get ahold of it.

"Marisa?"

Perhaps there was a back room—but no, as soon as he looked he saw that there was a rear door, but no other compartment in the wagon. He was alone. Neil stood up, still plucking at the mask. He thought he could feel the edge of it, but his attempts to push or roll it back failed.

"Marisa!"

It was a trick, just the kind of thing she would do. To tease him. He could imagine her laughing, then acting sheepish, the naughty girl. He would undoubtedly forgive her, but right now he felt angry. It seemed impossible to get the mask off his face. She would know how to do it, some simple method, or perhaps you had to use a liquid solution of some sort.

He tried the door, but the bolt wouldn't move—it was rusted in place and didn't budge. Neil kicked at it repeatedly, until he was out of breath. He stood in the little room, gasping, trying to think.

The mask felt hot and very tight on his face—it seemed almost to be alive in itself. On him. He tore at it in a rage, trying to dig his nails into it and rip it away. Neil felt the sudden raking pain in his cheek. It was as if he were scratching deeply into his own skin, but his fingers slid uselessly along the smooth, unyielding surface of the mask.

BY THE RIVER SAVA

The wagon rocked. The rear door splintered, tore loose and crashed to the floor. Neil was stunned. He had no idea at all what was happening. He could only stand there and gape at the sudden terrifying eruption of noise and violence. Three men in dark uniforms rushed through the open doorway. Two of them carried pistols, while the third had a short, wide-blade sword. Their boots thudded heavily. The men shouted angrily at him in a language he didn't understand, though it did sound familiar to him, probably the language of Marisa's parents.

Neil had no doubt that they meant to kill him. Fear paralyzed him, but he opened his mouth to protest. The first man hit him hard across the side of the head with the butt of his gun. Neil was dazed and fell against one of the side walls. Before he could recover his balance, two of the men set on him. They pummeled him about the head and face with their weapons. Neil held his arms up in an attempt to ward off the flurry of blows. The men kicked at him, yanked him across the room, and flung him out the door.

Neil flew through the air and landed painfully on hard rough ground. He was outdoors. He moaned and couldn't move for a minute. His head was pounding and he could taste his own blood in his mouth, but—absurdly—his mind still tried to calculate: the rear of the wagon had been backed up against the cellar wall, so there had to be an entrance to the outside there that he had not been able to see, one large enough to admit wagons, and—

But the immediate reality overwhelmed attempts at thought. Someone kicked him again. Neil jumped to his feet.

The night air was full of shouting voices, loud cries and sporadic gunfire. He saw that he was in a group of a dozen or so men. They were in an open area, a kind of courtyard bordered by wooden barn-like buildings—none of which resembled Marisa's house. The area was illuminated by a few street lamps mounted on wooden poles and by some rooftop spotlights that slowly swept through the darkness. The armed men in uniform—were they the police, or soldiers?—quickly herded Neil's group across the square. He saw a similar group of men ahead of them—but then it vanished into an alley between two buildings.

One of the men near Neil suddenly stumbled and lunged a couple of paces out of the group, trying to regain his balance. A guard stepped toward him and almost casually stuck his knife out, into the man's throat. The man fell, gagging, spurting blood and clutching uselessly at his throat. The guard stood over him and shot him once in the back of the neck. The man's thick hair fanned like wheat in a sudden gust of wind. He fell flat on his face and didn't move again.

Neil's eyes frantically scanned the area as he ran with the others. He saw numerous bodies on the ground. Off to one side a man struggled with a guard, but two other guards hastened to converge on him, and he fell beneath a torrent of knife thrusts. Then the first guard stomped on the man's throat several times with his boot.

The narrow alley was directly in front of them. The guards smoothly funneled Neil's group into the dark passage with more angry shouts and kicks, and by jabbing at them with their knives. At the other end, twenty or thirty yards ahead, another cluster of guards took control of the group and marched them across a much larger piece of open ground—though it was not actually open, Neil realized, when he saw the barbed wire fencing. The area was lit by more spotlights and several scattered bonfires. A three-quarters moon emerged from behind some clouds and added to the garish lighting. He saw a wide ribbon of water in the distance. For an instant he could even see that it was moving—a river.

But nearer, all around, were the bodies of dead men.

Neil and the others were made to lie face down on the ground. Here every guard—and there were many more of them—carried both a pistol and either a sword or a club. One man raised his head to look around and a guard swiftly stepped in and kicked the man in the face. Neil was careful, moving his head only fractions of an inch at a time to see as much as he could of what was happening. A kind of low-level pandemonium reigned. No one seemed to be in charge, but it was obviously a killing ground.

Suddenly Neil had to restrain himself to keep from shouting because he recognized someone. He had a clear view as two guards were leading a man past Neil's group—it was the same man who had brought the water for the radiator of Neil's car the other day. Perhaps he ought to shout to the man, even if it brought some punishment. The man would recognize him, perhaps he would say something, tell someone—but then the man and the two guards disappeared from sight.

Now someone from Neil's group was hauled to his feet and brought a few yards ahead, where he was engaged in an apparently heated conversation with three of the guards. He was a young man, in his twenties. He repeatedly shook his head at whatever the guards were saying. Then a priest arrived on the scene. Neil again wanted to shout—an instinct learned in childhood, that you can always turn to a priest for help. But it was so startling to see one in all of this madness—what was he doing there? The priest spoke briefly with him, and then walked briskly away.

The guards immediately began to stab and hack at the young man with their swords, slicing off pieces of his shirt and chunks of flesh from his back and arms. One of them pushed a knife into the man's midsection and slashed downward, spilling organs in a huge gush of blood. His scream was cut off when another guard swung a club and smashed it into his mouth, sending teeth and more blood through the air. The helpless man was still twitching wildly and gasping raggedly as they dragged him out of sight. Neil turned his face downward and away.

What lunacy was this? He knew from the sharp grit

pressing against his face on the ground that it was no dream, no hallucination, and yet his mind did not seem to be functioning clearly. He'd been in the wagon with Marisa, they had put on the masks and made love—twice, three times? But then Neil realized he still had the mask on his face, he could feel it there again, tight on his skin, the taste of honey and wintergreen. He reached to touch it, to pull at it—a club blow on the side of the head rocked him.

A few moments later, when he opened his eyes, he saw a priest again, but a different kind of priest. Eastern or Greek Orthodox, perhaps. He was fifty or sixty feet away, he had an unusual hat or vestment on his head, and his beard was full and squarish. The guards were talking to him in an animated fashion but the priest simply ignored them. He looked about forty years old. He didn't move or acknowledge the guards in any way. His eyes remained locked onto an invisible point no one else could see—the priest appeared to be focused entirely on his own thoughts.

One of the guards suddenly grabbed the priest's beard and hacked at it with a knife. Patches of wet redness opened on his face, but he sat still and had the same distant, stoic look in his eyes. The others were laughing along with this or else silently watching with smirks of mild amusement. After the guard had slashed off several chunks of hair and skin, he stepped behind the priest, knocked the headpiece off, pulled the man's head back by the hair and slowly dug a knife through his throat. The priest's eyelids fluttered open and closed a few times, then remained half open. After a few moments, when the eruption of blood slowed, the guard dug in harder with the knife. He couldn't manage it and became increasingly angry. Then one of the other guards came up with a hatchet and attacked the back of the neck, where the spinal cord and the brain meet, and after a few swings—flesh in the air like chips of wood—the priest's head was finally cut loose. The guard shouted happily and held it in the air, while the body sagged and toppled to the ground.

Think. Try to think. If I could only think—

He was aware of others in the group being moved, lifted up

and taken somewhere beyond his line of vision, one at a time. Neil thought again of the man who was supposed to fix his car. Was he a prisoner too, like the rest of them? Or was he with—

A shout and a painful kick in the ribs told Neil it was his turn. He got up, feeling certain that he was about to experience his own death. He had no idea why, and there was apparently nothing he could do about it but go along with it. As two guards pushed and steered him roughly, Neil wondered if he could somehow break free, run and dodge their bullets. Run toward the river and escape? But he had already seen others try that and he knew that it would be a pointless gesture.

They passed a small group of guards tormenting a man who staggered blindly in circles. His hands were tied behind his back. The guards had put a strange wooden box with bolts and leather straps over the man's head. It seemed to fit tightly and was probably smothering him. They cut his belt and tugged his pants down, and then jabbed their knives at his genitals. The man jumped and twisted, trying vainly to avoid each cutting thrust, but he couldn't see anything. His cries were muffled by the wooden box. The last glimpse Neil had— one guard was furiously slashing off a thick strip of flesh from the doomed man's pale buttocks.

A short distance farther, they came to a large cluster of guards. The circle parted to admit them and Neil was held tightly by two guards. He was allowed to watch a teenage boy, who seemed to be begging for his life. Neil couldn't see the people the youth was addressing, but he saw the desperation in his face. The boy made the sign of the cross, bowed his head, looked up hopefully and invoked the name of Jesus Christ, and then repeated the same sequence of gestures and words. One of the guards nudged Neil and nodded, as if to say that this was what he would be expected to do. Neil assumed that it meant he was to make his peace with God before he died.

The crowd tightened and necks craned, and Neil couldn't see what was happening. Everyone was quiet, but one voiced intoned softly. Then the guards began to laugh and clap, and suddenly Neil saw the boy's face again. He stood up, smiling cautiously. For just a moment, an air of bizarre gaiety seemed to prevail. But then two guards seized the boy. A third one held him tightly by the hair, pulling his head back. A fourth stepped forward to hit the boy's face with a metal tool—pliers. As soon as the boy's mouth opened, the guard clamped the pliers on his tongue. The boy struggled and tried to close his mouth, but couldn't do anything. With his other hand, the guard carefully slipped the blade of a knife between the boy's teeth. One of the other guards kicked the boy in the groin to make things easier. The boy's mouth opened wider involuntarily and he gave a strangled cry. The guard quickly flicked his wrist and came away with the boy's tongue in the pliers. This brought an enthusiastic burst of applause and more cheers. The boy was dragged off, his mouth foaming red, and a few seconds later Neil heard a gunshot.

Then he was hauled around to the center of the circle and flung to the ground. In front of him, torn and muddied, covered with gobs of spit, was a book in some unrecognizable language. Neil tried to think. The script was Cyrillic, he knew that much. When he looked up, Neil saw Marisa's uncle, Father Anton, smiling down at him.

The priest showed no sign of recognition. He was speaking softly and calmly, his hands making small gestures in the air, as if explaining things. When he finished, he pointed down to the book on the ground. Father Anton gazed at him with implacable indifference. Neil sensed that he had just a few seconds to reach some decision, and he understood. Marisa told him that her uncle was doing a study on conversions. That's what this was, a conversion. He was expected to renounce the book on the ground, whatever it was, and to proclaim his faith and allegiance to the one true Church.

The teenage boy—so that was what he had done. He had given in, he had renounced his faith, spit on the book and sworn himself to Christ. That's why they had cheered. But then they had cut out his tongue. Why? Probably so that he would not be able to recant—in the brief moment when he saw the pistol being aimed at him.

"*Padre Anton,*" Neil said anxiously. "*Padre Panic. Sono gia un cattolico.*"

The priest registered mild surprise, perhaps at both the words and the use of the Italian language. Neil could sense a flutter of curiosity among the guards around him, who fell silent and edged closer.

"*Sono gia un cattolico*" he repeated firmly. "*Dove e Marisa*? She will tell you. I'm a friend of hers." That involuntary lapse into English only seemed to confuse the priest. "*Devo vedere Marisa! Dove e Marisa, il mio amico, il mio caro?*"

Father Anton laughed as if he had just heard something ridiculous. A young man elbowed his way through the circle of guards and stood over Neil, who recognized him immediately—here was the person he had seen lying in the alcove bunk, in the house. Now this handsome young man glared at Neil. He wore a black leather coat over a gray suit. He swung his arm back. Neil saw the blackjack coming all the way.

Wow, a genuine leather blackjack—he thought, before it hit his head and sent his brain reeling into darkness—imagine that

STARA GRADISKA

The moon danced wildly in the sky above him. He was still there. He could hear the shouts, the screams, the random gunshots. His head rolled painfully on bare boards. A dark building floated by, then a tower. He was moving—he was being taken somewhere. When Neil finally got his eyes to focus he saw that he was lying in the back of a small open truck. It was kind of like an old army jeep. The driver and an armed guard sat a couple of feet away, in front of him. They passed a bottle back and forth between them and were talking loudly. Neil closed his eyes when he saw the guard start to turn his head to look back and check on him.

His head throbbed and his body ached, and every bounce on the dirt road only added to his pains. But they were nothing compared to what he had already seen there. He felt charged with fear and impatience—his body was shrieking at him. He had to act fast and somehow get away.

The vehicle slowed and turned a corner. The buildings on either side were dark or dimly lit. They seemed to be in a part of the place where there were few people about at present. As the jeep gathered speed again, Neil pushed himself up with his feet and slipped over the side. He rolled on the ground, got some balance and rushed toward the shadows. A few seconds later he heard the squeal of brakes and a shout, just as he ducked around the corner. The unhappy sound of reverse gear.

Neil looked around. He was in another patch of open ground that was surrounded by ramshackle two-story wooden buildings. Spotlights swept the area methodically. He could see more guards stationed or walking patrol, no matter which direction he turned. There was nowhere to go, they would grab him in a minute if he tried to flee.

The building beside him was dark—and the door opened when Neil tried it. He slipped inside. There was no lock, but he was out of sight for the moment. He knew it was only a temporary refuge. Sooner or later he would be found if he stayed there. Then he heard a loud noise and felt the building shake briefly. The driver and guard were cursing unintelligibly, and then they began to laugh. In trying to take the corner they had backed into the building itself. From the window, he saw them glancing around. Then they drove off, apparently deciding that someone else would catch Neil.

He was safe, for now. He sank to the floor and sat in the darkness. It felt good to rest his back against the wall, to be alone. But his mind was still swarming with unbearable images and raging confusion.

And then he became aware of the mask again. It was still on his face. As soon as he thought about it, he could feel it seem to tighten, choking his pores as if it were trying to enter his body through his skin. Suppressing panic for a moment, Neil tried again to remove it. Be calm, he told himself, find an edge and work it back. But he got nowhere with it. He could feel his fingertips on it, he could even make a small portion of it move slightly—but then it always slipped away from his hand and back in place. It was impossibly filmy to his touch, but on his face it felt heavy and oppressive.

He finally gave up, sobbing once out loud and banging his head back against the wall in frustration.

Someone laughed.

Neil froze. The shocking human sound had come from only a few feet away. He could hardly think at all now, let alone know what to do. He heard the soft pat of childlike footsteps on the floor, followed by a very loud click, and then an overhead light went on. There were piles of clothes everywhere, the floor dotted with random heaps of them. Nothing but clothes. The woman grinning hideously at Neil was the same dwarf he had seen on the balustrade when he arrived at Marisa's house.

She was one of them, she would alert the guards—

The woman read his panic and immediately made calming gestures to stop him from doing anything foolish. Neil was thinking that he ought to kill her and turn the light off. Her voice sounded like that of a toy doll, but there was something soothing in her tone. She held her finger to her lips. Neil sat where he was. It occurred to him that he was dead anyway, so what was the point of resisting, much less killing someone else? He felt tired. All of the energy he had somehow summoned up in escaping from the guards and then hiding in this barn-like building was now gone. His head ached and the mask felt like a huge clamp on his face. Let it be. Roll into it.

Noise, the sound of activity outside. The woman went to the window to take a look, then quickly turned away. She gestured with her hand for Neil to follow her. They went up a large, open flight of stairs to the second floor, which was covered with more mounds of clothing. There was no sorting, no order, just random tilting piles of ordinary clothes, as if they had simply been thrown down where they were.

The woman kept gesturing and Neil followed her to the front side of the building. There were two windows overlooking the open ground outside. She went to one and pointed Neil to the other. He no longer thought of her as a threat to him, and yet he didn't feel that she was a friend or ally. This place was like a concentration camp, but without the Nazis. The dwarf woman was perhaps a prisoner, but one allowed to live because of the work she did with these clothes, or because someone liked her—some insane reason. He didn't know, he had no idea, just fleeting guesses.

Why was he there?

Dozens of guards had assembled in the yard outside. The spotlights were fixed, illuminating the whole area in a harsh light. Everyone seemed to be standing around expectantly. Neil could feel the sense of something about to happen, and yet it was such an utterly barren scene—his novelist's instinct found it completely unworthy. Of anything.

A moment later, three large trucks arrived, each one full of women. They ranged from teenagers to the elderly. The guards immediately swung into action, pulling or flinging the women off the trucks. The older women were dealt with summarily, either shot in the head, stabbed or clubbed to the ground. Within moments, there were bodies everywhere and the spurious air of order had given way to chaos and mayhem.

It was worse for middle-aged women. Guards hacked at their skulls with axes, chopping off clumps of hair and flesh. They were pulled out of their clothes, beaten, slashed and kicked. Long knives or wide swords were inserted into them, then twisted, and yanked. Pistols were roughly forced into their mouths, vaginas or anuses, and then fired. Ears and noses were slashed off before their deliverance.

Neil sagged against the window frame. He gazed at the guards who were doing all of this. They didn't look angry, so much as determined. Like homeowners who had a job to do, because they could not bear to live with a certain pest. Whether you sprayed them in groups or crushed them beneath your heel one at a time, they had to go.

Two guards held a woman face down on the ground. Another guard pulled her hair so that her head was raised up a few inches. A fourth guard came and stood over her. He had some tool in his hand. A saw. He began to saw the back of her neck, like a log. The woman's body quivered like wire strung too tight, electric, and then collapsed. The guard swung her loose head and rolled it away like a bowling ball.

The youngest fared worst of all, their breasts hacked off, knives thrust into them, their loins doused with gasoline and set afire. Or they were fucked first, repeatedly, until someone decided they were no longer worthy. He saw one girl held bent over at the waist and entered from behind. When the guard in her was about to climax, he waved his fingers excitedly in the air. Another guard stepped up, swung a hatchet and decapitated the girl. It wasn't clean, it took three blows, but that only seemed to enhance the pleasure of the one who was coming in her. Then the guard with the bloody hatchet held up the girl's head and pushed her lips back to expose her teeth—evoking loud cheers and laughter. She had long straight hair, parted in the middle. A style that would fit in easily in Rome, Paris, London, New York or San Francisco.

Neil turned to the dwarf woman perched on a pile of clothes at the other window. It was as if he wasn't there. Her expression was blank, but she was totally caught up in what she was seeing. She gazed outward, like someone watching the crucial scene in a gripping movie. Understandable, and yet—how could *anyone* watch *that*?

Neil had felt such fear, but now he saw fear as something shallow, a surface ripple. In his blood and in his bones, in his whole body, he felt his own death now, and he knew it didn't matter. Not even to him.

He looked outside once more. It was like a Bosch painting, except that Bosch lacked the imagination or nerve for this horror. In some forlorn part of his brain Neil heard Abba singing "Fernando" in a tinny voice. And there, almost directly below him—he saw Marisa. She was watching the scene, close up. She was in a group of six or eight people, all of whom wore civilian garb. She had on a long black dress and leather coat. Her hair was done up in braids that were coiled tightly to her head.

Marisa ...

The dwarf woman gagged and giggled.

Marisa turned and rested her head on the shoulder of the young man standing beside her. His arm went around her, then rubbed her shoulders and back comfortingly. She looked up and he kissed her. No doubt about it, Neil was certain that it was the young man he had seen in the alcove, the same one who had knocked him out with a blackjack.

A little implosion, that's all.

Opera.

Neil turned and ran.

MISERERE

As if he should be surprised! Neil felt angry at himself. He had seen Father Anton at work. If her uncle, a priest, could be implicated in this, how could Marisa not be? Still, it was crushing to see her out there, calmly taking everything in. Kissing her lover. Was that Hugo?

The dwarf woman called out to him. Neil's foot snagged and he fell onto a large pile of clothing. He rolled over and came to rest, lying on his back. For a moment he thought he might never move again. He wanted only to remain there, burrowing in, hiding in the drifts of old clothes. He inhaled deeply. He could detect the whole range of human smells that lingered in the dresses, skirts and blouses, even terror and death.

He closed his eyes, allowing himself to imagine for just a second that when he opened them again he would be somewhere else. In the Italy that he knew. In his car, which worked. On a road, to somewhere.

But where was the house, where was his car?

What had happened to him?

He opened his eyes and saw the dwarf woman smiling down at him. But she wagged her finger and shook her head. Neil understood. She was right. If he just ran impulsively like that, he would inevitably give himself away and soon be captured. That wasn't the way to do it. Neil nodded in agreement and almost managed a faint smile.

She had seemed positively deranged the first time he had encountered her, but now he understood the mad, antic gleam in her eyes, the grinning and harsh laughter. He was where she lived.

The woman took his thumb in her pudgy little hand and tugged. Neil pushed himself to his feet. Outside, the screams and gunshots continued. He followed the woman through the mounds of clothing, toward the back of the upper room. It was much darker there, no windows, no electric light. They came to a door in the side wall. She opened it. Neil saw stairs disappearing down into complete darkness. No, he didn't like that.

The woman made a series of gestures, and Neil realized that she was trying to give him directions, to tell him which way to go. To escape? What else could it be? She would have called the guards and turned him in by now if that was her intention. She pointed to the front of the room and held her hand to her ear—Neil noticed that the sounds of the bloody rampage outside were slowly diminishing. The woman was telling him to hurry now, while so many of the guards were still preoccupied. This was his best opportunity. Okay, he understood. The directions were simple, which probably meant that his chances were almost nil. But he would try.

He stepped through the doorway and turned to nod appreciatively to the woman. Her head bobbed, she waved, urging him to go, and she closed the door. Neil put his hand on the wall and made his way slowly down the stairs in complete darkness. He had no trouble and he found the door at the bottom. He listened carefully for a few seconds, and heard nothing but the muffled sounds from outside.

The door opened directly into the adjacent building. The room was dark, but enough light penetrated from the front windows. Neil saw that this building was almost identical to the one he had just left. A large room and piles of clothing—though they were smaller and fewer in number. He moved quickly to the far side of the room, at the back. He found the next door that he was looking for, but it wasn't where it was supposed to be. He expected to find a door that would let him out at the rear of the building, but this door was in the side wall again and it clearly led into the next building. Neil wondered if he had misunderstood the woman. He must have. Well, he had no choice but to go on.

The ground floor room in the next building contained

dozens of bunks, cots and bed mats on the floor. They looked too mean and wretched to be for the guards. But there were no inmates, the beds were all empty. The room was bathed in the same eerie gray-white light from outside. Neil hurried to the other rear corner. He groaned aloud when he discovered that once again the door was in the side wall. Then he noticed the quiet—there was no more gunfire. He had to keep going, and hurry.

He opened the door a crack and saw that there were lights on in the next room. His view was blocked by a wood partition. He opened the door a little more and eased himself quietly inside. There was a strong smell of alcohol in the air. Then he heard the sound of someone moving about. Neil had never fought with anybody in his life, not even in grammar school in Southie—a remarkable but, he sometimes felt, dubious achievement. One person he could deal with—*maybe*. Two or more? Ha ha.

Then he saw it, on the other side of the room—the door in the back wall, the door he needed, to get outside. It was about thirty feet away. Neil stared at it. The floor was bare, aside from a few small wood crates and boxes lying about. There was nothing at all between him and the door that he could crawl behind or use to hide himself if he had to.

Neil moved carefully and slowly, testing each step, edging along the partition. The sounds he heard were slight, impossible to figure. He inched his face along the wood. Then a sigh, and a woman's voice, just a few words that were answered briefly by another woman. Neil was puzzled by this, but also vaguely encouraged. If these women were prisoners too, like the dwarf, they might be willing to help him.

Neil crouched and slowly expanded his angle of vision into the room. He saw some worktables that were cluttered with jars, boxes, hand tools and clumps of packing straw. Then the back of a woman's head came into view, gray hair tied up in a bun. She was seated on the other side of the tables, her back to Neil.

He leaned a little farther beyond the partition and saw the other woman, also gray-haired. She was bent over, apparently engaged in some chore. She was about ten feet away from the woman seated by the tables. Two older women. It occurred to Neil that they could be sorting out and packing up any valuables taken from the victims, like coins and rings. If that was the case, there might well be a guard in the room, watching them, still out of Neil's sight.

But then the woman straightened up and he recognized her as one of Marisa's relatives, her mother or one of her grandmothers. So the other one, with her back to Neil, was probably also a relative. Of course, they were all in on this madness. That seemed to make it a little less likely that there was a guard with them.

Neil took a deep breath and stepped around the partition—it was the back wall of some wooden shelves. He scanned the room quickly, saw that there was no guard, just the two women. He moved around the worktables. There were no front windows—an unexpected help. The women looked at him, then at each other, and they began to laugh. Neil stopped as if he had run into a brick wall. The open floor of the large room was strewn with the dead bodies of small children. There were dozens of them, boys and girls, infants and toddlers, some dressed, some naked, their skin color ranging from bone white to a pale gray-blue.

The old woman who was seated on a long bench was the grandmother who had been sharpening fruit spoons. In fact, she had one of those spoons in her hand now. On the bench beside her was the body of a small girl, her head resting on the woman's lap. They were laughing louder now. The woman pushed the girl's eyelid back and deftly used the spoon to scoop out the eye, which she then held out for Neil to see. He couldn't move. Then she reached toward the table, turned the spoon and dropped the eye into a large glass jar of clear liquid—the alcohol. There were already dozens of eyes in the jar, like shiny blue and brown pearls. Neil saw two other jars on the table, full and capped. He looked at the bodies on the floor and saw those that had been done—their empty eye sockets dark, thin strands of fleshy membrane trailing across their faces. And the rest, all around him, waiting.

He felt like a piece of ice, or stone, but he walked carefully toward the woman on the bench. She was still laughing, but her eyes were watchful. As he drew closer, she stood up and quickly scooted a few yards away. The child's head thumped on the bench, and then the body slid off. Neil went to the worktable. And there was grandma's favorite set of spoons, a dozen or fifteen of them, in different sizes. He took one in his hand and ran his finger along the edge. Sharp enough for the grisly work at hand, but was it sharp enough for him?

Neil put the spoon in his pocket and, without even glancing at the two women, went quickly to the back of the room. He opened the door, slipped outside and looked around. Arcs of light, moving zones of exposed ground. But there were also wide, shifting pockets of darkness, and Neil ran into the darkness. He expected to feel a bullet in his back at any moment. He kept running, veering off, swerving back, always hugging the darkness.

No alarms went off, no shots were fired, but Neil had a sense that he wasn't going to make it. His breath was ragged now, his chest and legs were tightening in pain, and a cramp was stitching through his abdomen. He kept on, gasping loudly but driving himself forward. Don't stop.

Then he hit the fence. Barbed wire raked across his scalp and dug into his throat, belly and thighs. He bounced back, hit the ground, and now he couldn't move. He couldn't even breathe. Flat on his back—there was the moon again. It wasn't his asthma, he realized. He'd had the wind knocked out of him, but that was all. Slowly his chest began to move again—oh, the sweet, sweet taste of air.

But he knew that the light would find him soon, he had to move. Neil dragged himself under the fence. Another twenty tortuous yards of dangerous open ground, and then he was in the woods, safe for the moment. He tried to follow the general direction the dwarf woman had indicated. Before long, however, he could sense the river nearby, and that was all he needed. For a few minutes he stumbled around, struggling in the darkness with thick brush, saplings and swampy ground underfoot. Finally, Neil found a clear patch of solid land at the water's edge. He sat down to let his body rest.

The idea was to swim to the other side and thereby escape. But what was on the other side? *Where* was the other side? The river looked so wide that he doubted he could make it across. What if he gave up and surrendered? If he begged to see Marisa, would she come?

Would she recognize him, and save his life? But Neil immediately felt a sense of shame and anger. How could he even consider that possibility? He had seen her world, and the only alternatives were to flee or to die.

He took the spoon out of his pocket and began to scrape his face with the edge of it. He dug in hard, not caring when he felt pain and his own fresh blood. Then the pain blossomed across his face and into his head, and he had a sense that he was breaking the mask in places. Hope electrified him and he gouged at his cheeks and chin and forehead even more energetically. It was like fire breaking out in his skin and then penetrating his brain. He bent over in agony. The spoon fell from his hand.

He saw the water in front of him and it looked so sweet and soothing. That was where he was supposed to go. The other side. He waded in and began to swim. Cold, too cold. But he didn't care. Neil swept his arms and kicked feebly. Then the body of a dead man bumped into him. He pushed it away, but another one bobbed against him, and another, and suddenly he saw that he was surrounded by countless bodies floating in the river. They moved slowly, drifting along at the edge of the current.

Go with them.

No ...

You're one of them.

No ...

You are. This is where pain ends.

No. Let someone else kill me. I want to see it happen. Neil turned and splashed his way back to land. He dragged himself under a clump of thick bushes and nestled close to the ground, curled up protectively. His face felt as if it had long jagged strips of raw exposed flesh. Had Neil broken the mask, ripped parts of it away? He couldn't tell. His brain wouldn't focus on anything, and that didn't even bother him. He didn't care anymore. He was so cold and wet, and he had nothing left.

REVIVAL

Neil shivered so violently it seemed as if his whole body was trying to shake itself to pieces. His clothes were wet, clinging to him. He felt the dank cold deep in his bones. His limbs were stiff and had no strength. He was on the ground, lying in tall grass.

Daylight. So much easier for someone to see him. At first he thought it was morning, but when he cautiously raised his head and looked around, Neil saw the big house—Marisa's house—shimmering with golden light. It must be late afternoon. He felt a tremendous sense of relief, but it was soon followed by a wave of confusion. How had he come to be there, outside the front of the house, and at this hour of the day? What had happened to him last night? Why had Marisa left him? Where was she?

The mask—fear and panic boiled up in Neil again as he realized that the mask was still on his face. For a brief moment, he had begun to consider the possibility that everything he'd experienced there had been nothing more than a long bizarre hallucination, or dream. That he had arrived there, fallen into a mysterious trance or had a brain seizure that somehow unleashed him on a journey into deep corners of his own subconscious mind. That seemed unlikely, and the presence of the mask disproved it.

Unless the mask was merely another imaginary sign of his continuing mental breakdown. Is this dementia?

Neil stood up and looked back, away from the house. He saw his car, still where he had left it. The hood was raised and the front end was partly dismantled. He moved a few steps to get a better angle and then he could see the radiator lying on the ground. That appeared to clinch it. There was no way Neil would have tried to take the radiator out by himself. He wasn't mechanically adept, he had no tools with him, and there was no point to it, especially in this remote spot. Someone else had done it, Marisa's workman, just as Neil remembered.

But he also noticed that the cluster of shacks and huts visible on the nearest ridge were half-collapsed, with doors gone or hanging loose, roofs caved in, all of them utterly dilapidated. No one lived or worked in them. And the grounds immediately around the house looked even more overgrown with weeds and brush than he seemed to remember—thick coils of brambles and briars sprawled about, slowly spreading, creating impenetrable thickets around the building.

The windows were gone—another small shock. The sun still caught the tiles and lit them brilliantly, but all of the windows were vacant, dark and empty rectangles in the face of the house. In some of the frames he could see jagged shards of glass that hadn't yet fallen away, but most of the glass was gone. So was the front door—not just open, but gone. The house stood open to the elements, and to anyone who happened to come there.

Like him. Neil walked along the crumbling balustrade, gazing at the old house and its surroundings. There was no sign of human life anywhere, nor any indication that there had been for many years. Again he wondered if he had somehow imagined everything—Marisa, her family, the workmen, the passion and fantastic sex, the billiards room, the cellar, the wagon, the horror and savagery he had seen. If only he had imagined all that. It was just a big crazy dream. Ha ha.

But how could he have conjured up all those peculiar details, like the bird skulls in the stew? And the sensory memories that were still so vivid to him—how it felt to be inside Marisa, the touch of her wet mouth on his skin? No, it wasn't possible. Besides, his car and the awful weight on his face told him it was something else, something unfinished.

Neil hesitated. He glanced back toward his car again. He could just walk away. Follow the gravel road until it brought him to another road, take that one and keep going until he either flagged down a passing car or reached the next town.

Then find a doctor—please take this thing off my face.

No. Not yet. He walked into the house. It was gloomy, but enough sunlight reached the interior for Neil to find his way around. Instead of going upstairs and trying to get to the bedroom where his things were, he began to check the ground floor rooms. The house was silent, except for the rush and swirl of the mountain wind as it blew through the corridors and passageways, which only added to the feeling of emptiness.

He went through several rooms that were almost bare, containing a few pieces of rotting furniture. The floors were littered with broken glass, gray grit, and mats of damp dust. Paper wasp nests clung to the upper walls, the empty ceiling fixtures and dangling sconces. Wide bands of wallpaper had peeled off and crumpled to the floors.

So far, everything he saw argued that the house had been abandoned years before. But he couldn't be sure yet. These might be some of the rooms that had been left unused by the family, as Marisa had explained to Neil. He was beginning to think that he would find nobody, but he also believed that he would find *something*—something that made sense of all this to him.

Then Neil opened a door and recognized the dining room. The long table and the sideboards were gone, but some of the chairs remained, dusty and scattered, lying on their sides. The wall tapestries were shredded and black with mildew. It was impossible to imagine that anyone had eaten there in years.

Neil walked quickly to the far end of the room, opened the door and made his way along the short, unlit passage. The windows in the billiards room were shuttered on the inside, but thin lines of fading daylight allowed him to make out various objects in the prevailing gloom. The billiards table was still there, and apparently in good condition. It startled Neil to see the sofa where he and Marisa had spent time. And the little television, the radio. Even their wineglasses—he stood frozen, staring at them. Finally, he went closer and lifted one. A small pool of red wine swirled at the bottom. Neil immediately recognized the strong tannic bouquet.

It was no dream or hallucination—none of what he had

seen—unless he was experiencing it all again. Or it had never ended. The mask was still on his face, after all. But the mask didn't explain anything. He'd encountered the dwarf woman, Marisa, the workers and servants, Marisa's family—all of that— well before they got to the masks. Neil felt like a dog chasing his own tail. It was a waste of time. It wasn't possible to make sense of experiences that seemed to arise from some lost pocket of reality, a place that had its own logic and reason—all of which escaped him. He had the irrational feeling of being caught in someone else's dream world. But that would mean he had no chance of escape, which he knew was absurd.

He turned the television on, but the screen stayed dark and there was no sound. The generator was off. He tried the radio, and the sexy, breathless voice of a woman singing in French squiggled out of nowhere. Neil laughed. There were batteries in the radio, and they still worked. He almost switched it off, but didn't. The radio station and the song reminded him that there was still an outside world. *His* world. He increased the volume, and it sounded good, it was like bright light and fresh air.

Neil picked up the box of matches Marisa had used and lit a candle. He carried it with him as he crossed the room and ascended the circular iron staircase to the second floor. In the corridor, he turned and made his way to the bedroom he had used. The door was closed. Before he tried to open it, he went into the bathroom. His toiletries were missing.

Neil looked in the mirror and saw himself—bruises and lumps on the side of the head, scratches, crusted spots of blood, all the signs and marks of what he had experienced. And his features were subtly different, younger and smoother, but also more drawn, tightened, as if with pain and deep inner hurt. He scared himself. The mask. He turned quickly away.

The bedroom was different. The furniture was still there, each item exactly where he remembered it. But there were no sheets on the bed and no blanket. Neil's things were gone—his overnight bag, the shirt and jeans he'd left out, the Rose Tremain novel he was reading—all gone.

Movement—he heard a sound outside. More than one— there were sounds in the house, both above and below him.

Neil cupped his hand around the candle and walked quickly back into the main corridor. He saw the faint blue glow down the corridor at once.

As he approached the alcove, one of the servant women came down the steps into the corridor and walked right past him without a glance, as if he didn't exist. Now he even heard the sound of people outside, carried through the open window at the end of the corridor. Nothing unusual, just the distant, ordinary sounds of people at work, talking among themselves.

The young man was in the bunk. The same young man he had seen the first time there, and who had struck him with a blackjack, and who had kissed Marisa at the scene of that unspeakable atrocity. But now he wore the black uniform Neil recognized. It was not the uniform of any police force or army, at least none that he could recognize, but it only seemed the more frightening for its lack of definition.

The young man's skin was bone white, puckering at the corners of his mouth and eyes. His body didn't move at all, there was no sign of breathing. Neil grasped one hand and felt for a pulse. Nothing. He let it drop back onto the black-clad shirt. The blue votive candle flames danced in a brief flick of the wind.

Neil was about to turn away, but he saw the young man's face seem to turn ruddier, flushed with sudden color. The slack skin on the face tightened, the chest rose slightly, and a soft sigh of breath broke the silence. Neil could not move. The eyes opened, and turned.

The handsome young man smiled as he reached for Neil.

ZUZU

Neil backed away instinctively, but then he noticed the expression on the face of Marisa's lover: his smile was warm and loving, his eyes were filled with—gratitude? His hands grasped feebly at Neil's arm and then his cold fingers brushed Neil's skin and rubbed his palm tenderly

Neil yanked his hand away The candle slipped out of his grip and was extinguished when it hit the floor. Now the tiny space was lit only by the votive candles, the air suddenly colored a chilly blue. He was fascinated and horrified by the look of pain and sorrow on the young man's face. It was as if he could not bear to be parted from Neil's touch.

Fear and hatred welled up within him. Neil lunged forward, grabbed the young man's throat and began to squeeze as hard as he could. But now Marisa's lover smiled gratefully up at him again. His eyes blazed with light, his smooth cheeks glowed with a rush of life and color. Neil felt a terrifying sensation, as if his own strength and energy were flowing through his hands, into the body of Marisa's lover, who was gaining vitality and starting to push himself up from the bunk.

Neil forced him back down, and moved away. A hand gripped his shoulder. He shook it off and spun around. Father Panic. The old priest grinned at him. Then he spread his arms wide and stepped closer, as if to take Neil in a comforting paternal embrace. The alcove seemed impossibly small, a death-box in which he was trapped. He could feel Marisa's lover behind him, clutching and tugging at his shirt.

He shoved the priest back against the wall in the landing and rushed past him, down the short flight of stairs, into the dark corridor. Neil's brain teemed with confused thoughts. It seemed as if his presence alone brought these people back. Were they real in themselves or was his deranged mind creating them before his very eyes? He had to get out of the house as fast as possible, and then far away from there.

"Ustashas!" Somewhere outside but close by, men shouted gleefully and triumphantly. "Ustashas! Ustashas!" Then he heard gunfire. Had war somehow broken out in Italy and fighting engulfed even this unlikely corner of the Marches? But that was an absurd idea. The madness was *here*, either a part of this house or a part of himself.

Neil felt trapped on the second floor. He heard the sounds of Father Panic and Marisa's lover in the alcove. The only sure quick way he knew to get out was back down the circular staircase into the billiards room. He shut the door tight and then descended the stairs as fast as he could. It wasn't until he reached the bottom step that he noticed that the lamps were all on and dozens of candles were lit, filling the room with a warm soft glow. As Neil walked slowly toward the bar he realized that all the shouts and sounds of movement about the house had vanished. The only thing he heard now was music, a dreamy mindless techno burble from the radio.

The television was on, but silent. A handsome young man wearing only pajama bottoms and a sexy young woman in a revealing nightie were talking, their faces and gestures overly expressive. The stage set was meant to suggest an expensively decorated ultra-modern bedroom, but everything was so polished and tidy that it resembled a display in a furniture store. An episode from an Italian soap opera, Neil thought absently. Then the pretty couple on the screen hurled themselves into each other's arms, pressed their bodies tightly in a feverish embrace, mashed their open mouths together and tumbled backward onto a huge bed.

Marisa was stretched out on the sofa. She was wearing only a black bra and a half-slip, and the large blue opal that hung from a ribbon at the base of her throat. Her hair was wild, her eyes shiny, her mouth wet. She raised one leg, bent at the knee, and held her hand out to him. Turn around now and leave, or stay forever. Neil sat down beside her.

"My lover ..."

"Take it off me."

"What?"

"The mask. Take it off my face."

"What mask? There is no mask."

"Please."

"Silly."

"Marisa, *please.*"

"Zuzu."

"Zuzu ..."

She smiled, caressing his cheek. "Kiss me."

"Let me go."

"No one is keeping you." She looked hurt, pouting, and she turned her face slightly to the side. "Go, if you want."

The sense of urgency and fear within him disappeared. He couldn't leave. She understood things he didn't, things he had to know. She was the only one who could show him the way—to anywhere, or nowhere. He felt as if he knew nothing, and she knew everything.

But even more than that, he wanted her again, he wanted to kiss her and touch her and enter her, be one with her. The room was golden, the air was sweet with her fragrance. He wanted to taste her again. He felt the heat from her body, like a deeply soothing radiance that reached into him, giving him comfort and peace. He put his hand on her thigh, his fingertips moving lightly over her beautiful skin.

She turned her head and smiled at him again. Neil kissed her and he felt her arms come around his shoulders. Their eyes closed as their tongues touched, their faces pressing together, skin to skin—mask to mask—and he felt once again as if they were a part of each other, sensation fusing them in a fire of infinite wholeness and pleasure.

He saw a child, a boy about seven or eight years old, dressed in rags, looking thin and frightened. Then a hand grabbed the boy's hair and jerked his head to one side.

Neil tried to open his eyes, but couldn't.

Marisa was dressed in black. She was the person holding

the boy by the hair. Her face alive, wild. She swung a ball peen hammer into the back of the boy's skull, the crack of bone creating a million screaming fractures in Neil's nerves and brain.

Zuzu's mouth sucked at his—and he had the distant, almost abstract sensation of flying slowly into her.

The boy's blinking and vacant eyes were replaced by those of a girl about the same age. Her round face was gaunt and hollow. Her eyes closed and she turned her face away slightly, and then Marisa drove the axe blade into the back of the girl's neck, at the top of the spine.

He still couldn't open his eyes, nor could he pull his face away from hers. His body churned and he kicked violently. He pushed against her and rolled away, peeling her arms off him. His face felt as if it were being eaten and burned with acid as he broke away from her and fell off the sofa. Neil quickly got to his feet. She looked like a big cat, holding herself up half off the sofa, her arms straight, her hands flat on the floor. Zuzu grinned at him through the long black hair that hung across her face.

"My lover," she said. "Without me, you're lost."

Neil turned and ran, bouncing off the walls of the dark passage into the dining room, and then into the next room. Broken glass cracked beneath his shoes. Open windows. Neil grabbed a sill, swung his body out and then let himself drop to the ground.

He didn't know which side of the house he was on. The air was gray and full of moisture. He was in a thick wet fog—*il morbo*. He could barely see five feet in front of him. Still he ran—staggered—as fast as he could in the circumstances, his eyes fixed on the ground just ahead. He hit saplings and tripped on rocks, pushed through thickets and crawled over rocky ridges that suddenly loomed before him, blocking his flight.

Finally he had to stop. He bent over, gasping for breath.

When he looked up, two men wearing black uniforms stood in front of him. They laughed as they took him in hand, and they didn't even bother to draw their pistols.

GROTTA ROSSA

They walked for some distance. Neil couldn't make out anything in the fog that swirled and blew around them, but the two guards knew where they were going. He tried to speak to them, a few words in Italian, and then German, but they merely laughed at him. Their hands were like iron clamps on his arms.

Neil's face was raw and the cold air grated painfully across his skin. He couldn't tell whether the mask still clung to him or not. In certain places it seemed to be gone, but he felt a lingering tightness and weight around the eyes and mouth. Nonetheless, it hardly seemed to matter anymore. Real or not, there or gone, the mask was almost irrelevant to his situation now. The guards had him and could do whatever they wanted with him. He thought about resisting, struggling, perhaps breaking free and fleeing, but he sensed that it was useless to try. He would simply wander around in *il morbo* until he fell off a cliff or they caught him again.

Then they were on a smooth wide path, and a high stone outcropping in the side of a hill appeared before them. The guards force-walked Neil to a cleft in the rock, and then inside. Within a few yards the path turned, and they emerged in a large, roughly circular open area. A limestone massif ran through the Marches, Neil knew, and limestone lent itself particularly well to the formation of caverns.

They were in the grotto Marisa had mentioned to him. It was lit by mounted torches and banks of candles. There was a simple wooden altar on raised ground. Behind it stood a rusty iron cross that was taller than a man. A few plain benches served as pews. A narrow stream of water bubbled out of the rock and flowed in a cut channel through the makeshift chapel. There were several plaster statues of the Virgin Mary around the place, the largest of which stood beside the source of the stream. Mary's robes were blue and white, and her face was painted with unnaturally bright enamel colors—red lips, blue eyes, shiny white skin.

Several people sat on the benches and another group stood in a tight huddle behind the altar. Neil recognized Father Panic and other members of Marisa's family. Then he noticed a third group of people, in a side area that was not as well lit. They were the workers and farmhands, dressed in rough clothes or rags, kneeling submissively on the damp bare rock. There were a couple of dozen of them. Their heads were bowed, their hands clasped as if in prayer. He saw the dwarf woman. She was the only person in that group who knelt with her head up, looking around calmly. When she saw Neil she grinned maniacally at him, and then shook her head.

Guards were posted all around, but they looked relaxed and they had their pistols holstered. They stood, watching, waiting.

Neil was brought to the area between the benches and the altar, and forced to kneel beside the fast-moving stream of water. His hands were tied behind his back, and then his ankles as well.

The same lunacy again, Neil thought. A conversion and baptism, but then what? His only fear was that they might cut his tongue out, as he'd seen them do with others. Could he pre-empt it—if he recited the Apostles' Creed, for instance, demonstrating that he was already a Catholic? Neil was not even sure that he remembered all of the Apostles' Creed anymore, and he knew it only in English. But if they would listen to him again, if he had a few seconds to explain, appeal ...

The circle of people behind the altar fanned out a little and gazed at him. Father Panic in his vestments, Marisa in a black blouse and black skirt that reached just below her knees. Her lover, also in uniform. A few guards and older people stood with them. She looked so young and beautiful—but the sinister black uniform made her look like a girl scout from hell.

Neil watched her hopefully. When Marisa finally looked

directly at him, her expression showed no flicker of recognition, or even of interest in who he was or what was happening. She turned her head and spoke quietly with the young man, who smiled, nodded and replied to her. Neil opened his mouth to address her by name, but a guard immediately shoved a thick rag between his teeth, rammed it halfway down his throat. A bitter alkaline taste filled Neil's nostrils and lungs—it was the same hideous fungus that he had experienced in the box room. He began to gag, trying desperately to spit, push and force the cloth out of his mouth. His body jumped wildly but the guards held him in place.

The handsome young man turned slightly and reached down to pick up something from the floor behind him. It was a wooden box with leather straps and metal bolts. He came forward and shoved the strange device over Neil's head. The straps were cinched tight under his throat. The bolts were turned—and Neil felt flat metals plates tighten against the sides and back of his skull. He could hardly breathe, his lungs were in extreme distress. His brain reeled. Then men were grunting close around him as they turned the bolts forcefully, relentlessly.

The last thing Neil heard—before he felt the bones in his head begin to crunch and splinter—was the sound of men and women laughing.

NOTES

1. In an apparent attempt to ape the Germans the [Croatian] ustashas set up a number of concentration camps. Being far less organized than their mentors or lacking the technology, they often resorted in these camps to knives with which to murder Serbs, Jews, Gypsies and undesirable Croats. The most infamous camp was at Jasenovac on the Sava River, on the border of Bosnia. Tim Judah, *The Serbs: History, Myth & the Destruction of Yugoslavia* (Yale University Press, 1997).

2. Seven hundred thousand men, women and children were killed there alone in ways that made even the hair of the Reich's experts stand on end, as some of them are said to have admitted

when they were amongst themselves. The preferred instruments of execution were saws and sabres, axes and hammers, and leather cuff bands with fixed blades that were fastened on the lower arm and made especially in Solingen for the purpose of cutting throats, as well as a kind of rudimentary crossbar gallows on which the Serbs, Jews and Bosnians, once rounded up, were hanged in rows like crows or magpies. Not far from Jasenovac, in a radius of no more than ten miles, there were also the camps of Prijedor, Stara Gradiska and Banja Luka, where the Croatian militia, it's hand strengthened by the Wehrmacht and it's spirit by the Catholic Church, performed one day's work after another in similar manner. The history of this massacre, which went on for years, is recorded in fifty thousand documents abandoned by the Germans and Croats in 1945...WG Sebald, *The Rings of Saturn*, translated by Michael Hulse (New Directions, 1998).

3. In *Kaputt*, his memoir of World War II, the Italian journalist Curzio Malaparte recounts the following incident when he and Raffaele Caserto, then the Italian minister in Zagreb, met Ante Pavelic, the Poglavnik (*fuhrer*, or leader) of the Croatian forces:

"While he spoke I gazed at a wicker basket on the Poglavnik's desk. The lid was raised and the basket seem to be filled with mussels or shelled oysters -- as they are occasionally displayed in the windows of Fortnum & Mason in Piccadilly in London. Casertano looked at me and winked.

"Would you like a nice oyster stew"

"Are they Dalmatian oysters?" I asked the Poglavnik.

"Ante Pavelik removed the lid from the basket and revealed the mussels, that slimy and jelly-like mass, and he said, smiling, with that tired good-natured smile of his, "It is a present from my loyal *ustashis*. Forty pounds of human eyes."

Curzio Malaparte, *Kaputt*, translated by Cesare Foligno (E.P. Dutton, 1946).

ABOUT THE AUTHOR

Thomas Tessier is the author of several novels of horror and suspense, including *The Nightwalker, Phantom, Finishing Touches, Rapture* and *Fog Heart*. He received the International Horror Guild Award twice and was a finalist for the World Fantasy Award and the Bram Stoker Award. He lives in Connecticut with his wife Alice.

John Langan is the author of two novels and three collections of shorter fiction. His novel, *The Fisherman*, received the Bram Stoker Award. He is one of the founders of the Shirley Jackson Award, for which he served as a juror during its first three years. Currently, he reviews horror and dark fantasy for *Locus* magazine. He lives in New York's Hudson Valley with his wife, younger son, and a house full of animals.

Curious about other Crossroad Press books?
Stop by our site:
http://store.crossroadpress.com
We offer quality writing
in digital, audio, and print formats.